"I hear you are going away early tomorrow morning. I thought there might be something I could pack for you," Carolan said as she leaned against the door.

"Pack? No. I do not think so. Pack? There is nothing to pack," Mr. Masterman replied.

"I see. Good night." Her voice was a breathless whisper.

He said, "Good night!" very steadily, and then, "Carolan!"

Her master was standing before her, looking down at her. "You should not have come," he said.

"No," she answered, "I should not. But tomorrow you are going away. . . . I will leave you now."

But he would not let her leave him now. He lifted her up; she put her arms around his neck. She was not sure whether this was her revenge on the men in her life who had betrayed her, or whether she had been unloved too long. . . .

Jean Plaidy

Beyond
the Blue
Mountains

A FAWCETT CREST BOOK

Fawcett Publications, Inc., Greenwich, Connecticut

BEYOND THE BLUE MOUNTAINS

THIS BOOK CONTAINS THE COMPLETE TEXT OF THE
ORIGINAL HARDCOVER EDITION.

A Fawcett Crest Book reprinted by arrangement
with G.P. Putnam's Sons

Library of Congress Catalog Card Number: 75-7951

Printed in the United States of America

First printing: April 1976

1 2 3 4 5 6 7 8 9 10

To

G. P. H.

CONTENTS

Kitty Kennedy

It was hot in the coach. The June sunshine was merciless, and the dust raised by the horses' hoofs powdered the hedges, penetrated the coach, tickled the throats of the travellers, and set their eyes smarting. They had dined adequately at Brentford off salt pork and malt liquor, but now they were crossing Staines Bridge and their thirst and peevishness more and more inclined them towards slumber. They were aware of the hardness of their seats, of the jolting of the coach, of the increasing tedium of a journey that with luck would go on for four days, and without luck longer; they were aware of the proximity of each other, not always pleasant; they thought, not without uneasiness, of Bagshot Heath. They should get over it in daylight, but they sat fingers crossed, guarding against ill luck, lest some mishap should befall the coach on its way across the Heath.

The merchant in the corner began to snore, his wife to nod. The middle-aged matron kept an unnecessarily watchful eye on her two daughters who were both fast approaching thirty, mousy-haired, one pimpled, the other pock-marked, and who seemed to be holding themselves in readiness for an attack on their virtue. It amused the girl of seventeen in the big straw hat, and the young man of eighteen with the leather brief-case across his knees.

They had been watchful of each other, these two, since he had boarded the coach at Kensington. He had sat opposite her; his eyes had tried to catch hers, but whenever he looked her way her charming oval face would be hidden by the brim of her hat. Her clothes were elegant; she had a mingled air of simplicity and sophistication which he found enchanting. Who was she? Why was she travelling alone by stage? How could her family allow it! He was intrigued and excited.

Her hair was golden like the corn in August, and when the sun caught it, it turned to the gold one saw in the goldsmiths' shops. He had not seen her eyes; the ridiculous hat hid them every time he would look straight at them. There was a dimple in her chin; her mouth was lovely, frightened yet bold, full, a little sensuous—just a little—and childish too. She was a very attractive young person, and alone! He himself had thought it quite an adventure to leave the home he shared with his Uncle Gregory in the little town just beyond Exeter, and to visit his Uncle Simon in Lincoln's Inn. An adventure for a young and adventurous man; but for a beautiful young woman! He studied her from head to foot. Her long green cloak almost enveloped her, but it was possible to see the striped poplin dress beneath it which at her tiny waist fell away from the gaily coloured quilted petticoat. Who was she? He was determined to find out.

The merchant was awakened suddenly by one of his own snores which was more violent than those which had gone before. He glared at his wife as though accusing her of having made the sound which had disturbed his slumber. She was meek, almost apologetic; she gave the impression of having taken as her due over a number of years any blame he cared to lay upon her.

The merchant began to address his fellow passengers. He was a garrulous man, and abject meekness in his wife had led him to expect it in all.

"Wars! Wars!" he declaimed. "There will be wars as long as there are men to make them!"

He glanced expectantly at Darrell Grey, the young man with the brief-case, and Darrell answered that indeed it looked as if there must always be these quarrels between nations; but his attention did not really stray from the young woman sitting opposite him.

"War with America!" went on the merchant. "War with France! War with Spain!" Oratorically he began to enumerate the events of the past year. "It is true Rodney put the French to flight, but what of the Americans and their independence. . . .?"

The knees of Darrell Grey touched the green cloak momentarily, and hot colour crept up the fair neck and was lost in the biscuit-coloured straw of the hat.

"War is indeed a terrible thing, sir!" said the matron. "Why, I can assure you, sir, that were it not for the wars my daughters would be married. Betrothed, both of them, to sailors and gentlemen of the quality at that! I will not mention names. Were I to, I should startle the company. Great names! Fine names! And both fallen in battle! Ah, sir! You cannot tell me anything I do not know of the horrors of war!" She turned to the merchant's wife. "Have *you* any daughters?" she enquired, but the merchant's wife merely shook her head and glanced from her questioner to the merchant as though to say: "Do you not hear that *he* is talking? How can you interrupt!" The matron was, however, so sure of her own importance that she had little respect for that of the merchant. "It is good to have daughters if they are a credit to you!" she said.

The coach lurched suddenly; the girl in the poplin dress was thrown forward and Darrell Grey stretched out to catch her. For a moment his hands touched her shoulders. She smiled and he saw that her eyes were blue, her lashes golden as her hair.

"I am sorry," she said.

"Please do not be," he answered. "You are staying with the coach for its entire journey?"

"Yes."

"And after?" he asked.

"I shall be met. My aunt perhaps, or her servants, will meet me."

He leaned back in his seat. She travelled alone, but she was not easy to know. He could wait. She was travelling all the way to Exeter, and Exeter was quite four days off.

The coach stopped suddenly. The matron and her daughters moved closer to each other. The merchant looked out of the window and cursed.

"We are stuck in a rut!" he said. "Confound it!" And his wife looked wretched, as though it were her fault.

"We shall not cross Bagshot before dark if we stay here long," said the elder of the daughters, and shivered.

"And they say," said the merchant's wife timidly, "that there is a very good inn on the other side of the Heath."

"I could not bear to cross the Heath at dusk!" said the second daughter. "They say there is much boldness in those rogues nowadays."

The girl in the poplin dress raised scared eyes to Darrell. He smiled reassuringly; he rather hoped they would cross the Heath in twilight. He would look after her and she would be very grateful.

"I do hope . . ." she began.

He leaned towards her. "They are desperate fellows, but you need have no fear of them."

"Nonsense!" said the matron. "Of what use are fine words when a man is armed! I tell you that Bagshot Heath is the most notorious hunting-ground for these men."

"My good lady," said the merchant, "it is obvious that you are unacquainted with my part of the country."

"They say," put in an elderly woman from a corner of the coach, "that they play odd tricks."

"They well may, Madam," boomed the merchant, "but they never forget to relieve one of one's purse, and they are always ready with their pistols."

One of the daughters shrieked, and at that moment the coach began to move forward. There was a little laughter then, but it was uneasy laughter. There was silence for some little time. The sun was a red ball declining westwards as they came to the edge of Bagshot Heath.

Darrell leaned forward, and the straw hat lifted momentarily.

"It is fortunate that there are so many of us," she said softly. "I confess I should be frightened were there less."

Fear was unleashing her reserve. She lay back against the woodwork of the coach. The cloak opened slightly to show the tiniest of waists and a ripe young bosom under striped poplin.

Darrell said: "You are on a visit?"

"No."

"Then you are staying . . . near Exeter?"

She nodded. The coquetry faded from her eyes; she had the tremulous mouth of a child. He found her enchanting.

He said: "That is good."

"Why good?"

"Because I am returning to my home near Exeter. Perhaps you are staying near my home."

"Perhaps." She turned her head now. He saw her girl's profile and her woman's throat; there were already signs of a voluptuousness to come.

Where was she going? he wondered. Who was she? She might be a young gentlewoman. Was she a lady's maid? He tried to think of someone in his neighbourhood who might be

12

requiring a lady's maid. The only person who, to his knowledge, had ever had one, was the squire's lady, and she had been dead two years. Mystery surrounded the young woman. Was she innocent or sophisticated? A gentlewoman or a serving woman dressed in her mistress's clothes? And why was she travelling alone?

He had to find out, and here on Bagshot Heath was the place for boldness.

He said: "My uncle is a lawyer. I work with him."

"You have no parents?"

He shook his head. His mother had died of the smallpox when he was five, he told her; his father, of he knew not what.

"My father?" she said, and wrinkled her nose very prettily. "He died long ago. I never knew him. My mother?" Again her mouth trembled. "She has just died . . . of what I know not." She added: "I go to my Aunt Harriet, five miles out of Exeter."

"Your Aunt Harriet!" he cried excitedly. "Can it be Miss Harriet Ramsdale who is your aunt?"

"The very same."

He was laughing, not with amusement but with pleasure, and his pleasure changed suddenly to concern. Harriet Ramsdale the aunt of this charming creature! It was impossible to believe. And she was going to live with her. He was delighted and dismayed.

"Her house," he said, "is but a few miles from my uncle's. We shall meet, I hope."

"It is good," she said demurely, "to have found a neighbour already."

"It delights me," he told her, leaning forward.

This explained everything. Harriet Ramsdale would rather let her young niece face the dangers of lonely travel than spend the money to go and get her. He was filled with tenderness. Poor little girl! To live with Harriet Ramsdale!

She said eagerly: "If you know my aunt, you can tell me something of the life that is before me."

He answered with a question: "Will you tell me your name?"

"Kitty Kennedy."

"Mine is Darrell Grey."

The golden lashes shone against her pale skin for a moment. It fascinated him to see the way she could play coquette and frightened child at the same time.

"I . . . I am glad we know each other," he said.

"Shall you call on my aunt?"

13

He smiled, thinking of calling on Harriet Ramsdale.

"We shall meet—be sure of that!"

They fell silent, not because they had nothing to say, but because there was so much to say, and they did not know how to begin to say it.

The Heath lay behind them; the passengers had ceased to talk of the terrors of the road; they talked of inns, inns they had heard of and inns they had stayed at. And then they talked of war . . . and uneasy peace.

The sun was setting as they drew into the yard of the inn.

Kitty was too excited to sleep much that night. The depression of the last weeks had left her suddenly; life was not going to be so dreary after all. She had some idea of what life in Aunt Harriet's house was going to be like. Her mother—gay, attractive, clever, beautiful, laughter-loving—had told her about her sister. How she had imitated Aunt Harriet! Though, as she said: "Bless you, Kit, it's nigh on twenty years since I last saw her. But I can imagine what twenty years have done to Harry, poor soul!" And she would purse her lips and frown, and her face would cease to be her own, becoming that of another woman, a woman who had not been blessed with her own gay spirit. "She was good, Harriet was; she was Father's daughter. I was all Mother's."

Kitty knew the story of her mother's flight from the country parsonage; how the atmosphere of piety had stifled her. Morning prayers. Sermons. No laughter. No singing. No acting. And Mother had loved to act. How vividly she had talked! It was possible to have a picture of the grey stone Devon house with the creeper climbing over its walls and the tower of the church looming over it, its graveyard just at the end of the garden, frightening Mother when she was a little girl. Years and years ago that had been. Why, Mother had not seen the place for twenty years, and that took one back to 1763 when another war had just ended. Kitty could picture her growing up, no longer afraid of the grey tombstones, playing in the graveyard with Squire Haredon's son who was wild and reckless and haughty as Mother herself. She could picture the parsonage dining-room with its big windows and air of cleanliness and the family gathered there for morning prayers, the serving maids at one end of the table in sprigged muslin and mob-caps, and at the other end of the table Grandmother Ramsdale, very pretty and restless like a brightly plumaged bird in a cage, and Grandfather Ramsdale, stern and pious. Jeffry the eldest and Mother the youngest had both

14

taken after Grandmother Ramsdale, but Harriet the middle one took after her father. Kitty thought of Mother and her brother always in mischief, helped by the squire's boy to tease poor Harriet who had not their gay spirit and attractive charm. Grandfather Ramsdale was of the quality and it was in a mad moment that he had made a most unsuitable match with Grandmother Ramsdale who was the daughter of a blacksmith; she had plagued and tormented him until he, being pious, must marry her. Kitty had seen a miniature of Grandmother Ramsdale, had seen the exquisite little face with its crown of fair hair; had seen the wilful eyes and passionate mouth so like her own and her mother's, and it was not so difficult then to understand how even a man such as Grandfather Ramsdale had been plagued into marriage. Extraordinary marriage it must have been. She had been unable to endure that country parsonage, and as soon as her youngest was able to walk and button her own clothes, like a bird which has taught her young to fly she no longer felt any ties held her to her nest; she flew off with a young lord who was passing through Exeter and saw her and was plagued by her, just as the parson had been. She was never heard of again. So the children grew in an atmosphere of pious gloom. They were beaten mercilessly by their father, for he feared his son and younger daughter had inherited their mother's bad blood. There was no fear in his heart for his favourite, Harriet. She was *his* daughter. And he was right to fear too, for at the age of eighteen Jeffry went to Oxford and in a year had run himself so deeply into debt that it meant several years of cheese-paring to extricate him; in his last year there he was killed in a tavern fight. And Bess, Kitty's mother, had grown to look just like the blacksmith's daughter, with the same fair colouring, the same laughing eyes, the same wanton mouth. A match had been arranged for her with George Haredon, but when a party of players came to Exeter there was among them one Peter Kennedy, and when the players left, Bess went with them.

She often told the story, lying back on her couch with her fair hair flowing about her shoulders and her rich wrap falling open to disclose her over-luscious charms.

"Poor Peter! How I adored him, swaggering on the stage with his red cloak and his moustaches! But, Kit my dear, I was just a country wench then; I soon saw what a mistake I had made. Besides, was I to spend my life with a company of strolling players! I wasn't sorry—I have never been sorry for anything. And, once I'd set eyes on you, I had a soft spot for

15

Peter Kennedy for evermore. Well, my dear, that's the secret of life—never stop to look back and sigh; go on and find something better. That's what I did. There was Toby after Peter, and after Toby my Lord James. It has been a good life and we've enjoyed it, eh?"

They had enjoyed it. There was always plenty to eat, good clothes to wear. No beggary for them. And Bess grew plumper and more luscious with the years, and Sir Harry took the place of Lord James, and it went on like that. A pleasant little house, a serving maid or two, and many fine gentlemen who always had a friendly pat for Bess's little girl. There was the academy for young ladies where one learned to read a little and write a little, to speak French and do fine embroidery. Occasionally there were slightly unpleasant incidents. A look, a gesture, a disparaging remark overheard about her mother. Kitty did not care; she was completely insensitive to these things. She was a modern replica of her own mother and the blacksmith's daughter; she was kindly, gentle, ready to be moulded by a stronger will, and these qualities, coupled with striking physical beauty, were at the root of her appeal to the egoistical male of all types and ages. In her firm, strong, flawless body and her pliable mind they saw perfection. She had her mother's gift for looking forward, stifling regrets for the past. The old life was done with; the new one, presided over by the stern Aunt Harriet, lay before her. The prospect was not pleasing, yet because she was herself she must always expect good things from life, and here already, on the journey westwards, she had met a young man whose admiration excited her, who was pleasant of countenance, charming of manners, and who was apparently to be a near neighbour.

Her mother had known death was coming to her; a certain breathlessness, a heightening of colour in her face, fainting fits; these were the forerunners of death. The doctors and apothecaries could not save her; perhaps she did not wish them to. She was thirty-eight years old, and that seemed to her no longer young. She had had her life and enjoyed it; she was ready to go. But what of Kitty, who was just on the threshold of life and had much to learn? She, who had never been afraid for herself, was suddenly fearful for her daughter. She thought constantly then, with a never-before-experienced respect, of the sheltered life in a country parsonage. Affectionately she remembered quiet fields and the glistening gold of buttercups in noonday sunshine; she thought of lanes shaded by leafy trees, of homely fare and morning prayers and strict surveillance. There was safety in these things. She had not heard from her family since leaving it, in the company of Peter Kennedy, but it did not occur to her that her old home was not exactly as she had known it, so she dispatched a letter to her sister Harriet at the parsonage, and waited anxiously for a reply, while the fainting fits grew more frequent and the fight for breath a losing battle. It came at length, but not from the parsonage. There was a new parson now, Harriet wrote, for their father had been dead ten years. Harriet had her own house; did Bess remember Oaklands? The little house just a stone's throw from the parsonage, and a mile or so from Haredon? Harriet was far from rich, but however exacting her duty, she could be relied upon to perform it. That letter conjured up such a picture of Harriet that it made Bess laugh until she began to cough so violently that she thought her last moment had come. The same Harriet! Grim and virtuous, determined on duty. However much she disapproved of Bess, Bess's daughter was her niece, and while she, Harriet, lived, it would always be her duty to see that any member of her family did not starve. Bess would have preferred to live a few years longer, to have seen her daughter safely married and settled for life; but that was not to be, and who knew that, by returning to the place from which her mother had escaped, Kitty might not make a more brilliant marriage than her mother would ever have been able to arrange for her in London Town? Respectability counted; Harriet was all respectability, and sometimes some very fine gentlemen went down to Haredon. So Bess began to convince herself that this was probably the best thing possible for Kitty's welfare, and she died, as she had lived, happily.

And here was Kitty on her way to Aunt Harriet, a little alarmed at the prospect of her new life, but not so very alarmed, because she was so like her mother. And when she at last fell asleep her thoughts were not of the lost life in London, nor of the new life which lay before her, but of Darrell Grey.

The next day passed, and the next and the next. They crossed Salisbury Plain and entered the fine old town of Salisbury. They yawned and slept and laughed and chattered, were irritable and gay, taciturn and garrulous as they passed the milestones. The journey was a tedious business for all but Darrell and Kitty; to them there was pleasure in each moment as it passed. There was joy in the shaded lanes; there was excitement at dusk when a lonely stretch of road or plain had to

17

be traversed; they were enthralled by each other. They loved the meals in the old inn parlours; they was joy in getting out of the coach to stretch cramped limbs, in settling in again to continue the journey. It was a voyage of discovery; to Kitty each town through which they passed was new; but there were more exciting discoveries to be made, and how exhilarating it was learning of Darrell's life, telling him about her own. He had heard of the parson's daughter, Bess, who had run away from home. He had heard how Squire Haredon had been in love with her; how half the neighbourhood had been in love with her; it did not surprise him, if she had been anything like her daughter. They wished, how they wished, the journey would never end! The weather was perfect; it was all blue skies and unclouded sunshine, wonderful sunsets. Even the garrulous merchant and the disapproving matron added to their enjoyment. To Darrell's amusement Kitty imitated them, for she had inherited her mother's talent for imitations. He had never known anyone like her. She was different from the country girls of his acquaintance, and even had she not possessed such startling and alluring beauty, her gaiety and her vivacity would have made her the most charming of all the females he had ever met. As to her, she was equally delighted with him. He was just a little naïve, so adoring, so longing to play the bold philanderer, and yet so awestruck and a little shy. With each hour he plunged deeper and deeper in love with her; and she followed at a respectable distance. It was an enchanting idyll, charming, delightful, but when they reached Dorchester it changed subtly.

It was a comfortable inn. The landlord came out to receive them, his honest red face beaming a welcome. He had rooms for all and to spare. A fire burned in the open grate of the parlour; throughout the inn was a delicious smell of roasting meat, appetizing to hungry travellers.

A serving maid showed Kitty her room, and when she was alone in it she flung herself down on the four-poster bed. She was tired after the day's journey; it had been even hotter than usual and the atmosphere inside the coach had made her sleepy. She was pensive too, thinking that tomorrow she would see her Aunt Harriet for herself. Already she had made plans for meeting Darrell again.

From below there was a sudden clatter of horses' hoofs and the sound of wheels on the cobbles. New arrivals? Curiosity sent Kitty flying from the bed to peep through the window. It was an elegant carriage and the horses which drew it were

18

beautiful indeed. The landlord, the ostlers, even the potmen were hovering about the carriage. Some personage evidently. Then she saw him . . . a big man, possibly in his late thirties—a red-faced man with powerful shoulders, well dressed though in a country fashion. He was scowling and was decidedly out of temper. Now the reason was obvious; one of the horses had turned lame. He was cursing his postillion as though it were his fault; he waved aside the landlord, he was cursing the roads, cursing the fools who were his servants, cursing all of them who stood there gaping at him.

"Bring me a drink!" he shouted, and the landlord fled to do his bidding. He stood there, cursing. A most unpleasant personage, thought Kitty; a hateful creature, ugly too, with his red-purple face and his rough words. The serving maid who had shown Kitty her room came out with a glass of ale on a green tray. She stood before the man, curtsyed awkwardly and waited with downcast eyes while he seized the glass. He drained it, complained that it was poor stuff and roughly commanded her to bring him another, and be quick about it unless she wanted a whip about her shoulders. She hastened to obey. Kitty drew back disgusted. She had never seen such a man before; he behaved as though he were king in this small world; he lacked the manners which she had come to expect in men, because the men who had visited her mother had always possessed them. He stamped his way across the courtyard, and when he had reached the door of the inn the serving maid again appeared with another glass of ale on the tray. He drank it, not quickly as he had drunk the first; he stood back, smacking his lips. His face was still purple with rage, but now the very way he stood there showed that his rage was receding. His voice floated up to her.

"Ah! That's better, eh, Moll?" He gripped the girl's shoulder roughly, and with one hand drew her to him and kissed her loudly on the mouth. The ale spilled from the glass in his other hand. Kitty heard the girl giggle. She turned away from the window. She no longer felt in the mood to lie on her bed and dream. She called for hot water, and when it came she washed the dust of the day's journey from her hands and face and went downstairs. She was hungry, and the smell of roasting meat was indeed pleasant, but as she turned the handle of the dining-room door, the landlord's wife came running towards her.

"Ma'am," she said, "if you will but go into the parlour, in a very short time . . ."

The woman looked harassed; Kitty hesitated.

"I thought," she began, "that you said it would be ready . . ."

"Your fellow travellers, Ma'am, are in the parlour. The moment the dining-room is disengaged I will let you know."

There was the sound of a chair being pushed back. A voice cried: "God damn you! Shut that door!" The door was how-ever pulled from Kitty's grasp, and the man whom she had seen in the courtyard was standing in the doorway; he did not see Kitty immediately; he glared at the landlord's wife, who stammered: "The passengers from the coach, your Honour . . ."

"Passengers from the coach! Let the scum wait! I tell you I won't sit down to eat with coach passengers." He stopped for he had seen Kitty now. "Aha!" he continued, putting a hand to his mouth to wipe away the gravy clinging there. "Who is the lady?"

The woman said: "The lady arrived with the coach this evening . . . the Exeter coach, your Honour."

"The Exeter coach." His eyes were large and brown; he had been an exceptionally handsome man less than ten years ago. He turned to the host's wife. "Come, woman!" he said, and there was a hint of laughter in his voice. "The lady will think me churlish." He bowed to Kitty. "You will come in, Ma'am. I should deem it an honour if you would share my table."

Kitty noticed his hands; they were large, and dark hairs grew plentifully on the backs of them. She thought of the way in which one of them had seized the not-unwilling serving maid, and she drew back into the darkness of the corridor.

"Thank you," she said, "but I am not travelling alone. I will call my fellow travellers; we are all very hungry."

In the parlour the matron was holding forth angrily.

"I never heard the like! We must wait because some impor-tant person is to be served first and prefers to dine alone! I would like him to know that I have mixed with the quality. Is a lady to be insulted because, having fallen on evil times so that it was necessary to sell her carriage, she must take the coach . . .?"

Kitty went to Darrell.

"The food is ready," she said, and they all went into the dining-room.

The man did not look up as they entered. He went on sto-lidly eating his dinner. The serving man brought in the joint and put it on the sideboard; the landlord appeared, and began to carve nervously.

The roast lamb was excellent, and there was no sound in the room except that made by hungry eaters. The big man had finished his dinner; he had turned his chair, and every time Kitty raised her eyes he was looking in her direction. Colour mounted her cheeks; she kept her eyes downcast, but she felt his were on her. He frightened her in a way she had never been frightened before, and she felt suddenly that to go upon a long journey alone and unprotected was something of an undertaking. She glanced at Darrell. How handsome he was, with his rather gentle scholar's face and the love for her in his grey eyes! He was very slender, and looked almost frail when compared with the arrogant, red-faced, alarming man sitting there in pompous state alone at his table. She stole another glance in his direction. He smiled and tried to hold her eyes. She lifted her head haughtily and turned away.

She said in a whisper to Darrell: "He seems a very coarse creature—this man whom the host is so eager to please! Let us get out of here to the parlour; it will be better there."

They went back to the parlour and sat down in the window seat.

Darrell said: "That is Squire Haredon. He is in a vile temper tonight!"

"Haredon!" she said. "George Haredon!" And she thought of her mother's playing in the graveyard with that red-faced man.

Darrell said: "You have seen him at his worst; he is in a bad temper. His horse went lame and he has had to put up here instead of getting home as he intended. He is a good squire, but when he is in a rage he can be terrible; everyone avoids the squire when he is in a rage."

"I should hate him, rage or no rage," she said.

The door opened and in he came.

"Bah!" he exclaimed. "These inns are draughty places." His rage had left him now; he smiled at them benignly. "Bless me, if it ain't young Grey! It is young Grey, ain't it? And the lady?"

Darrell got to his feet, but it was Kitty who spoke.

"My name is Kitty Kennedy."

"Kitty Kennedy!" said the squire. He brought his black brows together. "By God!" he went on. "Is it to your Aunt Harriet that you are going?"

"It is to my Aunt Harriet."

He slapped his thigh and laughed deeply.

"I thought I knew you. Why, my lady, you and I are not strangers."

21

He towered over her, and she drew farther back in the window seat, pretending not to see the huge hand extended towards her.

"I do not think," she said with dignity, "that you and I have met before." And she made an almost imperious sign for Darrell to take the seat beside her; there was not room for three on the window seat.

"The squire means," explained Darrell, sitting down, "that he knows your aunt and knew your mother. That is why he does not feel you to be a stranger."

"Trust a lawyer for putting his finger right on the point!" cried George Haredon. "That's right, I knew your family, Kitty. And you're Bess's girl! By God, I knew it! You've got Bess's looks."

She resented his familiarity. She slipped her hand into Darrell's, and because of a certain fear that had come to her she held her head higher.

George Haredon leaned forward.

"I could almost believe it was Bessie herself sitting there," he murmured. He breathed heavily, excitedly, and his eyes glistened.

"I have always heard," said Kitty, coolly, "that I much resembled my mother."

"And, by God, whoever told you that was right!"

He was so close that she could feel the warmth of his body; a smell of spirits was on his breath, and that of horses on his clothes. She wrinkled her nose in disgust, and she did not care that he saw this. She turned to Darrell and began to talk of the towns through which they had passed, and when George Haredon joined in she turned the subject to that of their fellow passengers of whom he could know nothing. Darrell was embarrassed, for he was a good deal in awe of the squire. She thought how beautiful, how cultured, how gentlemanly Darrell was, compared with this man, and because she sensed that he was a little afraid of him she wanted to put her arms round him to protect him; it was a new feeling, this tenderness, a new and wonderful feeling. She made up her mind in that moment that she was going to marry Darrell whatever obstacles had to be overcome. He needed her and she needed him.

George Haredon stood, watching them, his great hands hanging helplessly at his sides. She was aware of those hands; she could not forget the way in which one of them had seized the serving maid, and she knew that he longed to seize her in just that way. He was repulsive; he was hateful; he was arrogant too; he tried to force his way between her and Darrell.

22

"Why!" he said, coming so close that again she smelt the spirits on his breath. "Bess made a fine lady of her girl. Trust Bessie for that! And I'll tell you something—I like it. I like it very much."

Here he was, the arrogant male, strutting in his plumage. *"I* like it very much! Are you not flattered? For here I am cock of the walk!" But Kitty would show him she was not one of his country wenches to be cursed one moment and kissed the next. Her eyes kindled; they rested on his flowered waistcoat, spotted where he had spilled his gravy. She wanted him to know that she hated the smell of stables that clung to him, hated his big, hairy, not very clean hands, hated even more his crude manners.

"It does not greatly concern me whether you like it or not," she told him.

He laughed, but he was nevertheless disconcerted. He was fascinated by the proud set of the head on her shoulders, by that fearlessness, to be expected from Bess's daughter. The likeness to Bess moved him deeply. She thought him coarse, did she! Bess, who had never minced her words, had found him so in the old days. Bess's contempt had pierced the armour of his arrogance, filled him with the desire to beat the pride out of her. That was why Bess had attracted him so strongly. Now it was happening again, with Bess's daughter in the place of Bess, and this enforced stay at the Dorchester inn was changed from a tiresome incident to an exhilarating adventure.

"So you made the journey all alone, eh?" he said. "Why, if Harriet had told me, damme, I would have travelled up to get you myself, that I would. You should not have been allowed to travel alone."

She lifted her eyes to Darrell and smiled at him very sweetly.

"Mr. Grey looked after me very well, thank you!"

"The devil he did! Trust a lawyer for getting the best out of a situation."

The door was opened suddenly, and the matron came in with her two daughters.

She said in a loud voice: "The lamb was mutton, but edible. Sit down, children . . . just for a little while. Then we will go to our rooms. I do declare that travelling in this way can be a tiresome business. But there, doubtless we miss our carriage."

George Haredon was studying the two daughters quizzically; they simpered, casting coy glances in his direction. Their mother was alert, while she made a pretence of great languor.

The squire went to them. "Travelling in one's own carriage can be a tiresome business, Ma'am," he said. "Here am I, stranded for the night because one of my horses has gone lame. A devilish business! May I introduce myself? Squire Haredon, at your service, Ma'am."

He was smiling at the two girls. Their mother presented them.

"My dear daughter, Emily—my dear daughter, Grace."

The squire was out to impress. He sat between the two girls.

"I could have taken another horse, but I'm fond of my horses. It's nothing much—a little lameness. I'll leave her here tomorrow if she's not better, but I've a fancy that a night's rest is all she wants."

The merchant and his wife came in, and the merchant began to talk of wars in general.

"It is so hot in here," said Kitty after a while. "Darrell, I shall go to my room now. I am tired; it has been a tiring day."

She said good night to the company and went up to her room. She undressed quickly and got into bed. Her face was burning. She could not shut out of her mind the thought of those bold brown eyes and the strong hands with the down of black hair on them. From below came the murmur of voices. She pictured them all in the parlour—George Haredon ogling Emily and Grace. She was grateful to Emily and Grace. How relieved she had been when those bold eyes had ceased to contemplate her!

There were footsteps on the stairs. They would be taking their candles from the table in the hall; they would be coming up the stairs. Sudden panic seized her: she leaped out of bed and turned the key in her door. She leaned against the door, laughing at herself; absurd to be so frightened of him! He had turned his attentions to Grace or Emily. She got back into bed. Moonlight streamed into her room. She felt happier now that the door was locked. She dozed, and suddenly she was awakened again. She sat up, startled. Some noise had awakened her. She listened. There it was again. A light rattling, like the sound ghostly fingers might make on the window-pane.

She covered her face with the sheets; it came again. She uncovered herself and looked round the room; then she got out of bed and went to the window. She knelt on the seat and looked out.

Standing below her window was George Haredon. He had just picked up another handful of gravel to throw at her window.

For a second or two they stared at each other; then she stepped backwards. Hastily throwing a cloak about her shoulders, she went to the window and secured the bolt.

She did not look at him again, but she heard him laugh softly. She got into bed with her cloak still round her; she was trembling, not with cold but with rage.

Harriet Ramsdale was in her still-room when she heard the carriage stop outside her gate. She hastily locked a cupboard door, untied the apron about her waist and smoothed the folds of her muslin dress. She was a large woman with fine dark hair which she wore simply; her eyes were grey under bushy eyebrows; her mouth was thin and straight. At the sound of the carriage on the road her mouth softened a little, for she guessed it was the squire's carriage, and peering out of the window she confirmed this. She saw him alight; she saw him push open her gate in that forthright way which she admired so much; she saw him coming up the path to the front door.

She was as excited as Harriet Ramsdale could be excited, but with a return of her primness of manner she went back to the jars of blackberry jelly on the table, and began writing on their lids in a very precise, neat handwriting, "June, 1783."

"Don't be ridiculous, Harriet Ramsdale," she said under her breath, for when she was quite a small girl and Jeffry and Bess had not included her in their games she had formed the habit of talking to herself and had never lost it. "You're turned forty, and don't forget it!"

She was essentially practical; she was dogmatic; she was just. She set a strict pattern for herself to follow—Harriet, the daughter of a dearly beloved father, the only one in the entire family who had not disappointed him. Her house with its tasteful furniture, its polished floors where never a speck of dust was allowed to remain for long at a time, was a credit to her. For what would Peg and Dolly be doing, without their mistress at their heels? A pair of sluts, if ever there was a pair of sluts! Workhouse girls, wasteful, indolent and Harriet suspected, immoral. But then, having lived in a family which contained her mother, her brother Jeffry and her sister Bess, she was apt to suspect everyone of immorality. She had borne the great shock of her father's death some ten years back with fortitude, for she was strong of mind and body, and her one great weakness was her unswerving affection for George Haredon; it was a romantic affection, and quite lacking in that common sense which she, no less than others, expected of herself. It had begun when she had just passed sixteen and Bess was nearly fourteen; George must have been about eighteen at the time, and so handsome, so dashing, such a man of the world, that Harriet had admired him fervently, even though he did occasionally join in with Jeffry and Bess to tease her cruelly. Bess, even at fourteen, had been a lovely creature, and George's interest had been all for her, for in spite of Harriet's boundless good sense, in spite of the fact that she had been endowed with all the qualities which go to the making of a sensible wife, George, in common with the rest of his sex, was foolish enough not to recognise these virtues. When men grow older they learn wisdom; that fact was in Harriet's mind hourly.

Poor George had been heartbroken when Bess ran away with her actor, and Harriet was sure that it was purely out of pique that he married his foolish little wife. She proved to be a very unsuitable mistress of Haredon, and had borne him four children, two of whom had survived. She had died soon after the birth of the last child, for she had caught a chill when she went to be churched.

George, so wayward, so in need of a guiding hand! If only he would ask her now! It was two years since his wife had died—quite long enough for his period of celibacy. She blushed a little. One heard such stories of the squire, but did not one always hear stories of persons in exalted positions? One heard rumours concerning the wild life of the young Prince of Wales, simply because he was the Prince of Wales. Servants chatter; you can whip them, you can threaten them with dismissal, but they chatter. It was whispered that even before that silly woman had gone to be churched and caught her death . . . but no matter—she, Harriet, was not one to believe the worst of an old friend.

There was the sound of running footsteps, a timid knock.

"Come in!" said Harriet, and Peg entered; her hair was tousled, her face flushed.

"Ma'am, the squire is here."

"Peg! Your hair! Your gown! Is that a fresh rent?"

Peg's fingers pulled at the new rent in her gown.

"Whatever will the squire think to see such a slut in my house! You disgrace me. Go now. I shall be with the squire in a moment."

She was disturbed. Even the sight of Peg disturbed her,

26

with her old dress, one of Harriet's throw-outs, pulled tightly over a bosom that seemed to long to show itself, so that one had a feeling that at any moment it would tear the stuff and peep out, inviting admiration. Harriet smoothed her dress over her own flattish chest and went to the drawing-room. George was standing with his back to the door, facing the window. He swung round when he heard her.

"Harriet!" he said, and came swiftly towards her. He took both her hands, and his large brown eyes twinkled; they always twinkled when they rested on Harriet. Her heart began to beat quickly, but her face remained unchanged; rarely did a vestige of colour appear beneath her thick white skin.

"George! How charming of you to call! A glass of wine? Shall it be my sloe wine which you used to like particularly? There's my cowslip too."

He said: "Make it the sloe, Harry!"

She nodded her head, a little primly, but the corners of her mouth turned up. His low, rather hoarse voice excited her. Bess had said, years ago when they had lain in bed together: "George is coarse; sometimes it's exciting, but at others it's horrible. I don't know whether I'll like being married to George or not." Harriet had been indignant then, and she could still feel indignant. Who was Bess, she would like to know, to talk of coarseness? Bess who had run away with an actor—and heaven knew whether he had married her or not! Bess who, from all accounts, had not stayed with her actor, but had had many men friends and a carriage to ride in, and silks and satins and laces and ribbons to deck her wanton person. For Bess had written to Harriet regularly—maliciously of course—and those letters had been peppered with the names of men. Harriet had never replied; she remained aloof, the virtuous daughter of a good man, whose enthusiasms went into jars of preserves and whose great moments were when last year's sloe wine excelled that of the previous year. Who was Bess to talk of George's coarseness! And yet . . . well, when she was with him it was impossible to deny that coarseness; she began to believe, when she was with him, the stories she heard about him. There were two Georges in her mind, the one she thought of in his absence and the one he was when he stood before her. The good squire—and the man. The good squire needed her help, for he was impetuous and his bouts of rage were a byword, and every intelligent, practical woman knows that bouts of rage are a drag on the energy and get one nowhere; there was the man who set wild thoughts running through her mind, thoughts which she was

27

afraid of, yet, incomprehensible as it might seem, thoughts which she was not sure whether she liked having or not.

With dignity she crossed to the door and opened it. Peg had obviously been listening at the keyhole. The manners of these girls! It was not often that she used the whip on them, not because they did not deserve it, but because they were such lusty creatures and a whipping had scarcely any effect upon them at all. She could have whipped Peg gladly then because, she assured herself, it was atrociously bad manners to listen at keyholes—and if she had told them once, she had told them fifty times.

"Peg!" she said, her eyes straying to the bodice with the rent in it. "Bring the sloe wine and two glasses. Bring the new seedcake too . . . And, Peg"—she bent her head to whisper— "see that the tray is *clean.*"

Peg departed; Harriet returned to George, who smiled at her in a secret kind of way.

She said apologetically: "One has to watch those girls all the time. I never saw such a pair."

"You're a wonderful woman, Harriet," he said, and he rocked backwards and forwards on his heels.

She was in a sudden panic. She thought he was going to ask her to marry him, and she could not shut out the thought of him and some of the stories she had heard about him. That nurse-housekeeper person who, it was said, shared his bed besides looking after his children . . . a small virago of a woman, with flashing black eyes and thin mouth which never seemed to close properly, a bad creature if Harriet knew anything about badness—and, of course, being a parson's daughter, she knew a great deal.

"Your house is a credit to you, Harriet, 'pon my word it is. Ah! Here comes the sloe wine. Your sloe wine beats any other sloe wine in the country, I always say!"

To Harriet's practical mind such remarks were a direct approach to a proposal of marriage.

"It is good of you to say so, George."

"Good? No! Only truthful, and you know it, Harriet."

Peg stood before him with the tray; he did not look at her, but he knew she was smiling slyly, the consciously impudent smile of the underling who knows herself to be desired. Desire levels all social barriers . . . momentarily. Momentarily, he would have her know; still, she would never understand however he tried to explain. There would be no need to explain. You could thrash her one moment, abuse her, treat her as the workhouse brat she was, and the next minute she would be

28

smiling at you like that. Impudent slut! He preferred the other one, though still he preferred this one any hour of the day or night to poor old Harriet.

He took the glass, ignored Peg, and lifted it.

"To you, Harriet! Long life and happiness; you deserve it."

"Thank you, George. I wish the same good things to you."

He cleared his throat. He was enjoying this. Even Harriet, flat-chested, prim old Harriet, wanted him. This was how he liked it to be. He needed something like it, by God! That haughty girl in the inn had unnerved him. Not coquetry, either; not urging him on. Just flouting him as, years ago, her mother had flouted him.

He was not given to self-analysis, but he did know that Bess had done something to him years ago when she had teased him and tormented him and promised to marry him; and then gone off with a third-rate actor. He had never forgotten Bess. Always he was trying for that satisfaction which he was sure Bess alone could have given him, and it never came . . . not with any of them. That was why there were so many; that was why he was brutal with them sometimes, and sometimes incredibly soft. Always searching, and all because of Bess. He had often thought that if he had Bess alone with him at certain times he would have put his hand round that white neck of hers and strangled the life out of her. She deserved it. Mustn't think of Bess; it made the blood rush into his face, made the veins stand out; too much of that and he'd have to be bled again. But there was something in him, a little sentimental something that held an ideal. Squire! It was a grand title. He was proud of it, proud of his lands and his horses, proud of the position he held there. He liked to see them curtsy on the road as he passed, their eyes full of reverence for him; but there were saucy sluts like these two from the workhouse who would smile a different smile and toss their heads; then he would be angry with himself for the dignity he had lost; for, though he could thrash them and take them when he wished, he could not drive out of their eyes that look which showed so clearly that they understood that he was a man who could not do without women. Whatever their station, they knew it; they held it over him . . . like Peg smirking there when her mistress wasn't looking. And it was all due to Bess. Bess alone could have satisfied him. He could see her now, never could forget her in fact, laughing as he chased her round the tombstones; long blue eyes with golden lashes, luring, tormenting him with the knowledge of him and of all men which she must have been born with and which was a gift from the blacksmith's daughter. Married to Bess he would have sustained his dignity; there would have been no sly scuffling, no stolen moments with the kitchenmaids, no humiliations. What a family they would have been! They would have had children, plenty of them, for Bess was made to bear children and he was made to beget children. He would have had to keep a curbing hand on Bess, but he would have liked that, just as he liked his horses to have spirit; and by now she would be close on forty; he would be seeing some of the wildness go out of her, and he would be glad of it. They would be popular. The best squire and squire's lady ever known in these parts! He was a good squire now . . . at times. Often he was ready to take an interest in his people; a helping hand here; a word of advice there. But if Bess had been with him all these years it would have been different. He knew they said of him: "Squire bain't a bad squire, for all he can't keep his lecher's eyes off our daughters!" They would not have said that if Bess had been with him. But now regrets were tempered with amusement. He drew himself up to his full height, which was close on six feet. His clothes were those of a country squire, sober in colour, useful rather than elegant, but today he was wearing fine lace at his throat and wrists. And Harriet, one of the few women who had never made him feel a spark of desire, was standing before him getting excited because he complimented her on her sloe wine.

Cruelty leaped up into his eyes. He was always most cruel when his pride was touched. Inwardly he laughed at Harriet, because Harriet's niece had scorned him. He foresaw fun; he was a man of his age, and fun to him meant laughing at someone in a weaker position than the one he enjoyed himself.

Life had been unkind to him. First offering Bess, then snatching her away; and then he had married Amelia. Poor long-suffering Amelia, whose mild submission to his passionate onslaughts infuriated him. She thought him coarse and vulgar; she had never said so; she was too deeply aware of her wifely duty to criticise her husband, but unspoken criticism had been more difficult to bear for a man of his temperament. He had determined to put her out of countenance; perhaps that was why he had flaunted Jennifer before her.

He thought of Jennifer now, as he smiled at Harriet over the sloe wine. Jennifer's fierce little body; Jennifer's parted lips. Jennifer was a devil, but she amused him more than anyone had amused him since Bess; she gave him something of that satisfaction which he had always believed he would have got from Bess. Passionate and calculating, she was clever, methodically clever; she wanted to step up from children's nurse and general housekeeper to mistress of the house. He knew it—it made him laugh. "What's the point of marrying you, Jennifer? What do I get out of it, eh? I mean what more do I get out of it?" He could be decidedly cruel and blunt. He liked to watch her rage; he liked to see her stalk to the door, threaten to leave his house; he liked all that. He had said: "Be reasonable, Jennifer. Why should I marry you? You want children? All right—have children!" What a rage she was in! But she wouldn't go; she hoped she would beat him in the end. Never, Jennifer! Never, my dear!

He rocked backwards and forwards on his heels, and looked at Harriet.

"How you manage this house so well, with just those two sluts, I don't know, Harry. I really do not. But soon you'll be having your niece to help you."

Harriet tossed her head.

"I'm not hoping for much from that quarter, I can tell you, George Haredon."

He smiled; then he thought of her sitting in the window seat, looking so like Bess that he wanted to kill or make love to her, or perhaps both. When he half-closed his eyes he could almost see the red blood in them. He opened them and saw Harriet, very proud of her neat and orderly home, straight from her still-room. She's got a body like a board! he thought, and tried to imagine himself married to her. Different from marriage to Amelia, of course, for however similar, no two women were alike. More spirit than Amelia, this one had. Would it be possible to raise the blacksmith's daughter in her?

Harriet cast down her eyes. He is thinking of marriage, she sensed; and she was faintly alarmed. The marriage in her thoughts would be very different from a marriage of reality. She took a step backwards.

"Ah!" he said. "I got the idea that you were having the girl here to help you in the house."

"Help me!" She was the outraged housewife. "I can run my own house, thank you, George. I'm having her because it is my duty to have her. Could I let her stay in London with the company her mother doubtless kept!"

"Nevertheless," said the squire slowly, "she has kept that company." A dull anger burned suddenly in him. Doubtless she had, and how haughty she had been with him!

"I shall be severe with her, if I find it necessary," said Harriet. "She will lead a sheltered life here with me, meeting only my friends."

31

"What a wise woman you are, Harriet!" He smacked his lips over the sloe wine.

"Another, George?"

"Thank you, Harriet. I could not say no to wine like yours."

When he took the glass from her his fingers touched hers. She was calm, though aware of that gesture, he thought. He wanted to laugh. Queer, how sane women like Harriet Ramsdale had their crazy moments! And she was crazy; he thought of the two of them together—like mating a bull with a hinny!

"You're amused, George. May I ask you to share the joke?"

"No joke really—just enjoying the wine and your company. But what I came for, Harriet, was this. She'll come to Exeter, I suppose?"

"Why, yes."

"The coach is due in this evening. You're meeting her?"

"I thought of driving in the trap."

"A long journey for you, Harry. How'd it be if I sent one of my coachmen with the carriage? Jennifer could go to bear her company on the way back."

Her eyes glittered a little as she raised them to his.

"It's a very kind offer, George. But what trouble to put you to!"

He laid a hand on her shoulder. Boney, she was; bonier than Amelia. Never did like thin women, thought the squire.

"I'd like to do it for you, Harriet."

"Well, George! Well!"

Coy as a schoolgirl, and immensely gratified! He felt suddenly flat.

"I'll be getting along, Harriet. I'll send Jennifer in to meet the girl."

She stood at the door, watching him go striding out to his waiting carriage. Why, she wondered, had he not spoken? She had been sure he was going to.

Leave-taking was difficult. They sat side by side in the coach now, their hands touching.

Darrell whispered: "I shall be thinking of you every minute until I see you again."

"And that will be soon," she answered.

He knew her aunt's house. It stood back from the road, and near it was a little wood; if she came out of her aunt's house and turned right she would see the wood. It would shelter them for their first meeting, and that should be tomorrow evening at eight o'clock. It would be better to wait for evening. He would come to her on his uncle's chestnut mare, and wait for her just inside the wood; he would tell her what his Uncle Gregory had said about their marrying, because that was a matter he would discuss with him at the earliest possible moment.

"It is not real parting," said Kitty, and smiled up at his clearcut, handsome face and rather delicate features.

The coach rumbled on. The merchant and the matron were discussing Exeter, and every occupant of the coach was excited because they were nearing the end of the long journey. Under cover of such conversation it was possible to exchange vows of eternal affection.

"I thought you were wonderful, when I first saw you. I could just see your mouth; your hat hid the rest of your face."

She laughed softly and pressed closer to him.

"You stared so!"

"How could I help that?" he murmured. "And Kitty . . . now I have got to know you I've learned that you are more wonderful than I ever thought anyone could be."

He kissed her ear, and they laughed and looked round the coach. Had anyone seen? Who cared if they had!

The coach rumbled into Exeter and pulled up in the inn yard. The door was flung open.

"Perhaps," whispered Kitty, "I had better not introduce you to my aunt . . . yet. Perhaps it would be better to wait a while and see . . ."

There was bustling to and fro whilst the luggage was unloaded.

Kitty stood with her bags beside her, looking around her for Aunt Harriet.

A woman was coming towards her—a small woman in a dark cloak and hood. She stood before her; she had sharp, darting black eyes.

"Are you Miss Kitty Kennedy, who is on her way to Miss Ramsdale?"

"Why, yes. Are you . . . my Aunt Harriet?"

Laughter shook the thin shoulders momentarily.

"No. But I have come to meet you. I have a carriage here to take you to your aunt's house." She looked round and beckoned; a man came and picked up Kitty's bags.

Kitty turned and smiled at Darrell who had stood by, watching. His face looked bleak, she thought, but there was no time to ponder on that, for her companion was hurrying her into a carriage.

33

The door was slammed. The woman sat back, studying Kitty, and Kitty studied her.

She had thrown back the hood of her cape and disclosed dark, rather frizzy hair; her brows were dusky, her dark eyes large yet alert. Kitty felt them taking in every detail of her appearance. She wondered if she were a servant of her Aunt Harriet's; her manner was a little arrogant, hardly that of a servant.

The carriage rolled out of the yard.

"Do tell me your name," said Kitty.

"Jennifer Jay."

"And my aunt . . ."

"I have come to meet you on Squire Haredon's behalf." She stopped, watching the colour flood into the girl's face.

"But," stammered Kitty, "why? I was going to my Aunt Harriet . . ."

"So you are. But Squire Haredon thought it would be helpful . . . to your aunt . . . to send his carriage."

"I see. He is very friendly with my aunt?"

A scornful smile twisted the woman's mouth.

"He has known her for a number of years." Jennifer leaned forward. "I expect you are very like your mother."

"I am supposed to be. You knew my mother?"

"Hardly! She left this place years ago, did she not? I am twenty-one. Besides, I did not live here as a child."

"It was good of Squire Haredon to send his carriage."

"He is a generous man . . . at times," said Jennifer.

Yes, she was thinking, why had he gone to all this trouble for Harriet Ramsdale? She wanted to marry him, the sly old virgin! And she thought no one knew it. She, Jennifer, knew it; even those half-witted sluts, who worked for her, knew it. The squire knew it; there were times when she could almost get him to laugh with her over it. There were times when it was possible to get almost anything out of the squire. But he was hot tempered; the last time she had mentioned Harriet's name he had shut her up roughly; she had thought he was going to strike her. It wouldn't have been the first time, brute that he was! Like a great bull sometimes, rushing at you angrily . . . and then getting amorous. A smile lifted the side of her mouth.

And now this niece. Disdainful beauty! He would surely be impressed, but he wasn't the sort to press where he wasn't wanted. And who was the young man with the girl when she had got out of the coach, looking at her with those dove's eyes? This was going to be exciting, if a little dangerous.

It might be a good idea to find out all she could. Knowledge usually came in useful. She had a sharp tongue—it was one of the things which amused the squire. It was an easy matter to get into his bed; any kitchenmaid could do that; the art lay in staying there.

"You had a pleasant journey?" she asked conversationally. "Good companions?"

"Very."

"I thought one of the young men who got out of the coach looked as if he might be a charming travelling companion."

How easy it was to make her blush!

"Did you?"

"Yes. I thought he had specially friendly glances for you."

"I think," said Kitty slowly, "that you must be referring to Mr. Grey. His uncle, he was telling us, lives in Exeter."

"Mr. Grey . . . I do not know him. You see, I came here only four years ago. I don't know Mr. Grey, but as I said, he is a personable young man and, I should think, a pleasant travelling companion."

She would garnish the story of this journey she would tell the squire with a description of the flushing young woman who had perhaps been a little indiscreet with a handsome Mr. Grey. She could always make Haredon laugh, and when she made him laugh she was the mistress of the situation . . . always. She even thought at such times that he really was imagining her at his table, entertaining his guests; after all, it would soon be forgotten that she had come to his house as governess to his children and had been his mistress before she became his wife.

Kitty said quickly, to turn the conversation from Darrell: "And you . . . you are a friend of Squire Haredon's?"

Jennifer's head tilted proudly.

"I am in charge of his children."

"That must be interesting. Tell me about the children."

"There are two of them. Margaret is nearly two years old; Charles is five."

Kitty smiled encouragingly. It was more pleasant to think of the squire as a family man.

"I am fond of children; and you must be too, since you have chosen the task of taking care of them."

"I did not choose it—it was thrust upon me. I was at a school for young ladies when my father died suddenly. It was a shock to me to learn that I was penniless. There was nothing to do but earn my living—it had not been intended that I should—so I acquired this post! Margaret was not born then."

Her eyes were sly, Kitty thought, and wondered what made them so. Jennifer was thinking of her arrival at Haredon, and of the interest she had aroused in the squire right from the beginning; hotly pursuing in those days; quite gallant; now he blew hot and cold. She had been sorry for poor Amelia, but that had not stopped her from thinking of Amelia's husband. Amusing! Great fun, keeping him at bay! He could be so angry when frustrated; he had no finesse, the great bull! But when Amelia had died that had seemed like fate. Good God, she needed luck, and in those days Amelia's death had looked like luck. He would marry again. Weakly, but with an element of cunning, she gave in to him; she had thought that was the way. Perhaps it was; she wasn't sure. She had that in her which could enslave a man . . . up to a point. She looked at the girl opposite with faint contempt. She was too sure of her beauty, that girl, to think of much else, and beauty was not all-sufficient; wit came into it; the power to make a man laugh, to find the vulnerable spot. Cleverness was every bit as important as beauty. When she thought of that she was stimulated.

"Oh . . ." said Kitty, "the squire's wife . . ."

"She is dead."

Now why did her eyes cloud suddenly like that, as though she were sorry Amelia had died? Soft, this girl! But those eyes, that skin and that mouth! He must be interested, if only momentarily.

"It was after the birth of Margaret; she went to be churched. It was in November, and November can be a damp, unhealthy month in this part of the world."

"Poor lady!" said Kitty. "And poor little children!"

"They are well looked after," said Jennifer almost tartly, and then the secret smile twisted her lips. And so is the squire, she said to herself.

"You know my aunt?" asked Kitty.

Jennifer tossed her head.

"I have not visited her," she said with scorn. "A governess does not visit the gentry."

The carriage rolled on. Kitty closed her eyes; she was not looking at the immediate future; she was looking beyond, to marriage with Darrell.

"You are doubtless tired," said Jennifer. "Close your eyes and doze a little."

Kitty smiled and kept her eyes closed; it removed the necessity of talking to Jennifer, for which she was rather pleased. There was something about the little woman, strange and unfathomable, that was almost anger, and Kitty never had any real desire to fathom. She thought of Darrell, of the fine down on his cheeks and the sudden hard pressure of his mouth on hers.

Harriet heard the carriage draw up, and went out to receive her niece.

She gasped at the sight of Kitty. A young woman, a sophisticated London young woman with clothes that were much too fine for the country, who appeared so startlingly like Bess that she felt the resentment she had always felt towards her pretty sister surging up in her. And with her, that creature from Haredon, looking demure enough in her sober cape; but whenever Harriet saw her she could not shut out of her mind the stories she had heard; imagination could be a mocking enemy—it forced pictures into your mind, and though you tried to ignore them and make your mind a blank, the pictures remained.

Kitty stepped out of the carriage, and the coachman brought in her baggage.

Most definitely, decided Harriet, that creature should not be asked in to drink a glass of cowslip wine. It was really very thoughtless of George to send her to meet a niece of Harriet Ramsdale. If the stories one heard of this woman were true, it was a wicked thing for George to have sent her. Unchasity in George himself was forgivable, because God had made men unchaste creatures; but the women, without whom of course the unchasity of men could not have been, were pariahs, to be despised, to be turned from, to be left to suffer the results of unbridled sin and wickedness. She hated to think of it; she would rather think of her cool still-room or garden laid out with her own hands. But when she was near women such as this one, pictures forced themselves into her mind and would not be ousted.

"Kitty!" she said, and took the girl's hand. Bess's eyes and Bess's mouth! Her skin was flushed and her dress was too low-cut and revealing. Harriet thought uneasily: Is this going to be Bess all over again?

She said: "I have a meal waiting for you." Then she looked through the carriage window. "I shall convey my thanks to the squire." Jennifer's head was tilted higher and her eyes were really insolent. The first thing Harriet would do, if she married the squire, would be to dismiss that girl.

As Harriet led her through the door to the cool hall, Kitty heard a movement on the stairs, and saw two young excited faces peering down at her. She took off her hat and put it on the oak chest there. Harriet looked at it—could not stop looking at it. It was such a ridiculous hat and, lying there, it spoiled the order of the orderly house. "I do not like litter, my dear. Take up your hat; you can hang it in a cupboard I have cleared in your room."

Kitty felt chilled by the neatness all around her. Tears suddenly stung her eyelids, and she thought of her mother's apartment with the cosmetics arrayed before her mirror, and the trail of powder across her dressing-table, and the fluffy garments flung down anywhere. Oh, to be back there! But then she would not have met Darrell, and loving and being loved by Darrell was going to be glorious.

She smiled dazzlingly. Harriet was a little shocked by the smile; it expressed such confidence in life, and she, a good and virtuous woman whose future was secure, had never felt that confidence. Bess had had it though; here was Bess all over again.

"Come and eat," she said.

Everything was spotlessly clean. There was cold mutton on the table and fruit pie. Kitty put her hat on her head, since there seemed nowhere else to put it, and sat down at the table.

"Peg!" called Harriet. "Bring a glass of ale."

"Peg?" said Kitty. "Who is Peg?"

"My maid. A lazy, good-for-nothing piece if ever there was one. And the same applies to Dolly, my other maid. I hope you have brought some recipes from London."

"Recipes?" Kitty found that so funny that she began to laugh, and because tears had been so near it wasn't possible to stop laughing. Peg came in and stared at the newcomer, then she began to laugh.

"Please, please!" cried Harriet. "I do not . . . I will not . . ."

But they went on laughing, and Dolly came and peeped round the door.

Harriet's face was full of anger. Kitty saw this, and stopped.

"I am sorry. It was just the thought of my mother jam-making. She never did, you know; she never thought of things like that. If she wanted jam she just got it out of a pot; she would never *think* of how it got there."

Peg and Dolly were staring in frank amazement at this young lady from another world. Dolly was even so bold as to come close and touch the stuff of her dress.

"Dolly! Peg! Leave this room at once," ordered Harriet, "and don't dare enter it until I send for you, unless you wish to feel the whip about your shoulders."

When they had gone, Kitty said: "I am sorry. I expect that was my fault—only the thought of my mother making jam was so funny."

"You are evidently amused very easily!"

Kitty began to eat. Poor old Aunt Harriet, she thought; she didn't look as if she had a very happy time. It must be wearying living in this place, with only recipes and clean floors to think of. How gloomy the prospect, if she had not met Darrell! But, of course, meeting Darrell had changed everything. Perhaps, if she hadn't met him, she wouldn't be saying *poor* Aunt Harriet, but would just be disliking her. You couldn't dislike anyone when you were in love; you were only sorry for people like Aunt Harriet.

She ate the fruit pie and drank the ale, and all the time Aunt Harriet talked. She talked of what she would expect Kitty to do; there was the garden; there was the house; so many tasks to be performed, as Kitty could imagine, and it was Aunt Harriet's pride and joy to keep her house clean and shining, and her garden beautiful. Was Kitty fond of fine needlework? No? That could be improved. Did she play the spinet? Dear! Dear! Her education had been neglected. Aunt Harriet confessed that she had been prepared for that, and she added, almost indulgently, she was not sure that she would not rather work on virgin soil.

Kitty watched a harassed bee buzzing and banging himself ineffectually against the window-pane. Her thoughts were on the bee, not on what Aunt Harriet was saying. And from the bee they went to Darrell . . . A whole day to be lived through before she saw him. She wondered how she would slip out of the house; she had an idea that Aunt Harriet would be a watchful person, not easy to deceive. The thought stimulated her rather than anything else. Perhaps she would run away with Darrell. She was sure Aunt Harriet was the sort of person who would never approve of their marriage.

"If you would care to see your room," Aunt Harriet was saying, "I will show it to you. You could unpack your things and then come down and take a walk in the garden. I could show you what I hope you will make your duties there. What a lovely thing is a garden! Do you not think so? I always consider it a privilege to be allowed to work in my garden . . ."

They went up the stairs; everything smelt of soap.

"Your room!" said Aunt Harriet. It was a pleasant enough room, rather bare it seemed after her room in her mother's apartment, but good since it was to be hers, and she would enjoy privacy in it. "I shall expect you to keep it clean your-

39

self. I cannot lay extra burdens on the shoulders of those two stupid girls. Heaven knows they drive me to distraction now with their follies."

Kitty unlocked her trunk. Aunt Harriet was kneeling beside it, thrusting her hands into the folds of gowns and mantles.

"What elegance!" She was both grim and prim. "You will not have need of it here in the country. We can alter these things though; are you handy with your needle?" She made a little clicking noise with her tongue. "Your mother was most unsuited for motherhood; it seems she neglected you badly."

"She never did!" cried Kitty in revolt. "I loved being with her. She was a lovely person. She was the best mother in the world!" Her hands were buried beneath silk and fine merino. She took out the miniature and looked into the lovely, laughing face portrayed there. Harriet, full of curiosity she could not understand, peered over her shoulders and gazed at the magnificent bosom and the bare white shoulders.

"It was done," said Kitty, "by an artist who loved her."

Harriet drew a sharp breath, and the jealousy she had felt for Bess was there in that room as strong as it had been twenty years before.

"It is . . . immodest! A man who . . . loved her! Oh! I can well imagine the life she led—I can imagine it! She was born wicked. A wanton creature!" Pictures crowded into Harriet's mind. The squire and the hard-faced woman who looked after his children, Bess and men . . . vague men. She put her hands to her face, covered her eyes, but the pictures remained. And when she uncovered them, a girl with blazing eyes faced her.

"How dare you!" cried Kitty, and tears spilled from her wonderful eyes and ran down her cheeks. "How dare you say those things about my mother! She was good . . . good . . . better than anyone else in the world, and I loved her . . ."

Kitty threw herself on to the bed and began to sob now as she had been unable to sob since her mother's death. Harriet stared in dismay, first at the girl's shaking shoulders, then at her feet on the clean counterpane. She wanted to protest; she wanted to whip the girl; but she did neither; she just turned on her heel and hurried out of the room. In the corridor she paused. What a handful! Bess all over again! She would subdue the girl, though. She would force the wickedness out of her, just as she would have forced it out of Bess had she been old enough.

Kitty was stifled in that house. It seemed that everything she did was contrary to her aunt's wishes. At first she tried hard to please; she sat stitching with Harriet in the drawing-room until her head ached; she bent over the garden beds until her back ached; she worked in the still-room but hated the stains of fruit juice on her fingers, and she had no aptitude for the work.

How can she be so stupid! thought Harriet.

How can she care so much for all these things that do not matter! wondered Kitty. And she dreamed of Darrell, and thought of meetings in the wood, and of the day they would go to London together, for his Uncle Gregory had said he was too young to marry, and Darrell was hoping for support from his Uncle Simon in London.

"Wool gathering!" Harriet would snap. "Head in the clouds! I do declare I've got an idiot for a niece."

Kitty would merely smile and hug her secret to herself.

Insolent! Harriet would tell herself. Not a bit contrite! I believe she's laughing at me! But Kitty was not laughing at Aunt Harriet; she was only sorry for her, because she had no lover to meet in the wood and must spend all her enthusiasm on preserves and her kitchen garden.

Every evening at dusk she slipped out of the house. Darrell would be waiting for her in the wood. He would kiss her and fondle her, and she would look up into his face and think how good to look upon he was and how much older he seemed than the very young man she had first seen in the coach.

"Why," he cried impatiently, "do they put obstacles before us? 'Wait!' says my Uncle Gregory. How can we wait! Kitty, how can we?"

It was difficult. There she was before him, very young, desirable and desirous, Bess's daughter. Very soft and so ready to yield; he dreamed of the way she quivered when he put his hands on her shoulders. He loved her tenderly as well as passionately. He had written to his Uncle Simon in London, and Uncle Simon was more human, more understanding than Uncle Gregory. A large, red-faced man, Uncle Simon, whereas Uncle Gregory was tall and thin. Uncle Simon was a free thinker; he liked to foregather with his cronies in coffee and chocolate houses, and listen to the talk; he liked a carousal in a tavern; he liked women. Besides, he was ready to approve of anything of which Uncle Gregory did not. So Darrell had written, "and we want to marry. Uncle Simon, we *must* marry! At the moment we meet in a wood. She has a strict old aunt, and I have Uncle Gregory . . ." He had tried to word it so as to make Uncle Simon laugh as well as to arouse his sympathy. He had great hopes of Uncle Simon. Still, he did not let his hands rest too long upon her shoulders, nor look too much at her red, soft lips; he tried not to notice how green was the grass and how soft and beautiful the bank with the violets growing there. It seemed to him too that the birds were urging him to love, mocking him a little. There was a song of Shakespeare's that kept running through his head:

> "And therefore take the present time,
> With a hey, and a ho, and a hey nonino . . ."

For himself he would take all the present had to offer, but he loved her very tenderly, and outside the wood with its soft carpet of grass, its sheltering trees and mocking birds, the world was a cruel place.

The two girls, Peg and Dolly, knew of the meetings with Darrell, but there was nothing to fear from this. Kitty had given Peg a girdle of silk and Dolly a lace handkerchief, and no one had ever given them anything but advice and blows before. The clothes they had worn in the workhouse were payment for hard work; their board and lodging with Harriet were payment for more hard work. But the girdle and the handkerchief were simply gifts, for she had given them, asking nothing in return. But even without the gifts they would have been on her side. She was beautiful and she was kind; they had no learning, but they did know it was natural to love. So they would carry messages for her, and whisper together about her, and try to be a little like her. They had made constant use of the pump in the yard since the arrival of Kitty; they washed their garments. Peg wore the girdle on her quilted petticoat of flannel; Dolly carried the handkerchief tucked inside her bodice.

Two weeks passed in this way. The squire was a frequent caller. He sat in the garden and complimented Harriet on her flowers, and he studied her vegetables with what seemed like real interest. It could mean only one thing, thought Harriet, and she lay awake at night thinking of it.

She thought it was a pity that Bess had had to die just at this time and force on her the duty of looking after her daughter. For she did not understand Bess's daughter; she was almost rude to the squire, and he never seemed resentful, never even seemed to notice it. Sometimes he would look at her from under his bushy brows as though he were puzzled and interested—but then, if you planned to marry a lady, you would be interested in her relations! Now and then, when Kitty was offhanded with the squire and made Harriet cold with indignation and humiliation, he would turn to her, Harriet, and be so charming, almost like an accepted lover, as though he would teach the girl a lesson in good manners. It was gratifying, intensely so. Once she said to Kitty: "I do not understand you; you are positively unmannerly towards Squire Haredon!" And Kitty turned on her with flashing eyes, and cried out: "I hate that man!" Hate! What a word for a lady to use! And what had the squire ever been towards Kitty but indulgent, ready to overlook her rudeness? "You will never find a husband if you persist in those manners, my girl!" she had said severely, for the girl was as vain as a peacock, and she thought that the best way of piercing her armour. And Kitty angrily turned on her with: "Your excellent manners did little to help you in that respect!" And then, just like Bess, all fury one moment and full of ridiculous demonstrations the next: "I'm sorry, Aunt Harriet. I didn't mean that, of course. I know . . . there must have been people who would have liked to marry you . . . if you had wanted them . . . but . . . I do hate Squire Haredon. I can't explain, but I do." And Harriet had said: "Indeed, you foolish girl, you cannot explain; but I will thank you to be more civil to my guests."

It went on like that for three weeks, with the squire a constant visitor, until one hot afternoon, a lovely afternoon when the roses were at their best and the lavender was full of fragrance with the bees dancing a wild delight about it.

Harriet, from her sewing-room on the first floor, thought she heard the sound of carriage wheels on the road; she looked from her window, but the trees were too thick with leaves for her to see the road clearly now. She returned to her sewing. At any moment now Peg or Dolly would come to announce the arrival of the squire, and perhaps this very afternoon he would ask the question which must have been on his lips for weeks now, perhaps for years.

But the expected tap on her door did not come, so, she told herself, it must have been someone else's carriage she had heard on the road. Feeling restive, she remembered how dry the dahlias had looked that morning. Poor things, they got little sun, tucked away near the summer-house. If she wanted a good crop when the more spectacular flowers had faded she must give them a little care. So she went downstairs and took her watering-can.

She heard voices as she approached the summer-house. Kitty's voice! The squire's voice! Then it *had* been the squire's carriage she had heard. She hastened forward, for she knew

43

how unmannerly Kitty could be. She hoped . . . She stopped suddenly and leaned against the laburnum tree, which in spring time showered its yellow blossoms over the roof of the summer-house. Their voices floated out to her; the squire's was thick, Kitty's shrill.

"Look here," said the squire, "be reasonable, Kitty. God knows I've been patient. Why do you think I've been coming here like this . . . nigh on every day? To see you! And you know it, you little she-devil! Think I haven't seen that look in your eyes? Now listen, Kitty, I'll marry you . . ."

Kitty cried: "Don't dare touch me! I tell you I hate you. Nothing would make me marry you. I think . . . I think . . ."

Harriet realised that the rough bark of the tree trunk, pressed against her forehead, was hurting her. She stopped to pick up the watering-can which had fallen from her limp fingers.

"I hated you," Kitty was saying, "that first evening at the inn at Dorchester. I tell you, I hate the way you talk, and I hate the way you eat, and most of all I hate the way you look at me. Don't dare to touch me! I'll scream . . . I'll call my aunt . . ."

He laughed, coarsely, horribly; Harriet could bear to hear no more. She sped past the dahlia bed, across the lawn; she shut herself in her bedroom, feeling numb, and as the pictures crowded into her mind she made no attempt to shut them out. He was a beast! Why had she ever thought . . . ? And all the time he had been laughing at her! Letting her believe that he contemplated marriage with her. Thank God she had never betrayed her own thoughts! Thank God her father's training had taught her restraint! "Little she-devil . . ." The slur in his voice when he said that . . . you could hear frightful things in his voice, lascivious things. Oh, this was relief. She would never sit at his table now; she would never be the squire's lady; but now she could look straight at the ordeal of sharing his bed and not be afraid, because it would never happen to her. She must suppress anger; she must nourish relief. That evening in Dorchester! Now she knew why he had sent the carriage. And Kitty, the sly creature, was her mother all over again, with wantonnesss in her eyes. It was a duty now to prevent the girl from following in her mother's footsteps. She should be guarded with vigilance.

Up and down her room paced Harriet. She took her keys and went to the still-room; here was comfort. So clean, so neat—what joy in regarding those labelled bottles! Here was

44

her life. All thoughts of George Haredon were to be thrust out of it for ever. Never again should she be so deceived!

Someone was knocking on the door.

"Come in!" she said calmly, and Peg came in and told her that the squire had arrived and was downstairs in the garden.

She went out to greet him. How grateful she was to her father! She had inherited no luscious charm from her mother, but she must be grateful for her father's serene spirit.

"How do you do?"

His face was red and angry; he looked bewildered and younger than he had for a long time, almost as though he could not understand why the world was so unkind to him.

"How good of you to call, George!"

He sprawled on the wooden seat under the chestnut tree, sullen, trying to pretend nothing unusual had happened.

"You will drink a dish of tea, George? Peg will be bringing it—I told her to, when I knew you were here."

"You're too good to me, Harriet!"

"Stuff and nonsense! Because I offer you a dish of tea?"

She noticed how thick his legs were; she shivered. He had coarsened since the days of her youth when she had built an ideal and called it George Haredon. She believed the stories about him now; yes, she did, and she would admit it. She was angry; she was hurt; but the feeling of relief was there all the same.

"I will send for my niece. Where does the girl get to? A lazier, more good-for-nothing creature I never set eyes on, unless it's Peg or Dolly. Curling her hair, no doubt! Of all the empty-headed girls . . ."

In a way she was trying to comfort him. She was quite sorry for him—almost as sorry for him as she was for herself. It was Kitty she blamed; just as she had blamed Bess. You didn't blame men for being what they were; you blamed women for helping to make them so.

She left him sitting, and went indoors.

"Tell my niece to come down to the garden," she instructed Peg. "Tell her I particularly wish her to come."

Kitty came. On her lovely hair she wore a hat which shaded her eyes and shielded her face. She greeted the squire coldly. Harriet was amazed to see that there was a certain humility in the manner of his greeting to her; she had never seen George Haredon humble before, except perhaps when he was very young and so much in love with Bess. Kitty was almost haughty—ridiculous creature, giving herself airs! How she would like to beat Kitty until the blood ran! Once, before the days of Peg and Dolly, she had almost beaten one of her maids to death; a child of fifteen, a trollop if ever there was one! Got herself with child by one of Squire Haredon's grooms. And Harriet had beaten her and beaten her and when she grew big had turned her out. No one knew what had become of her after she left the bridewell. She was probably leading the life most suited to her nature. Well, that was how Harriet would have liked to beat Kitty . . . only Kitty was no child of fifteen; she was a strong young woman, and probably would not allow herself to be beaten almost to death.

The squire scarcely touched his tea, and he forgot to compliment her on the excellence of her seedcake. He was discomfited, and all because of his carnal desire for a girl who would be a disgrace to his house; why, she had no idea even how to make raspberry jam.

The squire took his leave. Kitty carried in the tea tray and, in her agitation, broke one of the cups.

Harriet screamed at her: "You lazy, careless creature! I wish I had never clapped eyes on you. A pity you did not stay in London where you belonged. Doubtless you would have found the protection of some fine gentleman, as your mother did so admirably for herself!"

Once Kitty would have laughed at that; the words would not have hurt her at all. But now she was jealous of her virtue; Darrell was involved. Her aunt was suggesting that this love she was so willing, so eager to give to Darrell, could have been any fine gentleman's in exchange for his protection. She turned on her aunt with fury.

"You wicked woman!" she cried. "And more wicked because you think you are so good. I will not stay here; I shall go away."

"And where will you go, Miss?"

Kitty faltered. She was ready to blurt out: "I am going to be married. I shall go with my husband!" But even at that moment, hot tempered as she was, she realised what folly that would be.

"I . . . shall go one day!"

Harriet laughed. And for one moment she knew that her place in the squire's bed had occupied her imagination far more than her place at the head of his table; and she knew that she was a disappointed woman, and felt an insane desire to go to the still-room and smash every one of those neat bottles. She tried to calm herself; but she could not. In a moment she would be sobbing out her disappointment. Angrily she

46

strode to the wall where hung that whip with which she had beaten the fifteen-year-old trollop who had been so free with one of George's grooms; she seized it, and her fingers were white with the tension of the grip upon it.

"You . . . you . . ." she cried, and there was almost a sob in her voice. "Do you think . . . I don't know . . . your kind! Do you think I haven't seen the way you led George Haredon on? I believe you let him into your room at night . . . perhaps others. I believe . . ."

The pictures were now forming into words, and she must stop herself—for shame she must! But Kitty stopped her. Kitty's eyes were blazing. She walked straight towards her, raised her hand as though to strike her, then dropped it and said in a cold low voice: "You wicked, foul-minded woman! You and George Haredon would make a good pair, that you would!" And she threw back her head so that the fine white voluptuousness of her throat could be seen to advantage. Then she laughed and went swiftly from the room.

Kitty stayed in her room until close on eight o'clock; then silently she left her Aunt Harriet's house and went to the wood.

Darrell was waiting for her in that spot where the trees were thickest. She clung to him, crying.

He said: "My dearest, what has happened?"

She cried out: "I cannot stay here; it is hateful! My aunt thinks hateful things of me. Darrell, she is a cruel woman, for all her piety. How I wish that we were in London and that my mother was alive; she would have helped us."

He said: "Listen, my lovely one, my darling Kitty, listen! You will not have to stay. Today I have heard from my Uncle Simon."

Her smile was more brilliant for the tears that still shone in her eyes; her joy the greater for the fear it displaced. "You have heard . . . He has said . . . ?"

"He says we must marry. He says we must leave this place and go to London."

"When . . . oh, when?"

Darrell hesitated.

"There must be preparations, dear one. In a month, say. Kitty, can you endure this for just one month longer?"

"A month! It is a long time. I have not yet been in my aunt's house three weeks, and it seems three years. Cannot we go now . . . this minute?"

He laughed at her impatience. They sat on a bank, and the

grass was soft and cool, and the trees made a roof and shut them in.

"If we could . . . oh, if we could! But no, dearest, we must do what Uncle Simon says. He is going to make preparations for us. He is going to take me into his business. He is going to find a house for us, and that will take a little time. Then, my darling, we shall take the coach and go to London, and when we get there a priest will marry us and we shall be happy, and all this will seem like a nightmare."

"Darrell! It is wonderful. How I love your Uncle Simon!"

"You must love no one but me!"

"I should not, of course, except our children, Darrell."

"Our children!" he said.

How the birds mocked overhead! He thought of their love-making on the branches of the trees, building their nests and bringing up their young. It was like a miracle—it was the miracle of living. And how much more wonderful to be a man and love a woman, a woman such as Kitty!

She had lain back on the grass now, and her eyes made the sky he could see through the branches look grey. Lovely she was, with her white bosom and fair neck and her hair a little tousled now, and her hands that seemed to be reaching to him.

She was seductive and irresistible; and because she knew it, and because she, like the birds, was mocking that cautious streak in him, he could no longer bear it. He threw himself down beside her and buried his face in the whiteness of her shoulder.

She said: "What a lovely end to a horrible day! Darrell, that hateful Squire Haredon asked me to marry him today."

Darrell drew himself up and looked at her with horror.

"Yes," she went on. "Oh, darling, don't look so frightened! I told him I hated him. He came upon me when I was in the summer-house, and tried to keep me there and force his horrible love-making on me. What a beast he is! Scarcely a man, I think—and how I hate the noisy way he breathes! You should hear him drink his tea, and it is as bad with coffee or chocolate. Hateful! Hateful! And I told him so."

He leaned on his elbows. Here in the woods was perfect peace and happiness; but outside terrible things could happen. He would write again to Uncle Simon; he would say a month was too long—or perhaps they would go to London without saying anything.

"He is powerful hereabouts," he said. "If he knew you loved me, he could rake up some minor charge against me."

"That would be wrong . . . that would be cruel . . ."

"It is a cruel world we live in, Kitty."

"But how gentle you are, Darrell! Perhaps that is why I love you. All the time, you think of me; not what you want, but what is best for me. I see it, Darrell, and I love you for it. You would die for me, I know; I would for you too."

"I do not want us to die, but to live for each other," he said.

"You are clever with words—and how I love you! Let us not think of Squire Haredon and my Aunt Harriet and your Uncle Gregory, nor of the cruel world we live in. How lovely it is here! How quiet! We might be alone in the world; do you feel that, Darrell?"

Her lips were parted. She was her mother and the black-smith's daughter. She loved; she loved passionately and reck-lessly; she was the perfect lover because love to her was all-important. There was no room in her mind for tomorrow; let others think of that.

He heard her laugh, a little mockingly, as he thought the birds laughed—invitingly, irresistibly. He felt the blood run hot through his veins. He was aware of the letter he had had from his Uncle Simon, crackling in his pocket when he moved.

He put his mouth on hers; her arms were about him. Only a month, he thought desperately; everything was really settled.

Inside the wood it was heaven. Outside was the cruel world. But did one think of the cruel world when one was in heaven?

Meetings in the wood took on a new joy. Kitty lived for them, scarcely aware of the days. Harriet watched her slyly, watched the rapture in her eyes, and thought, I believe she will marry the squire after all. I believe all that talk of hating him was coquetry. Was that how Bess did it?

And because the greatest terror of her life was that it might be discovered that she herself had contemplated marriage with the squire, she talked to him of Kitty.

"I felt, George, that right from the time you set eyes on her she reminded you so much of Bess that you had quite an af-fection for her."

What a keen glance he had shot at her from under those bushy eyebrows of his!

"You're a fanciful woman, Harry!"

"I'm a woman with my eyes open. Why, sometimes I could almost feel it was Bess herself smirking before her mirror, curling her hair and making herself a hindrance rather than a help about the house!"

He laughed at that.

"So that's how it is, Harriet."

"Mind you, if that is what was in your mind, and she was to know it and make a pretence of flouting you, I wouldn't take her seriously. She's a coquette; a born one, and made one by that mother of hers. She's the sort who would want to lead a man a dance . . ."

There! That had him. He was puzzled. He was beginning to think that Harriet had turned matchmaker. And how excited those words of her made him! He was ready to grasp any shred of hope, so badly did he desire the girl.

His visits to the house did not diminish. Kitty, though, hardly seemed aware of him. She passed through the days like a person in a dream, the passion in her making her long for the evenings. Meetings took place earlier now, for the days were getting shorter; so they had longer together. What good allies she had in Peg and Dolly! Sometimes she stayed in the wood until close on midnight, but Peg and Dolly never failed to watch for her return and creep down from the attic to let her in.

The days passed. Darrell heard from his Uncle Simon again. Uncle Simon was enthusiastic; he longed to see the beautiful girl whom Darrell described so eulogistically; he longed to score off old Gregory. He was getting ready for them; he would be ready for them very soon.

"Next Monday," said Darrell, "we will take the coach. We will meet here at midnight on Sunday; we shall have to walk into Exeter. We shall catch the very first coach, and we must take care not to be seen."

"Monday!" cried Kitty gaily. "Oh . . . in no time it will be Monday!"

Darrell was excited, making plans.

"One day this week I shall go to Exeter for my uncle; then I shall book our places on the Monday coach."

"It's wonderful! Wonderful!"

"And," cautioned Darrell, "a great secret, to be told to no one."

"You can trust me for that, though I should have liked to say goodbye to Peg and Dolly."

"You must say goodbye to no one. If this went wrong, Kitty . . ."

She laughed at him.

"How could it go wrong?"

She was so full of joy that she wanted everyone to share it. She worked hard in the garden; she tried to please Aunt Harriet; she even had a brief smile for the squire. She gave Peg a scarf and Dolly a petticoat. She just wanted everyone around her to be happy.

She met Darrell as usual on Wednesday evening. What a glorious evening it was! The air soft and balmy, and no breeze to stir the branches of the trees.

Darrell said: "I shall be thinking of this all the way to Exeter tomorrow. When our places are booked it will seem as though we are already there. Kitty! You must not go back looking as happy as you look, or someone will guess!"

And she laughed, and they embraced; and then they lay there, talking of London and the future.

It was past midnight when Kitty returned to her aunt's house, but Peg, wearing her scarf, let her in.

All next day she was absent-minded. Harriet noticed.

"What has come over you, girl?" she demanded. "You are not even as bright as usual!"

Kitty smiled very sweetly; she could afford to be patient with Aunt Harriet. Her thoughts were all with Darrell, riding to Exeter on his uncle's chestnut mare.

She went to the wood that evening. He did not come. She returned home a little subdued. Why, of course he had not got home from Exeter; that was the reason he had not come. He had said he might have to stay the night if he could not conclude his uncle's business, but would certainly be home on Saturday.

On Saturday she was waiting for him. How quiet was the wood! She had never noticed that so much before. There were few birds now and the leaves were thick, some already beginning to turn brown at the edges. A gloomy place, the wood, when you waited for a lover who did not come.

She was anxious now; she was frightened. What could have happened to detain him? Business? Suppose he did not return by Monday; they had made no plans for such an occurrence. What should she do? Go to Exeter alone? But how could she take the London coach alone? She would not know where to go when she arrived. She had not the money to pay her fare.

She ran through the trees; she gazed up and down the road. Once she heard the clop, clop, of horses' hoofs, and when the sound died away, the disappointment was intense. Lonely and desolate, she returned to the meeting place; he was not there. It grew dark.

Why had he not come? Here was Saturday, and he had not come.

Sunday was like a bad dream from which she was trying

desperately to escape. Perhaps he would send a message; he would know how frightened she must be, and he had ever been mindful of her comfort and her peace of mind.

On Sunday evening she went to the wood, and still he did not come.

Peg and Dolly crept into her room and found her sobbing on the bed. They eyed each other sadly. Perhaps they thought it was unwise to trust a lover too far. They cried with her. It was a cruel world, they said.

Monday, which was to have been a day of great joy, set in with teeming rain, and Kitty's heart was more leaden than the skies.

It was Peg who got the news. She kept it to herself for a while; then she told Dolly. They cried together; they did not know what to do. But if they did not tell her she would discover in some other way. So in the evening of that black Monday they told her. They tapped at her door and went in to find her sitting at her window, her lovely face distorted by grief, her beautiful hair in disorder.

"A terrible thing has happened," said Peg.

". . . to Lawyer Grey's nephew who went to Exeter," added Dolly.

"Though," put in Peg quickly, "it may be a story. Such stories are."

Dolly shook her head sadly. "He was seen to be took!"

Kitty stared in bewilderment from one to the other.

"And his horse was left there for hours, pawing the ground," said Peg sadly.

" 'Twas in a tavern . . . in broad daylight. The wicked devils, to take a man!"

Kitty looked at them wildly. The unreality of the day had faded, and stark tragedy was all that was left.

"What!" she cried. "What is it you are saying?"

"He went in for a glass of ale and maybe a sandwich."

"He was not the only one that was took."

"Tell me . . . tell me everything you know," pleaded Kitty, suddenly calm with a deadly calm.

"Such news gets round," said Peg wretchedly, shaking the tears out of her eyes. "There were them that saw it. The villains burst in . . . he was not the only one that was took."

Kitty stood up and gripped the rail of her chair.

"Peg . . ." she said. "Dolly . . ." And her mouth quivered like a child's.

Dolly threw herself down on the floor and put her arms round Kitty's knees, burying her face in her gown.

"It was they devils as folks call the press gang. Lurking everywhere, they be, to take our men to the ships."

Kitty stared blankly before her.

Peg said again, and then again, as though there was a grain of comfort in the words: "He were not the only one they took."

Kitty was numb with misery; listless, without spirit.

Harriet said: "Are you sickening for the pox, girl?" And she examined her body for some sign.

She went about the house, doing just what she was told. Harriet thought, I'm shaping her; she's improving. And when she knelt on the coconut matting beside her bed at night, she offered thanks for the change which had come over her wayward niece.

The squire was a more frequent visitor than ever. Kitty did not move away when he sat beside her on the garden seat. She listened to what he had to say, and gave him a listless yes or no.

The squire said: "It is quiet for you here, Kitty. Day after day going about the house and the gardens with your aunt—it is no life for a young girl. Now look here, we do a bit of entertaining now and then up at Haredon; why, sometimes I've got a houseful. Would you come, some time like that, eh, Kitty?"

She said: "I am all right here, thanks. I do not wish for a lot of people round me."

"Then a small party! Just you and your aunt . . . I'd like you to get to know my children."

She smiled.

"They are very charming," she said. "I have seen them driving with their governess."

From under his bushy eyebrows he looked shrewdly at her. What did she mean by that? Was she telling him she knew about his relationship with Jennifer? She was clever of course, this girl; clever as Bess had been. And he had never been sure what Bess might be thinking; why, right up to the end he had believed she was going to marry him, and all the time she must have had it in her head to run away with that actor fellow.

Women knew a lot about each other though. Harriet had said the girl was coquetting with him, leading him on. He liked to think that. He liked being led on. Cool and virtuous, holding him off, telling him she couldn't bear him, just to get him hot enough to offer marriage. He *had* offered marriage;

and she was still holding him off. She had been brought up in London Town where they were devilishly sly, and clever too—and, by God, he liked them for it! There were plenty of country wenches ready to fall into his lap; but Kitty was apart from that. Kitty was Bess, and Bess had haunted his life. Now here was compensation—he couldn't have Bess so he would have Kitty.

Sitting beside her, it was all he could do to hold himself in check. She had changed now; not the spitfire any more; calm, sad, wistful . . . womanly, you might say. She appealed now to something sentimental in him, as well as to his senses.

"I'll get rid of the woman!" he said, just in case she was jealous of Jennifer. "She was never much good as a governess."

"Oh! She looks capable enough."

Disdainful! It is nothing to me if she is your mistress! That was what she meant, confound her! He wanted to slap his thighs with delight. He knew the signs; he was like a small boy looking up at luscious fruit just out of reach, with the knowledge that sooner or later its very ripeness would make it fall right down into his hands.

"Capable . . . oh, yes. But why bother ourselves with servants on an afternoon like this!"

"I should have thought it was of the utmost importance to you, to bother with a servant who has the charge of your children."

"Now, Kitty . . ." His arm slid along the seat, but immediately she stiffened. He let his arm drop. No sense in rushing things; after all, he was not wholly sure that Harriet was right.

"Well, what about this visit of yours to Haredon?"

"You would have to arrange that with my aunt, would you not?"

"Why, of course, Kitty, of course!" His face was screwed up with delight.

Harriet came across the lawn. Her lips were pursed; they were always like that in repose. Peg followed her with the tea tray.

"A lovely day, George!"

"A perfect day," said George.

Daintily Harriet poured the tea. George took his and pressed his back against the seat. He was amused at himself, sitting here drinking tea with two women. He could have done with a pint of good ale. Still, here he was, doing the polite, and pretending to like it. He looked at the stiff figure of Harriet—poor woman! From her his gaze turned to Kitty and his

54

eyes were glazed with desire. But soon the fruit would fall into his hands; so much of the rebellion had gone out of her that it seemed as though the branch was already bending down to him. But he must go cautiously; he would say nothing now about this visit she would pay to Haredon. She was full of whims and fancies; she might refuse yet!

He sought for a topic of conversation.

"Lawyer Grey is in a fine to-do about that nephew of his!"

Kitty sat up straighter, but neither Harriet nor the squire noticed that.

"So I heard," said Harriet.

"A few years at sea will do the boy good. Roughing it never hurt anyone."

"I do agree," said she; "but will not Lawyer Grey try to do something about it?"

The squire laughed.

"What can he do? Fight the press gang? No! Mark my words, the young man's well out at sea by this time."

"He'll come back a man," said Harriet.

"If he comes back at all," said the squire. "There are dangers enough to be met with on the high seas."

Kitty lay in her bed and stared helplessly up at the ceiling. She was not thinking of Darrell now; she could think of nothing but the girl whom Aunt Harriet had whipped almost to death.

This could not be . . . not in addition to everything else! When she had heard them talking so callously down there in the garden, she had said to herself: I will wait for him! I will wait! And she had meant that if there were to be years and years of waiting, still she would wait. But those years had to be lived through, and how could she live through them, penniless, with a baby to care for?

How cruel was life! Darrell had been so anxious that no harm should befall her and it was only because they both believed so fervently that they would ride to London together that he had released his passion; and once he had done that he had been unable to stem it. She was shivering, but when Peg and Dolly peeped in to see how she was, they found her unnaturally flushed.

"Why, bless you, Miss Kitty, you have a fever!" said Peg.

She cried in panic: "Do not mention to my aunt that I am not well."

She got up and bathed her face. It was a good thing that Harriet, who had never been ill in her life, did not believe in illness. Unless it was a leg that was broken or a wound that she could see, she thought it was sham.

Kitty went about her tasks outwardly calm, inwardly in a tumult. She was forgetting her love for Darrell in her fear for herself. A terrible thing had happened to Darrell; but a still more terrible thing had happened to her.

If only her mother were here, she would know what to do. Nothing would ever turn her mother from her. She talked to her mother in her thoughts. You see, Mother, we loved each other so much, and we were going to London to be married. If only he hadn't gone to Exeter! If only he had stayed here, I should be married to him; we should be with his Uncle Simon in London, and we should be so happy because we should be going to have a child. But now there is no one to help me, Mother. Aunt Harriet is cold and distant, just as you said. She would never have done this thing which I have done; therefore she would think me wicked to have done it. There was a poor little girl from the workhouse, and she almost beat her to death. But what happened to her afterwards . . . when Aunt Harriet turned her out! That is what I think, Mother; that is what I cannot stop thinking.

And the very thought of her mother's face, lovely though ageing, and full of lazy kindness, soothed her. She would have understood; but she would have been practical too. She would surely have said: "We must find a husband for you, darling."

"Mother! Mother!" prayed Kitty. "*Do* something for me. Help me! Give me some sign that you know what has happened to me, and tell me what I can do."

She asked Peg and Dolly about the girl who had loved a groom. They had not known her but they had heard of her.

" 'Tis a terrible thing to happen to a girl," said Peg; and she and Dolly were silent for a long time thinking what a terrible thing it was to happen to a girl.

Kitty wanted to shout: "It has happened to me!" Something restrained her; she thought it was her mother, watching over her, restraining her. No one must know . . . yet . . . no one at all.

She and her aunt went to Haredon for a few days; the squire had sent the carriage for them.

A lovely house, Haredon; it had been built by a Haredon in the reign of Queen Anne. Harriet sat, lips pursed, as the carriage turned in at the drive. The gracious elms, the grey walls of the house had always filled her with pleasure. She thought of the land round Haredon, and especially the orchards; she thought of the staff of servants and the joy of running the place.

The squire came out to meet them, and from a window Jennifer Jay watched them.

Colour burned in Kitty's cheeks; her eyes were brilliant. Never, thought Squire Haredon, had she looked as beautiful as she did here in the setting which would soon be hers. She liked the house; perhaps she liked it so much that she was ready to take him, since he went with the house.

You wait! he thought. You wait, my beauty! And his fingers itched to seize her; and as they walked into the house he put his hand on her shoulder and gripped it hard; she turned her head and smiled at him, with her lips parted and a look of promise in her eyes. His hand slipped to her waist and touched the warmth of her bosom. She did not move away from him, and as they entered the house she was still smiling.

Dolman, the butler, brought drinks into the library. The squire touched her glass with his; she could see the veins standing out on his forehead—knotted they were, and blue, as if ready to burst. She felt more comforted than she had since she had lost Darrell, and it seemed to her then that this visit was her mother's answer to her prayers.

"I want to show Kitty round the place," said the squire, smiling into his glass. "I am proud of Haredon, Kitty."

"And rightly so, George," said Harriet with no trace in her voice of the wistfulness she felt; "it is a place to be proud of."

"Thank you, Harry. Now, Kitty!" He smacked his lips and licked the wine from them, and his eyes never left her. "Come now."

They left Harriet in the library with the squire's eldest cousin who had come to play hostess, and went over the house alone. It was indeed a beautiful place, so big that Kitty felt it would be easy to lose oneself in it. There were tall windows, ornate ceilings and deep window seats. Now and then Kitty heard the sound of footsteps hastily scurrying away; once a mob-capped serving maid, unable to escape in time, blushed hotly and dropped a deep curtsy; and in his free and easy way the squire made her stand before them, and he introduced Kitty as though she had already agreed to share his home. He seemed younger then, and she liked him better than she had ever liked him before. This was his castle and he was king; he was a showman watching the effect on her of his treasures.

"Do you like it, Kitty?"

"It is very grand!"

"Big though. Big for one man to live in . . . all alone."

She could laugh at that.

"As far as I can see, you are far from alone . . . here."

"You pick me up sharp, Kitty!" And he looked as if he liked being picked up sharp.

They were in the galleries, looking at portraits of the Haredon family.

"Do you think I take after them, Kitty?" he wanted to know, thrusting his face close to hers.

"I can see you better, not so close," she said, and he laughed and drew back. Wasn't that just the sort of thing Bess would have said! It was like having Bess here again. He thought of gripping the girl's shoulders and kissing her, and hurting her—hurting her for all the years he had been unable to forget Bess. "Yes," she went on, "there is a resemblance."

"Ah!" he said. "That's how it is with families; you are the spit of your mother, Kitty. There was a time, you know, when I was very fond of your mother."

"Most people were fond of her!"

"That was the trouble, Kitty! That was the trouble." He narrowed his eyes. He thought, by God, if you try any tricks with me, I'll well nigh kill you! Bess fooled me—I'll not stand for that treatment twice in a lifetime.

She said: "I want to see the children."

Jennifer stood up as they entered. She had been by the window, stitching something. He could see how violently her heart was beating under her tight bodice; she must learn to behave; more tantrums and out she would go; she gave herself airs because once he had found her amusing.

"Where are the children?" he asked curtly, and he wanted to give her a slap on the side of her face for her insolence.

She jerked her head towards the playroom, and his eyes looked straight into hers, cold and contemptuous. Kitty went forward. Jennifer almost barred his way; he pushed her aside without looking at her.

The children sat side by side on a window seat. The boy had a book of pictures on his lap, and the little girl was looking over his shoulder. She was a sweet little thing, thought Kitty; not yet three, she had large eyes not unlike the squire's but hers were blue and lovely and innocent. She smiled up at Kitty through dark lashes, and Kitty stooped and kissed her, feeling a sudden rush of tears to her eyes; for the first time she was not afraid of this thing which had happened to her;

she thought only of how wonderful it would be to have a daughter of her own.

The squire looked on, surprised. Real tears in her eyes, and all for little Margaret! He put out a hand and touched the child's shoulders; he felt suddenly happy. Now, after years of dissatisfaction, everything was going to be right for him. He had lost Bess, but he could laugh at Bess now. She would be getting old if she were here—too fat, the bloom all gone. In her place, Bess's daughter! Bess again, only young, just as Bess would have been had he married her all those years ago. They would have children; he would no longer be troubled by his desire for any attractive woman who came near him; he was convinced that he could find complete satisfaction with this girl, just as he would have found it with her mother. Now he would marry her, and he would grow into that squire he had always wanted to be. They would respect him hereabouts; they would love him. That was what he wanted; he wanted to be loved; to be a father to them all. Had he not often seen to it that deserving people in his domain did not starve—so long as they *were* deserving? He could be relied upon to give a man work and food, even if he did seduce his wife or daughter at the same time. Oh, yes, in the hard times, he had been a good squire! It was just that waywardness in him that he had been unable to control, but here was Kitty to subdue that . . . just as he had meant Bess to do. He had not been so near complete happiness since the day when Bess had said she would marry him.

They left the children and went on with their tour of the house.

The next day he asked Kitty to marry him, and she accepted.

Throughout the great house serving men and maids hurried here and there; there were so many preparations to be made, for the wedding must take place at Haredon. The squire was not a man to stick to conventions and the bride's home was not a grand enough setting for his wedding. Where would the guests be lodged? Where would the food be prepared? He was determined on a great feast. The neighbours should remember his wedding to the end of their days. It was the greatest day in his life; it should be a red letter one in theirs. He himself planned meals with the cook; he discussed beef and lamb and venison, cakes and pies, and wine and mead and ale. He was in a rare humour those days before his wedding. He felt his servants warm to him; he entered into an easy familiarity with them; already he was becoming their squire, their father and their friend. Only Jennifer did not come within the range of his friendship; he avoided her, and she had the good sense to keep out of his way. The servants said she brooded in her room, planning evil, for there was something of the witch in Jennifer Jay.

She did sit alone in her room, cursing her fate, looking into her mirror at the lines round her eyes and the thickening of her neck. She cursed the squire, cursed herself for her folly, cursed Kitty, and longed for the power to wreck this marriage. It was ironical that her best loved dream had been the marriage of the squire. This was like a nightmare, for he was marrying the wrong bride. As soon as he had seen that girl Kitty he had wanted her; she reminded him of her mother, sentimental fool that he was! Once she, Jennifer, thought of trading on that sentimentality, turning it to her own advantage, but now it had defeated her and here she was, living under his roof, the nursery maid who had been elevated to mistress and then reduced again to nursery maid. And possibly worse to come; because it was very likely that malicious people would whisper to the squire's bride of the place Jennifer had once occupied, and she, naturally enough, would send the nursery-maid-mistress packing very quickly. That was obvious; obvious to the squire, obvious to Jennifer, obvious to the lowliest serving maid in the place. They were laughing at her now, she knew, and she was fearful for herself and sick with envy of Kitty whose future seemed now so secure.

She need not have felt envious, for Kitty was far from happy. The day before the wedding she and Aunt Harriet, with Dolly and Peg, had set out for Haredon, and as Kitty went up the avenue in the carriage the squire had sent for them, as she entered the big house and was greeted by the squire and his elderly cousin, she felt as though she were entering a prison from which she would never escape. The exhilaration she had experienced when she had accepted the squire's proposal of marriage as a way out of her trouble was giving place to melancholy. For what would happen when he discovered the truth? The squire would never turn his wife out of his house, whatever her misdemeanour; but his wrath would be terrible. She thought continually of her mother. She was superstitious, and she fervently believed that her mother had shown her this way out of her trouble, for the suggestion that marriage with the squire would help her out of her difficulty had come to her suddenly, just as though it had been whispered into her ear by someone watching over her.

The wedding-day came—a hot September day with an early mist that promised more heat. Peg and Dolly dressed her. They squealed with delight over her beauty, and they wiped surreptitious tears from their eyes, for they knew that she did not love the squire; because she was beautiful as a princess and had shown them the first real kindness they had ever known, they wished everything to be perfect for her. And when, just before it was time to go downstairs and leave for the church, Peg threw herself on to the bed and began to sob bitterly, Kitty was very distressed.

She must not do this, she said. It was an evil omen. And why, she asked anxiously, did Peg cry? Peg murmured incoherently that there was something sad about weddings, beautiful though they were. But when Kitty put her hands on the girl's shoulders and looked into her eyes, she knew that Peg was not crying because of all weddings, but only because of this wedding. And Kitty was filled with a deep disquiet, for there was in Peg's eyes that knowledge of the fearful things that could happen to women, and though she said nothing she was thinking of the girl who had loved the groom; and perhaps too she was thinking of Kitty who had gone out each evening to meet her lover in the wood.

She knows! thought Kitty in panic. How long before others know?

The heat in the church was stifling, and the smell of September flowers seemed to overpower her with their sweetness. During the ceremony she was aware of the squire as a pair of hands—powerful hands that frightened her, for their strength was great indeed. She thought of Darrell's hands, long and slender . . . clever, kindly hands, and wondered if they were roughened now after weeks at sea. What was happening to Darrell? Terrible things? Cruel things? But not more terrible, Darrell, she thought, than this cruel thing which has happened to me.

And if he returned, what then?

"Wherever you are, Darrell," she murmured to herself, "whatever happens, if you need me I will come to you."

The ceremony was over. People crowded about them. The squire was blustering, full of good humour, exuberantly slapping people on the back; having a joke here, a laugh there. His hands longed to caress her, but there was in him a newly born tenderness which subdued his roughness just a little: it was an attempt to please her which was somehow pathetic, because obviously he had rarely thought of pleasing, but chiefly of being pleased.

61

She wondered then, if she confessed everything to him, whether he would be kind and tender and promise to look after her until Darrell came back. She laughed at herself. The gentleness in him was a frail plant soon to be hidden and stifled by the thick growth of other more natural emotions.

He whispered into her ear: "Cheer up, my dear. You're not going to the scaffold! Did you think you were?"

She forced herself to laugh. "No! Why should I? Is it a custom in Devon to hang one's bride?"

He guffawed with pleasure; laughter came easily to him when he was happy—as easily as rage came when he was irritated.

"Maybe," he said. "But I promise, if you please me, you shall be allowed to live."

"Thank you kindly, sir! You are indeed a bounteous squire and husband."

His great hand well-nigh crushed hers.

"A squire I have been for years, Kitty, but I feel I have never been a husband until now."

His face was close; there was moisture on his lips. She laughed; laughed at herself for imagining she could hold him off, could explain that he was not to touch her but to let her live in his house until Darrell came for her.

She sat beside him at the table. The smell of the food sickened her, and the warmth of his body as he bent close to her nauseated her. He drank a good deal; he filled her glass. He kissed her ear, and she could feel his teeth against her skin.

And the day passed into evening. The squire led her in the dance, and the musicians played gaily in the gallery round the hall. There was more drinking and singing and dancing, but the squire never left her side the whole evening. But the evening could not last for ever; she felt as though she were holding back the night with frantic hands while the squire beckoned it impatiently.

"The bride looks weary!" murmured the guests, and they whispered together and tittered, making references to the nuptial bed. The squire laughed with them, but the tenderness stayed in his eyes.

Peg and Dolly helped her out of her gown and prepared her for her bridegroom. She noticed that Peg's eyes were still red from weeping. They soothed her and patted her but they did not know how to comfort her.

She lay in the big bed and shivered, and called to Darrell, and prayed to her mother. She waited for a miracle, but all that came was the squire's step outside her door, and then his heavy breathing as he stood close to the bed.

Strange days followed for Kitty, warm days with evenings drawing in and autumn showing itself in the changing leaves and morning mists. It was a period of waiting.

Her feeling for George was not easy to define, nor did it occur to her to define it. His embraces could fill her with repulsion and yet excite her; his sudden change from an almost brutal passion to a gentleness which was pathetic because it sat so uneasily upon him, fostered in her a certain affection for him. Her need to be desired and possessed was satisfied, though her need to love was not; but she found it difficult to differentiate between desire and love, and did not understand herself.

As for George, he was delighted with his marriage. He thought her very desirable; shrinking at times, afraid of him —but then, he liked his women to be afraid of him; at other times there was a hint of passion in her that seemed reluctant to show itself but could not remain entirely hidden. It fascinated him; he longed to rouse it; it made him feel that, possessing her, he was still the hunter, and there was great zest in the chase. He played a game of make-believe with himself, pretending she was Bess—a Bess who had miraculously remained young for him. He was pleased with life. She was a wonderful toy, and because he did not understand entirely how she worked, his passion did not diminish; it was nurtured on the mystery of her. He was happy. He liked to be soft with her, indulge her, show her how truly gentle he could be when he loved; but there were times when he must show his strength; then he would catch her unexpectedly and crush her and force her and feel her resentful and wait for the sudden rising of passion in her. Sometimes when he was in a complacent mood, he imagined she feigned reluctance to please him; then he let himself believe he was the centre of her life and that her thoughts were occupied in his pleasure.

The days slipped into weeks. Kitty felt a fondness for the house growing in her; it was so big that she could hide herself in it; sometimes, when she heard George calling her, she would hide in one of the attics and felt completely shut away and safe; but one could not remain hidden for long, any more than one could keep a secret for ever. But she had her mother's gift of living in the present; something might happen, she told herself, so that her secret would never be discovered, and, wishing it, she began to believe it.

It was pleasant to be mistress of such a place as Haredon. The servants took to her; the housekeeper would discuss the running of the house with her in an indulgent way. "The dear little thing!" said the housekeeper. "She is not one to poke and pry." And indeed she was not; she could offer interest without interference. Peg and Dolly, whom she had brought with her, gave her an excellent reference in the servants' hall. "A dearer, sweeter creature never lived!" Dolly declared, and she and Peg showed the gifts Kitty had bestowed upon them, and never thought of whispering a word of those secret meetings with Darrell. There was one, of course, who was not pleased with her presence in the house; that was Jennifer Jay. Kitty heard whisperings of the squire's relations with Jennifer; that was inevitable. She was sorry for Jennifer. Jennifer's trouble was just another of those which beset the stormy lives of women. She tried to be friendly, but the glittering eyes of the woman alarmed her a little, and she had a feeling that Jennifer beat little Margaret for being so ready with kisses for her new mamma.

The time came when she must tell of the baby. It would be better to tell, she thought, than to be discovered. She decided that she must explain everything to her husband.

It was October. He had been hunting all day, and she had stayed in her room rehearsing what she would say to him. She had planned it all, beginning with the meeting in the coach; she had to make him understand how deeply she and Darrell had loved. "I should have told you before I married you," she would say, for indeed that was what she should have done, "but I was frightened, George, so terribly frightened . . ."

She knew just how she would appeal to him. She felt exalted, almost unafraid . . . until she heard his voice downstairs. Then she thought of his anger, and how terrible that could be; and she thought of being turned out of his house, and what had happened to the girl who had loved one of his grooms.

He came hastily up the stairs.

"Kitty!" he called in his lusty voice, and she trembled.

As he came in she stood up, her back to the window, so that he might not see her face.

"Ah!" he said. "There you are! Why the devil didn't you come down to welcome me home?"

He was laughing, not ill-pleased; his face was flushed with exercise and ale. It had been a good day, she saw.

He strode over to her and took her into his arms; he bent her backwards roughly and kissed her.

"Why, what's the matter?" he said. "You're white as a ghost!"

She was still trembling, and she could not hide it.

He said: "Why, Kitty?" and the tenderness was in his eyes again, and she felt her resistance weakening.

"George! There is something I must tell you . . . I do not know what you will say . . . I have been meaning to tell you for so long . . ."

His hands were on her shoulders, hurting her; he was always so rough with his great hands.

The words came out weakly: "George . . . there is going to be . . . a baby!"

Fearfully she looked up at him. Now was the moment. Now! His lips were moving, though no sound came from them. She stared. Was that a glaze of tears in his eyes? It was incredible. She had expected some crude remark; then she could have compared him with Darrell, have hated him, have said what she had prepared herself to say.

He murmured: "Kitty! It is the grandest news. We are going to have a family, Kitty!"

He threw off his sentimental mood. He was exuberant. He lifted her off her feet and gave her a great smacking kiss on the mouth.

Downstairs in the hall under the portraits of his ancestors he made the servants drink to the health of the child that was coming.

The children called her into the nursery.

"Jennifer is out for the afternoon!" whispered Charles.

"So you must come and tell us a story," added Margaret.

They climbed over her and touched the brooch at her throat. George had given her that only the other day; he delighted in giving her things. He had changed in the last weeks, since he had known of the coming of the child. He gave her little glimpses into his inner nature, told her of how he had felt about Bess, and how he had suffered when she had left him. It was unlike the squire to talk of weakness in himself, but he was so pleased with his life, so enchanted by the prospect of their both being parents of the same child, that he let her peer now and then behind his defences. He was not a monster, after all; just a man, very human, full of hopes and desires and aspirations.

"You are our new mamma," announced Margaret; and she and Charles laughed because it seemed so amusing to them that they should suddenly be presented with a new mamma.

"You see," explained Charles, "until now Margaret never had a mamma at all, and I only had one for a very little time."

"Jennifer says you're not a real mamma."

"She says you're a stepmamma!"

They watched her from under their eyelashes. Jennifer had said stepmammas hated their stepchildren, beat them and made faces at them in the dark.

They could not talk of these things, but they were there between them and their desire to love Kitty. For minutes at a time they forgot them though. They showed her their picture books and toys. They had opened Jennifer's cupboard, when Jennifer came in. Kitty actually had the love potion in her hand when the door opened.

Jennifer stiffened, and her face went dark red with hatred.

"Good afternoon, Jennifer," said Kitty.

Jennifer said: "Good afternoon, Madam."

It was Kitty who apologised.

"The children so wanted to show me round . . ."

"And you so wanted to see, Madam. I quite understand that." She was staring at the bottle and her rage got the better of her. "And you wanted to see what was in my private cupboard, so you . . ."

"Not at all," said Kitty with dignity. "I did not know this was your cupboard. The children showed me . . ."

The children stood awestruck, aware that this was a battle between two powerful grown-ups.

"My own possessions are private, Madam; I will thank you not to pry into them."

Kitty's temper flared up.

"You are insolent," she said, "and I will not tolerate that. You shall go at once!"

Jennifer retorted: "Perhaps you will speak to the squire about that . . . I myself will speak to him!"

Kitty was really angry now. She had not sought this opportunity, but now that it had come she would take it. "You may pack and go at once," she said. "I shall myself tell the squire that I have dismissed you."

How insolently the woman stared! Knowledgeably? What did she mean . . . ? Could she know . . . ?

Kitty began to feel very frightened. She was dizzy with fear; the room swayed; she clutched at the bureau. One of the children began to cry. Kitty saw Jennifer's face close to hers, and Jennifer was smiling; her cunning black eyes were like monkeys' eyes. Jennifer's arms were strong about.

When Kitty opened her eyes, she was lying on the sofa and Jennifer was kneeling beside her, holding hartshorn under her nose. The children were not there.

Jennifer said: "Madam should be more careful . . . her condition . . . I had not thought that it would be possible for Madam to be so far gone in pregnancy! The greatest care must be taken . . ."

Kitty managed to get to her feet.

"I am all right now."

"Oh, yes, Madam, you are all right now. It was just a little faint . . . so natural really. But Madam must take care . . ."

"That will do," said Kitty. "And do not forget—you are to pack your bags and go at once!"

Jennifer's eyes were downcast, but her mouth mocked. Kitty went unsteadily to the door. In her bedroom she bathed her face; her hands were hot and clammy, for she knew now that the moment had come. She prayed silently to her mother: "Mother, what shall I do now? What can I do now?"

She thought of the new tenderness which had sprung up in the squire. Words came into her mind. "We loved each other; we were going to marry. It seemed so safe, so right. He was always so careful of me, so eager that I should not suffer any hardship. Do not be cruel to me now! If you will only help me I will try to love you."

It seemed to her that she stayed in her room for hours . . . waiting.

She heard his horse's hoofs in the courtyard. It was some time before he came into the room, and she knew, as soon as she saw him, that Jennifer had waylaid him, had spoken to him. His big eyes bulged and there was a knotted vein on his forehead. Fearful as she was, it occurred to her that he was both like a dog that had received a whipping and an enraged bull.

His eyes searched her face, and his hands moved as though they would tear her secret from her.

There was no need; she would tell him now.

He stood before her, and she was aware of his hands again; now they were hanging limply at his sides.

He said: "What's this I am hearing? What's this that girl is saying? By God . . ."

And he wanted her to deny it, and he wanted to send Jennifer from his house; he wanted her to lie to him . . . anything so that he need not believe these suggestions of Jennifer's. He could still hear her voice, soft and insinuating: "I think I should tell you . . . Madam fainted clean away in the nursery

67

this afternoon. She must take greater care of herself. I feel—and I am no fool in these matters—that she is farther advanced in pregnancy than it seems possible to believe . . ."
The fury that had surged up in him! He had gripped the girl's shoulder and glared down into her impudent face. "Do not be angry with me. Is it my fault that she should use you so cunningly because her lover has deserted her?" Jennifer's eyes were full of the light of battle. She had been told by the mistress of the house to pack her bags, and if she did that and went away she would have lost everything she had fought for; but here was a chance of regaining a good deal. She was bold therefore; and she even laughed when he brought up his great hand and hit her on the side of her head so that she fell to the floor.

And well she might laugh, for he was a fool indeed! He had only to look into Kitty's eyes to see what a fool, for her guilt was there and she made no attempt to hide it. What was this she was saying? He could not hear properly because his blood was pounding on his eardrums, but he grasped its import. "We loved each other. It was so *right* . . . And then the press gang took him from me . . . We should have been so happy . . ."

He shrieked at her: "I'll kill you for this!"

And he would have killed her if he had not felt so miserably brokenhearted.

She said: "Please, George . . . I was wrong . . . I was wicked. But I will try, if only . . . There is the little baby to think of . . ."

He pushed her from him, and she fell on to the bed and lay there staring up at the terrible line of his mouth and the red tinge in what should have been the whites of his eyes.

He said: "So that was why you agreed to marry me, Madam!" He laughed and his laughter was horrible to her ears.

She hated him; and she hated herself for not hating more violently the last weeks during which he had been her lover. She answered with spirit, just as Bess would have answered: "Why else should I have married *you!*"

He had his riding-whip in his hand now; he thought of beating the life out of her for what she had done to him. He would take her life, for she and Bess between them had taken all that mattered in his.

He saw himself as a complacent fool; and later, people would know, and they would whisper together and laugh at him. "Poor Squire! Caught proper, he were!" His own people laughing at him! He was going to kill her; he would beat the life out of her.

He let out a string of epithets, but his voice broke suddenly. He was afraid that he was going to blubber just as though he were a schoolboy; there was nothing to be done but get out quickly.

He strode from the room.

Kitty lay there, dazed. The storm had broken; it was passing over her head. She buried her face in her pillow, and began to cry ineffectually.

Carolan Haredon

They were all going to pay a visit to the rectory.

Charles said: "Jennifer, *must* we take that silly little Carolan?"

Carolan made a face at Charles, for it was safe to do so since his back was turned to her. Charles was eleven—almost a man; Carolan was only five—quite a baby by Charles's standards; even Margaret thought her very young.

Carolan struggled with her sash; Jennifer never helped her to dress; she would come along afterwards and do up a button perhaps; then she would say: "I do declare you are a little slut!" And she would repeat the word slut, as though it gave her pleasure. And Carolan would retreat a pace or two and grimace at Jennifer, for grimaces were her only method of registering defiance, she being so small and they so big. Sometimes Jennifer merely laughed and said: "Go on! Make yourself uglier than you already are!" Sometimes though she would fly into a sudden rage and slap Carolan's face or beat her with a slipper.

Margaret and Charles were talking about Everard, who was twelve and wonderful. Everard must be very good, thought Carolan, for one day he was to be a parson like his father. He was taller than Charles, and he had kind eyes; and although he never took much notice of Carolan, he had never called her silly or a baby; he had never pushed her nor pulled her hair nor teased her about being afraid of darkness. Carolan was tormented so much that she felt quite a fondness for people who ignored her. Mamma was the only person whom she could really trust; Margaret next, she supposed, only she never knew when Margaret, even after a show of friendship, would say: "Oh, go away! You are such a baby!" And if there was one thing Carolan hated more than the dark it was being called a baby. Mamma sometimes said: "My baby!" but that was a secret between them and it did not hurt at all; it just meant that Mamma was her mother, and once she, Carolan, had been her mother's baby. Why, perhaps dignified Mrs. Orland called Everard *her* baby sometimes. She laughed at the thought.

"Here!" said Charles. "Are you laughing at me?"

He caught her arm and dug his nails into her skin; he was rough, Charles was; he could not pass her without pushing her aside; when he touched her it was like a blow. He has the eyes of a pig! she thought.

"No," she said with dignity, "I was not laughing at you."

"That's lucky for you!" He put his face close to hers. "Do you know what I would do to you if you had been laughing at me?"

"No," she said, and she was filled with a morbid desire to know what he would do.

"I would beat you till the blood ran!" said Charles. "Then I would cut you into little pieces and tie you in a parcel and send you to our stepmamma."

Silly! thought Carolan. As if he could! Now, if he had said he would creep into her room at night and pretend he was a ghost, he would really have frightened her.

"They would hang you on a gibbet if you did!" she said.

He pulled at her sash, which she had tied at great pains, and it fell to the floor.

Jennifer came over.

"Good gracious me!" said Jennifer. "What are you doing with your sash? A nice state you will be in, Miss! And talking of gibbets at your age!" Jennifer slapped Carolan's face, not roughly, just insultingly. "Come here . . . baby!"

Charles retreated, grinning, satisfied that he had left his victim in the hands of a more subtle torturer.

"Stand still! Or I swear I'll put you to bed and call the squire up to whip you."

That started a train of thought in Carolan's mind. Why did Jennifer always say "Your papa" to Charles and Margaret, and "The squire" to her? It was something to do with that mystery she had never been able to solve. She could never resist trying to find out.

"Jennifer, why is Charles my stepbrother and Margaret my stepsister?"

Jennifer was never angry at such questions; Carolan was yet to learn that she provoked them.

"Stepbrothers and sisters have not the same papa or mamma."

Carolan stood on one leg and considered this.

"My mamma is not their mamma!" she said, pointing at Charles and then at Margaret, who at that moment came into the room.

"Silly!" said Margaret. "You know your mamma is not our mamma!"

"But is papa my papa then?" Carolan's wide green eyes looked eagerly at Jennifer.

"Do I have to tell you again to stand still, Miss Impudent? I shall tell the squire I really cannot cope with all your impertinence. Then I shall go away."

Carolan looked hopeful, and Jennifer put her face close to Carolan's and said: "And you will have a new nurse who will not let you share Margaret's room, but put you in a dark room all by yourself."

Carolan was silent with horror. She had never known anyone who could convey so much as Jennifer could in a few seemingly commonplace words.

Margaret said: "Oh, Carolan's a silly baby; she is scared of the dark!"

Margaret did not mean to be unkind like the others did; she was merely stating a fact.

"She is afraid of ghosts and hobgoblins," chanted Charles.

Jennifer, pretending to take Carolan's part, said: "Well, in a house like this where so many people have died there is bound to be a ghost or two."

"Are there ghosts at the rectory?" asked Margaret. "I shall ask Everard. Everard would know."

The door opened then and Mamma came in; her eyes went straight to Carolan, just as though the others were not there. Carolan ran to her and flung her arms round her neck.

"Carolan . . . Miss!" cried Jennifer in reproach.

But Jennifer could say what she liked now. Mamma was soft and warm and smelt sweetly.

"So you are going to see Everard, darling?"

"Yes, Mamma. How nice you smell! You come too."

"No, I cannot do that, but you shall tell me all about it when you come back."

Carolan kept her arms round her mother's neck, and

73

laughed with pleasure. Over her daughter's brown head with reddish tints in it, Kitty looked fearfully at Jennifer Jay.

Is she unkind to Carolan? wondered Kitty. It was not easy to know. Of course there had to be certain corporal punishment for all children, and especially for a high-spirited child such as Carolan who could at times be very naughty. But was she really unkind?

"Come, Miss!" said Jennifer. "The carriage will be here at any moment."

"Yes, Carolan, you must go."

How I wish, thought Kitty, that I could get rid of that woman! She knew now that she ought to have got rid of her years ago, before Carolan was born—before George had known that Carolan was going to be born. It would have been easy then. But now Jennifer was back in the position she had occupied when Amelia was alive; it amused George to give Jennifer a certain influence in this house. It was a way of humiliating Kitty as she, to the knowledge of the whole neighbourhood, had humiliated him.

When she was in the nursery Kitty was full of love for little Carolan. Such a lovely creature with her brown hair that glinted quite red in the sunshine, and whose wide green eyes were alert with interest in everything that went on around her. She had a heart-shaped face and a sweet mouth that was going to be rather like Kitty's own; she had charm and appeal which Charles and Margaret, good-looking as they were, lacked. The years had left a certain mark on Kitty. She was modishly dressed—almost showily; indeed there were those in the county—and among them her Aunt Harriet—who thought her fast, flamboyant; a characteristic which displayed itself in her clothes. But the squire liked to see her thus, so there was a handsome enough dress allowance. She had a French maid, Thérèse, and a little black boy, Sambo, whom she petted. She spent a good deal of time before her mirror, while Thérèse tried new hair styles and discussed clothes. Once George, coming into her room suddenly and seeing her before her mirror with Thérèse combing her hair and the black boy sitting at her feet eating sweetmeats, had said: "You were born a harlot, Kitty!" and he dismissed Thérèse and the boy and made love to her there and then. She was so angry that she fought him, and he seemed to like that; but now she was indifferent to his humiliations. He did things like that, getting great satisfaction from them. Openly he lived with Jennifer. He was the same squire who had always been chasing the prettiest village girls, for he had lost his dreams of becoming the perfect squire, and when he remembered them he blamed Kitty and tried to hurt her. She was impregnable. At first she had had Carolan, and Carolan had been all-sufficing; how she had loved the little girl with the dainty hands and feet and the wide wondering eyes! She had bathed her and powdered her, and lived for her. But motherhood could only be a secondary emotion with Kitty, and there were lovers. First there was the young son of a neighbouring squire, who had reminded her of Darrell because he was so gentle and grateful. Later there were others. Thérèse was an adept at intrigue; she made the deception of the squire an adventure which was always on the point of being discovered, but never was. So Kitty loved Carolan when she was in the nursery, but when she was not there she forgot her for hours at a time.

Carolan did not know this. She adored her mother; she thought that she longed as deeply as Carolan for them to be together always, to go away somewhere, right away from Haredon, where they would live alone and never see Charles and Jennifer and the squire; though sometimes Margaret should come to see them and bring some of the servants—those whom Carolan liked best.

Carolan usually lost herself in this dream when she and her mother were together, even in the nursery with others around them. Perhaps, she thought now, Charles and Jennifer should come and she would say all the things she had wanted so many times to say to them; she would tell Jennifer that she was ugly, and Charles that he was silly. And they would not be able to do anything about it, because the cottage in which she lived with her mother would be a magic place and she only had to snap her fingers and two great dogs, breathing fire, would spring from nowhere and drive Jennifer and Charles away. Such a lovely cottage it was, with fruit trees all round it; and in the cottage it was always daytime. Only on very rare occasions should the squire come there, because she was frightened of the squire in much the same way as she was frightened of the dark. This fear was inexplicable, because she did not always want to run away from it. It called her to it, even as it terrified her. She always thought of George Haredon as the squire, because both her mother and Jennifer referred to him by that name when they spoke of him to her. He was a colossus of a man; he wore the biggest riding-boots in the world, and his hands were not like human hands; they were covered in black hair like the hair he had on his face. And his black eyes had a lot of red in them which she could not stop looking at. Sometimes he would lift her on to his knee and caress her as though he loved her; he would stroke her hair. He had a hoarse voice; often he said: "By God, Carrie, you're going to be such another as your mother!" His face would look very ugly when he said that, and he would put it so near hers that she could see each thick black hair of his eyebrows, and the red in his eyes formed itself into shapes like rivers on a map. Then he would say: "And if you are, girl, I'll break every bone in your body before I've finished with you!" which sounded very frightening coming from him, but was not meant to be perhaps, because he laughed when he said it. And sometimes he would kiss her in the hollow of her neck which Jennifer said was like a salt cellar, she being so thin and ugly, and sometimes he would put his great mouth on her eye so that she had to shut it quickly. A terrifying person, the squire. She hated the smell of him. Once she had wrinkled her nose, and he had said: "What does that mean?" And she had answered: "You have a horrid smell." And because she thought that might be very rude, she added: "The Squire!" She had called him that once or twice, as though it were his name, and it had amused him. But it did not amuse him then; he put her from him in a tantrum and strode away, and she hid herself thinking that if he found her he really would break every bone in her body. And next time he picked her up and set her on his knee, she made a great effort not to show that she did not like his smell. But for all this he fascinated her, and sometimes she would deliberately get in his way just to see whether he would be angry with her or caress her; and either was equally terrifying to her. Aunt Harriet should come to see them at the cottage too, and she, Carolan, would call up the dogs that breathed fire, very quickly if Aunt Harriet was unpleasant, for Aunt Harriet could be very unpleasant. She had hard hands that hurt when she slapped, but Carolan did not mind that so much; it was Aunt Harriet's cold eyes and grim mouth that Carolan hated. They seemed to be holding a secret—a horrible secret about Carolan.

But the dream of the cottage and its visitors and fire-breathing dogs was over, for Kitty was gently disengaging her hands and Jennifer was gripping her shoulder.

"It is time the children went now, Ma'am." Jennifer released Carolan, and going over to the mirror put on her bonnet.

Kitty thought how desolate Carolan looked, standing there. So much smaller than the others . . . And *was* Jennifer kind? Margaret took Carolan's hand and pulled her to the door. It was pleasant to think of the older girl's keeping an eye on little Carolan, and Kitty had always liked Margaret. Now Carolan was looking over her shoulder at her mother, and her face puckered a little; she looked such a baby, scarcely her five years now, though one was apt to think her older at times; she was such an old-fashioned little thing. Kitty wondered whether she would give up her afternoon to the child, keep her with her. But no! She had an engagement. Besides, children were moody; you were apt to think them unhappy when they were just a little peevish. And, in any case, all the children had been invited to the rectory; it would seem rude if one of them stayed behind. So Kitty eased her conscience; if Jennifer was unkind to her, surely Carolan would *say* so!

She watched their getting into the carriage, and told herself how good it was to know that Carolan was being brought up with other children. Jennifer would not be different from what she was to the others; she would not dare.

The carriage rattled over the stony roads. Carolan began to bounce up and down on the seat for the sheer joy of riding along country roads in a carriage.

Jennifer slapped her.

"Still, Miss!"

She was going to be the image of her mother, thought Jennifer; not so beautiful perhaps—she would be darker for one thing and her eyes were green—but those thick red-tinted lashes and that provocative tilt of the head! She had . . . what her mother had, and if one could believe the stories one heard, what her grandmother and great grandmother had had too. Jennifer wanted to beat that small wriggling body, but what was the good! There would be trouble if she went too far in that direction; the artful little imp already had some sort of influence with the squire; Jennifer believed he was more interested in Carolan than in his own children. Sometimes he could not keep his mouth from smiling when he spoke of her. What witchery was this she had inherited, when at five years old she, the very sight of whom should have enraged the squire, could command a special indulgence?

"Now you must all be very good at the rectory," said Jennifer. "You must not let your crumbs fall upon the floor. And when Mr. or Mrs. Orland speaks to you, you must answer up promptly and very respectfully. And if Everard should take you into the graveyard, you must be very quiet." She gripped Carolan's arm, for the child who had been staring out of the window before she had mentioned the graveyard, was now sitting up tense in her seat. "Don't go prying around too much in the graveyard."

Margaret, who was very matter-of-fact and without much imagination, said: "Why mustn't you pry round the grave-yard? I can't see that it matters; everybody there is dead."

"Hush!" said Jennifer, and looked at Carolan.

"The vaults are interesting," said Charles. "Full of dead people!"

"They put the coffins on shelves," added Margaret.

"So that one family can keep together," said Jennifer. "I've heard stories about what happens in the graveyard at night; it would make your flesh creep to hear them!"

"They are like little houses," said Charles.

"Houses where the dead lie," said Jennifer. "Now, Carolan, there is no need to look so frightened, Miss. Nobody is going to put *you* there. But mind you don't go prowling round where you should not go, and get shut in with the dead. A nice thing that would be!"

Carolan was white to the lips at the thought of it.

"Baby!" said Margaret contemptuously.

Carolan shut her eyes and tried to tell herself that she was not in the carriage at all, but in the cottage with Mamma. "Sparks!" she murmured to herself. "Rover!" For those were the names of the dogs which breathed fire.

The carriage had drawn up outside the rectory gates, and Mrs. Orland and Everard came out to greet them. Mrs. Orland was very gracious. She was sure, she said, that Jennifer would like a chat with her friend, Mrs. Privett. Mrs. Privett was the housekeeper at the rectory, and Jennifer hated her. This was one of the humiliations which made her so angry. She might have been riding in her own carriage to pay a call, had her plans not gone wrong; now she was here in the role of governess, and Mrs. Orland's drawing-room was closed to her; she must go to the housekeeper's room and chat with that stupid Mrs. Privett whose talk was all of apple jelly and inferior servants.

"Well," said Mrs. Orland, "and how is little Carolan?" Carolan was quite the most charming of the Haredon children, even though she had made such a distressing entry into the world. Mrs. Orland was afraid she was a little too broadminded, but one could not help liking the child.

Carolan put her hand in Mrs. Orland's and they went into the drawing-room.

Everard looked very handsome today, and bigger than Carolan had been thinking him. He sat down, and his feet looked just like a man's feet; Carolan's did not reach the floor, and she longed for her legs to grow so that they would. Margaret sat staring at Everard; she was always like that in Everard's company; she doted on him, and he did not like it very much. Margaret knew it, but she could not help staring at him. Carolan stared a little at him too, but there were other things to stare at in Mrs. Orland's drawing-room, because it was such a wonderful place, and Mamma's mamma had lived here once, when she was Carolan's age, which made it a very exciting place to be in.

Mrs. Orland talked to them very brightly while they ate seedcake and drank their milk. She talked of lessons, but that was not to Carolan who was too young to know much about them, but to Charles chiefly, occasionally bringing in Margaret. Carolan did not mind being ignored; she was quite happy; she loved seedcake and the milk was delicious, and on a stand near her chair was a fascinating ornament which represented a woodland scene; it was set on a wooden stand, and there was a glass shade over it. It was wonderful. There was green moss and some trees, and on one of the branches a real stuffed bird. When she pressed her face close to the grass she could imagine she was standing under the trees, and that her cottage was not far away, and that her dogs would come leaping out at her from behind those trees.

Mrs. Orland was saying: "Would you like me to take off the glass shade?"

Carolan had no words to express her delight. One plump finger stroked the bird's feathers. "Pretty, pretty *pretty!*" cooed Carolan.

Such a baby, thought Mrs. Orland, although sometimes she had the air of quite a sophisticated young person!

Margaret was standing near Everard, saying shyly: "Everard, *please* show me your books; I do want to see your books!"

Everard almost scowled, but Mrs. Orland said: "Take Margaret to your study and show her your books, Everard."

Everard said: "I do not want to Mother. I . . ."

"Everard! Margaret is your guest!"

Everard went very red, and led Margaret ungraciously towards the door.

"And when you have seen them, you may join the others in the garden. And remember . . . not *too* much noise. Papa is writing his sermon."

Carolan said: "Is he always writing sermons?"

But no one answered that, and she supposed he was, because whenever she was at the rectory she was always told to be quiet on that account, and she could not imagine the rectory unless she herself was there.

"Now, Charles, suppose you take your little sister into the garden and show her the nice flowers until the others come down. You would like to see the nice flowers, Carolan?"

Carolan would have liked to stay with the wood on the stand, but Charles was eager to escape from the restraint of Mrs. Orland's drawing-room.

"Come on, Carolan!" he cried, just as though he really wanted to show her the flowers, so that Carolan thought he had changed suddenly, and liked her after all.

It was lovely in the garden.

"Who wants to see her old flowers!" said Charles, but he said it in quite a friendly way, and Carolan laughed because she had always really wanted to be friendly with Charles. "Do you want to see her old flowers, Carolan?"

"No," said Carolan.

"Nor do I!"

He laughed as though it were a great joke, and Carolan laughed too because she was never sure about jokes, and always laughed when she thought there was one.

Charles led the way to the end of the garden, and at the end of the garden was a low stone wall . . . and beyond the wall was the graveyard.

"They look funny, those gravestones!" said Charles, and he laughed; so, thinking it was another joke, Carolan laughed too.

Charles was being very nice this afternoon.

"See me leap that wall!" he cried, and did so. "You could not do it!" he challenged.

She knew she could not, but she tried. He stood on the other side of the wall, laughing at her, but not in a spiteful way.

"You are too little, Carolan; you will be able to when you are bigger."

"I wish I was bigger!"

"Oh . . . you will be one day. Give me your hand and I will help you over."

She scraped her knees getting over, but it was exciting being on the other side of the wall. She liked it. The gravestones were like ladies in grey cloaks, but they did not frighten her; the sunlight glinted on them, making them sparkle, showing her that though they might look like people they were only stones after all. How she loved the great blazing sun up there! It was such a comforter; she was not afraid of very much when she felt that to be close by.

"See if you can catch me," said Charles, and he walked quickly amongst the gravestones. "I walk!" he called over his shoulder. "You run. That is what you call handicaps, Carolan. Oh . . ." For she had nearly caught him. Carolan shrieked with delight; she forgot all the unkind Charleses she had known, and remembered only the kind one who had helped her scramble over the wall and let her play touch with him in the graveyard. She caught him, and they stopped, laughing, by the side of what to Carolan looked like a little house covered in ivy.

"Do you like it?" asked Charles.

She shook her head.

"It is like a little house," she said, "but it has no windows. I like windows."

"Do you know what it is?"

"No."

"It is what we were talking about . . . you know . . . a vault. . . . It is our family who live in there—our dead grandpapas and grandmammas and uncles and aunts . . ."

"Oh!" cried Carolan. "Walk, and I will catch you."

"Later on perhaps," said Charles. "Now I am going to look in there!"

"But you must not!"

"I can if I want to, and I do want to."

He tried the door, but it was locked, and she was filled with relief.

"You cannot," she said gleefully.

"Carolan, *you* would be afraid."

She stoutly denied it. She could do so happily, for how was it possible to go through a locked door?

He said: "Carolan, if that door were open, would you go in? I would. I would want to go in."

"So would I!"

He put his hand in his pocket and brought out a key. She stared at it in dismay and horror.

"But Charles . . . How can you have a key . . . for that?"

He took her hand; he held it tightly, just as though they were friends. Then he opened the door; there was a short flight of steps that led down into darkness.

He looked at her over his shoulder.

"Papa keeps the key," he said. "I have seen it often in a

drawer in the library with other keys. I took it because I wanted to see what it was like in here. You do too, Carolan. You said so!"

She was silent. It was a different world in there; it was damp and it was dark and there was none of her well-loved sunshine to defy the darkness.

"Come on!" said Charles. He was excited; he had meant to enjoy this adventure with Everard, so he had taken the key and hidden it in his pocket. He was almost sure once that Jennifer had felt it there, but she had said nothing so she could not have noticed it; and then her words in the carriage had made him see the possibility of another adventure with Carolan instead of Everard whose years made him inclined to be superior.

He took Carolan's hand, and she descended the stairs with him reluctantly.

"What an odd, nasty smell!" she said, and her teeth began to chatter.

"Earth and worms and dead people!" said Charles. "That is what you smell." His voice was shrill with excitement. Now Carolan's eyes had grown accustomed to the darkness; they were standing in what was like a room, very cool and quiet, she thought.

"On the ledges," said Charles with his mouth close to her ear, "are the coffins. Oh, does it make your flesh creep, Carolan?"

"No!" lied Carolan. "But I like outside best."

"But you wanted to come, Carolan. You said you did."

"Yes, but we have been. I can catch you; you cannot walk faster than I can run."

"Would you be scared to stay down here all night, Carolan?"

"I would not stay here all night."

"But if you did . . . ?"

Her show of courage deserted her; she made for the steps.

"Listen!" said Charles. "What was that?"

She stood still; she could hear nothing but the wild beating of her own heart and Charles's breathing. He caught her shoulder suddenly; he gave her a little push backwards; her fingers touched the clammy wall. She shrieked, and then horror silenced her, for Charles had leaped up those steps and had shut the door on her. She scrambled up the steps as fast as she could, but the door was already closed. Now there was no comforting light at all . . . nothing but the damp darkness. She beat her fists on the door.

"Let me out! Let me out! Please . . . *please* let me out!"

There was no answer. She went on beating her little hands against the heavy door. She found the lock. She pushed, she kicked. But Charles had locked the door; he had taken away the key.

Carolan shut her eyes tightly and pressed her face against the door; she felt that a thousand horrors were rushing up the steps after her; she waited for something terrible to happen. She went on waiting. Nothing happened but the awful stillness pressed in on her, and the cold damp darkness was more unendurable than anything else could have been.

She could not keep her eyes closed for ever; she must open them. Fearfully she looked over her shoulder. She could just make out the dark entrance to the room; she turned and pressed her back against the door, her eyes fixed on the entrance to that room. Whatever was coming for her would come from that direction, she knew. She remembered the stories she had heard whispered by the servants; Jennifer had told her some horrible stories about dead people. Would they be angry with her for venturing into their home? She had lied; she had said she was unafraid, believing she would not be called upon to prove her lack of fear. Jennifer said liars went to hell; but what was hell, compared with this dark home of the dead?

"Charles!" she screamed; but the sound of her own voice, echoing about her, frightened her so much that she pressed her lips together lest any sound escaped to terrify her.

She did not know what to do. A sob shook her. She began wildly kicking the door again, but the hollow sound of her kicks echoed through the place as her voice had done.

"Mamma! Mamma!" The words must escape. She shut her eyes and began to pray. "I did not want to come here. I took only one small piece of sugar yesterday. It was not I who put my finger in the apple jelly. I did not! I did not! If I could get out of here, I would never do anything wrong again. I would never make faces at anyone . . . not even Jennifer . . ."

What was that? Only some small animal scuttling along down there in the gloom. She started to shiver, and her face was wet, but not with tears, for strangely she had shed no tears. Tears were soft and comforting things, and there was no comfort for her in this dark place.

Would they come out of their coffins? What would they look like? She shut her eyes tightly. I will not look at them . . . I will not look. Perhaps they would force her to open her eyes, and they would be horrible . . . horrible and angry with her for coming into their house.

"Oh, let me out, let me out!" she sobbed.

She found she was lying on the damp ground, her head pressed against the door, her hands over her ears, great sobs shaking her. Something must happen soon. Now she lifted her hands; she must hear. She was sure strange noises were going on all about her. Was it better to hear or not to hear? To see or not to see?

A ghostly voice whispered: "Carolan!"

She trembled.

"Carolan!" said the voice again. She stared at the entrance to the room which was the home of the dead, and she heard the voice again: "Carolan! Carolan! Are you there, Carolan?"

It was Everard's voice, coming through the door, and she was almost fainting with the joy of hearing Everard's voice; but she could not speak though her lips were moving. Frantically she tried to find her voice; he would go away; he would leave her. He was there, but she had lost her voice and could not call to him.

"Carolan! Carolan! Are you there, Carolan?"

She tried to get to her feet, but she was shaking so much she could not stand.

"Please . . ." she managed to utter, but her teeth chattered, and the words would not come out.

She tried again and again, and then she heard Everard's footsteps going away.

Despair seized her. She could shriek now.

"Everard! Everard! I am here. Oh, please get me out, Everard!"

But she was too late, for he had gone, and she would have to stay here all the night. The night? But here in this dark place it was always night. There was the faintest gleam of comfort in the thought, and it gave her the courage to raise herself and to turn her gaze on the dark entrance to the room.

It began again now—the staring about, the closing of her eyes; one moment alert, the next shutting out all sound and all sight.

Every movement about her set her heart pounding afresh. Sometimes it was the rustle of the trees outside; sometimes it was the call of a bird.

"Everard, come back!" she prayed. "I can talk now . . . I can talk." And she went on talking, just to assure herself that her voice was still hers to command.

Surely Everard would come back! Why had he said her name if he had not thought she might be there?

"Carolan!" A key turned in the lock, and Everard almost fell over her, lying there. He picked her up. She stared at him, still terrified, wondering if one of the dead ones had come for her and, as an additional torture, had made himself look like Everard.

Everard sat down on the top step, just as though it was anybody's step, and held her in his arms. She thought he looked frightened, but she only seemed to see things through a haze.

He said: "Everything is all right now, Carolan. I am taking you out of here."

She was shaking so much she could not answer him.

He was very tender. Jennifer said he was a mollycoddle. He did not play games; he liked his books; one day he would be a parson like his father, and write sermons all day long. But one thing Carolan knew instinctively about Everard; he would never lock frightened little girls in with the dead; and to Carolan, newly released from hell, he was wonderful.

He went on talking while she lay in his arms, which was just what she wanted him to do.

"There is nothing to be afraid of, Carolan. The dead cannot hurt anyone; besides, they are your own dead here. They would love you if they were alive, just as people at home love you."

Just as people at home loved her? Charles? Jennifer? The squire? But did it matter what Everard said! She only wanted his protecting arms round her and to listen to his soothing voice.

"There!" said Everard softly, like somebody's mother. "There! You feel better now."

Then her tears began to fall, and she could not stop them.

"Oh, I say!" cried Everard in real dismay. "Oh, I say, you know, it is all right now, you know."

But she could not stop the tears, and to show him that they were not really sad tears she began to laugh, and she was laughing and crying all at once, which frightened Everard. He kept saying her name, "Carolan! Carolan!" and rocking her to and fro as though she were a baby. And eventually she stopped laughing and was only crying. Then Everard said: "I hope I have hurt him badly, I do!" She was so interested that she stopped crying and asked: "Who, Everard?"

"Charles!" said Everard. "Let us get away from this place. We ought not to have stopped here; it is a dismal hole."

They went out and he locked the door after him. She stared round-eyed at the key.

He said: "Your eyes are red!" And she began to sniff again. Then he added: "I don't mind admitting I should not have liked being shut in there alone myself . . . much."

And saying that was almost as wonderful as letting her out. He was twelve years old and she was five, and yet she felt a wonderful companionship spring up between them.

She could see the sunshine glinting through the trees, and she stared up at it, at the lovely sun itself. And when she blinked and shut her eyes she saw red suns on her lids, as though it were saying to her: "It is all right. It is all right. You see I am here, even when you shut your eyes!" And she was suddenly wonderfully happy; she leaped up and kissed Everard. He did not much like being kissed by a little girl of five, but he was faintly aware of the charm of Carolan, of green eyes shining between swollen lids and a sweet and tremulous baby mouth.

"I say!" he said. "I say!" and wiped off Carolan's kiss, smiling at her as he did so to show that he was not as annoyed as he might easily have been.

"You should bathe your eyes," he said. "I will take you to the pump in the yard, shall I?"

She nodded. Willingly she would have followed Everard to the end of the world.

Just as, a little while ago, everything had been dark tragedy, now everything was very gay or extremely comic. She laughed when Everard pumped the water and gave her a lace-edgd handkerchief, which she held under the water. Then he stopped pumping, and said: "Here! Give it to me." And he took it and bathed her face with it, and again she thought he was like somebody's mother.

"Everard," she asked him, "how did you get the key?"

"I knew he had it," he told her, and that was another delightful characteristic of Everard's; he did not say, as the others would: "Oh, shut up, baby!" or "You wouldn't understand." Everard went on: "He showed it to me this afternoon. Then, when I saw him without you and asked where you were, he looked sly and I guessed; so I came and called you, and when you did not answer I was afraid you had fainted."

"I did not faint," said Carolan proudly, "but when I tried to speak my voice would not come."

"Well," he said, "you are all right now."

86

She leaped high into the air to show him that she was indeed all right. She was happier than she had been all the afternoon or for many days; she was not sure why, but she was a mercurial little creature, often very sad, often very happy; but rarely had she been as happy as she was now. Perhaps it was because Everard, twelve years old and admired and respected by the others, was being so kind to her.

While they were at the pump, Charles and Margaret came up. There was a cut right across Charles's forehead and it was bleeding. Charles and Everard glowered at each other, and Margaret looked frightened.

Everard said contemptuously: "You can say you fell over one of the tombstones and cut your forehead. Carolan can say she was with you and she fell first, and you went down after her. That will do."

He went on bathing Carolan's eyes, and there was a deep silence. After a while they went into the house.

Mrs. Orland was distressed that the children had come to harm at her house. She bathed Charles's forehead and looked in dismay at the strange appearance of Carolan. She sat down and wrote a note to Kitty, which when she had summoned Jennifer from Mrs. Privett's room she gave to her to take to her mistress.

Everard said: "It is nothing much, Mamma!" and Mrs. Orland said: "For shame, Everard! Your guests . . . !" Then Mr. Orland left his sermon for a little while and came out to say a few words before they left, but he noticed nothing unusual. Mr. Orland would not notice, Margaret had once said, if you walked on all fours. It was altogether a most exciting afternoon for Carolan, until they were riding home in the carriage; then her elation vanished:

Jennifer said: "Now, what was all the fuss about?"

They told her the story they had told Mrs. Orland.

"It was her fault!" said Charles, pointing to Carolan, and Margaret did not defend her. She was disliking Carolan almost as heartily as the others did. The silly baby! Why, Margaret had been looking at Everard's books, and then suddenly he had escaped from her, which had wounded her deeply, for she always tried to pretend that Everard wanted to be with her as much as she did with him; and then when she found him he had been bathing Carolan's eyes because the silly baby had been crying! He had escaped from her to go to Carolan's aid. She felt impatient with Carolan, so said nothing when Charles laid on the child's shoulders the blame for the afternoon's disturbance.

"I'll warrant it was!" said Jennifer, and decided to ask for no more details. "She shall be punished; she shall be taught that it is very ill-bred to make trouble in other people's houses. Ill-bred, indeed! Well, and what else can we expect?"

Carolan's happiness gave way to despair. She wondered whether Jennifer would whip her when they were back in the nursery. Perhaps she would content herself with a threat that she should be moved from the room she shared with Margaret to a dark one of her own. Suppose that her threat was followed by that action which Carolan dreaded more than anything else in the world. Carolan prayed fervently that it would only be a whipping, but from the way in which Jennifer was smiling, she was filled with fear. She could not bear it if she were sent to bed alone in a dark room. It would be almost as bad as being shut in the dark this afternoon, and it would not end suddenly with the kindness of Everard, but would go on night after night.

She was frantic, thinking of it, and by the time they arrived home she had decided she must go to her mother and beg her to see that her bed was not moved away from Margaret's room. It was not often that one could talk to grown-ups of one's troubles; everyone realised that. Even people like Everard, who was almost grown-up, knew that incidents like that of this afternoon must never be communicated to the grown-ups. But this time she could not help it; she would have to ask her mother to save her from the dark.

As soon as she was in the house she ran to her mother's room. She knocked. Thérèse opened the door, and when she saw who it was, lifted her shoulders.

"Ah! The little one. There is no time this hour for the little one."

But Carolan ran past Thérèse, for she had seen her mother sitting by the mirror. She wore a satin petticoat, and her hair was hanging about her shoulders. Carolan took a deep breath at the sight of so much beauty, and was very proud of having such a lovely mother. Now she would turn and say, "Hello, darling, tell me all about this afternoon." Then she would notice that Carolan's eyes were red-rimmed, and she would put her arms round her and kiss her and say: "What happened to my little Carolan?" Then, without saying anything about the afternoon's adventure which was too horrible to be discussed with anyone, Carolan would ask that her bed should never, never be moved from Margaret's room. That was how she planned it.

But it did not happen like that. Kitty saw her own lovely

88

face vividly reflected in the mirror; Carolan was vague as a shadow standing beside her.

"Hello, darling," she said. Then: "Thérèse, I will have the mauve ribbons in my hair, I think."

She held the ribbons up to her hair. "Do you like them, Carolan?"

Carolan nodded.

"They match my dress, darling, you see; there it is, on the bed. You may go and look at it. You can feel how soft and silky it is . . . Are your hands clean, darling? Show! Yes, you go and feel it."

Carolan felt the stuff of the dress. It was very soft and love-ly, and would match the mauve ribbons beautifully. Carolan forgot to be frightened. Dark rooms and Jennifer's anger seemed nonexistent when you were in this room, so full of bustle, the bustle of Thérèse and her mother; and Carolan, quick to catch a mood and share it, listened to the discussion as to whether it should be mauve or pale pink ribbons for Kit-ty's hair, and it seemed as breathlessly important to her as the request she had come to make.

"And now," said Thérèse, "the little one must fly away. There is much to be done, and so little time to do it in!"

"Did you hear that, Carolan? Thérèse is mistress here!"

Thérèse smiled; so did Kitty; so Carolan smiled too, and it was only when she was outside the door that she remembered she had not asked that which she had come to ask. She went back to the nursery and hid herself in a quiet corner, but no-body spoke to her, so she went over the adventure with Everard again and again, beginning at that part where Everard put the key in the door and let in the sunshine. Everard was her special friend, she kept reminding herself; he had talked to her as though she were older than five; and he liked her, she believed, better than he liked Margaret and Charles—which was a triumph.

She went to bed, and her bed was still in the room which she shared with Margaret; and when the candle was out and Margaret was sleeping and it really was rather frightening even though she could hear Margaret's breathing in the next bed, it was not with her mother that she, after her usual fash-ion, held a whispered conversation, but with Everard.

The year that Carolan was nine was one of the most event-ful of the century. France declared war on England, and Charlotte Corday assassinated Marat in his bath; Louis XVI was executed that January and his queen followed him in October; that year saw the beginning of the Reign of Terror in France and the wave of uneasiness which swept over England because of it. But Carolan was unconcerned with events outside her nursery. She awoke on the morning of her birthday in great excitement. She now had her own room, but she had lost much of her childish fear of the dark. Sometimes, of course, when she had heard an eerie story she had nightmares, but that was not often; then she would dream she was locked up with the dead, and that dream persisted. But it was a dream with a happy ending, and when she awoke, perhaps screaming, trying to fight off queer dark shapes, she would think of Everard's coming through the door, picking her up and talking to her so kindly. Then she would have a long imaginary conversation with Everard, and picture his face so clearly and hear his voice so distinctly that all fear would leave her. They were friends, she and Everard, and it was extremely exciting to have a friend who was so much older than oneself. It did not matter about being ugly. Her hair had kept its reddish tinge; her eyes had stayed green. Jennifer was for ever saying: "Green eyes for greedy guts! I do declare you grow uglier every day." Charles took up the refrain: "Greedy guts! Greedy guts!" It was not a very pleasant name. But when she said to Everard: "Everard, how ugly am I? As ugly as old witch Hethers?" Everard had laughed. "Silly! You are not ugly at all; you are all right—as good as most." "As good as Margaret?" "Oh, better than Margaret!" and Margaret, fair haired, blue-eyed Margaret was the prettiest person Carolan had ever known except Mamma, of course, who was lovely as a picture. But then Everard hated Margaret because she would try to talk to him and be with him; so that was why he thought her ugly, just as Jennifer thought Carolan was ugly, because she did not like her.

What exciting days birthdays were! She imagined what they would all give her; a dress of lace and ribbons from Mamma, because one always thought of lace and ribbons when one thought of Mamma. From Everard a riding whip to be used when she rode Margaret's pony. From Margaret a saddle of heavenly-smelling leather. She could not lie abed when so many beautiful gifts were awaiting her. She sprang out and danced to the window. What a lovely morning, with an April sun that was so beautiful because it had remained hidden so long, and an April freshness in the air, and the blossom just beginning on the fruit trees, and the daffodils under the oaks, and the birds wild with excitement because it was Carolan's birthday!

She stood, her head on one side, listening. "Carolan!" sang the birds. "Car-o-lan!"

"Here I am!" she cried. "Did you know it was my birthday?"

She pressed her nose against the glass, laughing. Then she danced to the cold water jug, poured out some water into the basin, and washed.

When she was dressed, she opened the door and looked out into the corridor. There was no sound from either Margaret's or Jennifer's room. She stood uncertainly in the corridor. If Jennifer heard her about so early, there would be trouble. She grimaced at Jennifer's door and tiptoed past it. Down the flights of stairs she went, to Mamma's room. How rich it seemed down here, compared with the shabby nursery quarters. Here was her mother's door, with Thérèse's next to it. She turned the handle and stood on the threshold, looking in. Mamma was sleeping, her fair hair in disorder on the pillow. Carolan tiptoed into the room and stood by the bed, watching. Mamma's lashes were long and gold coloured, and her full lips were parted. Carolan stood for some minutes, watching; then she whispered: "Mamma, I am here."

Kitty opened her eyes. She had not altered very much in four years; she preserved her beauty with the greatest care, and Thérèse, with her skin lotions and tonics, was a wonder. True, she had put on flesh, but as Thérèse assured her, it was in the places where it was well to put it.

"Carolan," said Kitty drowsily.

Carolan leaped on to the bed and knelt there.

"Mamma, do you know what today is?"

"Tell me, darling."

"Oh, Mamma, do you not know?"

"I am so sleepy yet, Carolan. Kick off your shoes, darling, and come in."

So Carolan kicked off her shoes and came in; she snuggled close to her mother.

"Shall I tell you then?"

"Yes, tell me."

"It is my birthday! I am nine years old today."

Kitty held the small body closer. Nine years ago that she had suffered so deeply. Nine years of humiliations from George Haredon. She put her lips against Carolan's cheek, and Carolan lay still, contented. Kitty lay still too, thinking of the wonder of her first love. Had I married Darrell, thought Kitty lazily, I would have been a true and faithful wife to him. I have always been searching for someone like Darrell—

91

that is it. Now she was wishing she had been a better mother to the little girl lying beside her. She would see more of the child from now on; she would look more closely into the nursery life of Carolan. Was Jennifer Jay cruel to her? She had never asked Carolan that question, for if Carolan said Yes, what could she, Kitty, do about it? George paid his children's governess; he would be the one to decide whether she should go or stay. How she hated George Haredon!

Ah! If only Darrell had not gone to Exeter! If they had gone to London together and married, there would still be this dear little Carolan—and how they would have loved her, both of them.

Am I to blame? Kitty asked herself.

Carolan's little body was quivering with excitement. Her birthday, of course, Kitty thought in panic, and I forgot. She will be expecting me to have remembered. Peg always used to remind her of Carolan's birthday, but Peg had married one of the farm labourers two years ago, and left Haredon. Then Dolly had taken it upon herself to remind her, but six months back Dolly had run away with a gipsy whose band had made their camp near by. And how could she tell this little daughter that she, her mother, had relied upon two of the lower servants to remind her of this great and important day!

Kitty resorted to subterfuge, for subterfuge came easily to her.

"Carolan, I am very unhappy about your present. It is not ready, darling. They have disappointed me."

"Mamma, when will it be ready? Tomorrow?"

"I hope so, darling."

Carolan squealed: "Then it will be like another birthday tomorrow, Mamma!"

What a sweet child she was! Kitty's eyes filled with tears. She stroked the unruly hair with the red in it; she kissed the smooth childish brow.

"I was so afraid you would be disappointed, darling; that it would be spoiled for you."

Carolan's hands round her neck were suffocating.

"No, Mamma, not spoiled . . . not spoiled at all. Tell me, is it blue . . . or pink?"

"Ah!" said Kitty. "That would be telling."

"It is pink. I know it is pink!" Carolan's eyes were dark with hope. "It might be green though!'Mamma, is it green?"

So she wanted green, did she?

"Well," said Kitty, suffused with mother-love, "as a matter of fact . . . it is . . . well, I ought not to tell you, ought I?"

Carolan was laughing hilariously now; she put her ear close to her mother's mouth. Beautiful, a child's ear was, soft and pink like a sea shell.

"Whisper, Mammà!"

"It is green," whispered Kitty.

"Is it silk or satin?"

So she wanted a dress. She was growing up, to want a dress. A dress she should have. Kitty must . . . simply *must* remind Thérèse to go out and buy one this morning. A white dress it should be, with green ribbons.

"I shall tell no more!" said Kitty, and Carolan knelt on the bed and rocked backwards and forwards in ecstasy.

Perhaps, thought Kitty, she would not send Thérèse; perhaps she would go herself to buy the dress.

"My little daughter!" she said. "My dearest little daughter."

And Carolan, overflowing with love for her, flung her arms once more round her neck.

Soon, thought Kitty, there will be another birthday, and another and another. Soon she will be fifteen, sixteen, seventeen. I was seventeen when I met Darrell.

Kitty held her child to her sharply. What had Carolan heard about her birth? Anything? Was it possible that there had been no hint, no whisper of what had happened? It was hardly likely. Wicked Jennifer Jay might have said something. Aunt Harriet's thin-lipped disapproval? George's ribaldry? Had any of these been noticed by the child?

Kitty raised herself and looked down into the face of her daughter. A sensitive face, very like Kitty's own; very attractive it was going to be one day—it was now—with a slightly different attractiveness from Kitty's, less obvious perhaps; but then it was not easy to tell. There was a look of Darrell in the child's eyes. Kitty thought, She must hear it first from me! And impulsive as Kitty always would be, she decided there and then to tell her something.

"Carolan, lie still beside me. I want to talk to you. Has anyone ever said anything to you about—about me . . . and . . . the way you were born?"

Carolan said quickly: "Yes, Charles says I am a bastard and not the squire's bastard at that. He said it is well enough for a squire to have as many bastards as he likes, but I am not even a squire's bastard."

Kitty cried out to stop her. "Oh, the wicked boy! I hate him! He is like his father."

"I hate him too," said Carolan happily.

"But I want to tell you, darling, about how you were born. It will not be very easy for you to understand, but will you try?"

Carolan nodded. How lovely it was in her mother's bed! There were sweet smells of powder and ointments in the room and the ornate posts of the bed enchanted her. She would have liked to draw the curtains tightly and be shut in with her mother.

"Darling, please listen very, very carefully. Years ago I loved your father."

"Not the squire!" said Carolan. "He is not my father, is he, Mamma?"

"No, not the squire. You see, I loved your father very dearly, and we were going to London to be married, and we were going on the coach. He went to Exeter to see about our going but he went into a tavern there, and while he was in that tavern, the press gang took him."

Kitty was crying at the memory, for she cried as easily at twenty-seven as she had at seventeen.

"Mamma, who is the press gang?"

Kitty clenched her hands and answered vehemently: "A wicked gang of cruel men who take men wherever they may be and force them into the Navy."

"But why, Mamma?"

"Because they need men for the Navy."

"And would they take any man at any time? Perhaps they will take Charles."

Kitty whimpered: "How different my life would have been but for the press gang! We should have been together, your father and I. How you would have loved your father, darling!"

Carolan's eyes were wide and dark; she could not grasp this very clearly. Her father—not the squire—in a tavern and a mysterious group of men called the press gang; they had cruel faces and they dragged him away while he screamed to be released.

"Oh, Carolan," cried Kitty, "do not blame me, darling. Do not listen to evil tales of me. Remember only that I loved your father; I loved him too well."

"Mamma, is there still the press gang?"

"There is still the press gang!" She added wildly: "There always has been; there always will be! Oh, my darling, the wickedness . . . the wickedness. And when you were born, my precious child, you would have had no father, so I married the squire in order to give you one."

"But how could you give me one if I had none, Mamma?"

"Carolan, my own daughter, try not to blame me!"

Carolan, whose nursery days were full of taking blame for real and imaginary sins, did not understand for what she should blame her mother. But it was pleasant in bed, and she was indeed sorry when Thérèse came bustling in to lift her hands and murmur: "What is here! What is here!" in her funny accents.

"It is a birthday little girl!" said Kitty, all tears gone, full of smiles.

"A wicked one," said Thérèse, "to spoil her mamma's beauty sleep!"

"Ah, but it was sweet of her to come. Carolan, my darling, come again, and we will talk often of . . . you know what. It is our secret, and we will talk together of it."

Carolan nodded. What a wonderful birthday morning! She had come, hoping for a present, and had discovered a secret. But then, were not secrets as amusing and exciting as presents?

"I will come," she said.

"And now," said Thérèse, lifting her from the bed, "you will go, yes?"

She ran to the door, looking back once to smile at her mother, and the look that passed between them was an acknowledgment of a secret shared.

She ran along to the nursery, where Margaret and Charles were already having their bread and milk. Charles stared down into his plate, eating hurriedly. He always ate hurriedly in the nursery. He was fifteen, and going away to school shortly; he thought eating in the nursery was beneath his dignity. Margaret was looking excitedly at the parcel she had put by Carolan's place. Jennifer sat at the head of the table.

"Ah!" said Jennifer. "And where have you been, Miss? I have been to your room once for you!"

"That," said Carolan, "is no business of yours, Jennifer!"

"Come here!" said Jennifer.

Carolan tossed her head and went to her place at the table.

"I'll tan the hide off you after breakfast!" said Jennifer. She always felt ill in the morning—too tired to put any energy into whipping the child.

"Perhaps!" said Carolan.

"No perhaps about it, Miss!"

Charles looked up, interested, as though he hoped Jennifer would begin now.

Carolan said boldly: "You could not tan the hide off anybody, Jennifer Jay. You are not much good at tanning; you are getting old!"

Jennifer stood up. Charles put out his foot, so that if Carolan tried to run she would have difficulty in getting past it. Carolan, feeling concerned, shouted in bravado: "You are getting old, Jennifer Jay! In the kitchen they say you are getting too old, Jennifer Jay!"

It was worth any whipping, to see the colour run out of Jennifer's face.

"Yes!" said Jennifer. "It is to be expected; you would talk to those sluts in the kitchen, you! That is your place—down there with them. I can tell you what will happen to you, Miss Carolan!"

"What?" said Carolan, who really wanted to know.

"You will end up on a gibbet, or in Botany Bay!"

Margaret was looking at Carolan in shocked wonder. Charles was laughing his agreement. Carolan quailed; there were those who said that Jennifer Jay was almost a witch.

"No!" cried Carolan, feeling rather frightened. "It is you who will end up on the gibbet, Jennifer Jay!"

Charles put his face close to Carolan's.

"Do not forget it is a birthday, young Carolan!"

"I do not forget. I am nine today! Yesterday I was eight. Today I am nine!"

"Nine is not much to be!" said Margaret. "But here is a present for you, Carolan. From me to you. A happy birthday! See, I have written it on the paper there. 'A happy birthday from Margaret to Carolan'."

"Oh, thank you, thank you!" Carolan hunched her shoulders with delight.

Margaret said impatiently: "Open it! Open it!" And, fingers trembling with excitement, Carolan opened it. Inside the packet was a book-mark in silk, with flowers embroidered on it, and "Carolan Haredon, April 19th, 1793" worked in red and blue. One of Carolan's great gifts was to be able to disperse elaborate expectation and find complete joy in the reality. She forgot the saddle she had dreamed that Margaret would give her; now she was completely absorbed in the beauty of the book-mark.

"Margaret, it is lovely!"

"You do like it!" cried Margaret eagerly. "I did those flowers myself!"

"They are beautiful!"

"There are a few bad stitches in the red ones," said Margaret modestly.

"*I* cannot see them!" Carolan warmly assured her, and they smiled shyly at each other.

Charles said: "Here! Margaret's not the only one who's got a present for you, baby."

Carolan stared incredulously at Charles, for from his pocket he took a brown paper packet.

"Oh . . . Charles! Thank you."

"Happy birthday!" said Charles.

"Thank you! Thank you!" Carolan smiled at him very sweetly. She felt ashamed that she hated him when she came into the room. She took the package; it was soft. There was no sound in the nursery but the crackling of paper. Beneath the first wrapping was a second one.

"Go on!" said Charles. "You are slow."

"I wonder what it is," said Margaret. "Charles, you did not tell me . . . though I told you the book-mark was for Carolan!"

"Oh," cried Charles, "she will love this better than your silly book-mark. She will take it to bed; she will keep it under her pillow; she will carry it wherever she goes. She will love it so much."

"Margaret," said Carolan, "the book-mark *is* lovely." And she thought: What would I take to bed with me? What would I keep under my pillow? What would I carry wherever I went?

What a successful birthday, with even Charles remembering it!

The parcel was open. Carolan squealed, and dropped it; her face was ashen. Lying in the paper was a tiny shrew mouse which had been dead some days.

Jennifer began to laugh shrilly.

"She will take it to bed with her! She will keep it under her pillow! She will carry it wherever she goes!"

Carolan raised her eyes and looked at Charles—looked at him with such utter loathing that momentarily his laughter was quelled.

Margaret said: "That was beastly . . . to pretend it was a present!"

"Be silent!" said Charles.

"Bah!" said Jennifer. "You cannot see a joke. Look at the little Greedy Guts! Ready to burst into tears, I do declare."

Carolan hated death; she ran from death. If she saw a funeral in the village, with all its black trappings and the mourners all covered in black, she could not sleep that night, and when she did, her sleep was disturbed by frightful dreams. Birds, animals, people . . . when they were dead they

97

changed subtly; they were not birds, animals, people any more. She could never be happy, thinking of death. And here, on her birthday, was death presented to her in the shape of the small limp body of a shrew mouse.

But the fun had only just begun for Charles.

"So you would throw my present on the floor, would you? You ungrateful little beast! Pick it up . . . Pick it up, I say! Do you not love its soft silky body? Stroke it, baby. Its name is Carrie—named after its new mistress, you see. Pick it up, I say! Kiss it!"

"I will not touch it," said Carolan.

He caught Carolan in his strong arms; she began to kick.

"Nine years old, she is!" he said, looking at her derisively. "One would think it was nine months!" He narrowed his eyes. "Carolan, are you going to pick up my nice present? Are you going to carry it in your pocket, take it to bed with you, my child?"

"No," cried Carolan. "No!"

Margaret looked unhappy. She hated to see Carolan tormented; but what could *she* do about it? She was not yet thirteen herself, so what could she do against Charles and Jennifer?

Charles gravely put Carolan down; his brown eyes that were flecked with yellow were the cruellest eyes in the world, thought Carolan, and when they blazed in anger they were not so cruel as they were when they laughed in this quiet way.

He picked up the mouse by its tail; then he caught Carolan. Carolan shut her eyes tightly, that she might not look into his face.

"Open your eyes," said Charles.

"I will not."

"You will," said Charles. "Do you think I bring you presents that you may haughtily shut your eyes and not look at them?"

"I hate you!" sobbed Carolan.

"Stop this," interrupted Margaret. "It is so silly."

Jennifer said nothing; she just sat there, leaning her arms on the table.

"Carolan," said Charles, "must learn not to be a silly baby."

With a mighty effort Carolan, taking Charles off his guard, wrenched herself free. She ran towards the door.

"Mamma!" she screamed. "Mamma!" But Charles dashed at her; she fell, Charles sprawled on top of her. Carolan beat at him with her fists; Charles was helpless with laughter, and

Carolan's sobs and Charles's laughter mingled oddly together. George Haredon, opening the door, stared at the scene in amazement.

"What is this?" he demanded, and there was sudden quiet in the nursery.

Charles and Carolan got to their feet. The squire did not look at Jennifer; he was heartily sick of looking at Jennifer. He looked from Charles to Carolan.

"What is this display?" he said, and he put a heavy hand on Carolan's shoulder and turned her face up to his. "Tears?"

"She is such a baby, master," said Jennifer.

Carolan stamped her foot.

"I am not a baby!" She faced the squire furiously. "I do not cry because I am a baby. I cry because I hate him."

"Nice words! Nice words!" said the squire, and sat down heavily on one of the chairs at the breakfast table. It creaked under his weight. Jennifer cursed her ill-luck. There was grease on her gown which she had not bothered to remove; her hair was limp and in need of a combing. How was she to have known that the squire would visit the nursery so early! Could it be because of the brat's birthday? Had he come to the nursery early for Charles's birthday . . . for Margaret's?

"Now," said the squire, "I will hear why there is all this kicking and screaming at this hour of the morning."

"Miss Carolan is a silly little baby,". began Jennifer. "She wants a good whipping . . ."

George Haredon said, without looking at her: "I am not addressing you."

Ugly colour flooded Jennifer's face. He could talk to her like that, after . . . everything?

"Charles," said the squire, "tell me why you think it so amusing to make a little girl cry."

Charles said: "She is such a baby! It was a joke. That was all, and she could not take it."

"I will hear the joke," said George.

"Oh, it's a silly joke really, sir," said Charles.

"I have no doubt of that. But when I say I will hear it, I mean it. And listen, boy, I will be judge of whether it is silly or not. Carolan, come here. Margaret too."

They stood before him, all three of them, Carolan in the middle. The squire looked from his own two children to Kitty's child. Why, he thought angrily, do I have to have those two, and why shouldn't she be mine! He had tried to dislike her, God knew; he had tried to ignore her. But she would not be disliked, nor ignored; she intruded into his mind at odd moments. Her skin was like the bowls of rich cream that were served at his table—cream with the bloom of peaches in her cheeks; now there was angry red there, like roses. And the eyes that glittered with tears were decidedly green. The red in her hair delighted him. What was it that she had, and Kitty had, and Bess had had, and no one else in the world seemed to have? Why was she not his child, instead of these other two? Unnatural father that he was! When a man got older he was more given to self-analysis than in his younger days. There were days when he did not feel like hunting—not the fox, nor the otter, nor women could make him want to hunt; then he sat in the sun or by a fire and thought about himself . . . not what he wanted to do, nor what he wanted to eat, but what he *was*. Searching, searching for something that was George Haredon, and the tragedy of it was—or perhaps it wasn't a tragedy, merely an irritation—that he did not know for what he searched. First he had sought it in Bess. Ah! If only he had married Bess! But Bess had run off with an actor. Then he had sought it in Kitty, but Kitty was a wanton. And now he sought it in the child. Little Carolan—as near his daughter as made little difference really. Little Carolan, green-eyed, red-haired, with that elusive and mysterious quality which had been Bess's, which still was Kitty's.

"Well?" he questioned.

"It's her birthday," said Charles, "and I thought she would enjoy a joke, so . . ."

Margaret cut in: "He gave her a dead shrew mouse wrapped up in paper."

"Is that all?" said the squire, and glared at Carolan. He was filled with delight to see the colour fade from her cheeks and rapidly flow back again, to see her eyes flash and her head tilt up.

"She is a silly baby!" said Charles. "Mamma's pampered baby."

Carolan stamped her foot angrily.

"I am not. I am nine. I am not a baby."

The squire drew her towards him. He held her small body imprisoned between his great knees.

She said: "That hurts me!" and put her hand on his knees to try to force them apart. He laughed; she delighted him, this funny little child. Perhaps, he thought, it was safer to love a child than a woman. He loosened his grip.

"Why, damme, Carrie," he said, "I thought you were my chestnut mare, not a little girl!" And his eyes glistened with laughter. A smile turned up the corners of Carolan's mouth.

"I am not a bit like the chestnut mare."

"What!" he said. "With this carroty hair?" And he pulled her hair, not unkindly though. "Now then," he said sternly, "what made you lie on the floor and scream like that?"

You should not tell tales, Everard had said; at school it was the worst offence. So now she could not speak of the cruel thing Charles had done to her. She said nothing.

But Margaret answered. Margaret hated trouble, and unless something drastic was done, she could see this affair of the shrew mouse drifting on interminably. Margaret was a dainty creature; she loved fine needlework and good manners; she disliked the sight of the shrew mouse as much as Carolan did, only for different reasons. She did not fear dead things; she thought them unpleasant—and she hated the unpleasant.

So Margaret said: "Father, Charles gave Carolan a shrew mouse for her birthday, and it was dead and wrapped up in a parcel. Carolan hates dead shrew mice, and she thought it was a real present. And then he tried to make her kiss it."

The squire's eyes narrowed as they rested on his son. There were times when he disliked the boy. He reminded him irritatingly of what he was himself at Charles's age. He could imagine Charles, blundering through life, making the same mistakes as he had made.

"Ah!" he said. "Bullying, eh?" He stood up ponderously and caught the boy by his ear. "How old are you, eh? Fifteen, is it? And you think it funny to tease little girls of nine?"

"It was only a joke," said Charles sullenly.

"Then, sir, it is time you were taught what is a good joke and what is a damned bad one!"

Now Carolan was very sorry for Charles. It was amazing with what speed she could slip from one mood to another. A moment ago she could have killed Charles, she had hated him so; but now to see him there, so red in the face, his eyes so full of shame, she was sorry for him, because humiliating him like this in front of her and Margaret was the worst possible thing that could happen to him.

The squire turned to Jennifer.

"Get the girl ready. I am taking her for a ride."

Jennifer answered as sullenly as she dared: "Yes, sir." Then: "Margaret, you heard what your father said; you had better go and get into your riding kit immediately."

"Not Margaret!" roared the squire. "I mean Carolan!"

Jennifer bowed her head; she had no words, for if she had tried to speak then she would have burst into tears.

The squire turned to his son. "And you," he said, "will go

101

to my bedroom. I have something to teach you, my boy! Go!"
he shouted suddenly. "Go at once!" He watched Charles go
from the room. Then he turned to Jennifer. "You heard what
I said. Get the child ready." His eyes rested briefly on Carolan, and he tried to prevent a softness creeping into his voice.
"It'll be the worse for you, girl, if you keep me waiting!"

Then he strode out of the room.

Jennifer stood up and jerked Carolan by the arm.

"Come on, you little tell-tale! You have to be got ready to
go riding with the squire. I hope your horse throws you! I do. I
do indeed."

Margaret shrugged her shoulders. She was used to scenes.
She gave one disgusted glance at the brown paper and its contents still lying on the floor, and went into her room.

Jennifer pulled Carolan along the corridor to the room
next to Margaret's, which was Carolan's. She threw her in
and shut the door. Jennifer leaned against the door; her eyes
were brilliant, and there were dark patches under them.

"Get your things off," cried Jennifer. "Did you hear or did
you not hear the squire say you were to go riding with him?"

Carolan did not answer. She went to the cupboard and
took out the fawn-coloured riding habit which had been Margaret's and which Margaret had said she could have. It was
still a little too big for Carolan.

She took off her frock.

"Skin and grief!" jeered Jennifer, and hated the green eyes
and the red hair which the squire was so taken with. The
beast, she thought; trust him to be taken with a girl not his
own daughter! She watched Carolan's struggling into the
habit. There she stood, shabby yet devilishly attractive. Nine!
She had the same look in her eyes as her mother had had. Did
she know, the little harlot, that she looked like that? Could
she, at nine? Oh, to be nine again! thought Jennifer; nine,
with no knowledge of the terrible problems that beset one's
later days!

"Better comb your hair," she said. "It looks like a bird's
nest!" She came over and stood by Carolan. "Do you know
what the squire is doing to Charles now?" she asked.

"He is whipping him," said Carolan.

"Yes. Because of you, you little harlot!"

Carolan paused, the comb in her hand. "What is a harlot?"

"Well enough you know," said Jennifer, and whispered
venomously: "It is someone like you, and like your lady
mother. That is a harlot."

"Like me and like my mother!" Carolan screwed up her

102

face in concentration, trying to imagine in what way she was like her mother.

"I saw you!" said Jennifer. "Smiling at the squire! Egging him on!"

"What?" said Carolan, puzzled.

"Ha!" said Jennifer. "I wonder that Charles's dear mother does not come and haunt you—that I do!"

Carolan put out her tongue. In broad daylight it was not so terrifying to think of Charles's dead mother.

"You can be saucy, Miss. If tonight she came into your room . . ." Jennifer made claws of her fingers and stared down at them.

"Everard says there are no such things as ghosts."

"Doubtless it was because his mother told him not to frighten little girls. There are ghosts, so there!"

Tired and wearied was Jennifer, too tired for tormenting. She thought longingly of the gin she kept locked up in her room.

"You had better not keep the squire waiting, unless you want a whipping."

Carolan went down to the stables. She would rather have ridden alone than with the squire; she had never before ridden with him. They said he was a marvellous horseman. Carolan shivered in an ecstasy of terror.

One of the grooms came up to her and touched his forehead.

"Morning, Miss Carolan."

"Good morning, Jake."

Jake's chin was wagging, which it always did when he was amused; he was very amused this morning.

"Happy birthday to you, Miss Carolan!"

Carolan smiled dazzlingly. Fancy Jake's knowing it was her birthday!

"Oh, thank you, Jake! Is the pony ready?"

Jake's chin began to wag again.

"Is it, Jake?" she asked; she was fearful of another scene. If she was to ride with the squire, and her pony was not ready, there would be trouble; the squire hated waiting.

"Well, Missie, the pony bain't ready . . ."

"Oh, but Jake, did you not know . . ."

"I weren't told to get no pony ready, Miss Carolan."

"Well, let us get him ready now . . ."

"No, no, Missie, you durst not go in there!"

She stared at him, round-eyed.

"What is in there, Jake?"

" 'Twouldn't be for me to tell you, Miss Carolan."

Then the squire came into the yard. He was whistling jauntily. He had enjoyed thrashing that arrogant youngster; it made him feel oddly young again.

"Ah!" he said, in ripe good humour. "Ah! Mistress Carolan, eh? And Jake." He winked at Jake, and Jake's chin started to wag all over again.

"Very important day today, did you know, Jake?" The squire was waggish. Jake chortled; he looked as if he was going to burst with suppressed laugher.

"Aye, sir, I do know what day it be!"

"Very important indeed. Now, Jake, lead the way, man! Stop standing there like a plaguey donkey, and lead the way."

They went into one of the stables, and there already saddled up was a smallish mare, strawberry roan in colour. She was a lovely little creature, spirited and full of personality, and as they came in, her ears pricked and she whinnied.

"Well, there she is! And a nice little thing at that, eh, Jake?"

"Aye, sir . . . a pretty little thing, and no mistake!"

"And what do you say, Mistress Carolan?"

"She is beautiful," said Carolan, a sudden possibility occurring to her which could not, simply could not, be true. She could not bear the suspense, so she said: "Whose is she?"

The squire laughed.

"Well, Jake," he said, "is it your birthday today, Jake?"

"No, master, bain't my birthday."

"Well, it bain't my birthday either!" The squire slapped his thigh.

"Do you mean . . ." said Carolan, looking at him very direct. "Do you mean . . . she's *mine?*"

"That's about it," said the squire.

"A birthday present?"

"Well, as Jake says, it bain't his birthday, and it bain't mine!"

"Oh!" cried Carolan. "Oh!"

And when she looked up, the squire's eyes were swimming with tears. She could see the red in them behind the tears.

"Thank you!" she said in a small voice. "Oh, thank you."

Then, because she was so happy, she forgot to be afraid; she forgot everything but that the strawberry roan was hers—no more ponies for her! Charles had a horse; Margaret had a pony; and she, Carolan, had this lovely strawberry roan. She could hardly believe it. She leaped high into the air, threw

104

aside that restraint she had always worn in the presence of the squire, and said: "I wanted a pony! I wanted a pony . . . I didn't *think* of a horse."

The squire said briskly: "Not much good having a horse, if you cannot ride it. Think you can?"

"Ride it!" screamed Carolan.

"Well, let us see."

It was strange to be riding alongside the squire. Always before, she had been out with one of the grooms; usually with Charles and Margaret too. And perhaps it was because she had ridden with Charles in those early days that she had learned to ride so quickly, and sat her horse so well and with such confidence. In the early days when she had been a little frightened, Charles used to whip up his horse to a furious gallop, and in a little while he would have her mount and Margaret's galloping wildly after him. Charles thought it good fun to see Carolan, white-faced, clinging to her saddle.

The squire watched her as she rode beside him; the sight of her straight little back delighted him. A good little horsewoman! Charles was good on a horse, and fearless enough, but he did not really like Charles. How pleased with the mare the child had been! The squire did not know when he had enjoyed anything so much. She had not expected a present from him either. There was a rare smile on the squire's face; it was pleasant to look into the future. A daughter to dote on her old father. He pictured them, riding together through his estate. Why should they not be the best of companions? The squire and his daughter—a good squire now, because he had no longer a roving eye for every village slut; he had eyes only for his daughter who was growing into a young woman more beautiful than any of them.

He broke into a canter, and then into a gallop. Carolan kept beside him, her red hair flying out behind; fine she looked, sitting her strawberry roan with distinction. Damme, thought the squire, if I don't take her along to the hunt with me! Why not? She can sit a horse with the best.

"Come on, Carrie girl," he shouted. "Why are you lagging behind?" And he laughed inwardly to see her spurt forward, her little chin set and determined.

Proud of her, he was. He wanted to show her off. A pity there was no meet today. Like to see her there among the pink coats. But not in those disreputable cast-offs of Margaret's. She should have a new riding habit; she should be grateful to him. He would say: "Come on, Carrie girl, what about a kiss for your old father?" When she was little more than a baby she had called him The Squire; now she called him nothing. She had to begin calling him Father; she had to think of him as her father. If anybody let her know he was not her father, there was going to be the devil to pay. After all, suppose he was her father; there was such a thing as a seven months child! She had been a little thing when she was born; suppose she had been born prematurely. Not impossible. How he wanted to believe that! The squire . . . and his daughter . . .

The parsonage was down this road along which they were trotting. Why not call on the parson and "Mrs. Parson"? Be a good start. Let people know that he looked on Carolan as his daughter. He went riding with her on her birthday; he had given her a horse. Charles had had a horse on his ninth birthday, and Margaret a pony.

"Oh!" said Carolan, when he drew up. "Are we going to see Everard?"

He had not thought of the boy of course. He was thinking chiefly of the parson's wife; old Orland did not count for much. The important thing was that Mrs. Orland should receive them and talk about the visit.

He signed curtly to her to dismount, and she did so neatly, he noticed with pleasure. They made fast their horses to gate posts.

Mrs. Orland suppressed her surprise at the call.

"Good morning, Squire. This is an unexpected pleasure!"

He was bubbling over with good spirits.

"As long as it is a pleasure, does it matter that it is unexpected?" he asked archly.

Mrs. Orland tittered sharply.

"We were out riding," said the squire, "and as we were passing . . . well, Carrie and I did not feel we could pass old friends without calling in to say how do you do."

"Of course not. Of course not. You will drink a glass of my cowslip wine, Squire?"

Cowslip wine! Elderberry wine! These old ladies! Champagne he would have preferred in his present mood.

"Nothing would delight me more!" he said, and he let his rather bloodshot eyes roam over her. Skinny, was his verdict. A proper parson's wife. Poor Orland! He reckoned he did not have much of a time with her. She flushed now at the boldness of his stare. Inwardly he chortled. These old women! Full of pretence. They thought they hated the way he looked at them because it was lechery; what they really hated was the fact that they had such skinny unattractive bodies. If they had something worth offering, they would be all a-simpering like any pot-house trollop.

But he had forgotten his new role; he was a father today, not a hunter of women.

"It is the little girl's birthday," he said, as they all sat drinking the cowslip wine.

"I know that," said Mrs. Orland, smiling. "Carolan, my dear, if you will go into the library you will find a parcel with your name on it. You may open it."

"Thank you, Mrs. Orland."

"Now run and get it."

Everard came into the library just as she found the parcel.

"I heard your voice," he said.

Her eyes were dancing, her cheeks red as berries, her hair glinting like the bronze ornaments on the mantelpiece.

"What has happened?" asked Everard.

"It is my birthday. The squire has given me a horse . . . all for myself. And now . . . Mrs. Orland has said there is a parcel here for me . . . I have it." On the brown paper was written "For Carolan on her birthday from Sophia, Edward and Everard Orland."

Everard came over to look. He had not known it was Carolan's birthday; he did not know what was in the parcel. Until this moment he had not been very interested in Carolan. She was just a little girl who was shamefully bullied by her half-brother whom Everard disliked intensely.

Inside the parcel was a cedarwood box.

"Oh . . ." cried Carolan. "What a lovely box! Oh, Everard, isn't it lovely to have a birthday!"

She leaped up suddenly and, putting her arms round his neck, kissed him.

Everard said: "Here . . . I say . . . I say!" But he was blushing, perhaps because she had kissed him, perhaps because he had known nothing of the cedarwood box.

"It is lovely . . . lovely of you, Everard, to remember my birthday."

He was filled with shame; heartily he wished that he had remembered. He was going to explain, but that would be tantamount to saying his mother told a lie. He was full of chivalry; he could not expose his mother's deceit, any more than he could allow that beast Charles to bully his little half-sister.

"I must go to thank your mother," she said, and together they went back to the drawing-room. The squire was sprawling on the sofa, his great legs apart.

"Ha, ha! Here is the heroine of the day!"

Carolan was hugging the cedarwood box.

"Thank you, Mrs. Orland. It is a beautiful box! May I go and thank Mr. Orland?"

"He is writing his sermon, dear; I should not disturb him. I will convey your thanks to him."

"Let me see the box," said the squire, and Carolan went over to him. She listened to his breath coming noisily through his great nostrils. The hairs in his nostrils fascinated her; they had frightened her when she was younger.

"Ha! A nice little box, eh, daughter?" He thought with satisfaction—cheap though! Picked up from some plaguey pedlar! And he laughed to think of the strawberry roan, impatiently stamping her foot outside.

Some new intuition told Carolan that he wanted to be thanked again for his gift, and because she was truly grateful and wanted to show her delight, and because, in some way she did not understand she was sorry for him, she said: "May I show Everard my lovely, lovely horse?"

The squire gave her a contented push.

"Go on!" he said. "Go on!"

And she and Everard went out. It was good to be with Everard. Everard was old, nearly seventeen; a man, of course; she had to remember that and not be too silly, too childish.

Everard patted the mare and said she was a beauty.

Suddenly he said: "Carolan, we'll ride together one day."

"Oh, Everard, shall we?"

He wondered why he had suggested it. He, almost seventeen and destined for the church, to want to go riding with a little nine-year-old girl! It seemed silly; but he had spoken on impulse and now he would have to go, for he was much too kind to go back on his word.

"And Carolan," he said. "Wait here a moment, will you? Do not go indoors. Just wait here. I will be back."

She caught the excitement in him, birthday excitement.

"Yes, Everard, I will wait."

She patted the mare, and stroked her soft, velvety muzzle.

"You are mine," she whispered. "You are mine! Carolan's strawberry roan mare, you are! Nobody else's."

The mare showed her pleasure in being made much of, and Carolan thought, She knows she's mine and I love her.

Then Everard was beside her. He held out to her a paper-knife of wood which he had made himself.

"The box was from all of us," he said shyly, "but I wanted to give you something special."

"Oh, Everard! Another birthday present. But you gave the box . . ."

"Ah, but this is different. From me alone."

"From you alone," said Carolan solemnly, and she knew that it was a very special present because Everard had given it to her. She was too young to keep that knowledge to herself. "I love it. It is the loveliest of all my presents." She fondled the mare, and she knew she understood that this was no reflection on her value as herself, but merely as a birthday present.

"It is not really very good," said Everard, and showed her a flaw in the wood.

"I love the flaw," she persisted stubbornly, and he laughed and noticed, as the squire had done, that her eyes were deep green as the sea sometimes is.

He said slowly: "If Charles ever hurts you, Carolan, you are to come and tell me. Do you understand?"

She nodded.

"I will tell him what you said," she promised him, looking up at Everard's tall figure and hunching her shoulders in delight. "I think he will take very great care when I tell him that."

"It will be better for him if he does!" boasted Everard, and she played with the idea of telling him about the shrew mouse. How angry he would be, and what delight in seeing his anger! But her pity for her enemy was strong within her, for he was a vanquished enemy; today he had already been beaten for his cruelty, and, worse still, humiliated. So she did not tell.

Mrs. Orland and the squire watched them coming across the lawn, Carolan dancing beside Everard, dancing round him—a dainty creature with flying hair and uncurbed spirits. Quite the most attractive of the Haredon children, thought Mrs. Orland, and Everard obviously liked her, more, it seemed, than he liked Margaret. But what did that matter, they were young yet! He would marry Margaret; both she and Edward had decided on Margaret for Everard, for Margaret would make an ideal parson's wife, a sweet girl, skilled in the domestic arts, gentle and pliable. Mrs. Orland foresaw a happy life for her son. This living would be his, and two others besides; a life of leisure should be Everard's, with curates to help him. But Margaret was of course the wife for him, so he must not get too fond of the little girl. Her birth for one thing was against her; people in a small place did not forget these things; besides, her high spirits, her lack of decorum—

charming as it was—were not suitable for a parson's wife. One had heard stories of a certain blacksmith's daughter who had married a parson. History must not repeat itself as neatly as that.

The squire watched them too, and wondered why anyone with as much spirit as his Carolan could admire a pale-faced scholar as this boy seemed to be. He felt jealous too. Damme, there will be a bit of trouble with her when the time comes, he thought, and he did not know whether he was pleased or angry that there would be this trouble. He was disturbed anyway.

"We must be going," he said, and he roared: "Carolan! Come here, girl. Come and say goodbye to Mrs. Orland, for we are going!"

Mrs. Orland and Everard walked to the gate with them. They stood waving as Carolan and the squire trotted down the lane.

"Bah!" said the squire. "White-faced milksop of a boy that! A parson in the making!"

He began to laugh derisively, looking at her from under his bushy brows as he did so.

She flushed a little.

"He is not," she said. "He is very brave. Why . . ." It was on the tip of her tongue to tell him how once, quite a long time ago, he had fought Charles for locking her in with the dead, and how, ever since, Charles had been afraid of Everard. But how could she tell that story without telling of the part Charles had played in it?

"What?" said the squire. But she would not tell; she merely repeated: "He is very brave."

The squire chortled uneasily.

"Damme if you are not impressed by his pretty face!"

She said: "He is not pretty, is he?"

"I saw you," blundered on the squire, "playing the coquette there on the lawn. Damme if you were not flirting with the boy!"

She turned a look so cold upon him that he was faintly alarmed, which was of course absurd. He had given her a magnificent present; she was his daughter; she should be fond of him. He would beat her till she was black and blue if she was not. She had ridden on a little ahead of him, like a queen showing her displeasure. By God, he thought, will she be haughty with me, eh! He spurred his horse until he was level with her; but the delicacy of her child's profile turned his anger into something he did not understand. Harshness was no way to win these creatures; he had to learn to be soft. For here was Bess and Kitty all over again; he saw it in the tilt of her head. Damn her! If he took the horse away from her she would doubtless toss her head and let it go rather than hear a word said against her friend Everard. They were like that, these female creatures who fascinated him. This was his third chance and he had to learn his lesson. If he wanted their affection—and God damn him he would be a lonely man to the end of his days without some affection—he had to win it, not stretch out and take it; it had to be given, not grabbed.

"There!" he said, with his voice soft enough to please her. "You have a silly old man for a father, Carrie—that's what you're thinking?"

She turned towards him. Her eyes were like green jewels and her brow above them was like ivory. All anger had faded before the softness in his voice. She said indignantly: "Of course you are not silly!"

"Father!" he said. "You talk to me as though I am a post. Am I to have no name?"

Now the colour rushed into her face. She knew then, did she! That sly Jennifer had doubtless told her; by God, he would have her out of that nursery. How he wished he had never clapped eyes on the woman.

"Carrie," he said, "why should you not call me Father?"

She said: "I will, if you wish." And he was not at all sure then that she knew.

"Well, see that you do in future, and begin now. Come on!"

"Yes . . . Father."

"Look here, Carrie, we are friends, you see. I like you, Carrie." His horse was so close to hers now that he leaned over her and she could feel his breath against her cheek. "If anything goes wrong up there in the nursery, you come and tell me all about it, understand?"

Two champions in one morning!

Her lips parted and she nodded.

"Thank you . . . Father!"

He roared with laughter. He slapped his thigh. She wished he would not do that; it irritated her strangely. But he was constantly doing it; it meant he was pleased in a particular way.

Lightly she touched the strawberry roan with her heel, and together she and the squire broke into a canter up the slight incline.

"Carrie!" he cried. "I'll tell you what we will do! We will pay a call on your Aunt Harriet!"

He was full of fun and mischief. Fun to see old Harry again! Besides, she had a present for the child; she had sent a note over to say so. He would enjoy comparing this young beauty with that dry old spinster, particularly as Harriet did not like the child.

"She has a present for you."

"Another present!" Carolan brought her mare down to a trot. Those little hands, he thought, who would believe they had such power in them!

He put his face very close to hers to see more clearly the soft texture of her skin, for his eyes were not what they had been.

"Hey, girl," he said, "it will not be a strawberry roan she has for you. What do you think?"

"A Prayer Book."

"Or a Bible!"

It was good fun to share a joke with your young daughter. Damn it, she was his daughter; she was a seven months child. Had not Kitty had some trouble in rearing her? His daughter! His! There would be trouble for anyone who dared suggest she was not!

Oaklands looked neat and trim, and the blinds had been drawn to shut out the sunshine. Emm from the workhouse opened the door; she was not a bad-looking girl. Possibilities there, the squire had often thought, if one had the time to develop them; he certainly had no time this morning; he was paying a call with his daughter.

Harriet came into the drawing-room.

"Why, George, how delightful of you to call!"

"I am not alone. I have brought someone with me who has a birthday."

He winked broadly at Harriet, who tried to smile. She did not believe in pampering children. She looked much the same as she had the day Kitty had come to her; there was perhaps a little more grey in her hair; she had never really recovered from the disappointment the squire had given her, though she tried to tell herself that it was a matter for congratulation. George had not improved with the years; he had coarsened visibly, and he had never been a refined man. Once she had caught him kissing Janet in the hall; Janet was the workhouse girl who shared the work with Emm. Disgusting sight!

"Carolan," roared George, "come and say how do you do to your Aunt Harriet."

"My gracious!" said Aunt Harriet. "Whatever has the child been doing? Look at your hair, girl! Look at your hands! I cannot have you in my drawing-room in such a condition."

The squire put out a hand and rumpled the reddish hair.

"This child," he said, with what Harriet noticed was a fondness almost touching on imbecility, "could never be tidy. She was not made that way!" He began to laugh as though it were a great joke.

"Run along, child," said Harriet severely. "Find Janet or Emm, and one of them will give you water to wash your hands, and do please comb your hair!"

The child, she thought, was very like her grandmother—the same pertness, the same way of twisting a man like George Haredon round her fingers.

"And," she called after Carolan, "tell Emm to bring two glasses and the cowslip wine." She turned to George, and she was smiling now. "I know you always like my cowslip wine better than anyone else's."

"Ah!" said George. "Your cowslip wine, Harry—no one can touch it!"

The woman almost dimpled. He sat down heavily in one of her chairs.

"I hope," she said severely, "that that child is not in danger of being spoiled."

"Who, little Carrie?"

Harriet frowned in an exasperation from which she could not keep a certain tenderness. Was it not typical of George to call Carolan Carrie, just as he called her Harry! Even now she thought of George as a big-hearted, blundering and misguided boy. The right woman would have made all the difference in the world to George, and she, Harriet, knew full well who that woman was, though she would never whisper it to a soul.

"Yes," she said, "Carolan."

George was serious suddenly. "I do not think there is much spoiling done in the nursery. Jennifer Jay is not the woman to spoil a child, and Charles, I am sorry to say, can be a brute."

"She seems to me to be a pert creature in the making."

"She is going to be a regular little beauty, eh, Harry?"

"I sincerely hope not, George."

"You mean that?"

"I think a woman is a better woman for not being . . . a regular little beauty!"

"You would know more about that than I would, Harry," he said wickedly.

The cowslip wine was brought in and poured out by Emm. Absently, but with interest, the squire's eyes rested on Emm's young body beneath the old-fashioned muslin dress which had once been Harriet's. Harriet noticed his look, and sighed.

"Thank you, Emm!" said the squire, and he took his glass and drank noisily. "Good stuff, Harry! Good stuff!"

He felt amusement bubbling up inside him; he was in good spirits today. Have a bit of fun with old Harriet! It appealed to him, that, in his new chaste mood. He was a father today; so he would have a bit of fun with old Harry, because in no circumstances could he be tempted.

"Ah!" he murmured. "A pity you never married. You would have made some man a damned fine wife!"

Her lips quivered slightly.

"Yes," he said, letting his lids fall over his eyes to hide the twinkle there, "a damned fine wife. Cannot think why you never did, Harry. 'Pon my soul, I cannot think why!"

"Well, George, there are other things in life than matrimony. And if a woman remains a spinster, it may not be for the want of asking."

"He would have been a lucky man, Harry, a lucky man!" He had infused his voice with a wistfulness which almost made him choke.

"Thank you, George," she said quietly and gently.

"But men," went on the squire, "are fools sometimes, Harry. Damned fools men are!"

She lifted her face, and he saw how brilliant her eyes were. Her skin was pale, but it seemed to glow, and he could see the fluttering of her heart beneath the prim bodice.

"I know," went on George, "because I happen to be one myself!"

Harriet got to her feet and went rather shakily towards the cowslip wine.

"Another glass, George?"

"I could never say no to your cowslip wine, Harry!"

Oh, this was the greatest fun, this was! Here she was, standing before him, her eyes downcast, her hands not quite steady. She had taken it in, the sly old puss. Why, she was as ready and willing as any pot-house wench, for all her prudery. Ah! thought the squire, what is virtue? Where is it? There is nothing real in virtue. It is a phantom, and women like Harriet pride themselves in possessing it, because they know no one will ever attack it. Oh, you silly old woman; it would be the greatest joke of a lifetime to take her here and now, with one of those workhouse girls likely to burst in at any moment and catch their mistress eagerly relinquishing a virtue she had cherished for years. Better than that, take her to her still-room and violate her virginity there! Damn it! That would be the greatest joke he could think of. She had preserved it as zealously as she preserved her plums, and all because she had known there would be no one to take it! When he got home he would split his sides with laughing. It would have been good fun to tell Kitty all about it, if Kitty had been what he had always wanted her to be. But Kitty and he were far apart —as far apart as he and Bess were really.

He took the glass from Harriet, and let his fingers touch hers sentimentally. Then Carolan came into the room, her hair combed into some order.

"Come here, child," said Harriet, "and let me see your hands."

Carolan showed them.

"Not very clean," said Harriet.

"They do not come quite clean," said Carolan, smiling disarmingly.

The two of them, side by side . . . What a contrast, he thought! Why, the child was more of a woman even now than Harriet could ever be.

"You are nine years old today," said Harriet. "You are leaving childhood behind you; it should not be necessary to tell you to wash your hands."

Carolan looked up at Harriet, and saw the squire standing just behind her; he winked at Carolan, and Carolan began to laugh.

"Really!" said Harriet. "Really! Why do you laugh?"

"I do not know," said Carolan, for she could not say she laughed because the squire had winked at her. "I just laughed."

"Indeed, Miss. That was very unseemly. In my young days I should have been beaten for such rudeness. But nowadays there is much licence!" Harriet turned to George. "You have heard, have you not, that to spare the rod is to spoil the child?"

George laid his great hands on Carolan and lifted her up.

"There shall be no sparing of the rod nor spoiling of the child," he said, and he tweaked Carolan's ear to show her that he was making another joke.

"I had a present for you," said Harriet, as though she were wondering whether Carolan still deserved it.

"Oh, thank you, thank you, Aunt Harriet!"

Harriet sailed over to a little table and unlocked a drawer.

"And I hope, my child, that you will read it every day."

George stooped down and whispered: "A Bible, I will bet you, young Carrie. A Bible!"

And so it was. Carolan was laughing so much she could scarcely say thank you.

"If everyone," said Harriet, "read their Bibles every day, there would be less trouble in the world." And she was looking at George as she said this. He and Carolan stood side by side like two children. He was enjoying this; he had not been in such spirits for years.

"That's true," said George. "Remember it, young Carolan!" And now he had had enough of this visit. They must go, he said. "Thank you, Harriet, for the wine. Thank you for *everything.*" He kissed her hand. A most interesting morning.

They rode home slowly. He dismounted first and went over to Carolan.

"Well," he said, "what do you think of your father's birthday present?"

"It is a lovely present! Thank you!"

"Thank you—who?"

"Thank you, Father."

He shook a big finger at her, which made him look very wicked.

"And do not forget, please, or . . ."

She moved from him a little.

"I will not forget, Father. And I love my present . . . It is a lovely, lovely present."

He was satisfied.

"I was right about the Bible, Carrie!"

She hunched her shoulders and laughed. Oh, she had charm. Why? She was not really pretty, though she might be later. But even now she had all Bess's charm and all Kitty's charm, though it was without their beauty.

"Do not forget it was a bet," he said, and he was breathless with emotion.

"A bet? What . . ."

"I said, did I not, 'I bet it is a Bible'?"

"Oh, yes, you said that."

"And it was; so because I was right you owe me something."

She was bewildered, wondering what he meant.

"What . . . should I owe you?"

"Well, as we did not stipulate, shall we say . . . a kiss?"

"A kiss!" She was a little startled, and he saw that and was

116

suddenly angry. God damn them, they were all alike. He had given her a valuable mare, and she did not want to give even a kiss in exchange. But, God damn her insolence, she should! He lifted her out of the saddle, and put his face close to hers. He kissed her on the mouth. It was such a soft baby mouth. She gave a little cry of dismay for he had hurt her with his roughness.

He shouted at her: "By God, girl, you would take everything and give nothing—your mother all over again! Kiss me or I will give you the biggest thrashing you have ever had in your life."

Her little mouth trembled. She shut her eyes tightly, so that he could see the fringe of reddish-tipped lashes jutting out; she shut her eyes so that she should not see his face, he knew. She kissed him and his heart was heavy within him.

He set her down angrily.

"Get in!" he said. "Get in before I put a whip about your shoulders."

She went, and he looked after her, and he knew that the morning had not been a success but a miserable failure. She was not his daughter any more than he was the man he sometimes pretended he was because he longed to be that man.

"Jake!" he roared. "You lazy hound, where are you?"

Jake came out and touched his forelock. Jake was jumpy as a two-year-old, eager to anticipate his master's wishes when he was in this mood.

"Take those damned horses away!" cried the squire. And he turned sharply and went into the house.

Carolan went up to the nursery happily enough. She had had an abrupt dismissal from the squire, but she did not attach much importance to that. It had been an agreeable morning, except when she had had to kiss the squire. That had been most unpleasant, but Carolan's life had never run smoothly for very long at a time, so she was prepared for sudden storms.

But, going upstairs, she thought what an extraordinary morning it had been. First her talk with her mother, then the horrible affair of the shrew mouse, then the present of the horse, then Everard who had said they must go riding together, then the horrid way the squire had kissed her. And now . . . back to the nursery, and she did not know what she would find. Charles and Jennifer might have something fearful in store for her as a punishment.

Cautiously she went in. There was no sign of anyone. She

117

breathed with relief, and went along to Margaret's room because she wanted to tell Margaret about the horse and the Bible and the paper-knife and cedarwood box.

"Margaret!" she called, and tapped on the door. There was no answer and she opened the door. Margaret had been sitting at her table by the window, for there was her quill pen and some sheets of paper lying on it.

She thought she heard Margaret in the garden below, and went to the window to look out; as she did so her eyes fell on the paper which had fluttered to the floor. On it was written "Margaret Haredon. Margaret Orland."

Carolan picked it up. Margaret Haredon was Margaret, of course, but who was Margaret Orland? There was no Margaret Orland! Then on the other side of the paper she saw that Margaret had written that many times. "Margaret Orland. Margaret Orland."

Why, Margaret could only be Margaret Orland if she *married* Everard!

What a strange morning! So much had been discovered, and yet more than ever seemed hidden. Margaret wanted to marry Everard! That was the latest discovery, and it disturbed Carolan, for though it seemed silly to think of such things when you were nine years old, she had imagined herself, some day, in the vague future, married to Everard.

Margaret was coming up the stairs and Carolan hastily threw down the sheet of paper; she went out into the corridor to meet Margaret, and though she told her about the strawberry roan, the cedarwood box and the Bible, she did not mention the paperknife.

There was one summer's day in Carolan's thirteenth year which she was to remember all her life. It was a hot day with a haze in the sky and scarcely a breath of air; she was old enough now to feel an uneasiness in the atmosphere about her. She knew that Napoleon was scoring success after success on the Continent and the squire grumbled a good deal and watched his villagers closely for the least sign of insolence. One awoke each morning wondering if something fearful would happen that day, but life went on much as usual until that summer's afternoon.

Charles was away in another part of the country staying with a school-fellow; Margaret and Carolan breakfasted together as usual, and after breakfast did their lessons with the governess who had been engaged for them last year. Miss

Scanlane was drowsy on that day, as indeed were Margaret and Carolan. Outside the schoolroom the wasps were buzzing noisily, and Carolan longed to be out with them; but when the afternoon came and she was free, she found it too hot to ride, too hot to walk over to the parsonage to see if Everard was at home, too hot to do anything but lie under the oak tree in the park and drowsily peer up through its leaves at the heavy sky. Margaret had gone off in the direction of the parsonage. Poor Margaret, at sixteen she was very intense and very tragic! She read poetry in her room every night; Carolan could hear the rumbling of her voice, and she knew it was all about love—tragic love. She even wrote poetry; she had shown Carolan some of it, and it was all about the sadness of love, and very melancholy; about people who died for love because they were broken-hearted. And Everard was somehow at the bottom of it. Poor Margaret! She would hang about outside the parsonage in the hope of seeing him, instead of going straight in and asking if he were home, as Carolan would. Carolan adored Everard too, but completely without melancholy.

And from Margaret, Carolan's thoughts slipped to her mother. How strange she had looked yesterday, her eyes bigger than ever, looking right beyond Carolan, far away, as though she were seeing something Carolan could not! When Thérèse had spoken to her, she had said, "Yes!" idly, and the answer should have been "No!" Thérèse had shrugged her shoulders impatiently, and grumbled in French. Mamma lay on her couch as though she were not really there, but somewhere else.

How complicated were the affairs of grown-up people!

Footsteps were coming along the path which ran close by. Carolan lay still in the long grass and hoped that whoever it was would pass by without seeing her. She had no wish to be disturbed, and it might be someone to tell her that the squire wanted to see her; least of all grown-ups did she understand the squire. He was either very affectionate or very angry, and one could never be sure whether he was going to scold or attempt to caress.

She saw Thérèse then, and Thérèse turned off the path and came across the grass towards her.

"Ah!" said Thérèse conspiratorially, but then Thérèse was often conspiratorial. She managed to breathe a certain amount of intrigue into going into town to buy ribbons. "I saw you from the window, Mademoiselle, so I knew where I could find you. Your Mamma wishes you to go up to her this minute."

"Why?" said Carolan, getting to her feet.

Thérèse shrugged her shoulders.

"That you will find out, will you not? Now, please, quick. She waits."

Hastily, Carolan followed Thérèse across the park and into the house.

Kitty was lying on a couch. She looked very beautiful, Carolan thought, for she was carefully dressed in a gown of blue silk which matched her eyes. She stretched out a hand.

"Ah! There you are, Carolan! Come here, darling."

Carolan went, and Kitty stretched out languid arms and took the girl's face in her hands.

"Mamma," said Carolan, "is anything wrong?"

"No, no! Thérèse is going into the town to do some little errands for me, and I thought it would be charming if you and I had some tea together. What do you say? I saw you being very lazy down there, so I thought—let her come up and we will be lazy together."

Carolan was completely under the spell of the charming and fascinating Mamma; she was delighted that she should have some time to spare for her; there had been very little recently. Charles and Jennifer goaded her with stories of her mother's intrigues; she always declared she did not believe them; but there were things one could not help knowing, however loyally one tried not to see.

"Well, Thérèse, my dear, ring for tea, and Carolan and I will have it while you go to shop."

Thérèse rang and the tea was brought, and after a while Thérèse put on her cloak and went out.

Kitty's hands were shaking as she held her cup. She lay on her couch like a lazy goddess with secrets in her eyes, and when they had finished the tea she said: "Carolan, I can trust you, darling. You are the only person in this house whom I can trust."

Carolan's green eyes were wide with wonder.

"Yes, Mamma."

"Will you swear to say nothing, nothing whatever, to anyone of what I am going to tell you . . . not until it would be safe to tell, that is?"

"I swear, Mamma."

Kitty took Carolan in her arms, and held her against her soft voluptuous bosom.

"Go to your room now and get your cloak," she said. "We are going out—just the two of us. If you see anyone and you

120

are questioned, do not say that you are going out with me. Say anything but that. Do not put on your cloak, but go down to the shrubbery by the main gate and see that you are well hidden. Wait there till I come."

"Yes, Mamma," said Carolan.

"Do not forget. Not a word that you are waiting for me. Go now, my darling. Go carefully and quickly. I do not want to wait. And I want no one to know—no one at all."

Carolan sped to her room, took her cloak, and hurrying down by a back staircase went swiftly to the shrubbery by the gate. In a very short time Kitty joined her.

"From here," said Kitty, "we can see the road, and we can hide ourselves from view very quickly. We are going to the woods, darling. Put on your cloak. There! Put the hood right over your head. Now you might be anybody; so might I. See? It is only a little way to go along the road; then we shall cut across the field to the woods. That will be safer."

"Mamma! What will happen if we are caught?"

"Terrible things!" said Kitty. "We must not be caught." She added, with a fierceness which was alien to her nature: "Terrible things happened once to me; they shall not happen again. One day, my darling, I shall tell you in detail of the terrible thing that happened to me."

"But, Mamma, today you are happy, are you not?"

"Happiness has come back, darling, as I never dreamed it could come back to me."

Kitty was breathless with the walk; she had put on a good deal of weight in recent years, and she was not given to exercise. She could not talk and hurry too, so she gripped Carolan's hot little hand and silently they went across the grass in the direction of the wood.

"Mamma," said Carolan, distressed by her mother's breathlessness, "why did you not come in the carriage?"

"My dear," said Kitty almost sharply, "how could I? Do you not understand that this is a secret? Did I not make that clear?"

"Oh, yes," said Carolan, and blushed at her own stupidity.

They went on over the grass until they reached the wood. The first thing Carolan noticed was a saddled horse tied to a tree. It was very quiet in the wood; their footsteps crackled on the bracken; there was a tenseness everywhere; Carolan felt that something very exciting was going to happen.

A man stepped out from behind the tree. Carolan had a blurred vision of a pair of grey eyes, of dark hair, of bronzed

121

skin. He said: "Kitty!" and Mamma dropped Carolan's hand and ran to him, and he put his arms round Mamma, and she was crying and laughing on his chest. Carolan stood uncertainly waiting for them to notice her.

Kitty took the man's face in her hands and looked into it searchingly. She said: "My darling, if only I had known that you would come back!"

He answered: "While there was breath in my body I would come back to you."

"The years . . ." said Kitty. "The long years! Thirteen years, Darrell, and what could I have done! I would have waited; I would have waited twenty years. But there was the child . . ."

She remembered Carolan then, and stretched a hand to her.

The man said: "We could not help what happened to us, Kitty. The past was not in our hands, but the present is, and the future shall be!"

And Kitty was crying as she knelt down by Carolan.

"This is the child, Darrell. See, she has a look of you!"

He knelt down, so that they were both kneeling by Carolan.

"Darling," said Kitty, "this is your father, my Carolan."

Carolan studied him eagerly. She was too young to realise that suffering and hardship had put those marks on his face.

"Now," said Kitty, between laughter and tears, "we are here together . . . the whole family . . . my family!"

The man touched Carolan's cheek gently with a rough finger.

"I like our daughter, Kitty," he said.

"Tonight then . . ." said Kitty.

He shook his head.

"Not yet, my darling." He took the stuff of Carolan's cloak between his fingers and felt it, as though appraising its value. "It will be hard at first, Kitty mine."

"What do we care?" said Kitty.

"But for the child?"

Kitty said earnestly: "She is our child, Darrell."

He stroked her cheek.

"We will send for her when we are ready."

Carolan cried shrilly: "Mamma! Mamma, you are going away with . . . with my father."

"Hush, darling," said Kitty, "you said you would keep a secret."

Darrell Grey took Carolan's hand, and smiled down at the small fingers.

"Did you tell her," he asked, "did you tell her how we met here in this very wood, and how we made our plans? Did you tell her how I went to Exeter and never came back till now?"

His face hardened into lines that were almost cruel, when he said that, and Carolan knew now that terrible things had happened to him as well as to her mother.

"I have told her something of this," said Kitty.

"Carolan," he said, "I will tell you something. It is a cruel thing to be poor in this world, for if you are poor you are helpless . . . and it is a cruel world, Carolan . . . a cruel world to be helpless in. Carolan . . . my daughter . . . have you ever seen the lame duck in a farmyard? Have you ever seen how its strong companions savage it to death because of its weakness? A poor man is a lame duck, daughter. That is why I would not take you to poverty."

He frightened her; he spoke with such feeling; but his dark face and the adventure in his eyes fascinated her. Besides, he was her father.

"You will be brave, Carolan, I know," he said. "You have bravery written on your brow. Listen, I am going to take your mother away . . ."

"But, darling," put in Kitty, "you shall join us. Shall she not, Darrell? As soon as possible she shall join us."

"As soon as possible she shall join us. You understand, Carolan? I am a broken man. Once I had dreams of a future that would be good. Now I start again. I am not so young, but then I am not so old. I have much to work for though. It will be good to have my family around me."

"Tonight," said Kitty, "your father and I will leave for London. Until we are well on our way, no one must know. You understand that, Carolan?"

Carolan nodded.

"So you tell no one, eh?"

"I will tell no one."

"It will be all right," said Kitty, "because no one shall know I have gone, till morning; then I shall be far away. Carolan, I am going to ride away on that horse with your father; not by coach, darling." She shivered. "Was it not because your father went to Exeter to book for the coach that our lives lay in ruins about us! Now we are going to build a fresh life for ourselves on those ruins, Carolan, and you are ours, and you shall be with us. You will come to us, darling, as soon as we are ready?"

Carolan nodded.

"I shall send a letter to the housekeeper who is a good

123

friend of mine, and in it will be a letter for you, Carolan. It will tell you what you must do. On no account let the squire know; he is vindictive, that man. Ah, what I have suffered these last years . . . while I waited, waited for the return of my love!"

Carolan thought fleetingly of her mother's lying back on her couch, with the black boy, Sambo, feeding her with sweetmeats, and Thérèse discussing what dress she would wear, she thought of the tales of the lovers she had had. But this picture did not stay long in Carolan's mind; she was now believing with her mother that there had been thirteen years of waiting and suffering.

Kitty looked about her.

"It would never do for us to be seen, Darrell," she said. "Oh, my darling, I could not bear that anything should go wrong for us again."

"No," said Darrell, "it must not! Go now, Kitty. And tonight, an hour before midnight, you will be here at this spot?"

"An hour before midnight," she repeated. They kissed. Carolan stood bewildered, watching. Then it was her turn to be kissed. Darrell lifted her and looked into her face.

"It is not goodbye, little daughter. I shall see you soon. Soon we shall send for you, and then we shall be together, one happy family, eh?"

Carolan nodded, received his kiss, and was put down. Kitty took her hand and led her away; they kept glancing over their shoulders, and Carolan's father stood there watching them.

"Now, Carolan, you know!" said Kitty. "And you see how I trust you?"

Carolan said with dignity: "Of course you can trust me, Mamma! Did he not say that we were one family?"

Kitty pressed her daughter's hand.

"Dearest Carolan, all through the long years you have been my comfort, my only comfort."

Tears filled Carolan's eyes; it was rather wonderful to have been Mamma's comfort through all the years.

"And very soon we shall be together in our lovely London home, darling. That will be wonderful, eh, Carolan?"

"Yes, Mamma."

"Oh, darling, how glad I am that I decided to trust you and let you meet your father!"

"I am glad too," said Carolan.

When they reached the shrubbery, Kitty said: "Let us take

off our cloaks now, darling; it would look odd for us to be walking in the grounds, clad in them in such heat, would it not?"

They took them off; while they were doing so, the squire came upon them. Kitty pressed Carolan's hand to warn her of his approach, and Carolan looked over her shoulder guiltily.

"Ah!" said the squire. "So my lady wife is taking a walk with her daughter, eh?"

Kitty's heart was fluttering uneasily under her blue silk dress; Carolan looked at the ground.

"Is there any reason why I should not?" asked Kitty.

"No reason at all," said the squire. "I merely remark on the fact because it is so unusual. I believe it is not often with your daughter that you amuse yourself?"

There was an insinuation in his voice which brought a flush to Kitty's face. She lived fully in the moment as it came along; she had just been with Darrell, and she was believing that for thirteen years she had waited for him, submitting only to the necessary embraces of the squire. It was unpleasant therefore to have that picture of herself wiped out so crudely, and another picture held up for her to see. The others? They had not really counted. She was just affectionate, eager to please, unable to deny; and the poor boys had needed her so badly. There was nothing in that. With Darrell it was different. If she had married Darrell she would have remained a virtuous matron to the end of her days. She was sure of that.

The squire pulled Carolan's cloak out of her hands.

"How well wrapped up you are for such a hot day! Your mother too? Did she think it well to conceal her charms? Of course, of course, her virtue would demand that!"

Carolan very boldly took her cloak from the squire's hands, but he did not seem to notice—he was looking at Kitty. She was dishevelled, but none the less attractive for that; she was shapely still; as for the weight she had put on, he liked it; he never could stand a skinny woman.

Carolan knew that her mother wished her to go, and quietly she slipped from the shrubbery and ran across the lawns to the house and up to her own room, there to stretch herself on her bed and think of the strange things which had happened to her that afternoon.

Meanwhile Kitty faced her husband. How loathsome he was, she thought! He breathed with his mouth open, and the hairs protruding from his nostrils were coarse and black. She hated him and he hated her—but differently, for his hate must always be tinged with desire and with the dreams he had had of a life with Bess and then with her.

He came towards her and put heavy hands on her shoulders. He saw a new flush under her skin, and anger only added to the sparkle in her eyes. She was like a girl in love.

He said: "But for the child, I'd say you had just returned from a tumble on the grass with your latest!"

It was his sardonic amusement that made her flush hotly.

"Oh, Kitty, have you?" he said. "Have you?"

She stepped back from him, but as she did so he stepped forward; her eyes were dilated with fear, the fear that he might have followed Carolan and her, have watched her meeting with Darrell. She wondered what he would do . . . the brute who, she told herself, had ruined her life; for she had forgotten that she had chosen to marry him as a way out of her difficulties. There was so much he could do; his power was real; he was king in his little neighbourhood. He thought the fear he saw in her eyes was that he might make love to her; it was many months since he had done that. And, damme! he thought. Why the plaguey hell should I keep off! I married her!

"Come to think of it," he said, "there is a good deal to be said for a tumble on the grass."

She began to tremble, and that sickness of defeat came over him. He tried to stifle it, tried to be the ruthless squire he liked to imagine himself at times when the sentimental mood was not upon him. But it would not be stifled.

She said coldly: "Keep your coarseness for the serving maids!"

He wanted to shake her. Who had driven him to serving maids? She had! She and Bess between them. He began to whistle, to show her that he did not care for what she said. If he wished to, he would have her as surely as he would have any serving maid that pleased him. But, he wished her to know, it did not please him . . . not at the moment.

"Do not think I am eager for you," he said with nonchalance. "Not me! Too many you have had, my dear. It takes the bloom off, believe me."

He let her walk past him; he watched her hurrying across the lawns and into the house. It might have been Bessie—so alike they were.

Damn Kitty and damn Bess! He kicked the earth under his feet and wondered what he would do. He went to the stables, still undecided, and called to Jake to saddle his favourite horse. Then he rode out of the grounds and into the road, and galloped furiously; the thudding of his horse's hoofs and the feel of the sweating body between his knees comforted him. He could do what he wanted to with this animal; he almost wished it were not so docile. He would have relished using his whip, but he was too good a horseman to do so without a reason. He wanted to slash out at someone though, so he went to Harriet.

Here he could laugh and be brutal in a clever, subtle way; queer that the prim spinster could give him the comfort denied him by the voluptuous Kitty!

"You're a wonderful woman, Harry!" he told her. Cruelly he laughed within himself and if her skin had not been so yellow, he would have kissed her there and then. But he could never bring himself to that; besides, it would spoil the fun. And good fun this was; baiting poor old Harry was as good as baiting a bear or the pitching of two cocks one against the other.

He stayed long with Harriet; he stayed for a meal, sat at the long table in the cool dining-room and carved the saddle of mutton for her. And how she twittered about him, and how she worried that he would defy the proprieties and stay all the evening; how she dreaded he would and longed that he would!

Emm waited on them at table and afterwards brought coffee, and Emm was brown as a berry and smooth too—a real country wench, ripe enough, sly enough. He watched her when Harriet wasn't looking, and he touched her bosom with a careless hand when she bent over him to serve him from the dish of potatoes. She quivered as a horse does; rippling through her body. Ripe and sly, he thought. And his mind was full of Emm as he looked at Harriet, and Harriet saw thoughts there that made her shudder, because she felt they were for her.

He sat, sprawled out in her drawing-room, and the candle-light flickered about the room, and the clock ticked on. Inwardly he laughed, and was soothed for the slights he had suffered from Bess and from Kitty. He sat on, drinking elderberry wine until the clock struck ten.

"Good gracious me!" said Harriet. "Did you hear that, George? Ten of the clock, I do declare, and you with that ride home before you!"

"The ride is nothing to me, Harry."

"But I was thinking of what you might meet on the road, George. I do declare the roads get worse and worse."

"Bah! I would like to see the man who would dare ask me for my purse! He would not get away with it and his life."

She eyed him with a wistful softness.

"Doubtless you would be reckless, George," she said softly, "but that does not ease my mind."

"By the Lord Harry!" cried the squire. "Are you going to offer me a bed?"

He could scarcely stop the smile curving his lips. It was such a good joke that; but she did not appear to hear it.

"There are beds and to spare in this house," she said. "I will tell Emm to prepare a room. Emm!" she called. "Emm!"

"My good Harriet," laughed the squire, "you're to put all such thoughts out of your head. A ride in the dark has no terrors for me, I can tell you. I enjoy it!"

"I know, George. I know."

He felt himself aglow with her admiration. He was glad he had come; he was glad he had stayed. Why let Kitty humiliate him? Why have let Bess? There were women in the world who thought very highly of him.

Emm appeared in answer to the call. Candlelight softened her, hid the grime of her. Her eyes were large and soft like a fawn's eyes.

Harriet hesitated. The squire roared out: "Get a lanthorn, girl, and light me to the stables!"

Emm said: "Indeed I will, sir!" and went out.

The squire rocked backwards and forwards on his heels, smiling at Harriet, well pleased with himself.

"Good night, Harriet, m'dear."

"Good night, George. It has been most pleasant."

"We will repeat the pleasure, Harry. No, no! You shall not venture out into the night air. I'll not allow it. There is deadliness in the night air, Harry."

Ah! he thought, laughing, and magic too! Starlight could throw a cloak of beauty even about such as workhouse Emm.

Emm appeared in the hall, holding a lanthorn in her hands.

"Come you on, girl," he said. "The hour is growing late." He did not look at her, but he was aware of every movement of her body as she passed him.

"Goodbye, Harriet."

Harriet stood in the doorway. The lanthorn, like a will-o'-the-wisp, flickering across the grass on its way to the stables.

"I shall not move till you have shut yourself in from this treacherous night air, Harriet."

"George, you are too ridiculous!"

"Is it ridiculous then to care for the health of one's friends?"

She closed the door. She thought how charming he was, under the right influence. What a certain woman could have done for him!

The lanthorn flickered against the darkness of the stables. It was a lovely night. There was no moon, but a wonderful array of stars. They seemed bigger than usual, like jewels laid out for show on a piece of black velvet. He began to hurry across the grass.

"Emm," he said softly. "Emm! Wait for me!"

She was beside him, and as he laid a hand on her shoulder, she stepped back a pace. Sly, silly girl, he thought. But he was in no hurry; he preferred a little dalliance.

He said: "Lead the way, girl. Lead the way!"

And she went before him, holding the lanthorn on a level with her youthful head. His eyes were fixed upon her appraisingly; all young creatures were beautiful by starlight.

"You are a nice girl, Emmie," he said. "Often have I noticed that."

She did not speak, and he roared out: "Did you hear me?"

"Yes, sir," she said, her voice trembling. "Thank you, sir!"

"You like me, Emmie, don't you?"

"Oh, yes, sir."

She had a grace, this girl; the fawn-like quality was very much in evidence. She seemed to him to be poised for a fleet and startled withdrawal.

Damn it! he thought, his veins swelling. She was willing enough. Brown as a berry, and ripe as plums in September. He would have fun with her, right under Harriet's prim nose.

"Emm!" he said. "Put that plaguey lanthorn down, and come here."

She came and stood cautiously before him. He put out his hands and felt the quiver run through her.

"Now, Emmie, girl, nothing to be afraid of, nothing to be afraid of, eh?"

He talked soothingly as he talked to his horses.

"Come on, Emmie girl; come on, now!"

Then he seized her and kissed her, and felt his blood run hot through him. She was not too clean, and she smelt of the dinner she had cooked—the dinner he had eaten with Harriet.

He was exultant, laughing at Bess and Kitty really, getting the better of them in some queer, subtle way.

But Emm was panting; she wrenched herself from his grasp suddenly; she was as agile as a young monkey.

129

Damn her! he thought. Wanted chasing, did she? These workhouse girls were giving themselves airs indeed! By God, did she forget he was the squire, about to confer an honour upon her! Had she been listening to that other one, that Janet who was saving up her virtue for some blundering farm labourer? No, no! She wanted a chase—some of them did; liked to lead a man a dance. But that was the ladies. The workhouse girls were giving themselves the airs of ladies these days! She would lead him a dance, make him chase her over the garden, taking good care not to escape from him, and be caught conveniently when they had both had enough of the chase; and laughing and panting, and perhaps biting and scratching, she would give way. Well, well, he was in a good humour and the night was before him. He set out after her across the lawn. She was fleet though. She was in the house! She had shut the door on him! And what could he do, confound the girl, but tap timidly for fear of Harriet's hearing, and then when she said from the other side of the door, "Please go away!" he had to plead: "Emm! Emmie, girl! What is wrong with you? Come out, I say! Come out, I tell you!" But she did not come. And how could the squire stand pleading at the back door with a girl from the workhouse!

Wild fury possessed him. It was all he could do to restrain himself from breaking down the door. That would be sheer folly, of course. He had to do better than that. By God, did the girl not know that he could have her brought before him, could have her whipped in public, could have her sent off to a convict ship . . . and, yes, could no doubt have her hanged if he cared to! He was the squire, was he not? A magistrate! A Justice! He felt the veins in his head would burst; his eyes burned with his anger. Doubtless the slut had committed many a crime which only had to be discovered. By God, he would show her! But there was nothing he could do this night. He forced himself to walk slowly back to the stables, trying to quell the angry beating of his heart. He did not want to be bled again . . . he must not work himself into such a fury over a mere workhouse slut. But it was not the workhouse slut— well he knew that—it was Bess again, jeering at him . . . Bess and Kitty, confound them!

It was good to feel the horse between his knees, responding to every pressure—a noble creature who knew his master. He had no wish to go home; he rode for miles, galloping and cantering across the fields, through the country lanes; and when he had had enough it was past midnight, and when he reached home it was nearly one o'clock.

He himself rubbed down his horse, for though he was a stern master he was a good one. Then he went into the house and poured himself a glass of whisky.

"I will get the taste of Harriet's plaguey concoctions out of my mouth!" he said, and he laughed afresh at Harriet's feeling for him, and drank more whisky, for there was nothing like whisky for keeping a man's spirit up—and he was going to Kitty. He had stood off long enough, and, damn it, he had to get the taste of that bit of foolery with the workhouse chit out of his mouth as surely as he had to get rid of the taste of Harriet's wine.

He went upstairs. The door of her room was not locked as he had half expected it to be, but if it had been he would have had it down; he was in that mood.

"Kitty!" he called. "Kitty!"

There was no answer.

"Ha! No use pretending to be asleep, girl." He sat down on the chair by her dressing-table. "Curse this plaguey darkness!" he said. "Where do you keep your candles, girl? Get out of that bed and light one. I have had enough of your lady ways . . . Tonight I am going to show you that I have had enough. From now on things are going to change in this house . . ."

His voice was a little shaky. The mood of sentimentality was creeping in on him. In a moment he would be saying: "Kitty, let us start again . . . Could we, girl? I will forget what you have been, and you forget what I have been . . ."

He wanted Kitty. Damn it, he was getting on in years. He had done with the chasing; he wanted to settle. A man felt like that—settle and look after the children. And perhaps have more children. Three was no family for a man. More children like little Carolan. Kitty's children—that was what he wanted—Kitty's and his this time.

"Kitty!" he said, his voice soft and pleading. "Kitty, girl."

He groped his way to the bed and felt for her. It took him some seconds to realise that the bed was empty.

He was shouting, rousing the household.

"Here! Everybody! Where the hell is everybody! Come here at once, I say!"

And while he stood there, listening to his own voice, he thought: By God, she is paying a midnight visit to a lover! What a fool I am going to look! By God! By God, I'll make her pay for this!

A fool he was, a fool, to act without thinking. He imagined the tittering of the servants after this. If he heard any titter-

131

ing, saw any sly glances, he would have them whipped, that he would.

Mrs. West, the housekeeper, came first, her dressing-gown pulled around her, her teeth chattering, her candlestick shaking in her hand.

"Where is your mistress?" he barked at her.

Mrs. West peered at the bed.

" 'T'as not been slept in, master!"

"I see that. Do you think I am blind!"

He looked at her narrowly; she had always been Kitty's friend, he knew. Was she hiding something?

"Look you, woman, if you have any idea, any idea whatsoever, of where your mistress is, you had better tell me at once or it will be the worse for you. Do you hear me?"

"I have not the faintest idea, master."

He knew that the woman was speaking the truth. Other faces appeared in the doorway, among them Jennifer's. Jennifer was smiling secretly. She was thinking, as he was thinking, that Kitty had gone out to meet a lover. In a moment he would be slapping that secret smile from Jennifer's face.

He said: "Call her maid!" and Jennifer went away and brought in Thérèse. Thérèse's black hair hung in two plaits and her black eyes glittered.

"Where is your mistress?" demanded the squire.

Thérèse looked towards the bed and lifted her shoulders in surprise.

"That I do not know, Monsieur."

"Come," said the squire, "I think you do know."

"But no, Monsieur!"

"Did you not dress her for an outing?"

"But no, Monsieur! She retired early this night. It was 'eadache!" Thérèse held her own head and closed her eyes, then opened them and lifted them to the ceiling. Jennifer laughed. The squire said: "Get outside, all of you . . . Except you!" he added to Thérèse.

He did not watch them go, but he heard them, shuffling out, and he cursed himself for a fool to have aroused the household like this.

"Now," he said to Thérèse, "no secrets! It is no use telling me that you did not share your mistress's secrets and take part in her intrigues."

"Oh, but no, no, no, Monsieur! Intrigue? What is he?"

Plaguey foreigner! She did not understand when she did not

132

wish to. Neat she was too, and cheeky with her flashing black eyes; and not too old. Her gesticulating hands were beautifully shaped.

"Damn it!" he said. "Get out. I will speak to you in the morning."

She went out daintily, and he sat alone in the bedroom. He would wait here for Kitty's return, and when she came in he would take his riding crop to her. He had been soft. It was no way to treat a woman, to be soft with her. He would punish her now, in the way that would hurt her most. He would beat her white skin until the blood ran; then she could show that to her lover, and they would say he was a brute, but they would know he was master. He would beat her for what she had her now, in the way that would hurt he rmost. He would beat her for a hundred insults, even the one he had received tonight from a workhouse brat.

Jennifer came silently into the room. She stood close to him, thin and tall; the candlelight on her slanting eyes and pointed face made her look like a witch.

"George . . ." she said humbly.

"Get out!" said the squire.

She knelt beside him and lifted her face.

She said: "*I* have always been faithful to you . . . We used to be happy."

By God, he thought, she has! And I believe we were happy in a way.

"All right, Jenny," he said. "All right."

"George," she said again, a high note of excitement in her voice, "why cannot we try to be happy once more?"

He was so tired; he let his hand touch her hair. She nestled close to him. He thought of past scenes; she was a passionate, strange creature, this Jennifer; he had liked her well enough once; she had been a great contrast to cold Amelia. There had been a time with Jennifer when he had almost ceased to think of Bess.

"All right, Jenny," he said again.

Closer she came, and he smelt gin on her breath.

He said: "You have been drinking, Jenny!"

"No," she lied. And he thought: Damn her, I cannot trust even Jennifer!

She nestled close to him. She was fuddled, too fuddled to think clearly. She tried too quickly to press home her advantage.

She said: "Oh, George, if you could know everything that has gone on in this room! If I could tell you!"

"Why the hell did you not tell me?" he demanded.

"How could I . . . of the mistress? There was not one lover, George. There have been scores!" She tittered. He hated tittering women. "There are things I might tell you, George, if you were to ask me."

Vivid pictures crowded into his mind, and Kitty figured largely in them all. Red mist swam before his eyes. He was so wretched and miserable and lonely, but Jennifer was too foolish to help him; a drunken sot of a woman she was nowadays. He stood up suddenly and sent her sprawling. He laughed at her and touched her with his foot, not violently, but contemptuously.

"Get out, you drunken slut," he said. Jennifer got up; she stood before him pleadingly.

"Get out!" He put his face close to hers. "And do not let me see you in this state again. It is bad enough to have a harlot in my nursery—I will not have a drunken harlot, do you hear!"

She crept out of the room.

The candle guttered. The clock ticked on. And as he sat there he knew that Kitty was not coming home.

The dawn was beginning to creep into the sky when he remembered seeing her that afternoon with her daughter. He went suddenly cold. Had she taken Carolan with her? Hastily he went to the child's room. With great relief he saw that she was still there.

He sat heavily on the bed. He could just see her face in the early dawn light—a child's face with a smudge of lashes against her pale skin, very sweet, very innocent.

He shook her.

"Wake up, girl! Wake up!" She awoke startled.

"Oh . . ." she said, "the squire!"

He frowned. He had told her she must call him Father, had threatened to whip her for not calling him Father; and it was only in unguarded moments that she slipped back into the childhood habit of calling him the squire.

"Carrie," he said sternly, "where is your mother?"

"Mother!" she said, and the events of the day came crowding back to her.

"You heard! Where is your mother? You know, do you not?"

She was too bewildered to deny her knowledge.

He said: "You know then, you know!"

She did not answer.

"By God," he said, "so you are in this conspiracy against me, eh? Where has your mother gone?"

"I . . . I cannot say," stammered Carolan.

"You cannot say! And why can you not say? Tell me that."

She was silent.

"You have been sworn to secrecy, is that it?"

She nodded.

"It would be better if you told me now, you know."

"I cannot tell."

He looked down at her, livid with fury; not because Kitty had left him now, but because Carolan was in league with Kitty against him.

He gripped her by the shoulder and tore her nightgown. She was very small, he noticed, such a child.

"Look you here, Carrie, I will have no more disobedience in this house. You will tell me where your mother has gone, or I will whip you myself. Will you tell me?"

But she knew she must not tell . . . not yet. They would not have gone far enough yet. She must wait a while, a whole day at least. Then he could never find them and bring them back. Mamma had married the squire because of her, Carolan; she had gathered that much; now it was her painful duty to save Mamma from the squire. So she pressed her lips tightly together and shook her head.

"You admit you know then?" he said, and she had known it, there was a pleading note in his voice; he wanted her to say she did not know; he wanted to put his great face close to hers and kiss her and say: "You are completely my daughter now, little Carrie." But she knelt on her bed, her hands clasped behind her back, her face white and frightened, but her lips pressed firmly together. She was going to be silent for Kitty, and she would not speak for him.

"Very well," he said cruelly, "we shall see whether you will speak or not. Margaret!" he roared, and Margaret, who had heard the commotion and had been awake for a long time, came in. "Go to my bedroom, Margaret, and bring my riding crop. I will not have disobedience from my children."

Margaret hesitated and wished she had pretended to be asleep. But he roared at her again: "Go! Or you will be the next. God damme, am I to be thwarted in my own house?"

Margaret went, and he pushed Carolan on to the bed.

"Now, Carrie," he said almost wheedlingly, "you tell your

135

father what happened this afternoon. Where did she take you, eh? Eh, Carrie?"

Carolan said nothing. He bent down and gave her a stinging blow about her ear. He lifted her by her hair and pulled her up. Her lips quivered.

"Are you coming to your senses, Carrie? Are you going to tell me?"

Carolan could only shake her head.

He threw her face downwards on to the bed and began to slap her body with his great hands. Carolan cried out, and he laughed.

"I will teach you, my girl!" he said. "I will teach you!"

Margaret came back and stood trembling on the threshold, the crop in her hand. He snatched it from her, and with it poised in his hand, stood staring down at the quivering body of the child.

"Damme!" he cried. "What do I want with this? I have strength enough in my hands to deal with the brat." And he picked her up and shook her, and he saw that her eyes were tightly shut and that tears were squeezing themselves through her closed lids. Emotions mingled in his mind.

Then he saw Jennifer. She was looking in at the door, and her mouth was working. She had been at the gin bottle again, and she was laughing because he had beaten the child.

He picked up the crop and went towards her; she ran, her arms stretched out before her, into her room. He stood in the doorway, laughing at her. Then he looked over his shoulder at Carolan, who lay still on the bed, her nightdress in ribbons about her bruised body, a sob shaking her now and then.

How loyal the child was! Loyal to that slut of a mother. And nothing for him but defiance.

"Carrie!" he said. "I'll see you in the morning. Then we will hear whether you persist in your folly or not."

But he would not beat her again. He was the beaten one, not she. He had to get out or he would be petting her, telling her he did not mean that after all, and that whatever she had done mattered not, because he loved her.

He went to his bedroom, but not to sleep. And in the morning he sent for Mrs. West.

"The child had to be whipped last night," he said, and though he felt her disapproving eyes upon him, he did not resent that. He warmed to Mrs. West. He said, almost apologetically: "I was upset myself. Perhaps I laid it on a bit too strongly . . . But I will have no more disobedience in this house. Go to her. And take her something tasty to eat . . . And see that she is all right."

In the evening of that day he sent for Carolan. She came to him, her head high, defiant.

By God, he thought, is she asking for another whipping? But how he admired her! She had something in her that Kitty had not had, nor perhaps Bess either.

"Well, Madam Carolan!" he said, with an attempt at lightness.

"Well?"

"Well what? Have I not told you to use some respect when addressing me? Did I not tell you to call me Father? You had better do so, unless you so like the feel of my hands about you that you are asking for more of what you had last night."

She was frightened, he saw with satisfaction.

"You are not my father," she told him boldly enough. "So why should I call you such?"

"Look here, Carrie," he said. "I *am* your father. You had better tell me immediately who has said I am not."

"My mother has said it. And I will tell you now what I would not tell you last night . . . She has gone away with my father."

His face went white, then hideously purple.

"Ah!" he said at length. "And Madam Carolan knew, and would not tell, eh?"

"No," she said, "I would not tell."

"For fear I should have gone after them?"

She nodded.

Brave little girl! Bold and defiant and disobedient. His eyes were filling with mawkish tears. Why was she not his daughter! He would have given anything to know she was.

"You need not have feared that, girl."

"Oh!"

"And you might have saved yourself a whipping. Carrie, come here, girl. It did not please me to whip you like that. How do you feel?" He looked at his hands. "They are big and clumsy, eh, Carrie?" He took her hand, and laughed comparing them.

She said: "I did not mind. It is all over now."

Queer position. Am I asking pardon of Kitty's bastard? It looked to him as if he were; he did not understand himself.

"Then," he said, "we will forget last night, Carrie, eh? I was in a foul temper."

"Of course," she said. "I know." And she smiled, and when she smiled she was the image of Bessie . . . more Bessie than

Kitty. "And it does not hurt much now. Mrs. West was very kind."

"Good for West!" he said. "We will have a ride together tomorrow. Not West and I!" He roared with laughter at the thought, and put out a great hand and pinched Carolan's cheek.

"These two, Carrie. Squire and his daughter, eh?"

There was nothing sullen about her. She was adorable, this child. Kitty had left her; that made her solely his.

After that Carolan's life slipped on smoothly enough. She saw more of the squire; they rode together almost every day. He was eager to make up for that beating, and he tried to do so in lots of ways which on account of their very clumsiness were endearing. He was like a father to her; indulgent, though violent enough when crossed, and afterwards almost pathetically sorry for his violence. She avoided him when she possibly could, but when she could not she tried very hard to be fond of him, and after a time she began to find his companionship tolerable, even amusing.

Often she dreamed of joining her father and mother in London, because she was sure that that was what she was going to do one day. She waited for the promised letter which was to be enclosed in one for Mrs. West, and she was disappointed for weeks, but eventually it came.

She took it to her room and read it through many times. Her mother had given an address in London but she said it would not be possible for them to have Carolan with them just yet. They had their way to make and prospects at the moment were not very rosy; they would prefer their daughter to wait until they had a home to offer her which would be as luxurious as the one she would have to leave to come to them.

As if I care for luxury! thought Carolan, but she did realise that if she went to her parents in London, it would mean leaving Everard, and that most decidedly she did not want to do.

Carolan's first ball dress was of green brocade trimmed with coffee-coloured lace. Its skirt was full and swept the floor; its bodice was tightly fitting and very dainty, falling from her shoulders, with tiny sleeves caught up with green ribbons. Her eyes matched the colour of her dress; and her hair, parted in the middle, hung in soft curls about her shoulders; it looked very natural and fashionable, unpowdered as it was, for powdering had gone out of fashion some four years before with the coming of the tax.

The squire had given her the dress; he had taken great pleasure in doing so. There was to be a ball, he whispered to her, and it was a great occasion—Carolan's first ball; she was to stop being a child when the old century ended and start her adult life with the new. The disreputable clothes in which she tore about the countryside were unsuitable for a young woman though they might do well enough for a child, so there must be a new dress and new slippers, and as the money for these were to come out of the squire's purse, he hoped young Carrie was going to be suitably grateful. She was grateful; she gave him a kiss without being asked, which seemed to please him mightily.

Carolan, studying herself in her mirror, thought about the kiss she had given the squire. He still made her uneasy, as he had when she was a child. She could have liked him so much more but for his hearty caresses. He was kind to her, indeed more kind than he was to Margaret or Charles, which amazed her. He liked to ride with her, to take her round the estate, to make the cottagers curtsy to her. Queer man, but kind!

Carolan bent her head and kissed her own white shoulder in an excess of excitement over this occasion of her first ball and the delight in herself dressed up in her first ball dress. Everard would be at the ball tonight. He had said: "Now, Carolan, I shall expect you to save plenty of dances for me!"

How beautiful was Everard! With his finely chiselled features and his courteous manners, he was aristocratic and gentle, elegant without being foppish; never really angry except on someone else's behalf; never unkind. So calm he was, aloof, never excited by her as she was by him; she loved to sit on the wall between the Orlands' house and the graveyard and listen to Everard's talk of his future; and how he loved to talk! She twirled round ecstatically to glimpse at the back of her dress; she danced round the room and imagined she was dancing with Everard.

She came to an abrupt stop by falling against the old bureau in the corner; she was laughing at herself. Did everyone get ready much too soon for their first ball?

She was so happy she had to dance. Indeed the last year had been the happiest of her life. In the bureau were letters from her mother; there were several which had come via Mrs. West over the last four years. Mamma was very happy in London; soon Carolan must join her and her father, but not yet; they were not quite ready . . .

Ah, thought Carolan, let them enjoy their happiness without an intruder!

And she knew in her heart that she did not really want to

join them; she was too happy here. It was true that the rough caresses of the squire sometimes perturbed her, and she understood him as little now as she had done when a child. But that was a small matter in the midst of such contentment, and Everard was the rock on which all this contentment was built. To go to London would mean to lose Everard; therefore she was glad when her mother wrote that they were not *quite* ready for her.

Life had changed for her. Everywhere it seemed good. Charles, who was at Oxford now and home only occasionally, no longer tormented her. He scarcely seemed to notice her at all. Jennifer Jay had drunk too much gin one night last year, and had fallen from the top of a flight of stairs to the bottom; that was the end of Jennifer Jay. With Mrs. West and the servants she was a favourite, more so than Margaret, which surprised her, for Margaret was lovely to look at and the squire's own daughter. But one of the deepest reasons for her contentment was Margaret's sudden change of feeling towards Everard. Margaret had loved Everard a little while ago; now she was almost indifferent to him. If Carolan talked of him, she was scarcely interested, and that made Carolan very happy, because she knew Everard had never wanted Margaret to care for him so blatantly, and he seemed to like her better now that she was more or less indifferent towards him.

Margaret came into the room, looking delightful in her favourite blue, with her fair hair dressed high on her head.

"You look beautiful!" cried Carolan enthusiastically.

Margaret looked wistful, and said: "You always exaggerate."

"How do I look?" asked Carolan, her head on one side pleadingly.

"All right!" said Margaret.

Carolan grimaced, and Margaret wondered why a dress, which had been merely pretty hanging in the cupboard, should, when draped about Carolan's slender person, become provocative, seductive, all that in Margaret's opinion a dress should not be.

Carolan quickly dismissed the disappointment which Margaret's cool comment had aroused in her, and said: "Oughtn't we to go down . . . since you will have to receive people, or something?"

"You need not come yet," said Margaret. "I must go."

"Of course I shall come!" giggled Carolan. "Do you know, I have been ready for at least half an hour, waiting! If I have to wait much longer I shall burst with impatience."

"You are a silly child," said Margaret, "and you say such silly things! I am going down now."

Carolan followed her from the room. The squire from the hall below saw them descending the staircase, and stood there watching them.

By God, he thought, she is growing up. She is a woman. She is not much like Bess and Kitty—smaller altogether, brighter, with more vitality. She has all they had though. Carolan . . . my daughter, Carolan!

His eyes went to Margaret. Nice enough—just the wife for young Orland. Margaret's place was in a country parsonage. Amelia's girl! And, by God, no one could have any doubt of that. And tonight that young milksop would come to the point, he hoped. The young fellow was a plaguey long time deciding that he wanted to take the girl to bed with him. Still, there was nothing like a ball to bring a young man to the point; show him Margaret's people knew how to entertain, by God! Show him what sort of a family he would be marrying into. She was nigh on twenty! Time she was off his hands. How the children grew up! Carolan next. No, not Carolan— she was his girl, his little daughter. This last year he had been happier than he had been for a long time. He was beginning to shape into that pattern he had cut for himself. He scarcely ever flew into one of the wild rages that had come to him so frequently at one time. People might think he was getting old, but it was not that entirely; he was not getting old; he was getting what he wanted. He had his little Carolan. Why did not Margaret's eyes sparkle as Carolan's did? Why did not her hair glow with that vitality?

His hand came down on Carolan's shoulder.

"By God!" he cried. "What have we here? I thought it was a child, but it is a young woman!"

She glanced at him through those thick lashes.

"Children are not given ball dresses, are they?" she said.

"Pampered ones might get all sorts of things out of their old fathers."

She was scintillating. And this at sixteen! He was faintly worried, seeing her like this. He wanted her to remain a child.

"Well, sir," said Carolan, curtsying, "this child is a child no longer."

He touched her nose with a clumsy forefinger, made her take one arm, offered Margaret his other. Now he was proud and happy, standing with Margaret—Carolan in the background—receiving guests. He was the good squire now; he had been wild in his day, but what young man is not wild in

141

his day? His cottagers could bring their troubles to him nowadays; he might roar at them; he might lose his temper now and then; but he did what he could for them; he was a good squire.

A girl in the uniform of a parlourmaid flitted through a door and across the room. His eyes followed her. That was Emm; and he glowed again with satisfaction. He was not a bad squire really . . . large hearted and tolerant. Good squire, people would say when he rode by with his daughter. Wild in his day, but a fine master! So many men would not have had Emm in their houses after Harriet had turned her out. Emm! He could laugh at the thought of one starry night when she had run from him and locked the door on him. She had saved her virtue for a young labourer who had promised her marriage and then deserted her. So virtuous little Emm had found herself with child and nowhere to turn. But the squire was a good squire, and Emm would never cease to bless him to the end of her days. He had not said: "Now you see what it is to trust a labourer; better far to trust a squire!" He had never deserted a woman. If there was a child he had seen that it was put out somewhere and a lump sum paid for it. Poor little Emm! What would have happened to her if she had lived in a neighbourhood where the squire was just a squire! But Emm had her baby at the cottage of Jane Lever the midwife, and a man and his wife who had no children looked after it; and Emm came to Haredon to be parlourmaid under Mrs. West. And she was shapely, a personable enough young woman; and she was grateful to the squire; but not once had he looked in her direction. That was the man he had become. He was bowing over Mrs. Orland's hand, well pleased with himself and with life.

Carolan watched the guests arrive. How lovely the old hall looked, decked out like this, the beautiful dresses of the women, the elegant garments of the men—a blaze of colour and lights and beauty! And here was Everard, more elegant, more beautiful than any.

He stood before her, his eyes shining.

"Why, Carolan, you have grown up overnight!"

"That is what everyone is saying. You like the change, Everard?"

"I like it very much."

She smiled her pleasure.

"The dress is beautiful, is it not?"

"Very beautiful."

"It cost a good deal, but the squire insisted on my having something really good for my first ball."

Mrs. Orland came swiftly to them.

"Hello, Carolan! It is going to be a wonderful evening, I am sure. Now Everard, the squire was going to open the ball with Margaret, but he feels unable to and he wants you to do it for him, Everard. Look, dear, do go over to Margaret right away. It is time to start, and the musicians are waiting. I will look after Carolan."

Everard smiled over his shoulder at Carolan. He was docile always.

"And, Carolan," said Mrs. Orland, "here is Geoffrey Langley coming over. I know he wants to dance with you. Ah . . . Geoffrey, my dear boy, you have come to ask Carolan to dance, have you not?"

Geoffrey Langley, rather portly, middle-aged and bucolic, said he had been coming to them with just that idea.

"There!" said Mrs. Orland, with the air of one who has worked very satisfactorily on behalf of others. "You will look after our little Carolan, Geoffrey; this is the dear child's first ball!"

Geoffrey Langley's small eyes smiled appreciatively as he held out his hand.

Now Margaret and Everard were dancing together down the centre of the hall, and other couples were falling in behind them and the fun was beginning.

Geoffrey Langley was not sorry to relinquish his partner to another. She was an enchanting child but her feet had wings, and his ageing body could not keep up with her frolicking. Her next partner was a young man who told her she was beautiful and tried to urge her out into the grounds because he was sure there was a wonderful moon. But Carolan wished to stay in the ballroom until Everard came to dance with her; but she was enjoying herself, waiting for Everard. It was fun to note the effect she had on this very young man, particularly when she remembered that last week, riding with him at the hunt, he had not given her a second glance. Oh, what a difference a ball dress can make! So she was coquetting, flirting in as natural a manner as her mother had before her. People glancing her way, noting her brilliant green eyes, her flushed, enchanting little face, thought, There will be trouble there! What is it those women have? The squire must watch out.

But there was in Carolan something neither her mother nor her grandmother had possessed, something more spiritual, less voluptuous; pleasure loving, certainly—but something finer too.

The evening was wearing on when Everard found her. There was a faint colour under his skin, and he looked as exasperated as it would be possible for Everard to look.

"Oh, Everard!" she said. "How nice to see you! I hoped you would come to dance with me before the evening was over."

There was the faintest reproach in her voice. This evening had taught her that she was not the child, Carolan, waiting to be noticed by grown-ups; she was a woman, to be sought after. That she had learned, and it was intoxicating knowledge.

Everard said: "I have been trying to get to you the whole evening. There were so many things I had to do. My mother said that, since this is Margaret's dance and the squire suggested I should open it with her in his place, I must dance quite a number of dances with Margaret. And," he added severely, "when I did come to you, you were very busily engaged elsewhere."

The flattery of this to one who, such a short time ago, was but a child in a nursery, bullied by Charles, tormented by Jennifer, whipped and made to realise that she was of no importance whatever, was intoxicating.

"Well," she said, "could I sit waiting for you all the evening?"

"No," said Everard. "Let us dance."

They danced, and all arrogance dropped from her shoulders then; she adored Everard, and this was the great moment of her evening.

"How pretty you are, Carolan! I did not know how pretty until tonight."

Little waves of pleasure ran all over her. She tossed her head.

"Then it is my gown you find so pretty!" she challenged.

"Your gown! My dear Carolan, I have not looked at it."

"Ah!" she cried. "Shut your eyes, Everard, and tell me what colour it is."

He closed his eyes; she looked up at him. Oh, he was wonderful—beautiful and wonderful! And she had never been as happy in her life as now.

"Blue," he said.

"You are thinking of Margaret!" she told him.

"No," he said, with a seriousness that made her heart beat

144

very fast, "I am thinking of no one but you. Carolan, when I saw you flirting so outrageously with that young man . . ."

"Everard! I . . . flirting!"

"Exactly!" said Everard. "Flirting! Inviting compliments —perhaps demanding them! Oh, Carolan, what has happened to you? You are different tonight."

"I am a young woman at her first ball, Everard. Yesterday I was a child in a nursery."

"Carolan, you alarm me. You are being a little silly tonight, Carolan."

"Let me be silly, Everard. I am so happy! I have never had a ball dress before. I have never before been to a ball. Is not a little silliness pardonable?"

"Perhaps," said Everard, "but it grieves me."

"Then I will be silly no longer, because I hate to grieve you, Everard."

"Carolan . . . you say such things!"

"Everard, you too are different tonight."

"No," he said, "I am not—or if I am it is entirely due to the difference in you. I have been very, very fond of you for a long time."

"And I of you, Everard."

"You are not very old, Carolan."

"You forget . . . I grew up overnight!"

"Ah! How I wish you had!"

"But you said you were fond of me as I was."

"Carolan, there are times when you frighten me. You are so impulsive."

"And you, Everard, are far from impulsive; that is why you do not like that in me."

"Who said I did not like it? Perhaps it is that I like. Carolan, I had not meant to speak to you tonight . . . but I am going to, because I must. I am afraid, Carolan."

"Afraid? Of what?" She looked over her shoulder as though she expected to see something fearful there.

He laughed.

"You baby!" he said.

"I do not like being called a baby," she said with dignity.

"But you are one. And such I will call you if I wish to."

"Everard, you look most unlike yourself."

"I have learned something, Carolan. I cannot talk about it in here; let us go outside. Let us go to the summer-house; there we can be alone and talk. Will you come?"

Would she come? She would have followed him to the end of the earth if he asked.

Daintily she picked her way across the grass, lifting the grreen brocade, feeling not Carolan the child, but a lady who found life intriguing and full of adventure.

Everard shut the door of the summer-house, and when he spoke his gentle voice was hoarse.

"Carolan, I told you that, seeing you tonight, I was afraid."

"Yes," she said.

"Carolan, dear little Carolan, do you remember when Charles locked you in the vault?"

"Yes, Everard."

"And I came and found you there, and you lay across my knees and were so frightened? Oh, Carolan, that was when it began . . . That was when I began to love you."

"Did you, Everard?"

"Yes. Just as a child then, as a little sister. You were so frightened and I was angry, more angry than I had ever been in my life."

"You gave him a black eye, and he had such difficulty in explaining!"

He caught her hands, and they laughed.

"What do you feel for me, Carolan?" he asked.

"Would I not love the person who rescued me from that horror?"

"But love is more than that . . ."

"But that was the beginning. I loved and loved and loved you, Everard. You did not show any sign of loving me."

"Did I not?" he asked in surprise, and she laughed with pleasure, thinking of those days; and it was all part of the pleasure of this evening that Margaret had ceased to love him.

"Not a bit!" she said, and laughing, moving nearer to him, she murmured: "And do you now, Everard? I am not so sure."

It was invitation, and Everard took it; he put his arms about her. He would have kissed her gently on the mouth, but there was no gentleness in Carolan. Everard was a little shocked, and because it was exciting to be shocked, he was enchanted with her. He had meant to explain, as one would to a child, that he loved her, that one day he would marry her—perhaps in one year, perhaps in two; he had meant to be gentle; but it was Carolan who was leading the way—and she sixteen, while he had lived twenty-four years. Carolan was no child; she was a woman because she had been born a woman.

146

She said: "For so long I have wanted you to kiss me, darling!"

And he drew back, still shocked, but mightily intrigued. This was so different from what he had imagined; he had rehearsed little speeches . . . "Do not be frightened, Carolan. You are too young to understand . . . You will be safe with me. I will wait until you are ready . . ." And she put her lips to his, and there was a quiver of passion in her as she said: "For so long I have wanted you to kiss me!"

He said rather hesitantly: "Carolan, let us sit down." They sat, and he put his arms about her; she caught his fingers and held them fast against her breast. He thought, she is so innocent, this little Carolan! And he made up his mind to marry her soon and look after her. Wayward she might be, as her mother evidently was, but she was sweet and impulsive and loving and passionate. She needed a curbing hand; and it should be his gentle hand. "You know I shall be leaving here soon, Carolan. I shall have a living and . . . and . . . I shall want you to come with me as my wife."

Through half-closed eyes she saw the moonlit garden, the outline of trees and hedges. There was a scent of lime trees in the summer-house, and this was the happiest moment of her life.

"Everard," she said, "I will come. Any time you wish, I will come. I will come tomorrow."

He laughed gently and put his lips to her mouth, because he longed to feel the eagerness rising in her. It delighted him, alarmed him a little.

"My darling," he said, "I shall not ask you to come tomorrow. These things need a good deal of arranging, you know."

She lay back in the seat, and he saw her wide eyes, her parted lips. "Ah, but I meant if you wanted me to come tomorrow, I would."

"My sweet Carolan! But think, there is your family and mine!"

"But, Everard, what do we care for them? It is you and I . . . is it not?"

She was like a wild bird, he thought. She was enchanting; she was delightful. He wanted to fall on her and kiss her, and blot out the rest of the world as surely she was inviting him to. He remembered his sober years. I am a man; she is but a child, for all her exciting ways, her ball dress and her passionate love. The exciting things were so often forbidden, were they not? The things that appealed to the senses must be eschewed. Oh, yes, that was what he had always thought. In the days of his boyhood he had thought of entering a monastery; suffering hardship for his faith; he used to think up forms of self-torment as other boys invent new games. In those days he had told himself he would never marry, and he had meant it too, until Carolan came, with that peculiar quality in her which turned his thoughts from his religion to sensual love. He had compromised then; a priest may take a wife, may he not? He was no Catholic—no monk! He shivered to think of the predicament he might have been in, had his mother granted his wish to enter a monastery.

And now Carolan was beside him. Carolan! Carolan! A man, even a man who is a parson, may enjoy his wife.

"Everard," she said, clasping her hands, "I shall be such a good wife to you. I shall have my work to do, shall I not? There are special duties of the parson's wife. Do you think I will suit, Everard?"

He gripped her shoulders hard, trying to fight the excitement that was coming on him again.

"You will suit Everard perfectly," he said, and she laughed, and her laughter was that of a child.

"I must give up climbing trees, must I not, Everard?"

"Indeed you must!"

"I shall have to behave with the greatest decorum? Shall we have a grand wedding, Everard . . . and when?"

"Soon," said Everard. "It must be soon."

"Yes, I think so too. Soon . . . and I shall wear white and there will be a grand ceremony. Your father will marry us. Everard, do you think they will mind your marrying me?"

"Mind! Our families have always been friends, have they not?"

She clasped his arm.

"Of course! Of course!"

They were silent; he could feel her fingers pressing his arm, and her face was white in the moonlight.

"Is not life wonderful . . . wonderful," she said. "Happiness like this . . . such as I never dreamed of! Oh, what a mistake it is not to be happy when there is happiness all around you waiting to be taken!"

"We may not take what is not meant for us, darling," said Everard gently.

"May we not? I would. I will snatch at it when no one is looking if need be."

"You are a baby still, Carolan."

"No. Really I am very wise. But I am not good, like you,

Everard. You would never take what was not meant for you. And it is because you are so different from me that I love you."

They were silent while he kept his arm about her. She was holding his hand, kissing it, setting it against the cool skin of her shoulder. She was full of innocent provocation. He was alarmed for her and for himself, and it was he who said they should go in; they had been in the summer-house for a long time, and people would notice. Carolan herself had lost all sense of time; she had forgotten that others existed to notice.

But if Everard wished to go in, they must go in. As they walked across the lawn, she said fervently: "I shall be a good wife to you, Everard. I shall do everything you say . . . always. Oh, you will be surprised in me! So good I shall be . . . sedate and careful—everything that you wish."

Everard said: "But perhaps I would not wish you to be different from what you are."

Her laughter echoed round them.

"Then, my sweet Everard, that will be very easy, very easy indeed."

They had been gone a long time, and when they were back in the ballroom, curious glances were cast in their direction. Their flushed faces told their own story. Women smiled behind their fans; men's eyes lighted up with amusement. Mrs. Orland's face was blank with disapproval and disbelief. The squire's was black as thunder. When he was in a rage he had no thought for the proprieties; he went across the ballroom to Carolan, and spoke to her in a voice which several people standing round him heard. Mrs. Orland drew Everard aside.

"You will go to your room at once," said the squire. "I will have an explanation of this disgusting behaviour."

Carolan's green eyes opened very wide.

"Oh, but . . ."

The squire lowered his voice slightly, but the fury in it was unmistakable. "Go at once," he said, "or I will take you."

"I do not understand," said Carolan. "The ball is not over yet, and it is my first ball and I . . ."

"Evidently," said the squire, "you have to learn how to behave, before you go to a ball. You behave like a kitchen girl. Get up to your room at once!"

She stared at the blue veins standing out on his forehead. And then Everard turned from his mother.

"Allow me to explain, Squire," he said. "It was entirely due to me . . ."

"Allow me to look after my own family, sir!" retorted the

149

squire with murder in his eyes. Mrs. Orland, who above all things dreaded gossip, plucked Everard's sleeve.

"Everard, come with me quickly. The squire knows best where his daughter is concerned."

Eyes were watching. The music was playing; couples watched as they danced; their eyes were full of amusement and speculation. The naughty little girl and the parson's son! It was rather a good joke.

"If you do not go to your room this minute," said the squire between his teeth, "I will tear that contraption of lace and ribbons off you, and lay about you with my own hands here and now. I mean it, Madam! I repeat, go to your room."

Mrs. Orland's eyes were pleading; Everard was undecided.

"I am going," said Carolan, and the anger of the squire could not quell the happiness in her.

She went to her room. So this was the end of her first ball! She looked at herself in the mirror. Changed, she was— grown up. She loved, and was loved; that had put colour into her eyes, a radiance on her face. Everard . . . wonderful, beautiful, clever, kind, *good* Everard loved her and they would be married.

I will be so good, she thought, so good.

She had almost forgotten her undignified retreat from the ballroom; she had almost forgotten the anger of the squire, until she heard his step outside her door. He burst in angrily, so that the door crashed against the side of the wall.

"Ah!" he said. "Preening in front of the glass, eh?"

And never, never in all her life at Haredon, had she seen him so angry.

He shut the door behind him, and leaned against it, breathing heavily.

"Well?" he said. "You absented yourself from the ballroom with that mollycoddle for nigh on two hours. What were you doing all that time?"

He came towards her threateningly.

"You had better tell me the truth!" he added. And his eyes rested on her bare shoulders, as though, she thought, he were seeing weals leaping up there as he applied the whip.

But happiness gave her courage, and even now she could not think of him so much as the sudden roughness in Everard's voice, and the sudden quiver in his lips as they touched hers. This was nothing. Soon she would be Everard's wife and out of reach of this brute whom she had tried to love and whom, she knew now, she had always hated and feared.

"I *will* tell you the truth!" she cried out. "There is no need to hide it. Soon I shall be gone from here. Soon you will have no right to order me about as you did just now. I hate you for that . . . in front of them all. Everard and I are going to be married . . ."

"What!" His laughter was horrible. "A chit of a girl, and without my consent! Ah! That is what he told you, eh?" He put his face close to hers, in that crude way he had. "That is an old trick, my girl . . ." Horrible words came to his lips; he was saying foul things about her and Everard, and parsons and foolish girls. He was ugly, hateful, satanic. She flew at him suddenly, and struck him across his face. He roared with laughter, but not healthy laughter. He reached for her, but she was quick and agile; she had the bed between them.

"Oh," she cried, panting, "what a wicked man you are! I always knew you were. None but the wicked could think such thoughts of Everard. You lie! I wonder your lies do not choke you. How I wish they would! How I should laugh! I hate you . . . I always have hated you. I hate you when you kiss me. There is something horrible about you . . ."

He interrupted her: "Girl! You forget yourself. Do you realise that you owe everything to me?"

"To you!"

"Yes," he retorted, and his face was so full of blood that she thought it would burst, "to me! But for me you would have been born in the workhouse. You do not know your father. You were born ungrateful . . . you were born a harlot! I have brought you up as a lady, in comfort; I have given you all you could desire . . ." His voice broke with self-pity, but Carolan had no pity for him; she was as violent in hate as she was in love. And how she hated him for saying what he had just said about Everard!

"All I could desire!" she said. "You! Do you think I forget how you treated me the night my mother went away!"

"You forget all I have given you. Was not that very dress you are wearing a present from me? You kissed me for it; it was cheap, was it not? Such a dress, and all for a kiss!"

"I wish I had never had it."

He was trembling now. She was no longer a child—he saw that, and he could have wept for it. He was losing her as surely as he had lost Bess and Kitty. Why did he always lose? He had tried so hard . . . first with one, then with the others.

"What happened in the summer-house? Tell me that!" His voice was calmer now. He hoped he sounded like a father, anxious for his daughter.

"Everard asked me to marry him, and I said I would."

"You . . . marry him! My dear child, he is going to marry Margaret."

"How can that be, and he know nothing of it!"

"It has been arranged between our families for a long time."

"He will not. He loves me."

"Listen, Carrie, God knows I am fond of you . . . Carrie, you have no doubt of that, have you?"

She was silent.

"Carrie . . ." He began to move slowly towards her, but as she edged away he stopped.

"If you were, could you have behaved as you did tonight?" she demanded.

"Yes," he said, "for that very reason. I thought he had taken you out there . . . You know what I thought—and you no more than a child! I was angry with him and angry with you. I have been a father to you, Carrie. Do you not appreciate that?"

She wished he would not talk as though he were weeping. She wanted to be angry with him, and she could not.

"A father to you, Carrie," he went on. "Anxious for you, wanting the best for you. I do not think he would offer marriage; indeed I do not see how he can. It is known, my dear, that you are not my daughter; none knows who your father is. Your mother deceived me. It would not be well for a parson to marry you, Carrie. And he is all but affianced to Margaret."

"Nothing will stand in our way," said Carolan.

The squire murmured: "We must be calm, Carrie. We must talk of this. I must see Parson Orland. Damme, I do not know; I do not know, I am sure."

She was smiling now. This was nothing, this scene. The squire had been drinking too much, that was all. It was just a display of his violent temper.

He was rocking backwards and forwards on his heels.

"You can be sure, Carrie, of one thing. I shall do what I can for your happiness."

He was looking at her pleadingly, but she was in no mood to forgive him. His horrible words still rang in her ears, spoiling the heavenly moonlight of the summer-house. Her hands still tingled from the blows she had given him.

"Look here, Carrie, I lost my temper. Damme, it is not the first time you have seen me lose my temper."

She was laughing. She was not really the sort to nurse an

injury. She would always be essentially generous, too generous perhaps.

"No," she said with a charming gravity, "it is not the first time."

"And will not be the last, I'll warrant!" He slapped his thigh; one should not take his words seriously—he was just a coarse old man.

"I suppose not."

"Then I am forgiven?" he asked, and thought, God damn it, is this Squire Haredon, asking a woman to forgive him? "Then we are friends again?"

He looked so old, standing there, that she had not the heart to tell him she had never looked on him as a friend.

"Oh, yes," she said, "friends. But never say such wicked things about Everard again."

"Then come and kiss me just to show we are friends."

She hesitated. How she hated these embraces! The roughness of his gestures, the feel of him, the smell of him—repulsive!

"Come on, Carrie! I tell you I am going to help you. And, mind you, this is not going to be an easy matter with the Orlands."

She went to him slowly, and lifted her face to brush his cheek with her lips, but he caught her suddenly in a grip that was like a vice about her slender body, and he kissed her full on the mouth; and even then he would not release her. She could feel his hot face against her own, smell spirits on his breath, hear his heavy breathing.

She tried to wriggle free, but he held her fast, laughing. She struck out then, for a panic had seized her.

"Put me down!" she said in a voice of ice. "Put me down at once!"

He put her down; he was laughing thickly, and his voice seemed drugged and slurring. "God damn it, Carrie, you have a temper. I could almost believe you are my daughter after all!"

He went out, and she ran to the door, leaning against it, listening to his footsteps as he went downstairs. He was thinking: Why not? She is no daughter of mine—there is no relationship. Carrie, Carrie, little Carrie . . . lovelier than any of them.

And he knew then that he had never wanted her as a daughter, but as a woman.

Carolan was going away. Not openly but secretly. No one

153

knew; not Margaret, not the squire—most definitely not the squire—not Mrs. West nor Mrs. Orland, nor even Everard . . . yet. But Everard would know, for of course she would tell Everard.

Who would have believed that such glorious happiness as she had known momentarily in the summer-house should so quickly become tinged with grey! Everard's love for her, she told herself, was like the sun shining on a grey day. It was there; obscured temporarily. For Everard had gone away; for three months he had gone away.

How could he! How could he! she demanded of herself when he had told her. Would I have gone away?

Everard had said: "Always remember, Carolan, I love you. I shall come back for you. Whatever they say, I shall marry you, but just at present I must do what my parents wish. After all, Carolan, what is three months?"

Three months, Carolan could have told him, is an eternity when you love. But when he said "What is three months?" just as though to him it could be no more than a matter of so many days and nights, he had wounded her deeply. And he had given in to his parents.

She would have been all for a midnight flitting, elopement, a speedy marriage anyhow, anywhere.

"My sweet Carolan!" he had said. "You are hasty, but you are a child. What do you know of the world? I would have us begin our new life together in a seemly fashion."

And she stamped her foot and laughed and cried.

"Seemly! Is love to be a seemly matter then?"

"To us, Carolan, yes; for love is marriage, and that is indeed a sacred thing."

There she stood before him, her lips parted, her eyes ablaze. And he turned from her because there was something pagan in her that touched something pagan in him, and a man who has given his life to the church cannot be a pagan.

But the first great blazing glory had departed even before that. It was when the squire had come to her room—no, it was not, for what did she care for the squire! It was when Margaret came and stood at the foot of her bed, her face ashen, her fingers plucking at the blue silk of her gown.

"So!" said Margaret slowly. "You have taken Everard!" And then Carolan had known that she was indeed a child, for she had not understood that Margaret's seeming indifference meant that her love for Everard was greater than it had ever been before.

Margaret had burst out passionately: "How could you!
154

How could you, Carolan! It was my ball; it was to have been the night of my betrothal. And you took him, and you went out and everyone noticed you had gone, and when you came in . . . people said 'Poor Margaret!' "

Poor Margaret indeed, for what could Carolan do now to help her? What could she ever have done, loving Everard? For was it not for Everard to decide?

Now here was misery. They were all against her—Margaret, Mrs. Orland, Mr. Orland—not the squire. He watched her with a queer brooding smile on his lips, and she began to be frightened of the squire.

What wretchedness! To have hurt Margaret like this—Margaret, who had almost always been kind to her. What unhappiness to see Margaret growing thin and wan each day because of her.

Mrs. Orland said: "My dear Carolan, I must talk very seriously to you. It would be tragedy for you to marry Everard. You are old enough now to know that the squire is not your father. How could an Orland—and one who has given his life to the church—marry a woman who was born as you were born? It would be as though he condoned immorality. It would kill the career he has planned for himself; one day he would reproach you if you married him."

Could that be so? She did not know. She asked Everard. "I would never reproach you," said Everard. He was young and very earnest, very earnestly in love, very earnest about his career too. Marry Carolan he must, for his need of her was sinful; he would never forget her as long as he lived, and only by marriage and the getting of children could he be Christian. He could not talk of this to his mother, nor to anyone. But thus it was. And yet . . . why had she to be born in that sadly immoral way? Why had she to have a wanton for a mother? Would she have been Carolan if she had not? Would she have had that wild quality, that queer fascination, from which he could not escape?

His mother said: "But, Everard, think, my darling, think!"

He said: "Mother, I love Carolan . . . I must marry Carolan. I could never love anyone else."

His father said: "You have a duty, my son, to God and the church. Such a marriage would be pollution. Is the girl suited to be the wife of a parson?"

"She is suitable to be my wife!" said Everard.

"The obstinacy of youth!" wailed Mrs. Orland. "After all we have done for you . . ."

But Everard knew that, had he not been bewitched, he

155

would not have chosen Carolan. They were right when they said Margaret was the wife for him. Docile, religious-minded, gentle, loving was Margaret. Sweetly pretty, without that wild beauty of Carolan's which was hardly beauty at all. He knew, and he was wise and serious in all things except in love. But how could a man be wise, loving Carolan!

"I must marry Carolan, Mother, I must!"

Mrs. Orland loved her son dearly; he was all her life, for her husband she had never loved. So she set about saving Everard from the disaster of marriage with Carolan, and she set about it wisely.

"I would not wish to spoil your chance of happiness, dear boy. I would want only to make sure of it. You are very young yet; Carolan is even younger. Why, only yesterday she was a baby in the nursery. I am very fond of Carolan; she is a wild, sweet child. But, darling, haste in all things is inadvisable; in marriage it may well prove disastrous. Will you do one little thing for me, darling?"

Everard kissed his mother's hand. He loved her deeply, and the strong sense of chivalry in his nature made him long to protect her from any unhappiness he might cause her by this consuming passion for Carolan.

"I will do anything except give up Carolan—and that I cannot do!"

"I would not ask that. I begin to see how you love the child. It is only your happiness that I think of."

"You are an angel, Mother." His face was alight with happiness, so that he looked just a boy again.

"Listen, darling," she said. "You have your new living; go to it. There will be plenty of work for you to do. Go to it for three months. Do not see Carolan during that time."

"Not see her . . ."

"You could write, my darling . . . Believe me, it is wise . . ."

And eventually he had agreed to do that.

"Three months? What is three months, Carolan?"

An eternity! said Carolan to herself.

She let him go. And he had gone fifty miles away to the new living, and he wrote to her often and told her of the events of his days.

With Everard gone, and Margaret pining, and the strange secret silence of the squire, life was grey indeed.

Charles came home. A big man of twenty-two, very like his father, causing a flutter among the females of the countryside. He too watched Carolan with something of the secret silence of the squire. From under his heavy lidded eyes he watched her, and there were traces of that childhood cruelty about his mouth.

Once he found her in the stables grooming her horse, and he stood leaning against the door watching her.

"Damn it, Carolan," he said, for he used oaths like the squire, "you have grown quickly!"

"Naturally," she said, "I am older."

"And good to look at too!"

She was silent, wishing him gone.

"Everard evidently thought so," he added.

She was still silent.

"You are a sullen devil, Carolan! Have you no welcome for your . . . for your . . . what am I, Carolan? I am not your brother, am I? I do not mind that though, do you?"

"I do not mind in the least," said Carolan coolly.

"Why should you? Do you still bear grudges for past offences?"

"I dislike you intensely, just as I always did, if that is what you mean."

"Hoity-toity!" he said. "What a little Miss she is! I could make you like me, Carolan."

"You would set yourself an impossible task."

"Would I? Would I?" He pushed through the half-door. "Not impossible at all, Miss Carolan. By God, you have a damned pretty face! And cheeky too. But I always liked a bit of cheek."

"Stand back!" ordered Carolan. "I am not a child of five now to be teased by you."

"Oh, no, not five. Almost a wife, eh, Miss Carolan? Almost the parson's wife! Still, is that going to stop you having a little fun?"

"Fun? Do you think dallying with you would ever be fun for me? I assure you it would be far from that—in fact quite the most unpleasant thing that had ever happened to me."

"Good God, Carolan! Do you think I will stand for that?"

"Stand for what you will. I want nothing of you!"

He caught her suddenly.

"Little prude! Are you such a prude with Everard, I wonder?"

She kicked his legs angrily, and he released her.

"What a spitfire!" He grimaced, for she had hurt him, and all the desire to kiss her had vanished momentarily; he would have liked to hit her. He almost did, but the thought of the squire's anger if he heard of this reminded him that he needed money from the squire, and he had to sing small for a while.

He said: "Do you imagine that you are so very attractive that you can kick and still be kissed?"

"You are ridiculous! Conceited fool, that is you, and always was!"

"By God, there are those who are only too pleased to kiss me."

"There are those doubtless, but you probably have to pay them well."

She walked past him arrogantly, her chin up, her eyes flashing her contempt. But her heart quailed a little at the expression in his eyes; it reminded her of the squire's eyes.

So there was Charles, a hateful presence in the house; and that scene in the stables had brought home a sudden and horrible realisation. She would not face it, for quite a long time; but she did eventually. She dreamed once that the squire gave her a horse for her birthday—as indeed he had many years ago—and they went riding together, and he said: "Kiss me for my present, Carrie!" And he seized her, and he had two heads, and one was his own and the other Charles's, and he would not let her go. She awoke from that dream, screaming, and then she could no longer hide the truth from herself.

Sometimes at mealtimes she would watch the big hands of the squire, peeling a peach, cracking a nut; sometimes she would find his eyes fixed upon her.

She would wake suddenly in the night and think she heard footsteps in the corridor outside her door. Once she thought she heard the door handle turned. Her door was locked; she had long ago taken to locking her door.

Panic grew on her. She was afraid to be alone, afraid of his coming on her suddenly, afraid to sleep, afraid to be off her guard, afraid to ride out in case he rode after her. The squire was a great shadow over her life, and beside it was the smaller shadow of Charles. Terrified she was. Nervous and pale. The storm was gathering; one day it would break. Something frightful was going to happen to her if she stayed . . . something inevitable and inescapable.

She could write to Everard, but it was only three weeks ago that he had given his word to his mother that he would not see her for three months. She was terribly frightened and lonely and inexperienced, bewildered by the passion she aroused in the men around her.

She sought for escape. There was only one way of escape—she would go to her father and mother in London. She would write to Everard from London. It was simple—it was the only solution. All that was needed was a little courage. So, late one night, she packed a small bag and crept out of the house; all through the night she walked, and early next morning reached Exeter and caught the London coach.

"Are you going far?" asked the merchant's wife.

"To London."

"To London! It is a long way to go alone."

"I am going to my father and mother," said Carolan.

"Ah! You have been on a visit to the country then?"

"Yes. On a visit."

"And you are looking forward to joining your parents, I can see."

"Very much."

The merchant's wife decided to keep a watchful eye on the child during the journey, for the melancholy young man who had drunk too freely at luncheon was casting many a speculative glance in the young traveller's direction.

"I am surprised," said the woman disapprovingly, "that you are allowed to travel alone."

"I had to come," lied Carolan glibly, for she had made up the story lest she should need one, and could not but congratulate herself on her foresight in having prepared it. "My aunt was taken sick, so she could not accompany me. I can take care of myself."

"You may believe so," retorted the merchant's wife, and noted that her own husband was more than a little interested in the child. She resolved with redoubled fervour to see that the girl came to no mischief during the journey.

So much for the first day, but as they left Honiton behind them Carolan wondered whether she had not been a little impulsive. Her parents would be delighted to receive her of course, but perhaps they would have liked to prepare for her in advance. If only she could have gone to Everard! Surely, had she told him what she feared from the squire and Charles, he would have been glad to receive her! But how could a young parson take a girl into his household? He would have to despatch her at once, and what good would it be to go to him if it were only that he might send her away? And where could he send her but to his mother, and was his mother really a friend of hers?

She had done the only possible thing then in coming to her mother; and once there she would write to Everard and explain everything to him, and by and by he would come for her and there would be a wedding, and she would go to that home which Everard had prepared for her. She felt gloriously wise, very competent to manage her own affairs; and by the time they reached Dorchester her spirits had risen, and her gaiety both amused and delighted her fellow travellers. She was very sure of herself, believing all her difficulties to be over; she was intoxicated with the success of her venture, and she took a wicked delight in inventing stories of her home and her past life for the entertainment of the inquisitive merchant's wife. It was exciting to feel that at sixteen one could make great decisions and possessed the wit to carry them through.

She enjoyed the journey. The thrill of crossing Bagshot Heath . . . even in the morning! She almost wished it was twilight, and the heath full of terrors. She was sure if a highwayman attempted to get her little bit of money she would manage to fool him. But it was absurd to think of highwaymen at eight o'clock of the morning, with the sun brilliant and not yet too hot. By afternoon they would be at the Oxford Arms and the journey done; she would say goodbye to all these people who had been her constant companions for the last few days. This night she would spend under her parents' roof. And the first thing she would do would be to despatch a letter to Everard, telling him what she had done; and, who knew, Everard might decide he could not wait the stipulated three months, and come for her right away. They would be married in London from her father's house.

"We are passing Turnham Green," said one of the travellers, startling her out of her dreams.

It was afternoon when the coach trundled into the yard at the Oxford Arms. It was strange, thought Carolan, how people on a journey were somehow different from the same people at the journey's end. There they had sat, these people, making idle conversation through the long days, over meals in communal dining-rooms; but when the coach unloaded and they stepped out on to the cobbles of the yard, looking about them for their friends, they were like butterflies emerging from the chrysalis stage. The melancholy young man, who had scarcely spoken throughout the entire journey, was greeting a friend; he was no longer melancholy but voluble, talking of lousy beds and dratted inns and the slowness of the coach. The merchant's wife was being greeted affectionately by her sister, and seemed to have forgotten Carolan's existence. But with Carolan the process was reversed. The gay butterfly crept back to her chrysalis. There was no one to meet Carolan, and indeed how could there be? But so childishly had she believed the charming fables she had told the merchant's wife,

160

that she had almost expected her father's carriage to be waiting for her. So now she stood there, forlorn, cramped from the long hours in the coach, hungry and alone.

The merchant's wife saw Carolan, and stopped her chatter. Carolan said quickly: "My father has not yet arrived; something must have occurred to delay him."

The merchant's wife looked faintly perturbed, but Carolan saw with relief that her affairs had ceased to be of paramount importance to the good woman, who was eager to be gone with her husband and sister.

"I shall take a little refreshment while I wait," said Carolan. "It may be that he has left a note for me at the inn."

The merchant's wife kissed her affectionately.

"Take care of yourself, my child! And while you are waiting for your father do not talk to strangers; that is most unwise in London Town. And do not forget, my dear, if ever you *should* be Clapham way, you must bring your family to see us."

The invitation was vague, for the girl was attractive and the merchant had a roving eye; and even the kindest of women must give thought to these matters.

"You are very kind!" said Carolan, for so the woman was, though old-fashioned and over-cautious and sentimental and middle-aged.

Carolan went into the inn. It was cool in the parlour. She sat in a deep window-seat, and looked about her at the gleaming brass over the open fireplace. The pleasurable excitement was returning. She would engage some vehicle to take her to her parents' house; it would be quite simple. In the glass on the sideboard she caught a glimpse of herself, small head held high, eyes a-sparkle. This was adventure as she loved it; she wished that Everard was here to enjoy it with her.

A serving maid came in, buxom and pretty, with ribbons in her gown and a mob-cap on her fluffy hair. Carolan asked for refreshment. It would have to be bread and cheese with a glass of ale to wash it down, said the maid, for that was the best the inn could offer in between meals. Carolan could think of nothing better, since all she needed was a little light refreshment before she set out to find her parents' house. She would enquire about a conveyance later.

When the maid had disappeared, a woman came into the parlour and sat down in one of the chairs near Carolan. Carolan scarcely noticed her, so deep was she in her own thoughts, and when the maid returned with the food and drink, she took the little velvet purse from the pocket of her

161

cloak, paid her, and wondered whether to ask then about the best way to get to her mother's house; but before she could speak, the newcomer had engaged the maid's attention and was asking for a glass of ale.

There was plenty of time, thought Carolan, and meanwhile the bread and cheese were delicious and she was hungry; the ale was cool and refreshing, and she was thirsty.

"A warm day," said the woman, and Carolan noticed that the maid had slipped out and they were alone.

"Very warm," agreed Carolan, "but the ale is cool!"

"Ah! Indeed." She was a tall woman with white hair, very dark eyes and a pleasant smile. Carolan warmed to her, for there was something in the very vastness of the City that chilled her, and it was good to discover so soon that its people were friendly.

"You travelled by the coach, my dear, did you not?"

Carolan nodded.

"And you have come far?"

"From Exeter."

The woman smiled.

"That is a long journey for one so young . . . and forgive me if I say it . . . so beautiful."

"Oh!" said Carolan, protesting but well pleased. "You flatter!"

"Not I! Have you looked in the glass recently? There is one!"

The maid came in with the ale. The woman paid and sat back in her chair sipping the beverage.

"As you say, it is cool enough!"

The maid left them. The grandfather clock in the corner ticked loudly, and every now and then Carolan could hear distant voices crying wares. It was indeed pleasant in the old inn parlour, with the adventure well-nigh over and so successfully carried out, and the glass on the sideboard showing Carolan her reflection and assuring her that though the woman had exaggerated a little, there was some truth in her words.

A smile appeared about the woman's mouth as she watched the girl's smiling at her own reflection.

"You are visiting relations?"

"I am going home . . . to my parents . . ."

"Ah! Then you know London well?"

"No. I have been living in the country . . . not with my parents. Now I have come home to them."

"They were to be here to meet you perhaps?"

"Oh, no . . . It is a surprise visit. They will not be here to meet me."

The woman watched her speculatively.

"You have a lucky face," she said.

"A lucky face?"

"Indeed you have! As soon as my eyes fell on you, I knew good fortune awaited you."

"But how could you know that?"

"There are some of us to whom such knowledge comes."

"Do you mean . . . you are a fortune-teller?"

"Oh, come! Do I look the sort? A lady does not call herself a fortune-teller; that suggests a gipsy, does it not, one who must have her palm crossed with silver before she will ply her trade?"

Hot blood rushed into Carolan's face.

"I am very sorry . . . I should have known."

The woman threw back her head and laughed. Her teeth flashed. Carolan caught a glimpse of gold ear-rings.

"Bless you, my dear," said the woman, "I did not mean to embarrass you. In a measure you are right; nature does not discriminate when she bestows her gifts. I can see into the future; only . . . I do not ply my accomplishment as a trade."

"I . . . see . . ."

"Ah! But not so clearly as I see a wonderful fortune for you!"

Carolan was breathless, eager, lips parted, eyes shining; her hood fell back from her glowing hair.

"You can see that for me?"

"There is mystery about you."

Carolan blushed; she was sure the woman knew that she had run away.

"Are you by any chance going to join your lover?"

Carolan was silent. Very soon of course she would join Everard; perhaps it would be sooner than she expected.

"You are running away from your home," went on the woman, her dark eyes shining with prophecy. "I see you are greatly loved."

"You are indeed clever!" said Carolan.

"I will tell you what I will do. I will read your palm; that will tell me more than your face. Come and sit nearer me, my dear. No! I will join you on the window seat."

Wonderful things could happen to you if you were bold and took from life what you wanted; that was what Carolan

163

was learning. How much older she was now than that girl who had left Haredon but a few days ago! How much wiser than Margaret who would never undertake such an adventure! The kindness of people! The merchant's wife who had befriended her; this lady, who, for no payment at all, would tell her fortune, and just because she had a lucky face!

She sat on the window seat beside Carolan. She smelt of musk.

"Give me your palm, my dear. There! Why, what a little hand! A pretty little hand; and scarcely any hard work has this little hand been forced to do. Perhaps it has gripped a pair of reins, eh? Ah! You lived quietly in the country, did you not? And a little pet among those with whom you lived. There is much love in your life, child. And in the country you met your lover." A very long thin finger touched Carolan's palm. "And there was some disagreement, eh, some little bit of trouble? Disapproval of the match from those who loved you and wanted to keep you with them a little longer?"

Carolan was red and white by turns, for surely she was in the presence of a seer! So it was all written there, was it? Everything that had happened to her.

The woman's fingers closed about her hand.

"Never fear, all will be well. Very soon you will be a wife. Do not be dissuaded from true romance. It is a headstrong little girl you are—fond of your own way. Am I not right? Already you know something of the charm those green eyes hold. Well, well, that is natural. One thing, my dear, do not be so ready to trust those around you. I think perhaps you are over-trusting."

Carolan's eyes were dreamy. It was true, absolutely true. How readily she had trusted Charles at the first show of friendship! How innocently had she believed in the fatherly affection of the squire! London was indeed an enchanting place; how glad she was that she had come! How wise she had been!

"Thank you!" she murmured. "Thank you!"

The lady's laughter rang out and echoed in the rafters of the inn parlour.

"Do not thank me, my child. Thank fate that gave you your beauty and your charm."

"You should not say such things," protested Carolan, longing for the lady to repeat them. "They are not really true."

"So you doubt my word?"

"Oh . . . no . . . no! I know you are speaking the truth . . . about what is happening, but . . ."

"Ah! So modest? Or not so modest, eh? Which is it?"

And the keen black eyes seemed to look right through Carolan, making her blush for very shame.

"But, my child," said the lady, "you must not think I am laughing at you. If I laugh it is because there is something beautiful about youth and innocence. How I hope that your dearest wish will be granted! Come, I will see what I can do to give you that wish. Give me your hand. See! I will hold your wrist lightly, thus. Now close your eyes. Keep them fast shut until I say you may open them. Now wish. Just repeat the wish over to yourself—not aloud. None but yourself must know your dearest wish. There! Have you said it to yourself? Then say it again. Your dearest wish. Open your eyes. Perhaps now it will come."

Carolan opened her eyes. She was still saying to herself: "Let Everard come at once to me in London. Let him leave everything and come!"

"Your wish will come true," said her kind friend. "I know your wish will come true."

"You are so kind to me, I do not know how to thank you!"

"It is not I who am kind—it is life. And I do not like thanks."

She drained off her ale.

"You are going?" said Carolan, disappointed.

"I must be on my way. Goodbye, my child, and one word more before I go. Guard that impulsive nature of yours. Do not be so ready to trust. Remember that, will you, my dear, and little can go wrong with you, for you have a high good spirit, and it is such as you that Life loves. But remember— not too trustful!"

"I will remember," said Carolan. "And you are right, wonderfully right. I shall never forget you."

"No, my dear, I do not think you will. Our meeting must have been ordained. I feel it here." She touched her bosom, and a smile that was oddly mischievous sat upon her face.

She went out, and Carolan saw her make her stately way past the window. She did not look in though, and Carolan remembered that she was hungry, and sat back to enjoy her bread and cheese.

Life was wonderful. Very soon she would be married to Everard, for had she not wished that he would leave everything and come to her, and was not her wish to be granted? And in the meantime she was to enjoy this adventure of getting to her own dear Mamma and the father she would surely love. Would it be possible to hire a carriage to take her to the house? She wondered how much a carriage would cost. She would ask the landlord or one of the ostlers what would be best. And she would go now, for she was eager to see her mother and her father.

She drew on the hood of her cloak and went to the mirror on the sideboard to pat the tendrils of hair at her temple.

Excited like this she was certainly pretty, as pretty as Margaret perhaps, but in a different way. She was staring at her dress, for the pearl and turquoise brooch which the squire had given her on her last birthday was not there. Her fingers flew to her dress in dismay, she could not believe the mirror was telling the truth. The brooch had gone. She began to ask herself if she had put it on that morning. Had she left it in the inn on the other side of Bagshot Heath? But no! Distinctly she remembered she had the brooch pinned in her dress when she came into this parlour.

Well, she had lost it; she must resign herself to that. Did it matter? Every time she put it on she thought of the squire's hot fingers fastening it at her neck, as he had done on the day he had given it to her. But though she was young she was no fool. The lady had come very close to her when she had made her wish. She had *felt* her close while she murmured the wish over and over again to herself. Oh, how wicked she was to think such evil thoughts of one who had been so kind! But, wicked as she was, she was feeling in the pocket of her cloak to make sure that she still had her purse.

The purse had gone . . . had disappeared as surely as the brooch!

Hot anger burned in Carolan's cheeks. Not for the loss of her brooch and her purse . . . oh, no, that was a loss certainly, but there was something that went deeper than that. Oh, the wickedness! To say such things! The deceit! The pretence! The hypocrisy!

I'd have her beaten! Carolan said to herself furiously. I'd have her jailed, sent to Newgate! I'd have her hanged! The wicked old thief!

Carolan ran out into the yard. She was young and fleet, and the woman had been neither. Eagerly Carolan looked about her, but there was no sign of her quarry. Out in the street people glanced curiously at her, noting her flaming face. If I catch her, thought Carolan, oh . . . if I catch her! She thought she had a glimpse of her, and started to run, but even before she had collided with an old woman selling bunches of lavender, she realised she had been mistaken.

"Look where you are going, lady!" scolded the lavender woman, and then seeing Carolan's good clothes she held out her wares and chanted: "Sweet blooming lavender, lady. Won't you buy my sweet blooming lavender . . . ?"

Carolan looked into the seamed face before her, ugly from the pox, and lined with cares.

"I have no money," she said. "I have just been robbed of my purse."

With some, that might have been an excuse not to buy, but one does not sell lavender outside the Oxford Arms day in and day out without learning something of human nature; and here was a young face, a young and lovely face with wonderful green eyes that flashed anger and pity together, and a tremulous mouth that had not yet learned to give the ready lie to a pestering street crier.

"A bad business, lady," said the woman. "I hope you'll not be incommoded . . ."

"And my brooch," said Carolan. "My brooch and my purse . . . by a creature who said she would tell my fortune and take nothing for it."

"Why, bless you, lady, it is few there are that gives and take nothing in this world."

"Indeed, it seems so," agreed Carolan, and hated the teller of fortunes afresh, for she longed now to give a coin to this poor old woman.

"I am on my way to my parents' house," she said, "and as I have been staying in the country for a long time, I have never seen the house in which they live. I shall have to walk there. Please, could you tell me the way? It is Grape Street that I wish to go to."

The woman was silent for a moment while she sniffed her lavender. Then her eyes rested on Carolan's dress and cloak and the good shoes she wore.

"Grape Street, did you say? Grape Street? 'Tis not so very far, but are you sure it was Grape Street?"

"Quite sure," said Carolan.

"Well, then, you walk straight on till you get to Holborn. Then I think mayhap you would do better to ask again. 'Tis one of the streets that run behind Holborn. Not so far to walk, if you have the feet for walking. And lady, are you new to London?"

Carolan, chastened by recent experiences, said humbly that she had never set foot in the city before in her life.

"There are more rogues to be met in London in one half-hour than in a year in your country towns, lady. Be careful who you should ask the way."

"Thank you," said Carolan. "Thank you."

The woman looked after her as she went up the street, scratched her pock-marked brow, shrugged her shoulders, giggled a little, and murmured: "Grape Street, eh? Grape Street!" And then, seeing a likely customer, forgot the unusual sight of a well-dressed young girl from the country asking the way to Grape Street, and sang out in a high quavering voice: "Will you buy my sweet blooming lavender . . . ?"

Carolan hurried on, looking about her eagerly. Here was a lively spectacle on which to feast the eyes—people everywhere; gay people and sad people, some who talked incessantly, some who were silent, some who shrieked with laughter, some who mumbled to themselves. Everywhere there were people; they thronged the street, jostling one another, so that unless one was young and determined to have a share in it oneself, one was pushed out into the dirty carriage-way. At street corners were whining beggars, their diseased and dirty flesh visible through their rags. Street vendors peered into Carolan's face as she hurried along. Would she buy a China orange, an apple? Would she buy a ballad, muffins, some branches of lavender? Down narrow side streets she caught glimpses of stalls and even greater crowds of people. She heard the shrill voice of the cheap-jack on the corner; carriages rattled over the cobbles—and what haughty, elegant passengers they contained! Never had Carolan seen such clothes, such brilliant colours, such sumptuous cloth. A gentleman, riding by in his carriage, gazed appraisingly at her through his eyeglass; he made as if to stop the carriage, and Carolan hastened on in alarm. But the gentleman was too languid to give chase; when Carolan turned, she saw the tail end of his carriage disappearing in the stream of traffic. Ladies, holding nosegays to their faces went by in their carriages; disdainful and very, very elegant were those ladies; some, less elegant, walked the pavement, generally, Carolan noticed, with an escort, lifting their skirts that they might not trail among the dirt, taking care not to touch those who passed by them. Exciting, exhilarating scene! Carolan had never witnessed anything like it. Noise all round her; conversation mingling with the vendors' cries and the sound of carriage wheels. And thus she came into Holborn. Now she must ask again for Grape Street, and decided to follow the advice of the lavender woman; so with the greatest of care she selected, for her look of honesty, an old woman who was selling papers of pins. Carolan blushed to see how new hope leaped into her eyes as she approached her. The woman sang out:

> "Three rows a penny pins
> Short whites and mid-di-lings."

Hastily Carolan explained: "I have not come to buy: I have no money. My purse has just been stolen . . : Could you tell me where to find Grape Street?"

"Off with you!" said the woman. "Off with you!"

"But, please . . . I only want to know . . ."

The woman turned away, grumbling about the tricks of the well-to-do who must torment a poor, nay, starving woman.

Carolan was so hurt she could have burst into tears. She caught at the woman's ragged sleeve, but she was turned upon with such ferocity that she desisted immediately and walked on. She felt frightened now, a stranger in a strange city. It was difficult to understand the speech of these people; they were all in such a hurry, except those who quizzed her with their speculative glances and frightened her more than those who ignored her. She must find Grape Street and her parents quickly.

Somewhere a clock struck four, and out of Hatton Garden a flying pieman came running. There were only a few pieces of baked plum pudding left in his basket.

"A piece for a penny," he called as he ran. "Buy, buy, buy!"

He had a kind face, Carolan saw, and she was getting desperate. She ran beside him for a second or two.

"Please," she panted, "I cannot buy, but please could you tell me where is Grape Street?"

He stopped. His eyes, she noticed, were brown and full of laughter, and into them crept that puzzled look which she had seen in those of the lavender woman.

"Why, lady," he said, "Grape Street is not so far, but are you sure you mean Grape Street?"

"Quite sure," Carolan told him.

"Well then, if you are quite sure it is Grape Street that you are after, you go down this turning and you take the first on the left, and then take the second turning on the right. Then you will find yourself in Grape Street . . . if it *is* Grape Street you want."

"Thank you!" she said. "Thank you!"

169

He stood looking after her, as the lavender seller had done. Carolan hurried along. Now she was in a narrow street with tall, dingy houses on either side. She took the turn to the left and was in an even narrower street. The stench from the gutters was appalling; she hurried on. Surely she could not be far from her parents, but this was so different from her imaginings. She had pictured a charming house by the river with a garden extending to the water's edge, from which it would be thrilling to watch the ships and barges pass by; and here she was, hurrying past alleys in which dark shadows seemed to lurk, while through grimy windows unfriendly faces peered at her with half-hearted curiosity.

Someone was walking very close behind her. She turned to look, and there was a man, a young man not much taller than herself, with a face which, though far from handsome, was attractive. He had the brightest, merriest blue eyes she had ever seen; they showed up startlingly in his brown face.

"Could you spare a penny, lady?"

His voice was the most surprising thing about him; it was cultured, even charming; and it seemed to her a very sad state of affairs that such a man as he apparently was should be reduced to begging in the streets of London. She had never been able to hide her feelings.

He looked straight into her face and some of the merriness left his eyes.

She said: "I am sorry I have nothing to give. I have had my purse stolen."

"Your purse!" he said. "That is bad. And did you see the thief?"

"Indeed I saw her, but I did not know her for a thief until too late."

"New to London Town, that is you, lady!" His eyes darted from the fine lace at her throat to the good leather of her shoes. "You are bound somewhere?"

"To my family in Grape Street. Perhaps you can tell me if I am near?"

"Grape Street! You cannot mean Grape Street . . . but if you do, it is just around the corner."

He leaned towards her and touched her sleeve as he pointed the way.

"Thank you," she said.

"What part of Grape Street were you after, lady?"

"Number sixty."

"Ah!" he said, and his eyes were merry again. "It is number sixty then! You cannot miss it—the number is plain over the door." And he seemed consumed with some joke of his own. "Good day to you, lady."

He bowed rather mockingly, she thought; he swaggered along the street, and was soon out of sight.

As she turned to follow his directions, a man approached her. He was tall and spare of figure, and as he came nearer he slackened his pace. She was suddenly afraid. She looked about her at the deserted street; the man with the merry eyes had already disappeared.

"Forgive me," said the newcomer, his eyes taking in every detail of her appearance, "but are you aware that the man who just approached has made off with your handkerchief?"

She stared at the man. His face was very white, and the skin seemed to be drawn too tightly across his sharp features so that they gave the impression of trying to burst through it. He had the face of a dead man, Carolan thought, apart from his eyes, which were dark and alert—strange, excited and inquisitive eyes. She thought fearfully, What now, I wonder?

"You have lost a handkerchief, I believe?" he insisted.

She stepped back a pace, suspecting some trap. She felt in the pocket of her gown.

"I have," she said.

"He took it."

"You saw him?"

"One looks for these things in this part of the town."

"Then, why did you wait to tell me until it is too late to retrieve it?" she demanded.

She did not realise it, but all the time they were speaking she was stepping backwards, putting distance between herself and the man.

"It would have been unwise to try to retrieve it. Think yourself fortunate that it was merely a handkerchief. These streets are as full of thieves as a warren is of rabbits. They work together; it is not always wise to raise a hue and cry in these streets. You have got off lightly. Would you allow me to help you?"

She was suddenly angry. She had felt so sorry for the man with the merry blue eyes, and he had known it and laughed at her for it! Were there none but thieves and rogues in this wicked place? Humiliation and anger made her forget her fear of the newcomer; besides, his respectable garments of black that were a little shiny, suggested an honesty in some odd way.

"I am looking for Grape Street," she said. "My parents live there, and I am visiting them."

"Your parents live in Grape Street!" he repeated as though stupefied.

"That is what I said. I wonder if that rogue who stole my handkerchief directed me truly."

"Tell me," he said, "where in Grape Street your parents live."

"The number is sixty."

"Sixty! Let me see. I believe that is the second-hand shop, is it not?"

The dark eyes searched her face eagerly. Strange eyes—beautiful eyes in an unbeautiful face; that was what made them look so incongruous.

"Second-hand shop! My mother did not say . . ."

He spoke slowly, as though checking over the items in his mind.

"You have never been to London before, have you? You have come on a visit from the country; you are visiting your parents. And it is your mother who lives in the second-hand shop at number sixty Grape Street."

It was kind of him to express such interest, but she had been robbed twice in a very short time, and she was in no mood to trust a living soul.

"When I saw you," he said, "I was of the opinion that it was some prank that had brought you here. You are not dressed for these streets, if you will allow me to say so. That makes you very conspicuous."

"It is far from a prank," said Carolan. "I have been in this wicked place little more than an hour, and already I have lost my purse, my brooch and a lace handkerchief."

"That is because you have doubtless acted unwisely. Will you allow me to walk with you to number sixty Grape Street? I am sure I can protect you from further annoyance."

She hesitated.

"If you would feel happier, I would walk in front and you could follow. I understand that you are not inclined to trust strangers, and that means that you have acquired some wisdom in the last hour."

She was sorry for her seeming churlishness; she was absolutely certain that this man was no pickpocket.

"If you would show me the way, I should be most grateful," she murmured. "And please do not walk in front."

He walked beside her, so that he was nearer the road to protect her from splashes of mud and filth if any vehicle came along the street. He kept a certain distance between them, as though he were trying to inspire her with confidence in him.

"Would you think me impertinent if I asked you your name?"

"Indeed no! It is Carolan Haredon."

He seemed to be searching a list of names in his mind.

"Carolan Haredon," he repeated. "Let me see, I believe it is a Mr. and Mrs. Grey who keep the second-hand shop."

"My . . . mother is Mrs. Grey," said Carolan quickly.

"I see . . . I see . . ." Odd, the impression he gave of making a mental note of information!

But Carolan was too bewildered by all that had happened to give more than a passing thought to him. Her mother in a second-hand shop! Had she changed? She thought of Kitty . . . in her boudoir with Thérèse to dress her, and Sambo to sit at her feet . . . That Kitty . . . in a second-hand shop!

"My name," the man beside her was saying, "is Jonathan Crew, at your service. And here is Grape Street . . . and see, there is number sixty!"

Number sixty was a small dark shop, and in its window and doorway hung garments of all descriptions. It was dingy and depressing, thought Carolan; her heart sank, and with her first glimpse went all the pretty pictures she had built up in her imagination. She stepped down into the dark interior of the shop, and Mr. Jonathan Crew followed her.

Almost immediately a door opened and a man appeared. He was the man she had seen in the wood.

"Father!" she cried.

He stared at her, without recognition.

"It is Carolan . . . your daughter," she said. "Is my mother here?"

"Carolan!" A smile broke out on the man's face. "Why . . . little Carolan! So it is!"

He took her face between his hands; her hood fell back, and her reddish hair gleamed even in the darkness of the shop. There were tears in the man's eyes. He held her against him as though he loved her very dearly. He said: "Little daughter! Little daughter!" Then: "Kitty!" he called. "Kitty!"

And all this time Jonathan Crew stood close to a bunch of old coats hanging in the doorway, and watched them.

Kitty came into the shop; she had put on a good deal of weight, and had changed subtly. She was the same beautiful Kitty, but the hair, without the ministrations of Thérèse, was untidy. She wore a pink frock with fine lace on it, but the pink material and the lace were none too clean. She saw Carolan, and screamed with delight.

"My darling child! My own darling child!"

173

Carolan ran to Kitty, and they embraced.

"Mamma, I could not stay away longer."

"No, no, my love, of course you could not!"

"Mamma, you are truly glad to see me?"

Kitty laughed; it was the same spontaneous laugh that Carolan remembered well. Kitty held her at arms' length and looked at her.

"How you have grown, my love!"

"Have I, Mamma?"

"Why, when I left you were only a baby."

"Oh, no, Mamma, not a baby!"

"Then a very little girl."

Kitty held out a hand and drew Darrell into the magic family circle.

"Now I have both my darlings with me."

Carolan looked from one to the other.

"Is not your daughter a regular beauty, sir?" demanded Kitty.

"She is a sweet creature, and I am proud of her," said Darrell shyly.

"But, darling," said Kitty, "why did you not let us know you were coming?"

"There was not time." A dark shadow crossed Carolan's face. "It is too much to talk of now, Mamma. I will tell you later. Mamma, there is one thing I must tell you . . . and you too." She smiled shyly at Darrell. "I shall not stay long, because I am going to be married."

Kitty wiped her eyes.

"My own sweet darling, to marry! But you are but a child."

"Rising seventeen!" said Carolan.

"Can you believe it, Darrell, my darling? And whom have they chosen for you, sweetheart?"

"They did not choose. Indeed they are not happy about the choice. Everard and I chose."

"Everard! Everard Orland! The parson's son?" Kitty laughed gaily. "Well, he is a dear boy, and I am happy. He will make a good husband."

"So I think," said Carolan. And they all laughed, though Carolan noticed that there was something hollow about her father's laughter, as though he had not learned how to do it properly.

"I have been robbed . . . twice!" cried Carolan, and then remembered Jonathan Crew. "Oh . . ." she cried, and turned towards him; he emerged from the doorway and came slowly into the shop.

Darrell hastily took a step forward. "Can I help you, sir?" he asked. But Carolan rushed in with explanations.

"This gentleman was kind enough to bring me here. I was the victim of a second pickpocket, and he said the streets were unsafe and that he would show me the way."

"Then we have to thank you, sir," said Darrell.

"Carolan, my sweet!" said Kitty. "You must be hungry; come along and we will eat."

Darrell turned to Jonathan Crew.

"And you, sir—you will take a glass with us? We would have you know that we are indeed grateful to you for bringing our daughter through these streets."

"It is a kindness, and would be a pleasure," said Mr. Crew, and all four of them went through a door into the shop parlour.

Pale sunshine, streaming through her window, awakened Carolan next morning. Just at first she could not remember where she was, for the room and its furniture were unfamiliar; a strange room indeed, full of shabby grandeur. The two armchairs, with their brocade coverings, had been splendid once; the carved table was a beauty; the curtains were rich though torn in places and a little dirty.

The incidents of the day before crowded into Carolan's mind. She remembered coming through the streets of London to her father's shop; she remembered drinking a glass of ale with their new friend, Mr. Crew, who had volunteered a little information about himself. He had a clerkship in a shipping company's office on the river bank; he lived in the Grape Street neighbourhood because it was cheap and he found it interesting. He had little money, he said oddly, for any entertainment save the study of human nature—and indeed there could not be a more interesting study, nor one that was kinder to the purse.

They had talked of him a little, after he had gone.

"An honest man," said Darrell, "and one without pretensions."

But Kitty had added: "A little on the dull side. Now I would have preferred my Carolan to have been brought here by a nobleman!"

"A nobleman in Grape Street!" laughed Darrell indulgently. "That, my dear, is like looking for an apple on a pear tree."

"Indeed it is not!" retorted Kitty. "Often enough I have heard of noblemen coming down to the poor parts of London,

175

disguised as clerks or journeymen, or tinkers, or what you will. It is a new sport among the aristocracy."

She was the same Kitty, painting rosy pictures of the life around her as she wanted it to be, not as it was.

Carolan stretched herself in bed and thought, I do believe she is trying to conjure up a romance for me and Mr. Crew, who, she is assuring herself, is a prince disguised as a clerk. And this in spite of what I have told her of Everard! Dear, inconsequent Mamma, to whom fidelity is an elastic quality to be stretched by her according to her need and mood of the moment.

Last night she had brought Carolan into this room, and had sat at the dressing-table, twirling her hair while the candlelight played about her face.

"Of course, darling," she had said, "this is no permanent home! It is a stepping-stone to better things. Your father has told me so, and well you know your father is not the man to lie. He has said to me: 'Kitty, my own love, this is not what I would wish for you!' And indeed I understand that, for is it what I have been used to! 'No!' he said. 'One day I shall make a fortune here, and then you shall have a fine house, a worthy setting for your beauty.' And, Carolan, do you think me still beautiful? What do you say? Have I aged much since you last saw me?"

She had indeed looked lovely with the candlelight to soften her face.

Carolan had laughed at her vanity, but had been unable to resist pleasing her charming, illogical mother.

Then Kitty cried a little, and laughed a good deal, and said she was happy, happy, happy that her own darling daughter had at last come home to her mother. She had kissed her tenderly; insisted on waiting until she was in bed, and tucking her in as though she were a little child. Carolan remembered sharply that when she *had* been a child, Kitty had not come to tuck her in. But such thoughts she quickly dismissed, because when Kitty was with her it was always difficult not to fall in with the bit of play-acting she was putting over at the moment.

Carolan put one bare foot out to the rug beside her bed; then the other. She pattered across the floor to the narrow window. Now she was looking down on the mean street. It was deserted, no doubt because of the earliness of the hour. The dingy houses opposite were so close that but for the curtains it would have been possible to see into those rooms behind them. When she leaned out of the window she could see the façade of the shop, but the door was shut and the old clothes which had hung in the doorway had been taken in.

She thought of Jonathan Crew's words—"These streets are as full of thieves as a warren is of rabbits." She wondered why her father, if he had wanted a shop, did not have one in a busy thoroughfare such as some of those through which she had passed yesterday on her way from the Oxford Arms. Surely more business could be done in those busy streets. She thought of the ladies and gentlemen riding by in their carriages. They would not want to buy old clothes, of course, but there were other things in the shop.

She left the window and washed her hands and face in the basin. The water was cold and refreshing.

When she was dressed she opened her door and listened. There was no sound in the house; evidently her parents were not early risers. She smiled to herself, thinking what a good idea it would be to prepare breakfast and take it up to their room. Her mother, she was sure, would enjoy that. She tiptoed downstairs and along the passage to the shop parlour. There was a sour smell in the place, which she decided probably came from all those secondhand goods in the shop beyond.

A clock began to strike. One, two, three, four . . . right up to seven. She opened the parlour door and looked in at the shop. Light flickered through the shutters and fell on a pair of brass candlesticks; they glittered brightly among that hotchpotch of articles. Chairs and carpets, chinaware and silver, oddments of furniture, usually broken and decrepit; and everywhere old clothes. The striking, she saw, had come from a grandfather clock in one corner of the shop.

Carolan thought indulgently of her parents. She was beginning to suspect that her father was no shrewd business man. Why did he not arrange his goods more attractively? That confidence, which she had lost owing to her encounter with two thieves during her first hour or so in London, was returning. While she was awaiting Everard she would look after these two dear simple parents of hers. Oh, she could imagine them with their shop! No doubt her mother went through the stock and kept the most attractive articles for herself; and her father, poor sad man, would not say her nay. Oh, they needed looking after, these two parents of hers! Mamma was a child at heart . . . and Father? Terrible things had happened to him. His gentle expression and his smile were like a mask he drew down closely over his features lest you should read there what he did not wish you to. Kitty would never read anything she did not want to; but Carolan would read the truth if he as much as lifted that mask for a moment. And he was afraid that she would, poor darling.

She looked up at the bell over the door, which would warn her father of the approach of a customer; that was well enough. But why did he hang garments outside the door, in a place which was as full of thieves as a warren was of rabbits? Carolan clicked her tongue indulgently; he had probably lost lots of things that way, and most likely did not know it!

She heard a movement in the shop parlour, and turning, saw her father entering the room.

"Good morning!" she said.

"Good morning, Carolan! Is this a little tour of exploration?"

"Yes. I thought I would get breakfast for you and Mamma."

"That is a kind thought, but your mother does not open her eyes until midday; I shall have mine now, because I have to go out this morning on important business."

"You were going to get it yourself then?"

"Ah!" He had a very charming smile. "I am a handy man, daughter." He looked down at his hands, and she followed his gaze. They were gnarled hands, and one of the fingers of his right hand was missing. They seemed to be telling her so much, those hands; they made her want to weep.

There was a very tender note in her voice when she said: "You will sit down this morning, and I will get your breakfast."

"It is difficult to work in a strange kitchen."

"I shall discover very soon where things are kept."

"How would it be, Carolan, if we got it together?"

"Excellent!"

He led the way. The kitchen was stone-floored and untidy. He watched her survey it with a faint pucker on her brows.

"Carolan," he said, "you are like your mother . . . though different. I wish . . ."

"Well, Father, what is it you wish?"

"That I could have given you riches and luxury. And Carolan, but for this thing which happened to me, I could have given you both comfort. Behold me, Carolan, a most unfortunate man!"

She laid a hand on his shoulders.

"We are here now . . . all three of us together. That is good."

"Yes," he said slowly, "it is good; but it will not be for long, Carolan, for your lover will come for you."

She turned away from his incomprehensible eyes.

"He will come for me, yes, but when we are married we shall see you often."

"That," he said, "will be delightful. Here is cold bacon and bread; a little pickled onion and ale. How does that appeal to you, Carolan?"

"Admirably! I am hungry. London air evidently agrees with me."

He cut the bacon into slices; she cut the bread; and when they were seated at the table, she said: "It is exciting—getting to know your father when you are a grown-up person. I do not suppose that happens to many people."

"Fortunately, no," he answered.

"I might say 'Unfortunately, no!' Just think! Had you known me when I was one, two, three, four, five, you might have had to punish me now and then."

"I cannot imagine myself punishing you."

"I was a very wayward child."

"All the same, you and I would have come to an understanding about your waywardness." He looked down at his hands again. How very sensitive he was about them! she thought tenderly. "No, Carolan," he went on, "I think it was well you spent your childhood in a fine old place like Haredon. I could never have given you so much luxury."

"I was not very happy there. I should have been happier with you and my mother."

She watched the colour come into his face.

"Ah!" he said, very eagerly. "You would have preferred me as a father, to Squire Haredon?"

It was her turn to flush, remembering the presents, hearing the slurring voice—"Now, Carrie, give me a kiss. By God, you are your mother all over again! Take all and give nothing." Not the voice of a father! It was horrible.

"I hated Squire Haredon. You I could have loved."

He said: "I'll remember that, Carolan. I'll remember it." His heart was beating violently; it would be so good to tell her everything, not all at once of course, but gradually. Odd how he had wanted to talk! He had tried to talk to Kitty. He had told her a little, but she cried and said it was horrible, and he could not bear to make her cry, even though she would have

179

forgotten it all by the morning. With Carolan it would have been different; she would have seen with him; she would have felt with him—humiliation, hunger, torture, desperation. He could not forget what had happened to him, and sometimes he craved to talk as a man will crave for drink. There she sat before him, with her small charming face so vital—more so than Kitty's had ever been—and those wonderful green eyes that would flash in anger and sympathy simultaneously; the anger would be for his tormentors, the sympathy for him. No! Talking to Carolan would be a luxury he must deny himself.

He said: "Have you written to your lover yet?"

"No. I intend to do so today."

He said: "Do so now; and I will take the letter and see that it is dispatched at once."

He found her writing materials, cleared a space for her on the table, and went out to prepare for a journey, leaving her to write.

Carolan sat at the table and conjured up a picture of Everard, and then began.

> "Dearest Everard,—No doubt you will be surprised to hear from me that I have left Haredon. I found it impossible to stay there. Charles and the squire made it impossible. Please understand me; there seemed but one thing to do, and that to get away quickly; there seemed to be one place to go to, and that the house of my parents. So I am here, dearest Everard, as you will see, at number sixty Grape Street. My father is very, very kind, and my mother is glad to see me. They have the oddest shop, and I hope to help them, but I also hope that it will not be long before you come for me or tell me to come to you. I think of you continually, Everard, and if you should think it was wrong of me to leave Haredon so hastily, please try to understand that I *could* not stay; I can explain more fully when we meet. My father is going to take this letter and despatch it for me; he is ready to go out now. Darling Everard, it is only one month since you said *au revoir* to me; it seems like one year. Two months seems an age. I am longing to see you, darling.
>
> Your ever constant Carolan."

It took a long time to write the letter. She wanted to show him, without actually asking him to do so, that he must break his promise to his mother because her need of him was urgent.

When she read the letter through it sounded cold; it did not adequately express her feelings. She would have written another, had she not known that her father was ready, waiting to go out.

He took the letter and put it into his pocket. He sat on the edge of the table, looking down at her.

He said: "Do you think he will come for you before the two months are up, Carolan?"

"I do not know. He has given his promise . . ."

"I do not understand how he could give such a promise; not to see you for three months . . . that seems to me incredible."

"You do not know Everard. He does not get excited as I do. He thinks clearly; he measures his actions. He loves me; indeed he must, for I shall have to try very hard to be a suitable wife for him; he knows this, but he wants to marry me all the same. He loves his parents . . . though not as he loves me but, because beside his love for me his love for them is insignificant, he would try to hide that and be doubly eager that they should not be hurt. So he gave this promise, much as it grieved him to give it. Do you understand, Father?"

He nodded.

"My child, I hope that you will be very, very happy; that you will know a happiness which was denied to me and to your mother."

Her eyes filled with tears of pity. She could understand their agony now that she knew what it was to love. To be separated for three months from a loved one was sad, but to be separated for years . . . that was torture. Impulsively she took his hands—his tortured hands—and covered them with kisses.

"My sweet Carolan," he said. "My sweet daughter!" He tapped the pocket containing the letter. "I will despatch this immediately. Carolan, did you beg him to come . . . at once?"

She shook her head.

"He has given his promise, Father. I could not ask him to break it."

He said: "My daughter, life can be cruel; delay is dangerous. You know—in a small measure—what happened to me and to your mother. I could not bear that you should lose your happiness. Love is all; what is a paltry promise compared with the love of two young people! Take the letter. Add a sentence. Say 'Come to me without delay! I need you!' Say that, Carolan."

There was almost a command in his burning eyes. She broke open the letter, and wrote at the end of it: "Everard, please, please come for me . . . at once. Don't wait, Everard, please!" And there was a frantic appeal in those words, for the burning eyes of her father frightened her.

She re-sealed the letter and handed it back to him.

"He will come," he said confidently. "He would not be able to stay away from you . . ." He went on: "Carolan, what shall you do today?"

"I shall find plenty to do. Remember I have never set foot in London before, and from what I have seen I find it most exciting."

"Do not go out, my child. Wait; I shall show you London. But do not go out unaccompanied. It is unfortunate that today I have urgent business, but that will not always be so. I shall take you to Ranelagh, my child. I will take you to hear the talk in the coffee-houses. We shall sit by the river and watch the barges go by. We shall go to the playhouse."

"I think I am going to enjoy my stay in London, Father."

"I intend that you shall, child. But for today, promise me this—stay in. The neighbourhood, as you have gathered, is not one in which a gentlewoman should walk alone—nor, my dear, are many places in this big city. But give me your word that you will not venture out until I can accompany you."

"Of course I give my word."

"Why do you smile?"

"Because it is so good to have an anxious parent. No one bothered whether I went out or stayed in before."

"London is different from the country."

"Still, nobody ever cared before."

"Millie will be here at nine, Carolan."

"Millie?"

"Our little maid."

"Ah! I wondered how the work was done. I could not quite imagine Mamma . . ."

They smiled together.

"No," he said, "I should not care for your mother to soil her hands. So there is Millie."

"She does not live here?"

"No, she lives at the end of the street. She comes in at nine o'clock and goes at four. We like it better that she should not spend the night here; we prefer to be alone. She is a little simple, poor Millie."

"I see."

"She will be here soon, and will open the shop."

"But can she she deal with customers?"

"There are few customers."

She looked at him anxiously. That would account for the worry lines about his brow. He was finding it a terrible struggle to make ends meet. And no wonder! Not only was the shop in the wrong neighbourhood, but there was no one to attend to customers—when he had to go out—no one but a girl who was "simple". How could he hope for a prosperous business!

He saw her thoughts and patted her hands.

"Do not frown, little daughter. I am doing very well; this is a fine business, and very soon I shall retire. It will be to a house in the country, a house which my daughter and her husband . . . and their children . . . will not be ashamed to visit."

"Your daughter and her husband and their children would not be ashamed to visit you here," retorted Carolan.

"I know. I know. But you wait, Carolan, and see the fine house in the country I shall have!"

"I am glad the business is prosperous, Father."

"You need not worry your head about us, Carolan. Well, when Millie comes, the shop will be opened. You and your mother need not think about it. Listen! I think that is Millie's step; I will go and let her in."

Millie was a sandy-haired girl of about Carolan's age. She had a pale face and closely set eyes; her skin was pock-marked, her mouth perpetually open; she seemed vacant.

"Millie," said Darrell, "this is Miss Carolan, my daughter."

Millie nodded, without looking at Carolan.

"And now," said Darrell, "I must be going. Carolan, do not forget what I have said about going out alone."

"I promise. I shall wait for you to accompany me, Father."

She kissed him and went to the door of the shop with him. She stood there watching him; as he turned the corner he waved.

Carolan went back into the shop. Millie had taken down the shutters now, but it was still gloomy. Strange, thought Carolan, if her father was doing such a prosperous business here. But when he had said that, he had not met her eyes; she had a feeling that things were not as glorious as he would have her believe. When she married Everard they would have her father and mother to live with them; or perhaps they would give them a little cottage close by. Her father would be happy enough with a little garden in which to grow flowers and vegetables, she was sure. But in the meantime she would make things a little more comfortable for them here. She went into the kitchen, where Millie was bending over the sink.

"Let us have a real clean-up today," she said. "This place is very dirty."

Millie merely pushed a strand of hair out of her eyes by way of reply.

"Do you not think so?" demanded Carolan, a little irritated.

"I dunno," said Millie.

"Well," said Carolan tartly, "you can take it from me that it is! Those shelves are full of dust; the floor needs washing. When did you last wash it?"

"I dunno," said Millie. "Forget."

Enthusiasm burned in Carolan's eyes; she was a crusader; she was going to make this home of her parents fit to live in. They were like children, both of them; and Millie was worse than hopeless. Very slowly the girl was washing the breakfast dishes. There was nothing domesticated about Carolan; that had been Margaret's forte. How she longed for Margaret's advice now; she imagined Margaret's dainty nose wrinkling up at the sight of this kitchen. The kitchen should be made so that even Margaret would approve!

"Good gracious!" she said. "Do you take all the morning to wash a few dishes? Then it is no wonder that this place is so dirty."

Millie regarded her from under bushy eyebrows.

"I am going to change all that," Carolan continued. "I will help with those dishes, then you can wash the floor and we can . . . arrange things."

Millie was a most irritating person. If she had been sullen or if she had burst into protests, Carolan would have found her attitude understandable; but the complaints seemed not to touch her at all. Slowly she went on with the dishes.

"Millie!" said Carolan sharply, and caught the girl's arm. Millie let out a cry and dropped the plate she was about to plunge into the water. The sleeve of her dress was so rotten with sweat and age that even Carolan's light grasp had torn it, but it was not at the tear that Carolan stared, but at the weal on the flesh beneath it.

"Why . . ." gasped Carolan. "Who did that?"

Millie looked at her arm, and then a faint expression crept into her face—the first Carolan had seen there—and it shocked her that it should be one of fear.

"Me father," said Millie.

"Your father did that! You mean he beat you . . . and that's why you are so slow? Are you in pain? Why didn't you tell me . . . It ought to be dressed . . . you should have said so."

184

Now Carolan's irritation had melted before the warmth of her pity for Millie and the heat of her indignation towards Millie's father.

Millie said: "S'nothing. He's always doing it."

"You call that nothing! Does it hurt? Of course it must hurt. It ought to be bathed; it's very dirty."

So, instead of cleaning out her parents' house as she had intended, Carolan spent the morning washing and dressing Millie's arm, making her hot chocolate to drink, and trying, without much success, to get the story of Millie's life from her. All she discovered was that Millie lived with her family of ten or eleven—Millie did not seem altogether sure of the number—in one room at the end of Grape Street, and that Millie's father drank too much gin with results of which this was a good example.

"When he attacks you," said Carolan, "you should hit back. If he is as drunk as you say, he should not be so formidable."

Millie only stared at Carolan with vacant eyes.

"You should not stay there!" said Carolan. "Could you not get a job where you could live in?"

"I dunno," said Millie.

"Then you should find out."

"How?" asked Millie surprisingly, but Carolan really had no suggestion to offer. She said: "I will think of something. And tell your father if he dares to hurt you again I . . . I . . ."

Millie waited expressionlessly, but when talking to her, Carolan had discovered that, if a sentence became too complicated to finish, it was possible to trail off without comment from Millie. She did this now, but she was determined nevertheless to add Millie to those people whom she must help during her stay in London.

The morning was speeding up, and Carolan did not notice until later that not once had the shop door bell rang.

At midday she carried a tray upstairs to her mother's room.

"Come in!" said Kitty sleepily, and Carolan went in.

It was something of a shock, remembering Kitty's room at Håredon. Then of course there had been Thérèse to fold up her things. Now, the dress Kitty had worn the previous night lay on the floor, and undergarments were strewn beside it. The room smelt musty.

Carolan said: "You are shutting out the sunshine; I'll draw the curtains better than that."

"Don't open the window, darling," said Kitty fearfully. "I do not trust the morning air."

"Scarcely morning now, Mamma! Did you not hear the clock strike twelve?"

"Did it? I am a lie-abed. And you have brought me a tray; that is nice. Much nicer than that foolish Millie's bringing it!"

"A cup of chocolate to begin with," said Carolan. "Do you like that?"

"I adore chocolate, darling. Bring it here. Hand it to me, there's a love . . . But first give me the mirror . . . Goodness gracious! I do look a sight, do I not?"

She looked old, thought Carolan, untidy; and she had put on so much weight. The lace of her bedgown was draggled, and there were chocolate stains on it. But her voluptuous bosom, showing through the lace, was white as ever. She looked the picture of indolence, the beauty who is ageing, who has fed too well on the sweets of life and shows signs of it in her face.

Kitty grimaced into her mirror.

"How do you find I look, darling? Have I aged much?"

"Scarcely at all, Mamma," lied Carolan. "You have put on flesh though."

"Ah! But in the right places, as Thérèse used to say! What happened to Thérèse?"

"I do not know. She went."

"And poor Sambo?"

"He went too."

"And that beast, Jennifer?"

"She fell down the stairs one night . . . dead drunk."

"Serve her right, the wicked creature! Carolan, there is one thing I always wanted to know. Did she beat you?"

"Sometimes."

"You should have told me . . . Why did you not?"

"I do not know," said Carolan, and thought of Millie and felt inadequate and suddenly humble.

"She will never beat you any more, Carolan. Give me my chocolate, child. I do not care for it cold." She drank greedily. "Ah! This is good! You make better chocolate than mad Millie does."

"Mamma . . . you are not sorry you ran away?"

"Ran away from Haredon? My child, how can you ask? Of course not. I would follow your father to the end of the earth!"

There she sat leaning back on her pillows, carefree, thinking of nothing but that Carolan made better chocolate than Millie.

"But, Mamma, this is so different from Haredon!"

"I do not wish to return, nevertheless. Of course, I miss Thérèse. What a wonder she was! Certainly I miss *her*. But I hated the squire, darling. Your father is my true husband."

"He is a dear," said Carolan.

"You are fond of him already?"

"He is so gentle, so . . . everything that one would hope a father might be. But, Mamma, this place . . . is it . . . is it . . . a good business proposition?"

Kitty laughed.

"La, child! Do you expect me to understand what is and what is not a good business proposition? I was never clever enough; I leave that to your father."

"He seemed to me a little worried."

"Worried! Indeed he is not! He is very happy here . . . with me . . . and I am happy. All those long years I waited for him, did I not? Waited and grieved, and he came for me as I knew he would . . . but the waiting was hard . . ."

Carolan smiled at her with tolerant affection. How fortunate to be able to believe just what you wanted to believe. Dear Mamma! No wonder she had had so many lovers; she would make each feel that he was the best, the only one that mattered, while the others were mere episodes. And she would make that belief possible, because she herself believed it so sincerely.

Carolan tried again.

"Everything down there is in such a jumble, Mamma, so untidy. The shops I passed on my way here had wares displayed temptingly in their windows. Ours is not very attractive . . . not even very clean!"

Kitty leaned on a plump elbow and surveyed her daughter. She began to laugh.

"What a little wiseacre you have become, Miss Carolan! So solemn! It is no use trying to make me solemn, I warn you. I positively refuse to be. Why, what should I have been now, had I allowed trifles to worry *me*? Old! Haggard! With a million lines about my face!" She picked up the mirror and looked at her reflection smilingly. "Whereas . . . I am . . . I refuse to tell you how old I am, Carolan! And you should be ashamed to ask me! When I think of all I've gone through . . . the weary waiting for your father . . . and then, after we came together again . . ."

"Yes," said Carolan eagerly, seating herself on the bed, "afterwards, when you came together?"

"There was a terrible time I went through! Poverty! My child, you have no conception of what poverty I suffered. I

. . . who had always previously been so free from want. Even when I was with Aunt Harriet—and I can tell you I suffered in that hell-cat's house, my dear—even then I had enough to eat!"

"Mamma! Were you and my father starving, then?"

Kitty was rocking to and fro on the bed in an agony of remembrance.

"It was terrible! Terrible! The filthy lodging-houses! The dreadful food . . . and then no food at all. Your poor father used to say: 'Kitty, it would have been better had you stayed at Haredon!' I answered: 'Indeed not! My place is by your side, Darrell. No matter what I must suffer, that is where my place is!' "

Was it really true, wondered Carolan, or was she playing another part—the faithful lover? No! There must be a modicum of truth in it.

"Did he do no work then, Mamma?"

"He worked for a merchant. He worked along the wharfside." She shivered and covered her face with her hands. Then she removed them and smiled radiantly. "But why do we talk of it? Now all is well."

"Ah, Mamma! Are you sure all is well?"

"My child! Oh, my solemn little darling! Of course all is well. We have the shop now. Your father says the shop will make our fortunes, and your father was never a man to adorn a tale. He says that after a short stay here in this perfectly frightful neighbourhood . . . And let me tell you, Carolan, it is frightful, and you must always remember—should I and your father forget—to lock up the doors and lower windows every night . . ."

"There is so much I do not understand," said Carolan. "It is such a queer sort of shop . . . without any customers."

"You must not worry your head over it, Carolan—I do not. I trust in your father. He has promised me a house in the country with servants to wait upon me, and he is not a man to make promises lightly, that much I know. Oh, Carolan, what a happy day when we leave this place! I can see the house I shall have . . . I can see it clearly . . ." Her manner changed suddenly. Now she was gracious, full of dignity, receiving her guests at the top of a wide staircase; and that image was more real to her than this tawdry room and her daughter, sitting there on the bed.

Kitty stopped dreaming abruptly and said: "My dear, pass me that wrap, and I will have a little more of the bacon."

She ate heartily.

"I am glad," said Carolan, watching her, "that you do not regret leaving Haredon."

Kitty laughed.

"That place! That beast there! Ah, how he tormented me! And should I be the one to pine for a country life? No! No! Now if I had a carriage . . . I cannot get about as I would, but your father will not get me a carriage; he says we cannot afford it. He has said we must save . . . save . . . save . . . so that we can leave this wretched business behind us! But when I get my own house, servants to wait on me . . . ah! Then you shall see. Perhaps I could get Thérèse . . . Dear Thérèse! With her lotions and concoctions, what she could do with me now! In the country I shall bloom again." She smiled at her daughter appraisingly, a little complacently. "You have charm yourself, my dear, but you will never be what I was. Your looks are modern. Looks are not what they were in my young days. Ah! We knew how to be beautiful then. But you have a look of me about you, Carolan. A pity your eyes are so green; blue would have been so much more appealing. And if your hair had been fair like mine . . . But you have my nose, darling, and my chin, and—though not quite—my mouth. You have a lot of me in you, Carolan."

Carolan curtsyed.

"Thank you kindly, Mamma." She stooped and kissed her mother. "I will leave you to dress now, and perhaps soon my father will be home, and he will take me walking."

"Do not expect me too soon," warned Kitty. "I miss my dear Thérèse. And, darling, bring me hot water, please. I loathe cold, and I declare that if either your father or Millie did not bring me hot, I often could not resist the temptation not to wash at all."

"You shall have hot water, Mamma."

"Thank you. I will wait for it. Ah, my darling, how good it is to have you home! If you could but know how deep was my longing to have you here during those years of separation!"

It was during the afternoon that the idea came to Carolan. Not a single customer had come into the shop. She had listened eagerly for the sound of the bell all the afternoon. Kitty sat in the parlour, idly turning the leaves of Madame D'Arblay's *Evelina*, and talking now and then to Carolan. Millie was dusting the upstairs rooms.

Carolan said: "Mamma! I have an idea. I am going into the shop; I want to tidy things a bit. It is very gloomy out there, and I am sure it is wrong to go all day without a single customer. It will be a surprise for my father."

Kitty laughed.

"My darling, how difficult you find it to sit still, do you not! You are not like I was . . . even at your age; I was not nearly so restless. But if you would like to . . ."

"Do you think my father would be pleased?"

"Of course he would be pleased, dear man!"

"Then I shall go. Leave the parlour door open and I can talk to you as I work."

"Yes," said Kitty, "leave the door open."

Carolan stood in the dark interior of the shop, and wondered where to begin. Such a hotchpotch! And how typical of her father to show the most unattractive of his goods in the most prominent positions! Those old clothes hanging in the doorway; shabby things green with age! And the window chock-full of unwholesome looking garments, while in odd trays he had quite an assortment of pretty, though apparently cheap, jewellry. And if some of the old silver were polished up, what an attractive face the little shop could show the world!

First of all she would take the old coats from the doorway; then she would clear the window. Cheerfully she set to work, and in a short time she had a pile of unsavoury garments laid out on the floor. The window space was clear, but very dirty. She would dust it for today, and tomorrow she would get Millie to help her and they would get to work in earnest.

"Darling," wailed Kitty, "such a dust is floating through!"

"It shows how badly it needed cleaning!" called Carolan excitedly.

There was a smear of dust on her nose; her eyes were brilliant. Now and then she would click her tongue indulgently, as some fresh example of her father's carelessness came to light. She found a piece of black velvet and enjoyed herself, laying out the jewellry on it. The shop was going to be tasteful, as alluring as the shops she had passed on her way here. She tried to visualise her father's pleasure when he saw the alterations.

She stood, her head on one side, surveying her handiwork. She frowned at the great bunch of old coats hanging against the wall just behind the counter. An eyesore! As soon as she touched them a moth flew out. She began to pull them down, but they were heavy and not easy to move. She had to get a chair to stand on and unhook them. And when she had them down, a door was disclosed; she tried it, but it was locked!

"Mamma!" she called. "What door is this?"

190

"What door, my love?"

"A door here in the shop. There were a lot of coats hanging over it. It is locked!"

"A door . . ." mused Kitty. "Oh, I remember. We never use it; we always keep it locked. At least I think your father uses it sometimes . . . I do not know."

"Where does it lead to, Mamma?"

"I think to a basement room; I'm not sure."

Carolan went to the door between the shop and the parlour. She surveyed her mother with exasperation.

"Mamma, do you mean to say you have never been through that door?"

"Why should I go through it?" asked Kitty.

"But surely, when you came to the house . . ."

Kitty yawned indolently.

"My darling, shut the door. The dust is worrying my throat, and my throat was never really strong. I often thought that, had it been, my mother would have had me trained to sing. She said my voice was exactly like Elizabeth Sheridan's." She smiled, flushed with the applause of an enthusiastic audience.

"But when you looked over the house," persisted Carolan impatiently, "did you not open that door and see what was beyond it?"

"My dear," said Kitty, "I was not as inquisitive as you! I do not worry myself where this leads, and what is beyond that. It is a mistake to worry about things that are of no importance."

Carolan sat on the table.

"Mamma, tell me about how you came to the shop. Where did you get all this furniture? It is by no means new; did you pick it up through the business?"

"When we came to the shop . . ." began Kitty. "Well, it was just as it is now, when we came to the shop; I do not remember it any different."

"Ah!" said Carolan, swinging her legs. "I can guess what happened; my father bought the place just as it was—furniture and all. He must have had a windfall, if before you were so poor that you had nothing to eat!"

"Yes, that was it," said Kitty.

Carolan took her mother's face between her hands and kissed it. She was thinking of Darrell's trying to explain his business affairs to this adorable, inconsequent creature.

Poor darling Mamma, and poor darling Father! she thought. She leaped off the table and went back to the shop.

191

She decided to heap all the clothes into a corner and consult her father about them when he came in; and as she was doing this the bell tinkled and a man walked in. A customer! she thought jubilantly. But almost immediately she recognised him as Jonathan Crew.

"Good afternoon!" he said.

"Good afternoon, Mr. Crew."

His great dark eyes went all round the shop, from the window to the newly exposed door.

"You are very busy . . ."

"Indeed yes. And you? You are not working this afternoon?"

When he smiled, his skin seemed tighter than ever. He exposed a row of strong white teeth.

"Sometimes I am sent from my office on certain commissions. If I execute them with speed, why should I not have a half-hour to spend as I will! You are well, after your adventures of yesterday?"

"Very well, I thank you."

"And making good use of your time, I can see."

"Do you notice any difference in the shop? But I suppose you do not; it was dusk when you saw it, was it not?"

"I notice some alterations; I have always been told that I am an observant man."

"And the change is for the better?"

"Very much for the better!"

Kitty called through the door: "Who is that, Carolan?"

"It is Mr. Crew come to enquire how I am after yesterday's journey."

"Come in!" cried Kitty. "Come in, Mr. Crew."

Carolan led him into the parlour.

Kitty, sitting upright in her chair, extended her hand; she was like a queen graciously receiving an honoured subject.

"It is indeed kind of you, Mr. Crew."

He bowed courteously over Kitty's hand.

"I was anxious to know how your daughter was today, Ma'am. London gave her a rough welcome, I fear."

"Not all London!" mused Kitty. "And she has you to thank for that, sir!"

"It was the greatest pleasure to be of some small service."

Carolan's eyes strayed back to the shop.

"There are one or two things I must clear up before my father returns. If you will excuse me, Mr. Crew . . . You talk to Mr. Crew, Mamma, while I finish."

Kitty pouted. Was this the way to treat a gentleman caller! Carolan must learn better. There was a smudge of dirt across her nose and her pretty hair looked most inelegant.

"Run to your room, darling," said Kitty severely. "Wash, and change your dress. I will entertain Mr. Crew while you do so."

"No, no!" insisted Mr. Crew. "I see I make a nuisance of myself. Miss Carolan is a young lady who, having started a job, will wish to complete it. I admire her for it; moreover I will help."

"There is no need," said Carolan. "There is little to do now."

"Nevertheless, I insist on helping!" And help he did; he worked very hard, stacking the old clothes together in a corner of the room.

"This kind of shop interests me greatly," he said. "You never know what you will find!"

When they had finished, Carolan said: "I long to see my father's face when he comes in."

"He will be astonished, I am sure. How long do you stay, Miss Carolan?"

"I am not certain. Two months, or possibly less."

"Two months can be a long time. And your idea is to turn this shop, before you leave, into what it was surely meant to be?"

"That is my idea."

"I sincerely hope that you will achieve it."

"There is my mother calling; let us go to her."

Kitty, the mother, a little shocked at the unconventional behaviour of her daughter, but smiling indulgently because she was such a child, said: "Now, Carolan, go to your room and wash your hands and face at once. To please me . . . go. I insist!"

When Carolan returned Mr. Crew was talking of London; and how vividly he talked! Carolan was ready to listen as eagerly as her mother. He told of the pleasure gardens, the coffee and chocolate houses, the plays. He had seen Mr. Sheridan's *School for Scandal* years back; he had seen the great Mrs. Siddons herself. He often caught glimpses of the Prince and Princess of Wales; and when he was a mere boy he had once seen the Prince with Mrs. Perdita Robinson; that was in the days when the Prince was young and handsome and had not put on weight so distressingly, before he had married Maria Fitzherbert. And yes, Mr. Crew confessed he had set

193

eyes on the fair Maria too. He seemed to know everything and have been everywhere. Kitty loved such talk and drank it in eagerly. She told Mr. Crew that someone had said she was remarkably like Sarah Siddons, though for the life of her she could not see where! Mr. Crew put his head on one side and made a play of studying her critically. Yes, he said, there was a resemblance, but he thought it was chiefly in the expression.

"My little daughter is all agog to see the Town," said Kitty.

"I trust, Ma'am," answered Jonathan Crew, "that some day I may be allowed to show her a little of London . . . to show you both of course."

"That is most kind. My poor husband is such a busy man; he is here and there on business, and there is little time for pleasure."

"But perhaps," said Carolan, "Mr. Crew is also a busy man."

"I have some leisure," he answered.

"And it is gracious indeed to offer to spend a little of it on us," said Kitty.

"It is you who are gracious."

"Flatterer!" laughed Kitty.

Oh, Mamma! thought Carolan, *Don't!* He is not a bit like that. Can you not see?

But Kitty did not see; she gazed at the visitor admiringly, and fluttered her long golden lashes. Carolan was uncomfortable, over-silent and a little gauche.

Kitty thought: I am still attractive then! Here is a young man who calls to see my daughter and finds me more interesting. Does not a woman become more attractive as she grows older—providing of course she is not too old! What she gains in flesh she loses in gaucherie. For all we know, this man may be a great gentleman—a rich merchant—perhaps even a lord! How I wish I had put on the black velvet! Black is becoming to a fair skin. But perhaps this blue is more enchanting . . . Thérèse used to say blue was my colour.

"I must go," said Mr. Crew. "But I trust you will allow me to come again."

He bowed over Kitty's hand, and Carolan went to the door with him.

"I hope to see more of the interesting things in your interesting shop," he said.

"Please come whenever you want to. My father has lots and lots of things tucked away, I'm sure. I vow he most likely keeps the best locked away in the basement."

"I think that very likely. You are going to be his guide and counsellor—that much I see, Miss Carolan. Then I may call again?"

"Please do!"

"Thank you! Thank you! Goodbye."

Kitty was smiling when Carolan returned to the parlour.

"My dear, an admirer so soon!"

"Not an admirer at all, Mamma."

"La! child. You are but a baby."

"To my mind," said Carolan, "he admired you more than he admired me."

"Nonsense!" said Kitty, smiling to herself. "I am an old woman, though I do admit I was very, very young when you were born, Carolan."

It was an hour or so later when Darrell came into the shop. Carolan waited in the parlour, listening for his exclamation of surprise and delight. She peeped through the parlour doorway at him. He was staring about him as though he scarcely recognised the place.

She ran out to him.

"Do you not think it a great improvement?" she asked demurely.

"Why . . ." he stammered. "What . . . what has happened?"

She slipped her arm through his.

"You had so many pretty things tucked away, and you showed all the most unattractive of your stock. Now, Father, that is not the way to manage a shop!"

He was silent for a long time; she tried to see his face, but he had a gift of drawing the mask so firmly down that it was impossible to see behind it.

"Father . . . Father . . . you are not pleased then? You think I am an interfering, stupid creature? You are not pleased?"

He turned to her then. He took her hand from his arm and kissed it tenderly.

"You are a sweet daughter for a man to have, Carolan."

"Then you *are* pleased!"

"We will have a talk. I can see you have the makings of a business woman!"

He went to the shop door and locked it.

"But, Father . . ." she began.

"There will be no more customers today," he said.

"I think you are very tired."

He smiled his slow sweet smile.

"A drink and a rest would be very welcome, I admit."

They went through into the parlour.

"Ah!" said Kitty. "There you are, my love. And have you done good business? And would you like a drink? We have had a visitor today . . . Carolan and I. He is quite a presentable young man, that. Carolan, a drink for me too; I declare my throat is as dry as a bone."

"A visitor?" said Darrell slowly.

"Mr. Crew," said Carolan. "He just came to inquire how I was after yesterday's excitement."

Kitty smiled slyly, and Carolan felt she wanted to escape from her sad father and slyly smiling mother.

Darrell twirled his ale round and round in the tankard.

"Carolan," he said, as though choosing his words carefully, "business is complicated. Odd as it may seem to you, those old clothes are more important to the business of the shop itself than the jewellry. But my main business is not done in the shop; I do not sell much over the counter. This is how I do my business—my chief business, you understand—I meet a man who wants something: I try to get it for him. Do you understand? It is not a matter of showing goods in a shop window. This is not so much a shop as a store-room. That door you have discovered; I would rather have it covered. Listen, Carolan, I will tell you something. This is a very poor neighbourhood in which we live; it is a dangerous neighbourhood. Beyond that door is a flight of stairs which leads down to a basement room; and in this room I keep my more valuable stock. You understand? A man may come into the shop to ask the price of a second-hand coat, but he may be a burglar spying out the land. I would rather people did not know of that door. That is why I have kept it covered with those old clothes."

"I see," said Carolan humbly, "that I have been rather foolish. Oh, Father, why do you not tell me that I am an ignorant girl from the country who, because she knows so little, thinks she knows much!"

He put his hands over hers.

"You are sweet," he said, "and I love your solicitude. But this business is too involved for you to understand in a few weeks. While you are here I want you and your mother to enjoy yourselves. I am going to plan some excursions for you. Do not worry yourself about dull commerce!"

"I am sorry, Father."

"Bless you," he said. "God bless you and keep you out of harm all the days of your life!"

A week passed, and it was a full one for Carolan. When

196

her father went out on business she insisted on looking after the shop; it was now as she had first seen it, the old clothes huddled in the doorway, the door to the storage basement concealed by musty coats. Carolan did not think of altering it now. She understood that her father was no ordinary shopkeeper; he was known in the coffee and chocolate houses of the town as an enterprising merchant. If a rich man wanted an ornament for his wife, sweetheart, mother or daughter, he would get into touch with Darrell, and Darrell would do his best to procure what was wanted. He told Carolan that he had started in this humble shop, and because he wished to save quickly that he might retire to the country at the earliest possible moment, he did not see why he should take more expensive premises. He liked, too, to keep up the business of selling old clothes. The poor in the neighbourhood knew they could get what they wanted at a fair price from his shop.

"One day," he said, "I may take you along to the coffee house with me." Then he added quickly, as though his pride and common sense were having a struggle from which common sense came out triumphant: "No! That would be foolish; though I should have liked to show them my daughter."

She went through Kitty's wardrobe with her, and helped to make alterations. They sat for hours together in the little parlour while Kitty talked, chiefly of the day when they would retire to the country and she would have her own house. She would not be house-proud like her Aunt Harriet; she would be no goddess of the still-room. No! But she would entertain, and there would be servants to wait on her and her guests, and a full larder always. Thérèse should come back and set about the task of resuscitating her beauty.

On one occasion Darrell hired a cabriolet and they all drove round London. Then they had a picnic on Hampstead Heath and took a trip to the Bald Faced Stag in Epping Forest. It was all delightful and full of interest—the best way of making the days pass quickly while one waited for news of a lover.

"You are very good to me," Carolan told Darrell. "But is not all this very expensive?"

"It may be," answered Darrell, "but a visit from a daughter can be a most special occasion. I shall tell you now, I am planning a visit to the playhouse, and then of course we must all go to Ranelagh . . . or do Vauxhall Gardens appeal to you more?"

Carolan put her arms round his neck and kissed him,

which made him flush with pleasure. He, who was undemonstrative himself, loved such gestures in his wife and daughter.

Jonathan Crew came to the shop often. He would sit in the parlour and talk to Kitty and Carolan. A most interesting man, he was, and how well he knew London! There was no place one could mention without his knowing a good deal about it; and in his quiet, unimpassioned way, he was a vivid talker.

"Has it struck you," said Kitty one day, "that Mr. Crew has a good deal of leisure?"

"It had not until you mentioned it," replied Carolan. "Mamma, why do you look so full of wisdom?"

"For this reason, my dear. The hours of a clerk are very long. Does a clerk get so much leisure for visiting ladies?"

"He has explained; he comes here when sent out on some commission."

"Ah!" laughed Kitty. "*I* was not born yesterday!"

"Oh, Mamma, why must you see intrigue in the most ordinary things!"

"Intrigue? I? My dear, I would have you know that I am a few years older than you are. I have lived; why, I could tell you . . . but no matter. It is an extraordinary thing to me, if not to you, that Mr. Crew has so much time on his hands. Has he the air of a clerk, think you? Those eyes of his—do they look as if they have stared at rows of figures? Does he look as if he has spent long hours on an office stool?"

"The elbows of his coat were very shiny, I noticed!"

"La! What a baby it is! What could be easier, for one with means at his command, than to acquire the shiny-elbowed coat of a clerk! I have a theory; suppose he came here to explore these parts. He might be a most important person! You laugh, Carolan, but do you or do you not know more of the world than I?"

"I do not dream, as you do, Mamma."

"Stuff and nonsense! It might well be that he belongs to the quality and poses as poor Mr. Jonathan Crew in order that he might make our acquaintance."

"Why ever should he do that, Mamma?"

Kitty patted her hair.

"Because, my child, he may be tired of sycophants; he may want friends for his own sake. My dear, you are not without attractions."

Carolan laughed, but Kitty only smiled. She had her own private thoughts on the matter, and these she would not admit to anyone.

Carolan was in the parlour one day when the shop door bell rang. It was morning; her mother was still a-bed, and Darrell had gone out for an hour or so, he said. Millie was working in the kitchen.

Carolan went into the shop. A man was standing there. He had his back towards her, and, as she approached with a bright "Good morning", he turned and she was looking into a pair of blue eyes that twinkled merrily. She had seen them before, and they must have made a vast impression on her, for she recognized them at once as belonging to the man who had stolen her handkerchief.

"Good morning," he said, and she knew that he recognised her, for a look of embarrassment passed quickly over his face. He added quickly: "I came to see Mr. Grey."

She answered: "He is out; I will attend to you. What is it?"

Now the embarrassment had left him; he was mischievous, amused.

"That is very kind of you."

"Not kind at all. I am here to serve my father's customers. What is it you want?"

His eyes went round the shop and fell on some oddments of jewellry lying in a tray.

"A ring," he said. "A ring for a lady . . ."

He moved towards the tray, but she was before him. She put her hands over the tray and faced him squarely.

"Please touch nothing! I might tell you that I recognise you. You stole a handkerchief of mine some days back."

He laughed. He had good white teeth, and though his face was far from handsome, it was attractive.

"You think that extremely funny, I gather," said Carolan coldly.

"I find it extremely gratifying that you should know me again."

"I should have thought it would be merely embarrassing . . . for a thief!"

"Will you believe me," he said, "if I tell you that that was my one and only lapse?"

"No!"

"But you are cruel!"

"I hope I am not a fool."

"Do I look like a common thief?"

"I do not know how a common thief should look. I only know you are one."

"You are brutal . . ."

"Do you think an honest man would be tempted to steal a

199

girl's handkerchief just because it was a pleasant and dainty affair?"

"He might because *she* was a pleasant and dainty affair!"

She flushed angrily.

"Sir! You are offensive."

"My manners are rough, but my heart is soft," he said. "I assure you the theft of the handkerchief was my only lapse."

"Then you had better return it."

He looked sad.

"No!" she cried. "You have doubtless disposed of it to a fellow criminal! I should be obliged if you will leave this shop, but not before you have turned out your pockets to show me that you are taking none of my father's goods with you."

"What a spitfire you are! But a fine daughter to your father, I'll be bound."

"I shall very certainly not allow him to be robbed under my nose."

"And it is such a charming nose!"

"Turn out your pockets, sir!"

"And if I say no, what then, lady?" He stretched out his arm. "Feel those muscles; feel those biceps! I'll warrant you have nothing like it."

"Do not dare to touch me."

"Certainly I would not presume to touch your ladyship."

"Then turn out your pockets."

"Before you make me?"

"I am not joking. I warn you that sooner or later you will end up in Newgate."

"Ah, who can be sure that that evil fate does not await him!"

"An honest man can. Now, pray, sir, turn out your pockets and be gone."

He thrust his hands into his pockets. He began laying out the contents on a small table; a clasp knife, a leather purse, a bandanna handkerchief. As he did so he looked at her puckishly, as though consumed with some private mirth which, try as he might, he could not repress.

"You say that an honest man need not fear the dark shadow of Newgate," he said. "Never be too sure of that! Newgate is an octopus; it stretches out ugly tentacles to catch the unwary."

"To catch the dishonest," she said. "Hurry."

"I would like to talk of that one lapse."

"But I am not interested."

"It is a mistake not to be interested in your fellow men."

"It is a mistake to listen to the tales of robbers."

"You are harsh. Sad that such harshness should exist behind that lovely face of yours!"

"Do not think that your absurd flattery moves me in the least."

"Flattery? It is not flattery. Come, do you ever use your mirror?"

She began to laugh suddenly.

"You are amused?"

"Enormously. You speak the language of thieves; those very words were said to be by a cheat in an inn parlour just before she relieved me of my purse."

"A purse is a purse. A handkerchief is a very different matter."

"I see no difference."

"Would you believe me if I told you I have preserved that handkerchief, that I look at it often and think of you?"

"No," said Carolan. "Pray take up your things and be gone."

"The next time we meet I shall convince you."

"There will be no next time."

"Do not be sure of that."

"I am absolutely sure."

"It is never wise to be sure of anything in this world. How old are you?"

"A most impertinent question which I shall certainly not answer."

"Not yet seventeen, I'll warrant. Do you know how old I am?"

She looked at his face now, for there was in him an irrepressible charm which, in spite of distrust, she could not ignore. She saw that his face was as brown as a berry, and wrinkled, but not with age; his teeth were good; and his smile and his merry eyes made a pleasant thing of his rather ugly face.

"Thirty years old, I'd say," she answered. "Old enough to have trained your hands to keep off property which does not belong to them."

"Twenty-four. That's no lie, and it surprises you. I do not wonder at that, for it is not the number of years that leave their mark upon the face, but the contents of them."

The shop door opened to admit Darrell. He stared at the pair of them for a moment; then advanced into the shop.

"Why, Marcus!"

"Darrell . . . my old friend!"

They clasped hands.

"I was not expecting you," said Darrell.

"A chance call, that is all. Your charming daughter and I have been making each other's acquaintance. But I for one should be glad of a more formal introduction."

"Why yes," said Darrell, still looking a trifle dazed. "My daughter, Carolan. Carolan, Mr. Marcus Markham."

"You did not say you knew my father," said Carolan with an angry glint in her eyes.

"I was coming to that," he told her; his smile was broad and yet secret. "You did not give me much time, you know."

"Well, come in! Come in!" said Darrell.

"I did want to buy a ring I see there. A gold ring, is it not? And of good workmanship? Perhaps Miss Carolan will serve me."

"Certainly I will," said Carolan.

Darrell said: "You will eat with us? What is there, Carolan?"

"Boiled mutton with caper sauce . . . but not ready for half an hour."

"You will stay, Marcus?"

Marcus let his eyes rest on Carolan.

"Wild horses would not drag me away, Darrell my friend! But pray do not disturb yourself about this little matter of the ring. Go on in; take off your boots; take off your coat. Miss Carolan and I will settle about the ring."

Darrell said: "As you will," and went in.

Carolan looked up into the man's face.

"Why did you not tell me you were a friend of my father?"

"I did not think you would believe me."

"Tell me, are you a thief?"

"The stealing of your handkerchief was my only lapse."

"But that makes you a thief!"

"Indeed it does. Shall you denounce me?"

"How can I . . . for such a paltry thing?" She began to laugh. "I suppose you think I am a foolish creature."

"I think you are a charming creature."

"And a spitfire! You said that."

"Such an honest little spitfire! No, my dear, you were angry in a good cause . . . I like you for it."

"Well then, shall we forget the whole stupid business?"

"Forget it! I shall never forget my first meeting with you. Instead we will say that the stormy beginning of our friendship is over. There is a trite saying that sunshine is brighter after the storm, but like most trite sayings it is true."

"I am sorry for jumping to conclusions. What did you think when I asked you to turn out your pockets? And you a guest, a friend of my father's!"

"I thought it fun."

"Did you think it fun to steal my handkerchief?"

"Certainly—fun with a smack of danger in it. Men have hanged by the neck for stealing a handkerchief!"

"I see. I am, you notice, from the country. London ways are very new to me."

"You are the sweeter for that."

"You wished to see a ring . . . was this it?"

"It was. Slip it on your finger that I may see the effect."

"There! It is attractive, is it not?"

"Delightfully so, there."

She put her head on one side, surveying it, wondering about the person for whom he was buying it; his wife, his sweetheart? I would not care to be either, thought Carolan, remembering the warmth of his merry eyes as they smiled into hers. A gay man, a man fond of the pleasures of life . . . and yet very different from the squire. Not furtive; not sly; not lecherous; just amorous and eager and merry and very gallant. She liked him, in spite of the fact that he had made her feel foolish.

He took the ring and put it into his pocket.

"I will settle with your father."

She bowed her head. "And now shall we go inside?"

"I would prefer to look around here with you. Who knows, I might see something else that attracts me."

"Then I must call my father, for I have the dinner to attend to."

"Then let us go and find your father."

They went into the shop parlour. Darrell was sitting in an armchair; he had removed his boots and wore soft down-at-heel slippers. His feet, like his hands, were mis-shapen, had become so, Carolan knew, during that tragic period of his life which he was forever trying to forget.

"Father, here is your friend," said Carolan. "Now I must go to the kitchen to see how Millie is getting on."

In the kitchen she absently lifted the lid of the stew-pot and sniffed the appetising smell which rushed out. She was thinking of the man in the parlour. He had aroused in her a longing—not for him, but for Everard.

Kitty had heard that there was a visitor. She came down resplendent in black velvet; it was low cut, too magnificent. Carolan thought it incongruous for the shop parlour as she came in carrying the steaming dish of mutton.

She listened to Kitty's talking to Marcus Markham.

"So you have already met my little daughter? She thought you were a customer—an ordinary customer. Do you think she is like me? Tell me that."

"No," said Marcus, "not greatly like you, though there is a resemblance."

"Rejoice, Carolan, you are only a *little* like me!"

"Nay, Ma'am, that would assuredly not be a matter for rejoicing in the ordinary way, but may I say that your daughter has beauty of a different kind?"

"Marcus! Flatterer!"

It was a little foolish, thought Carolan. Why could Mamma not resign herself to growing old! She had Darrell; he was, she was fond of saying, her true love. Why must she always be seeking for stupid compliments which did not mean anything! She felt a little angry, not only with Kitty but with Mr. Markham. Everard would not pay such stupid compliments. But Everard was different from all others; there was no one quite like Everard—there never had been and never would be. Soon, soon there must be a letter.

They sat round the table, and Darrell served the mutton.

"How silent is Miss Carolan," said Marcus.

"Ah!" said Darrell. "Dreaming of Everard, I'll be bound. Eh, daughter?"

"Everard?" said Marcus lightly. "Is it permitted to ask who this most lucky person is who so occupies Miss Carolan's thoughts?"

"The man she is going to marry . . . very soon!" said Darrell, and he said it firmly, almost as though he had chosen him for his daughter and was determined that she should marry him, if he had to drive her to the altar.

"I might have known," said Marcus, "that such a prize would be quickly appropriated."

"He is a parson!" said Kitty.

"And the marriage," put in Darrell, "is to take place in a few weeks' time. We are expecting Everard to call here soon . . . in a week or so. Then he will have the arrangements for the wedding complete."

"I sigh with envy!"

"La! Sir!" put in Kitty. "*You* should not find it so difficult to persuade a girl to marry you!"

"You mistake me, Ma'am. I am full of envy, not for Bridegroom Tom, Dick or Harry, but only for Bridegroom Everard."

Kitty lay back in her chair, her fingers curled lovingly about her glass.

"In my days men were different. They did not envy long; they took what they wanted."

Carolan's heart was beating wildly; an angry flush came into her cheeks. There were times when she felt really angry with Mamma.

"It is a good thing then," she said tartly, "that men have changed. Nowadays we are not taken; *we* decide!"

"Bravo!" cried Marcus. He lifted his glass. "To the modern generation! The march towards civilisation is slow but steady. Each generation is a little less savage than the last."

"I like savages," said Kitty.

"But you are a pagan," said Marcus, caressingly.

"I like pagans, and I must confess I am not over-fond of parsons. Nor do I think our Carolan will make an ideal parson's wife; she has too much of me in her."

"You know nothing of the matter, Kitty," said Darrell sternly, and Kitty pouted at being so spoken to. Angry lights leaped into her eyes. She to know nothing! She who had been loved by many, married to a lascivious brute who had however provided her with a comfortable home; she who had left that home to run away to squalor with Darrell, and had taught him how to make love and be happy! He was her true love, of course, but there were times when his unworldliness drove her well-nigh crazy. They had this attractive daughter who had rashly betrothed herself to a parson; there were better fish in the sea than parsons! And a man who came to the shop in the course of business might well be rich—a merchant or a nobleman. Who *was* Marcus Markham? She had never thought very much of him until now. When they had come to live at the shop, he had come into their life; or about that time —Kitty was not sure. How could she be sure of unimportant details! Darrell never talked about him much; the few idle questions she had asked had never been really answered. She had thought Jonathan Crew might be posing as a clerk, but Marcus Markham had an air which Jonathan Crew would never have. The burning question of the moment was—Who was Marcus Markham?

"Mr. Markham," she said, fluttering her eyelashes demurely, "do you agree that I am an ignoramus?"

Marcus flashed a smile at Carolan.

"Certainly not! You exude wisdom. But one thing I am absolutely certain of—in whatever generation Miss Carolan had lived, *she* would choose and not be chosen."

"Thank you for that!" said Carolan.

Kitty shrugged her shoulders.

"And what have you been doing recently, Mr. Markham?" she inquired, turning the conversation. "Have you been to the races lately?"

Darrell stirred uneasily in his chair.

"I must explain," said Kitty to Carolan, "that I suspect Mr. Markham of being a gay dog. He is a regular gad-about. He does not mean us to know that, but it slips out. He has been here, there and everywhere!"

"It seems to me," said Carolan, "that Mr. Markham is a somewhat mysterious gentleman."

"There is no mystery whatever," said Marcus.

"I am glad of it," retorted Carolan.

"I do not believe that," put in Kitty. "I believe he is a gentleman of fashion . . . when he is not wandering about Grape Street."

"Oh," said Carolan, "do *you* spend your time wandering about Grape Street?"

"Why not! An interesting neighbourhood, is it not?"

"If you have a taste for squalor and poverty, yes," said Carolan.

Odd, she was thinking, how both he and Jonathan Crew had said they found the neighbourhood interesting.

Darrell said: "Marcus came in to buy a ring."

"Ah!" said Kitty. "For a lady friend, I'll be bound!"

"If she will accept it!"

"You see, Carolan, I was right when I said he was a gay dog."

Marcus grinned at Carolan. "In some society it is necessary to be a gay dog. In other society it is only necessary to be one-self."

"But," said Carolan, "the two might add up to the same thing."

"You are a cynic!"

"Is one a cynic for stating what one believes to be true?"

She was trying hard to dislike him, as she felt she ought. He was too bold; he was flirtatious, and with every flicker of his eyes he was telling her that he found her desirable.

"Carolan," cut in Kitty, "you must not take him too seriously. He is trying to impress you with his wickedness. Nowadays to be wicked is a greater asset than to be good."

"But, Mamma, you said a little while back that it was in your generation that pagans flourished."

"I am not clever like the rest of you! You tie me in knots. But then I will say this—it was not always thought necessary for a woman to be clever."

Darrell said: "Marcus, come with me to the store-room. I have something to show you there."

The two men departed, and Carolan began to gather up the dishes. She paused suddenly and said: "Mamma, who is that man?"

"That is what I would like to know. He has an air, has he not?"

"I am not sure that I like his airs."

"No?" said Kitty, oddly piqued and not knowing why. "One would not expect you to—you who have a fancy for parsons!"

"What I meant, Mamma, was—why does he come here? Is he one of the rich merchants for whom my father procures goods to sell?"

"That would be most likely," said Kitty.

Carolan went into the kitchen and washed-up with Millie. Then she went upstairs and changed her morning gown for one of grey merino with a green belt and green silk at the neck and throat. Her hair was sleek and shining.

"My darling," said Kitty when she returned to the parlour, "I am parched with thirst; what about making some tea? Doubtless the men would join us."

"Are they still talking business?"

"They must be. They have been shut up in the basement for an age! I do declare there is no gallantry left in men these days; I have been sitting here for ages waiting for them to come."

"Mamma! You are a very naughty woman. Why do you think my father works so hard, is so eager to do business? For you, of course! That *you* may leave this place at the earliest possible moment, that *you* may have comfort, that *you* may have the life to which you are suited! And then you accuse him of lack of gallantry because he shuts himself away with a client to talk business. Is it not more gallant, more loving, to try to give you what you want, than to smirk and bow over your hands and say stupid things that have no real meaning?"

"La! How you bully me! And doubtless think me a stupid old woman to boot. Now I must say 'Of course, of course, wise Carolan!' And you are right, and I am a foolish old woman . . . though not really old . . . not old for a long, long time. And, my dear, I'll whisper something—you look *most* enchanting! You put me in the shade with Marcus, did you not? I do not like being put in the shade . . . but as it is my own daughter who does it, perhaps I do not care so much. You liked Marcus, did you not, my child? Oh, do not protest! I saw that you liked him. And how he liked you! How his eyes danced to contemplate you!"

"Oh, Mamma, please! Do you not see that he would make his eyes dance for anything in petticoats?"

"But they danced more brightly for these petticoats, my dear Carolan. How do we know who he is!"

Carolan sighed.

"It is funny! A man only has to appear in Grape Street to be endowed with mystery, with romance, with intrigue. Who is he? What is his business here? Mamma, have you found another nobleman who, tired of the sycophancy of his friends, seeks real friendship in Grape Street?"

"You have a lively tongue, Carolan."

"But not nearly so lively as your imagination! Now Mamma, let us stop this foolish talk. Mr. Markham is a client of my father's—nothing more. Nor could he ever be to me, however merrily he should make his eyes to dance. Please remember I am engaged to marry Everard."

"Oh . . . but a parson!"

Carolan stamped her foot angrily.

"Yes! A parson! And please say no more. Is it not an honourable calling?"

"I would not have dared to stamp my foot at *my* mother, Carolan!"

Carolan stooped and kissed the soft cheek of her mother.

"But this, dear Mamma, is a new age, and I am far removed from the paragons of your generation, remember?"

"You tease me. Why should I be teased?"

"Because you are an old darling, and it is no use trying to pretend you're a cross patch. And now I shall prepare the tea."

Kitty called through the door: "Carolan, you are in love with that parson, are you not?"

"I am indeed."

"Then you shall marry him!"

"Generous of you, Mamma," chuckled Carolan, "but did not your friend Marcus tell you that I would decide for myself? That was a point on which he happened to be right."

"Wayward child! What a handful you are!"

208

Carolan came in with the tray.

"I will go and call the men," she said, and she went through to the shop. The door behind the coats was open, and beyond it was a flight of stone stairs; she went down these.

"Father!" she called.

At the bottom of the steps was a door, and, as she called, this was opened abruptly. Her father appeared; he shut the door behind him as though there were a wild beast in there instead of Marcus.

"Tea is prepared, Father," she said.

He smiled indulgently. "Not for us, Carolan; we have to go out."

He stood at the door, watching her mount the stairs.

"They are not coming," she told Kitty. "It is business."

"It is always business!" said Kitty, tossing her head. "But never mind, we can get along well without them."

Kitty talked. She described the sort of house she would have when they left the shop. She talked of the dresses she would have and those which now filled her wardrobe. Did Carolan think her black velvet could do with a slightly lower neckline? Did her chocolate brown sweep the floor too much?

They heard the men go out through the shop.

"I should have thought Marcus could have called farewell," said Kitty, pouting.

"He is a strange man," put in Carolan pensively.

"Strange indeed! He does not belong to these streets, that I'll swear; he is here to amuse himself."

"What an odd way he has of amusing himself then!"

"Gentlemen get tired of the old ways of amusing themselves. The faro table, racing, betting, even love affairs can pall. At any rate a new setting is needed."

"You think he is here to find a new setting for a love affair?"

"Carolan, how you pull me up! I said no such thing. He is here for novelty; that I could swear to! He is no more of this world of sordid streets and trading than . . . than . . . I am. It would not surprise me to hear he was a friend of the Prince himself!"

Carolan laughed, but Kitty turned away from her to pursue a dream. The Prince was being entertained at her house and paying such attention to his hostess that everyone remarked upon it. Why not? Was it not known that it was the matronly charms which he ardently admired?

The shop door bell rang.

"They have remembered it is tea-time!" said Kitty. "They could not have got much farther than the end of the street."

Carolan opened the door between the parlour and the shop. Jonathan Crew stood there.

"Good afternoon, Miss Carolan!"

Inside the parlour, Kitty heard that voice and patted her side curls.

"Come in, Mr. Crew! Come in!"

He bowed low over Kitty's hand.

"But how radiant you look today, Ma'am!"

"I am well enough," said Kitty.

Carolan poured out a cup of tea and handed it to the guest. He smiled his thanks. How cold his eyes were, after the warm admiration in those of Marcus!

"I was passing," he said, "and I thought I could not do that without calling in to see my very good friends. I did not dream that I should be just in time for a cup of this delicious beverage."

"We are glad you came at this moment. We have just been deserted by my husband and his business colleague."

"Indeed, Ma'am! You are very kind to welcome me thus."

"You take sugar in your tea?" asked Carolan.

She watched him help himself; his fingers were short and stubby; unlike Marcus's, which she had noticed were long and delicate.

Kitty lay back in her chair. Her mind was still in a rosy dream of the future; the only difference was that she had substituted Jonathan for Marcus. Marcus certainly had an air of breeding which Jonathan lacked, but Jonathan flattered her more. Jonathan, she felt, would if he had such intentions offer Carolan marriage; Marcus might not. Jonathan was safer. Yes, Jonathan certainly fitted into her future very satisfactorily, even if he would not bring the Prince of Wales to dine under her roof.

"So comfortable you are here," said Jonathan. "I often think of the cosiness of this little parlour behind the shop."

"Do you?" said Kitty. "And might I ask, sir, if it is only of the parlour you think, or do you sometimes spare a thought for its inhabitants?"

Now his eyes were on Kitty, turned away from Carolan; they smiled straight into Kitty's eyes, glittering oddly.

"You know the answer to that, Ma'am," he said slowly, and coldly it seemed to Carolan, who could not see his eyes. The

210

Prince, thought Kitty, was not the only man who liked a little maturity in women and found the youthful very tame.

"Indeed," he turned to Carolan now, "this is a most interesting house. I often think that the property in these parts is very interesting . . . drab as it may sometimes seem."

Ah! thought Kitty. He is interested in property; perhaps that is his business, and the clerkship he talks of is just a blind. Men who own property are rich men, though they may lack the polish of gentlemen of fashion.

"Perhaps, sir," said Kitty archly, "you know more of such matters than do two ignorant females."

"I will not allow you to call yourself and your daughter ignorant, Ma'am. But these properties must be nigh on two hundred years old; think of that, Ma'am!"

"That takes us back to the dark ages."

"It does indeed. I am interested in property; perhaps one day you would be kind enough to show me the house."

"You would be bored to tears," said Kitty.

"You would certainly find it rather dull," said Carolan.

"The matters that interest never bore us. I am interested in old houses. Will you please show me this place . . . one day? Those narrow windows in your upper rooms have always intrigued me from the street. Tell me, do the ceilings slope right to the floor?"

"In the attics, yes," said Carolan.

"Ah, my dear," cried Kitty, "I see that our miserable house interests him far more than we do! Let us show him it."

"No more, Ma'am . . . not *more!*" he insisted.

"Come along," said Kitty. "Now."

Carolan piled the crockery on to a tray and carried it to the kitchen. As she washed the cups she heard the footsteps of her mother and Mr. Crew mounting the stairs, and she ceased to think of them, for she was telling herself that it was high time she received a reply from Everard.

When she had dried and put away the cups she busied herself with some preparation for the evening meal before going back to the parlour, and she had sat there some time before she realised quite suddenly that the house seemed very quiet. What on earth were her mother and Mr. Crew doing all this time? They were probably in the attics, she thought, and went upstairs to find them. They were not there, and she came down again; she explored the lower part of the house, and they were not there. She peeped into the shop, and stared; for

211

she saw at once that the door, which her father had taken such pains to conceal with those old coats, was open; in its lock was a key. She thought quickly that he must have left the key there this afternoon when he went out with Marcus, and that her mother and Mr. Crew must have slipped through the parlour to the shop while she was in the kitchen.

She took four strides across the shop, went through the door and shut it carefully behind her.

"Mamma!" she called. "Mamma!"

The door of the basement-room was open. She looked in. The room was small and dark; there was no window, but a grating high in the wall. There were a good many trunks and boxes in the place, and over one of these bent her mother and Mr. Crew.

Kitty turned and laughed at her.

"Your door was open, Carolan!"

"Oh . . ." stammered Carolan. "But this is . . . Father's store-room. He always keeps it locked. He . . ."

Kitty wagged a finger.

"Now, Carolan, you reprimanded me the other day for a lack of curiosity; now you would reproach me with being too curious! You see what an exacting daughter I have, Mr. Crew."

Jonathan Crew turned, and in the dimness of the room Carolan noticed particularly the white flash of his teeth. He was holding a silver ornament in his hands.

"Mamma!" said Carolan. "Have you a key then?"

"Oh, no. Your father left the door of this room unlocked and the key in the door at the top of the stairs when he went out. Careless man! He must have gone in a hurry. Mr. Crew found the door; he said he saw it when he helped you clear up the shop."

"Why, Miss Carolan," said Jonathan Crew, " you seem put out. I hope I do not intrude here . . ."

"No, no!" cried Carolan. "It is of no importance; merely that my mother and I have never been down here before . . . and my father has always kept the doors locked and . . ."

"I can understand that! With such articles as these about . . ."

Carolan went into the room towards them, and looked at the ornament in Jonathan's hands. She watched him as he caressed the polished surface. They were ugly hands, red, and cold-looking.

"Ah, yes," he added, "handling articles like this in such a

212

neighbourhood, he would need to be careful. I am sure he is quite unaware that he left the doors unlocked."

"Both keys were in the doors!" said Kitty. "I shall tease him about this . . . Naughty man!"

"And did you find the house interesting, Mr. Crew?" asked Carolan.

"Enormously! Beyond my wildest expectations."

They went back to the parlour, and shortly afterwards Jonathan Crew took his leave.

Kitty said: "Darling! Tighten my stays. There now, I have put on flesh. Darling, do you think with Thérèse that it is in the right places? And how thin *you* are, child! I do wish you could take some of mine; you could do with it and I should not miss it. It was a great idea to add the ruching to the neck, do you not think so, Carolan?"

Kitty regarded her daughter from under lowered lids. Quiet, secretive, brooding almost. Was she, like her mother, wondering whether the life of a parson's wife was the best she could choose? London did strange things to you; it had done them to Kitty, so why not to Carolan? It was not a town so much as a personality; it intrigued while it repelled. It had fascinated her from the first, and oh, the squalor of those rooms she had shared with Darrell! Lousy lodging-houses and the people in their rags, and the smell of the river and the back streets, and the empty feeling inside, which was hunger, and the lightness in the head which was part of it too. She had been something of a prophetess. "Darrell," she had said, "we never know what is waiting for us round the corner!" And how right she had been! She, whom they thought just a frivolous woman. For, one day he had come in full of excitement, and told her he had met a friend; she did not know who that friend was, but now she had come to believe that he was Marcus, for from that time Marcus had come to the house frequently enough. A good business proposition had been made to him, Darrell had said, and he was going to take it. It would mean saving hard at first; it would mean living simply, but there was money in it, and after a while they would come out of business and be rich, free from want for the rest of their days.

She patted the ruching at her neck. Life was strange, promising a good deal, withholding much. How she had longed for reunion with Darrell! How she had dreamed of it! And now here it was, but he was not the same man with whom, years

213

ago, she had coquetted in a coach; he was not the lover whom she had met in the wood. Ah, no! There were years and years of experience between that man and the Darrell of today. He was moody, easily depressed, and indeed the depression came upon him suddenly, out of the blue, for no reason at all. Kitty wanted gaiety all the time; admiration she wanted, fine clothes to wear, men about her telling her she was beautiful, all that she had been years ago. Since the coming of Carolan life had certainly become more intriguing; there were the outings with Darrell which previously he had not felt inclined to give her; and there was the company. Marcus calling in nigh on every day. And what a man was Marcus! And how his eyes glistened as they rested on Carolan! Who knew, he might abduct her one day! He was that kind of person, she was sure. The love of adventure sparkled in those merry eyes of his, and his long tapering fingers itched to touch Carolan; Kitty knew the signs. There was little of such matters she did not know. Exciting indeed! And Marcus . . . often dressed so poorly that he looked the typical loafer of Grape Street and its environs; but once when he had come to the shop unexpectedly for a conference with Darrell, she had caught a glimpse of Marcus in the rôle of an exquisite gentleman of the Town. What fun! What excitement when one was an attractive woman with a daughter who was almost as attractive! What enchanting rivalry! And Jonathan Crew, that strange, quiet man who looked at her so oddly that she felt he saw behind her smile and knew that she was wondering whether he wished to be her lover; Jonathan Crew, who whispered such compliments in her ear and spoke them so strangely that afterwards she wondered whether he meant to compliment her at all; who watched Carolan with a glitter in his queer eyes sometimes, so that she wondered whether after all it was not Carolan in whom he was primarily interested. But then, he had always contrived not to come when Darrell was about, which rather showed he had his eyes on Darrell's wife.

"These stays will give me the palpitations, Carolan; I swear they will!"

Carolan laughed.

"Oh, Mamma, Mamma, they are indeed too tight! Why, you will faint in the arms of Mr. Jonathan, or perhaps Marcus, if you persist in wearing them thus."

"Unlace them . . . just a little. And, my dear, do you think that would disconcert either of them greatly?"

"Marcus would not be disconcerted, I am sure of that," said Carolan, unlacing the stays with deft fingers. "Of Mr. Crew I am not so sure."

"You think it would annoy him then?"

"Indeed I do not know. There! How is that? Breathe in, Mamma. Now!"

Kitty smiled at her reflection in the mirror.

"Ah! That's better. You think Mr. Crew does not like me then?"

"Mamma, I cannot say. He may like us all a good deal, or he might like us not at all. It is not easy to tell."

"Come, come! Does a man visit a family whom he hates?"

"I should think not, Mamma."

"Well then?"

"By the frequency of his visits I should say that he likes us very much."

Kitty put her head on one side and laughed gaily.

"Have you noticed, Carolan, that he endeavours to call mostly when your father is out?"

Carolan smiled at the big, fleshy face reflected in the mirror. What a vain old darling she was! And her eyes were the colour of speedwells with the velvety quality of pansies; and her face was like a flower, big, overblown, rich in beauty before the petals began to fall.

"I had noticed that," said Carolan.

Kitty fluttered her long, golden lashes.

"To you, I suppose, I am an old woman!"

Carolan bent her head and kissed her mother's forehead.

"No," she said. "A very fascinating one—ageless. Like . . . like . . . well, like no one but yourself!"

When Carolan stooped over, Kitty could see the letter she had tucked into the bodice of her dress. From the parson! It had come that day. And though, thought Kitty, I am supposed to be a foolish and frivolous woman, there are some matters which it is easy for me to understand. Carolan was not very pleased with that letter. What if there was an estrangement? Might that not be the best way for things to work out?

"Ah!" said Kitty. "As if a man would look at an old woman when there is a young and lovely one about the house!"

Carolan laughed.

"Come, Mother, you must not talk thus, for I know you

215

too well, and we both know that for many years men will continue to cast glances in your direction, whoever else may be about."

"Flatterer!" said Kitty gaily, for truly it was a fact that Mr. Crew made a habit of calling when Darrell was out.

"Now Marcus!" said Kitty, trying to make her daughter believe that Jonathan Crew had not been the one in her thoughts. "What do you think of Marcus?"

Carolan was silent, surveying their faces side by side in the dusky mirror. What did she think of Marcus? She did not know.

"There is a certain mystery about that fellow," went on Kitty. "La! There are times when I could think him a veritable simpleton . . . and at others, there he is—the man of the world!"

"I, too," said Carolan, "sometimes feel that he is not all that he would have us believe."

"There! Do you not find life interesting here, my dear?"

"Very interesting, Mamma."

"More interesting than Haredon, I would say."

Why did the girl shudder? What had happened at Haredon? Charles? He was a little beast, that boy. Could it be . . . Something had made her run away; and that parson had not been there to help her. A pox on that parson! Why in God's name did a high-spirited girl like Carolan want to pledge herself to a parson? Why did she want to wait on his letters? Why, when one arrived, did it fill her with melancholy? How Kitty wished that she could put a spoke in this arrangement of Carolan's with her parson! Everard Orland! She remembered him well; a tall, lanky, pale-faced boy . . . fastidious! A nincompoop! And betrothed to Carolan!

And what a lover Marcus would make! Kitty sighed for the passing of the years. If she were but Carolan's age . . .

The letter was showing above Carolan's bodice. I wish I knew what the nincompoop has said to her, thought Kitty.

"Marcus is indeed an amusing man," she said aloud.

Carolan went to the dressing-table and stood there, smiling at her mother.

"And *you* seem to find *me* most amusing, Carolan."

"Most, darling!"

"I am not at all sure that your mirth pleases me."

"I laugh because of your tremendous interest in these men."

"And why should I not be interested in my friends?"

216

"But, Mamma, you do not know the first thing about Millie."

"Millie? And why should I, pray?"

"If you were interested in human nature as such . . ."

"Indeed I am interested in human nature."

"But only when it is of masculine gender!"

"Well, and what do you know of Millie?"

"More than I know of Marcus or Jonathan."

"Indeed! I am sorry to hear you profess such interest in a scullery maid!"

"Mamma! You have the dignity of a queen!"

"And you, Carolan, have the vulgar curiosity of a serving-girl. Tell me, is Silly Millie your bosom friend, your confidante?"

Carolan came to her mother and touched her cheek with her finger. Now Kitty could see the paper more clearly and the black writing upon it. His handwriting was thick and bold, as though he were very sure of himself.

"No, Mamma, she is not. But I discovered that she and her family live in one large room at the end of Grape Street, and that there are many of them, and often no coal to make a fire, and often nothing but stale bread to eat."

"She told you that?"

"It came out . . . she did not exactly tell me. Mamma, could we not have Millie to live here?"

"Your father is all against it; he says we cannot afford to keep a girl in the house."

"It would surely cost no more; and in the circumstances . . ."

"Your father says no. Though it would suit me well to have the girl about the place."

"I cannot understand my father; he must guess what Millie's home is like. I will speak to him."

"There you go. You see, I am right when I say you have more interest in a serving-girl than in friends of your own standing."

"No, Mamma, you misunderstand. I *am* interested in those two men. But, Mamma, do you not feel it . . . there is something in both of them . . . something remote . . . something . . . I feel I express myself badly, but do you not feel they are keeping something back?"

"Something in check! That is it. My dear, beware of Marcus."

"How . . . beware, Mamma?"

"He is a very passionate man, and I have seen how his eyes glitter at the sight of you. I have heard stories of abductions . . ."

Carolan laughed, and the letter fell from her bosom to the floor, but she laughed so much that she did not notice this, and Kitty was able to drop a lace handkerchief over the letter and pick them both up unnoticed.

"You may laugh, my dear," said Kitty, putting the letter and the handkerchief on a small table, "but be careful! Never ride alone with Marcus. Never walk alone with Marcus. I could tell you some stories, I vow."

"I have no doubt that you could." Carolan leaned across the dressing-table, and in the dust on the mirror sketched two faces. In one she accentuated the lean features of Jonathan, and in the other the rather large ones of Marcus.

"There, Mamma! There they are—one either side of your mirror. You may study them and probe into their minds as much as you wish."

"And very good likenesses too. Particularly of Jonathan!"

"He lends himself to caricature! There is a leanness about the man. Something of the bloodhound . . ."

"Anyone less like a bloodhound I never saw!"

Carolan twisted her features into a grimace and by some artistry she captured the expression of Jonathan Crew. She sniffed around after the manner of a dog. "And what have we here? I declare this is a fascinating house . . . And then he looks at you, Mamma, as though he finds you almost as fascinating as the house. Almost . . . but not quite!"

"Nonsense!" said Kitty.

"Nonsense indeed that he should find a gloomy old house more fascinating than you. The man must be crazy!"

"At least he is not a bit like a bloodhound."

"Well, that is of what he reminds me. Then Marcus . . . sometimes his eyes are like a spaniel's . . . in expression, I mean. Sentimental, pleading. But sometimes they are mischievous as a terrier's and often as vapid as those of a pekinese."

"I trust," said Kitty, "that you are not so critical of Everard!" Then she could have slapped herself for such folly, for was that not the way to remind Carolan of the letter? She went on in a panic: "And now, my dear, be off with you. Run down and tell your dear friend Silly Millie to put the kettle on."

Carolan smiled over her shoulder and went out. Kitty ran

to the table and waited, listening to the sound of Carolan's footsteps. She took the letter from the folds of the lace handkerchief, and ran her eyes hastily over it.

"I will come for you," he had written, "as soon as the three months are up. I work very hard here, and plan what we shall do when you are here with me. I trust you are enjoying your stay with your parents. Do not get such a taste for Town life that the country will seem dull to you. Oh, how I wish the three months were up! Were it not for breaking my promise I should be with you there now . . ."

Carolan was coming back. How quickly she had missed the letter! Cunningly Kitty threw it on to the floor near the door; she was struggling into her dress as Carolan came in.

"Well, dear?"

"I thought I dropped something. Oh, yes . . ."

She pounced upon the letter, and tucked it into the bosom of her dress. "Can I help you, Mamma?"

"No, dear. I am all right, thank you." Her face was red with guilt, and Carolan had such penetrating eyes. She was relieved when Carolan went downstairs again.

"Bah!" said Kitty aloud. "A milksop! 'How I wish the three months were up!' . . . 'were it not for breaking my promise . . .' A lover should never make promises to others than his mistress! Why, were I Carolan, I would say: 'Forsooth, sir, if your promise to your mother is of more importance than the vows you would make to me, well, then is it so important to you that I should be your wife?' "

Kitty tossed her head. She was playing the part now. She was Carolan, young and defiant and desired. Invitingly she smiled at the drawing of Marcus. "I would know more of *you*, sir, before I pledged myself!"

Her eyes went to the sketch of Jonathan who came when Darrell was out. Now she was Kitty again. Not the young and lovely daughter, but the mother whom the years could not wither, but who seemed only to gather greater charm as time rolled on.

Down in the parlour behind the shop, the teapot stood upon the table. Kitty took her seat.

"Come, Darrell," she called. "A cup of tea, my love!"

He came up from the basement, looking tired, with the furrow on his brow. How he had changed from the boy she had loved in the wood! But how faithful she had been to him . . . always! The darling! The poor suffering darling!

"Carolan, my dear, hand your father his cup."

"I cannot stay long," said Darrell. "I have business to attend to; in five minutes I must be gone."

"Father," said Carolan, "I was talking to Mamma about poor Millie. Could she not live here? I fear it is a dreadful life she leads in her own home."

"We cannot afford to keep the girl," said Darrell.

"But, Father, it need not cost more. I have heard such a sad story of her. So many of them all in one room! And I heard that her father gets drunk on gin every night, and they are terrified of him, simply terrified! Could it make much difference if she lived here?"

"I did not intend . . ." he said.

She had gone to him; she sat on the arm of his chair. Kitty watched them. He loved this daughter of his dearly, though he scarcely knew her. He was afraid of her in an odd way—or perhaps afraid for her. I must remember, thought Kitty, to ask him if he, like me, is disturbed by this suggested marriage.

Carolan said: "Father, can you imagine what it is like in that one room where they live?"

"Indeed I can," said Darrell grimly.

"Then, Father, surely . . ."

He took her hand; there was an odd, defensive quality about him when he touched either of them, as though he were watching to see if they would flinch from being touched by those poor hands of his.

"You have a kind heart, daughter," he said slowly, "and that is what I would wish. Millie shall come here."

She kissed his cheek, and Kitty watched the colour run up under his skin. Dear Darrell! It was good to see them thus, and to know that it was her suffering, her endurance which had brought him this daughter. Squire Haredon . . . Brute! Lecher! What a man! She shivered deliciously, remembering incidents with him. What I endured! She laughed inwardly and stroked the soft skin of her arms.

"I shall tell her today," said Carolan.

"I do declare," said Kitty, pouting prettily, "that you can twist your father around your finger. To me it was always 'We cannot afford this! We cannot afford that!' And now, at your request, we are to have a maid to live in the house; we are to go here and there. Did you not say that we should go to Vauxhall, Darrell?"

He smiled fondly across at her.

"I did indeed. We must show Carolan around, must we not?"

"Oh! Did you think I should be the one to say no to a little gaiety?"

They were smiling, a happy family party. How I love them both! thought Kitty. It was worth going through what I did, for their sakes.

"Vauxhall Gardens on Saturday afternoon then, Darrell?"

"If you wish it then."

"I do wish it!" How Carolan's eyes sparkled! A pity to waste those sparkling eyes on a parson! I shall wear my black velvet, thought Kitty, and we shall have a carriage to take us there.

She looked across at them, smiling lovingly, but instead of their faces she saw herself sitting under the trees in her black velvet; she heard an elegant man whisper to his companions: "Gad! Who's the beauty in black velvet?"

Darrell put down his cup and said he must go.

"Do not be long," said Kitty.

And he smiled his well-pleased smile as he went out, and the wistful look was in his eyes, which meant that he was longing to finish with business and retire to the country.

Kitty sat back in her chair.

"Another cup, please, Carolan. My dear, what shall you wear for Vauxhall? You must look smart, my dear, because it is a veritable fashion parade there, I do hear. My black velvet is most becoming . . . I think I shall add a fichu of lace, something delicately coloured in a pastel shade. How glad I am that I have the colouring to suit black velvet!"

The shop bell rang, and there was the sound of a footfall out there.

"Now who in the world can that be?" said Kitty, but her eyes were mischievous; she could guess, of course. By the Lord, I believe he waits outside the shop until he has seen Darrell go. Naughty man!

Carolan went through the parlour door. Kitty heard her say: "Oh . . . how do you do, Mr. Crew?"

Then she led him into the parlour. He looked pale, and his skin seemed to be drawn more tightly than ever across his prominent bones.

He came swiftly to her. Languidly she lifted a hand which he took courteously and pressed to his lips. They were feverishly hot, those lips. Kitty found that piquant—such hot lips, such a queer cold face—unfathomable! Mysterious! Perhaps when a woman grew older she liked a subtle lover. Too much sweetness could be cloying—too much petting, too much fondness. A strange man, Jonathan Crew!

"Carolan," said Kitty, "perhaps our guest would like a cup of tea."

"Indeed, Ma'am, you are too hospitable."

"Now, sir! Should I refuse a cup of tea to a thirsty man?"

Carolan filled the cup and handed it to him, and now his eyes rested full on the girl. Oh, she was attractive with her eyes that deep green, and her reddish hair, and the soft roundness of her cheeks. But would he wait until Darrell was out of the way, to call on Carolan? So ridiculous! And there was nothing foolish about Mr. Crew . . . except perhaps his rising passion for a woman older than himself; though it might well be that he did not know this, for truly she did not look her age.

She said: "We are going to Vauxhall on Saturday, Mr. Crew. My little daughter here is in a fine state of excitement about the jaunt."

"That will be delightful," said Mr. Crew, turning his eyes upon her. He seemed to be summing her up. If his manners were not always so perfect, that appraising glance of his might be offensive.

"You have been of course, Mr. Crew?" said Carolan.

"Many times," he told her.

"Then it would not hold the same thrill for you as it does for us?" Kitty inquired archly.

"That would depend, Ma'am."

Here, Kitty was in her element. Her eyes were wide and innocent.

"Depend on what, sir, may I ask?"

"On the company I had the privilege to enjoy!"

"And if the company was all that you could desire, you would enjoy a visit to Vauxhall?"

"Indeed I would!"

Kitty was silent. Another man would have asked outright if he might join the party; not so Jonathan Crew. All his movements were mysterious; he would leave one guessing. Would he or would he not join their little party at Vauxhall? Wretched man! Yet exciting man! For, Kitty asked herself, what was there about him except that mysterious quality? Take that away, and what had you—a tall, thin man with a skin the colour of old parchment drawn so tightly across his bones that they looked as though they would break through it, a man whose peculiarly prominent eyes and somewhat receding chin gave him the appearance of a fish. And yet that peculiarity, that soft tread when he entered the shop, that timing of his entrance—attractive, yes! Or it may be, thought Kitty, that I have been shut away so long that I find any man attractive. Now Marcus . . . there is a different sort of man. Not good-looking, it was true, but with a charm and an air . . . But his merry eyes could see none but Carolan.

She found they were talking of Marcus. Jonathan had seen him leaving the shop a few days ago. Was he well? asked Jonathan. Very well, as far as she knew, Kitty replied.

"A man whose chief object in life is to amuse himself," Jonathan said a trifle severely. "That was the impression he gave me."

"You are an observant man," Kitty told him. " 'Tis my belief our friend Marcus comes from some great family and likes to haunt our poor neighbourhood for the amusement it gives him!"

Jonathan talked on, asking questions about Marcus, but he did not seem to care very much whether or not he received answers. Kitty had never noticed before what long arms he had, what strong-looking, ugly hands.

Carolan sat by the table, not attending; now and then she touched the letter in the bodice of her dress.

Kitty turned the conversation back to Vauxhall. She was sure Jonathan would come upon them, supposedly by accident. When a hot-blooded man is roused to passion, that is natural enough, but when it happens to a cold man, why then it can be catastrophic and most entertaining.

Kitty patted her hair and smiled slyly across the table at Carolan. Odd that he should prefer her, surely; but then perhaps it was not so odd!

At the end of that day when they visited Vauxhall Gardens, Carolan sat at her window, looking down on the moonlit street.

It was just on midnight; her mother had gone to bed worn out with the day's excitement, but Carolan could not sleep. She was too disturbed. Her eyes felt hot and weary, as though they had stared too long at some over-bright light, and her emotions were mixed ones.

The illuminations, like constellations, had been wonderful. They had enchanted her; and indeed there had been much in the sylvan scene to enchant her; the delightful paths, the hedges, the trees; and in addition the picturesque pavilions and colonnades; the porticos, the statues, the paintings, the ornate pillars. There had been so much on which to feast the eyes that they grew weary. And the people . . . a never-ending stream of them, loud-voiced ladies and their gallants, merchants, apprentices; everyone there had been bent on pleasure.

And then that ugly little incident to spoil it all! Who else had seen? Had Kitty? No, definitely not. She had been too enthralled by the glamorous scenes about her. Darrell? She did not think so. But she, Carolan, had seen . . . and so had Jonathan Crew.

Now she must go over it all again—leaving the shop in the hired cabriolet, laughing a good deal at nothing in particular, because the excursion put them all in such high spirits, Darrell included; and so to Vauxhall.

It had been late afternoon when they arrived.

"Wait," Darrell had said, "until the lamps are lighted; it is then that Vauxhall can enchant the eye."

It had enchanted Carolan right from the beginning; also Kitty. Dear Mamma, in her hat with the big plumes which she imagined made her look very much as Mrs. Fitzherbert had looked in her heyday.

"They say, my dear, that I am the dead spit of what she was! And in this hat . . . and in this gown . . . Look! Are not people glancing this way?"

"We must see everything," said Darrell.

"We must miss nothing!" countered Carolan.

Delightful it was to sit in carved wooden seats under gracious trees, eating sliced ham and sipping syllabub. She had told herself then that she would enjoy telling Everard all about this when she was with him in the country. "The day we went to Vauxhall!" It would stand out in her memory as a golden day, and she would remember Darrell faintly flushed with the pleasure he was giving his family, and Mamma, proud in her plumed hat and the knowledge that her resemblance to Mrs. Fitzherbert was indeed remarkable; and herself from the country, drinking in all the excitements of the place.

Such a lot of people seemed to know Darrell. There were nods from some; others exchanged a few words with him; and not one of them did he introduce to his wife and daughter.

"Business acquaintances, my dear!" he whispered. "Not the kind for you to meet."

"Ah!" Carolan laughed. "Big ideas you have of your family since bringing them by cabriolet to Vauxhall Gardens!"

They were sitting at a table under the trees when they saw Jonathan Crew coming towards them. Even he, thought

Carolan, was affected by the scene. The faintest colour showed beneath his tight skin; excited, he seemed, and his eyes glittered more brightly than usual, or perhaps that was the light, for the lights had been lit at that time.

He was almost shy with Darrell, half apologetic. Kitty had watched them from under her long lashes. Piquant scene! she was thinking, Carolan knew. Poor darling Mamma, who had been so very beautiful and sought after in her youth that her confidence in her charms was as sturdy a growth as that of the young oak tree behind them!

"Unusual to meet you here!" said Jonathan. "Do you often pass an hour or two in the gardens?"

Darrell said it was a treat for the little girl, who would so soon be returning to the country.

Kitty was demure, eyes cast down. She did not say that she had told Jonathan they would be here. This was intrigue such as Kitty loved. Carolan did not greatly care for it, but it seemed harmless enough.

"May I join in your feast of ham and syllabub?" Jonathan asked humbly, and Kitty looked modestly askance at Darrell as though, without his consent, she would not dare to ask the newcomer to sup with them.

They talked lightly of the weather, of the gardens, of the poor quality of the champagne which was served here, of the elegance of the grottoes and rotundas, of the charm of the music to be heard from not far off.

Perhaps, but for her sharp eyes, Carolan would not have seen what she did see. It had seemed a trivial incident. Kitty did not notice it; she was too busy noting the dresses of the women, the glances of the men; Darrell's eyes were short-sighted, so he contented himself with admiring his Kitty in her Fitzherbert hat.

On the other side of the portico sat a lady, her face half covered by a mask. Now Carolan knew she was a lady of fashion in spite of the long, dark, concealing cloak she wore. Carolan had had a glimpse of a fine leather slipper and a rich gown. She was talking to a man who sat beside her, leaning towards her as though to catch every word she uttered. Carolan guessed that the lady was here clandestinely meeting her lover, and the concealing cloak and the mask pointed to the face that she did not wish to be recognised. That would account for her choosing Vauxhall Gardens as a rendezvous, for so few of her own class would come there on a Saturday evening. She was wondering about them when the man came by. He was a thick-set man wearing the most elegant of coats, and his breeches were so tight that they seemed like a dark skin about his legs. So deep in thought he appeared, that he walked straight into the table where the lady and gentleman sat. The lady gave a little cry, while the man in the elegant coat gripped the table as though to steady himself. For half a second Carolan saw his hands, and then looked up at his face. She was about to speak, but he had apologised and moved on. Then she was aware of Jonathan's watching her. Not a word did she say of this. If she told Kitty, Kitty would say: "In an elegant coat, did you say? Ah! I knew it! Then Marcus Markham is a gentleman of fashion who amuses himself by taking a cup of tea with us now and then." And she would weave fresh dreams about the man.

There the incident would have ended, had they left the table and gone on their way as they might so easily have done, having finished their repast. But they sat on until that moment when the lady started up from her seat and cried: "My purse! I swear it was here a moment ago. Where can it be?"

Then Carolan went cold with fear, for she had seen those long, tapering fingers resting on the table, and she remembered that occasion when she had first seen Marcus and he had pointed the way while he so deftly extracted her handkerchief. There was now no doubt in her mind; Marcus was a practised thief!

She wished they had gone before the lady had cried out that she had lost her purse; she wished she need not know. That was foolish and illogical; Everard had once said she was illogical. But I liked him, she thought, I liked him! I did not want to *know* that he was a thief. She seemed to hear the cool voice of Everard saying: "But if he was, it was better to know it."

"No, no no!" she persisted illogically and ridiculously.

So he went about stealing, and she had thought of him as her friend! He had said to her, of the handkerchief: "This was the first offence." He was a liar; he was a rogue; but he had such merry eyes, and she had laughed with him as she had never really laughed with Everard.

Everard was perfect in her eyes; Marcus far from perfect. But she had liked him; perhaps she was vain and foolish, but his admiration had pleased her. The throbbing note in his voice, the passionate glances . . . well, she had not wished to respond to them in the slightest but it had been good to know that he thought her comely. And now she was angry, not so much perhaps because he was a thief, but because he was a

226

cheat. He had lied to her about the handkerchief; so therefore it was most likely that his admiring glances, the note of tenderness in his voice, were just a part he was playing. He was a libertine, a thief and a rogue; and he had fooled her.

If he were standing before her now, she would flay him with her tongue, she would tell him she despised him.

But she could not get out of her mind the picture of Marcus, hanging by the neck, and a crowd of laughing, jeering people looking on. Then her anger melted before her fear, and she wept for the folly of Marcus, for the stupidity of the man.

The gentleman had said: "Genevra, calm yourself! You cannot make a fuss here. Forget your purse . . ."

"Forget it! I had taken my pearls off because the clasp was weak; they were in my purse."

"Hush, Genevra! You cannot stir up trouble here. Remember . . ."

And listening, Carolan felt glad . . . glad that those two were engaged in some clandestine intrigue, that they dared do nothing . . . glad . . . glad, and all for that rogue, Marcus!

When they left their table, Jonathan put his hand lightly on her arm, to detain her, and Kitty and Darrell walked ahead.

He said to her: "I wonder if you saw what I saw?"

"And what was that?" she asked, trying to force a note of unconcern into her voice.

"The little fracas at the table near us. Did you see it? Did you hear it?"

"It would have been impossible not to—and we so near."

"Her purse was stolen. Did you see by whom?"

"If I had," she said defiantly, "I should have called stop thief! I should not have sat by and watched a thief make off with the lady's purse!"

"We saw the thief," said Jonathan slowly, "but we did not actually see the theft. They are clever, those rogues, and sleight of hand is the first lesson they learn."

Carolan shrugged her shoulders. "An incident that must happen time and time again in such a place as this."

"Indeed you are right, but this particular incident would interest us more, since . . . we are aware of the identity of the thief."

Carolan was too guileless to hide her dismay.

He said: "May I speak to you frankly?"

"Of course."

"We recognised him, did we not? He is the man who stole your handkerchief. He has called on you since; I have seen

227

him, leaving your house. Your mother has mentioned him to me; he is, she says, a friend of your father's. Now we have discovered that he is a rogue, a common thief."

"I am not at all sure . . ." began Carolan, but he interrupted her.

"Come! Let us be frank with each other; we have to be, if we are to help him. You recognised him, did you not? I knew him at once. Do you not understand that when I discovered he was visiting your house, I felt I had to know something of him? There have been other times when I have seen him."

Carolan shivered. There was a burning self-righteousness about Jonathan now; a certain fire was creeping into his words; he moved nearer to her.

"Do not think," he said, "that I wish to condemn him. I wish to stop his career of crime; do you understand? I was wondering . . . Could you speak to him? Your mother has told me that he sets a certain store by you . . ."

"Oh!" cried Carolan angrily. "Is there anything my mother has not told you!"

He smiled. "She has a nature that is scarcely secretive. Listen, dear young lady. Could you plead with him? Could you make him see that to pursue a life of crime means the gallows or transportation? I think he may listen to you, whereas he would not to others."

Now she was sorry that she had been angry with Jonathan, when all he wished to do was to help Marcus. Marcus was a lovable fool; but Jonathan was a wise, good man.

"Speak to him," went on Jonathan. "Perhaps he has some good reason for behaving as he does. Perhaps he was led into temptation and finds it difficult to extricate himself. Ask him. Try to understand, for it is only by understanding that you can help him."

"You talk like a preacher."

"I wish to help the friends of my friends."

"You are very good. I will think about it . . . Perhaps I will speak to him."

He pressed her hand; his fingers were cold, and yet they seemed to tingle. He was a very good man, she thought, to feel so deeply for poor, foolish Marcus.

She was remembering it all so vividly as she sat, looking down on the street, that when Marcus appeared suddenly she felt for a second or two that he was part of her imaginings.

She stared down at him. He was strolling along the street, as though well pleased with himself. He had changed his elegant clothes for coat and breeches of worsted. How he angered her! The complacent fool! No doubt he was congratulating himself on a fine haul. Angrily she got to her feet. She would speak to him; she would tell him that he was a fool—a ridiculous fool—nay, a criminal and a rogue, and she and her family had done with him.

She sped downstairs. There was no one in the parlour. Her mother had retired to bed; her father was probably working down in the basement and would not hear him. She was glad of that.

She opened the front door, and Marcus was standing there.

"Why . . . Miss Carolan!" he said.

"Indeed, yes!" She spoke severely. "Pray come in. I would have a word with you."

He looked alarmed.

"I trust I have not offended you."

"Offended me! That is a mild way of expressing it."

"You alarm me."

"You should be alarmed! Speak quietly; I do not wish my father to hear. He would not have you in this house if he knew . . ." She drew herself up to her full height—she was almost as tall as he was—and her eyes flashed in scorn. "We have just returned from Vauxhall."

"I trust you spent a pleasant time there."

"A most pleasant time, until one incident spoiled the whole day for me!"

"I am sorry to hear that."

She noticed with a grim satisfaction that he was shaken.

"And well you may be! Please lower your voice. Come over here behind these old clothes; they will muffle our voices."

"It is you who are speaking loudly, Miss Carolan!" He smiled at her tenderly. "My dear, how upset you are!"

"Upset!" She was finding it difficult to keep back the tears. "I was sitting near a masked lady who lost her purse."

"But why should you care so deeply for a masked lady's loss?"

"I saw you. Oh! You were elegant, a young gentleman of fashion, but I saw through your disguise! All the fine coats in the world would not deceive me into thinking you were anything but a thief! If my father knew, he would never allow you to set foot inside this house again."

He stared down at his hands. He was guilty but unrepentant. disturbed only because he had been found out.

"You are a fool, Marcus," she hissed at him.

"Well I know it, Carolan."

"Where do you think this life is leading you?"

"Well, can any of us see the end of the road we are treading?"

"We can at least guide our footsteps upon the safest paths!"

"One day I shall retire from this life. Then I shall be a rich man, and the only way to be a safe man is to be a rich man. Did you know that, Carolan?"

"I know that the way to be unsafe is the way you are going, Marcus! I would not have believed it of you. Had you told me you had not taken the purse, I should have believed you."

"But you said you saw!"

"I did not see you take it."

"You did not see me take it!" There was relief in his eyes. "I was afraid my hands had lost their cunning."

She looked down at his long white hands.

"It is a pity you do not put them to a better purpose."

"Carolan, do you despise me now?"

"I am deeply disappointed in you."

"That is a pity. I had my dreams."

"Dreams? What dreams?"

"Of the days of my safety . . . But what matter?"

She clasped her hands. "Oh, Marcus, *must* you do these things?"

"I live by them, Carolan."

"You live by robbery?"

"I have tried other methods."

She pictured Everard's face then, cool, a little stern; she could hear his calm voice.

"A man's life," she said, quoting him, "is surely what he makes it?"

"He has a hand in shaping his destiny certainly."

"Well then . . .?"

"There are other considerations. There are people who are born in mansions; there are people born in Grape Street. It is not easy to be an honest man in Grape Street, Carolan."

There was banter in his eyes, but they had lost some of their merriment.

"Carolan," he said, coming closer to her, "I would like to tell you what I have told no one else. Will you listen to me?"

"Of course."

"I want to give you a brief outline of my life. I am wicked; I am a criminal; I am unworthy to be called your friend. That is the truth, but I would have you know how it is I have sunk so low. Perhaps, later on when I am a rich, safe man, I shall call upon you and your husband in your happy home. I

230

should like to do that, Carolan. I should like to see if you are happy. The parson will accept me because he will not know the secrets of my past, and his wife will accept me because, I hope, she will understand why I took to such evil ways. That will warm my heart, Carolan if *she* will understand."

Carolan was silent, her heart beating rapidly. She was realising now how fervently she had hoped he would deny all knowledge of the purse.

"I must make it brief, Carolan. But you must understand that I cannot convey everything in the short time I have. You must see beyond my words. You must visualise a happy childhood; you must see everything that was mine. A good home, tender parents, an excellent education . . . right up to the time I was fourteen. Then my father died. My mother was a dear woman, a tender woman, but an unwise woman. A year after my father's death, she sought to replace him. My stepfather? Ah! What stories I could tell you of that man! But I waste my words. Suffice it that, in less than a year after that disastrous marriage, my mother was dead. Her money was his; I had nothing. He had arranged it so. Sometimes I think he arranged her death. That sounds melodramatic, Carolan, but it is nevertheless true. I was alone; I was penniless. I stole some money from my stepfather and came to London. What dreams I had! You can well imagine what they were. I would make a fortune at the gaming-table, for were there not fortunes to be made in London! I will not harass you with my adventures; perhaps one day, in the secure, rich times ahead I may tell you. I will not tell you how I sank and sank. There is a life here in this great city of which I hope you will never know. I shall not tell you. Have you ever heard of a thieves' kitchen, Carolan? It is a place . . . they abound here . . . where one is taught to pick pockets. These hands of mine— sensitive, are they not? Once they were to have been a musician's hands; now they are pickers of pockets. They learned well. Ah! I was as apt a pupil with a pocket as I ever was with the spinet. I was caught, Carolan." He paused to smile at her. He laid his hands on her shoulders. "Why, you tremble, child! I am safe now; I am not such a fool as I was . . . I shall not again be so easily caught. I am too wily now. The memory of that is too strong within me. You thought I was thirty, Carolan, and I am barely twenty-four. You see the lines about my face, do you not? That is what transportation does to you, Carolan. That is what stifling in the stinking hold of a convict ship for months on end does for you, Carolan. Oh, Carolan . . . Carolan, see me as I might have been had my father lived.

231

A happy youth . . . for twenty-four is not so very old. A young man of substance, a fit companion for you, Carolan. And see me now . . . see me now. See me as I should have been . . . not as life has made me!"

Her eyes were swimming with tears.

"You have suffered very much, Marcus. And I have hurt you; I am so stupid, so ignorant! There is so much I do not know."

"And never shall know! I am sorry I had to speak of these things to you, Carolan. I would have it that you never knew of their existence."

"Life is very cruel to some, Marcus."

"It is also kind."

"You can say that?"

"I can say it now, because I see that though I have told you so little, you have seen beyond my words. I see that when I come to that happy parsonage home I shall be welcomed in like an old friend."

"You will," said Carolan. "You will! But, Marcus, this is folly surely! To go on with this . . . after that . . ."

His eyes lit up.

"The risk! The excitement! The adventure! And the hope, of course, that one day . . . one day . . . I shall settle down to security; that is when my eyes are not so sharp and my hands not so quick. Tonight you have made me wonder if that day is not approaching!"

"Marcus, how I wish I could do something! Words are such inadequate things; it is easy to talk sympathy . . . but I feel it, Marcus, I feel it."

"You are right when you say words are inadequate; there can be so much behind them . . . or just nothing at all. If! What a word! *If* my father had not died! *If* I had been an honest man, and *if* you had not been engaged to marry a parson. Ah, Carolan! What a word it is!"

He had moved closer to her, and his eyes were brilliant.

"Oh, come!" she said coldly, for she was a little afraid of that passion in him. "I know you well, Marcus; you have had many adventures of all kinds. You seek adventure right and left; at Vauxhall Gardens and here in my father's shop among these musty old coats. Do not think I cannot understand."

His hands hung at his sides, and a smile turned up the corners of his mouth.

"An adventurer! That is what you think of me, eh?"

232

"I fear so, Marcus. What would happen to you if they found the purse in your possession?"

He made a gesture to indicate the tying of a rope about his neck. "Or," he added, "I might be sent back to Botany Bay."

"Marcus, you have suffered a good deal. You would prefer the hanging?"

"Never! Life is sweet; it is only those who have been in danger of losing it who know how sweet. Carolan, but now you know this, what now?"

"I cannot say. But of one thing I am certain; you must give this up. If you were caught, Marcus, if you were caught . . ."

"You would care so much?"

"One does not like to think of a friend with a noose about his neck!"

"You still think of me as a friend?"

"What rubbish you talk!"

"Carolan, I shall always remember."

"And you will not . . . run these risks?"

"I will think on it very seriously."

"You have some money?"

"A little."

"It is cheap, living in the country. You could work."

He looked down at his hands, and grimaced.

"Ah!" he said. "A little cottage under the shadow of the parsonage! A pretty picture, that. Perhaps your children will look over my garden wall and talk to me as I work in my garden. Perhaps there will be one very like you, Carolan."

"I think you do not take this very seriously."

"It is a mistake to take life seriously. Is it not by laughing at things serious that we render them ridiculous?"

"I wish you had not lied about the handkerchief you stole from me."

"I . . . lied?"

"You said it was the first offence."

"Indeed it was!"

"And the purse? And the many, many others?"

"Those were stolen from society, a society which is rotten and decayed, a society which made me what I am. The handkerchief was stolen from you."

"Then you are sorry for having stolen it?"

"I could wish that you had given it."

"You anger me, Marcus. You are no fool; surely there are ways in which you could earn a living!"

233

"A man who returns from Botany Bay has not much chance, Carolan."

"But surely, having taken your punishment . . ."

He smiled at her wistfully.

"Carolan, one day I shall tell you the story of my life. It will run into many chapters."

"I shall look forward to hearing it. I want to understand. But in the meantime you frighten me . . . What if . . ."

"Never fear, Carolan! I shall not be caught; I am too old a hand! It is not the hardened sinner who is most frequently caught, believe me!"

She shivered, and he went on softly: "Carolan, it is sweet to see you so concerned for me. I could almost be glad I am what I am, to so earn your sweet sympathy."

She stamped her foot.

"How foolish you are! How ridiculous! I dislike that exaggerated talk, those honeyed compliments. You are glad you are a thief so that I can be sorry for you! I assure you I am not . . . not in the least, when you talk in that strain!"

"Now I adore you! Why is it that an angry woman can be so enchanting . . . if she is beautiful? Of course an ugly angry woman is a vile object, but if she be beautiful . . . *If* again, you see . . . that little word!"

Carolan turned away, tears smarting in her eyes. She felt weary and depressed.

"Why did you come here tonight?" she demanded. "To see my father?"

"When I come here," he said slowly, "it is always in the hope of seeing you."

"I believe I hear his footsteps. He is coming up from below."

"Carolan . . ." He caught her hand and looked at her pleadingly. "Let me tell you more fully, Carolan. Let me explain everything. There are terrible things I could tell you, Carolan."

"Oh, Marcus!" Her lips trembled. "Marcus, I will do everything I can to help you. Please, you must believe that, Marcus."

"I will believe it, Carolan. I will carry the memory of this moment with me to the grave."

"And you will promise . . . ?"

"I will explain."

"But I *must* have your promise. Marcus, be careful. What if you were caught again?"

"I will explain. Tomorrow we must meet, Carolan. Quick

. . . where shall it be? Tomorrow afternoon at three? I will be waiting outside the shop. I shall take you somewhere quiet, and we will talk. For there is much I must say to you . . ."

"Here is my father," she said, and went towards him. "Father, here is Marcus to see you."

She ran to her room; she was trembling. She threw herself on to the bed; she shut her eyes, but she could not shut out the face of Marcus. I should have nothing to do with him, she told herself. He is a thief, a convict! He should not be in my father's house. But I must help him—I must!

She spoke into her pillow.

"You would see that, Everard, you who are so good. That is what our life together will be, Everard; helping others, will it not? *That* is religion . . . not the beautiful sermons you will preach, not the prayers you will say. . . It is helping others, Everard."

How she longed for a sight of his calm and beautiful face! How she longed to tell him the story of Marcus!

It was wonderful what comfort, what hope the thought of Everard could bring.

She slept, and dreamed of a country parsonage, and Marcus was there and she was leaning over the wall of a cottage garden. Distinctly she saw his long tapering fingers curled about a garden spade.

The shop door bell tinkled. Carolan said to Millie: "I will go."

She had an idea it was Marcus. He had agreed to meet her at three that afternoon, and it was only eleven of the morning, but her thoughts were full of him. She was glad her father was out; he had gone off early that morning, having most urgent business, he said. Kitty was still a-bed. And Millie did not count; she was humming to herself while washing the dishes in the kitchen.

Carolan hastened through the door which led into the shop. It was not Marcus standing there, but Jonathan Crew.

"Good morning," he said. "I was passing . . ."

"Good morning! It was good of you to call. Will you drink a cup of chocolate? Mamma is not yet up."

He said: "A cup of chocolate sounds most inviting."

"Then come in, do! And I will make it."

Millie put her head round the door, her lips formed into a round O of alarm, but when she saw who the visitor was, the O became a smile. Poor Millie was always afraid her father would come for her and take her back with him. The attic with the sloping ceiling, and the tiny window, which she occupied, was paradise to Millie.

"Here is Mr. Crew, Millie," said Carolan, "come to drink a cup of chocolate."

"Oh," said Millie, "I will make it, Miss Carolan."

There was nothing she would not do for Miss Carolan, for it was she who had given her that paradise under the roof up there, Millie knew. There were those who called her silly, but Millie knew.

"I can make it, Millie," said Carolan. She was disappointed, in no mood for light conversation. She had hoped to see Marcus, to hear more of his strange story.

Through the kitchen doorway she could see Jonathan Crew; he was leaning back in his chair, his eyes closed as though he were very, very tired. She thought his clerkship on the wharf must be an exacting job. He often looked tired and . . . what was it? . . . lifeless, lacking in vitality. But was that because she had unconsciously compared him with Marcus? Marcus was full of life; he was born rogue, for whatever had driven him to the perilous life he lived, he enjoyed it, she was sure. Why did she have to like Marcus so much? A thief, a rogue and an ex-convict. And Jonathan, who was a steady clerk, a kind and sympathetic man, she did not really like.

She carried the tray into the parlour, and set it on the table.

"Ah!" said Jonathan. "This is very pleasant."

She handed him the cup, and he lifted his eyes to hers. It seemed to her then that there was something behind those eyes . . . something that was trying to break through, and perhaps was being stopped from breaking through. She could swear he was excited.

"Would you like me to tell Mamma that you are here?" she asked.

"No, no!" He spoke so eagerly that she thought then that he had come to ask her to marry him. She could think of nothing else to account for that excitement, that eagerness to speak to her alone.

"She will be sorry to have missed you. Do you know, this is the first time you have visited us in the morning?"

"My work usually engages me in the mornings."

"It must be very tiring work, and bad for the eyes."

"Do you know, I did not sleep at all last night!"

Now she was sure it was going to be a declaration. Why else should he have that air of suppressed excitement?

"No," he went on, "I could not sleep. I was thinking of . . . that poor young man."

She breathed a deep sigh of relief. It was good of him to have such sympathy. "Yes," she said, "I thought of him too."

"I cannot understand it; it seems so short-sighted of him. Is he completely unaware of the risks he runs?"

"He is not unaware."

"Ah! You have spoken to him!"

She did not want to talk of it, but how could she help it when he spoke so sympathetically, so earnestly, and she, impetuously, had already given away the fact that she had spoken to Marcus!

"Yes," she said, "I have seen him!"

"And taxed him . . . with that?"

"Well . . ."

He did not pursue the question. He said, as though talking to himself: "I would help him. If he had a good job . . . well, a moderately good job . . . would not that help him to . . . to be honest? I mean, there is a vacancy in my office. Perhaps if I put in a word . . . What do you think?"

Carolan turned to him with shining eyes.

"Oh! That is good of you! I am sure he would be so grateful. I know that it is just because of what happened to him that he has found it difficult. Do you think you could . . ."

Jonathan leaned forward in his chair. Then he sat back and thoughtfully stirred his chocolate.

"I suppose," he said very slowly, "he has not been in any sort of trouble before?" He lifted his eyes and saw the hot flush run from the lace at her neck to her creamy forehead. He saw the disappointment in her eyes.

"Well," she said reluctantly, "there was some trouble."

"Newgate?" he questioned. "That is where that sort of trouble leads."

"And more . . ." she began.

"He was not transported! You must tell me this, because it adds a complication; but perhaps we can get over it."

She nodded. "Does it matter so much?" she asked earnestly.

"It matters a great deal!"

"You do not think they will engage him? Is it necessary to tell them?"

He was weighing up the situation carefully. "It is a responsibility to introduce a thief into a respectable business."

"I believe we could trust Marcus."

"I wonder. Once a thief . . . I only thought that if that was his first offense . . ."

"But . . . could you not explain to your master? Perhaps he

237

would be willing to help. If you knew the whole story, you would realise as I do that Marcus would be saved."

"You know his story then."

"He told me last night. He came here to see me. I . . . I told him outright what we had seen."

"You mentioned me?"

"I . . . I don't think I did."

"That is well. It would have embarrassed us both."

"He told me a little," she said, "about losing his money and coming to London, and falling in with terrible people, and then being caught and sent to Newgate and Botany Bay. He says that, if I meet him outside the shop at three o'clock today, he will tell me more."

"When you meet him, do not speak of our conversation. I would prefer to make sure that I can help before telling him so."

She seized his hand and looked into his eyes. Why had she thought them cold?

"You are so good!"

"I am trying to do something worth while, that is all."

"I shall always be grateful to you."

"But if I am unable to help him?"

"Then I shall remember that you tried."

"Do not tell him of this at three o'clock, remember."

"Of course I will not."

He stood up and laid his cup upon the table.

"No," he said slowly, "of course you will not."

He walked to the door.

"Thank you," said Carolan. She stood at the door, watching him go up the street. He did not look back; he was so intent upon his thoughts. A good man! He trod softly, like a cat, but that was because he had to work all day in a dark office; and he probably walked quietly in order not to disturb his superiors.

"I have misjudged him somewhat," said Carolan to herself. She would be careful not to mention this to Marcus, for it was a secret and she must guard her tongue. Impetuosity was a grave fault of hers; and so eager would she be to impart good news!

Poor Marcus! How wonderful if she could do this for him, put him on the right road before Everard came for her! Then she would know there was some meaning in life. All she had endured at Haredon would have led her to the saving of Marcus. It would be like a pattern; it would give her a great faith in life and living.

In spite of her cultivation of serenity, she was full of eager excitement as the hands of the grandfather clock crept up from the half-hour to three o'clock. On the stroke of three she opened the door and looked out into the street. There was no sign of Marcus. She stood there at the open door while the clock ticked away the minutes. Ten minutes past three! Fifteen minutes past! Twenty minutes past! And at half past he had still not come!

Kitty peeped round the door of Carolan's room.

"Ah! Not ready yet? I declare you take longer than I do."

Carolan turned from the mirror, before which she had been sitting for the last ten minutes, without being aware of what she saw there. She had fallen into a reverie from which her mother's knock at the door had aroused her.

"I am ready, Mamma!"

"I am glad to hear it. I should hate not to arrive for the start." Kitty sat on the bed and eyed her daughter appraisingly. "You look very charming, my child. And how does it feel to be going to the play—the real play—for the first time in your life?"

"Very exciting," said Carolan.

"We have good seats, and the carriage will be here at any moment. I could wish that we had another gentleman escort. Mamma, papa, and the young daughter! It is not quite as exciting as it might be. What do you think?"

"I like it very well," said Carolan.

"And what," demanded Kitty, "has become of friend Marcus these last days, I should like to know?"

Carolan would have liked to know too, but she was silent, for she could very well guess. He had left the Grape Street area. Had she not gone to the rooms he occupied, and boldly asked for him! A slut with hair that hung about her shoulders, like black snakes, and a coarse mouth, had whispered that she did not know what had become of her lodger. He had been there, and he had gone . . . disappeared, owing a week's rent. Tenants did not usually owe just one week's rent; they more likely owed ten, for such was what a poor honest woman had to put up with. He had left in a great hurry, indeed he had, and if the lady were a friend of his, could she see her way to paying a poor woman who needed it, that one week's rent? Carolan explained that she had no money, and with that was quickly made to understand that her presence in the lodging-house was redundant.

Yes, it was only too obvious to Carolan what had happened

239

to Marcus. He had no intention of giving up his life of crime. He was probably under suspicion, so he had moved to a fresh district. There was no real good in him. He was a thief and a liar. Perhaps the story he had told her had had no truth in it. But he had charmed her oddly; but then, the perfidious often had the power to charm. She would forget him as soon as she could. But often during that week she had dreamed of his calling out to her because he was in trouble, and once she dreamed that she saw him on the platform outside Newgate prison, and that the hangman was putting the rope about his neck.

If only she could have seen him once, have told him that Jonathan Crew was going to give him a chance! She had seen Jonathan only once in the past week; that was the day after Marcus had failed to keep his appointment.

"You have no idea what can have happened to him?" asked Jonathan.

"I can guess."

"Ah! A life of crime can only lead to one end, Miss Carolan." She had lost her temper then.

"Oh, it is easy for you to talk! How can you know what he had suffered, what temptations came in his way?"

"You are too sympathetic towards the rogue, Miss Carolan; too sympathetic by a long way."

She had felt really angry until she remembered all he had tried to do for Marcus, then her anger vanished as quickly as it had come.

"Perhaps you will see him again one day," said Jonathan.

She shook her head.

"Very soon I shall be leaving here. My affianced husband is coming for me very soon."

Then Kitty had come in and had chatted brightly about the play which Darrell had promised them they should see. And now here they were, ready to set out for it.

"Now, tell me how I look," said Kitty, turning round and about to show her gown.

"You look very lovely," said Carolan. "And what a handsome brooch!"

Kitty dimpled and put a finger to her lips.

"Does it not match the blue of my gown?"

"Admirably, Mamma, I have not seen it before."

"Indeed you have not! And I still have to get your father's permission to wear it."

"Ah! You have taken it from his stock of valuables!"

"This afternoon, while he was out, I found he had left the

key of his precious storeroom behind. My dear, this gown called out for an ornament. The neck does not fit with that elegance with which it should. An ornament to hold it in position was a necessity; but it had to be the right ornament. So into the storeroom I went, and in a case there I found this brooch. Now, tell me, is it not the very thing?"

"Indeed it is! And how it sparkles! It is a sapphire . . . or so near it that it might be taken for one. Mamma, you will be a grand lady tonight! Listen! Is that the shop bell?"

"I do believe it is!" Kitty's eyes were twinkling wickedly. "Now, who in the world . . ."

They were silent, listening. Carolan went to the door and looked out on to the landing. She could hear a rumble of voices below.

"Your father is down there," said Kitty, "so we need not worry ourselves. Come! Put on your cloak. Let me see how you look. My dear, how glad I am that you can wear that shade of green! So few can, but on you it is mightily becoming."

Millie was coming up the stairs.

"Millie!" called Carolan. "Millie . . . just a moment, Millie."

Millie came in. Her lips sagged open at the sight of the grandeur of their costumes.

"Millie," said Carolan, "who is down there?"

"It is Mr. Crew."

Carolan looked at Kitty, and saw the demure expression, the downcast eyes.

"Oh, Mamma, did you tell him we were going to the play?"

Kitty went to her dressing-table and peeped slyly at her reflection in the mirror.

"I may have mentioned it."

"A mention which was an invitation, I expect!"

Kitty said: "Listen! Is that the carriage! I declare, we are doing things in style tonight. Millie, you had better go and open the door."

Without a word Millie went.

They heard a scream from below, Millie's scream. Carolan went to the door and listened.

"I do hope the girl hasn't fallen down and broken her leg," said Kitty. "It would be very inconvenient."

Carolan started downstairs. There was the sound of raised voices now, a scuffling, the noise of heavy furniture being overturned.

She rushed into the shop parlour, from whence the noises

241

came. Her father was lying on the floor and Jonathan Crew was kneeling on him with his hands about his throat.

"Father!" shrieked Carolan, and ran to him.

"Keep off!" shouted Jonathan Crew.

Carolan flew at him; it was like a crazy nightmare, for she knew suddenly that she hated Jonathan Crew and always had distrusted him without realising it.

Her father's eyes were on her; they looked too large and protruding, unlike his eyes. His lips said: "Carolan . . . Carolan."

With a slight movement of his arm, Jonathan Crew threw Carolan off; she fell, striking her head against the table, and the blow had the effect of stunning her slightly so that the room whirled round and the sounds in it were confused.

Darrell was lying very still on the floor. Jonathan Crew got slowly to his feet. His eyes were now on Kitty, who was standing there, ashen-faced and trembling. There was a hammering on the shop door.

Jonathan Crew went to Kitty; he dragged her into the room. Roughly he seized Carolan and in a second he had them handcuffed to each other.

"In the name of the law," said Jonathan Crew, "I arrest you on a charge of receiving stolen goods."

Kitty screamed: "Darrell . . . Darrell . . . my love! What has he done to you?"

Jonathan Crew had turned from them and seized the frightened Millie. He pushed her towards Carolan and Kitty. Then he touched Darrell with his foot.

"He is dead, I fear," he said.

"Then *you* killed him!" cried Carolan passionately. And she knew that he had waited long for this moment, had planned it, had thought of nothing but it ever since he had first met her in the street.

"He tried to resist arrest," said Jonathan Crew coldly.

Carolan stared down at her father's mis-shapen hands, now still, lifeless. He would never look at them again; he would never reach that peaceful country home for which he had schemed and longed.

Kitty said in a surprisingly cool voice: "It was blood-money you were after then, you rogue! You pig!" And great hot tears rolled down her cheeks, tears of sorrow and humiliation. "My love!" she moaned. "What will become of us now?"

Carolan was not thinking of the future but of the past. Words rushed into her mind, words that evil man had spoken; she began to tremble, for now she was seeing clearly what had led to this. *She* had brought her parents into this. *She* was responsible for the death of her father, for the betrayal of Marcus—for now she knew without a doubt what had happened to Marcus; and she wished, in that moment, that it was she who lay dead on the floor in place of her father.

Jonathan Crew opened the door and two men came in.

"Here are the prisoners," he said, and they were taken out to the waiting van.

Oh, why had she not fought him as he bent over her father! Why had she not picked up a knife from the table and plunged it into his wicked heart!

He sat opposite her, his eyes alive, amused.

"Ah! How beautifully you played into my hands, Miss Carolan!" he seemed to say, and black misery was in Carolan's heart as the jolting van carried them through the streets of London to Newgate Prison.

Dazed, bruised, with the taste of blood in her mouth, and the permeating, inescapable and foulest of all smells in her nostrils, Carolan lay on the hard platform which was her bed. Around her, women breathed noisily in sleep, snoring, sighing, groaning, muttering, cursing. Carolan lay still, saying over and over to herself: "This has not really happened to me; I shall awake in a minute. Please God, let me wake now!"

Kitty was beside her; Kitty's beautiful hair hanging matted round her face; Kitty's voluptuous body naked beneath her torn cloak; blood on Kitty's face, mingling with tears and dirt. Kitty was not quite conscious now. Carolan could almost say "Lucky Mamma!"

Millie was there, sleeping with her hand curled round Carolan's foot. Millie's clothes hung about her, tattered and torn, for Millie had fought for her clothes, fought and become exhausted; and, like an animal, as soon as she had laid herself on the floor beside Carolan, she had slept. Perhaps Carolan could say "Lucky Millie!"

Carolan tried to raise herself on her arm, but so bruised was she that this proved too painful. There was an itch about her body which was beginning to madden her. She buried her face in her hands to shut out the dark shadows about her, to try to free her nostrils from that sickening smell. Impossible! One could shut one's eyes, but whatever one did, the smell remained. Unclean human bodies, foul air, slop pails, the evil-smelling breath of diseased women.

High up in the wall were two barred windows through which came scarcely any light or air. On the window-sills whale-oil lamps burned. A small child was creeping silently towards Carolan. A little girl? A little boy? She did not know. It was more like a dark little animal . . . or a scarecrow. Tiny hands were feeling for her pockets, very deft hands, and very, very small.

"Go away!" hissed Carolan, and the small figure darted back whence it had come, and was lost to her in a maze of sleeping bodies.

Carolan, remembering what had gone before, began to cry softly. Anger and bitterness were a pain that constricted her throat so that she breathed with difficulty. She would have sobbed with rage, with fury, had she not known that she, and she alone, was responsible for their being here. She it was who had had Millie leave her home and come to live at the shop, and, but for her, poor half-witted Millie would be sleeping in the crowded room with her family and her drunken father; it had seemed horrible enough when Carolan had first heard of it—now it seemed paradise indeed.

I brought Jonathan Crew to the shop! *I* betrayed my own father, my own mother, and poor little Millie. *I* . . . with my folly!

The knowledge of her weakness sustained her; it was rough justice somehow. Folly was as deserving of punishment as crime.

She went over it all, from the moment that odious, that wicked man had slipped the handcuffs on her wrist and had dragged her and her mother, who was half-fainting, into the van which had come to take them to Newgate. She had struggled, she, Carolan, for wild, reckless, impossible thoughts of escape had filled her mind; and one of the men had struck her on the side of her head so that she became semi-conscious for a while, until she was shaken roughly and told to get out.

It was an imposing building that loomed up before her, and she had stepped into the filth of the gutter and been angry because her shoes were splashed. Absurd . . . when Newgate was opening its doors to her! Queer things one noticed in moments of distress; she remembered the French cap of Liberty and the overflowing horn of Plenty. Queer things to see at Newgate's door; like a horrible joke! And then the design over the porch, of fetters and chains, explaining maliciously that the joke was done with. Newgate did not look out on the street; the windows showed only her narrow, filthy court-yards, as though she were ashamed that the world might look beyond her imposing façade and see into her evil soul. And the first thing that rushed to greet one was the stench—that Newgate smell which made one retch in those first moments, and wonder how one could live for an hour in its company.

What courteous treatment they had received from the guards! And why not? thought Carolan in her innocence. Their guilt was not proved. They were no criminals.

How anger had surged up in Carolan then! Jonathan Crew, that sly murderer, should hang by the neck. She would appeal to the squire, to Everard. And these people should see that gentlefolk could not be clapped into prison in this manner!

But the courteous treatment of the guards was dispensed with when it was found they had no money.

"Receivers of stolen goods," wrote the turnkey slowly and laboriously, in the book of records. Carolan protested, but a man with a horrible, blue-tinged face and ugly red hands leered at her, and told her to be silent while their irons were adjusted.

"Triple irons," said the guard, and then resentfully: "Ladies and gents buys off their irons . . . all, barring the one lot. One lot of irons is comfort, ladies, compared with three."

Carolan said stonily: "We have no money for such luxuries!" and the guard murmured, disbelievingly and hopefully, that there were many who came to Mother Newgate protesting their poverty, but the old lady had a way of worming the coin out of their pockets.

They went, clanking their irons, through corridors and down dark staircases, Carolan supporting Kitty on one side, as Millie did on the other. Perhaps it was well that she had Kitty to think of.

Kitty was moaning, crying, not fully aware of what had happened. Poor Mamma! Carolan kept thinking of her at Haredon, sitting by her mirror with Thérèse twittering about her. There is nothing so frightful in this world as poverty, thought Carolan.

But the most horrible moment in that night of horror was when the guard unlocked a door and they were face to face with the companions with whom they were to live in the closest intimacy during their sojourn on the Common Side of Newgate Jail. What were they? thought Carolan in horror. Not people? Not women? They shrieked unintelligibly, like untamed animals. They could not be women . . . not our own species. Their eyes were too dull, too cunning, too lacking in intelligence. Their hair was not like human hair; it hung matted over their faces like the manes of wild animals. Surely these were not human beings! So degraded, so vicious, so cunning, so sly, so lacking in everything that lifted man above the level of the lower animals!

The guard laughed softly, wickedly. He gave all three a push. Kitty first; Millie next; then Carolan.

"There you are, my beauties! New lady friends to join you!"

What a queer silence it had been! Tense and dramatic! Then, from somewhere among that crowd of sub-human creatures there came a wail that was like a battle-cry. One creature, a head taller than the others, came swinging towards the newcomers. She was hideous; she was something Carolan had dreamed of in the days of childhood at Haredon. A nightmare . . . something that lurked in the darkness. She laid filthy hands on Kitty.

"Garnish!" she muttered. "Now, lady, pay up and be cheerful!"

"Listen!" shouted Carolan. "We have no money!"

The woman was pulling at Kitty's cloak; and watching, while a red mist swam before her eyes, Carolan remembered now that as she lay back only partly conscious in the van which had brought them to Newgate, Jonathan Crew had leaned forward and taken the sapphire brooch from her mother's dress.

Kitty screamed. There was the sound of tearing cloth. Carolan tried to get to her, but she was surrounded.

A face close to Carolan's, a face with yellow fangs in a mouth through which came the foulest of breath, chanted "Garnish!" And the rest of them took up the cry till it was like a barbaric chant echoing through the place.

Carolan tried to repeat that if it was money they wanted, neither she nor her mother had any; but she could say nothing. She saw Kitty go down; she fought then as desperately as she could. She hit out at the yellow fangs, and the thing swayed and fell before her. She turned, her eyes blazing, and saw Millie laying about her with a strength that was astounding. For these creatures, these ugly, gaunt things that inhabited this vile underworld, had not much strength left in them; their poor stinking bodies were lacking in vitality. Carolan and Millie were young and strong; it was only Kitty who had gone down before them.

They fell back from Carolan. They were falling back from Millie. There was the big woman, who had started it, facing her now, and she fought but half-heartedly, for her thoughts were with Kitty, that easier victim, who lay on the floor with a crowd round her stripping her of her clothes. But whereas the thought of Kitty weakened her opponent, it strengthened Carolan. She gave the woman a blow which sent her sprawling against the slimy wall; she clutched at it for a moment, then her eyes slewed round to where Kitty lay. She got up and, looking over her shoulder to see if Carolan followed her, she loped over to the crowd round Kitty.

Carolan was there as quickly as she was. Millie came leaping up, her eyes ablaze with the light of battle won, alive as she had never seemed to be before.

"Get away!" cried Carolan. "All of you!"

She seized a woman by the shoulder, and part of a dirty shift came away in her hands. The woman wore nothing but the shift; beneath, her skin was rough with gooseflesh where the dirt allowed it to be seen. Her breasts were full, and it was obvious that she was a nursing mother. Carolan felt sick.

Someone tittered, and in a second the crowd had dispersed, leaving Kitty there, stark naked, her eyes tightly shut, and blood running from her mouth.

Carolan's eyes were blinded with tears of rage. She wondered what she could take off to cover Kitty, for her own garments now hung upon her in ribbons. Millie plucked at her arm and pointed to a corner where a big woman was squatting with Kitty's cloak wrapped round her.

Carolan, too angry to feel any fear, strode over to the woman. Eyes followed her; jeers escaped from the lips of many.

"A fight!" said one. "A fight between Poll and a lady of the quality what's come to stay a while!"

But Poll quailed before the wrath of Carolan. Poll, after a year in Newgate, knew the weakness of her body when matched against one well-fed; when the girl had had a month in the place, she would get the cloak back again; she would half kill her for this night; but in the meantime it would be better to hand over the cloak.

She took it from her shivering body and threw it from her. Carolan picked it up and ran back to Kitty, put the cloak about her, and then, turning away, was violently sick.

She thought of all this as she lay there, and as she was wide awake now, she was fully aware that this was no evil dream. Yesterday this place had been only a name to her; she had

247

heard whispers of its horrors, but had she ever really believed them? Had she ever bothered to enquire what happened to people who were brought here, some of them as innocent as she was herself?

She closed her eyes and saw the face of Marcus clearly. Some time—she did not remember when—he had said to her: "It is a mistake not to be interested in your fellow men!" Was it? she wondered. Was it better to have known nothing of this, so that when ill chance brought her here it should find her bewildered and unprepared? But, she thought, had I known of it I should never have been at peace. I shall never be at peace again, for even if I escape from here I shall always, at a moment's notice, be able to call up this frightful stench and remember Newgate.

She raised herself with an effort and leaned over Kitty. The faint light from a whale-oil lamp on the high window-sill showed her vaguely the outline of Kitty's face.

"Mamma!" she whispered. "Mamma!"

There was no reply. She put her hand on Kitty's heart; it was fluttering feebly.

There was a movement close to her, and turning sharply, filled with suspicion, for it seemed to her that all were her enemies in this evil place, but Kitty and Millie, she saw a shape rise up close beside her. She stared. It was a girl, and all she wore was a bit of rag wound about her like a loin-cloth. The light was dim, but Carolan could see a youthful, shapely outline and a mass of waving hair.

Carolan sprang to her feet with an effort, her fists clenched, anger, which now came so easily, rising within her.

"Please," said a voice that was neither strident nor cruel, but gentle and cultured. "I . . . I would like to talk to you." The girl sat down; there was something so disarming about her that Carolan's suspicions gave way to curiosity.

"What do you want?" she asked ungraciously.

"Only to talk to you. Is . . . she . . . your mother?"

"Yes."

"Poor soul. She is of gentle birth, I see. This must have been horrible . . . horrible . . . for her!"

"Yes," said Carolan and moved closer to the girl. "Have you no clothes?"

"No. They took them. I could not pay garnish. Besides . . ."

"Are you not cold?"

"At first I was very cold; you do not feel it so much after a while."

"How long have you been here?"

"I do not know for certain. As far as I can calculate— about a month."

Carolan shivered. "How do you endure it?"

"God helps me," said the girl. "He gives me wonderful comfort."

"Comfort?" said Carolan.

"Spiritual comfort."

Carolan laughed bitterly. "I will give you more than spiritual comfort. I will give you my petticoat."

The girl did not answer and Carolan moved closer to her.

"Did you hear me say I would give you my petticoat?"

The girl was weeping softly.

Carolan, tactless, impulsive, and ready to suspect all, said harshly: "Now what does this mean? You are happy when you are given comfort which is cold, hunger and other frightful things I have yet to discover, but the offer of a petticoat sets you weeping!"

"Forgive me!" whispered the girl. "It is so long since anyone has been kind."

Now Carolan was ashamed, for she saw that the girl was very frail. She stood up, slipped off her tattered dress and the petticoat beneath.

"There!" she said in an outburst of generosity. "You have the dress; the petticoat will cover me."

"I cannot take either," said the girl.

"You are a fool; you will freeze to death!"

"Yes," said the girl slowly, "in the winter, if I am still here, I shall freeze to death. I shall not be the first."

"You may not be here," said Carolan, her spirits rising through contact with someone more wretched than herself, new strength coming to her at the sight of another's weakness. "There is no point in freezing to death *before* winter!"

The girl put out eager fingers and stroked the petticoat.

"If I had it," she said, "they would have it off me tomorrow. I saw the way you stood up to them; you were magnificent; I cannot tell you how I admired you. You got strength from God."

"No," said Carolan, "from a more reliable ally—anger!"

The girl caught her breath, and folded her arms across her bare breasts. She looked, thought Carolan, like a saint, and felt humbled and feigned anger to hide her shame.

"Now do not be so foolish," she said. "Put on this petticoat at once. And if they try to take it from you tomorrow, they will have me to deal with."

The girl raised her eyes to the oil lamp, and Carolan saw that she was beautiful. "I prayed this day for a miracle," she said. "I believe it has come."

"Rubbish!" said Carolan. "And if you think that my coming with my mother and our poor serving-maid to this hell is a miracle, I can tell you we do not look on it as such. There, are you warmer?"

The girl looked up at her shyly, for Carolan was several inches taller.

"How kind you are!" she said. "It is wicked of me to be glad you have come to this dreadful place, but I cannot help it."

Carolan was happier then than she had been since that nightmare moment when she had stood at the threshold of the shop parlour and seen her father lying on the floor.

"There is not much warmth in that petticoat, I fear," said Carolan.

"There is a good deal of warmth in it. And will you really let me keep it? And will you stop them from taking it from me?"

"I will!" said Carolan. "Sit down beside me."

"I . . . I am unfit to sit too close."

"Come close," commanded Carolan.

"Is there nothing we can do for your mother?"

"What can we do? I would bathe the blood from her face, but there is no water. I would like a little spirit to revive her, but where can I get it?"

"You cannot get these things if you have no money. Have you friends . . . outside?"

Carolan said: "Certainly I have friends—friends who will see that justice is done. But they are far away in the country. I must get a message to them."

"How will you get a message to them without money?"

Carolan said in a frustrated tone: "Do not let us speak of my distressing affairs! Tell me of yours; what is your name?"

"Esther March. What is yours?"

"Carolan Haredon."

"May I call you Carolan?"

"Of course!"

"Why are you here, Carolan?"

"On a false charge," burst out Carolan. "I would not have believed there was such wickedness in the world!"

Esther touched Carolan's shoulders timidly. "Do not despair."

"Despair!" cried Carolan angrily. "How can one but de-

250

spair of this wicked place; in the country it was so different . . ." She stopped. Was it so different? She thought of Jim Bennett, the farm labourer who had stolen a rabbit from Squire Haredon's fields. What had happened to him? She had heard vague talk of fourteen years . . . Transportation of course; there had seemed nothing unusual about that; she had not given the matter a thought. There was a sob in her throat now. "I have been blind," she said. "Blind!" She cried out: "Do not talk of me! Later I will tell you; but now I would hear of you. What brought you here? You stole nothing! You did no crime!"

"It is good of you to believe that, and even before I have said a word."

"I am no fool!" said Carolan, and laughed inwardly at herself, for was she not the biggest, the most easily duped of all fools who had ever led themselves and others to destruction!

"I would like to tell you of myself," said Esther. "It is an ordinary enough little story, I fear. My father was a curate, and we were very, very poor. There were six of us. But he taught me, and when I was sixteen I was given a post as governess in the family of a squire . . . and the squire had a son." She looked down at her hands, and Carolan was aware of the deep shame that beset her. "He . . . made advances . . . which I could not accept, and that made him very angry. I did not know what to do, and I sought the protection of his parents. They did not believe me . . . and when the squire's lady lost a valuable ring she accused me . . . and the ring was found in my room, and I was brought here. But I swear I knew nothing of the ring!"

"But did you not explain?"

"The ring was found in my room."

"She put it there—that wicked mother of a wicked son! Oh, how I hate this world!"

"Whom the Lord loveth. He chasteneth. We must bear our sufferings with fortitude. That is what my father used to say. They were sent us for a purpose. We must be meek, for it is the meek who inherit the earth."

"That is a doctrine I will never accept. I will tell you something; I am going to marry a man who is a parson."

"Oh!" Esther exclaimed with delight. "I am glad . . . Carolan."

"But," said Carolan, "there are matters on which we cannot agree. I do not think we should accept our sufferings and the suffering of others. Everard and I almost quarrelled about that. He said I was headstrong, illogical. He believes that people should be contented with their lot in life because that lot has fallen to them through God's will. I do not! I never will!"

"Godliness," said Esther, "is humility!"

"Then I'll have none of it!" cried Carolan. "When I think of what has happened to me . . . and my poor darling Mamma . . . and Millie there . . . and what has happened to you, I want to set faggots in this place, and pour oil on them, and I want to see this evil place go up in smoke. And yes . . . I would throw Jonathan Crew, who betrayed my father, into the flames . . . and with him your wicked squire's son and his mother . . ."

"Ah, Carolan, you must not say such things, for truly it is the will of God that we are here."

"Since you are obviously a saint, you had better steer clear of me!" said Carolan.

"I love the fire in you. It warms me. And I am so cold, so lonely and so frightened! I am wicked too, for I have had more comfort from your presence than from my prayers. There! That shows how wicked I am, does it not? Are you crying too? We must not cry, Carolan. This is our cross, and we must bear it. You see, I who have been so wretched these last weeks—and it is the loneliness that makes you wretched, Carolan—have had my prayers answered. I have now a friend, someone who talks to me, listens to me, who doesn't laugh at me, who does not pinch me and kick me and scratch me, who gives me clothes to cover me."

"Why did they take your clothes . . . all your clothes?" demanded Carolan. "The others have some rags to cover them."

"When I came in," said Esther, "they cried at me, as they do to all. 'Garnish!' I had no garnish, I had nothing . . . nothing but the clothes in which I stood. What could I do, therefore? They tore them from me as they did from your mother. But they left me my shift. And that night I knelt down and prayed, because my father has always said to me, 'Never mind where you are, whatever you are doing, you must always kneel down and say your prayers.' I always had; and I did. And as I prayed they crept closer to me. Carolan, I am so feeble; I have no godliness in me, though I try to be good like my father. I knelt over there; you see, near the sill there. Through my closed lids I was aware of the flickering light from the whale-oil lamp, and, Carolan, I tried so hard to go on with my prayers and not notice them. But I was afraid; I was more afraid than I had ever been before in the whole of my life. I could feel them creeping up to me; I did not know what they would do to me. I could smell their mingled breaths very close to me, and it was horrible, horrible, Carolan. You who are so brave could have no idea. Closer, they came; they were all round me; then one of them laughed. It was terrible laughter, Carolan. I trembled; I stopped praying; I covered my face with my hands, for I knew the most terrible moment I had ever known was upon me. There I knelt in my shift, saying under my breath, as my father had taught me, 'Courage, O Lord; give me courage!' Then they started." She stopped, and covered her face with her hands; she began to sob.

"Silence there!" snarled a drunken voice in the darkness.

Carolan whispered: "Don't cry! Don't think of it—telling it brings it back."

"But I want to talk to you. I have talked to no one for weeks, and the silence is more than I can bear. I must tell you what I had to suffer here; I must make you understand why I could not be brave. I did not kneel again, after that night. I prayed silently. You see, Carolan, I denied my God. That's why He had forgotten me."

Carolan said: "When I was little, my half-sister and I used to go to the curate for Bible lessons; he was the curate to the father of the man I am going to marry. I never listened to those lessons; my cousin Margaret did though."

"Poor Carolan, then you have been denied the comfort of God."

"I," said Carolan, "would rather rely on the comfort of my own ability to stand up to these beasts! Tell me more, if it does not distress you too much."

"They jeered at me, Carolan. That was not all; they . . . took my shift, and when I stood before them in terrible shame, they laughed at me. They touched me, Carolan . . . They did obscene things to me, Carolan. They said things that were coarse and horrible; I cannot talk of them; I cannot tell you. And next night I . . . did not kneel and pray. They would not give me any clothes to cover me. I have found pieces of old rag and tied them about me, and worn them for a day or so . . . perhaps longer . . . until they notice and remember, and then the rags have been torn off me . . ."

"If you have been here a month, you cannot surely stay much longer. You will have to stand for trial surely."

"Some day, I suppose; I do not know when."

"How can people be so cruel, one to another! Do you know?"

"I do not, Carolan. But I believe that when life gets too bad something happens to help you along. Today I had felt so weary, so tired, so cold, so hungry; and I have thought of the winter coming on, and I have said to myself: 'I cannot bear it. If I could find some means of ending my life, how gladly would I take it!' And then, just as I thought these wicked thoughts, the door opened and you came in, and your courage and the way you held your head made me ashamed of myself."

Carolan said: "There must be some way of getting a message to my friends!"

"You need money. All the time in Newgate you need money. They say that a stay in Newgate is not too unpleasant if you have money. Money will buy you a separate room, food, coals, candles. Without money you get your pennyworth of bread each day, and water from the pump to drink. That is how things are here on the Common Side."

"Something will be done!" said Carolan. "I will see to it. Somehow I will get a message out. Why . . . there is Everard! He will surely come for me. There is the squire; when he hears where I am, he will not tolerate that for a day. He has money; he has influence; and so has Everard. They will come for me. I know they will! And listen, Esther. This I swear. I will not leave this place unless you come with me. You are innocent, more innocent than I, for I was a fool, and folly must be paid for. I shall not let them keep you here . . . !"

Carolan broke off. Esther was kneeling now, with her eyes tightly shut, and the palms of her hands pressed together. Through her closed lids tears trickled down her cheeks. Her lips were moving. "I thank thee, O Lord!" And Carolan knew that till the end of her days she would remember that scene, the sleeping bodies around her, the wail of a hungry child, the dismal gloom, the hateful stench . . . and the kneeling girl, offering thanks to her God.

Carolan could not define her feelings; she was too worn out to cry; she was angry; she was moved; she was full of exaltation, for she was going to help this Esther, as a little while ago she had planned to help her parents; she was, too, full of sorrow and misgivings.

Esther's hands fell to her sides; her face, in the light from the lamp, looked radiant.

"How old are you, Esther?" asked Carolan.

"Sixteen."

"My poor child!" said Carolan. "I am seventeen."

"We are much of an age then," said Esther shyly.

"Yes, but I am older. I am going to try to sleep now. Can you?"

254

"May I stay near you?"

"Of course. You will join us now, Esther, will you not? We are all friends?"

Esther settled down beside them, and both girls lay for a long time, eyes open, staring at the grim walls enclosing them.

"Esther," said Carolan, "you must not cry so much."

"No. I have not cried so much until tonight."

"You must not cry! You must not cry!" said Carolan, and silently wept.

Morning came, exposing fresh horrors. Now it was possible to see more clearly the depraved faces of those about her. Carolan kept thinking: I shall wake up. We went to the play last night. This is a nightmare. I shall wake up in my bed.

But she could not go on indefinitely thinking it was a dream. Soon that other life, the serene, happy, free life would seem the dream, and this horror the reality.

Kitty was sick that morning, and the irons cut into her flesh; she cried with the pain. She was not sure where they were yet, and Carolan was glad of this.

"Carolan, how my back hurts! It's bruised. This bed is so hard. Carolan, where are we? There is something horrible near me . . . something dead; I smell it."

Carolan sent Millie for water, and Millie got it . . . with Esther's help. Kitty drank, and Carolan bathed her face and then Kitty fell into a deep but troubled sleep.

"She will recover," said Esther. "She is healthy . . . that much I see. She has had enough to eat; it is those who come in starving, who are quickly starved to death. I wish we could loosen those irons; they are too tight. See how the flesh is swollen . . ."

"What can I do about that?" demanded Carolan. "Cannot the irons be taken off? There is no fear of Mamma's trying to escape."

"They could be *bought* off . . . all save one."

An assistant keeper came in; he was carrying ale and bread which he had bought for a prisoner who had had a little money sent in to her.

Carolan went to him.

"My mother's irons must be removed. Otherwise I fear there will be trouble."

Bleary eyes studied her. Her clothes were good. "One set 'as to remain," said the man, "but . . ."

"Money, I suppose!" said Carolan. "Then I have none. You will do this for the sake of decency!"

He chortled.

"Decency, eh?" He scratched his head. "Now I can't say as how I've heard of irons being struck off for decency. Money's the only thing that'll strike off irons, my lady. And then the one must be left. Fair's fair . . . that's what we say in Newgate. One pair has to stay on."

"I will get money . . . somewhere!" said Carolan.

But the man was no longer interested; he had passed on.

"I cannot endure this!" cried Carolan, returning to her mother.

"She still sleeps," said Esther. "And look! She is smiling in her sleep. That means good dreams."

Carolan said angrily: "I will not stay here! I will get out! But shall I? How do I know? Everything I have done since I have been in this accursed city has made trouble. I am more likely to lead you into trouble than get you out of it. Millie! Why don't you reproach me? I brought you into this. You . . . my mother . . . my father . . . myself! It was my folly. I do not think I shall ever get out. I shall stay here for the rest of my days . . . for I am a fool . . . a crazy fool who not only brings trouble on herself, but on all those around her!"

Millie stared, open-mouthed. Esther sought to comfort her, and Esther could do that, for when Carolan looked through her tears at the sweet face of the girl, so pale and thin, she wondered how she could speak of her misfortune when before her was the greater one of Esther.

The day began to wear on. Now the door was unlocked, and the prisoners had the use of one of the yards. The scene was more sordid by daylight than it had been by the light of the whale-oil lamps. The faces of the women were more clearly seen, and in consequence more horrible. But already Carolan was not feeling the horror of the place so acutely; her eyes had grown accustomed to the sight of vermin; her ears to the obscenity of the conversation in which these creatures seemed to find some relief from their misery; she did not feel now that the smell of the place would make her retch. She had learned that the feeling one may have for a fellow being is in some strange way a more precious thing than it would otherwise have been, if that friendship is nurtured in misery shared. She was drawn to Esther more than she had ever been drawn to anyone in so short a time. Esther was so weak, and that pioneer spirit in Carolan, that leadership which was so essentially a part of her character, was stimulated.

Carolan found that she could not eat the bread that was given her. Esther ate hers ravenously; so did Millie. Millie was like an animal, adaptable, accepting the cruelty of life as her natural due.

"You must eat," said Esther.

"I cannot!" said Carolan. "It is filthy stuff."

"It is all we shall get. Only those who have money can eat better food."

"I would rather starve than eat that."

"Save it," said Esther. "You will be glad of it later."

"It will be crawling with maggots by that time. You and Millie eat it between you."

Millie's eyes glistened hungrily; Esther tried to prevent hers from doing the same; and Carolan broke the loaf in two and gave them half each. She felt rather sick to see the eagerness with which they consumed the mouldy stuff.

Kitty stirred. She murmured,

"Carolan, is that you? Don't draw the curtains . . . How my head aches! I will have my chocolate now."

Carolan bent over her.

"Mamma . . . you are not at home now."

Kitty opened her eyes very wide. Memory came back. She tried to raise herself.

"Carolan, what is this . . . ? Why, Carolan . . ."

Kitty had raised her head and was looking about her.

"Oh . . ." she said. "I . . . remember . . ."

"We are in Newgate, Mamma. You remember what happened last night?"

"Darrell . . ." said Kitty, and began to cry.

"Mamma, Mamma, you must have courage. We will get out of here. Then we will avenge him! I will get a message out to Everard and . . . the squire . . . We shall get out, never fear!"

Kitty said: "My darling, of course we shall get out. But . . . your father . . . Oh, Carolan, I cannot bear it! I cannot bear it! That man . . . that vile beast . . . and I thought . . . and it was my folly. . . ."

"Listen, Mamma! We were foolish, all of us. We are paying for our folly now. Let us not look back. My father would not have wanted us to do that."

There was no comforting Kitty. She wept bitterly and her sorrow was great, for she did not even notice that her clothes were torn and her body bruised, though now and then her hand, as though unconsciously, strayed down to where the irons cut into her flesh.

Esther whispered: "Poor, lovely lady! How unhappy she is! And you see, her sorrow for her husband wipes out all other pain. She does not feel her own sickness; she does not feel the pain that iron is giving her; she only feels one sorrow, and that is the loss of her husband. That is proof of the goodness of God."

Carolan, sick with grief like a wounded animal, spoke sharply to the girl.

"Do not talk to me of God! What have any one of us done that we should suffer in this way! That is what I should like to know!"

"Hush!" said Esther. "Oh, hush!" And she looked so calm, so serene, that it was Carolan's turn to be comforted. Carolan had physical strength; Esther had spiritual strength. They could lean on each other; they had much to give, and much to take.

With the passing of the day their spirits rose a little. Kitty's natural optimism was fighting its way to the surface. This, she said, was not the sort of thing that could happen to people like them. What had they done to deserve it? The thing to do was to get a message through to Squire Haredon and Everard Orland. She tried to walk out into the yard with the young people, but she walked painfully and each step made the irons cut more severely into her leg. She was horrified at the discoloration which was already beginning to show itself.

"They must be removed at once," she said.

"As soon as we can get some money they shall be," Carolan assured her.

Kitty pointed out her grievance to one of the guards, showing him her swollen ankle. Queer, thought Carolan, how natural the role of coquette came to Kitty; she would play it even in her moments of direst misery. But the man was dour; he shook his head. Irons could be bought off; he had never heard of them coming off for any other reason. Kitty was shocked at the refusal of her request, but the man's indifference acted like a douche of cold water in her face. She brightened. Of course, she was looking frightful! Carolan seemed to see her reasoning to herself . . . Her cloak was torn, her skin scratched, her hair . . . oh, her beautiful hair! These things could be remedied . . . and when had Kitty ever failed to get what she wanted from mankind? Carolan's heart was filled with pity for this poor foolish Mamma.

During the second day a turnkey came into the prison room and called: "Haredon! Who is Haredon here?"

Carolan started to her feet.

"Carolan Haredon," he said. "Are you the one?"

"I am," said Carolan.

"Then you had better come with me."

"Why?" said Carolan.

The turnkey shrugged his shoulders.

"Orders was to bring you; not to tell what you're wanted for."

"Suppose I refuse to go!" cried Carolan, incensed by the cruel eyes of the man, and of all these men who found amusement in the torture, both mental and physical, of their fellow beings.

Esther caught at Carolan's hand; Esther's eyes were pleading with her. Never would she make this hot-headed, courageous, magnificent friend of hers understand that when you are helpless arrogance is a mistake.

The turnkey scratched his head.

"Orders has to be obeyed," he said. "Come on!"

Kitty began to cry softly. Millie stared open-mouthed; Esther's lips were moving in silent prayer. Carolan turned to look at them; they thought something more fearful than what had gone before was about to happen to her. A flogging perhaps. Carolan's courage began to quail.

"Who gave these orders?" she demanded in a loud, blustering voice, hoping that she was hiding her terror from her friends.

"Come along with you!" said the turnkey roughly, and would have laid hands on her, but she said, suddenly subdued: "Very well. Lead the way."

Eyes followed her as she went through the room, watchful, speculative, excited eyes.

She was led through corridors, up steps and down again. She would never forget the mental suffering she endured on that walk! She could feel the lash about her shoulders. She had heard the prisoners say that blood sometimes came at the third lash . . . and that as the lashes went on, the victims fainted, and often when they did, the lashes were suspended until consciousness was regained.

The turnkey paused before a door. He hesitated; his little eyes looked full into her face; the corners of his lecherous mouth twitched as though he found it difficult to control his laughter; he was enjoying himself; he knew something of what her thoughts had been as he led her slowly through those dark corridors.

He threw open the door. Beyond him was a small room, and in it was a table, and on the table food was laid out; there was wine and cold roast chicken. That much she saw, and the sight of food made her dizzy. But a man had risen from the table; he was coming towards her. He took her hands, and said: "Carolan, my darling! What have they done to you?"

The turnkey snickered as he closed the door. She was alone with Marcus.

Marcus had not changed in the least; he kissed her hands.

"I heard, only an hour ago, that you were here," he said. "I hear the news, you know! And when I heard I sent out for this, and I sent for you to be my guest."

"Marcus!" she said. "Marcus!"

"No," he said, "not Marcus now. William Henry Jedborough, who was sent to Botany Bay for fourteen years, and came back Marcus Markham after three. And now here is William Henry again . . . your friend who hopes to make your stay in Newgate a little more agreeable than it has hitherto been."

"Marcus . . . who are you?"

"Not Marcus, darling. I always hated the name. William— William Henry, a thief and a rogue, an escaped convict. Here I am . . . awaiting the death penalty."

"The death penalty!"

"Ah! You grow pale at the thought. It is worth being sentenced to death to know you care so much."

"You are the same! Such foolish extravagant words!"

"And you are the same. So quick to anger, and no attempt made to hide it . . . even from a poor man who is to be condemned to the gallows!"

"You joke about it."

"Is it not a matter for joking? Let me whisper to you, Carolan—the gallows are not going to get me!"

"How will you prevent it? You seem to have much power, Marcus."

"William, darling . . . William Henry."

"I have thought of you as Marcus."

"Then call me Marcus. It will always remind me that when I went abruptly from your life you thought of me."

"Do you imagine one forgets one's friends and never thinks of them when they have gone out of one's life?"

"My sweet Carolan!"

"Please tell me what happened to you."

"What is there to tell, my sweet? I came to meet you, as we arranged, and the man Crew met me at the corner of the street. He had his van and his accomplices waiting for me."

"Did you think I had betrayed you?"

"I knew you had betrayed me."

"How you must hate me."

"On the contrary, my sweet Carolan, I love you."

"How foolish I have been! I brought it on us all."

"You have never been anything but adorable."

"Do not talk so foolishly. I brought him to the shop the very first day I came home. I betrayed my father and you . . . and now my father is dead, and you are about to die . . ."

She covered her face with her hands, and he lifted her in his arms and carried her to the table. He sat down on one of the wooden chairs, still holding her. He wiped her eyes tenderly.

"He would have got us, darling, sooner or later. He was waiting, you see. He knew I was a thief, but he wanted the highest ransom for me. He was waiting till I 'weighed my £40.' As for your father, he would have got him too. No! It is you, my sweet Carolan, who have been so wronged; you who do not belong here. Look, Carolan, we must discuss what is to be done. First of all let us eat, for I hear you have been in this filthy place for two long days, and I know you must be hungry. See! I sent out for this chicken, it is tasty. And the wine is good. Now, child, we will eat together and we will talk."

"I am bewildered," she said. "You have such power . . . you, a condemned man!"

"Certainly I have power. I have my business associates outside Newgate. I have money! Money is power; it buys me this room; it buys me this food. It buys me your company . . . There is not so much to fear from law and order when you have money, Carolan."

"I cannot sit here and eat with you," she said, her eyes on the chicken. How good it looked! Golden brown! How hungry she was . . . faint and sick with hunger! "Did you not hear that my mother is in Newgate with me?"

"I did hear. We will send for her."

"She could not walk here . . . the irons . . ."

"They shall be struck off, my dear. Yours too. All but the one pair, and that is not so hard to bear when you have had to drag three about with you. Your mother shall come and share our meal."

"I don't know how to thank you. It is noble of you, when it was I who . . ."

"Hush! There is nothing noble about me. Did you not know that? I will see to it that your mother's irons are struck off, and that she is brought here at once."

"'There is Millie too. And Esther . . . They must all come, or you must give me the chicken and I will take it back and eat it with them."

"Ha! You would be torn to pieces if you went back with that chicken!"

"I! Indeed I should not! I can defend myself."

"That you can, I swear! Oh, Carolan, Carolan, how I love you, Carolan!"

"This is not the time to talk of love! Nor do I admire your light treatment of the subject."

"How like you! I offer you release from discomfort—or comparative release from it—and all you offer me in exchange are harshness and cold words."

"I do not mean to be cold, Marcus . . . but your flippancy seems out of place."

"I never felt less flippant in my life. Do you know the thought of your being here makes me burn with rage. You believe that, Carolan?"

"Oh, remember my own folly has brought me here. Please will you have the irons struck off my mother . . . and could you do the same for Millie and for Esther . . . ?"

"Esther?"

"A poor girl who has become a friend of mine."

"What! Making friends so soon?"

"If you could see her you would like her. She is innocent, and her case is far more to be deplored than my own."

"How I adore you, Carolan, for your anger and your enthusiasms, for your harshness and your kindness!"

"Then please make haste, for every moment spent in those irons is torment for my poor mother . . . and Millie and Esther are so hungry! But . . . can you do these things?"

"You shall witness the power of money, darling. But first we will have those irons off yourself, for it makes me very angry to see you fettered, Carolan."

He went to the door. The turnkey appeared immediately. He must have been waiting there, thought Carolan, speculating on further opportunities of earning money.

In a short while all but one pair of irons were struck off Carolan.

"There!" said Marcus. "You see my power, Miss Carolan! I am a magician . . . the magician of Newgate. I wave my wand . . . in this case it is coin . . . and it is as I say!"

"But Marcus . . ."

"Perhaps you had better call me William, for Marcus was a flippant fellow, never very much to you, your thoughts being all of a certain parson. But William is a different kettle of fish. He came into your life when the parson had left it . . ."

"How foolishly you talk!"

"No, Carolan! Do you think your parson will marry a wife who has been the guest of Newgate?"

"What difference does that make?"

"A hell of a difference, sweet Carolan, to a parson!"

"Rubbish!"

"Sound sense, sweetheart."

"Please do not call me by those endearing names. I find it excessively irritating. I want to know . . . is it true that you are condemned to die?"

"The fate of all who escape from Botany Bay to be caught again—generally."

"You joke about it!"

"I can afford to, Carolan. It shall not happen to me, I promise you; or I should be very surprised if it did. You see, I have money, and money can buy almost anything a man can desire. It can buy love; it can buy life."

"I do not agree with you."

"Of course you do not. You would not be Carolan, whom I love, if you did. But, bless you my child, one day you will learn I am right. Not, I grant you, that it can buy these things in full measure. I can buy my life, but I doubt if I can buy my liberty. And as for buying love . . . let us not talk of it though, for I see the subject distresses you."

"Do you think it will be long before the others can come to us?"

"It will be done as quickly as money can do it."

"You talk incessantly of money!" She must keep the conversation going somehow, and she averted her eyes from that table, for there was in her a wild longing to sit down and fall upon the food laid out there.

"Naturally! Money, money, money! One thinks of little else in Newgate. Now on my last visit I had no money. That, I said at the time, shall never again happen to me. Here, darling, eat one of these bread rolls while we await the others."

She said faintly: "I would rather await their coming. Will they be much longer?"

His eyes glistened, she saw; they were very tender. She was suddenly aware of what an unkempt spectacle she must present to those eyes. She touched her hair.

"What would I not give for a tub of warm water and a change of clothes!" she sighed. "I wonder you recognise me."

"I would recognise you, Carolan, whatever the disguise! But do not think of it. Let us sit down and eat while we wait the others."

"I said I would rather wait. The food would choke me when I thought of them in that foul place."

"You are too sentimental, Carolan. Sentiment is well enough in its rightful place; but never let it stand in the way of common sense. Come, my child!"

There was a tap at the door which flew open without any response from Marcus. Eagerly she turned but it was not those for whom she had hoped, but two turnkeys with more food which they set out on the table.

Carolan stared at the table.

"Come!" said Marcus. "These little rye cakes are appetising."

He held one out to her; she could not resist it. She seized it and ate it ravenously. He watched her, well pleased. Then he went to her suddenly and seized her by the shoulders.

"Carolan! Carolan! I don't despair," he said.

"What do you mean?" she demanded, her mouth full.

"You are so sweetly human, but you were ever one to set yourself impossible tasks. And how I love you when you fail!"

"You talk the most arrant nonsense."

"Do I! Well, now I shall do something useful. I will carve the chicken."

She watched. She felt faint with hunger. She ran to his side, and he, the carvers poised, looked over his shoulder and smiled mockingly into her eyes. He cut off a piece of the breast and put it into her mouth. Never had food tasted so good.

"More!" he said, and continued to feed her. And as she ate he laughed and kept murmuring her name. "Carolan! Carolan! Oh, my sweet Carolan!"

"Here!" he cried. "Wine to wash it down! We will both drink. Here, Carolan! To the future! To our future!"

The wine did strange things to her; made her light-headed. The room swam round and Marcus . . . Marcus only was the one steady thing in a topsy-turvy world. She clutched his arm, half laughing, half crying.

"Marcus!" she said. "Oh , . . Marcus!"

The door opened. There were Kitty and Millie, and behind them, Esther. Carolan was ashamed that they should see her eating, with the glass of wine in her hand. She put down the glass unsteadily, and went to them.

"Why . . ." cried Kitty. "It's Marcus!"

Millie and Esther could only stare at the food.

"Come along!" cried Marcus. "Sit down. We won't waste time on formal greetings; we'll talk as we eat."

There he sat at the head of the table, watching them all . . . smiling queerly.

Kitty recovered herself almost as soon as she had drunk her first glass of wine. The striking off of all save one set of irons had brought great relief to her; she began to see daylight after the long dark night of torment. Marcus was delightfully familiar. To sit here, eating and drinking, the guest of a charming man, was stimulating. She was still in Newgate, she was still a prisoner, but things had changed.

Esther felt she was in a dream which had begun with the coming of Carolan into her life. Anything that was wonderful might happen now—she was sure of it. She tried to suppress the unsuppressible desire to eat too quickly and too much.

Millie settled down at the table more naturally than any of the others; Millie was an animal who had suddenly come upon a patch of fertile land where grew the food she needed to keep her alive.

"What I want to know," said Kitty, "is why you, a prisoner, can entertain guests in this manner and with such food and wine in Newgate?"

"That is what I have been explaining to Carolan. It is the power of money. I merely send out for the food, and the turnkeys are paid well for their trouble in bringing it in."

"I always thought you were a wonderful man, Marcus. I always knew you weren't what you said. You were always too distinguished to be an inhabitant of Grape Street!"

"Too distinguished to be anything but a thief in fact!" he said.

"Tell me," said Carolan. "Did you set my father up as a receiver of stolen goods?"

"I did. I must tell you both that he was very reluctant to enter into such a life. It was only starvation that drove him to it . . . not starvation for himself, but for his wife."

Kitty began to cry softly. Marcus leaned over and filled her glass.

"Do not cry, Mamma!" said Carolan. "I cannot bear it. Let us forget the past."

"I am to blame for bringing it up," said Marcus. "I am a fool as well as a rogue!"

"I could not bear it," said Kitty, "that he should be dishonest. He had always seemed to me so . . . noble. And then to know that he . . . even though he did it for me, which I do not doubt . . ."

"He was noble," said Marcus. "There are two kinds of roguery—his and mine. He becomes what the law calls a criminal, for the sake of his family; I, for the sake of . . . myself! Always remember that. This is a cruel world in which we live. For some it is impossible to live, impossible to eat. Those men have a right to have a family, but what can they do? What *can* they do? There is stealing *and* stealing. There are criminals *and* criminals. A society which is indifferent to so many of its members should not feel outraged if those of its members are indifferent to it. That is my law of life. It is wrong. I am wicked. But that is what I think. So, I cheat, I steal. And when I come to Newgate I see to it that I enjoy as much comfort as it is possible to enjoy; and I see that I entertain my friends."

Carolan said: "I agree, I think. I am not quite sure, but I think I do."

Esther spoke then for the first time. She lifted her head, and her blue eyes were brilliantly beautiful in her poor emaciated face.

"It is written—'Thou shalt not steal.' Therefore, whatever the provocation, it is wrong to steal."

Marcus looked at her, and the colour rushed into her cheeks, and showed momentarily the beauty which health would have put into her face.

"Ah! You are an idealist, Miss Esther; I am but common clay. I adjust myself to the world in which I live; you dream of a society which could never be . . . at any rate not in our time."

"It might be, were we all of the same mind," said Esther.

"Esther," said Carolan, "is a saint. Not all of us have her way of thinking. No, Esther, Marcus is right in a way. I did not think so until I came here, but here I have learned to think differently. A society which can tolerate this vile place . . ."

"People know little of it!" protested Esther. "Did we know before we came?"

"Ignorance is no excuse. And come, can we say we had never heard of Newgate? We had, and we chose not to think of it; it was unpleasant. So we went on living our pleasant lives, and it is because of our indifference and the indifference of thousands like us that it exists. And so . . . innocent people, such as you and Mamma and Millie and I, can be forced to come here, to starve here, to freeze here, and perhaps to die here. We, the innocent, must suffer because we are poor and friendless, while the real criminal . . ."

Marcus bowed his head ironically.

"I'll finish, Carolan. A real criminal can buy the best Newgate has to offer. That's true! Life is a wicked old strumpet;

she's devilishly sly and mercenary; but laugh with her and she'll laugh with you. Even in Newgate, laugh at her and she likes it!"

"Your words hurt Esther," said Carolan.

"I am sorry, Esther." His eyes, Carolan noted, were almost caressing as they rested on the girl. "But it is necessary always to face facts. Where shall we be if we do not? The answer is obvious . . . in Newgate most likely without a penny piece to buy a bit of extra bread. Carolan agrees with me. Carolan, I think you and I are of the same mind on lots of subjects. The thought warms me. You and I . . ."

Carolan broke in impatiently: "We are certainly not of the same mind! Do you think I admired your way of life? You are a thief! You are . . . It is that people should be sent to this vile place before they have been found guilty . . ." She broke off angrily. "Oh! How I hate that creature, Crew!"

"Do not hate him, Carolan. He was following his trade. He probably relies on what he gets by these activities of his. I doubt whether he enjoyed the whole of the forty pounds he got for betraying an escaped convict; or even what he picked up on account of you and your mother and Millie. And he worked very hard for his reward and his Tyburn ticket."

"You would make excuses for him!"

"For him and for us all," said Marcus.

"Absurd!"

"Doubtless."

"You wish, I think to be contrary. You excuse a man who has brought Mamma . . . to that!"

Tears filled her eyes; all the blazing indignation had left her; there was only hopelessness in her now.

"Carolan!" he said tenderly. "Carolan . . ."

The door was pushed open slowly, and a tousled head appeared. It belonged to a black-haired, black-eyed young woman with large gilt earrings swinging in her ears, and a red silk blouse stretched tightly across her full bosom. She raised heavy black brows, and surveyed them.

"Hello, Will!" she said in a drawling voice. "Is it company then?"

"Rather an unnecessary question, Lucy, since I have always been led to believe you have a very sharp pair of eyes!"

His voice was silky with suppressed anger; hers was rough with it. Instinctively Carolan guessed at the relationship between them.

"Well," said Lucy. "I was never one to intrude. I will say good night!"

"Good night, Lucy."

The door slammed.

Carolan met Marcus's eyes; he smiled briefly.

"A friend of mine," he said. "In for passing counterfeit coin."

"Obviously a monied friend," said Carolan. "Like you, she seems to enjoy her freedom!"

"She seemed angry with us," said Esther. "She seemed as if she knew we came from the Common Side."

Carolan smiled tenderly at Esther. How innocent she was! It would not occur to her that this Marcus, who had been so kind to them, was a rake, a philanderer, a libertine. Poor Esther! Her upbringing had been such that the bad and the good were divided into two distinct lots—all bad and all good. Esther had much to learn.

"I do not think I liked her very much," said Kitty. Kitty had drunk a little too freely of the wine; she felt pleasantly drowsy. She leaned her head on her hands and closed her eyes. Esther had drunk but little of the wine, but she too was sleepy. Carolan felt wide-awake, excited by the change in her circumstances, by the presence of Marcus who now, more than ever he had, aroused in her mixed emotions.

He twirled the wine in his glass and leaned towards her suddenly.

He said: "Come, Carolan! Out with it! You are thinking with great disapproval of my friend, Lucy, are you not?"

"Why should I?"

"I do not know why, Carolan; I only know you do."

"I cannot see why I should concern myself with your friends."

"Darling Carolan," he whispered, "you were so angry; you flew to such conclusion that you made hope soar in my wicked breast."

"You talk in riddles."

He caught her wrist; his fingers were warm. She looked down at them; his hands had always attracted her, the hands that picked pockets so deftly, that were his stock in trade.

"No, Carolan. We understand each other well enough. We might understand each other better. Carolan, it will grieve me very much to think of you and your mother and friend Esther, and poor Millie, going back to the foul felons' side."

She shuddered.

"Do not let us think of it. It has been a great treat for us to taste real food again, to eat it in comfort."

"Were you very angry about Lucy?"

"Angry?"

"Sparks flew from your eyes."

"Ridiculous! How could they?"

"A figure of speech, of course. But I saw all sorts of things in your eyes. I myself was angry with her for coming in like that; and then I was glad she did."

"You are very imaginative."

"No . . . merely observant. See how your mother sleeps. And poor little Esther, she is nodding too. What a difference one meal had made to them! Perhaps, too, it is the quiet of this room. What say you?"

"I am frightened for my mother; she is brighter now but there is a terrible change in her."

"I will be frank with you, Carolan, because, although I am a fool and a rogue, I have sense to know that one must always be frank with you. Lucy was my friend . . . a great friend. She is a generous soul, and life has dealt cruelly with her as it has with us. We helped to give each other a few home comforts here in Newgate . . . do you understand?"

"Of course. But is it necessary to explain this to me?"

"It is very necessary. Carolan, from the moment I first saw you I knew there was something different about you."

"So you stole my handkerchief! There was not much else, since I had already lost my purse. You must have been very disappointed."

"How you fly into a passion, my dear! Look!" He put his hand inside his jacket and produced the handkerchief. "I carry it always."

"Why?"

"Surely you know."

"Sentiment? You should never let sentiment stand in the way of common sense, and does it not show a lack of common sense to carry a worthless handkerchief about with you?"

"You are quick! Do you hate me, Carolan?"

"How absurd! Of course not."

"Then since you cannot hate me, perhaps you could love me."

"I think this is an absurd conversation which does not lead us anywhere. Look at that poor child Esther!"

"Poor child Esther! She is not strong, and yet doubtless before she came to this place she was well enough. Newgate gnaws the strength out of a man or woman."

"Unless he knows how to live there!"

"Wise Carolan! Do you know?"

"I do not understand you."

His grip on her wrist tightened.

"Stay with me," he said. "Stay with me here. No! Do not fly into another passion. Listen! Be wise. I will strike a bargain with you. Stay here with me, live in as much comfort as money will buy in Newgate. Your mother, your friend Esther and poor Millie shall have a room like this one; food shall be sent in to them. And you . . . share this with me."

She leaped to her feet, her cheeks flaming red.

"Do you think I am one of your Lucys?"

"No! Assuredly I do not."

"Have you forgotten that I am to be married in a short while?"

"You will not marry your parson, Carolan."

"I think it is time we left you. I think it is a pity we ever accepted your hospitality."

"Listen! How will he know what is happening to you? If it were possible to get a message to him, then he might know, but whether he came for you would be another matter. Money would send that message, Carolan. Suppose I held that out as a further inducement?"

"You are vile!"

"I am, alas! And you are very desirable, which makes me my vile self."

"Mamma!" cried Carolan. "Esther! It is time we went." She nodded towards Millie, who had been watching them with bright, unintelligent eyes. "Wake them," said Carolan. "We must go now."

"Remember the misery of the felons' side, Carolan," whispered Marcus.

"Remember it! I shall never forget it as long as I live."

"And you will go back to it!"

"Assuredly I will go back to it."

"And allow them to go back to it?"

"They would not wish it otherwise—that I know."

"And do you hate me very much, Carolan?"

"Hate! That is too strong an emotion to waste upon such as you. Let us say that I despise you . . . that I never wish to see you again . . . And I heartily wish that I had never eaten your food!"

"It is easy to say that after the feast, Carolan. Would you have said it when you stood at my side and I fed you over my shoulder?"

"Oh, let me go!"

"You disappoint me, Carolan. You prefer that foul place and that foul company to this room and mine."

"Yes," she replied, "I do prefer it! Mamma! Esther!" she shook them. "It is time we went. Come along!"

Kitty opened her eyes.

"I dreamed," she said, "that we were in a beautiful house in the country . . . Darrell and I, and you, Carolan . . ."

"Wake up now," said Carolan. "It is time we were back."

"Carolan, must we go back to that frightful place? They won't put those dreadful irons back, will they? This one pair is bad enough. They cut my skin. It frightens me, Carolan. You know how white my skin used to be . . ."

"Esther," said Carolan, "help me with Mamma."

Kitty got slowly to her feet; on either side of her stood Carolan and Esther. Millie kept to the background.

Kitty said, with sudden graciousness: "Thank you, dear boy! It was a wonderful feast. I hope that some day we shall be in a position to invite you to dine with us."

"You must come again," said Marcus.

He was looking at Carolan, but she would not meet his eyes. He strode to the door; a turnkey came in and conducted them back.

How dingy, how gloomy, how foul the place seemed after that brief respite! Bright eyes peered at them as they returned. What had happened to them? There was no sign of lashes received. Here they were, back again.

Kitty, refreshed and with new hope springing up, became a pale shadow of her talkative self. A group gathered round her; she talked to them.

"We dined with a friend . . . a wealthy man. It was a wonderful meal . . . We shall go again, of course. It will not be long, I assure you, before we are out of here. We have friends, you know . . . It was all a mistake, our coming here . . ."

Carolan listened to her mother, and she was filled with fury against Marcus.

Esther said: "He was a charming man, a good man—although he spoke so wildly. It is hard to be in such a place and refrain from bitter feelings. But he is a kind man. Do you know, I think it grieved him that he could not afford to take us all out of here and give us a room to ourselves."

"You think that he wanted to do that?" said Carolan.

"Indeed I do!"

"Then if he wanted to, why did he not do so, do you think?"

"It was doubtless because he had not enough money to buy luxuries for us all."

271

Millie was fast asleep. Kitty was still talking excitedly. Esther's voice was dreamy.

"I think I have never experienced such joy as when I took my first mouthful," she said. "I feel I would have given my life, if it had been asked, for one mouthful of roast chicken. And there was never such a roast chicken as that one! Did you note how brown and crisp was the outside, and the flesh melted in your mouth like rich butter!"

"You talk of your God," said Carolan. "It seems to me your belly is your God!"

Tears filled Esther's eyes; Carolan turned away. Ought I, she was thinking, to have given them that room, food . . . real food . . . to eat everyday? Do I set too high a value on myself? It is not too late perhaps . . .

Her heart began to beat more rapidly; she put her hand over it; it seemed to be leaping up into her throat. He touched something in her, that man, rogue though she knew him to be. She loved Everard; she would wait all her life for Everard. But there was something in the man, Marcus, that moved her, that fascinated her, that tempted her now to say: "I will do it for their sakes!" and made her wonder whether, after all, she might not be doing it for her own.

It was a wicked passion, this racing of the pulses; something purely of the senses. When he had laid his hands on her she had liked that; she had been angry at the sight of Lucy and the knowledge of what her relationship was to Marcus. When he said her name over and over again—"Carolan! Carolan!"—with the vibrating note in his voice, she felt weak and wanton and very wicked, yet revelling in her wickedness. Everard had been shocked a little by her displays of affection. "My dear Carolan . . . my dear . . . how fierce you are!" He had liked it and tried not to like it. Marcus would never try not to like any affection she had to give him; he would offer passion for passion.

I am really very wicked! thought Carolan, and remembered her mother's procession of lovers. But she was different from her mother; her mother would have so willingly made the sacrifice for the sake of the others just now . . . and would have been able to believe it was a sacrifice. Carolan must see the truth. She tried not to. She thought—How can I let them suffer here in this hell when there is escape for them! How can I!

And she fell to shivering.

Esther leaned over her.

"Are you well? Have you the ague . . . or fever? Why, you are hot and yet you are shivering!"

272

"I am all right!" snapped Carolan.

One of the turnkeys came in; he was jangling a bunch of keys, and grinning.

He said: "This way . . . the four of you. This way . . ."

Carolan leaped to her feet.

"What do you mean? Where are you taking us?"

"Orders is orders," said the turnkey, and there was a hint of respect in his voice, which was not lost on the listeners. Carolan saw looks of envy leap up in several faces. It was true, they were thinking; all that Kitty had told them was true; they were of the quality, these people! But most of their envy was of Esther who had been chosen as their friend and was now sharing their good fortune. One woman sat down in a corner and wailed in her anguished jealousy like an animal in distress.

"Come on," said the turnkey, still respectful. "This way!"

They went along corridors and up staircases. They were shown into a room like the one where they had dined with Marcus. There was a bed in it . . . and rushes on the floor. It looked luxurious after the Common Side.

"Here you stay," said the turnkey. "Gentleman's orders!"

He took a piece of paper from his pocket.

"Gentleman says I was to give you this," he said, and handed it to Carolan.

She took it and read:

> "Of course I hoped you would submit to temptation. But you did not imagine that I would let you all stay in that place, did you? Come and dine with me tomorrow. Now you shall see what a good heart beats under my villainous exterior. Ask the turnkey for writing materials and write a note to your parson. He will see that it is despatched.
>
> William Henry."

Kitty said: "That is from Marcus?"

"William Henry, he calls himself now," said Carolan. She added petulantly: "How can we be expected to get used to this continual change of names!"

"My dear, you sound quite cross; what has come over you? This is luxury. A bed! I declare I long to lie on it and rest my poor leg."

"He says if I write a note it will be delivered . . . I am going to write to Everard." She said to the turnkey: "Will you please bring me pen and paper?" The turnkey nodded and disappeared immediately.

"What a wonderful man he is!" said Kitty. She lay back on the bed. "This is heaven! This is comfort! My poor leg . . . it is throbbing dreadfully."

"I will ask for water to bathe it, and a bandage, Mamma. It seems that nothing is too much for these people to do for Marcus's money!"

Esther looked at her strangely.

"You talk as though you hate him."

"What! Hate our benefactor! Lie down on the bed, Esther. Enjoy the luxury; I shall when I have written my letter. Look Millie, if you lie along the foot, the rest of us can lie the other way. A bit of a tight squeeze, but what luck . . . a real bed! Esther, why do you not lie down? Why do you not try our new bed?"

"You look strange. Did you drink too much of your friend's wine? There is a flush about your face. Carolan, are you all right?"

"I am quite all right. I am not tipsy either! Ah! Here come my pen and paper. Now hear me ask for water and a bandage. I can give orders now because I have a friend named William Henry . . . and he has money . . ."

It was some time before Carolan joined them on the bed. She had written to Everard; she and Esther had bathed and bandaged Kitty's leg; Esther had knelt down by the bed and thanked her God for this newly acquired luxury. Carolan lay very still; she was cramped, and it was impossible to move without disturbing the others. Millie was snoring; Kitty was breathing deeply; Esther, Carolan believed, was awake.

"Esther!" she breathed. "You do not sleep."

Esther's voice came to her in the darkness.

"It is the unaccustomed comfort. The bed is so soft . . . I am so used to hard planks."

"Why do you cry, Esther?"

"Because it is so wonderful. Because I have prayed for something like this to happen."

There was a silence, then Esther said: "He is very kind, our friend. He is a good man, though he tries so hard to pretend he is not."

"He is a thief!" said Carolan. "He is a rogue . . . Do not forget that. He was not brought to this place wrongfully."

"But Carolan, you have said that no one should be brought

274

to a place like this whatever their crime. You said it. Then he has been brought here wrongfully."

"Hush!" said Carolan. "You will wake the others."

She tried to sleep, but she could not. She lay there, cramped, uneasy, thinking of Marcus.

It was stiflingly hot in the women's quarters. When Carolan had stood at the top of the ladder and peered down into the darkness below, she had felt sick with hopelessness and terror. The women's quarters consisted of double tiers of bunks roughly divided into berths; and, sharing Carolan's was her mother, Esther, a crippled girl of twelve and a middle-aged woman. The little girl had cried intermittently ever since they had come aboard; she refused to talk to anyone, and would hide her face in her hands, peering through her fingers, if spoken to, suspicious and defiant. The woman had been drunk all the time the ship lay at anchor; gin had been smuggled in for her; now the ship had set sail and she no longer had her gin, she was either quarrelsome or over-friendly. She sang lewd songs for hours at a stretch; and in close confinement with this woman, Carolan knew that she, her mother and Esther must spend the next months. Millie they had not seen since leaving Newgate. Her sentence had been the same as Carolan's—seven years transportation—but she had been sent to another ship. Poor Millie! It was to be hoped she would not suffer too deeply. Carolan thought of her often, hating herself, for it seemed to her that never would she be able to forget that she had been the chief instrument in bringing trouble to these people.

But even in the depth of misery there is some comfort to be had. They were all together—she, her mother and Esther—and it might so easily have happened that they would be parted. She believed, though she was not altogether sure, that Marcus was aboard this ship. Marcus—she had told him that never, never could she think of him as anyone but Marcus, to which he had replied characteristically: "What's in a name? As long as you continue to think of *me,* what matters the label?"—Marcus had been sentenced to transportation for life, Kitty for fourteen years, and Esther, like herself, to seven.

She would clench her hands and think of the mockery of the trial, the weariness of the court, its automatic and careless sentences. It is so much easier to say, "Guilty!" than "Not Guilty!" And who is to care, save a poor prisoner of no significance whatever?

275

Always there would stand out in her memory the ride to Portsmouth. Chained, dirty—not Carolan Haredon surely, this creature, whose red hair, once so sleek and shining, was matted and filthy! Carolan, who had danced in a green dress at her first ball, now a grotesque scarecrow, her thin body hung about with rags. The van had been open and crowds in the street had watched its progress. They laughed; they pointed; they jeered at the van's most miserable cargo.

She had prayed then—she who had vowed never to pray again.

"Let me die. This I cannot endure." Then someone had thrown a rotten apple at her and she had stopped praying, for furious anger had surged up within her. She had seized the apple and flung it back into the crowd, which action had been greeted with roars of ribald laughter; and then rotten fruit, mud, dung came thick and fast.

I'll never forget it, she thought; and indeed the very memory of it set her heart pounding with fury.

In Portsmouth jail—with its Gentlemen's Side and its Common Side in fair imitation of its big sister, Newgate—they had dined with Marcus. His eyes had glittered with excitement because the last days of prison life had been lived through. There was the weary waiting before they set sail, there was the dreaded journey across the sea to the other side of the world, but the filthy Newgate days were over, and that in itself was a matter for rejoicing.

Marcus had said: "My darling, how it grieved me that you should travel down as you did! Believe me, I tried to move heaven and earth to get you with me in a closed carriage. There are some things that money cannot achieve—please understand that that was one of them."

She tried to tell him of that journey, but the words choked her, and she spoke only one sentence to sum the whole thing up: "I wished I was dead."

"Carolan, my sweet," he said, "never wish that. That is an admission that life has defeated you. Why long for death when you know not what it brings! Eternal sleep? Do you want it, Carolan? You, with your fine spirit, with your loves and your hates! That sort of death is not for us, Carolan, and the only sort of life we know is the hard life—and would such as we are want it soft? Would it not lose its zest?"

"Esther has beautiful ideas of death," she said.

And they had both looked at her. There was an unearthly beauty about the girl; her spiritual strength shone in her eyes for her belief was invulnerable.

276

"But Esther, how can you be *sure?*" demanded Carolan, irritated.

"How can you be not sure," asked Esther, "when you *know?*"

"You do not know!" said Carolan, impatient. "Who has ever told you? Your father? Your mother? But what did they *know?*"

"They knew," said Esther. "I could not bear not to believe."

"It is comforting, doubtless," said Carolan.

Marcus put his hands on her shoulders.

"But Carolan, do *we* want comfort? I do not think so; not unless we know it to be truth. We cannot accept things because they are comfortable. Why, damme, our forefathers doubtless thought it was comfortable enough living in their uncivilised way. It is the uncomfortable things which make the world progress."

Esther shook her head.

"I wish I could make you see it as I do."

"Ah, Esther!" said Marcus. "We are neither of us saints, Carolan and I!"

"No," said Carolan, "we are sinners . . . angry sinners. We cannot accept cruelty because God decided that we should. No, we will fight against God; we will fight for ourselves!"

Marcus laughed. How his eyes glittered! She thought, He is already contemplating escape when he gets to Botany Bay. And she warmed towards him; they were much of a kind, he and she.

Everard was of a kind with Esther. Everard was ever constant in her mind, Everard who had not come for her, who had accepted cruelty as God's will. Perhaps he had wanted to come; she imagined his mother's begging him not to . . . and Everard's fighting with himself. Everard the parson, Everard the lover. She had always suspected the parson of being the stronger of the two. Perhaps that was why she had suffered so deeply in the van which had taken her to Portsmouth, for then she had known that Everard was not coming; that was why, in the open van on the Portsmouth Road, she had despaired.

And when she had thrown that rotten apple back into the crowd, she had been throwing it at Everard and Everard's mother. Had she been unshackled, she would have leapt from the van and fought them with her hands. She was not the sort to suffer in silence, to pine away and die; she was the sort to fight, to hurt herself, to hate. . . .

277

"I wish I were dead," she said again, remembering.

And then there had been the comfort of seeing Marcus in the Portsmouth jail. That jauntiness of him, that glitter in his eyes! Rogue, thief, philanderer that he was he was more her sort than gentle Everard.

One pain will subdue another. There was poor Mamma getting weaker and weaker, and thinking of Mamma it was possible to forget Everard a little.

The last weeks had changed Kitty beyond recognition. She was like a flower that had been cherished in a hot-house, and is thrown onto a dung heap. No flower could be expected to last long in that condition. When they had come on board and had stayed on deck while farewells were said, Kitty had sat propped up against the rail unable to move. Her face was a greenish colour, her eyes bloodshot, her tongue thickly coated, and her lips twice their usual size. She was, Carolan knew, unaware of her situation, which was perhaps not a matter for regret in itself. All about them were their ribald companions of the voyage, men, women, boys and girls; murderers and highwaymen, people who had stolen a loaf of bread, river thieves, counterfeiters—the innocent and the guilty. Gin flowed freely. Old songs were sung. Some sang of their joy to be rid of their country; some were sentimental in a maudlin way about leaving it. Men and women embraced openly; young boys and old women, and young boys and young women, mere children, followed their example. Conversation was as obscene as they knew how to make it. Some danced; some sang; some wept; some laughed. And Kitty sat there, propped up, seeing nothing.

When the cry of "Clear ship!" went up, Carolan and Esther between them managed to get Kitty below. There they had all remained since in the fetid atmosphere, among the rats which were tame and insolent and had no respect for this rag-tag shipload of convicts. The hatches had been secured; and the only light and air came through one hatchway, and at night there were candles in iron lanterns. Sometimes though, the hatches had to be removed, for the captain did not wish to arrive at the settlement with a cargo of dead prisoners.

Days and nights merged into one. They ate their meagre allowances of food. Kitty had given up eating hers. She lay languid, with her eyes wide open . . . but they weren't like Kitty's eyes.

"Ah!" said the woman who shared their berth, and who had told them she was known to the taverns of Thames-side as Flash Jane. "She's a bright one! Hi! Wake up, me lady, and let's run me blinkers over you."

"Please do not touch her," said Carolan. "She is very ill."

The woman shrugged her shoulders, muttering something about fine ladies' manners. She would have them know she was of the real quality of a prison ship; none of your half and halfs. Why, curse them, she had been brought up before. She was no newcomer to Newgate. She had robbed many a fine gentleman, she had; ah, and slept with many more. Highwaymen and lords . . . they were all one to her. River thieves and gentry. Ah! There were things she could tell about them all, but why they wanted to coop her up with a gang like this, she couldn't be saying. She thought things were managed better than that at Newgate and on board. She had a friend outside who was looking after her, she had; he had come on board to take his last farewell. " 'Come back in seven years' time, Jane,' he said. 'I will not be the one to forget you.' He was good to me, Jem was. . . . And I was good to him. Here you. . . . Got long ears now, have you not?" She leaned over and pulled the ear of the trembling girl cowering in the corner. The child was mis-shapen, alarmingly ugly . . . almost not like a child. Flash Jane began to whisper to her of her adventures with highwaymen and lords and Jem and others. The child shrunk back into her corner, listening.

"Esther!" cried Carolan. "How can we bear this!"

Esther said: "We go through the fire, Carolan, that we may be tried, and if we come through safely are we not cleansed?"

"You make me angry. Do you call this a cleansing process?"

Esther tried to reason: "You are suffering more keenly now, Carolan. I have got over the worst. The worst for me was in Newgate when I was alone and friendless. Now I have your friendship I can never be so unhappy again."

Carolan fought back her tears. "Oh, be silent, Esther!" she snapped; and then suddenly, putting her hand over Esther's thin one: "Forgive me! I am so tired of living. I wish the boat would go down."

"Oh!" said Esther. "You waited for your lover, and he did not come."

"What a lover!" cried Carolan. "I was in Newgate, and he did not come for me. Esther, let me talk to you of him. Let me try to show him to you as he was. So tall, so clear-eyed, so gentle in his talk, so understanding, so mild, so good! I first loved him when I was a frightened little girl. I think I was no more than five, and my cruel half-brother shut me inside the family vault and I was frightened. Everard opened the door and came to me. I loved him from then on. I must go on loving him till I die. And, Esther, I shall never see him again. I am an exile from England for seven years, and what will those seven years bring, Esther? Why did he not come? They say people have escaped from Newgate; I used to dream that he came and rescued me from Newgate as he did all those years ago from the dark tomb."

"To rescue you from Newgate would have been well nigh impossible, Carolan."

"Still . . . some would have attempted it!" She was thinking now of Marcus with his jaunty smile and his blue eyes in his wrinkled face, and the glitter of those eyes . . . the recklessness of him.

"What use to attempt it, Carolan? Greater trouble would have followed."

"Oh, you and your doctrines! You make me weary, Esther. I will have none of them. Listen, I have to live through this, have I not? From now on I live for myself. . . . I will steal, I will cheat. I shall think of no one, care for no one . . ."

"Carolan, what rubbish you talk! While you are yourself you will always care for someone. You must not steal; you must not cheat; for that would not be *you*, Carolan. I'll never forget the way you stepped in amongst us with your head high. You looked to me like a leader. Do you know what I mean, Carolan . . . someone who can fight, but only for what is right. Someone, meant to show the way . . ."

Carolan laughed.

"What a leader! What a noble spectacle in my rags and my dirt!"

"Wilfully you misunderstand."

"I tell you, you are quite mistaken about me. I am weak and foolish, and I was largely responsible for bringing this tragedy about. I fought those women without any noble thoughts in my mind. They wanted my clothes; I wanted to keep them. Marcus is like I am. Circumstances affect us. Had fortune not changed for him, he would have been a high-spirited squire, fond of fun, whose life is made up of amours and gambling. I am like that too. We are very strong and very weak; things happen to us, and we are no longer the same people. . . . You are different, Esther; you have your faith."

"Oh, if you but had it too, Carolan!"

"I could not have faith in anything any more, Esther. I can never believe anything without proof. Do you hope to convert me, Esther? Do you hope to convert Marcus?"

A flood of colour rushed into Esther's face.

"Do you think I could?" she said.

"I think," said Carolan, "that if you looked as beautiful as you do now—in spite of rags and filth—Marcus would be only too willing to listen . . . in the hope, of course, of making you listen to him."

"You are hard on him. He means no harm."

Carolan turned away. Dear Esther, who thought that Lucy of Newgate was a mere acquaintance of his, and the dark-haired gipsy who was hanging round his neck while they said goodbye to friends on deck, was merely expressing her gratitude for some small kindness!

"You're sweet," she said suddenly. "I wouldn't have you otherwise. Stay close to me, Esther. Listen to me when I want to be listened to. Let me be angry with you when I want to be angry . . . and please, please do not let my ill temper make any difference to our friendship."

Kitty began to moan.

Carolan leaned over her: "Mamma, Mamma, is the pain worse then?"

"Is that you, George?" said Kitty.

"She is dreaming," said Carolan, "dreaming of Haredon, her old home, the place where I was born."

"Do you think her leg is worse?" said Esther.

Carolan lifted Kitty's rags and looked at the leg. When she had seen it on deck she had been deeply shocked. The discoloration and the swelling presented an alarming sight. Something ought to be done quickly; the irons removed, a doctor called. She had shouted to one of the Marines, whose duty it was to look in on the prisoners now and then, that her mother was sick and needed attention, but the Marine had orders not to speak to any of the convicts; any complaints were to be put before a senior officer; he had been warned that he was travelling with the equivalent of a cargo of wild beasts who, ignorant as they might seem, were possessed of beast cunning, who would be for ever planning violence since violence was second nature to them. Therefore he ignored Carolan's plea for help.

"It does not look any worse," said Carolan, and added, "as far as I can see. If only they would strike off these irons I am sure it would heal."

Kitty lifted her hand and Carolan took it; Kitty's was icy cold, which was extraordinary, for the fetid atmosphere of the prisoners' quarters was stifling, and Carolan's hands were burning.

"Mamma," said Carolan, "do you feel any better?"

"Yes, my darling, I feel better."

Carolan touched her mother's forehead; it was as cold as her hands.

"She is better!" whispered Carolan. "She knows me."

There was a haze in the atmosphere which came from mingled breath and the steam of sweating bodies; it was foul with the slime and muck of years, with disease and filth and the odour of vermin. There was a good deal of noise down below —the constant muttering and grumbling and shrieking and chattering and laughing that might come from a cage full of monkeys. Those above had found it impossible to insist on silence down below; there must be certain privileges even for wild beasts. So the prisoners talked and laughed and wept aloud, and they walked about in the narrow space between the tiers of bunks, like grim spectres in an underworld. They fought among themselves; they planned escape; they boasted of past successes in the worlds of crime and lust; and degradation was their god, to be bowed down to and worshipped, and those who had achieved most in his service were considered the cream of the prison society.

Carolan, holding her mother's hand, listening to the conversation going on around her, watched the ghostly figures prowling about in the dim light, stared through that hazy atmosphere and asked for death. An old hag with bare, pendulous breasts, hideous in the extreme, was squatting on her berth telling her berth mates how she had most successfully combined a life of lust and profit. Every now and then one of them would burst into shrieks of unnatural laughter. Another old woman, her back bent, her limbs gripped with rheumatism, was murmuring to herself of the revenge she was going to take on someone home in Wapping, when she had done her seven years. Someone else was singing in a loud, discordant voice.

"Carolan . . ." said Kitty.

"Yes, Mamma. Do you want to be raised?"

Esther leaned forward, and together they raised Kitty.

"Is that better, Mamma?"

Kitty said: "Climb in beside me, Carolan. What a little thing you are! Tell me, darling, is she kind to you . . . Does she beat you? You would tell me, if she did . . . surely you would tell me?"

Carolan whispered to Esther: "She is wandering. She is back in my childhood."

Carolan put her lips to her mother's forehead, and went

on: "There was a nurse whom I was afraid of. Now I see how weak she was . . . how I need not have been afraid. Esther, do you think . . . years hence . . . we shall see that we need not have been afraid . . . even of this?"

"Yes," said Esther, "I know. We shall look down on the suffering we endured here below and smile at what we were."

"Ah!" sighed Carolan impatiently. "I was not thinking of what would happen to us beyond the pearly gates! I mean . . . here . . . in this world. I talk of reality, not dreams. Oh, forgive me, Esther, I am a beast! I am wicked. Why do you not hate me?"

"Hate you! That makes me smile. What cause have I ever had but to love you!"

"Carolan!" said Kitty. "Are you there, my daughter?"

Carolan bent over her mother.

"Darling, does it not tire you to sit up so?"

"Carolan . . . you laugh, but do you know life as I know it? I tell you, he does not belong here . . . A gentleman of the quality he is . . . Have you not noticed the way his eyes look at you, Carolan . . . A parson! My daughter, the wife of a parson!"

Carolan began to cry.

"It is raining," said Kitty. "I must go now, Darrell . . . Peg will let me in; she is my friend . . . Aunt Harriet will be sleeping in her room . . ."

"I do not like to hear her talk thus," said Carolan. "It frightens me. And yet, she is more coherent than she was. I wish we had water. How hot it is in here! Esther, how long will it take to get to Botany Bay? How long have we been at sea?"

"I do not know," said Esther.

"Several days and nights . . . I think I have counted six, but I cannot be sure."

"I like the rain on my face, Peg," said Kitty. "It is so good for the skin . . . as good as your lotions, Thérèse . . . and you know it!"

Kitty attempted a laugh, but her lips were so thick and dry it scarcely came through, and it ended in a gurgling in her throat.

"It is well that she does not know she is here," said Carolan. "Esther, I wonder what is waiting for us on the other side of the world!"

"Nothing could be worse than prison and this ship, could it, Carolan? We shall have work to do, and surely any work is better than no work at all."

"That I cannot say. How will my mother fare there, do you think? She has been used to a maid to dress her hair; I remember well how the colour of ribbon could be the burning question of the day."

Kitty stirred in their arms. She began to sway a little, there was coquetry in all her movements. Now she was a young girl in a coach, and her broad-brimmed hat hid her eyes from the ardent gaze of the young man opposite. Now she was mischievous, slipping out of a house in late evening to meet her one true love in a wood. Now she was married to George Haredon, the sensualist who had desired her so strongly that he had married her and provided the solution of her troubles, and even when he had discovered how she had deceived him, still yearned to be her lover.

"George . . ." came through her cracked and swollen lips. "I . . . hate . . . you . . . George . . . Do not touch me . . ." Her heavy lids closed over her eyes; her lips curled up at the corners; she was excited. George was being as cruel, as exciting in her thoughts as he had been all those years ago at Haredon.

Her mood changed quickly. A gracious lady receiving the Prince at the head of the staircase of her country house . . . A fascinating creature who had thrown herself away on her own true love and must pass her days in the shop parlour of a second-hand shop . . . A young girl repressed in the household of a spinster aunt, a wife running away from her cruel husband with the man she loved . . .

"She is getting better," said Carolan. "Her mind is active. But how cold she is! I wish we had something with which we could cover her. How swollen her leg is! It is festering there. Oh, Esther, surely we can make them do something! I know they do not care how we live down here, or whether we live at all, but we must make them! I am going to do something, Esther. I will not endure this. When one of them comes down here again I will seize him; I will insist. I will make them do something!"

Flash Jane, who had been crooning to herself, sat up listening with sudden interest. When she moved, an indescribable odour rose from her.

"Going to make them, eh? He! He! Going to make 'em do something, eh?" laughed Flash Jane.

Carolan turned on her. "Do you think I am afraid of them?"

"He! He! You will be, I'll warrant, when you've had the lash about your shoulders. It ain't nice, lady, the lash ain't.

Ye're a pulp of bleeding flesh when they've done with yer . . . and then there's the maggots crawling in your sores, driving you well nigh crazy. I know. I've seen it, lady."

Esther began to tremble. Carolan said: "Bah! Do you think I am afraid!" But she was afraid, horribly afraid.

"We should not endure it!" she said fiercely. "Why should we? We are human beings, are we not?"

"We ain't 'uman beings, lady! We are only the poor!" The woman's eyes were like sloes, her teeth hideous yellow-brown stumps, her breath foul, her head alive with lice.

Kitty said: "Now, sir! You flatter! Do you think then that I was born yesterday?"

Flash Jane burst into paroxysms of laughter; she slapped Carolan on the back.

"Quite the lady, eh? 'Now, sir! You flatter! Do you think I was born yesterday?'" She leaned forward and peered into Kitty's face. "Yesterday! Oh, no, me lady . . . a good four and forty years ago, I'd be saying!"

Carolan pushed her off fiercely.

"Keep away!"

"All right! All right! We ain't so used to the quality, you know . . . if I don't get a drop of gin soon I'll go stark crazy!"

"Go crazy if you like," said Carolan, "but keep your distance."

Esther put out a warning hand. The woman crept up to Carolan, and put her evil-smelling face close to hers. Carolan gave her a push which sent her sprawling. Someone laughed. Eyes watched with interest, hoping for a little trouble to relieve the gloom.

But Flash Jane was not ready for a fight. Though, she thought, a few years back I'd have scratched the eyes out of the little she-cat! But today the she-cat was too much for her . . . young claws are sharp. Flash Jane turned her attention to the mis-shapen child beside her and began laying about her with fury.

"Snickering at me, snickering, are you? Take that, you imp! Take that!"

Flash Jane was soon exhausted. The girl whimpered and Flash Jane lay growling like a wild animal which had successfully fooled its fellows into thinking it is stronger than it is.

Somewhere in the gangway two middle-aged women began to dance; they took off their rags, bit by bit, until they were naked; and there they danced together amorously, lewdly, and the fetid hole of the women's quarters was filled with ribald laughter.

"I do declare," said Kitty, and Carolan had to put her ear close to her mother's mouth, so great was the noise, "I do declare that I could have rivalled Sarah Siddons . . . Listen . . . the applause . . . listen . . ."

The hatchway was thrown open suddenly. The eyes of the convicts were bright with interest. The monotony of the first days at sea was being broken at last.

"All on deck!" shouted a voice.

"What is it?" said Carolan, excited as the others.

"A hundred lashes apiece!" chortled an old woman. "Your back will be like a piece of butcher's meat before they be finished with you!"

"What do you know!" said a tall, gaunt woman who seemed to be something of an authority among the convicts. "I can tell you. We're well out to sea. It is 'all on deck' for the striking off of our irons!"

Carolan began to cry weakly.

"Thank God! Thank God!" She sprang up on to the berth. "Mamma! Mamma! They are going to strike off the irons. Now you will be well again!"

But Kitty lay in a heap, her eyes closed, her body cold, and Carolan, shaken with a sudden horrible fear, knew that it was too late, for whether or not the irons were struck off could mean nothing to Kitty now.

The sun beat down incessantly, pitilessly upon the ship, and there was no breath of wind to help her on her way. She lay, as though exhausted, her timbers creaking as she rolled and lurched; her sails flapped against her masts as though they reproached themselves for their uselessness. Birds cruised about her; in the glittering water a shark moved silently. There was an air of weariness aboard; there was a relaxing of discipline. On their part of the deck, shut in by barricades, the convicts lay about in groups, seeking a little shade from the merciless sun. The heat was so intense, they just lay about, too languid to talk very much; they looked a dirty, docile collection of tamed animals on this tropical afternoon. On the other side of the barricade the sentry sat, yawning. He had walked up and down, musket over his shoulder, until he could bear no more. What need to guard convicts in such weather! Who would want to do anything but seek a bit of shade and sleep on such an afternoon?

The men had had their two hours exercise; some had stayed on deck, sleeping, drowsing; and there had been no attempt to send them back to their stifling quarters. The Marines had possibly been too weary themselves to assert discipline. However, there lay Marcus, and beside him, Carolan and Esther. They were talking eagerly, for though they had caught occasional glimpses of each other they had not been able to converse in all the months since they had left Portsmouth.

Marcus said:"Ah! Thank God for a calm! Look at that sentry! The man's yawning his head off. I'll warrant there isn't a soldier on the ship who is not more concerned with taking forty winks than guarding a cargo of miserable convicts!"

"Marcus!" said Carolan. "You are not thinking . . ."

Esther burst in: "It would be most dangerous. They say that terrible things are done to those who try to mutiny."

"Bless you both!" said Marcus. "I plan no mutiny. I am awaiting the journey's end complacently. What chance would mutiny have here, think you? We should be caught, flogged and sent to solitary confinement. I know what it means!"

Carolan raised herself and looked at him. He seemed, she thought, impervious to misery. His grey convict clothes were filthy; he was unwashed, his hair matted, his skin grimy; but his startling blue eyes were bluer in the tropics than they had been under London skies; they seemed to borrow their colour from the cloudless sky and the brilliant ocean; and they were as unfathomable as the sky, as dazzling as the sea, and as unconquerable.

Carolan thought, I must make the most of this time I spend with him. I must discover what it is that makes him so hopeful, so courageous. I must borrow some of his hopefulness, borrow some of his courage.

She told him brokenly of Kitty's death.

"Oh, Marcus, she lay there for so long. They left her beside us . . . and in that hot and frightful place . . . Oh, Marcus, I cannot talk of it; it was hell. My Mamma . . . my beautiful Mamma! If you could have seen her in the Haredon days . . . in front of her mirror, with Thérèse trying a ribbon against her hair . . . and then, there in the stinking hold of a prison ship, herself no longer, just a decaying body . . ."

Marcus put his hand over hers; so did Esther, and the hands of Marcus and Esther met. They smiled at each other, as they comforted Carolan.

"You must not think of it, darling," said Marcus. "It may be better so."

"That is what I say," said Esther.

"Esther has talked to me of Providence and happy releases until I could scream. Marcus, please do not you talk like that!"

"I will not. But I will say this, Carolan. She is well out of it. What do you think would have happened to her on the other side?"

"I do not know," said Carolan. "How should I know! What will happen to us?"

"We can bear it," said Marcus, "because we are younger, and when we are young we look forward; it is the ageing who look back. What have you, Carolan, or you, Esther, to look back to? What have I? We must therefore look forward. We are luckier than those who have lived well and fallen on evil days. Hope is a happier companion than regrets."

"Oh, I do agree! I do agree!" said Esther.

"Tell us, Marcus," insisted Carolan, "what we must expect when we get there."

He was silent; his blue eyes watched an albatross rise from the water. He reached for Carolan's hand, and his fingers curled about hers.

"How should I know!" said Marcus.

"Neverthless, you do," said Carolan. "You have been before, have you not?"

"But the treatment of women is not the same as that of men."

"And you of course never spoke to a woman the whole of your time. That was like you, Marcus, never to speak to a woman!"

He moved closer to her; his eyes smiled at her.

Esther said: "Oh, Carolan! How can you . . . when he . . . has been so kind to us!"

"His kindness to us does not alter the fact, Esther," said Carolan. "I do not believe that Marcus has never heard the story of a female convict's adventures. For after all, would she not be eager to talk of them to her . . . friends?" She paused. "And I would rather know the worst . . . or perhaps the best, for I swear my experiences of the last months have led me to expect no haven of rest . . . nothing indeed but misery and starvation and humiliation."

"I know little," said Marcus, "but I will tell you what I do know. An advertisement announcing your arrival will be sent out—'A cargo of females . . .'—and those who want servants will come aboard and choose."

"There will be no alternative but to be chosen for a servant?"

"There will be other alternatives."

"Do you think they will try to separate us?"

"You may be lucky and keep together."

288

"And if we are not chosen?"

"Well, then you will be sent to the factory—a sort of clearing house. You will be put to work sooner or later."

"For seven years!" said Carolan. "I shall be twenty-four before I am free . . . it seems a lifetime!"

"Bah!" said Marcus. "What is seven years!"

"When I think how different my life might have been, had I never run away from Haredon . . ."

"Bah!" said Marcus again. "How different all our lives might have been, had we not done this and that!"

"Mine could not have been more wretched!" said Carolan bitterly.

He let his fingers touch her wrist.

"Never despair, Carolan. How do you know what is waiting?"

She turned her head and looked into his eyes. They were burning with desire for her. She looked away quickly, but she was thrilled. No! She was not despairing. It was good to know that Marcus was her friend.

She shaded her eyes against the glare of the sun.

Esther said: "Good and evil are so oddly mixed. But for the heat we should not be together again, the three of us!"

"Oh, Esther! How sweet you are! Then it means something to you, if not to this hard-hearted Carolan, that I am here to talk with you!"

Carolan said: "Marcus, tell us what happened to you when you got there before."

"I was a fool in those days. I was over-bold, not cautious enough. I got myself into a deal of trouble. I spent three months in the hulks before I sailed. I loathed the hulks. Why, here you do feel you are getting somewhere; you are moving all the time; you come on deck; you see the sea; you are aware of the motion. But a prison hulk is hell! It was for me. I was a rebel in those days, and looked upon as a troublesome prisoner. One day, dear Carolan, and you, too, sweet Esther, if you can bear the sight, I will show you the scars across my back. I could not count the lashes I have had."

Esther was blushing; Carolan scowled at him, and his answer to the scowl was a mischievous smile.

"Solitary confinement in total darkness! It drove some of them insane. I survived it. Oh, Gad! What a fool I was in my young days! And then I arrived and immediately planned escape. Oh, my youthful folly! Now, hope is good when there is some sound possibility to support it, but when it is propped up by folly, it is disastrous. Never nurture that sort of hope,

289

Carolan, nor you, Esther! I do not think you would, Esther, but my sweet Carolan—who is so like what I was at her age—might be tempted to do so."

"Oh, I am a fool of course!" said Carolan.

"With the devil's own temper. Odd . . . how one loves these foibles!"

"You were telling us . . ." said Carolan.

"Yes, my lady, I was telling you. I tried escape. I was brought back. I was given a thousand lashes . . . and I was put alone on an island outside the bay from which escape was impossible. The sea was infested with sharks. There was no shade from the sun, nor shelter against the cold night. My food was bread and water, rowed out to me each week. I thought I died a thousand deaths on that island, dear children, but it was only one foolish boy who died, and in his place was born a wiser man. I was brought back from there, and worked in a road party—which meant that I lodged in barracks and tramped daily to work. I worked hard and became an overseer. I earned a little tobacco. But the devil was in me and was not sufficiently caged, so I tried escape once more; and when I was caught, I worked in a chain gang, and that, my dears, was a living hell if ever there was one! The chains about my legs were never removed for an instant. I still bear the scars of those days about my body; but I learned much that was profitable."

"And the next time you escaped you were successful!"

"Third time lucky! But you see, here I am . . . and this time it is a lifer!"

Esther said earnestly: "You would not try again?"

He smiled at her lazily, and tenderly.

"I do not know, Esther. But this I can say. There would have to be a very good chance of escape before I took it. I am wiser now, but perhaps not really as wise as I shall be in five years time. That is the compensation of growing old, is it not? Wisdom accompanies the grey hairs, the flagging steps."

"What a moraliser you are!" said Carolan. "Tell us about the chain gang."

"It is ugly telling."

Esther shivered.

"Nevertheless," said Carolan, "I wish to know the truth. I never want anything dressed up to look pretty any more. Tell us, Marcus."

"No," he said. "Not before Esther."

"Oh, Esther is too squeamish! It is her way of looking at life. God is good! she says, when she sees the beauties in the world. When she sees the squalor and the wickedness, she looks the other way or forgets God had a hand in that too!"

"Don't be harsh with Carolan, Esther; try to understand our Carolan. She has suffered much; it hardens her . . ."

"Be silent!" cried Carolan fiercely.

"But I thought you wanted to hear of my adventures with the chain gang!"

"But you prefer not to tell in front of Esther."

"Ah!" He laughed a little, and his eyes were burning in his face. "I am between two fires, you see. How I long to please you both! And damme, I will. Carolan, we will leave Esther dozing here, and we will move just out of earshot, and I will talk to you of what you want to know."

His hand was about her wrist, burning hot.

"Come," he said. "Come on."

"I am not all that eager to hear."

"Carolan!" he said. "Come, please. At any moment now we shall be sent back to our holes. Carolan . . . please . . ."

"And you are eager that I should know of all the horrors that await us on our arrival?"

"I think it is better to have your eyes open . . . if you are strong enough to bear what you see."

He drew her a little along the deck. The exertion of the movement was exhausting. "Carolan, I had to speak to you alone."

"Of the chain gang?"

"That is past history. I had to talk of us."

"Oh. Why?"

"All these months I have longed to talk with you. I cannot talk in front of Esther."

"And yet, when she is there, you look at her as though you could bare your soul to her!"

"You are jealous, my sweet child."

"Jealous! I? I was about to say you may practise your arts on whom you will, but I will not have them practised on Esther! Do you not recognise innocence when you see it? Esther is a romantic little fool. She does not see you as you are, nor does she see me as I am. You are a sort of Robin Hood . . . the sort who robs the rich to help the poor. What poor did your thieving ever help?"

"William Henry Jedborough, alias Marcus Markham, of course! He was excessively poor."

"You put on a different personality for different people, do you not? To Esther you are the philosopher. To me you are the charming rogue. At least you think you are charming."

291

"And you do not?"

"I only know you for the rogue you are! Oh, Marcus . . . I did not mean that . . . not entirely. It was so good of you to buy us that room in Newgate."

"Even though you would not enter into a bargain with me, eh?"

"To me you pretend to be very, very bad, and to Esther you try to appear a sinner struggling towards righteousness. I do not believe you are either one or the other. Why did you try to make that stupid bargain, and then show clearly that you did not mean it?"

"I hoped you would fall into temptation."

"And what satisfaction would you have had from it?"

"Enormous satisfaction. I love you, Carolan."

"And you thought that your miserable money . . ."

". . . would have brought your submission! Come, Carolan, you know you hesitated."

"I did not!"

"You did. I saw it in your eyes. And how hope leaped in my savage breast!"

"I would rather you did not joke about the matter."

"Often a joke will hide our most serious feelings."

"Please do not be so sententious. I am not Esther!"

"No darling Carolan. The time is passing, and we are wasting precious moments in quarrelling. I love you, Carolan. I want . . . some hope that some day, on the other side . . . you and I . . ."

"What?"

"Convicts whose conduct is exemplary are allowed to marry."

"You are suggesting that I should marry you!"

"Please do not look as though the idea is repugnant to you, Carolan."

"I should be sorry for your wife. You would not be faithful to her for a week."

"If she were you, Carolan, I should be faithful to her for the rest of my life."

"Your conversational powers are truly miraculous, Marcus! I doubt whether you have ever been at a loss to say the right thing. Still, I fear long practice in the art of deceiving poor females who want to be deceived has made you such an expert."

"The last months have made you cruel."

"Did you expect them to make me soft? Children go into

292

Newgate innocent; they come out criminals. I went in, soft and foolish; I emerged hard, perhaps cruel. It is what life has done to me."

"Carolan, my sweetheart . . ."

She turned her face to him; tears were streaming down it. She burst out fiercely, because she could not bear the tenderness that leaped into his eyes: "You know I loved him. You know what his desertion has meant. You know it has cut deeper than those irons, than all the horrors of prison. And yet you . . ."

He put his hand on her shoulder.

"Carolan, do not look back. Look forward. You are young; you are beautiful. You were never meant to spend your life grieving for an unworthy lover." His hand slipped down to her breast. "You are beautiful, Carolan . . . *my* Carolan. You are vital; you are trembling now because you need me as I need you. Make no mistake, we were meant for each other!"

She tried to control her trembling limbs. She longed to lie against him, to lift her face to his. There was in his eyes that which she had tried to arouse in Everard; she had tried to make a man of Everard, the saint.

"Carolan!" he said. "Carolan! Darling, what is prison, what is transportation, what are chains? We can overcome them all. Promise, my darling. Promise to come to me . . ."

Her body urged her to lift her head, to let her brilliant eyes tell him of her response to the passion in him. But she could see Everard, his young face so different from that of Marcus, so beautiful, so saintly. What had prevented Everard from coming to her? How could she know what? Suppose he came? Suppose, when she landed on the other side, he was there waiting for her! Miracles could happen. In seven years time she would be a free woman. She would be twenty-four. Was that so very old? She fought against the almost overwhelming power of her senses. Because Marcus appealed to her body so strongly, she must guard against her body. What had Aunt Harriet slyly hinted? She was like her mother, like her grandmother . . . she had that in her, that immodesty, that sensuous desire which could, while it lasted, seem so important that it could lure one into ruining's one's life just for a momentary satisfaction. There he lay beside her, this man whom she knew to be a thief; he was unkempt; he was dirty; he was a convict sentenced to transportation for life! And because of that indefinable attraction he had for her, she had been ready

293

to give herself up to the sensuous dream of living beside him for the rest of her life, loving him, hating him, finding pleasure in him.

She said: "I love Everard. Who knows, he may come to me! I do not believe he has deserted me; doubtless his mother prevented his coming to Newgate . . . We must go back to Esther; whatever will she think?"

She got up and went back to Esther.

"Was it very bad?" Esther asked.

"What?" said Carolan.

"The chain gang. What a coward you must think me! But I cannot bear to hear of it." She appealed to Marcus. "Do you think I am a coward?"

"I think you are a very charming young lady!"

Carolan threw him a glance of distaste. She felt safe now. He could not put his hands on her, with Esther so near.

Esther said: "There was a lady looking over the barricade. I think she must be a passenger. She wore a beautiful gown; but how she scowled!"

"Do you not know," said Carolan, "that we convicts are performing animals? Our ways and habits are a source of amusement and ridicule to the free."

"She did not seem amused. Her dark eyes flashed. She seemed to me to be looking straight at you and Marcus. Her petticoat was satin; she had black hair and black eyes. She was very beautiful! She paced up and down . . . in this heat too, but she did not seem to notice it!"

Carolan said: "An admirer of Marcus's, doubtless!" She laughed at him. "Odd how, in his convict's rags, he can exercise that appeal of his!"

"Do not be jealous, darling," said Marcus. "I am not the man to be impressed by a satin petticoat."

"Oh, but Esther says she is beautiful! Do you not admire black eyes, Marcus?"

"What does it matter?" put in Esther. "This is the happiest hour we have spent since coming aboard. I could almost feel I was taking the trip for pleasure!"

"You must have strange ideas of pleasure, Esther," said Carolan.

"Oh come," put in Marcus. "A great poet once said 'There is some soul of goodness in things evil, would men observingly distil it out.' There is truth in that, do you not think so?"

"I do," said Esther. Then: "Look! There is the dark lady again!"

Marcus looked up and looked away quickly.

294

"Fie!" cried Carolan. "How coquettish he is! As coy as any maiden!"

"Carolan, please do not tease me." The seriousness of his eyes made her look at him sharply.

She demanded: "Why is it that there is always mystery surrounding you, Marcus?"

"Is there? I did not know it."

"You must know it. In Grape Street, one was never sure of you. And even here, on this miserable prison ship, there must be mystery concerning you."

"My dear Carolan, what are you saying? What mystery do you refer to?"

She was unable to reply. She stammered: "It was just . . . that you looked . . . oh, I cannot say. Secretive perhaps."

"Look!" said Esther. "That woman. She is talking to the sentry about us."

The woman's voice floated towards them, indignant and angry.

"I declare . . . such lack of discipline. One does not feel safe! They . . . so close . . . just as though they were ordinary people!"

"Oh, you dark-eyed beauty!" murmured Carolan. "If I had you here I would let you see whether or not we are ordinary people. I would have that satin petticoat off your back!"

"Yes, my dear," said Marcus. "Newgate is a good teacher; and found you an apt enough pupil, I'll swear!"

"And doubtless you would protect her from my violence, and tell her how becoming was her satin garment, and how you had always adored black eyes!"

"What if I do adore black eyes! I worship green ones . . . particularly when they flash in fury . . . and jealousy perhaps? Oh, Carolan, can you not see that you are my woman and I am your man? Do not stamp your foot or I shall be unable to resist putting my arms round you here and now and kissing your angry mouth and your angry eyes . . ."

"Hush! Esther will hear."

She turned from him.

The woman had walked away from the sentry; his face was red.

"You dogs!" he cried. "What the hell do you think this is? A pleasure cruise? Down to your holes before you're clamped into irons, every one of you!"

The black-eyed woman, for reasons best known to herself, had put an abrupt end to the hours of freedom.

Down in the women's quarters the heat was only just bearable. The convicts lay gasping in their berths, some of them reduced to semi-consciousness by the poisoned air. Half an hour ago two of their number had been taken away; they had died the day before. They did not talk of them, but in the minds of every woman and child was the thought, "Shall I be carried out like that before the journey's end?"

They were just out from Cape Town, and the weeks they had spent there had been a trying ordeal, hardened though they were. They had been kept down below for what seemed interminable days and nights. Fighting for air, listening to the creaking of the ship's timbers, with that foul odour of her stinking bilges in their nostrils which sickened even the most insensitive, most of them had longed for death. But now the ship had taken in her stores; sheep and fowls, pigs, goats, all sorts of livestock and fresh fruit and vegetables had been put aboard her; and now she was ready to complete her voyage. This was a matter of rejoicing, but the death of those two had sobered them strangely, had temporarily drawn them closer to each other.

Flash Jane, a good deal thinner than she had been since they entered Cape Town, dark hollows under her eyes like saucers in her yellow-green face, no longer Flash—just poor, sick, only half-alive Jane—turned to Carolan and said with her habitual aggressiveness: "You never tell us nothing about yourself. How did a lady like you come to be here with a lot like us, eh?"

Was she spoiling for trouble? wondered Carolan. But as she looked at the poor shadow of that Flash Jane who had come aboard all those months ago, she felt an unexpected tenderness sweep over her, and for the moment it smothered that bitterness which had eaten into her, tingeing all her thoughts and words.

"What do you care?" she said, but softly, gently.

Flash Jane spat neatly across the berth.

"Only wondered," she muttered. "Seemed a bit unnatural like . . . you and her . . ."

Carolan looked up into the blue-grey haze which always seemed to fill the crowded place; and she surprised herself by telling the woman what had led her here. She began with the visit to her father's shop, and as she talked, silence fell all about her, and lack-lustre eyes were turned in her direction. She felt sympathy there in that sordid place. Nobody laughed, nobody jeered; many listened.

When she ended, a woman from an upper berth raised her emaciated arms and began to shriek.

"It was a nark who got me, lady! If I had him 'ere I'd tear 'im to pieces, that I would. Boiling in oil is too good for narks. Them's my feelings."

The silence was resumed. There was more in that silence than the languor produced by fetid heat, semi-starvation and sickness. Carolan realised that she was living through a strange experience. It was as though the women drew together, forgot beastliness, forgot cruelty, forgot everything but that they were fellow human beings.

"What about her?" said Flash Jane, jerking her head towards Esther. "How'd she come?"

"Tell them, Esther," said Carolan.

"Do you think they want to hear?"

"Go on!" growled Flash Jane, and Esther told them.

It was a simple little story, but they believed it. It made them angry and it made them sad. Some of them may have been present when Esther arrived at Newgate; they may have been among those who tore off her clothes. But if they had been, they would have forgotten. Then and now had no connection with each other.

"Life's cruel, ain't it!" said Flash Jane. "I remember when I come to London. In service I was, where my Ma put me. Service! Not me, I says, and I come to London, and when I got there, there wasn't nothing for me to do but pick pockets, and I wasn't good at it. Then I met a girl who took me along to Mother Maybury."

"Mother Maybury!" cried a shrill voice. It belonged to the woman whose chief amusement seemed to be to strip herself, expose her gross body and fling it about lewdly in grotesque movements meant to be a dance. "You was at old Maybury's, was you?"

"Twenty-five years back!" said Flash Jane with a touch of honesty.

"Twenty-five! Why, it must be twenty-eight since I last seen the old lady. How did you leave her, Flash? The old trollop! She ought to have been strung up long afore she met me!"

"Well, believe it or not, she died a rich woman. Died in a feather bed with servants to wait on her, so I heard," said Flash Jane.

The other woman began to cry suddenly; not in the hysterical way in which Carolan had heard them sob during the last months, but quietly and regretfully. There was something heartrending about the shaking of that gross body.

Carolan said: "I've told my story; tell us yours."

The words had an instant effect on the woman. She dried her eyes; she laughed hoarsely and pulled open the ragged garment she wore. Carolan thought she was going to start stripping for her dance, the dance which seemed to drive the others into a frenzy of sensuality, which would set them recounting their adventures in lust. If she did, these moments would be lost; harshness, cruelty, would return. Carolan fought for these moments, fought for a longer glimpse beneath the horrible veil which the cruelty of life had drawn tightly about these people.

She said: "I'm sure it's interesting."

The woman's hands fell to her sides; her fingers plucked at her dress, miserably, not lewdly. She drew the dress tightly round her, and sat down heavily on her berth.

"Funny," she said, "looking back." Her voice was hushed; she was not speaking to them, but to herself. "Funny to think that was me. But it was me. Gawd! What life does to you!" She turned to face Carolan, and she smiled. "We all lived in the country. I loved the country. The trees . . . they was lovely. Never mind whether it was spring with the buds out and the birds up there—and what a row they used to make!—or summer with the leaves all thick and green; in the autumn they was golden brown and we'd sweep up the leaves and burn 'em. What a smell!" She began to cry softly. "And in winter, all black with the mist on 'em. I loved the country. My Gawd! I ain't been there for nigh on thirty years. Do it still look the same? Trees don't alter, do they? It's people that changes, it ain't trees.

"There was ten of us children! Me father worked in the fields. Me mother helped, but she was always having a fresh baby. I was the oldest. It was all right when we all got working. But Charley—he was me little brother—he was a cripple. No farmer wanted Charley. Him and me . . . well . . . I used to carry him everywhere on me back. But me father, he couldn't bear Charley, because Charley was doing nothing for his keep; and he wanted Charley out of the way. He'd belt Charley. I was twelve and Charley was ten when we run away to London. We hadn't never seen anything like London. It was wonderful. We thought there'd be work for us, but there wasn't work. We slept in alleys and under arches, and we was colder and hungrier than we'd been in the country. But we

298

was happier because there was no father to belt poor Charley. Then Charley stole a loaf of bread. We was together, and it was Charley who took it, and someone got hold of him and they took him, and I run behind, but they wouldn't take me too. I never see Charley no more."

Now everyone was listening, and the tears ran out of the woman's eyes and she did not seem to know they were there.

"Well," she went on, "I starved. I stole a bit, but no one caught me; and one day I talked to a girl a year older than me and she took me to Mother Maybury." She began to laugh.

"Mother Maybury! She had a rosy face and a little white cap; spotless it was. And she'd sit by her big fire; and she would pat you on the head, and she would tell you not to be frightened any more—you was one of her chicks. It would be 'Eat this, ducky! Another helping, chicky? You're with your old Mother Maybury, now, my poppet!' And you would eat; and you'd wonder if you'd died of cold by the river and gone to Heaven without knowing it. And then, when you had sat by her fire for a day or two with your belly as full as you could pack it, she would begin to explain to you all that you owed to Good Mother Maybury, and just how you would have to pay it back. She showed you how to tell fine ladies and gentlemen from the sort that aped them; she'd show you how to creep up behind them, swift as you like; she showed you how you went to bed with men. And if you didn't like it, there was always the cold outside and the hunger waiting for you. 'Don't be soft, my poppet!' Good Mother Maybury would say. 'My chickens have a rare time of it.' So I stayed, and I was with Mother Maybury nigh on three years, and if you looked after Mother Maybury she looked after you. And if you didn't look after her, she looked after you too! It was queer how many who didn't give up all their takings found themselves in jail. Good Mother Maybury! Kind Mother Maybury! It was pease pudding she gave me first; I can taste it now. It smelt that good! I can see the log on her fire; it was all blue and pretty. So I thought I'd died and was in Heaven; but I was only at Good Mother Maybury's!"

Silence fell, thick as the haze made by their breath. The mis-shapen girl who shared their berth sat up suddenly, her eyes brilliant.

"Keep still, you!" growled Flash Jane, but her voice held none of its old harshness.

"Do you want to tell us how you came to be here?" asked Carolan.

"It was the chimleys," said the girl.

"What?"

"Me brother done 'em. We was the eldest, him and me. The baby wasn't old enough. I was five. Me brother was four; he done the chimleys. Me father made him."

"What happened to your brother?" asked Carolan.

"He went down a chimley. He got burned to death. Me father came in and told us. He was wild . . . 'cause, if me brother was burned to death, who was going to sweep the chimleys?"

There was a stark horror in the halting words which had been lacking in the woman's more coherent story. Everyone was listening. The mis-shapen little girl was no longer a butt for their cruelty; she was a child who had suffered horrors such as even they had not experienced.

The child began to scream out: "They dressed me up in his clothes, so's they'd think I was a boy. I'd got to go, they said. I couldn't . . . I was frightened. I knew I'd be burned to death. Me brother was frightened of that, and he'd got burned to death. I knew I'd be burned to death . . . I couldn't . . . !"

"Try not to think of it," said Esther. "It is past now."

The child looked at her with wide eyes.

"He made me. I was too big. Me brother had done it when he was four. He wasn't too big. But I was bigger. It used to hurt. Once I couldn't get out, and I screamed and screamed. Then they got me out . . . and . . . I wouldn't go again. Me father beat me. Me mother beat me. I didn't mind beatings. I couldn't . . . I'll never go up again. It's black up there . . . it's so dark you can't see. Me father said he'd kill me if I didn't go up. Then . . ." Her voice broke on a sob. "I . . . run away . . ."

The dark chimneys would always haunt her dreams. When she screamed in the night it was because of those dark chimneys. If only they had known before, perhaps they could have comforted her.

Flash Jane put her face close to the child and said, not unkindly: "What was you took for?"

"For taking."

"Nicking, you mean?"

"Taking. I didn't mind. It's better than the chimley."

"Chimley sweeps has a terrible time of it," said Flash Jane. "I remember a man named Tom what was one. He was a rare one, Tom was. River thief and a regular swell. Done well for himself. Nice big man. He begun as a sweep though. He was smart. Said there wasn't much you couldn't hide in a bag of soot. He started on his own. Done well for himself. I wonder what become of Tom?"

The child said: "There ain't nothing so bad as a black

300

chimley with the fire down below. There ain't nothing so bad as that."

Esther stroked her hair, and she looked with wondering eyes up at the girl.

Esther thought: "I'll teach her to pray."

Carolan thought: "If anyone torments her again, they'll wish they hadn't."

Change came as suddenly as before. There was something so hideous about the picture that child had conjured up that they could not look at it. Softness was folly. Flash Jane went on to talk of her friend Tom, the big man, the river thief. Her reminiscences were as highly coloured as she could make them, the details as intimate. They listened awhile. Someone began to sing a bawdy song. The woman who had gone to Mother Maybury's wriggled off her berth and slowly began to take off her clothes.

It was January, and the summer evening was calm and warm. Esther and Carolan lay side by side looking across the sea, for it was the women's hour of freedom. It seemed to Carolan that years had elapsed since they left England, and here they were, almost on the other side of the world.

"Esther," she said, "how lucky we have been . . . so far!"

Esther said: "I cannot bear it if we are separated."

"Esther, do you believe in will power?"

"I believe in prayer."

"But I cannot leave our being together to prayers, Esther. Prayers are never answered. Do you know, when I was in prison I prayed. I prayed for Everard to come back to me. He never came. What good were my prayers?"

"Perhaps God did not mean him to come."

"Perhaps He does not mean us to be together. It would be cruel to separate us now, Esther. We must do everything we can. Who knows, there may be some opportunity. Esther, Esther, what will become of us on the other side?"

"That we cannot know until we get there, Carolan. But I would have you know, here and now, what your friendship has meant to me. I believe I should have died without it. You are different from the rest of us, Carolan. You are strong and brave. I think you were meant to be a leader."

"A leader! I should have liked to be a leader, Esther. I should like to lead people against cruelty and wickedness. Oh . . . not what you call wickedness. Not Flash Jane and her kind, but those who made Flash Jane what she is. I would be a crusader against those who made our laws, against your church perhaps which allows these things to happen . . . and more, applauds them. There, I have hurt you, Esther, I blunder. I am always hurting you. Wasn't there a parable about a man who was set upon by robbers. The Levite passed by on the other side of the road, like our churchmen, Esther, our politicians; those people know what is happening, yet pass by on the other side of the road. I like to think that I am the Samaritan of a different faith . . . the Samaritan who did not pass by. But what can I do . . . a prisoner? Besides, I know myself. I am not good enough. I am wicked, more wicked than you could understand, Esther. But that is what I would like to be, were it possible . . . the good Samaritan."

"You would be, Carolan. You would be!"

"No! I should be thinking of myself as I walked along. I should not see the poor man calling for help . . . Not until I myself was set upon should I see him, and then it would be too late."

There was a short silence, then Carolan said: "How good it is to breathe fresh air! I never thought of that in the old days at home. Fancy being grateful because you can breathe fresh air for one hour each day. We must be very strong, Esther, to have survived."

"We are not very old," said Esther.

"You are but a child. I wonder how Marcus is. Is he in as good spirits as he was, I wonder?"

"I should like to see him. He is a good man."

"He is a thief!" said Carolan roughly. "We are here through no criminal acts, Esther; do not forget that such is not the case with Marcus."

"Life was very cruel to him."

"Very cruel. But it will never conquer Marcus." Unconsciously she spoke his name softly, thinking of the glitter of his blue eyes, and the desire in them.

"Tell me," said Esther, "of how you went to Vauxhall Gardens, and how he was there, dressed as a fine gentleman."

"I have told you many times."

"Nevertheless I like to hear it again, I love to hear the stories of your life."

"I have told you so much, have I not? You must know it almost as well as I do myself."

"I lie in the berth and think of it all. Sometimes it helps me to sleep, and I forget I am there. I can smell the horses in the stables, and the mutton cooking before your Aunt Harriet's fire; and I can smell the perfume Thérèse is putting on your

302

mother's gown. When you came, you made me alive, Carolan. I wish there was something I could do for you."

"What should I have done without your friendship?"

"You talk as though this is farewell," said Esther with terror in her voice.

"Who knows, it may be! Look!"

Carolan stood up, excited. She pointed.

"I saw something. I am sure I saw something. It has gone now . . . but look, Esther, can you see?"

Their eyes were fixed on the horizon. For ten minutes they did not move, and then clearly and definitely they saw the dim outline of white cliffs.

There was bustle on board now. All convicts were ordered below; gratings were made fast over hatches. The air was more stifling than ever.

Carolan and Esther lay very close. They held hands in the darkness. Esther prayed: "Please God, having given her, do not take her from me."

Carolan murmured: "I will not lose her. I must keep her with me. She does not know it, but I need her as much as she needs me."

The ship lay at anchor, while the new land smiled under the morning summer sun. Forests of eucalyptus trees like an army of giants, had marched to the edge of the land and halted there. On the grassy hills stood out clearly the silver-barked gum trees freely mingled with cedar. The leaves of the great eucalyptus trees cast their shadows where in spring golden wattles and the white flowers of the dogwood bushes bloomed. It seemed a smiling, fertile country that welcomed the newcomers, but it aroused in them nothing but nostalgia for their native land. The warmth of the sun, the brilliance of the sea, the green foliage, the white-crested cockatoos and the gaudy parakeets which gave to the scene that picture quality, could only by their very contrast remind them of the crooked streets of St. Giles's, grey-white buildings looming up in fog, the clop-clop of horses' hooves on cobbles, the Thames enveloped in mysterious gloom—London, which had been home to them, and which always would be home.

The women were lined up in one portion of the deck. Some way off were the men. Carolan looked for Marcus; she could not see him. Esther stood beside her, terrified. Looking along the lines of faces whose skin had acquired that peculiar quality of bad cheese, Carolan thought what a contrast they made

303

to the sparkling sea and the colourful land. So beautiful, so straight, those trees; so ugly, so distorted, so stunted, this pitiful collection of human beings.

Flash Jane told the company that she had heard through a friend that there was a very comfortable brothel in Sydney, whose proprietress always came to look over cargoes in search of 'servants'.

"He! He!" laughed Flash Jane in anticipation. "If you play your cards right, they say the convict life ain't so bad . . . for a woman."

The little girl whose brother had been burned to death clutched at Carolan's fingers.

"Do they have chimleys there? Do they have chimleys?"

"You have grown too big," said Carolan. "If they have chimneys they would not think of using you to clean them."

The child's smile appalled Carolan; it was like the smile of an idiot. "I have growed. I have growed!" she said, and stood on tiptoe.

A Marine came walking past them.

"Quiet! In line there!" He dropped the butt end of his musket on a woman's foot. She screamed. He passed on, laughing.

Indignation rose in Carolan. The humiliation of this! Lined up on show, like cattle. She could have wept with the indignity of it, but she dared not weep. She held her head high, and Esther came nearer; their fingers touched. She could feel Esther's terror through her fingers. She knew Esther was praying silently all the time.

Boats had been rowing out to the ship ever since they had stood here, and that was quite an hour, Carolan thought. Her eyes ached with the unaccustomed brightness; she would have liked to have fallen down on the deck and slept. She looked at Esther's face. It had that queer look which they all had—that of cheese which is going bad, a little green and yellowish-white; the bones of Esther's face were very prominent; but starvation and confinement had not been able to dull the splendour of her hair. It was unkempt; it was dirty; but the sun's rays touched it and made it shine like a field of ripe English corn. People would notice that hair. She thought of Flash Jane's words and her evil grin. A procuress looking for servants . . . Oh, not that for Esther! Not that!

A man with an eyeglass and a very elegant coat had come aboard. He stood near them, exchanging a word with one of the Marines. He stuck his eyeglass into his eye, quizzed the rows of female convicts, said something to the Marine and they laughed coarsely.

"By gad!" His voice drifted over to Carolan. "A lovely crew! What beauties, eh?"

He approached. "By gad!" he drawled. "By gad . . ."

Flash Jane tittered. One of the women began to sing in order to call attention to herself.

"Silence, you old whore!" cried the Marine.

Carolan watched the eyeglass turn on one woman, then on another. It was getting near to her and to Esther. She gripped Esther's hand; Esther cowered close. The indignity of it! The humiliation! Hot colour flamed into Carolan's face; the eyeglass was approaching her; instinctively she knew that when it reached her it would pause.

Another man had appeared. He was very fair and very large, with big, irregular features. The captain was with him, and from the respectful attention the captain was giving him it appeared that he was a person of some importance. His mouth was a straight line; he looked as if he could be excessively cruel, coldly cruel. Carolan was alert now. Neither she nor Esther must fall into the hands of the man with the eyeglass. In her panic, Carolan told herself that anything would be preferable to that. She began to bargain, which was the only way of prayer she knew: "Please let the other one see us. Do not let that eyeglass find us. If You will only not let that happen, I will . . . I will . . . try to believe in You: I will try . . ."

"This way, Mr. Masterman," the captain was saying. "This way, sir. They freshen up, sir. Soap and water will work wonders, sir. A cargo always looks very frowsy on arrival; it's the conditions aboard."

"Frowsy is a very mild way of expressing it," said the man who had been addressed as Mr. Masterman. His tone was cold; his words clipped. The eyeglass was very near now.

"Hello, ladies."

The little girl began to scream suddenly.

"I won't go up a chimley! I won't! I won't! I'll jump in the sea. I won't be burned to death!"

Mr. Masterman and the captain had paused. They stared at the child who had thrown herself down on the deck and was sobbing wildly.

The Marine kicked her.

"Get up, you baggage! You ugly imp, get up!"

She did not move and he kicked her again.

"Get up, I say! Get up!"

"What is it that the child says?" enquired Mr. Masterman.

"It is giving themselves airs, sir, to call attention to themselves. A taste of the lash will do her good."

305

The man with the eyeglass stared down at the child.

"Ugly little devil. Cripple, ain't she?"

Carolan stepped forward unthinkingly.

"She has been badly frightened. She was nearly burned to death."

They were all looking at Carolan now. The man with the eyeglass quizzed her with insolent interest. The captain's face was scarlet; so was that of the Marine.

"Get back into your place. Speak when you are spoken to." He turned to Masterman. "These convicts have no shame, sir. They push themselves forward to get attention."

"Bless me!" said the man with the eyeglass. He rocked backwards and forwards on his heels. "I believe it is a redhead. And damme, I do declare a little soap and water would make a beauty of the gal!"

Carolan was limp with terror. Impulsively, foolishly, she had done that which she had most longed to avoid; she had called attention to herself. She remembered some of the stories she had heard of prisoners who were taken into households; she guessed the fate of anyone taken into the household of a man such as this one.

It was one of the important moments of her life, and she knew it. She was aware of everything about her, the rocking ship, the changing sea and sky, the bright plumage of birds, the green lush land before her. Perhaps she forgot her cynicism and prayed then, humbly; she did not know; all she was aware of afterwards was that some instinct made her turn her head towards Mr. Masterman, to hold him with her burning eyes, to beg, to plead.

"Save me!" said her eyes. And then as though from a long way off she heard his voice.

"My wife wants a couple to work in the kitchen. She looks a strong girl, that one."

Carolan thought she was going to faint. The smell of filthy bodies in that fresh air enveloped her. Desperately she fought her faintness. She took an almost imperceptible step forward, and she was dragging Esther with her.

Those queer grey eyes withdrew their gaze. It seemed like minutes before he spoke, but actually it was only a second or two.

He said: "Those two look all right. Those are the two I will take."

The man with the eyeglass dropped it. Carolan heard his exclamation—"Gad, sir! I saw the girl first. By gad, Mr. Masterman . . ." But there was defeat in his voice, which told her

306

that Mr. Masterman was an important person in the new land for which they were bound.

When Carolan and Esther went to Sydney it was little more than a settlement, for several years were to elapse before Lachlan Macquarie, with the help of a transported architect, was to replace its wood, wattle and daub with stone and brick, and straighten out in some measure the confused crookedness of its streets. The house into which Carolan and Esther were taken was one of the grandest in Sydney, standing on the corner of an up-hill road that branched out of Sergeant-Major's Row, now George Street, and which was little more than a track which drivers of carts had followed among the low hills. From the upper part of the house it was possible to get a perfect view of what has been called the most beautiful harbour in the world, with its sand and gravel beaches, and its many indentations fringed with green foliage. When Carolan had first seen it, having been sent to clean the attics, she was lost in admiration for so much that was beautiful; and then in one of the narrow, winding, up-hill roads she saw the bent backs and manacled limbs of a chain gang returning from work, and went quickly from the window, wondering if it were possible that one of those scarcely human creatures was Marcus.

She had been lucky, she and Esther. So much that was horrible might have happened to them, but they had had the good fortune to be taken into Gunnar Masterman's house; this man was a leading citizen with his eye on big rewards for the services he rendered the youthful town; a cold and calculating man by all accounts, but a wise and good man who went to church every Sunday. Upright, commanding, excessively virtuous, he was friendly with Governor Philip Gidley King; he had married the daughter of Major Gregory, a man of wealth and power in the town, and it was a worthy marriage, for everything Gunnar Masterman did was apparently worthy.

Being confined to the basement, it was only rarely that Carolan saw the upper part of the house. The servants were kept to the basement as much as possible, for they were convicts, all except Margery the cook, and she was on ticket of leave. Their bedroom—one huge room which every one of them shared—was in the basement. Its floor was of earth, and one of its walls was the side of the hill against which the house had been built. There was a small grating high in one

307

wall; and this place was considered adequate, even luxurious, accommodation for convicts.

It was at the end of January when they arrived, and in the next weeks the summer weather grew intolerable. The mosquitoes were a plague to torture English skins, and there were no sleeping nets available in the basement. The moist heat was intense and oppressive; there was no respite. It was too hot to work by day; it was too hot to sleep at night.

Esther, who was adaptable, was almost happy, but Carolan rebelled against this new life, and as the memory of Newgate and the convict ship became more and more remote, her dissatisfaction grew greater.

But Margery, the priestess of the kitchen, the ticket of leave woman, was drawn more towards Carolan than towards Esther. Margery had been sentenced to seven years transportation for bigamy, and had served four years of her sentence in Mr. Masterman's establishment when she had been given a ticket of leave and put in charge of the convict servants. Having just come into freedom she was ostentatiously aware of it. She flaunted that freedom; she boasted of it; and she was witheringly contemptuous of those who had not yet attained it. She wore blue merino, and when she worked in the kitchen, a white apron over it; she smoothed it happily, contrasting it with the yellow garments the others wore. She was not unkind, but lazy and selfish, sensual and mischievous. Her most precious possessions were her memories and the bunch of keys she wore at her waist, these latter the symbols of freedom. She talked incessantly of her past, and Carolan soon learned that she had begun by being the wife of a small tradesman; he was a good man, but he did not satisfy her for long, and she ran away with a travelling actor who deserted her after three months, when she took up with a pedlar. She loved all men; she couldn't help it, she told them; there was something about men that appealed to her. They were so strong, and yet such babies. She loved them all, from Mr. Masterman to James who did odd jobs about the house. And the pedlar had been a proper man with whom life had had its ups and downs but had managed to be excellent fun. She had travelled everywhere with him; he had said she was a wonderful woman at getting the men and girls to buy their goods, and so she was. She could sell anything . . . particularly to men. But the pedlar was a jealous man, and once he had seen her trying to sell a book to a farmer behind a water-butt, and he had been so angry, poor, sweet man, that he had walked

308

off and left her. The farmer had a wife, and would have none of her either; so she had wandered on and on until she came to a cottage, and in this cottage lived a curate all alone, and she had stayed with him; and the poor soul had had but one bed which he had wanted to give up to her, but she would not have that; so they shared the bed, and he, poor religious man, had wanted to marry her after that, fearing he might be damned if he did not. She had had to soothe his poor worried mind, and that was how she committed bigamy and came at last to be a ticket of leave woman in Mr. Masterman's kitchen. She had taken James, the odd-job man, for her friend now. He used to lean on the kitchen-sill and she would feed him with tit-bits. She was proud of her friendship with James, for he was a free man . . . free enough in this town of convicts, that was—on ticket of leave like herself. Mr. Masterman trusted James. He went about the place as he liked; sometimes he rode out to one of Mr. Masterman's stations and worked there for a week or two. At midnight he used to knock at the basement bedroom door, and Margery would let him in; they would whisper together, keeping up a pretence that the others did not hear, nor even guess at these midnight visits of James's.

Margery, who liked to talk of her own life, had a curiosity about the lives of others.

"What brought you here?" she demanded of Carolan and Esther.

Carolan told her.

"H'm!" said Margery. "I don't know as I like thieves in me kitchen."

"We were wrongly accused," protested Carolan. "We are not thieves!"

Margery and Jin, the parlourmaid, rocked with laughter.

"All convicts are accused wrong . . . according to them," explained Margery. "I can't think what Mr. Masterman can be thinking of to bring thieves into me kitchen!"

"Look here!" Carolan said hotly. "I never stole anything. If you think I did, if you think I'm not good enough to mix with you . . . I . . . I . . . I'll ask to be moved right away."

Margery put her hands on fat hips and rolled about in delight.

"Hark to her! Hark to her! Now who do you think you are, my dear? The Queen of England? The Princess of Wales? Just hark at her! She will ask to be moved. And listen to her, Jin; just listen, girl! The way she talks . . . all haughty, eh?" She turned to Esther. "And what about you?"

"I know it is of no use to say so," said Esther, "but I am innocent too."

Margery seemed overcome with merriment and at length gasped out: "I ain't laughed so much since my curate put his spectacles on his nose and said 'Well, if you really think I ought to come in with you . . . I will. Perhaps if we pray for great strength of mind . . .' No, I ain't laughed so much since then!"

It was Carolan she liked though. Not Esther. Mealy mouthed, that was Esther. Carolan, she fondly supposed, was something of what she herself had been at that age.

"Thieving was something I never could abide," she said. "I wouldn't have thought you would have been sent out for thieving; you don't look the kind. Still, you are here now and I don't mind telling you you are the dead spit of what I was at your age. I was married then though; we had our little shop. There I was, ladling out the sugar; we used to make love behind the sacks of flour. Funny it was when customers come in. I can laugh at it now. Look here, you see that whip hanging over the mantel? That's for them that can't do as I say, do you see? Do *you* see?" she asked Esther.

She looked with disfavour on Esther. Thin! Lovely hair though. Not one for the men, and the men wouldn't be for her either, because men were for those who liked them, and she didn't blame them for that!

Jin, the parlourmaid, was a good-looking girl of the gipsy type. She had flashing black eyes and vital, black, curling hair; in her ears she wore brass ear-rings, and she had tied a piece of string about the waist of her yellow frock to accentuate the smallness of her waist and the line of the bosom above.

"Now Jin here," said Margery, and her voice took on a note almost of reverence as she spoke, "Jin was transported for attempted murder. She stabbed her lover. Mind you, I wouldn't say but what he deserved it; he was carrying on with somebody else right under her very nose, so she stabbed him. Now I was never a one for violence myself—and a good deal I had to put up with particularly from my pedlar! He would go take his pack into a house, and, given half a chance, he'd take advantage of the lady of the house in the twinkling of an eye and scarce say thank you. There was a man to take up with, and mad he could make me, but I trust I'm a woman who can control herself. Still, I understand Jin."

Jin eyed both Carolan and Esther from under lowered brows. She was sullen, not inclined to be friendly.

310

"Jin's got a mighty temper, she has!" chuckled Margery. "Show 'em what you carries around with you, Jin!"

Jin did not answer, and Margery pulled at her skirt and chuckled throatily.

"Where do you keep it today, Jin? In your pocket, eh? There it is; take a look at it. She carries that knife around with her, and she'd as lief bring it out as look at you. That's what gipsy blood does for you! I know. I knew a gipsy once; he come to our door, a fine-looking man, flash as they made 'em. Baskets he had for sale, and he asked me to cross his hand with silver. 'Lady,' he says, 'there's a dark man coming into your life. You're going to be glad of this dark man, lady!' And believe me, I was . . . curate's being a bit tame now and then. Talk about temper, he'd got one! They was encamped near the cottage for days. I saw a lot of him. And his wife carried a knife around, just like Jin. You've got to keep clear of people what carries knives. I'm not so sure of what Mr. Masterman mightn't say if he was to know you carried that knife around."

"I ain't hurting no one," muttered Jin. "It's my knife, ain't it?"

"No!" said Margery. "It ain't. It's Mr. Masterman's. Everything here is Mr. Masterman's. You and Poll and these two here. Why, if he liked . . ."

"I did not know," said Carolan, "that he had bought us body and soul."

Margery rocked backwards and forwards, laughing.

"Don't it make you laugh, Jin? The way she talks, eh? Body and soul! Tell you who she reminds me of? The mistress! Talks just like that, the mistress does. And every time I looks at the poor lady I says to myself: 'Poor Mr. Masterman!' You would think . . . but there you are, men is funny creatures, no mistake. Well Miss, do you think we're going to suit your ladyship here? Speak up, lady. We've got to suit *you*, haven't we; now whether you was to suit us, that ain't no importance at all, it ain't!"

"Well," said Carolan, "you asked for my opinion; I have given it."

"I say, Jin, I do like to hear her talk. You'd think she was out for politics, not thieving. Here, you! Why don't you say something?"

"What do you want me to say?" asked Esther.

"How do you like us?"

"I . . . I think I am going to like it here."

"This is good, this is! A pair of 'em! Now my curate, he

spoke soft and gentle just like her . . . but soft and gentle, rough as you like, they're all the same between the sheets. That's men for you! Women's the same, I bet. Where's Poll? Poll! Polly! Come here and meet your new friends."

Poll came from the sink, wiping her hands. She was very thin and pale and ugly; her nose was large, her eyes small, and her mouth was crooked; her teeth were uneven and brown.

"Poor Poll," said Margery. "She came from the workhouse and was took advantage of. She murdered her baby; that's why she's here."

Poll started to cry.

"Now, don't snivel, Poll," said Margery sharply. "And it was your own fault for getting took advantage of. Come here and meet her ladyship. What do we call your ladyship, eh?"

"My name is Carolan Haredon."

"Really now! Are you sure it ain't Lady Carolan Haredon?"

"Quite sure."

"A pity! I'd have liked to have a ladyship in my kitchen."

When Margery heard Esther's story, she was a little more pleased with her.

"But you shouldn't have been cruel to the young gent, my love! That's why you got to Newgate . . . being cruel. Why, if you'd done what the young man wanted, you might have been ladying it in London Town instead of working in a Sydney basement."

So much for life in the basement. It was not so easy to know what went on in the upper part of the house. Mr. Masterman was engaged in much business. He owned several stations, but that strip of country shut in on one side by the Blue Mountains and on the other by a great ocean had not proved such rich and fertile land as the first settlers had hoped it would. While the mountains remained an impenetrable barrier, the activities of pioneers on land must necessarily be restricted, and Mr. Masterman was not the sort to endure restrictions. At one time he had taken a schooner to the Bass Strait Islands and done very well out of the venture, returning with many sealskins and tons of oil; but these did not attract him as the land did. He kept an interest in the sealing business, but did not himself go again to sea. He arranged for the putting up of houses and other buildings; he dabbled in the politics of the town, and was a friend and supporter of the influential John MacArthur, though he managed to keep clear of the man's quarrels with Governor King. He was clever and alert, a pioneer who had come to this country, not in the grip of the law, but in that of his own relentless and dynamic ambition. A new country had been discovered; he wanted to write his name boldly at the head of its history, side by side with that of Phillip, that man of genius and such patience who was the real founder of the colony and had brought out the first fleet; he wanted to write it beside that of MacArthur, him whom they called Kingmaker. There was little cruelty in his house; the lash was hardly ever used. But to him, Carolan was sure, the convicts were not people; they were merely a cheap and convenient form of getting labour. He had convicts on his sheep farms, convicts building roads and houses. Cheap convict labour was one of those stepping stones which were helping Gunnar Masterman to glory. But much of this was conjecture on Carolan's part, built up from scraps of conversation chiefly with Margery, the talkative, who saw all men through amorous eyes. "Poor man," said Margery, "with that sickly wife of his! And not a son, nor yet a daughter to call his own. And him not the man to go around whoring. And her, with her room all to herself . . . Poor Mr. Masterman!"

"I do not believe he minds that she has a room to herself," said Carolan. "He does not mind that he has no son or daughter. He is cold as ice. You feel it."

"So your ladyship feels it, does she! So your ladyship has been looking at Mr. Masterman, eh? Now Tom and Harry, riding in from the stations with the smell of cattle in their clothes, now they wouldn't be the ones to attract your lovely ladyship! Of course not! Why, your ladyship's eyes are all for Mr. Masterman!"

"How dare you!" said Carolan. "I . . . hate the man!"

"Hate your master, eh? Don't forget the whip over the mantel. 'Margery,' he says to me. 'I trust you to use it judicial.' 'You can trust me, Mr. Masterman,' I says. And so he can. And listen, my lady, if I hear another word against your master, I uses it. It's mutiny, nothing less!"

Margery would never use the whip, though she talked so often of doing so. Carolan laughed at her.

"Suppose I tell you all about my lover—how would that be?"

"There now, me love, I knew you'd got one. You tell Margery. I understand. You don't want this other scum to hear."

It was so easy to please Margery; she loved the story of the squire. "His rage, me love, when he found the bird flown! You was a sly one!" Carolan told of Everard. "Parsons, me lovely, they're men too. I can tell you that. I said to him:

'Now there ain't no sense in staying out there shivering. There's room in here for the both.' And what if he does mutter a prayer afore he gets in! Why, bless us all, it makes a change, now don't it?"

But Carolan never said a word about Marcus; yet she thought of him often.

Esther was almost happy. Each night she knelt by her bed to say her prayers. Margery chuckled at the proceedings; Jin looked on with cold distaste, and Poll watched with vacant eyes; but none molested her.

"If only," said Esther, "we could hear news of Marcus, how happy we could be!"

"You might be," said Carolan. "I could never be happy again. You forget I have lost Everard, and my mother is dead."

Esther was full of contrition.

"I am selfish! I think only of myself. Poor, poor Carolan!"

Carolan spent a lot of time talking to Margery, who loved to hear her talk. She told of the passion of the squire, who was not really her father; she told of Charles who had been cruel and had tried to kiss her; she told the story of how she had been locked in the tomb.

"Ah!" sighed Margery, rocking with glee. "You and me, me love, is as like as peas in a pod. You'll be the spit of me when you grows up to be my age. And one word in your ear, lovely —keep clear of pedlars!"

Carolan thought, Shall I be like her?

Her hands were rough with housework. She was an indifferent worker, and but for the fact that she was a favourite with Margery, the woman might have been tempted to get down the whip from above the mantel. Crockery seemed to slip out of Carolan's hands. " 'Tis a mighty good thing that poor lady's so sickly. Now if it was some ladies who took a pride in their homes, it would be the triangle for you, lovey, and the lash about your white skin." Margery liked to pull the yellow dress off Carolan's shoulders and stroke her. "Lovely white skin it is, lovey. Dead spit of what mine was when I was twenty, and it ain't so long ago neither."

Carolan, restive in the basement, hating the dirty water into which it was necessary to plunge her hands, washing dishes, peeling potatoes, hating the smell of cooking, was bored. She longed for the fields and lanes around Haredon, and the feel of a horse beneath her. She asked a good many questions about what went on above stairs.

"There used to be a good deal of entertaining," Margery

told her, "but the mistress don't often feel up to it nowadays. Her health's bad, and getting worse. I can't think that it's what you might call a happy marriage. There she is, spending half of her time on the bed in her room with one of her headaches. Now if I had a nice upstanding man like Mr. Masterman for me husband . . ."

"Do you think she is really ill?" asked Carolan.

"Illness is a funny thing. There's people who thinks they has it, and if they thinks hard enough they've got it. That's illness just as the smallpox or anything else is. Well, that's the sort of illness she's got. Why, I remember a year or so back there was an epidemic of fever and people was afraid of its spreading; bless me, if she didn't take to her bed and was burning hot, and the doctor coming. It wasn't fever she'd got, but it was something well nigh as bad, and if it hadn't been for Doctor Martin . . ." Margery smiled affectionately as she said the doctor's name ". . . if it hadn't been for him, she'd have had fever all right. That's her for you!"

They sat round the table, Esther, Jin, Polly, Margery, James and Carolan, eating supper of bread and cheese, which they washed down with ale. It was lax in Margery's kitchen. It might have been a servants' hall back in England. Where else in Sydney were convict servants treated like this! Margery was responsible of course. She sat at the head of the table with James on her right hand and Carolan on her left. She was well pleased, for the presence of James meant that she was still attractive enough to bring him round to the basement every night, though he had his own quarters with the other men in some outbuildings near the house. And there was Carolan, with her smouldering eyes and her lovely budding body to remind Margery of what she was a mere twenty years ago.

There was a dinner-party going on above stairs, and Jin wore a white apron over her yellow dress; she looked attractive in the lamplight.

Carolan said: "Tell us what the table looked like, Jin."

"It looked all right," said Jin.

Margery said: "The table looked beautiful. I done it meself. The linen! And the glasses! I took in the pudding meself, pretending it was to see all was well, but really to have a look at them. Now he was at the head of the table, and a handsome man he is, and mighty pleased with himself he was looking too, and do you wonder! Quite some of the best people in Sydney was at his dinner table. And her . . . well, there she was at the other end of the table . . . in blue. Her fair hair's getting thin, I noticed, and she was too pale. Too much lying a-bed, my lady, I says to meself."

"Lazy old woman!" said Jin. "Why should we slave like we do . . ."

Margery's eyes flashed.

"Now that's enough of that. I'll tell you why. Because you're nothing more nor less than a murderess, and she . . . she's a lady of the land. Another word from you and I ask James to get down the whip for me . . . aye, and to lay it about you for me. It's mutiny, that's what it is!"

Jin lifted a lazy eyelid and surveyed James. It was the first time she had glanced in his direction. There was something fiery and passionate about the gipsy, stormy and fascinating. James stared at her; Margery flushed a dirty pink; her jowls quivered. She looked very old, thought Carolan.

Esther said: "I saw her; she was coming down the stairs and the kitchen door was open. I saw her pass along the upper floor. Her dress was shimmering blue. She looked . . ."

"I know," said Margery curtly, "like one of them angels you're always praying to!"

Esther blushed and cast down her head.

"Here, Poll, you go and get me that bottle out of me cupboard," said Margery. "Go on! Don't gape. Look sharp."

"Tell us about her dress," said Carolan to Esther.

"It was blue, and there was some silver about it, and she had silver slippers. She looked like a fairy . . . she is so small."

"A sickly fairy!" said Margery, still angry. "And next to him at the table was that Miss Charters. A big, bold girl, she is, and looking for a husband if you'll be asking me. There she was, right next to him, and you could see how he would have been the one she would have chosen if it wasn't for the fact that he had a wife already."

"Perhaps they'll get rid of her," said Poll, dribbling in sudden excitement. "Perhaps . . ."

She came to the table and laid the bottle of gin beside Margery's plate.

Margery caught her by the ear. "Look here, girl! Don't you run away with the idea that because you commit murders, other people do. Decent folk don't, I tell you. There's something bad about people as takes life, and I always have said it."

Poll's lips began to quiver. Her mind was unhinged by the murder of her baby. Carolan had seen her in her bed, holding a roll of dirty towelling against her breast, crooning over it.

She had seen her in the light of morning, holding the towelling against her, asleep, with a smile of content about her face; she was dreaming of course that it was her baby she held; she could not go to sleep at night until she had assured herself that her baby was not dead and that she held it in her arms. Poor Poll, she talked incessantly of murder; during the day she tried to pretend that it was a natural thing . . . people did it as easily as they laughed or sang. It was the only way she could console herself.

Carolan had deftly worked a piece of flannel into the shape of a doll. She had sewn buttons on it for eyes, and had drawn on it a nose and mouth with a piece of charcoal. It had been touching to see the way the girl seized it. She took it to bed every night. How cruel of Margery to speak in that way to the girl! But Margery was put out because Jin was still regarding James from under those heavy lids of hers.

Carolan longed for the comparative peace of the bedroom, with Jin lying on her back, her hair a black cloud on her pillow, and Poll cuddling her doll and thinking it was her baby; and Esther, having said her prayers of thanksgiving, lying sleeping in her bed, while Margery and James groaned and giggled, and sighed and chuckled together in Margery's creaking bed.

Now here in the kitchen the atmosphere had become sultry with the tumble of coming storm. Margery's big brown eyes, usually soft with reminiscence, were hard in her red face; she kept looking at the whip over the chimney-piece and she lifted her head proudly, flaunting her freedom.

"Here!" she said. "Let's have a drop of gin. There's no kick in this grog. Now gin's the stuff. Why, back home you can get rolling blind for twopence. Bring up your glasses."

"Not for me," said Esther.

"Oh, not for you, eh? Too good, are you! But not too good to thieve from the lady you works for. I'll have to keep my eye on you, me lady. You takes from one, you takes from the other."

Carolan said: "Give me your glass, Esther." She took it, flashed a warning glance at Esther, smiled at Margery.

"There!" said Margery. "Drink that up, you sly little cat! And don't think you deceive me for a minute with your praying to God."

Carolan wanted to comfort Margery, poor Margery to whom youth meant a good deal because love went with it.

Esther took the glass with trembling fingers. Her nerve had been broken in Newgate; temporarily she was lulled into a certain security, but she could be jerked out of it in a second. Here in the Masterman kitchen she could do the work allotted to her, the convict garb did not hurt her because she was meek of heart and she was innocent; she took on a good deal of Carolan's work, and enjoyed doing it, for she felt she owed to Carolan a debt which she would never, never repay as long as she lived. She said her prayers each night, before she slept the sleep of a quiet conscience. But embedded in her mind was the memory of the agony she had endured in Newgate when those women surrounded her, stripped her of her clothes, and did to her what she preferred to forget and never could as long as she lived. Sometimes she would awake in the night, screaming, because she had dreamed that that ring of hideously cruel faces was closing in on her. Then Carolan, strangely gentle, unlike herself, would lean over to her bed, take her hand, waken her. "It's all right, Esther. It's all right. You're not there now. You're here . . . It's all right here, Esther." What she owed Carolan she could never repay, and what joy it was to do the hardest tasks for her! In it was the glory of the hair-shirt, of the stony pilgrimage, of hardship and suffering. And now, with Margery's hard eyes on her, saying "Drink that up!" she caught again that spirit of Newgate, the tyranny of the strong over the weak, the hatred of the impious for the pious. And Carolan, her protector, was urging her with her eyes to sip, to feign to drink. Carolan, her eyes alert, Carolan grown wiser, sensing danger.

"You too, me love!" Margery's eyes caressed the face of the girl beside her. It was pleasant to turn back to memory. Might be me own young daughter, thought Margery. Like her to be! We'd get on. Only, if she was my daughter I wouldn't have had her so haughty. Fun it would have been to listen to a daughter's romances, rather than suffer the uncertain glory of romancing oneself.

"Fill up," said Carolan.

"Come, Jin! Come on, Poll! Come on, James," cried Margery.

The bottle was empty before she had done. She lay lolling back in her chair.

Carolan twirled the gin in her glass. The effect of it was strange. It made her want to cry, cry for Haredon and its comforts, cry for Everard. For Marcus? She was not sure which.

The lamp flickered up suddenly. The oil was running low. Jin folded her hands on the table and glanced at James; James fidgeted and started to talk to Margery, who laughed heartily

318

over nothing and pathetically tried to reassure herself that that slut, Jin, wasn't there. Poll was crying softly for her baby. Esther had drunk too much gin; it gave her a look of fever; Carolan thought her very beautiful tonight.

Margery said suddenly: "Shut up snivelling, Poll! Why, what Mr. Masterman would say if he was to come down here I couldn't think. And what of her bath? Good gracious me, look at the time. She'll retire at eleven, if the others don't. Doctor Martin's orders if you please. And a hot bath she wants, before getting to bed. It's a wonder to me she don't catch her death. Jin! What are you thinking of? Get up, you lazy slut! Get her cans of hot water. There'll be trouble in a minute. Why, it only wants five minutes to eleven!"

Jin drained her glass. From under her sullen brows she watched Margery. She was a little afraid of her. Jin's stay in prison and again on board the prison ship had taught her the folly of flouting authority. Margery had not used the whip yet, but she might for some offences. Jin did not like the thought of the whip. She had often shuddered at the sight of the triangle in the yard. She had seen one of the men convicts whipped; she had run away, but she had heard the sound of the whip swishing through the air, and the sickening thud of its fall; she had heard the agonised screaming of male voices. No, no. There was not one of them in the basement kitchen who would dare to flout authority completely.

Jin stood up. She clutched the table. She swayed. Margery was beside her, gripping her shoulders, breathing gin fumes over her dark face.

"Ye're drunk, me lady! Drunk!" She caught the girl's ear and pinched it hard. She laughed almost with relief. If Jin was drunk, that would account for her boldness. Drink and love! she reasoned. If you were under the influence of either you couldn't be taken too much to task for what you did. She pushed Jin back into her chair.

Carolan said: "Shall I take up the cans of hot water?"

Margery nodded, and fell into the chair next to James.

"Let me do it," said Esther. "They are heavy, Carolan. And you know how you hate carrying things!"

"No!" said Carolan. "You have had too much gin. I can see you have, Esther, so it is no use saying you have not!"

"Ha ha!" cried Margery. "These praying people! Just show them a gin bottle, and they are as bad as the rest. Look sharp with the cans, me love. I don't want complaints."

A queer excitement filled Carolan. She had seized on the

opportunity of getting upstairs. She wanted to be caught up in the excitement of the party. She longed to go to a party, to wear a beautiful dress. But first of all it would be necessary to have a bath. She grimaced at her hands; they were grimy and beneath the nails were black rims that it was impossible to eliminate.

She filled the cans. Esther came to her. "Are you sure, Carolan?"

"Oh, go to bed, Esther! I am absolutely sure."

When she carried the cans through the kitchen, Jin and Esther and Poll had already gone into the bedroom. Cautiously, for the cans were heavy, Carolan mounted the back staircase.

On the first floor of the house was the suite occupied by Mr. and Mrs. Masterman. She had seen it once when she went to help Jin clean up. This was the first time she had been allowed to roam about the house by herself, for newly acquired convicts were rarely allowed upstairs alone. It was the unwritten law of the establishment, and was a sensible enough rule, she had to remind herself. A Sydney servant would very likely be a desperate creature. She smiled, thinking of Mr. Masterman. She supposed he had a dossier of them all. They would all be neatly labelled; for example, "Carolan Haredon, thief."

Outside the suite of rooms she paused. Mrs. Masterman's room was at the end of the corridor, and between it and Mr. Masterman's there was a smaller room where they made their toilets. The house had been planned with care. There were doors connecting the two larger rooms with the toilet-room, and that itself had yet another, opening on to the corridor. Mr. Masterman had planned the house, Margery said. One had to admire his methods.

Carolan set down the cans outside the door of this toilet-room, and knocked. There was no answer, so she went in. It was a fairly large room, for all the rooms in the house were large. There was a hip-bath in the corner, and a long mirror. There were several cupboards. On a table near the mirror were cosmetics and bottles of perfume. It was pleasant merely to be in such a place.

But she must not stand about, letting the water get cold, or she would not be allowed to come up here again. She went across to Mrs. Masterman's door, and knocked.

She heard a sigh, then a very weary voice said: "Come in!"

Mrs. Masterman was in bed. The blue frock lay on the floor, and beside it the silver slippers. Mrs. Masterman's thin fair hair was spread out on the pillows. She looked very tired.

She said, without turning her head: "Oh, is it my bath? I'm too tired now. . . ."

"I will take the water away," said Carolan.

The sound of her voice, cultured, unlike the husky tones of Jin, made Mrs. Masterman turn her head slowly.

"Oh . . ." she said. "Oh . . ." And then: "Take my frock and put it away, will you? It goes in the cupboard in the toilet-room."

Weary eyes watched the yellow-clad figure walk across the room and stoop to pick up the dress.

"Have I seen you before?" asked Mrs. Masterman.

"I do not know," said Carolan. "I have seen you."

It was not like a conversation between mistress and convict servant. It was like one lady paying a call on another.

"I think I should have remembered if I had," said Mrs. Masterman. "Give me one of those pills on the table, will you? A glass of water is what I have with the pill."

Carolan was aware of Lucille Masterman's very white hands lying on the counterpane.

"Thank you. I have very bad health."

"I am sorry," said Carolan.

"Sometimes I scarcely sleep a wink all night."

"That must be very unpleasant."

"It is. Thank you. Dr. Martin says these pills are wonderful."

"I trust you find them effective?"

"I do. Although of course one gets accustomed to taking anything. Good night. Hang the dress up in the cupboard, please."

"I will," said Carolan. "Good night."

Lucille called her back when she reached the door.

"Lock it, please. And when you have locked it, will you push the key under the door?"

"Yes," said Carolan, and went out and did so.

It was rather an extraordinary experience. She felt intoxicated with success. It was the gin perhaps; it was such heady stuff. It made her excited because for the first time since she had been thrust into Newgate someone had treated her as she used to be treated in the Haredon days; and this the mistress of the house!

She opened a cupboard door. It was filled with dresses. Velvets and brocades, soft wools and silks. She rubbed her hands over some of them, and shuddered at the rasping sound they made as they caught in her rough skin. It was like a protest.

She held the blue and silver dress against her, and looked at herself in the long mirror. Carolan Haredon of Haredon! All that suffering, all that misery, had scarcely changed her at all. To wear that dress . . . only for an instant! To recapture the joy of going to one's first ball!

Colour burned in her face. She tiptoed over to the door of Mr. Masterman's room. Very cautiously she tried it. It was locked. This was safe. Mrs. Masterman was in bed. Mr. Masterman was still with some of his guests. It would only take ten minutes. Ten minutes of joy, and no fear of discovery . . . or very little, and she was reckless . . . reckless for the feel of warm water on her body and the caress of silk against her skin. She went to the hip-bath; she would be quick. She slipped off her clothes. She turned to the mirror so that she could see herself, tall and shapely, youthful, graceful. What joy it was to be free of the convict garb!

She scrubbed herself gleefully. She kept her eyes on the two doors. She could not help it, but the fear of discovery gave her an added sense of excitement.

When she stood before the mirror, clean, she felt she had washed off all the grime of Newgate and the prison ship. Perhaps some other time, when the coast was clear, she would bring the cans of water for Mrs. Masterman and use them herself.

Now just a glimpse of herself in the blue frock, and then back to the yellow.

She took it up; she slipped it over her head. She had forgotten that Mrs. Masterman was a smaller woman than she was. She struggled, and as she stood there, the frock over her head, she heard a footstep quite close. She was not sure which room it came from, Mr. Masterman's or his wife's. Panic seized her, she struggled. She must get into her yellow frock quickly; she was sobered suddenly; she realised what discovery would mean. Punishment . . . and what was punishment for a convict servant? The whip? She began to shiver, and as she stood there, with the dress half over her head, the door opened. Frantically she pulled at the dress; it fell about her bare feet, and through the mirror, for she dared not face him, she saw Mr. Masterman standing in the doorway of his room. He stood very still, like a great idol carved out of stone, awful, terrible.

He said: "What is this?" And his voice was harsh. It had a trace of the London streets in it; a hint of studied culture.

She had no words; she was dumb with terror. She could

only think of the sound the whip made as it descended through the air.

"Who are you?" he demanded, and took a step towards her. "I don't recognise you."

Still she could not speak. Her mouth was dry, her throat parched.

She noted clearly the fairness of the hair about his face; the pale skin beneath it; the eyes that were grey-green like the sea on dreary days. Now those cold eyes had seen the garments lying by the hip-bath, had taken in the significance of it all.

"You're from the kitchen," he said.

"Yes." Now her voice had come back she felt better. To hear it gave her courage; she felt herself once more. If she were going to be punished, she would accept punishment, and she would not let him see how frightened she was.

"And why did you do this?" he asked.

She answered simply: "She did not want her bath. I did. She told me to put that dress away; I wanted to see myself in it, so I . . . put it on."

"You are a pert young woman," he said. "And very disrespectful."

"You asked me," she flashed, "and I answered."

His eyes went over her, slowly, from her flushed face and tousled hair to her bare feet. It was the coldness of him that exasperated her, that aroused her fury; and when that was aroused, she could never give a thought to the consequences. A lump was in her throat; she was choking with anger and self-pity.

"I suppose you will have me whipped for this," she said. "I don't care!"

"Oh? You do not mind the lash? You have experienced it? No? Is it not rather rash then to speak so lightly of it? Perhaps when you know something of it you will not be so contemptuous!"

"It is well for you to be so calm. You have not been dragged away from your home. You have not seen your father murdered, nor your mother die of neglect and cruelty. You have not lain in stinking Newgate and nearly died on a foul prison ship! You have not been taken into . . . into someone's house as a slave . . ."

Her voice broke; tears began to stream down her face. He walked away and stood with his back to her.

"Doubtless," he said, "you are quite innocent of any crime."

"I am innocent!"

"Of course! So is every convict I have ever met. They only rob and murder; that is perfect innocence. Now perhaps you will be good enough to get out of your mistress's clothes and into your own. Perhaps you will be good enough to keep to your own quarters."

If only he had shown a little anger, she would have liked him better. It was that coldness in him which exasperated her beyond endurance.

He turned his head slightly and gave her a swift look as though he found the sight of her too loathsome to be endured for more than the briefest second.

"Please wait," he said, "until I have gone. I notice you have the charming modesty of our Newgate friends!"

The door closed; she heard the key turned in the lock. She looked at herself in the mirror. Her cheeks were scarlet; her eyes brilliant with tears. How long had he stood there, watching her struggle into the frock. She put her hands to her cheeks, and a burning shame was in her eyes. The beast! The cold-blooded beast! How she hated him! There were none quite as loathsome as the cold-blooded. Anger one could forgive, but that cold, calculated sarcasm . . .

She took off the dress quickly. She was terrified he would come back. She got into her own clothes; she could not help noticing, even in her distress, how different she looked. She tried to stifle her sobs. He would hear; he would smile with satisfaction, the loathsome brute! She imagined his coming to the yard to witness her punishment. It made weals on your back, Marcus said, weals that left their mark for ever, that branded you.

She poured the water back into the cans, spilling a little on the floor, and hung up the dress, terrified all the time that he would return.

When she got back to the kitchen, she found the others had gone to bed. She emptied the water away and went into the communal bedroom.

There was a candle burning. She saw James and Margery clasped in each other's arms; Poll was crooning over her doll; Jin was snoring slightly.

Esther was awake though. She whispered: "What a long time you've been!"

Carolan answered quite steadily: "I had to put her clothes away."

"I'm glad you've come back; I was frightened."

"You are too easily frightened."

"I know, Carolan, I know! I wish I were brave like you."

324

"Well, get to sleep now. Good night."

Brave! That was funny. She was trembling all over. She could feel the lash cutting into her flesh.

How I would love to put it about his shoulders! she thought, and hated him afresh. Cold eyes that betrayed no emotion. How I should love to make him suffer!

She thought suddenly of Marcus, of warm, friendly, passionate eyes.

Oh, Marcus! Marcus! I want you. Of course it's you I want.

"Carolan, what is wrong?" Esther was anxious. This morning when Margery had called to them to get up, Carolan had been so fast asleep that Esther had had to shake her to awaken her, and when Carolan did awake, her eyes were dark-ringed with sleeplessness.

"Wrong?" cried Carolan irritably. "What should be wrong? Just everything . . . that is all! Do you enjoy this life of slavery?"

"But Carolan, today there is something more wrong than usual. Will you not confide in me?"

"Oh, Esther, how foolish you are! Nothing is any worse today than it was before. How could it be, when before it was as bad as possible?"

They stood at the sink, peeling potatoes. The dirty water ran up Carolan's arms. Every time the kitchen door opened, she trembled with fear.

He would spring suddenly, she was sure. He would not come into the kitchen himself. Perhaps one of the roughest of his men would be sent to take her to the yard. They would tie her hands and feet to the triangle. He would not be there; he would not even bother to look on. There was no fire in him; he would coldly, calculatingly mete out what he considered justice. Crime—Using mistress's bath water, dressing up in mistress's clothes. Punishment—Fifty lashes. She imagined his keeping a little notebook, and writing such things in it. I would rather Jonathan Crew, she thought, than this cold, inhuman creature.

The morning wore on.

Margery said: "Are you in love, me lady? You're as droopy as a sleep walker."

"In love!" said Carolan, hatred shining in her eyes.

"Ha! Ha! In hate, eh?" said Margery, observant, shrewd. "Not in love? Has one of the men been disrespectful to your little ladyship? Is that what makes you look so fierce?"

"I am not looking fierce. Why cannot you let me be!"

"Tut-tut! Give yourself airs with the men if you must, but not with Margery. Don't forget there's the whip over the mantel, put into me hands by Mr. Masterman himself."

The whip! Mr. Masterman! Try as she might, she could not keep her lips from trembling.

"Come over here and watch the meat. Jin'll finish them taties. Go on, Jin! And don't you give me none of your sullen looks, me girl, or it will be the whip for you as sure as I'm Margery Green."

Real sparks of anger were in her eyes now. She would show the girl that she could not cast those eyes of hers on Margery's men. James had been mealy-mouthed enough last night. "Why, look ye, Margy, d'ye think I want to take up with silly bits of gipsies! Not when I can get a bit of all right like you, girl!" Ready as you like, it came, and when a man's tongue was so ready, could you trust him?

Margery's fingers itched for the whip. She would have liked to lay it across the girl's face! Very pretty she would look with a weal across her gipsy face! But Mr. Masterman would want to know what had happened, if Jin served at table with a face like that. Margery was afraid of Mr. Masterman. Queer, cold man, he was, so that you all but forgot he was a man. Funny how the very thought of him kept them in order down here. Jin was afraid of him; she would not like him to know she carried that knife around with her. Jin had cast glances in his direction, but he wore a thick mask through which the arrows of desire could not penetrate. "Bah!" murmured Margery, contemptuous yet with a certain awe, "he's only half a man!"

She let her hand rest on Carolan's shoulder as the girl watched the spit. Lovely skin, like peaches warmed and touched with the sun. She had been washing her hair under the pump this morning, and the sun played about it, loving it you might say, making it more beautiful because it loved it so much.

In love? With which one? James, Tom, Charley? No! Don't make me laugh; her haughty nose would go up in the air at the thought of any of them.

The kitchen door opened. Margery saw the girl's face whiten. This was very strange; something was afoot . . . what? She sat very still, her eyes downcast. Margery had never seen her so pale. Her eyelashes were incredibly long, and her pallor, oddly enough, made them look longer. They were tipped with reddish-brown. She was a beauty!

It was James at the door.

"Hot coffee at once! With biscuits. The lady has a visitor."

326

Margery got up, grumbling.

"Morning visitors, I hates 'em. Why does people have visitors in the mornings! All right, all right! Come on, you. You can help me. Not you, Jin . . . you get on with them taties, and keep your eye on the spit at the same time, will you?"

James went out. Margery touched Carolan's arm.

"Look here, me girl. You can take their coffee up to 'em. It ain't often servants is allowed the run of the house, but you ain't like the rest, see? It's funny, but I don't believe you had nothing to do with that thieving they sent you out for."

"Oh . . . Margery . . ." Carolan caught the woman's arm. She had great difficulty in keeping the tears back.

"Here! Here!" said Margery, herself moved unaccountably. She wished she was a man so that she could love the girl physically; Margery played with the idea while she made the coffee. It fascinated her.

"Now up you goes with it! Mrs. Masterman and her lady friend in the drawing-room. Steady, girl! For God's sake don't drop the tray, or it'll be the last one you'll carry into Mrs. Masterman's drawing-room, I'm warning you. Now don't be shy. Wouldn't be surprised if Mrs. Masterman asked for you to wait at table. You're a lot nicer to look at than that saucy Jin . . . Gipsies is dirty things, no mistake! Go on with you. Here's the biscuit barrel. I'll come up with you and knock. Ready?"

They mounted the stairs. Would he be there? wondered Carolan.

Margery knocked at the door of the drawing-room.

"Come in!" said Mrs. Masterman.

Margery pushed open the door, and Carolan went in. Mrs. Masterman was lying back in her chair, looking wan. She wore a fleecy jacket that made her look like an invalid.

Margery said from the door in a hoarse whisper: "Better pour it out for 'em."

Carolan, relieved that Mr. Masterman was not present, put down the tray and started to pour out.

"Bring it over here," said Mrs. Masterman, and Carolan, her hands steady, carried over the tray. They helped themselves to brown sugar. There seemed to Carolan something slightly familiar about the dark-haired visitor.

The visitor said: "You seem to be well served, Mrs. Masterman. I must say I have the most shocking trouble with my servants."

"Gunnar is so careful," said Mrs. Masterman.

"Ah . . . yes. That is it. When you have a man to arrange

your affairs . . ." Dark eyes studied Carolan appraisingly. "I always think it is such a pity, when I see these young criminals."

Carolan went out, wondering where she had heard that voice before. But that seemed a trivial matter. The main thing was where was the master, and what was he going to do about a rebellious and disrespectful convict servant who had behaved shamefully in his toilet room? Had he forgotten? Was that possible? Wild hope soared up. A very busy man, was he not, with so much to attend to? Could it be that he had forgotten?

Something was happening in the kitchen. She heard Esther laugh. She had never noticed before that Esther had such joyous laughter. It came floating through the open door. Perhaps people's voices were different when you dissociated them from their faces. If Newgate had left its stamp on Esther's face, it had not been able to touch her voice. Margery spoke, excited, giggly. And then . . . another voice, a voice that made the blood rush into her head and beat like the tattooing of a jungle drum in her ears. The voice of Marcus.

She almost fell down the last steps to the kitchen. There he was, jaunty as ever, debonair, wearing riding breeches and leggings of leather, leaning in at the kitchen window.

She stood on the threshold of the room; he looked up and saw her, and she forgot the awful fear of punishment that was hanging over her, because the look in Marcus's eyes dispelled all that.

He said: "Carolan!" and his voice was husky with emotion.

"Marcus!"

He held out his arms and she ran to him. He kissed her, first on one cheek, then on the other, then on the lips.

"My sweet, sweet Carolan!"

"Marcus . . . all this time . . . what has happened? Where have you been? You are free . . . Surely you are free? Oh, what happened? What happened, Marcus? Have you come to take me away?"

He laughed and held her from him.

"So much you want to know," he said. "So much I want to know. Why, your eyes are wet, my darling. Does the return of the wanderer mean so much to you then?"

Margery was laughing, holding her sides, while the tears ran out of her eyes.

"Come in! Come in! Mr. Masterman would be the first person in the world to want to show hospitality to the servant of his lady's friend. Come in!"

328

"Servant . . . Marcus, you?"

He leaped over the window-sill. And Carolan was laughing now; they were all laughing.

"And you too, my haughty Carolan!"

"Poll!" cried Margery. "Don't stand there gaping, girl! Bring out glasses. A little drop of ale would go down well here, I'm thinking."

Marcus put his arm lightly round Margery's shoulder, and planted a light kiss on her hair.

"What angels have you fallen amongst, my darlings?"

"Go on with you!" Margery pushed him away. "You keep your kisses for them as asks for them, young man!"

And she was laughing as she had not laughed for a long time. That was the charm of Marcus. His warm eyes embraced them all; Carolan first, Carolan his woman, then Esther, nice sweet Esther, and amorous old Margery, sullen Jin and even Poll standing there plucking at her dress. Every one of them could feel the charm of Marcus.

The glasses were on the table. They sat round it. Esther was on one side of him, Carolan on the other. He put an arm round them both.

"Marcus," said Carolan, "you must have been very lucky. Why . . . you seem not like a convict at all. You seem . . ."

". . . A thorough gentleman! My luck held, my dears. I was taken into the service of a Miss Clementine Smith. She discovered I could manage a horse, so I drive her buggy; it is now standing in your yard."

"You knew we were here, Marcus?"

"Do you imagine I would not make it my business to find out where you were?"

"Marcus! I am so happy. If only I could go away with you! If only Esther and I . . ."

"If only! Do not forget we earn our rewards by good conduct. One day . . ."

She said: "I can wait now. I can bear anything. Esther, can you?"

"Yes," said Esther, eyes shining. "Yes, I can bear anything."

"You are a pair of angels!"

"Drink up," said Margery. "It ain't often I has guests in my kitchen, it ain't!"

"That's a pity, Ma'am, for it is right welcome you make them."

Margery simpered and wriggled in her chair. Her eyes glistened. What a man! And he loved the girl. How he loved the girl! He was right for her. What had brought them out together? Imagine them ... imagine them loving ... And bless him, he had more smiles to give to Margery than to the dark-skinned gipsy. Dark-skinned gipsies were not to everybody's taste!

Marcus told them what had happened to him.

"I went into the service of Miss Clementine Smith almost immediately. She had only just arrived in Sydney, and wanted a manservant. She said I was just the man for the job. I was lucky. I have been treated well."

"Like a human being, I trust," said Carolan, thinking of a pair of bleak, grey-green eyes.

"Like a human being exactly."

"You are living near us?"

"In Sydney."

"Oh, Marcus, it is over a month since we came here."

"I know, I know. Do not forget I am not a man of leisure. I must wait on the pleasure of her who has taken me into her service. So when she arranges a visit to Mrs. Masterman, I can scarcely contain myself."

"Oh, Marcus! Marcus! This is wonderful."

"How much more wonderful it is to me! You look better, Carolan, than when I last saw you."

Old Margery said: "She had luck to be brought into this house. Mr. Masterman's is the best house in Sydney, though I say it myself."

"I am glad, Carolan," said Marcus. "I am glad, Esther. I don't know how to thank the gods for placing my dear friends in such excellent hands, Ma'am."

"What a caution!" giggled Margery. "I don't know what the Old Country's coming to, when it starts transporting the gentry."

"Your smiles warm the cockles of my heart, Ma'am. May I come often to your kitchen?"

"What do you think this is, might I ask, a convicts' club?"

"Just now it seems something like paradise to me!"

Margery twirled the drink in her glass. The voice of him! The words of him! Never, in the course of a man-haunted life, had she known anyone like him. And the girl loved him too, and if she was not mistaken, so did Miss mealy-mouthed Esther! But what chance would she have, beside Carolan, bless the girl! That white skin, that red hair, those lashes tipped with reddish-brown. Margery shivered with ecstasy, which the mere thought of love between them could give her. If ever two was made for one another, she mused, it's them!

330

Come to her kitchen? He should come whenever he could; and they should have the basement bedroom to themselves any time of the day. And she herself would prepare a bit of something to eat and drink for them, for there was no denying that love-making could be a hungry business . . . thirsty too! She chuckled, musing on memories that seemed suddenly touched with more romance, more beauty, in the presence of Marcus.

Now he was whispering to the two of them. He had an arm round each of them.

"I'll whisper a secret. I shall not stay with Miss Clementine Smith much longer. There is someone else after my services; his name is Tom Blake, and he comes from Seven Dials. He was a friend of mine in dear old London Town. Carolan, Esther, did I not tell you that I should know how to make my bed soft, even here! I am going to do it, my children. Tom is here; he has just arrived. He is what is called a warm man; money, has my friend Tom. He is going to set up in business here, and I believe there is money to be made in this country by those who are prepared to work for it. Tom will become a squatter; he will buy land and a flock of breeding ewes. He will start business in a big way. But he will want a man to help him, a man who is prepared to work hard, to be a partner to him. You understand; it will be his old friend Marcus. He will take me away from the household of Miss Clementine Smith. According to the records, I am William Henry Jedborough, convict for the term of my natural life; but I shall, as servant to my good friend Tom Blake, to all intents and purposes be a free man. And do you know that after eight years of exemplary conduct a man can get a ticket of leave . . . even if he has been sentenced for life?"

"Oh, Marcus, Marcus!" cried Carolan. "How clever you are!"

"I am, am I not!" He laughed. "My experiences have taught me how to be clever. And do you know, my darlings, it has taught me something else—the astonishing fact that honesty is the best policy."

"Oh, Marcus! How glad I am!" cried Esther. "Everything that has happened to you is worth while if it has brought you to that way of thinking."

Marcus smiled and caressed Esther's hand.

"Sweet Esther!" he murmured. "How right you are! From now on . . . when I get to Tom, that is . . . I shall be perfectly honest. Why not? There are opportunities in a land like this; do you not sense it? Do you not feel it? Here there is a certain equality among men, which was missing in England. Once I can throw off the convict's taint I will be an honourable man. This is God's country . . . His own country, for it is a country made for men to be free and happy in. Here the sunshine is more beautiful than at home. I see a great country here . . . not yet, but later. On the other side of the mountains I feel there is grass for millions of sheep, and not to be stored in barns for winter either, but growing here under the sky all the year round."

Jin, the gipsy, watched him with wide eyes and parted lips. She would have run away with him there and then, had he asked her. Poll listened, plucking at her apron; she did not understand what he said, but it was pleasant to hear him talk, and when his roving eyes fell on her, there was a tenderness in them that she had not had from anyone else in the whole of her life—not from haughty Carolan who had made a doll for her, nor from the man who had briefly been her lover.

Carolan was aware of the effect he had on them all. Marcus, philanderer and thief, the most charming man in the world! All the time he talked, his fingers were on her arm, pressing lightly, urgently. His eyes told her he loved her, and behind this talk of grass and sheep was the picture of their home together on some station not far from Sydney. He conjured up in her mind complete pictures of their riding together, of their living together.

She wanted Marcus, and she thought that everything that had gone before was worth while when set against that picture of them on the station together.

"You planned it!" she said. "You were planning it all the way out!"

"Tom used to come to see me in Newgate," he answered. "We worked it out."

"He sent the money for the privileges you enjoyed!" said Carolan.

"Who else? And it was my money, darling."

"It will be your money he brings out."

He touched her cheek tenderly.

"It will buy us a place in the sun, in the sunniest country in the world, my darling."

"When will you go to Tom?"

"We have to go cautiously."

"You will manage it, Marcus. You are so clever."

"I shall certainly manage it. And when I am with Tom we shall need some young women about the house. Tom and I were never ones for the pots and pans!"

332

"Marcus! Marcus!"

Esther said shyly: "Oh, Marcus!"

"One word in your ear," put in Margery. "What about Mr. Masterman?"

"What about him?" said Carolan lightly, reminded of him suddenly, and hating and fearing him scarcely at all.

"He is a power in the city. Do you think you can pull wool over his eyes?"

"I have heard of this Masterman," said Marcus.

"A beast!" said Carolan vehemently. "A cold-blooded beast!"

"I would rather have you in a house with a cold-blooded beast than a hot-blooded one!" He turned to Margery: "You think he will not let these two go?"

"I'm sure he would not. He is all against the sort of thing you think of doing, young man. And let me tell you this—he has quite a lot to say as to the way things are run in this town."

"He would be 'All for Justice'! cried Carolan. "He would hate it if anyone did not pay the full pound of flesh."

"Do not forget he is the master!" said Margery.

"Master!" cried Carolan. "Master!"

Marcus gripped her hands tightly.

"We must wait of course. I talk impetuously. I lose my head because I am so glad to see you again."

"Marcus," said Carolan, "you have not been too unhappy then since we arrived?"

"My unhappiness has been in not seeing you."

"I am so glad. Those triangles! I wish I need never see another as long as I live!"

"There shall be none on our station."

"Our station!"

"Yes," he said. "Ours. Yours and mine and Esther's . . . and shall we remove the whole of Mr. Masterman's kitchen staff to work for us?"

From under his lashes he threw glances at them all; he saw, and Carolan saw too, the quivering excitement of them. He had been incautious. This was the way to ensure their secrecy; they would not babble of his affairs if they thought of sharing in his adventure. Whether he meant what he said, she did not know. Could one ever be sure that Marcus meant what he said? He was clever. Clever, clever Marcus! And she did not care whether he meant what he said or not. She only cared that he was back with her again.

He stood up suddenly.

"There calls my Clementine! It would never do to keep her waiting. Au revoir! Remember I shall see you again soon."

He kissed Carolan, then Esther. Then with an audacity which completely won her heart, he kissed Margery. He bowed to Jin; he bowed to Poll. Then he leaped through the window. He stood for a half second, smiling through the frame of the window at them. Then he was gone.

There was silence in the kitchen. They heard a voice say: "Where did you get to? I was a long time, I know; I certainly did not intend to stay so long."

Then they heard his voice, but they did not hear what he said. They listened to the sound of buggy wheels.

"Well, come on!" said Margery. "We ain't got all day. Jin, wake up, girl! Now then Poll! Good gracious me! We can't waste half the morning entertaining visitors and the other half standing about like great big gabies!"

When it was time to serve the meal, Margery came over to Carolan.

"She sent for me."

"She?"

"The mistress."

"Oh?" Carolan was only half attending; her thoughts were with Marcus.

"She says she wants you to wait at table. She likes the look of you better than Jin. You'd better look sharp, lovey. Tidy yer hair a bit, and nip out to the pump."

Carolan let the cold water trickle over her hands. A strange day! She felt that there was change in the air; anything might happen. Marcus might come riding over and take her away. It was a day when dreams might come true.

Margery called to her.

"Here! What are you doing out there? Does it take all day to wash your hands? Come here . . . quick!"

In the kitchen they were preparing a tray.

"She's took suddenly queer," explained Margery. "It'll be a tray took up to her room, she wants. The master ain't home; he's riding over to one of his stations. Here, Jin! Get on, girl, get on! Unless you'd like the feel of the whip across that smug face of yours. Is that plate hot? Then get it hot, and sharp about it."

"He's away!" said Carolan. "How long will he stay?"

"The questions! How am I to know? D'ye think he shares his little secrets with me? All I know is that when he rides over to the stations it's often enough he don't come back for days and nights at a stretch. Got that sauce, Poll? Why, if it was any other man I'd say there might be something more than his stations that was keeping him . . . but with him . . . Well, he's only half a man, if you was to ask me. Come on, Jin, girl. . . . Ain't that plate hot yet?"

Carolan's eyes were sparkling. He was away on business. It might be days and nights before he returned, and he had evidently not said a word about her escapade of the night before. It was truly a day when exciting things could not help happening.

She carried the tray upstairs and tapped at Mrs. Masterman's door.

"Come in," said the weary voice.

She was lying on the bed.

"It's one of my headaches," she said. "They come on so suddenly. I think I'll have my pills before I eat. What is it you've brought? Oh! I cannot eat a thing, that I know!"

Carolan felt intoxicated with success. She felt, as she often did in the presence of Marcus, that she had stolen some of his verve for living, for finding life amusing. She felt sly, able to plan for herself.

"You must try to eat, M'am!"

She began to understand the sickly creature on the bed. Her ailments were her life; the table beside the bed was full of remedies. She locked her door to keep out that brute, that cold-blooded brute. Surely he did not need much keeping out? They were only half alive, these two. Oh, Marcus! Marcus! she thought, and she could feel his lips on her skin, warm and eager.

"But I cannot. I do try. If you only knew how I feel?"

"I can guess, M'am."

"There isn't much sympathy I get here. What is your name?"

"Carolan Haredon."

"You speak like a lady."

"I was supposed to be one once."

"Yours must be a very interesting story. . . ."

But Carolan did not plunge into an account of it, because she saw clearly that Lucille Masterman did not want to hear it, but only to talk about herself.

"It is a frightful story," she said, and added artfully: "But in one thing I have been fortunate—I have had good health."

Lucille raised herself on her elbow.

"It is not often that people who have are wise enough to realise what a boon it is."

Carolan smiled and forced compassion into her eyes.

335

"Please, M'am, could you not try to eat a little?"

"I will try then. . . ."

She took the tray. Carolan picked up a bed jacket and wrapped it round her shoulders.

"You may take further cold, M'am."

"I do take cold very easily. No! Do not go. Stay a while. You may sit down and talk to me while I eat. But first give me my pills. . . . A little water to wash them down; it is there, in the jug."

"You must suffer very much, M'am, to need so many remedies."

"Indeed I do! I do not like that gipsy; she frightens me. She creeps about so; she is like some soft-footed animal. The other girl, Poll, is such a frightful creature; I could not bear her near me. You and the other new girl are much nicer types. But my husband has always said that you convicts should not be allowed to roam about the house at large until you have been with us a little time. How long have you been with us now?"

"Six weeks."

"It is a very short time, but you do not look vicious."

"You would not believe me if I told you that I was wrongfully accused?"

"Will you pack up my pillows a bit? I have a terrible backache. That is much better. These pills are so hard to swallow. Where did you live in England?"

"In the country near Exeter, and then in London."

"London! Do not talk to me of it, for the homesickness is more than I can bear. I feel that I cannot endure this dreadful country much longer. The heat is so appalling. Tell me what they were doing at the playhouses when you were there. Tell me what the shops looked like. How I would love to ride around the town in my carriage, seeing it all, smelling it all! Do you not feel the longing to go back?"

"No!" said Carolan. "When I think of London I think of horrible things. I was not very happy I think in the country."

"You speak very nicely. I shall certainly have you to wait at table. Everyone will be envious; they have such trouble with their servants. You are sympathetic too; you shall look after my clothes and give me my medicine."

"Thank you," said Carolan. "Thank you very much. It is very good of you."

"I have taken a fancy to you. That gipsy girl never speaks at all. She grunts, and she is so sullen. I have told my husband that I am terrified of her; her eyes flash so. But he laughs that to scorn; he is a most unimaginative man. He has never had a day's illness in his life, and he does not understand what it means to be ill."

"People who are healthy are so often like that, M'am."

"I shall tell Margery of the change. You can send her up to me at once. Take this tray down . . . why, I have eaten everything! Those pills are truly wonderful, and what I should do without dear Doctor Martin I do not know. Tell Margery to come up at once."

Carolan went slowly down the stairs. Had she ever been as happy as this, even in the days of freedom?

Margery was rocking backwards and forwards in her chair. She had thrown her apron over her face to hide the tears of laughter which for the life of her she could not stop flooding her eyes. It was the funniest thing she had heard for a long time. Should she tell the girl? She was not sure whether she wanted to or not.

What a change there had been in her in the last week! Her beauty had been veiled before, and now it was as though she had thrown aside the veil. There she was, radiant. A lovely, healthy girl. Reckless as they made 'em. The dead spit of what Margery had been at her age. In love if anyone ever was. Every time they heard the sound of carriage wheels, her head would jerk up, her eyes glisten, and Margery would see her heart beat faster under the yellow frock. Now that her skin glowed with the regular application of soap and water, the yellow suited her, brought out that red in her hair, that green in her eyes. Her body had filled out a little. She was ripe for the plucking. And what a plucking it would be! But what if she whispered what she had heard?

The girl was doing well upstairs. The mistress had taken a fancy to her. Carolan had asked if she could use the bath water after her mistress had done with it, and strangely enough permission had been given readily. A queer request, Margery had thought, but the mistress did not seem to think so. She had said that, when Carolan worked in the kitchen, she was not to be given the dirty jobs because she hated to see dirty hands serving her guests. The master had come home. Now for trouble, thought Margery; he was not one to see his laws flouted. But, queer enough, nothing happened. He probably hated the sight of the dark-skinned gipsy at his table as much as his wife did. For the first time since Margery's entry into the Masterman establishment rules were going by the board. There was excitement in the air, and if there was one

337

thing Margery liked almost as much as a bit of romance it was excitement. She hated to be outside the play too; she liked a prominent place on the stage.

This was the funniest thing she had heard for a long time. The rogue! she thought. The lovely, clever rogue! If I were twenty years younger, or even ten, I would be mad for him. And I'd tear his eyes out for this, which she will, I'll be bound. And when he puts his face in at that window and looks all round my kitchen for her and sees her, she'll spring at him like a tigress. I wouldn't miss it for a sack of gold!

But she was not sure. Would she rather see her run to him, soft and loving, wanting him? Or would she rather see her fly at him in her rage? Margery was not sure. Let him have her first, and let her find out afterwards. Serve her right! Such mighty airs Miss Carolan had been giving herself since doing so well with the mistress.

Margery pulled down her apron and composed her features, for Carolan had entered the kitchen. Carolan sat at the table; she was singing to herself.

> *"In Scarlet town where I was born,*
> *There was a fair maid dwelling . . ."*

Queer emotions fought each other in Margery's mind. Admiration and jealousy were uppermost. Wonderful to be young and beautiful, desirable and desirous. A little she-devil, this Carolan, and a temper ready to flare up at a moment's notice. Now the other one, Esther, with that shining fair hair of hers like a halo, reminded Margery of a saint in a holy picture. She wanted no truck with saints. Why was she, Margery, not young and beautiful like Carolan? What a time she would have! James? Awkward little man . . . no fire in him! He just knew what to do and that was about all.

Carolan was looking at her hands; they were small and beautifully shaped, it was now possible to see. She sat there, admiring them. The nails were beginning to lose that raggedness, and what had been a rim of immovable black was now light grey.

"Well," said Margery, "you look as if you've lost a penny and found a sovereign."

"Mr. Masterman came in while I was putting her clothes away."

"Oh, he did, did he!"

Was it possible? Why not? Even half a man could surely not be blind to all that budding loveliness. When she opened her mouth and showed those sharp white teeth, she seemed to promise all sorts of things if a man could get round her to give them.

"I am sure he hates the thought of my being there."

"Indeed, Miss, and why should he?"

"Just because he's a stickler for rules, and he hates to have his broken."

"And why shouldn't he hate to have them broken? What are rules for if they are to be broken?"

"Stupid rules should be broken." Carolan threw back her head and laughed. "How I despise that man!" She thought of his standing there, eyeing her coldly, the dress over her head. He would doubtless think she had merited some punishment, but he had said nothing, and she was sure it was because he could not bring himself to tell his wife that he had seen her almost naked. Squeamish! Cold as ice!

Now Margery was suddenly angry. Envy had stifled her admiration. Mr. Masterman might in her opinion be only half a man, but she respected him as she had never respected anyone else in her life. He was the master and a good master. She would have no disrespect shown towards him in her kitchen!

Ah, Miss Carolan, so sure of yourself, eh! she thought. Now you're in for a mighty big shock. Perhaps you will not sneer at a man of honour so easily in future. Perhaps you will wish that your gay Marcus was a little more like the master.

"You'll be seeing your lover very soon now, me lady, I'll be bound!"

Carolan stood up.

"You have seen him?"

"No, I have heard of him though."

"Margery! You know something. Tell me. Oh, please tell me."

Margery was trembling with excitement; she threw her apron over her head and rocked with laughter.

"Margery! Margery! What is it? Do tell me, please."

Margery brought her apron down to the level of her eyes; she peeped slyly over it.

"It makes me laugh. I reckon that man's about the biggest handful any woman ever had to look after. Promise you'll not be too hard on him."

"Margery! Margery! What do you mean?"

"He's such a sharp one . . . sharp as a needle, that's him! He'll get on in the world. I reckon he never wanted nothing but what he got it."

"If you will not tell me . . ."

"Hoity toity! What airs you give yourself these days! You'll be setting your cap at the master next. A regular pair you be. A regular pair!"

"Set . . . my cap at the master! What a ridiculous thing to say!"

"Aye! You laugh at that, me lady. I reckon you'll be wishing you had someone as reliable and as steady for a lover. There's something to be said for steadiness, I'll tell you."

"What is it you know?"

"Just this. Your fine lover has left his Clementine Smith. He's with his new friend and partner. He'll be coming to see you soon. He couldn't before; the lady was a jealous piece."

"What are you talking about?"

"Oh, you don't see, don't you? You ain't so sharp, are you, me love? Still, I'll tell you. When he came here, all gay and loving, and looked at you with his heart in his eyes, remember, eh? 'Oh,' he says, 'there's Clementine! Mustn't keep the lady waiting?' So after having kissed you on the mouth, off he goes home to bed with Clementine Smith."

"That's a lie of course!" said Carolan.

"Of course it's a lie. You only have to look at him to see it. There he goes. A kiss for you and a kiss for Esther and a kiss for old Margery. A bow for Jin and a smile for Poll. He'd give any number of women what they wanted, and all in just as long as it took to get from one to the other!"

Carolan said: "Where did you hear this . . . this . . . gossip?"

"Now, no need to get so worked up, dearie. I heard it from James, who had it from one of her servants. There he was, living in the house like the master of it. It was Darling Clementine and Darling William. . . . Why, he even changes his name like he changes his women!"

Margery was disappointed; Carolan was flying into no passion; she had sat down at the table and was picking up crumbs off the cloth with a wet forefinger and putting them into her mouth. True, her eyes burned; so did her cheeks; but she was very still. Margery laid a hand on her shoulder, suddenly penitent. She recalled how she herself had felt on discovering the first infidelities of the pedlar.

"I wouldn't take it to heart, lovely," she said. "Men is men all the world over, and there ain't so much to choose between any of 'em."

Carolan said slowly: "So that is where I saw her! I knew I'd seen her before."

"What's that, dearie?"

"Nothing."

"Look here, Margery'll get Poll to make us a nice cup of tea."

"If you think to comfort me," said Carolan harshly, "spare yourself the trouble. I always knew the kind of man he was."

"Poll!" cried Margery. It was Esther who put her head round the door. Poll was doing something in the yard, she said. "Then you make us a cup of strong tea, will you?" said Margery. "We've just had bad news."

"Bad news? Carolan . . ."

A smile touched Margery's lips. This girl was in love with him too.

"About your friend, your gentleman friend who come into my kitchen and made so free with his kisses, him that was . . . er . . . servant to Miss Clementine Smith."

"Bad news of Marcus?" said Esther, white to the lips.

"Well, not such bad news of him. He gets his fun out of the whole business and asks for more."

Carolan could not bear the telling to come from Margery.

"Oh, it's nothing, Esther," she said wearily. "Do you remember that woman on the ship? A dark woman who was very angry because we had such freedom when we were becalmed. Well, she was Clementine Smith. Either Marcus must have had some arrangement with her before he came out, or she must have taken a fancy to him on the ship."

"I gathered that he had been lucky. She took him into her household, and was quite a kind woman, I thought."

Carolan shrugged her shoulders impatiently.

"Oh, Esther it is time you stopped being so young and innocent. She was in love with him. She took him into her house as her lover. I do not suppose she would have taken him on any other terms."

The colour flowed under Esther's skin from the open neck of her dress to the roots of her hair.

She'd be lovely, thought Margery grudgingly, if she had a bit more life in her.

"Poor . . . Marcus!" said Esther.

"Poor, poor Marcus!" echoed Carolan ironically, and got up.

"And where do you think you are off to, Miss?" demanded Margery, feeling that she had not reaped half the fun she had expected from such promising seed.

"I have work to do for Mrs. Masterman."

341

Out she walked, like the mistress of the house, and none would guess, except by her heightened colour, that she suffered anything at all.

Margery set herself to enjoy teasing Esther. She conjured up pictures of the lovers to make the girl blush. But it was poor fun, and she kept thinking of Carolan, angry and unhappy upstairs in the mistress's room.

Carolan was thinking, What a fool I was! I do not seem to learn anything by my experiences. I knew him; I knew what he was, and I believed that it was luck that gave him a soft position in Miss Clementine Smith's household, driving her horses, while for others it was slavery and the lash. What a fool! And he doubtless laughing at me all the time. His affectionate words have no meaning behind them. He is shameless, graceless. He could come here, speak of marriage to me, when all the time he was living with her, using her for his comfort. All he cares for is his comfort; he will lie, bribe, steal for it. What a fool I have been! I should be thankful to have found out in time.

In time? What could ever quell this wild longing she had for him, rogue though she knew him to be? But he should never know how she felt.

Mrs. Masterman had spilt medicine down her satin dress. Carolan took it into the toilet-room and was sponging it when Mr. Masterman came through. He paused in the doorway and said "Oh!" Then he hesitated.

She did not lift her head, for she did not care what became of her now. She wanted something to happen to take her thoughts from Marcus.

"If you wish me to go, please say so," she said.

There was silence. She went on rubbing the frock, and when she glanced over her shoulder he had taken a few steps nearer to her. She looked at him coldly.

"It is of no importance," he said.

He stood watching her; at any other time she would have thought this strange, but she had no thought for anything but Marcus and Clementine Smith . . . together.

He ventured: "You . . . you like the change of work?"

She stopped rubbing and looked full at him. There was the faintest flicker of warmth in his eyes. She disliked his fairness; he had scarcely any eyebrows, so that he had a look of surprise.

"I hated the kitchen work," she said.

"I can see you have not been used to it, nor work of any kind."

342

She was silent, returning to her work; there was insolence in the gesture, as though she were dismissing him, and she was surprised at her own temerity.

"Usually," he began quite angrily, "with convict servants . . ." and he laid strong emphasis on the words, but faltered after them, for he had seen a tear drop from her eyes on to his wife's blue satin gown. She too stared at the tear and made to cover it with her hand. She looked over her shoulder and there he was, disappearing through the communicating door.

Marcus looked in at the window. Carolan was sitting at the table, cleaning silver. Margery shrank into her chair. She was frightened; she wished she had not told.

Esther, at the sink, turned, and what she believed to be a carefully guarded secret was written on her face for all to see.

"Carolan!" he said. "Here I am!" He was laughing; he had good white strong teeth, and never, thought Margery, was a man more sure of a welcome, never was a man going to be so swiftly disillusioned.

Carolan did not rise.

"Carolan!" he said again with a faint edge of fear in his voice, and leaped into the room.

"Jin!" said Margery, her voice sharp with agitation. "Poll! Go into the bedroom; it's shocking untidy. See you get to work, and don't you dare to stir till I say so!"

They went reluctantly, but Marcus had no glances for them, no smile, no bow. He was looking at the profile of Carolan, turned from him slightly, aloof, those beautiful lashes downcast, hiding the burning fury in her eyes.

"Carolan!" he said once more, and took two paces towards the table. She picked up a silver dish and seemed very earnest about the polishing of it.

"Are you not glad to see me?" he asked, and laid a hand on her shoulder.

She threw him off imperiously. "Please do not touch me. And please do not look so surprised that I do not wish you to touch me; I am not one of your Lucys and Clementines!"

It was out. She, who had intended to be so cold and haughty, had been betrayed by that tongue of hers. He recoiled as if from an unexpected blow. What had he hoped? That she would never discover? To tell her himself some day . . . years ahead?

I shouldn't have told, thought Margery miserably. In a minute he'll want to know who told her, and she'll tell him, and that'll be the end of me as far as he's concerned.

"You have been listening to evil tales of me."

"I have been hearing the truth."

"Will you not let me explain?"

"I have no wish for more explanation, Marcus. Please go away; I have this silver to clean."

He sat on the table. He would work himself out of this, he would, Margery knew it. With most women he'd only have to kiss and say that whoever he had had only made him appreciate her the more, and she'd be weak as water. But not so Miss Carolan! Strong and proud, and ready to cut off her pretty nose to spite her lovely face.

"Listen to me please," he said, his voice as sweet as honey.

"I prefer not to!" she answered, hers acid as vinegar.

"Esther!" he said. "You will listen to me?"

She came from the sink, wiping her hands. Her delight in him set colour in her face, made it young and very sweet, and her glorious hair was wonderfully beautiful.

Esther said: "Oh, Carolan, you should never condemn unheard."

"How wearying you are, Esther! You remember Flash Jane, the prostitute on board the convict ship? Here is the male counterpart. How shocked he looks! He need not be, need he, Esther? We have met many of his kind since we entered Newgate."

"Carolan . . ." said Esther, almost in tears. The silly little fool, thought Margery, didn't she see that *her* only hope was in estranging these two!

He was hurt and angry; he would not look at Carolan now.

He said to Esther: "You have some kindness in you, Esther. You are not the sort to condemn unheard. You cannot understand what I suffered when I was last in this country . . . the agony, the torture. Things have not changed much; the lash has lost none of its sting; it is applied as heedlessly. Chains about one's limbs, while one works on the roads in the heat of the midsummer sun! Just enough food to keep a man alive! Misery! Torment! Solitary confinement! Until one has suffered it, how can one understand! To have undergone a second term such as the one I endured before would have finished me, physically and spiritually. Anything was preferable, Esther."

"Of course," said Esther. "I understand. I do. I do. If you repent now, all your sins will be forgiven."

Carolan said: "He repents now; of course he repents! He has chosen the right moment for his repentance; he probably

344

knew before he left England that he would repent at this precise moment."

"Oh, please! Please!" said Esther. "Stop quarrelling!"

"We are not quarrelling. We are not speaking to one another, so how can we quarrel? Why should I bother to tell him that he is despicable!"

Marcus said hotly: "And why should I tell her that she has no softness in her, no loving kindness, no understanding; only a set of stupid morals!"

Carólan laughed cruelly.

"Yes, Esther, of course I am very stupid; but not quite as stupid as some people might think. I am not deceived as easily as some might think to deceive me. Do you remember a certain late afternoon when we lay becalmed in the tropics, Esther, and they seemed to forget that we were convict beasts to be battened down under our hatches? They let us lie on deck. To be sure the sun was unbearable, but we thought ourselves lucky to get a breath of fresh air. Do you remember that, Esther? And do you remember how we talked to him, the two of us, and a dark-haired, imperious lady had us ordered below? Do you know why, Esther? She was jealous. She was jealous because he was with us. She was coming out on the convict ship with him because she loved him so much. And when she arrived she saw that he was assigned to her as her servant, her very loving servant. I recognised her—or I thought I did—when I took coffee in to her and Mrs. Masterman. Now I know. Now it is all clear to me."

Esther looked at Marcus.

"It is true, Esther," he said. "Now she has told you what a rogue I am, will you turn from me?"

"Very pathetic, is he not!" said Carolan, throwing the words over her shoulder.

A shadow darkened the window then. They all looked towards it at once, and saw a man standing there, a man in a mulberry coloured coat and riding breeches. He was grinning.

"Ah!" said Marcus. "My friend, my master, Tom Blake."

The corners of the man's mouth were like the horns of a crescent moon. His teeth were small and white; his eyes small and shrewd; his hair so curly and shiny that it looked grizzled. His age appeared to be somewhere in the early thirties.

"Tom," said Marcus, with a swift change of manner, "meet my friends, Carolan Haredon, Esther March, and Mistress Margery their guardian angel."

Margery stood up eagerly. She wondered if he knew she had told; she supposed he might guess. There was no hint of reproach though in his eyes. Was he thinking Mistress Carolan was a virago not worth the pursuit? Was he noticing the loveliness born of love, in Esther's face? A man such as he was would have known many women; there would have been spirited beauties like Carolan before, like as not; but a modest violet, and innocent little blossom like Esther? They were rare enough! There was a lot of kick to be got out of despoiling the innocent. Didn't she know it! She had enjoyed her curate.

And now this new man . . . His eyes went round the room. Carolan, Margery, Esther, and Carolan again. No, no! No man could ever want the modest violet when the rich red rose was his for the plucking.

"You're Marcus's friend!" She was throwing sweetness all over her anger, dampening it down, though it smouldered through the sweetness. "He was telling us about you."

"Well now!" said the man, and he could not take his eyes from her.

She was for all the world like a lady receiving her guests. The man was of lowly stock; he hadn't the breeding of Marcus. He was quivering with pleasure at the sight of her; he was wondering why her smiles were all for him.

"Margery," she said, just as though she were the mistress and Margery rather a favoured servant. "Margery, couldn't we have a little celebration?"

It was queer how, if you were a servant by nature, and a lady or gentleman by nature, you slipped into your parts naturally enough, thought Margery. She wanted to say: "Here! This is Mr. Masterman's house, this is! You're only a servant . . . a convict at that! Who are you to give yourself airs!" But she didn't. She was reckless, and she didn't care if Mr. Masterman himself came in and found them and took her to task. She had to obey. She was sorry for her, anyway; she was sorry for having told her; because they were made for each other, and heaven knew there wasn't nearly enough loving in the world.

"All right then, but we mustn't make too much noise."

"The way of entry is a leap over the window-sill," said Carolan, and he leaped in.

"You are very hospitable," said Marcus, trying to catch her eye.

Carolan laughed, but she did not look at Marcus. "If those above knew we entertained our friends, there would be some severe reprimands, I feel sure."

Tom Blake said hesitatingly: "We wouldn't want to be making trouble for you."

His voice had the tang of the Thames in it. Margery thought it was like a breath of fresh air from home.

"Trouble!" said Mistress Carolan. "Who cares?"

That was her mood, reckless, angry and hurt.

Margery went to the cupboard and brought out a bottle of spirits. I never knew anything like this, she thought. Suppose someone was to come in? Suppose Mr. Masterman himself . . . not that he comes to the kitchen . . . but it might get to his ears. Convict entertaining convict!

They sat round the table. Marcus was talking to Esther, but it was easy to see he was thinking of Carolan. Carolan talked vivaciously to the newcomer; he was dazed. Margery could see he had never known anyone like her before. His experience of women would have been picked up in Thames-side taverns. His admiration was buoying the girl up while she swam away from the misery of loving Marcus. Margery joined in now and then, though she was content to watch them. It was as good as the play to sit here and watch them, and to know that she was the master-hand behind it all; she had jerked these people into action; in a measure she controlled their movements; it was balm to wounded vanity. Watching, laughing secretly, she forgot that James was missing a night now and then, that his love-making was getting more casual than urgent.

Tom Blake was talking to Carolan in his stilted way; in every tone of his voice, in every glance, he expressed his admiration. He had got the land; he had got a grant from the government. There was more money to be made in this new country than in the old. One day—and that day not far distant—he might be a rich man.

Marcus talked to Esther, their heads close together. He was tired of a criminal's life; he had seen a chance to escape it, escape it for ever. Could he not expiate his sins of the past by leading an exemplary life? Eventually he would get his ticket of leave; a ticket of leave man was all but free. And if he worked hard, became a respectable, honest citizen . . . why, what did this country need to exploit its riches as much as respectable, honest citizens? He had practised deceit, God knew, to get to this; but could he not work out his salvation?

Oh, he could! He could! Miss Mealy Mouth clasped her hands, and her eyes adored him. Margery laughed into her glass. She thought she loved him for his strivings towards the right; but she loved him for his merry blue eyes, and the movements of his hands, and the softness of his voice and the things he said, and the way he could caress a woman with a smile or a word. Did she not see that he was playing her off against Carolan, just as Carolan was playing off this other fellow against him? And all the time they wanted one another, were made for one another.

James put his head round the door; he jerked his head towards Carolan. "She's wanted upstairs . . . sharp!"

Carolan stood up, a hostess no longer, a servant, a convict servant.

"Goodbye," she said, all gracious again. "I shall see you again soon, I hope."

Tom Blake rose to his feet and took the hand she offered. He looked as if he would have bowed, had he not felt that he would appear ridiculous so doing. Marcus looked on superciliously.

"Goodbye," said Carolan, and her eyes flicked him hastily.

Marcus stood up. He bowed ironically.

"Such a pity you have to go when we were enjoying ourselves so much!"

She moved towards the door, gracious as a queen. A pity she hadn't a train to sweep instead of that faded old yellow!

When she had gone there seemed no longer any point in continuing the party. The men left. Esther went back to her sink. Margery started to scold her; she felt rather ashamed of herself and had to take it out of someone.

Carolan went slowly upstairs. She felt strung up, full of sadness and cynicism, thinking: First I loved a coward; then I loved a rogue. My own fault for loving the wrong people. Poor Everard, he had had a mission in life; he had had a family; they were too strong for him. And Marcus? Marcus had had bad luck and the cruelty of life was too strong for him, so he became a schemer and a rogue and a philanderer and a prostitute. I loved the wrong people.

She tapped at Mrs. Masterman's door. There was no answer, so she went in. The room was empty.

A voice called: "In here please!"

It was Mr. Masterman in the toilet-room.

Her colour heightened, a certain fear rising within her, she went through.

He was standing with his back to the door, and he was holding something in his hands. He did not turn. It seemed that he did not want to look at her.

"This coat of mine," he said. "I have spilt some wine on it. My wife tells me that you remove stains from her garments most satisfactorily . . ."

She approached. She took the coat from him.

"I will do my best," she said, and she could not prevent a cold dignity from creeping into her voice.

"Thank you," he said.

She took the coat, and as she took it she lifted her face and looked at him; he was looking at her. There was a trace of interest in his eyes. She felt the blush deepen in her cheeks. He had noticed her then! Even he! He was interested in her . . . mildly of course. It was funny. It made her want to laugh, and she had need of laughter. She smiled at him shyly.

He said: "Do you think you will be able to remove the stain? It is a good coat."

She said again: "I will do my best."

"That . . . that is good of you."

"I will sponge it first and see what happens. Velvet is not easy to treat."

"I should imagine it was more difficult than . . . than . . ."

He was bashful, bashful as a schoolboy. What was this power she had inherited from her mother and her grandmother and her great-grandmother, the power that could make cold Mr. Masterman bashful as a schoolboy? But it could not win Marcus's fidelity, nor give Everard courage; those were what she had wanted from those two. What did she care for this man! But she needed to laugh, and she could laugh at him.

She laid the coat out on a table, and touched the stain with a finger. She had a sudden suspicion that he might have spilt the wine purposely, because he wished for this interview with her. That would be like him, calculating. He was attracted by her; did she not know the signs? She thought of that sickly woman, his wife, locking the door, having the key pushed under it. There was a certain balm in teasing him, this cold, unemotional man who was suddenly not quite so cold, not quite so emotionless.

He said: "You are happier than you expected you would be?"

"Yes, thank you."

"You must have suffered a good deal."

She lifted her face to his, and the tears were in her eyes. They were real tears; they were born of anger and self-pity; but they were very effective, more so than tears of sorrow would have been, and in any case he was a novice in his knowledge of women and would not know the difference.

He quickly looked away from her, and said slowly: "If . . . if it is any satisfaction to you, I should like you to know that I believe in your innocence."

"Thank you," she said, and smiled through her tears.

Lucille Masterman said: "I am tired now, Carolan. It is not a very exciting book, is it! I am sure your voice is tired too. Draw the blinds; the sun hurts my eyes. Do you find this sun overbearing too? Thank heaven March will soon be out. How I look forward to the winter! Not that I shall be able to entertain much; I simply have not the strength."

Carolan closed the book. In the last weeks her status in this house had risen considerably. In the kitchen they regarded her with awe; she was not there often now. She still slept in the basement with the others, but she was not required to do any of those menial tasks which she loathed. Sometimes she polished the glasses. Mrs. Masterman said: "See that they come shining to the table, Carolan. You know what these people are . . . they have simply no idea . . ." Carolan this, Carolan that; and once, Carolan, my dear. And all due to that cunning she had learnt from Marcus. She had been sympathetic to Lucille, had listened to her talk with obvious interest; she had invented a disease which had killed her grandmother; it was something like the one from which Lucille imagined herself to be suffering. And now, she put away the clothes, she sewed them—not that she liked sewing; but she preferred it to peeling potatoes and washing floors. She read aloud to Mrs. Masterman; she kept her engagement book; she waited at table. Visitors said: "What a good-looking girl, and so refined! My dear, you were lucky." And Mrs. Masterman would sigh and say: "Oh, it was Gunnar . . . you know he's so clever, and of course he always gets what he wants." She had grown from a lower to an upper servant. Mrs. Masterman depended on her. "Carolan, where did I put those pills? Carolan, pour out my medicine; you know just how much water. Carolan, spray a little perfume on my handkerchief, and lay it across my forehead. You can have no idea how my head aches. Pull the curtains and read to me. I find it so soothing." She was not unkind by any means. She was rarely out of temper, and she could always be lulled into sweetness by a discussion on her health or on England. She had a nostalgia for England that was in itself a sickness. She said: "It hurts me here to think of it." And she would touch her heart and wipe away a few tears. "The river, all silver and shining in sunlight, and the barges floating down it. My grandmother had a house in Kensington, Carolan. Mamma was wrong to marry a soldier. Mamma had a wonderful time in her young days; she used to tell me of it. Walking in the park with her nurse! Going to Ranelagh! Going to the play! It was all fun and parties and balls. Such beautiful clothes she used to wear. She fell in love with my papa at one of the balls. They danced a minuet and were head over heels in love. So she married him, little thinking of all that a soldier's life entailed. Poor Mamma! She suffered as I do. There were no more children; she said I nearly killed her. I used to massage her forehead when she had a bad headache. I must show you how to do it. It is most soothing. I used to give her her medicine. She spent most of her days on a couch. And then she died, and papa came out here, and it was here that I met Mr. Masterman."

It was easy to piece together her story, to see her as the overserious little girl with the sickly mamma. Her childhood would have been spent among tonics and pills. That had had its effect upon her and she was like a little girl with her treasures when she talked of her medicines.

Carolan was cunning, feigning sympathy where she felt nothing but contempt.

"Really," Lucille Masterman would say to whoever cared to listen, "I do not know what I should do without Carolan!" And Carolan, feeling that life was cruel and that she had been selected for special persecution, suppressed all her natural softness and decided to play Marcus's game.

Before the finding of the laudanum, Lucille Masterman had been the mistress casting favours on a convict servant who pleased her; but the discovery of the bottle changed that.

Carolan went in one day and found Lucille sleeping deeply, and on her bedside table was the bottle and a glass. Carolan smelt the glass; then she picked up the bottle, took out the cork and sniffed its contents. For the moment she thought that Lucille had killed herself.

She sat on the bed looking at her. A year ago, Carolan would have been horrified by death; now to contemplate it left her almost unmoved. She was young to have arrived at such indifference, but it was due to her very youth that she had hardened so quickly. She had little pity for Lucille because Lucille was a fool who did not know what it meant to suffer hardship. Hunger, thirst, the lash—they were merely words to her, words which described the trials that fell upon people who deserved them. The way in which Lucille spoke of these people fully expressed her indifference to them. She chose to believe that Carolan was innocent because Carolan had not begun life by being poor, and because she could talk about ailments and England for as long as Lucille wished. It was convenient to believe in Carolan; it was pleasant to have her acting as lady's maid and parlour maid, because in a land like this the servants who usually came one's way were murderers, thieves, or prostitutes, petty criminals or hardened ones. It was the insecurity of Carolan's position that helped in the hardening process. She knew that at any time she could be passed on to another household; a word from a master or a mistress could mean the triangle. She had missed it so far, but there were nearly seven long years of captivity before her. She was playing cunningly, and softness did not blend very well with cunning. So she watched the woman and wondered about her life with her husband, and as she thought of the man, her eyes narrowed and the corners of her mouth quivered with cynical amusement. For this silent man was being slowly dragged from his virtuous ways by the eyes of Carolan, by his growing awareness of her youthful body beneath the yellow garment of slavery. She rejoiced in the feeling of power which that gave her. So demure she was in his presence, never looking at him if she could help it lest he should see the laughter in her eyes. She was angry with the world, and on whom could she better vent her anger than on these Mastermans who, so strangely, both wanted something from her! She was a young animal licking her wounds and growling all the time, ready to snap, ready to hurt others as she had been hurt. She held herself cruelly aloof from Marcus; she smiled ravishingly on Tom Blake, trying to make him believe she was the woman he had longed for all his life; she was short with Esther—she hated herself for that, for what had Esther done to her but be an exasperating saint!—and was sweet and patient with Lucille because she wanted her interest; she was alluring yet demure before that silent man who was Lucille's husband, because she felt that to nourish that flicker of attraction he felt for her into a mighty flame was going to be to her advantage. He, the master, would be the slave; that would amuse her; that would make life bearable. I am loathsome, she thought, as she sat on the bed and watched Lucille. And she tried to think of other Carolans; the little girl who had cried when a doll was broken, because she thought the doll was in pain; the girl who had ridden her first pony and flung her arms round the neck of the blacksmith because she loved everybody on that day; the girl who had gone to her first ball and been so in love with life because Everard loved her. They were lost, those Carolans. Mother Newgate had caught up with them, and like a mischievous child with a pencil had added a touch here, a touch there, and so altered them completely.

Lucille opened her eyes; her pupils looked strange, so that she was unlike herself.

She said drowsily: "Gunnar . . . Oh, Carolan . . ."

Carolan answered: "You were sleeping deeply."

The eyelids flickered.

"Carolan, if . . . anyone . . . should call, tell them I am not very well today. I shall sleep a bit."

Carolan took up the bottle and put it away in the medicine chest. She took the glass and tiptoed to the door.

"Carolan, where are you going?"

"To leave you to sleep."

"Do not go. I was very tired. I did not sleep a wink all night. Sit down . . . and pull the curtains together, Carolan; the sun hurts my eyes."

Carolan obeyed.

"I am an unhappy woman, Carolan." Tears rolled from the corners of her eyes. Carolan took a lace-edged handkerchief from under her pillow and wiped them. "Life is cruel, Carolan."

Carolan wanted to laugh. Cruel! What do you know of cruelty? Have you lain in the stench of Newgate? Have you tried to sleep in the fetid atmosphere of the women's quarters on a prison-ship? Have you felt the lice crawling in your hair? Have you seen rats so bold that they sit on their hind quarters insolently eating the food they have stolen from you, because they know you're not strong enough to stop them?

She veiled her eyes. "Yes, M'am!" she said softly.

"My husband . . . he does not really care for me."

"M'am, shall I lay a perfumed cloth across your head? I swear you have a headache."

"Thank you, Carolan. My head is whirling. Your hands are so gentle. It is good to have someone to look after me. I have come to rely on you. He does not care; it is obvious, is it not, even to you?"

"Come," said Carolan, "I would not say that. You have a comfortable house, M'am, servants to wait on you. You have beautiful clothes to wear."

"What are these things, Carolan!"

What were they indeed! Were you put in a shapeless yellow garment to brand you as a slave, you would know what it meant to feel silk against your skin! Had you lived in Newgate you would love your feather bed! Had you scrubbed floors and peeled potatoes and done a hundred menial tasks, you would know what it meant to have servants to wait on you!

"They are something, M'am," she said mildly.

"He is very angry that there are no children, Carolan. He is a very ambitious man. He was nothing . . . nothing in the beginning; he has risen up from nothing. He was not the man for me; not quite . . . a gentleman, you know. Papa did not want me to marry him at first, but when he saw what he was doing—climbing steadily, Carolan—he was not averse to the match. In fact he encouraged it."

How dilated were her eyes! Although she spoke Carolan's name, and although her eyes never left her face, she was like a woman talking to herself.

"When I married him I was twenty-four, and yet I knew nothing of what marriage would mean."

At Haredon one seemed to have been born with such knowledge. Conversations with servants, sly hints from Jennifer, the coarseness of the squire, the coquetry of Mamma, the intrigues fostered by Thérèse, even the primness of Aunt Harrict, had all seemed to teach one.

"He is not an easy man to live with."

Inwardly she laughed. You do not know how to treat him, Madam! Were I in your shoes . . .

She could scarcely suppress her laughter at the thought of herself in Madam's shoes.

"Carolan, can you keep a secret?"

"You can trust me with anything, M'am."

"Five years ago I was very ill. No one knew how ill. No one knew what I suffered."

Was that all! Another illness!

"I am so sorry. Your life seems to have been made up of illnesses." Sarcasm was lost on the poor drugged creature.

"This was different, Carolan. There is no one listening, is there? I was going to have a child. I was terrified. In my state of health, you see . . . Imagine it!"

"You could not face it," said Carolan.

"How well you understand; No, I could not face it. There was a man here . . . a servant to one of my friends . . . a superior sort of convict who had been a doctor. He . . . he did this for me. It cost a good deal of money . . . even a convict wants money for that sort of thing. And . . . he helped me out of my trouble. You see, I could not face it . . . the thought of having a child . . . out here in this primitive country. I was never meant to live here. At home in London I should have been terrified too, but here I could not face it; it was certain death.

354

And the pain I suffered even then was frightful, Carolan. And I had to suffer it in silence, for I was terrified that he should know."

Poor little coward, thought Carolan contemptuously, but she was glad he had been cheated of his child.

"I . . I could not go through that again." She sat up, her eyes staring wide. "Carolan, the bottle, where is it?"

"I have put it away," said Carolan.

"Oh . . ." She sank down on her pillows. "It is so soothing . . . and I could not sleep. I do not want him to find it."

Carolan stooped over and stroked the hair back from her forehead.

"He would be angry if he found it?"

"He never needs a sedative. He has no sympathy; he said once that if only I would stop thinking I was ill, I would cease to be ill. Oh . . . he can be coarse, Carolan. . . . But what am I saying! He is your master, Carolan, and a very clever man."

"Yes," soothed Carolan, "he is very clever. He has come very far, has he not?"

"He will not talk of what his childhood was like. He shuts up tightly if I ask. He has a cold way of suggesting one has no right to ask questions. He does not want to think of the past. But he is so clever; he may well be governor one day."

"Yes," agreed Carolan, "he will be a great man here in this country."

And she laughed to think of that appealing look, that helpless look in his eyes when they rested on her youthful beauty, her vitality. Was he comparing her with this faded, worn-out wife? She wanted to go on talking of him.

"He does not want you to take . . . that which is in the bottle?"

"He would be furious! He wants me to get well, to be strong . . . and why, do you think? So that I can give him a son! He lives for his ambition, Carolan. He wants to be one of the fathers of this new land, populating it with his children. That is one of his ambitions. He would say that . . . stuff was weakening. But I *must* sleep, Carolan. I cannot bear this perpetual wakefulness. It is so dreary here, and the heat and the mosquitoes and the brilliant sun . . . they are here all the time. How lovely it would be to wake up in England! 'Is it raining?' you would say. You would never know whether it would rain or not. Rain is beautiful, soft and gentle. And the greenness of it all! It will soon be April. . . . April in England. . . . Springtime! I have been ten years in this country, Carolan. . . . Ten years since I have seen an English spring."

"Do you wish me to hide the bottle, M'am?"

"Oh, Carolan . . . yes! You must not let him see it; he would be angry, and his anger is so cold it frightens me. He would take it away and forbid me to get more."

"Where do you get it?" asked Carolan.

"From the doctor I told you of. He is a free man now. He deals in medicine and so on; it is possible to get practically anything you want from him. I hear he is doing very well in Sydney. I think he must be, for his charges are exorbitant."

"You must try to sleep," said Carolan. "Try to sleep off the effects of the drug. If Mr. Masterman came in he might guess. I will hide the bottle in the top drawer of your chest of drawers. We will lock it."

She took the bottle from the medicine chest and locked it in the drawer. When she returned and gently put the key under Lucille's pillow, the metamorphosis had begun. Carolan was in command.

In the kitchen her manner had changed. While she remained in this house, she need not fear the lash; she need fear nothing. That knowledge was a balm laid on her wounds. She softened a little. Marcus had taken an easy way to solve his difficulties; she and Marcus were very much alike. Should she blame him? The thought of reconciliation was sweet. She pondered on it often as she lay in her basement room. Marcus's arms about her, Marcus loving her! She was going to him eventually.

He came to the kitchen often. He would look through the window and he would flirt a little with Esther and Margery, and sometimes Jin. He was cool to Carolan, but in her newly found power she knew that she could dispel that coldness with a glance. She, in her turn, would flirt with Tom Blake, and he, poor man, was only too happy to be flirted with.

She was acting for Marcus, he for her. That was how she saw it. She was angry, seeing him smile at Esther. She wanted him to stop this foolish game, to beg her to give him her favours. Imperious as a queen, she was, for every time she saw the master of the house she was more and more aware of the devastating effect of her charms. On such a man! she marvelled. How much stronger must be the desire of Marcus!

And still he flirted and philandered, played that game he knew so well how to play; and there must be occasions when she was with the mistress and he came and flirted with Esther.

Margery looked on and laughed, and rocked herself with laughter. Ha ha! Mistress Carolan! What airs you give yourself since the mistress took you up! Pride, even for a little beauty such as you are, goeth before a fall, so I've heard. And Margery chuckled and slapped herself and rocked herself, waiting for the fall. For James's visits were less and less frequent, and she suspected that gipsy Jin of trafficking with him in the yard. Stolen opportunities . . . she knew how sweet they could be, and a woman has to do something!

The climax of Carolan's triumph came with her possession of the green frock. It was an afternoon frock, sober enough, but becoming.

"I never liked it," said Mrs. Masterman. "I am too ill for green. Your hair looks really red beside it. My poor hair is falling out; that is a sign of great weakness."

"How I should love to wear it!" Carolan's eyes went to the chest of drawers, and Mrs. Masterman's followed her gaze. Carolan saw the thoughts come into her eyes. Carolan was more than a servant, a confidante, a friend. They shared secrets; she owed Carolan something surely. But what would he say? He hated his rules to be broken. A convict in an expensive green dress! But she was too tired to think of him.

"You must have it, Carolan. After all, I never wear it."

"Oh, thank you, M'am. How kind you are!" Carolan hugged the dress and skipped over to the workbasket in a corner of the room.

"What animal spirits!" said Mrs. Masterman. "How I wish I could feel so pleased with life, and all for a cast-off dress!"

"Shall I give you your pills now?"

"No, I think I will have a draught of the tonic."

Carolan poured it out, her fingers itching to get to work on the dress. She smoothed the pillows. She picked up the dress and set to work. She let it out a little; she lengthened it. And all the time she talked soothingly to Mrs. Masterman of her grandmother's illnesses. For an hour she worked on the dress; she slipped out of her own and tried it on. The change was effective. Never again, thought Carolan, shall I wear that hideous convict's yellow.

Mrs. Masterman began to be nervous. "What will the master say?"

"Do you think he will notice?" asked Carolan, slyly.

"Perhaps he will not," said Mrs. Masterman. "Read to me a little, Carolan."

She read, but she did not know what she was reading; she was longing to get down to the kitchen, to flaunt her new dress. Margery's face! Jin's, Poll's, Esther's! She hoped Marcus would look in at the window. She laughed inwardly. Life was turning out to be quite amusing after all. What other woman, arriving on the convict ship, had found such an easy way of life as she had! What others would be wearing a green afternoon frock such as this! Some of those in the brothels perhaps. What a life! She did not need to use her body; she could use her brains.

Mr. Masterman came in while she was reading. He often came in while she was there. He saw her in the green dress, her red hair falling about her face. She smiled at him demurely, yet with a challenge daring him to suggest it was not in order for her to wear it.

He said to his wife in his clear, pseudo-cultured voice: "How are you today?"

"Much the same I'm afraid, thank you."

"The Jenkinsons want us to dine there tomorrow if you are well enough."

"I rather doubt that I shall be."

"I thought so."

He stood by the bed. Carolan busied herself with her sewing, but she was aware of his attention focused on her, and she knew that the words were spoken automatically; he was not thinking of the woman on the bed, because he could not tear his thoughts and eyes away from her.

He went out.

Mrs. Masterman said: "He did not say anything. I do not believe he would notice anything outside business. He is a most unobservant man!"

Carolan was silent.

"Although," went on her mistress, "I did think I saw him looking in your direction rather curiously."

Carolan laughed. That was the supreme moment of triumph. She was the real mistress of the house; mistress of them both if she cared to be.

The girl, Margery told herself, was intolerable. What airs! Who ever heard the like? A convict, not three months in the house, and riding rough-shod over all! She had come to giving orders in the kitchen!

"Mrs. Masterman will not like the table laid this way. Mrs. Masterman hates dirty glasses!" Mrs. Masterman this and Mrs. Masterman that! Then Mr. Masterman . . . "Mr. Masterman is asking some friends tonight. This is the menu."

Who was in charge of this kitchen? That was the question Margery wanted to ask.

Once it was not Mrs. Masterman nor yet Mr. Masterman, but "I"! "I cannot have these flowers any longer in Mrs. Masterman's room. The water positively stinks!"

The airs! The graces! Wearing the mistress's cast-off clothes. Oh, she had bewitched the mistress completely. But what was wrong with the master? Why didn't he put down the foot of authority?

If you ask me, said Margery into her glass of grog—for whom else had she to talk to, with Jin, the slut, for ever creeping out to the backyard for a word or something more with James, and Poll with her slavering mouth and her doll, little more than an idiot, and Esther walking on air because she was in love?—if you ask me, he's only too glad to quieten the mistress; he'd put up with anything, even a convict servant, flaunting all over the house.

Oh, but she was lovely! So lovely it did something to your inside to watch her. Made you think of years and years back, and wish you were young again. And what was the good of getting angry, wouldn't most women have been the same?

Funny it was to see what love did to people. Herself and James, Jin and James, Poll and her doll, Esther with that Marcus, and Tom Blake with Carolan.

People do funny things when their emotions are aroused—didn't she know it! She hadn't known life and known men for nothing. And when you have been young and full of adventure, it comes hard to take a back seat. Fun too to try *your* hands at working things . . . not necessarily the way you want them to go, but just poking about here and there . . . a jerk at this one, a push at that . . . It gives a feeling of being something more important than just an old woman taking a back seat by the chimney corner, grumbling into her grog.

Pride goeth before a fall, Miss Carolan, and you're mighty proud; the proudest piece I've ever clapped eyes on. Oh, but so lovely to the eyes, soft skin and budding beauty, and eyes of green behind whose haughtiness passion could burn and tenderness glow. It wasn't surprising that Marcus loved her, and Tom Blake loved her, and the mistress had got interested in her. But she was walking with her head in the clouds, the silly puss, who thought herself so sly, she didn't watch her steps. You had to watch your step all the time in life. When you were eighteen and so beautiful your head got tilted too high so that you couldn't see the ground, you didn't know so much, you weren't so very wise—and the trouble lay in the fact that you thought yourself the wisest soul on earth. Now Marcus, he wanted her sure enough, for all his goings on with the other, but he was a man who could love half a dozen women at once, and that sort has to be watched. And Tom Blake, he might be the faithful sort, but he wasn't her sort; she'd tire of him in a month, that's if she ever liked him enough at the start. And the graces of a mistress are like a house built on shifting sands . . . there right enough one minute, and gone the next.

Margery laughed so much that tears fell into her puddings. Her eyes were beady black and sharp as needles. There were things she had suspected for a long time. She bided her time, waiting; it was good fun waiting. Is it? No, it ain't. By God, it is! By God, I'm sure it is!

This is funny. It ain't the things that happen; it's the people they happen to. It's people that make the drama and the comedy, not just events. It's her and him, and her again. Oh, this is funny; this is side-splitting! Serve her right, the proud hussy.

Esther—the mealy-mouthed, the prayer-maker—looked strange these days, peaked and frightened, exalted, queer. Her face beneath that cloud of glorious hair was drawn. She was frightened.

Is it? No, it ain't. But it *is!* Of course it is!

Oh, Mistress Carolan, Mistress Carolan! Here is a shock for you!

Tell her today? No, wait a little. Store your secret. Have fun with it, play with it. How to begin? Not an expression of her face must be lost, not an inflexion of her voice.

She came into the kitchen one late afternoon; she was wearing the green dress the mistress had given her and allowed her to alter. It was tight across her breasts and it made her skin glow and her hair, glossy from the brush, hung about her face. She walked like a lady . . . and her a convict, a thief!

But Margery always softened when she was there, liked to watch her eyelashes sweep up and down, liked to stroke the soft skin of her arms; her hands were whitening, growing soft, and she, unbelievably insolent, used the mistress's polish on her nails. When she was there, Margery put off telling; there were times when she felt she could not bear to hurt her, when she liked to listen to her all but giving orders, liked to watch the proud tilt of her head.

She said now: "Well ducky, have a cup of tea, will you, love? I'll tell Poll to make it."

"I cannot stay," said Mistress Carolan. "I have to be upstairs."

The airs! The graces! Too good to drink a cup of tea at Margery's table, Margery who had been good to her when she had come from the ship a poor, lousy, shivering creature!

"A word in your ear," said Margery, a dull flush rising to her cheeks.

"I have not very much time to spare," she said.

You'll have time to spare for this, me lady! Margery looked through the window to where Esther and Poll were pumping water in the yard.

"It's what the master will say that worries me. I always thought Jin would be the one. I didn't think it would be her."

"What do you mean?"

"What—ain't you noticed?"

"Noticed what?"

"What's happened to her!" She nodded through the window at the two girls at the pump.

"Poll?"

"The other one."

"Why," said Carolan, "what has happened?"

"Can't you see? You've got eyes in your head, ain't you? Oh, I know what it is, them eyes is too busy upstairs to notice what's going on down here among us humble folk."

"Esther . . ."

"She fainted clean away yesterday. Where's your eyes, girl? But, deary me, I reckon a lady wouldn't be noticing such things."

"Esther . . ." said Carolan again.

". . . has been up to what ain't respectable. That's about the long and the short of it."

Carolan turned on her.

"You're a coarse old woman! Esther fainted—then she is ill. How can anyone endure this sort of life . . . ?"

"Well, there *is* them that gets themselves a place upstairs, but it ain't so good for us ordinary folks, that I will admit. But if ever I see a girl in trouble, I see one now."

"But Esther . . . Esther . . . it isn't possible! She . . ."

"Ah! It's the quiet ones what go wrong; I've seen it before. One little slip and down they go, sliding down to perdition. Whereas our kind . . . you and me . . ." She nudged Carolan, winking one eye.

"I don't believe it."

"It's true as I stand here. I got her round all right. I had a good look at her. I wasn't born yesterday. I know a pregnant girl when I see one, and I saw one yesterday. I sent the others

361

out, then I made her tell me. All she could say was that she loved him and there didn't seem nothing wrong in it at the time. That's what they all say!"

"Marcus!" whispered Carolan.

"That's about the ticket. Been hanging round here a lot, he has. He's artful as a monkey, he is. It wouldn't be easy for a girl like her to say no to him. You see, he knows just how to get round her, him ... going all religious-like just to make her feel everything's all right, and talking about love being beautiful and sacred, I reckon; and then she gives way ... that's how trouble starts."

Margery watched her. She had to admire her. Her face was blank and white, so that you wouldn't know what was going on behind her eyes. They were hard and bright like precious stones. And how they glittered.

That's got you, my fine lady! That's pricked your pride. Thought he was all for you, didn't you? Thought he couldn't look at anyone else. You've got a lot to learn, my pretty. Men is men all the world over.

Carolan went past Margery right out into the yard. She went to Esther, and the way she dragged her from the pump showed what she was feeling. She could have murdered the girl, it was clear. She was wishing she had never met her.

That would teach her to give herself airs. Oh, but so lovely she was, lovelier in her rage than she was when she was soft. And just because she held her head so high, it made you want to cry for her, made your inside go all funny. It seemed there was some evil blight on her love-making. First that parson who didn't move a hand's turn to save her. Then Marcus, who was mad for her, and yet couldn't keep himself straight for her. There's men for you! Not worth a penny piece, the whole boiling of them. Ruining a girl's life like that! Oh, she was wild! Oh, she was angry! She was sad too. She was flaying the girl with her tongue, pouring contempt on her. Sly thing, all that praying, and then to go behind her dear friend's back ...

Margery wiped a tear away from her eyes. It was something that couldn't be helped. Margery had seen it coming. The girl's blossoming, washing her hair under the pump till it was all shining and made little curls all round her forehead; watching the window for a sight of him, listening for his step. A woman can't have such goings on in her kitchen and not get a bit of a kick out of it herself.

That evening, that was the beginning. Her ladyship flouncing down for something or other and seeing Marcus there at the table drinking a glass of ale, and her looking at him like

362

he was a bit of dirt beneath her feet, when all the time she was jealous because he was sitting so close to Esther. She didn't stay in the kitchen; she went upstairs again. And the way his eyes followed her, started making your own water. She was just a child really. Seventeen! It ain't so easy to remember what you was at seventeen. Pretty silly . . . making a fool of yourself. Well, that was what Mistress Carolan had done . . . made a fool of herself and Esther and Marcus too for that matter. Him and her! What a pair! They rushed at life; there wasn't any sense in rushing at life; you came a cropper sure as you were born. There was her ladyship wanting him, and there was him wanting her. But no, she has to be all pride and dignity just because he let a woman keep him to get started on his way of life; and he has to show his anger with her by pretending to be interested in someone else. If you've been young and in love yourself, you know. Silly children! Want a good smacking, both of them.

She had made Esther drink gin that night, a lot of it. It was easy enough to keep filling her glass. And he had drunk too, and got reckless, and that was the beginning. Esther was pretty enough when she was lively, when she wasn't saying her prayers, when she was wanting a bit of life like other girls wanted. He was never the man to miss his opportunities, it was as natural and easy as eating and drinking to him. He was made that way. That was how it happened . . . and give young people a taste for that sort of thing, and there you are. They don't stop at once . . . not if she knew anything about it! And there was her ladyship, tripping about upstairs, getting dresses out of the mistress, altering them, like some queen's favourite, making her lover wait a while to show her displeasure. Ha! Ha! It was funny, whatever way you looked at it.

Carolan came in from the yard. She looked like a sleep-walker, with all the life taken out of her.

"Now, lovey," said Margery, "it don't do to take these things to heart, and all this keeping a man waiting never did pay, to my mind."

But she had walked through the kitchen as though Margery was not there.

"Draw the curtains, Carolan. I think I will have a rest for a while."

"I will leave you, M'am; you will rest better without me." Her voice was hard, determined. She could not stay in this room; she could not bear it. She would scream, be rude to the woman, would cry out: "Oh, stop talking of your silly ailments! What do you think I am suffering. . . . I have lost Marcus! First Everard. Then Marcus!"

"I wish to turn out one of the cupboards in the toilet-room. If you need me, you can knock on the wall."

Docilely Lucille Masterman nodded, and Carolan went out.

She looked at herself in the long mirror. How strange she looked! If that selfish woman in there had been the least bit interested in anything but herself and her silly medicines she would have noticed. There was no one to condole with Carolan. Margery was laughing up her sleeve. Esther could weep till she could not see, but she was weeping for herself and her predicament. Esther! The virtuous Esther whom she had looked upon as something near a saint, creeping out to him like a servant girl. Esther! Her friend no longer. She wished she had never seen her, never listened to her whining voice. Esther and Marcus. Marcus and Esther. Together. Making love. "I hope you said your prayers, Esther, before you began!" The words had made the girl flinch, and serve her right. Sly, deceitful little hypocrite! And Marcus, the beast! She was well rid of him. Had she married him, what would her life have been? He would not have been true to her for a week. I hate them both. I hate them. She had said: "Mr. Masterman will be furious when he hears. He will want to know how it happened, who the man is. He will want to know how you came to be entertaining convicts in his house. I would not be in your shoes, Esther." She had had the satisfaction of hearing Esther's strangled words—"I wish I were dead."

Weak, snivelling Esther. What will become of her now? What will Mr. Masterman say? Momentarily she tore herself away from her sorrow to visualise the man. Cold profile, eyes that could glow warm enough for her; but his sort, when they knew what it meant to feel desire, were harsher to those who gave way to it.

I would not be in your shoes, Esther! But she would, of course. She, who loved Marcus, would have given a good deal to be in Esther's shoes, bearing Marcus's child, having been loved by Marcus.

Why does everything go wrong with me? she asked her reflection. First Everard, now Marcus. Why, why?

The answer was there in the headstrong line of her jaw, in the tilt of her head, in the shine of her eyes. She herself was the answer, and the losing of Marcus was more her own fault than anything that had happened to her.

She wanted Marcus. She loved Marcus. Only now did she know how much. Only now when it was too late; for it was too late. She must face that. She could never marry Marcus now. How could she? When Esther was to have his child.

Let Esther have the child; what did it matter! Queer thoughts darted into her mind. There was a doctor, an ex-convict; he had helped Mrs. Masterman—why should he not help Esther?

No! Let Esther find her own way out of her difficulties. She would not help her. She imagined Esther, standing before Mr. Masterman, explaining her guilt. What would happen to Esther! Who cared what happened to Esther! Esther had acted without thought of the morrow. Let the morrow take care of itself. All right, let it!

And meanwhile, what of herself? Lonely and sad, loving Marcus who did not love her whatever he might say, she sank down on a pile of clothes she had turned out of one of the cupboards. All her pride left her, and she sobbed broken-heartedly.

Quite suddenly she was aware of not being alone. She turned slowly, saw first his shapely legs in well-cut riding breeches, his good though sober coat, his fair face pale like a statue she had seen carved in stone at Vauxhall Gardens.

He did not move; he was embarrassed. He said: "I am afraid you are very unhappy. If there is anything I can do to help . . ."

She smiled sadly and shook her head. "There is nothing, thank you."

"Oh, but surely there is?"

He knelt down on the pile of clothes beside her.

"You are very kind," she said, and she thought, For seven years I shall stay here working in this house, for him and the woman in there. There will be no hope of escape now. And she realised how, even while she tossed her head and refused to be friends with him she had been longing for reunion with Marcus, for the life he had talked of, on the station. The thought of her blind folly set the tears gushing out of her eyes again.

"Oh, come," he said, "you must not be so upset. Will you not tell me your trouble?"

She saw the pulse hammer in his temple, and she knew that his general serenity was disturbed by close contact with her.

"It is nothing . . ."

He was still kneeling. He put out a hand to touch her shoulder.

"My poor child," he said. "How old are you?"

"Seventeen!"

"It is very young."

"It feels old," she told him, and her mouth quivered. "Just over a year ago I was young. Now I am old."

"You must tell me about it. Oh . . . not now; when you are feeling better. It is a momentary depression, I believe. Yesterday I thought you were the gayest person I had ever seen in my life."

There was great satisfaction in such solicitude. She began comparing him with Marcus. There was the same eager burning light in his pale eyes as there had been in Marcus's blue ones, but there any resemblance between them ended. Here was an upright man, kindly though cold. He seemed very youthful in his eagerness, although he was probably older than Marcus, but not old in experience; in experience, just a boy.

She put out her hand and he took it.

She said: "I cannot think why you are so good to me." Which was untrue, for she knew full well.

He gripped her hand more tightly, and said: "It grieves me very much that you should be unhappy here. You are homesick perhaps."

"No!" she said. "No!" Defiance returned to her eyes; they glittered behind the tears. "I do not feel homesick. I do not care if I never see England again. Why should I want to? What are trees and grass? Are they England? There are trees and grass here. No! England is Newgate, cruelty, injustice. I do not care if I never see it again."

"How badly they have hurt you!" he said.

She nodded. He drew her towards him.

"I am so sorry. I have wanted to tell you so before."

She lifted her face to his, until their lips were very close. She thought, Marcus is finished now; I will remember nothing of him except his rogue's philosophy. I will never love anyone again as long as I live.

He was staring at her. In a moment he would kiss her unless she moved away. She only had to repulse him once, and he would keep right out of her way for evermore; he was that sort of man. Now he was fighting with himself; he was thinking, I must not; I must get rid of this mad infatuation for one of our servants, a convict of whom I know nothing except that she is beautiful and more than beautiful.

Let him escape, and he would disappear for days; he would go to church and hold his head high and thank his God to have been delivered from temptation. Like Esther! Waves of anger swept over her. The cowards! They wanted what others wanted, and hadn't the courage to take it. They did not do these things naturally, gloriously; they did them because the temptation had been too strong for them to resist. Weaklings, all of them!

She moved nearer to him; he put his arms round her suddenly and kissed her. She kissed him triumphantly and angrily. Oh, you good man! she thought. Oh, you good, good man! How amusing to think of you here, kissing your wife's convict maid while she sleeps in the next room!

She struggled free. She saw that his face was pale pink; he looked comical kneeling there, with those arms, from which she had just escaped, hanging at his sides.

"I'm sorry," he said. "You must forgive me."

She regarded his downcast head. Mr. Masterman, the master! And she thought then of how he had come aboard, and how she had tried to will him to look at her, and how she had appealed to him with her eyes. The master! He was no longer that.

"It does not matter," she said. "It is of no importance."

"It is of the greatest importance," he insisted. "I am afraid that you will think I wished to insult you."

Inwardly she laughed. He was not grown-up at all. He might be Mr. Masterman, a power in the colony, but he was also a young man embarking on his first passionate love affair.

She shrugged her shoulders and stood up.

"One gets used to that . . . insults, I mean. You are sorry, I know."

He was standing beside her, and Madam's blue velvet dinner gown was a carpet beneath their feet.

"I must explain," he said. "You have disturbed me for a long time."

She opened her eyes very wide. "I . . . disturbed you?"

"You do not understand. The fault is entirely mine. It is nothing you have done, except to be so beautiful and so young and so different from other people."

In spite of herself she felt a tenderness for him.

He went on: "Many times I have wanted to do that . . . many times before."

"Oh, but . . ."

"It is wrong of course, very wrong. But I have told you now, and in future . . ." She watched him closely now; he was

367

uneasy. "There is so much unpleasantness here in this place. I would not wish anyone who comes under my authority to suffer from that."

He walked over to the mirror; he stood there, facing it, looking into it but not seeing himself. Seeing her perhaps, with his wife's dress half over her head.

"Therefore," he said, in the judicial voice with which he must surely address his committee meetings, "I want you to accept my apology. I must make you believe it will not happen again."

He walked slowly to the door.

She folded the dresses and put them back. The pain of her discovery about Esther and Marcus was less acute. She went back to the kitchen, and she tried to think of Mr. Masterman, that cold, stern man, who, kneeling on his wife's blue dinner dress, had humbly asked her to forgive him. She was cold to Margery, she was distant to Esther.

Esther tried to catch her hand once, but she made her own go limp, and she saw the look of pain and fear cross Esther's face.

James came in. Carolan was wanted in the mistress's room.

"Oh, Carolan, I have such a headache! Give me one of my powders. The master has been in; he is going away for some days, he says. To one of the stations. He says it is time he looked in on the men."

Carolan thought, Days of it, days of monotony; and it will go on like this for years . . . seven perhaps. Men grew out of desire. Marcus had. Everard had. I am so tired of being a servant and listening to her wearying talk.

"When does he go, M'am?"

"Early tomorrow morning. He will be up by sunrise; it's a good day's ride out to the station. He is so energetic!"

"You look very fatigued, M'am."

"Fatigued!" She closed her eyes. "I am worn out."

"It will be dark at any moment now, M'am," said Carolan. It was still light, and she had never got over the wonder of the sudden descent of darkness, the absence of the English twilight hour. "Shall I light the candles?"

"My powder first."

"Oh, yes. . . . I should rest all day tomorrow, M'am . . . with the master away. I have rarely seen you look so fatigued."

"Give me my mirror."

Carolan sat on the bed and held out the mirror. Oh, to recline on such a soft bed! How she hated the dampness of the basement! How she hated this life of a convict servant! So monotonous, and she should be grateful for its monotony when others, less fortunate, must endure horrors. Nothing to look forward to. She could still feel the imprint of that kiss on her lips. The master! The desire in his eyes had made them like Marcus's eyes. I am so tired of being a servant; so tired of being unloved. My mother had had lovers when she was my age. My grandmother. . . . It is not natural for the women of our family to go unloved.

Her heart began to hammer inside her; she thought it would burst. She was hardly thinking of Marcus at all now.

"I must get your medicine," she said. And she went to the drawer and unlocked it. She took out the bottle and shook it.

Lucille watched her with startled eyes.

"I said the powder."

"Oh, yes, the powder! I thought, as you looked so tired . . . But as you say, it is just a headache. The powder."

"No, no, Carolan. Give me that . . . I will have that. I never felt so tired in all my life, and what Doctor Martin said was that I needed to sleep more than anything."

Lucille drained the glass.

"I will wash it; then I will draw the curtains, shall I? And I will leave you to sleep."

"I do not know what I should do without you, Carolan!"

Carolan locked the bottle in the drawer, washed the glass, smoothed her mistress's bed, drew the curtains.

"Sleep well, M'am."

Lucille nodded drowsily.

In the toilet-room Carolan lit a candle. She held it high and looked at her face in the mirror. Her lips were parted, her eyes brilliant, recklessness was in her face.

I am so tired of being a servant!

Deliberately she went across the room and knocked at the door.

"Come in," he said. She went in. Two candles burned on the mantel shelf. She blew hers out.

"I hear you are going away early tomorrow morning. I thought there might be something I could pack for you."

She leaned against the door.

He said: "Pack? No. I do not think so. Pack? There is nothing to pack . . ."

"I see. Good night."

Her voice was a breathless whisper.

He said: "Good night!" very steadily, and then: "Carolan!"

He was standing before her, looking down at her.

369

"You should not have come," he said breathlessly.

"No," she answered, "I should not. But tomorrow you are going away . . . I will leave you now. I thought . . ."

But he would not let her leave him now. He lifted her up; she put her arms round his neck. She was not sure whether this was her revenge on Marcus, or whether she had been unloved too long.

"Carolan," he said, as they lay on his bed, "what are you thinking?"

"Of you . . . and of myself."

"What of us?"

"It was wonderful, was it not?"

"It was wonderful."

"You look exalted . . . and damned. Such a queer mixture!"

"You say such things! Adultery is one of the mortal sins."

"It is a great tragedy, my coming here." She put her arms round his neck. "If you could go back, back to where I came in with the candle, would you tell me to go?"

"I believe I would commit any sin rather than not have had that."

She smiled, but he could not see the smile, for her face was pressed against his. She was thinking of Esther in her passion for Marcus, as reckless as this man, denying her God with the ease that he denied his. Esther and Masterman. Herself and Marcus. That was how it should have been. Yet it was as though life had carelessly shuffled them like cards in a pack, and then had turned up herself with this man, Esther with Marcus, in the wrong places.

She stroked the fine hair on his hands. There was the glimmer of a scheme in her mind. She was not sure what it was; she was not even sure that it was a scheme.

It was amusing to see anxiety breaking through his ecstasy.

"What a brute I am! You . . . so young and innocent . . . To think that I . . . I have always wanted to do the honourable thing by the people who came into my house . . ."

She laid her lips gently against his. Like her mother and her grandmother and her great-grandmother, she had the arts of loving at her finger-tips.

"If I tell you something, promise not to despise me . . . Gunnar. It is such a queer name!"

His arms tightened about her.

"I like to hear you say it. My mother gave it to me. She was Swedish."

"Is it right for me to call you by it? Perhaps I will . . . when

370

we are alone! it will be necessary to remember when others are present. It will be necessary not to show by a look . . ."

She paused, wondering how he would take this suggestion that love between them was to be no isolated incident.

He said: "I have plunged you into this deceit—you who are so young and have been entrusted to my care."

She laughed softly.

"I said I would tell you something, if you would not despise me."

"Despise you! It is you who should . . ."

She laid a hand on his lips.

"No," she said, "the fault is with me. It is I who am wicked, abandoned. You see, I could not bear to think of your going miles away. I wanted to see you . . . so I came to your door . . . and asked if I could help . . ."

He was enchanted. He would not know that a woman could be like this. He thought her naïve, more innocent than ever. How repulsive were those women like Lucille, who stood guard over a virginity which one had no wish to assail, who handed out favours one did not greatly desire, as though they were the most precious gifts on earth! And here was this girl, this innocent child, giving so freely, and so naïvely confessing that she wanted to give. He was overcome with tenderness.

"Listen to me, Carolan," he said. "This must never happen again. I cannot understand myself. I must have been possessed by the devil."

She gazed at him. Physically he was magnificent; his features were not unattractive. She liked his simplicity; the puritan in him appealed to her because Marcus might be many things, but never a puritan. Marcus was a liar and a cheat; he would caress one with his eyes, with his words; he was full of artifice; he would suit his methods to the woman of the moment. Why think of Marcus, knowing him to be a cheat? Now here was Mr. Masterman . . . Gunnar, as she would think of him in future . . . a man of power in the colony, and a man who was more completely in her power than Marcus could ever be. A simple man, a puritan. A man who had strayed from his virtuous path because he could not resist Carolan Haredon, his convict servant. He did not seek passion; his love was natural and pure as the wind and the sun and the rain; Marcus's was something grown in a hot-house, cultivated, seeming delightful because so much care had been spent on it, completely artificial. Yet there was no natural recklessness about Gunnar. Why, he had locked both doors leading into his room before he had made love to her: Now Marcus

371

was the essence of recklessness. Marcus was unsafe, and that locking of the two doors was in itself a symbol . . . a symbol of safety and security which one must enjoy if one walked beside this man. She had learned cunning from Marcus perhaps.

"You see, Carolan," he said, his brow wrinkled, "that there must be no other time. It will be difficult, but I shall go away. I shall spend much time at the stations."

"Tell me about the stations," she said.

He was rather slow of speech, reluctant to enthuse, but he gave her a picture of a lonely station surrounded by grasslands where sheep fed and cattle were raised and wild horses tamed. It appealed to something in her. She imagined the two of them living there, cooking their own meals after a day in the open, making love out of doors. Mr. Masterman, the master. When men spoke of him there was awe in their voices. She thought of his trembling before her, whispering that there must be no more; and she smiled, for she knew it was for her to say whether or not there should be any more.

She listened to his description of a muster. She could feel a horse between her knees; she could feel the wind on her cheeks as they galloped . . . both of them together. He belonged to fresh air and camp fires, and it was pleasant to think of enjoying these things with him.

She was almost happy; if only she could forget this nagging ache for Marcus she could be happy. Gunnar Masterman offered such balm to her wounded vanity. The master who was in the power of his servant. The strong man who could only be weak with her.

She lay against him.

"Tell me more. I want to know all about you."

He told her about the Swedish mother who had died on the journey across the Atlantic. He had been born, he told her, just over thirty years ago, during that year—and this always seemed strange and very significant to him—when Lord North became Prime Minister of England, and Captain Cook discovered New South Wales. He was a man, he assured her, who forever tried to override superstition, but did she not see the significance? Who had been responsible for the loss of the American colonies? Chiefly Lord North and his half-crazy monarch. Who had been responsible for the opening up of this colony? Captain Cook! Did she see now what he meant? He, Gunnar Masterman, had been born in that year when the fate of America and of New South Wales was decided. He had always seen it that way. When he was quite a small boy, he and his sister Greta and his parents had left America for

England, for his puritan father had been a staunch loyalist and had no place in the New America. Gunnar remembered only little of his life before the journey across the sea, during which his mother died. It was a new life for them all on the other side of the water; it was a step from moderate prosperity to a desperate privation. The Old Country had little hospitality to offer those of her loyal sons who had fought for her three thousand miles away; there was little reward but vague promises of a chance in the new country discovered by Captain Cook, promises which did not materialise. His father was a strange man; he did not complain; he had tried to make puritans of those people who lived in the fever-infested huts and haunted the low taverns along Thames-side. It was a self-appointed task, and he starved and preached, though at the wharves and on the barges he did work sometimes. It was there by the river that he met his second wife. She was beautiful and abandoned; she picked up a living from the sailors and wharfmen who frequented the taverns. He took her to his shabby little home and married her, because he must have wanted her as his son now wanted his convict servant. Listening, Carolan felt a tenderness for the man and for his son twining itself about her cunning. She saw the eldest of that poor family, a tall, lean boy, almost hungry. They kept a lodging-house by the river at one time—a squalid place, but the step-mother could not be weaned from the gin bottle, and the father from the saving of souls; and thus they could not expect to become successful lodging-house keepers. They had several children, and Gunnar, who had hazy recollections of a sunnier life, soon decided that they could not go on living that way. He began to earn money, carrying parcels, loading barges . . . anything to earn some money.

"I never told anyone else," he said wonderingly. "Why do I feel I have to tell you? I think it is because I have fallen in love with you, and you are so generous that it seems wrong not to tell you the truth about myself."

Carolan felt tears prickling her eyelids and the tenderness within her deepen. I shall never fall in love again, she assured herself. It is well to be loved, but not to love.

He told of winter and the icicles hanging from the gables of the lodging-house, and a cold wind sweeping up from the east, all along the river; pumping water in the yard; chilblains, coughs, colds; some of his brothers and sisters dying off, and his father, preaching in the market place, and his mother, going to bed and refusing to get up until the weather changed.

He it was who must wash the children and feed them. Was this Mr. Masterman?

He told of summer. The appalling heat of houses crowded together, and the stench of decaying rubbish in the gutters. Of armies of bed-bugs that could not be kept down—himself a campaigning general, a candle his weapon—of rats that lived on the stores in the warehouses near the river and who overflowed into the house.

The candles flickered. They would be out in a moment. She had no idea of time, nor did she care. She thought of Lucille, sleeping her drugged sleep in the nearby room, who knew nothing of this man's life before he had married her; and if he had told her, what would she understand of stinking gutters, of rats and bugs, of a praying father and a drunken mother!

She saw his face, set, determined, and it was easy to see the young Gunnar there, the boy who made up his mind, as he looked across the ill-smelling river, that he would escape.

"You do not wish to go back to England, Gunnar?"

"No!" he said fiercely. "No!"

"Nor I! England for you is poverty, chilblains, and pumping water from a pump in the yard. I know. The water used to freeze, and it was slippery in the yard. You could have cried with the cold, if you had been anyone but yourself, Gunnar. You would never cry at anything; however bad it was, you would only say 'I shall escape from this.'"

He said: "Why did you not come here ten years ago? Why did I not find you here when I came?"

"You would have married me . . . a convict! Why, you married Major Gregory's daughter. It was a good match. It gave you a position in this town."

He flinched. Now he was uneasy. A moment ago he had forgotten Lucille. Now he must remember she was here, in this very house, a room dividing them.

She wished she had not said that, but she was tactless by nature, and she wanted to know him absolutely.

"I have made you sad." She moved nearer to him. "I am sorry. How can you know what you would have done?"

He said reproachfully: "Surely you know that if it had been possible to marry you, I would have asked you to before . . . before . . ."

"Before this happened!" she said, and she felt on safe ground now, knowing her man. "Tell me the rest," she said.

"When I was nearly eleven, I decided to get away. I felt grown up. My sister, who was nine, could look after the little ones. I hated the lodging-house; it was getting lower and lower. My step-mother was almost always drunk. My father wanted to teach me how to be a preacher; and I saw that if I followed in his footsteps there was nothing for me but poverty."

"So you ran away, Gunnar?"

"Not until I knew where I would run to. I had a job offered me in an inn in Holborn, and there I was a pot-boy. I was there for a year; then I took up with a travelling salesman. We went about the country with a packhorse; we sold all manner of things, and when I had learned how it was done, I thought how much better it would be if, instead of working for someone else, I worked for myself. So I saved money and I bought goods which I sold again. I was frugal. I never paid for a bed in summer; I slept under hedges and hayricks and in alleys, and so I saved money."

She compared him with Marcus. Marcus, choosing the reckless way, the way that led to trouble; Gunnar, choosing the safe and sure road that led to success. Marcus picked pockets and cheated; Gunnar made plans and went without food and bedding. Marcus was a convict, clever and cunning though he might be; Gunnar was a successful man. She had been right to hitch her wagon to this steady star. But she wanted Marcus. She wanted his merriment, his quick wit, his knowledge of life, his passionate eyes and his caressing hands. She half turned away from the man beside her, sick of the whole business, wishing she could go back to that moment when she had stood at his door with the candle in her hand.

She was not listening to him. He had made his little successes and had decided to come to Sydney. He had discovered the government was willing to help men possessed of some small capital who wished to emigrate to New South Wales. There was more hope for a rapid rise there than in the old country, where a man must have, in addition to determined ambition, a string of noble ancestry behind him. So he waited till a passage could be found for him, free of charge on a store ship, and out he came. And the rest was simple, for men such as he was were needed in New South Wales, and his flair for organisation had stood him in good stead. He had risen rapidly; he had married Major Gregory's daughter; he had a fine house in Sydney; he was accepted anywhere. He was Masterman of Sydney.

"It is interesting," she said, "particularly to me. You see, you went gradually up, which is so much more satisfactory than going down as I did." Briefly she told him the story of her life. He was shocked by the conduct of the squire—more so than he was by the injustice of her and her mother's being thrown into Newgate.

"My poor child!" he said. "How cruelly life has treated you . . . and to send you here . . . to such a monster!"

But she would not have it.

"Please!" With a pretty gesture she laid her fingers on his lips. "I believe you are the best thing that has ever happened to me."

"My poor child . . . My dear child!"

"Gunnar," she said, "you have no children. Did you want children?"

He did not answer, but held her tightly against him.

"I too," she said, and she thought, If I had a child, I should cease to think of Marcus, cease to think of Everard. A child . . . a child of my own! And a child should have a father to whom it could look up. Not a lecher like the squire; not a weak man like Darrell; not an attractive philanderer like Marcus. It was not men like that who made the best fathers. It was the calm men, the practical men, the puritans who would perhaps be a little stern, but firm and wise and kindly.

She wanted to show him how happy he might have been had he, ten years ago, met Carolan Haredon in Sydney instead of Lucille Gregory. How wicked I have grown, thought Carolan. Did Newgate do this to me? Or was the evil there, waiting to grow, and was the Newgate climate such as to nourish it?

He was saying: "There is something else I want to tell you, Carolan. You will despise me for this, you who are so truthful and honest."

"What! You have been dishonest then?"

"My name is really Morton. I changed it when I came out here."

She said soberly: "Masterman is a good name. I like it, and it suits you. Why should we not choose our own names! It will be a good name to pass on to your children."

"I shall never have any," he said. He added desperately: "You must go now, Carolan. You see, it is so difficult, and it was so wrong . . ."

She said: "Oh, my darling, it is not so easy for me." And she saw how the endearment delighted him and charmed him, who seemed unable to speak them himself.

"You must go," he said, "you must!"

She moved nearer to him; she put her arms round his neck and pressed her body against his.

"Carolan!" he said.

"My dear . . ."

He must know that it was not for him to say she should go; from now on, she would command. She liked him, this master of men. He appealed to her senses, if not to her heart, and her senses were important to her; she had gone too long unloved. She could accept his caresses, even if, as she did so, she might dream of Marcus. To see him, the good man, falling deeper and deeper into what must seem to him unbridled sin, stirred in her that bitter contempt of law and order which Newgate had nurtured in her.

Now he was throwing away every one of those good resolutions he had made but a second ago.

"Gunnar. Please, my dear, do not go away tomorrow. I could not bear that."

"No," he said fervently. "I cannot go. Of course I cannot go tomorrow . . . Just another day . . ."

Carolan went about holding her head high.

Not the woman who has just been thrown over, thought Margery. Not if I know anything about it. And talk about arrogance. She would flounce into the kitchen, for all the world as if she were mistress of the house. Lovely she was though, so that Margery forgave her. Her hair was soft and all shining . . . and if she wasn't dressing it up fashionable now! And she had a new frock; and she had secrets in her eyes. Hard as nails she was too. Bright and glittering and beautiful with her mermaid's eyes green as the sea . . . icy cold sometimes too!

Golly! thought Margery. Am I to be frightened of her, and that in my own kitchen? Why don't I have a talk with Mr. Masterman about her? Wasn't I put in charge down here in the kitchen?

But she was rarely in the kitchen now; she detached herself. She no longer slept in the basement. She had her own room upstairs.

"Mrs. Masterman wants me near her in case she needs me in the night."

Did you ever hear the like? The mistress doted on her; as for the master, he seemed struck dumb. Not a word in protest had he raised, and him such a stickler for his rules and regulations!

So up she had gone, and now she was demanding that Poll should take up her own special bath water!

And this, said Margery to herself is where I do put me foot down. Bedrooms is one thing; frocks is another . . . and

377

so is fashionable hair styles; but when it comes to having bath water sent up . . . that is where I has a word with the master.

But somehow it did Margery good to look at her, even though, when she came flaunting down to the kitchen, it was all she could do to stop herself boxing the girl's ears. Rather her any day, thought Margery, than that moping Esther. Miserable little slut, whining and praying, getting up every morning white as a sheet; scared out of her natural, that was what she was. Serve her right too! And one of these days the master would have to be told: "Now tell me, Margery," he would say, "what was this man doing in the house?"

"I don't know. I don't really!" muttered Margery. "A nice bit of trouble this is. Things is going to happen in this house and happens soon, or I'm very mistook."

She rocked backwards and forwards, laughing. She hadn't enjoyed herself so much for a long time.

He came often, that Marcus, and with him that Tom Blake. They couldn't keep away from Carolan, neither of 'em. And the haughty piece pretended not to care a jot about them, tossed her head, threw a smile at Tom though, and looked through Marcus as though he wasn't there. Funny. And funny-I-don't-think when the master gets to know they've been coming here. The cheek of them, coming into the yard to pay visits just like they was gentry. Marcus had a word with Esther, tried to cheer her, told her he'd look after the baby, tried to show her that what had happened wasn't much, nothing to get frightened about. He would go on talking to the miserable girl, and Mistress Carolan would flounce in, and if looks could kill she would have killed him, but Margery wasn't born yesterday and she knew how it was with both of them . . . crying out for each other, that's what they were. It made you feel funny to see them.

One afternoon Margery was in the shed near the pump when Carolan came into the yard. It wasn't often that Carolan went into the yard. The summer had faded now and the winter was on them. It was chilly in the yard, but something queer about the way she stood there as though she were waiting for someone, made Margery cautiously shut the shed door and decide to wait and watch. She did not have to wait long before Marcus came swinging into the yard for all the world as though he owned it; and peering through a crack in the door Margery saw his face and she guessed they had arranged this meeting.

Ho! Ho! thought Margery. So it's making it up, is it, me lovelies! So you're coming to your senses at last!

"Marcus!" said Carolan.

"Carolan! Carolan!"

The way he said her name was in itself a declaration of love. He had a beautiful voice. She's hard as nails to say no to a man like that, and her not cut out to do without men no more than I was.

"I want to talk to you about Esther."

"Is that why you sent for me?"

"She is very unhappy, Marcus. She is thinking of death. I saw her take up a knife and look at it in a longing way, as though she were thinking death would be a way out of her troubles, for life has become unendurable for her."

"What can I do about that?"

"What can you do? You are the cause of it; you will have to do something."

"Tell me what, Carolan."

"Marcus, you are a brute! I wish we had never met you. Poor Esther, you have ruined her life. You know how she feels. She believes herself to be utterly damned."

"You put all the blame on me, Carolan."

"Because that is where it belongs!"

"Now, now, me lady!" muttered Margery. "That ain't fair. It takes two to make a quarrel and it takes two to make a baby; that's my way of thinking. And to see the way you've been treating that Esther, it would seem you thought all the blame was with her!"

"Carolan! Carolan!"

"Oh, please stop saying my name in that way. If it is meant to be affectionate, it does not seem so to me. I see right through you, Marcus. You have no scruples whatever; you are completely without honour; you are absolutely despicable."

What a tongue she had! And a fool he was, for all that he seemed such a fine gentleman. She wanted him to take her now and not to mind if she kicked or yelled. Let her yell; it would do her good. Let her kick; she was a kicker anyway.

"There is only one thing to do. Esther will die of a broken heart, or she will kill herself. I know Esther. She can never bear the shame of this. You must marry her."

"Marry her! You talk as though we were in conventional England."

"Esther is conventional, as England made her. You are rotten, as England made you."

"And you are hard and cruel and cold as ice!"

"I am trying to do the right thing for you both."

"Carolan, have you no sympathy, no understanding?"

379

"No sympathy, but complete understanding, I fear. You must marry Esther. Nothing else will make her live. I know her, and I am sure of that."

"My dear Carolan, you are talking the most ridiculous nonsense. Marry Esther! Have you forgotten that we are convicts?"

"Convict! You! What an evil world this is, when such as you can feather their nests, and such as Esther, innocent Esther, can become your prey! I tell you you *shall* marry Esther."

"It is impossible, Carolan."

"You talked of marrying me."

"I should have had to arrange it very carefully."

"Well, this is arranged. I have arranged it."

"What do you mean? Carolan, you simply do not understand. We are slaves, all of us. We have been here but a short time. We shall have to wait, shall have to prove that we are worthy of marriage."

"Worthy of marriage! You certainly are not. If Esther were not such a little fool, I should tell her to have nothing more to do with you, to think herself lucky that, though she has been foolish enough to make you the father of her child, you are not her husband."

Margery chuckled. Ha! Ha! My beauty, you're giving it away. All that bitterness, and you pretending not to care! You're jealous . . . jealous as they make 'em, and of that snivelling, praying wretch. As for you, me fine gentleman, you're not so smart. You can't see what she's thinking, can you?

"But you see, Carolan, it is impossible; if it were not, I would marry her. She is a sweet girl, and I behaved, as you say, very badly. It is up to me to make amends in the way she wants me to. But it is not possible, for she has been assigned to this house. . . ."

"It is possible. I have spoken to Mr. Masterman, and I have his consent to your marriage."

"You . . . have what . . . ?"

He might well be surprised. Margery almost burst out of the shed. You spoke to Mr. Masterman . . . you! And who are you to speak to him? Didn't he put me in charge of the kitchen? Isn't it my place . . .

Carolan had folded her arms across her breast, and she stood there, rocking on her heels, laughing to herself, hating him in a way that was really loving him; and yet stubborn as a mule with the fierceness of a tigress.

"You have spoken to Mr. Masterman . . . you, Carolan?"

"Oh, yes. I, Marcus!" Her voice was edged with light laughter, bubbling laughter that was somehow sharp and meant to cut into his pride, murder any hopes he might have had. "Mr. Masterman and I are friendly . . . very friendly indeed."

Margery let loose an expletive. She clapped her hands over her mouth; her face was purple with fury; her hands itched. Had she been near the whip that hung over the mantelpiece she would have reached for it and she would have laid it about those insolent shoulders. She was speaking in that way of the master!

"I am sure," she said, haughty now, verily the mistress of the house and the yard and of the kitchen and of him and of herself, "that I can arrange it satisfactorily."

Marcus was taken off his guard.

He said: "I see." Then he burst out: "You . . . you slut! So that is it. I see. I might have seen before. How long?" And those two words betrayed his defeat, his love for her.

"What is that to you?"

"It makes me laugh!"

"I am glad you are amused; though why you should be I quite fail to see."

"You, my haughty Carolan . . . and that . . . puritan! His name stands for virtue in the town. Tell me, Carolan, how did you manage to seduce the fellow?"

She flashed out angrily: "How dare *you* talk in this way! He is a better man than you will ever be. I am happy now. Why should we not? He is in love with me."

"I do not doubt it, Carolan. Masterman! The prude! The puritan! I shall split my sides with laughing."

"It would be the best thing that could happen to you if you killed yourself with laughing. For Esther too, I am thinking!"

"Carolan . . . forgive me! It is so funny . . . so funny. You and . . . Masterman! You will have to play your cards very carefully, my dear."

"Do not dare to breathe a word of this to anyone!"

"Oh, Carolan, Carolan!"

"If you do, I will have it known that you are a cheat and a liar. I will see to it that you are punished. I will see. . . ."

"Ah! I see Masterman's mistress will rule the town!"

"You heard what I said. I mean it. Breathe a word of what . . ."

". . . of what you have so indiscreetly told me . . ."

"Breathe a word of it, and I will . . . I will have you beaten to death. I will . . ."

"It is blackmail! I keep quiet then about you, and you keep quiet about me. What a pretty pair we are, are we not? So admirably suited!"

Margery thought the girl was going to cry, for all she held her head so high. And as for him, he was heart-broken, for all the cruel lashings of his tongue. Oh yes, they were crying out for each other, and in spite of everything Margery could have wept for them.

"Enough of this," said Carolan, and turned from him. Through the crack in the corner of the shed, Margery saw her face, saw her lips quiver. "You and Esther can be married soon."

"Carolan!" He was beside her, his hands on her shoulders, forcing her round to look at him.

Now! thought Margery. Now! She's yours now for the taking . . . the wanton! The *master!* I don't believe that. I wasn't born yesterday. That's just to aggravate him, that is!

"Well?" her voice rapped out at him. "What is it? Please take your hands off me."

"And if I will not? Doubtless you will call your lover to horsewhip me!"

"You have no right to be here! You behave as though you are a free man instead of a felon."

"Would your mistress think you had a right to be what you are . . . did she know?"

"Please go at once. You are insolent."

"I am mourning, Carolan. I am mourning for a sweet and beautiful girl whom I loved . . . Carolan, whose handkerchief I still carry close to my heart."

"Were you carrying it when you seduced Esther?"

There was a confession, if he could but read the meaning behind her words. She was jealous as fury, that girl; and her daring to let the master make love to her!

"I carry it always. I shall burn it when I get back. It means nothing now."

"A pity to waste good linen! Give it to Esther, or whoever occupies your affections at this moment."

"I would not keep it now. Every time I looked at it it would remind me of you and your puritan together. But, Carolan, I can see you are a wise woman. Play your cards cleverly, my dear, and you may do very well for yourself."

"Thank you, Marcus. But I happen to be in love, and playing cards well or otherwise does not come into this."

She walked towards the shed, so abruptly that Margery thought she had seen her and was coming in to denounce her.

Margery's knees began to shake. Suppose she told Mr. Masterman that Margery was a very unsatisfactory person to leave in charge of the kitchen! Suppose she told of laxness, of James's coming into the basement at night! She was a power in the house. No wonder she gave herself airs and graces! She was mistress of the house.

She looked over her shoulder.

She said: "We will make the arrangements for the wedding. And we shall make them promptly. It will be well for Esther's sake to get done with the business as soon as possible."

She flounced into the house, and he stood looking at her, like a man who has lost everything he most wanted in life. Queer, Margery wanted to go out and comfort him, but she dared not. She was bewildered. She did not understand life in this place as she had thought she did. Things went on under her nose, and she did not see them. She had to be careful. The house had a new mistress.

She waited until he had walked away; then she went into the kitchen. She could hear Carolan in the communal bedroom talking to Esther.

"What I want is a good strong cup of tea," said Margery aloud. She made it, and all the time she was doing so she thought of her—red hair and green eyes—and the master, noticing her, trying not to let her get him at first, and then . . . and then . . .

Margery laughed. Perhaps he wasn't only half a man after all. Well she liked him for it, so there!

As for her, the arrogant piece, fancy making the master fall in love with her, and him always such a good man and always doing the right thing! But come to think of it the good ones were as bad as the others. Look at Miss Mealy Mouth saying Yes please, to the first man that asked her!

But the master and that Carolan! Well, could you blame him?

"I don't!" said Margery, stirring her tea. "And come to think of it, I don't blame her either!"

When Lucille Masterman came out of a drugged sleep she talked to Carolan.

"There is a change in him. Do you not see it?"

"A change? I see no change."

"Ah, but you do not know him as I do. There is a change, I assure you. He rarely comes in here now. He is very absentminded. He was never that before. Carolan, there are times when I have a feeling that he does not mind how ill I am, that he does not care whether I recover or not."

"You are talking nonsense," said Carolan.

"Am I? I do talk nonsense, do I not! I have been so tired; I am waking now. I feel as if I am struggling out of darkness, and that words are a sort of rope I cling to. Oh, you smile, Carolan; you are so strong and practical. You are very like him, Carolan, in a way . . . in a way. Once he wanted me to get well; he was very eager that I should. But that was not because he cared about me. Oh, no! He wanted me strong and well because he wanted us to have children. Sons he wanted. Big, strong men to go on living here when we are dead; to build up this country into a great place, independent of England. I am sure that is how he feels. He is such a strange man, Carolan. You would not know, because you always see him as the master, so careful, so right in everything he does."

"Why do you not try to sleep again?"

"Sleep! I have slept and slept. Do you know, Carolan, sometimes I feel the desire to go on sleeping, not to wake up. It is as though, when I lie in that deep sleep, hands are laid upon me, soothing me, bidding me stay there in the peaceful darkness for ever . . . not come back, you see . . ."

Carolan's eyes glittered.

"You took too much of the drug; you must be careful."

"I must be careful, Carolan. I will. When you are tired, it is so beautiful to sink into that deep sleep."

"I should not take it so often, if I were you."

"Oh, Carolan, do not stop me. Please do not stop me!"

"Who am *I* to stop *you?*" said Carolan.

The glazed eyes were lifted to her face.

"You are so good, so kind, so sympathetic. I do not know what I should do without you. You are strong; I have always been attracted by strong people. He is strong; that was why I was attracted by him, I suppose. I wish I could have been more the sort of wife he wanted. When I was not so ill, I must have pleased him. We entertained a good deal. It was only after our marriage that he was on such good terms at Government House. He owes me a little, Carolan."

"What would he say, were he to know about the child?"

"You would not tell a soul!"

"Of course I would not; you told me in strictest confidence." She laughed. "But he would be very angry, I do declare."

Lucille was awake now, wide awake; the thought of discovery could make her throw off the last effects of the drug.

"I should be terrified if he knew. He . . . is ruthless, Carolan. I often wonder what happened to him before he came to Sydney."

"Did he not tell you?"

"Never!"

"Not even when . . . when you were lovers?"

"Lovers! What do you mean, Carolan?"

Carolan wanted to laugh out loud. They had never been lovers; they had never been anything but a suitable match for each other. That accounted for his happiness now, for his complete simplicity, for the youthfulness of his love-making. Carolan felt she ought to have been amused, discussing her lover with her lover's wife, but she was only ashamed. She had to force herself to go on. "I mean during the engagement."

"It was very short; there was no reason why it should not be. I was so sure it would be a successful marriage then."

"Oh, come," said Carolan falsely, "is it not now?"

"That I do not know."

"You are thinking of the child."

"Oh, Carolan, please do not speak of that again."

"I will not, if you wish it so, but if he were to know . . . He would consider it a great wrong."

"Oh, I could not face it. Carolan, you know I am not strong."

"He would have thought it your duty to face it."

"I was very wicked, Carolan. That is what you are thinking." Lucille caught at her hand. "But now, Carolan, it does not matter. I am sure he is resigned . . . I am sure of it! He used to come in and look at me, and he would frown and ask me how I was, and I would know that he was thinking of children. But lately he has ceased to think of them. He has changed. He is a different man. He looks . . . as though he finds life good, no longer frustrated. He is a man who is always reaching for a goal. Now . . . perhaps I talk rubbish . . . but it seems to me as though he is no longer reaching, that he is satisfied with life."

"You think he has given up hope of children?"

"Carolan, I do. I have been careless of late. The bottle . . . it was by the side of my bed . . . on the table here, when he came in."

"What did he say?"

"He said nothing."

"He could not have seen it."

"He is usually observant of such things."

"But had he seen it, he would surely have said something?"

"He merely looked at it. He said: 'How are you today, Lucille?' very gently, almost tenderly. And I felt then that he loved me more than he had ever done."

"But should he not have been pertrubed at the sight of the bottle?"

"Why should he? Perhaps he did not know what it was; perhaps he thought it was some tonic. I was trembling all over. I was terrified that he would take out the cork, that he would discover what it was, that he would forbid me to take any more."

"You would have obeyed him?"

"I must sleep, Carolan. Doctor Martin says the best thing I can do is to sleep."

"But he would not give you this! You have to go to your shady convict doctor to get this, to the one who helped out about the baby . . ."

"I used to think you understood, Carolan," she said and her voice shook with fear.

"I do understand, but you wronged him deeply. To marry a man is to promise him children. You did not keep your promise. Come. Lie down. Do not distress yourself; you are not strong enough. You should never have married."

"But, Carolan, I do not think he minds now. He does not worry about my health as he did, and I know he was once waiting for me to get strong so that we could have children."

"He does not think of children now, you tell me."

"Sometimes it seems he does, sometimes not. He told me of that girl, Esther. Is it not good of him to concern himself with her? He is arranging everything for her, and when he talked of her I saw a gleam of something in his eyes. 'She is going have a child,' he said. 'I am arranging for her marriage to the man responsible.' I thought he was wonderful then, so good. He wants to make this place a beautiful country; that is what I think. He wants to set it in order; he is like that . . . he wants to set everything in order. He was envious of that man because he is going to be a father. He still feels it." She shivered. "If I could have given him children . . ."

"Listen," said Carolan. "You must not fret. It is bad for you. You must forget that you cheated him, that you killed his child."

"Killed, Carolan!"

"There! I have hurt you. No, no! That is not murder; it is only when a child is born that killing it is murder. I will put this bottle away. You must not take so many doses. They will cease to be effective if you do, and it would be dangerous to increase the dose. I will cover you up. There is a chilliness in the air. Now try and sleep gently, naturally, and I will go down to the kitchen and order your bath."

Carolan saw that fear drew down the corners of the woman's mouth. Murder! She had not seen it like that before. Her hands trembled. They often trembled. It was too much drugging that did that to her. Fool that she was! She deserved her fate surely. She had had everything, and she was afraid to live the easy life that had come her way.

Carolan went downstairs. There was a light in her eyes that might have been the light of battle.

"Poll!" she said. "Heat water for the mistress's bath."

Poll! Who had murdered her baby! A different sort of murder, it was true. For the rich one law; for the poor, another. Poll would never have been able to pay the convict doctor's price; so she had murdered her baby after it was born . . . with those skinny hands of hers. Lucille, the lady, had had it done for her. What was the difference? Poor Poll! Poor Lucille! Not for her to waste her pity on them; she needed all her resources to fight for herself.

Esther was not there; she was with Marcus now. Picture Esther working at some garment in happy preparation; happiness made Esther beautiful, and Marcus was very susceptible to beauty.

Margery, at the table, watched her slyly. She had a strange and grudging affection for the lecherous old woman.

Margery's eyes went all over her. Fear shot through Carolan's heart. Those sharp eyes would see whatever there was to be seen.

"Ha, ha! Not often we have the honour . . ."

"You put it very charmingly."

"Don't suppose you'd deign to drink a glass of grog with me now! Don't suppose it for a moment!"

Carolan laughed, showing her sharp white teeth in a rush of friendliness. The woman was more than ready to meet her half way.

"That is an invitation I cannot refuse."

"Jin! Bring out that bottle."

Jin came sullenly, and Margery made her pour it out for them.

Margery smacked her lips.

"Good stuff, eh?"

"You know how to get the best out of life, Margery!"

Now what did that mean? Who knew what she would be

387

saying to the master? Queer things women would say to men in bed o' nights!

Margery touched Carolan's breast with a caressing finger. "Now don't you too, me love?"

Carolan laughed falsely. They were suspicious of each other. Sly smiles on Margery's lips. Admiration, envy, excitement to have the girl sitting so close. You couldn't help your thoughts, now could you? And for all his funny ways, he was a fine figure of a man. And to think of her ladyship, going with him out of pique—for, not being born yesterday, Margery knew, sure as fate, that it was the other one she wanted. To use the master like that! The master! It was the best thing she had heard for years. And here was the girl, sitting right next to her, her lovely body close, the body the master was in love with! It made you feel funny, no mistake!

That slyness, thought Carolan, that knowledgeable slyness! How can she see? What is she thinking? She knows so much. It may be that she sees what I cannot. They were very friendly with each other, almost ingratiatingly so.

"Things ain't what they was, with you out of me kitchen, dearie."

"I shall often come down for a chat like this."

"And how do you like sleeping in a nice feather bed?"

Hot colour ran up under the girl's cheeks. Margery had a vision of her going in to the master. No, of the master's going in to her; she would see to that! Margery could have rocked with laughter.

"It is very comfortable, of course."

Margery nudged her.

" 'Course it's comfortable!"

Poll came in eventually with the water.

"Carry it up," said Carolan.

There she was, giving her orders in Margery's kitchen! Carry it up yourself, me lady, is what she ought to be told. But how can you say such things to a girl what's got the master where she wants him? And that in a house where the mistress goes for nothing!

Poll went up with the cans; Carolan followed. Margery stood at the bottom of the stairs, watching.

"Knock at the door," said Carolan, "and tell the mistress her bath is ready."

"What!" said Poll.

"Knock at the door, I said."

"What, me!"

Carolan went across the toilet-room. She knocked at the door, listened for Lucille's sleepy "Come in," then opened the door and pushed Poll in.

Lucille looked up. Poll stared at the woman in the bed; at the luxury around her.

"Y . . . yes?" said Lucille.

"Bath's ready!" said Poll, and fled.

A few minutes later Carolan went in. "Your bath is ready."

"Yes. A . . . that girl told me."

"Poor Poll! She's a sad wretch, do you not think so?"

"Dreadful!"

"More than a little crazy." Carolan smoothed the silk coverlet angrily. "Newgate! Transportation! They can be terrible experiences; none knows how terrible unless experienced."

"Carolan, my wrap please."

"She was sentenced for murder. She murdered her baby. Poor Poll!" Carolan arranged the wrap round Lucille's shoulders. "Why, you are shivering! It has turned quite chilly. Come now . . . while the water is hot."

Her room was just above Lucille's—a small room with a feather bed. If Lucille needed her in the night, she could knock on the ceiling with a long stick. She never did.

He came some nights, Carolan would lie listening for his step. He would knock lightly, and she would be at the door, opening it swiftly and letting him in. Sometimes this stealth amused her; sometimes it disgusted her. She seemed to be full of inconsistencies these days. Sometimes she saw herself as a scheming woman, a woman who has suffered much and is determined to lie on a feather bed for the rest of her days. Wild thoughts came into her head when she was in that mood— plans and schemes. But there were other times when she saw herself differently. She had gone to Masterman, she believed then because she had known Marcus must marry Esther, and only when she had taken her determined steps away from Marcus could she bear to give him up. Perhaps she did scheme; perhaps she had made a great sacrifice; she was not entirely sure. But whatever had been that primary motive, her feet were now firmly set upon the road she must take. That was why, if he stayed away for more than two nights, she grew frightened. Once he was with her, he was completely hers, and she could do with him as she wished. But when he left her she was afraid; she, who had made so many false steps, was afraid of making more. Love between them was to her intensely exciting, and his very shame in their relationship added a piquancy for her. But she was afraid always that one day he would say he was going away, perhaps to work on one of the stations for awhile, where he could avoid her attraction. It was exciting to know that he had meant to talk of ending their relationship, and to lure him into complete surrender, to make him admit that he would face anything rather than miss this happiness. There was power; in all but his desire for her, he was the strong man; that made his downfall more gratifying, that in itself made her enjoy these months, made her hold her head high, made her heart glad even when she heard of the birth of Esther's son.

He would lie in her arms, this master of men, and talk a little. She was sure he had never talked to anyone else as he talked to her. He wanted her, not only as bedfellow, but as companion to hear about his ambitions, to listen to the stories of early struggles. She was determined to be everything to him, to strengthen the bonds about him.

He was a strange man—cold and passionate; sometimes she felt she hardly knew him; at others he seemed as simple as a child; and ambition and idealism were the keystones of his character. He spoke shyly of his dreams. Himself and his family—a big family, a family of boys to cultivate this land which he loved with a passion that, until he had met Carolan, he had bestowed on nothing else; girls to breed more men to cultivate the glorious land. That was what he had wanted. Himself a man of importance in the town, Governor perhaps; though it was hardly likely that the government at home would approve of that.

He grew excited, talking of his adopted country. He liked to think of the arrival of the first fleet.

"Eleven ships, Carolan! Only that . . . to start a new world! What a glorious moment it must have been when they sighted land!"

Carolan thought of the convicts, battened down under the hatches, and she was silent.

"And Phillip . . . that great man . . . I like to think of his sailing into Botany Bay—that great wide-open bay—and turning from it into our own Sydney Cove. 'The finest harbour in the world, in which a thousand sail of the line may ride in the most perfect security.' It *is* the finest harbour in the world. Why should not this be the finest country? In years to come people will remember that it was men such as I who made this new world. Pioneers who left the home country to start a new life. Men like Phillip, that great genius, men who with small worldly goods, but great courage, set out to open up this great new world of the South!"

He was lyrical about the place. When his enthusiasms were roused they were prodigious. His love for her, his desire for children, his love of his adopted country—all were the enthusiasms of a strong man.

And below lay that useless woman, that selfish woman who had denied him his dearest wishes.

Carolan was waiting for him now. Tonight she must be seductive, cautious and wise, for much was at stake. Tonight she was fighting not for herself alone.

The mirror told her she was beautiful. There was a new softness in her eyes, and a new fierceness too. A tigress at bay, preparing her lair.

She was trembling with fear. What would he say . . . this puritan? What would he do now? Did she really know him very well? Could she be sure of his reactions? She was terrified that he would not come. All day she had rehearsed her speeches.

Her heart felt as if it had leaped into her throat when she heard his footstep on the stairs. She opened the door, and she was in his arms.

They would make love, and then he would very tenderly tell her that he was a monster and that he must think of some plan which would help them both. But before he could talk in that way she said: "Gunnar, I am frightened, terribly frightened!"

"Why?" he said. "What has happened?"

"Can you not guess?"

He was silent, but she knew by the hammer strokes of his heartbeats that he was deeply affected. So much depended on the way he felt about it—whether his joy would overcome his conventions.

She released herself from his embrace and sat up; she drew her knees up to her chin and put her arms round them; her hair fell about her face. She was aware of her own beauty; she could see herself in the mirror; she could see him too.

"It is a strangeness that has come over me. Gunnar, I cannot help but be happy . . . frightened as I am!"

He got up; he put his arm round her.

"Carolan . . ." he said brokenly. "Carolan . . . I . . . have done this . . . I . . ."

"It is my concern as much as yours, Gunnar dear. I will not have you take all the blame."

He worshipped her; she could see it in his eyes. He could forget the difficulties in his contemplation of the miracle of childbirth! His child, his and Carolan's!

He said falteringly: "My dear . . . my very dear . . ."

She turned and kissed him on the lips with a quiet confidence.

She said: "Life has always been difficult for me, darling. You must not be disturbed by this."

"My . . . dearest, everything must be done. I am bewildered. Your child, Carolan . . . and mine! We must get you away from here. But where? Where can I send you? You must not go out of Sydney. It would not be safe . . ."

She put her arms round his neck then; she was filled with triumph. *Her* safety! The safety of the baby! That was what concerned him; not the safety of his reputation. She had not been mistaken in him. He was the strong man, the idealist, the master. Crazy ideas began to whirl around in her head; wicked ideas. She was so excited that she could scarcely play the part she had set herself to play.

"Gunnar, I have thought of a plan. You shall not be worried at all. I would not have the most wonderful experience of my life spoiled in the smallest way."

"You are wonderful, Carolan. There is no one like you. So brave . . . so sensible . . . so . . . everything that I could desire in my wife!"

She buried her face in her hands; hot colour had flooded it; she thought for a moment that he had read her wicked thoughts.

She said coldly, and her voice was muffled coming to him through her fingers: "There is a man who would gladly marry me. His name is Tom Blake. He is a man who has come here to breed sheep. He was taken with me, and I know he wishes to marry me."

She felt him to be in the grip of cold horror.

"Carolan!"

"Do not look at me," she cried. "How do you think I can bear it!"

"I thought you loved me," he said.

"Ah!" Her eyes flashed as she raised her head. "You say that, you say it coldly! You thought I loved you! You had good reason to think so, had you not? I loved you . . . I did not think of the consequences to myself, did I? You know that. You know that I was virtuous before I fell so much in love that I . . . I . . ."

That was enough. He was embracing her, murmuring endearments. Did she not know that the thought of her marriage to someone else was unbearable to him? That was why he had said cruel things. But if it was unbearable to him, how much more so was it to her who would have to live it!

"Dearest, do not think of this marriage!"

"But I must, Gunnar, I must! How can I help it? This child of mine, it must have a father. Oh, I know it has . . . the dearest, best father in the world . . . but how can I tell the world that *you* are its father! Gunnar, you do not understand this. To you it is just a vague child. To me it is already living. I am its mother. Gunnar, I tell you this now, and I mean it as I never meant anything else in my life—I will not allow my child to be born nameless into a world which takes count of these things. I am wild; I am rebellious. I came to you without thought of what I might do to myself, what hardship I might suffer. I am not sorry I am to have your child; I am glad, gloriously glad! You wanted children, you said. So do I. Madly! Recklessly! That is how I want this child. It means so much to me that I will marry a man I do not love, in order to give it a name." She watched him in the mirror. "My child *must* have a name, Gunnar, no matter what its mother suffers to get it!"

He was heartbroken, crazy with the fear of losing her . . . and they were both thinking of the woman who lay below.

"Carolan, Carolan, if only it were possible . . . if only I could make you my wife . . ."

"Gunnar, my dearest, you are talking foolishly. You talk of making a convict your wife!"

"If they had sent you over for life even, I would have found a means of marrying you . . . if only . . ."

"If only . . . what Gunnar?"

"There is only one thing that stops our marrying. What else could there be but that I am married already!"

"Oh . . . were it but possible! But think of your position here in the town, Gunnar. Gunnar Masterman marries a convict! It would ruin you. Why, even were it possible, I would not accept such sacrifice."

He pulled her down, so that they lay side by side. He said, kissing her fiercely: "Do you think that my position here in the town means anything beside us? Do you think that I would not get to any position I wanted, whatever the handicap?"

"You would, darling. You would! You would do anything, you are so wonderful. Anything you want you could do . . . Nothing would ever stand in the way . . . of the things you wanted . . . you only have to want them badly enough."

He kissed her again, holding her fast to him. She knew he was thinking that never, never should she go to Tom Blake. She knew that he was thinking of their life together—Mr. and Mrs. Masterman of Sydney. No more creeping up the stairs. No more of that furtiveness which he hated. Nothing but the indulgence in that love which had become necessary to him, nothing but growing prosperous, procreating children, which was what the Prayer Book said marriage was for. She let him go on dreaming sensuously for some time before she mentioned the woman downstairs.

Then she said: "Life is ironical. She who could have had a child, would not. Oh, Gunnar, is it not cruel! To think of her . . . your wife . . . and not . . . and not . . ."

She had spoken softly, and he was still in the dream.

She said again: "I would not do what she did, Gunnar. Even I, in my position, would not do that! I think it is little short of murder . . ."

"Murder!" he said, aghast.

"You were not listening. Never mind. I was talking rubbish."

But he wanted to know.

"The baby," she said, "yours and your wife's."

"There has never been a baby."

"I mean the one . . . the one that wasn't born. Oh . . . I should not have reminded you. How stupid of me!"

"Where did you hear such a tale, Carolan?"

"It was she who told me. Really, Gunnar, I must say no more . . . No, no, please do not press me. It was just that it made me feel bitter. She . . . who is your wife . . . and deliberately . . . Oh, but I will say no more."

"You must tell me," he said. "I know nothing of this."

"Oh, what have I done! She told me . . . but it was when she was under the influence of that stuff . . . she did not mean to tell perhaps . . . Oh, how stupid I am! Please, Gunnar, do not ask me more."

"I do ask you, Carolan." She sensed his growing hatred of the woman who stood between him and his dreams. "You must tell me."

"I think she told me not to tell. I did not think she meant you, of course. I thought you would have known. But you see, she takes laudanum; it frightens me sometimes; it would be so easy to take an overdose. Sometimes I think she will, by mistake; it would kill her . . . she was frightened . . . frightened of having a baby here; she says it is so uncivilised. She said she would have been frightened in London, but here she was terrified, simply terrified. So she went to that doctor . . . the ticket of leave man who sells medicines which other doctors will not sell . . . and he did it for her. She was ill; she nearly died, she said. Do you not see what I mean? She could have had her baby happily . . . whereas I . . ."

He did see. There was a cold glint in his eyes now. He hated Lucille, and in his hatred there were no regrets for the child of which he had been deprived; he wanted nothing of Lucille now. He wanted Carolan and his child, which was chiefly Carolan's child. He was powerless; he did not know how he must act. He was a practical man who had never before been so foolish as to want something beyond his reach.

"It was frightful," said Carolan, and she shivered. "When she told me, it seemed to me that what she had done was little else but murder." She drew close to him. "Gunnar, you must not worry, my darling. Who knows, it may come right."

He said: "Carolan, you must promise me you will not marry that man."

"How I love you!" she answered.

"I would not have it. I would do anything to stop it."

"You will not let it be, Gunnar," she whispered. "You will stop it . . . I know you will. You are so clever . . . so wonderful . . ."

Something was wrong with the master. Margery knew it! He had a dazed look; his eyes burned; he wasn't eating his food. Something was wrong with Mistress Carolan; she was paler; her eyes were brilliant. When you spoke to her sometimes she did not answer, and it wasn't because she was playing the haughty lady either. She wore a black dress nearly all the time—a dress with a voluminous skirt, a concealing sort of dress that gave you a clue.

Quite sorry she was for the little ladyship. No snivelling about her. Her lovely head was carried a sure degree higher these days; but there was a pinched look about her mouth. Was she frightened? She wouldn't admit it! She wasn't that sort. Now, if only she would confide in old Margery!

She came into the kitchen for the mistress's bath water. She always made Poll carry it up and take it in. A nice spectacle, Poll, to go into a lady's bedroom! Why didn't she let Jin take it? Jin was a strong enough girl. One of these fine days Poll would be upsetting the water all over the stairs, and then there'd be a nice how-do-you-do!

"Get the bath water, Poll."

"Hello, me love! And how are you today?"

395

"Very well, thank you. Are you?"

"Now that surprises me, for you're looking a bit peaky."

She flinched a little. Suspicious? Come on, tell old Margery. How long do you think you can keep that sort of thing secret from a pair of knowing old eyes?

"I'm quite worried about you, lovey. You ain't looking yourself."

"Please do not worry then, for I am quite well. Poll can take up the water when it is ready. Tell her not to forget to knock on Mrs. Masterman's door before entering."

"Not so fast, me darling. I am worried about you. Have a glass of grog. There's nothing like grog at such times!"

"What times?"

"Times when you're feeling peaky."

Margery grinned. Not an atom of doubt either; it wasn't the girl's looks so much as her manner that gave her away. The master! What would happen now? Men were funny . . . could be funny . . . times like these. And when a man was as successful as the master, there were always those who were only too ready to pull him down.

Carolan hesitated. Obviously she suspected Margery of knowing. She sat down at the table.

"Jin!"

Jin came with the bottle, sullen as ever. Margery hoped Jin had noticed nothing. Didn't want her snickering. Not that Jin ever noticed much except men. She was born a harlot, that gipsy.

"There, dearie, drink up. It'll do you good. You know Margery's your old friend."

"Of course I do." Sharp, acid—that was her voice. Keep off! it said. I manage my own affairs. No doubt you do, me lady, but girls in trouble ain't so beautiful as girls out of trouble, and even men like the master is only human. They don't like trouble, though God knows they like what leads up to it well enough!

"'There!" Margery smacked her lips. "Good, ain't it? The master is a good master; not another like him in Sydney. We was lucky to get taken into his house."

There was a chance for her! Margery could have loved her, if she had fallen on her neck and burst into tears. But she didn't. She was hard as nails and cold as stone.

Anger surged up in Margery. All right, me beauty! All right . . . She laid a hand on the swelling bosom beneath the black folds.

"You're filling out, me lovely. You are filling out. Good living agrees with you, ducky. So that's what a feather bed does for you, eh?"

The girl had whitened.

She said, calmly enough: "Yes, I think I have put on a little weight." She drained her glass unhurriedly. You had to admire her. What a change, eh, from that snivelling little wretch!

Funny, the two of them, almost together too. But not so funny, for if Margery knew anything of human nature, which she did quite a lot, she would be saying that it was the one that grew out of the other.

Carolan sat there till Poll came through with the water. Then she led the way upstairs.

Carolan said: "Gunnar, I must talk to you. I *must* talk to you now."

They were in the hall together. He had just come in from riding. He looked tall and powerful.

He said: "In my room. You go now."

She went, and in a few moments he was with her.

"They know," she said. "It is getting obvious. Margery hinted . . ."

"You must go away from here at once, Carolan."

"Yes," she said, "I will."

"You must see that my plan is the only plan."

"You must see that mine is."

"You cannot marry this man."

"I can, Gunnar, and I will. I will tell him everything, do not think he will refuse. He will do anything for me."

She resisted the temptation to burst into tears, to throw herself on to his bed and sob out her defeat. Tom Blake! The man was repulsive to her, and yet if Gunnar forced her to it, she knew herself well enough to know that she would keep her word. She thought of rough hands touching her . . . And would even he be able to stop himself from reminding her of the conditions under which she had married him? At first he would take her at any price, but afterwards, when the humdrum life of the station began . . . the child would be a constant reminder. They would quarrel—the fault would doubtless be hers, for she would not be easy to live with—and he would remind her of why she had married him. A festering sore! What a way to embark upon marriage! And Marcus would be living in the same house . . . Marcus and Esther. It was sordid and horrible.

And beside that, think of life here in this house . . . mistress of this house . . . wife of Gunnar Masterman, one of the important men of the town. She did not love him perhaps, but she liked him. Physically he appealed to her as no one else had, except Marcus. To be his wife—that was safety, security. To be cherished, to have his children; that was what she wanted.

But it could not be, because of that woman, his wife.

"You shall not marry him, Carolan! You forget you would need my consent."

"You would withhold it! You would dare do that . . . when I an about to bear a child!"

"But my child, Carolan! Mine!" Even now he could not keep out of his voice the exulting note. His child! That gave her fresh courage, fresh hope.

"Listen," he said. He led her to the bed and they sat there side by side, his arm round her. "You cannot stay here any longer. I will make immediate arrangements. I know a family who will be the soul of discretion. There is nothing to fear. You shall go to them; they will look after you. You shall be denied nothing, my darling . . . you and the child. I shall come to see you often."

She touched his face with her fingers, but she was trembling with rage.

"It sounds very simple, Gunnar, but it cannot be."

"You must be reasonable, Carolan. We must both be reasonable and practical."

"I am being practical. I think I am being reasonable. I can see I must marry Tom. Cruel things happen to me; this is just another, but one grows accustomed to cruel things and able to meet them. My heart will be broken; my life will be finished." She put her hands against her body. "My baby is there. To me it is wonderful and precious. I would not alter anything . . . I am ready. And of one thing I am certain—my child shall be born in wedlock."

"But it is my child too, Carolan," he said gently.

"No, no, Gunnar! It is mine, entirely mine. And it will be Tom's too. If I married Tom I should never see you again. I would be faithful to the man I married. I will go now. There is nothing more to be said."

"Carolan! Carolan! What can I do?"

She took his face between her hands and kissed him tenderly. Tears were running down her face.

"There is nothing you can do, my darling, but say goodbye. Life has been cruel to us, but we have to be brave, my dearest. It is not only ourselves that we must think of now. It is the child. Say goodbye to it, Gunnar. Say goodbye to me. Tomorrow I will go to Tom and tell him, and you will give your consent to our immediate marriage. It is the only way."

He protested. She saw the anguish in his face, and came very near to loving him.

"Carolan, I cannot. I cannot."

He turned his face away. There were tears in his eyes, she knew, tears of rage and sorrow.

She stood up and walked over to the door.

"Do not make it harder for me, Gunnar. I cannot bear it. It makes me afraid. Wicked thoughts come into my mind. I think . . . if only she would take an overdose . . . if only . . . You see how much I love you, how I care and plan for my child. I must go now. I must go quickly. Goodbye, Gunnar. Perhaps we had better not see each other alone . . . again."

He stood up, and she ran to him; she kissed him wildly.

"Goodbye, Gunnar. Goodbye!"

He was trembling; he, the strong man, the master.

In the toilet-room Carolan took off the black dress and put on a green one. Her eyes blazed in her pale face. She surveyed herself. Oh, yes! Margery had noticed all right. In the green dress it was obvious.

She knocked.

"Come in," said Lucille.

She was sitting up in bed, a wrap round her. She always retired early these days. She had grown from a delicate woman to a semi-invalid since Carolan had been ministering to her.

"I have come to draw the curtains and light the candles," said Carolan.

She stood, the taper in her hand, willing the woman to look at her.

"Carolan," said Lucille, "you look strange. Have you been crying?"

"The shawl is slipping from your shoulders," said Carolan. "It would not do to catch cold."

"You are very good to me, Carolan."

"No, no, it is you who are good to me."

"I? Good? No, Carolan. Sometimes, particularly lately, I think of what a wicked woman I am."

"You must not take it to heart, you know. There must have been many women who have done . . . that."

"What, Carolan?"

"I am sorry. It is nothing. You must not worry. You know Doctor Martin says the last thing you must do is worry."

"It has occurred to me, Carolan, that in a way . . . it *is* murder. It is only a matter of months . . . and then it would have been murder. The baby was alive . . ."

"Please do not let us discuss it—it worries you so."

"No, do not let us talk of it. I have dreams about it, Carolan."

"It is worrying by day that makes you dream at night. No! You must forget it. He will never have his children, but what is to be, will be, and so many of us have to go without what we desire most in this world. It is time you had your pills. Did you have another dose this morning?"

"Oh, Carolan . . ."

"But in the morning!"

"I had such dreadful dreams, Carolan. I dreamed that it was alive . . . a real baby . . . and that I had killed it, and they found out and took me to the gallows. And he was there. He looked terrible. He kept saying . . . Murder! I could not sleep after that, and I was so tired in the morning. I longed to sleep . . . it is such a deep, dreamless sleep, Carolan . . . soothing and caressing."

"But," said Carolan slowly, "it makes you feel that you want to stay like that for ever, and that is dangerous."

"It is just like that, Carolan."

"Sometimes I think you may not resist the temptation to stay there for ever . . ."

Lucille laughed. "Is it not strange that that comfort should be there in a bottle?"

"Very strange."

"You look different tonight, Carolan. Is it because you have changed into the green dress? It looks gayer on you than it did on me. But it is too tight for you, my dear. I must find something else for you; you have been so good to me!"

Carolan laid her hands across her breasts. She looked wide-eyed at Lucille.

"What is it, Carolan?"

"Nothing . . . oh, nothing."

"I thought for the moment that something was wrong. I . . . I have had that feeling for some time. I thought you seemed absent-minded, and . . . you were always so reliable. If there is anything I could do to help you . . . But perhaps it is my imagination, for I thought the master seemed strange lately."

"Strange?" said Carolan. "The master strange?"

"He looks at me strangely. It is nothing. I have such a vivid imagination; I am so sensitive. He asks after my health more than he did. Perhaps he wants children again."

Carolan leaned over the bed.

"And if he did . . . ?"

Lucille shivered. "I should die. I know I should. I could not bear it. Perhaps I could arrange to go home; but the journey! I should die, Carolan. Sometimes I get the idea that my end is not far off, that I deserve to die . . ."

"Because you killed your baby? You must get such ridiculous nonsense out of your head. To have a baby is a wonderful experience . . . for a woman in your position."

Surely she must see now. But she was utterly selfish; she saw life from one angle only—life as lived by Lucille Masterman.

Carolan turned away, her lips trembling. Had Lucille sufficient insight to grasp the situation? An ailing wife, a beautiful girl, a man who wanted children—it was an old enough story. But Lucille was wrapped about with her own selfish needs— her pills, her comforts, her pains.

Lucille's eyes were glassy; the drug robbed her of strong emotions; strength was slowly seeping out of her body. Sleep she wanted . . . sleep, eternal sleep. She wanted it for herself, and Carolan and Gunnar wanted it for her.

"Read to me, Carolan," said Lucille.

Carolan opened the Bible. Her eyes were burning, her hands trembling.

" 'Now Sarai Abram's wife bare him no children: and she had an handmaid, an Egyptian, whose name was Hagar . . .' "

There was no sound in the room but that of Carolan's voice, very clear, high-pitched with emotion.

Suddenly Lucille cried out: "Stop! Stop! No more! I wish to hear no more."

Carolan put down the book and went to her. Lucille looked into her face and their eyes held each other's, Carolan's commanding, Lucille's submissive.

Carolan said softly: "You must not blame yourself. You were ill, and illness weakens the spirit. You did him a great wrong, but it is done with. Live . . . and bear him more children."

"I could not, Carolan. You do not know how weak I have become. If I was weak before, I am doubly so now."

"You must live! You must bear him many children, for that is what he wants, and that is the way you must expiate your sin."

"My sin . . . Carolan!"

"The murder of his child . . ."

"I am too ill, Carolan."

"Remember," said Carolan, and her voice was commanding, "no more drug tonight! You would need a double dose for it to be effective tonight, for you have taken one dose already today."

"Carolan, are you going to leave me now?"

"I am going to leave you to sleep."

"I cannot sleep."

"You must. Try to calm yourself. You need sleep."

"But I cannot sleep . . . without . . ."

"Good night," said Carolan. "Remember what I said, Good night."

Carolan went to her room, and lay on her bed, staring at the ceiling. She was exhausted.

Katharine Masterman

Katharine Masterman awakened early that December day, but the sunshine was already streaming into her bedroom. She experienced a disappointment, for as soon as she was fully awake she remembered that Christmas Day was still three weeks off, and realised that she had only dreamed that it was Christmas Day, and that she was at the breakfast table looking at the presents piled high beside her plate. Three weeks to go! It might as well have been three years, for three weeks is an age when one is ten years old.

She threw aside her mosquito net, and got out of bed. This was her own room, right at the top of the house where the nurseries were. From her window she could see the dazzling sea, and cockatoos and parakeets, white and so brilliantly coloured that it was sheer pleasure to watch them. She stood there, watching them now, and forgot her dream in her desire to fly as they could. She spread out her arms and swooped about the room, uttering cries of delight, until the exertion made her so hot that she remembered the boys in the next room. In a moment she would have them running in, swooping about her room crying: "I'm a cockatoo! I can fly fastest!" They always imitated her; they were so very young. James was eight, Martin six and a half, and little Edward just four. She felt superior in wisdom; ten was so very much older than even James, and she had heard Margery say that girls grow up quicker than boys.

She sat down on her bed, swinging her legs to and fro, wondering what she would do today. It must be a special day because she had dreamed it was Christmas. No day of course could be like Christmas Day, but it could be made exciting. But how?

She was tall for her age, rather thin, with blue-green eyes and a little more red in her hair than Carolan had had at her age; she had a quiet introspective air, reminiscent of her father, and her mouth was like his too. She drove the entire household to distraction with her capacity for asking questions, Where? Why? What . . . ? Almost every sentence she spoke began like that. She would sit quietly watching people, seeing behind them the background of all they had told her over a number of years, all skilfully fitted together by herself until it made a complete picture. At some time they had all felt a little uncomfortable before the candid scrutiny of those calm blue-green eyes. She would pull them up sharply over any small divergence from a previous story. "Oh, but before, you said . . ." It was disconcerting. But they loved her; she was the favourite of all the children, although James was the eldest son, and Martin and Edward were boys, and people wanted boys. She knew though, by the way Mamma looked at her and Papa looked at her, and the way Margery said: "Now, what do *you* want in my kitchen?" that they loved her best of all.

It was good to be loved; it gave one such a sense of happy security. Papa took her out to the stations with him sometimes; she would ride beside him in her neat outfit, and when they met people, who always had something to say to her, Papa got quite pink as though he liked very much hearing them say what a fine girl she was becoming.

She had a less clear picture of Papa than of anyone. She supposed that was because he was so important. "Your father is a very *busy* man!" "Your father is a very *clever* man!" How often had she heard that! But she didn't know things about him as she did about Margery and Miss Kelly and Poll and Wando. He was just Papa, a very clever man and a very busy man, who went pink when people stopped to talk to her. Conversation with him was not always satisfactory; he would not be lured into disclosures. Mamma could be lured more easily than he could. "Papa, do you wish I were a boy?"

"No."

"But don't you want boys?"

"Why . . . yes."

"The eldest is always supposed to be a boy. Why did you have me a girl?"

"You cannot choose these matters, Katharine."

"Why not, Papa?"

"Because they are arranged for us."

"Who arranges them?"

"Does not Miss Kelly teach you to read your Bible?"

"Yes, Papa, but there is nothing about arranging there. Do you have to pray hard if you want a first-born boy?"

"Yes."

"Then didn't you pray?"

Her questions were relentless, and Papa always, sooner or later, took the grown-up way out.

"Little girls should not ask so many questions."

"Oh . . . but Papa, didn't you pray? I should have thought God ought to have answered *your* prayers. I think it mean of Him not to have made me a boy if you wanted a boy."

"Hush, Katharine!"

"Why must I hush?"

"Because it is unsuitable for you to talk in this way."

"Of first-borns and God?"

"Yes."

"But in the Bible there is a lot about first-borns and God. God killed all the first-borns. Oh, Papa, suppose He killed all the first-borns in Sydney! That would be me . . . oh, but it wouldn't, because it would be the first-born boys. That would be James."

"Now look here, nobody is going to kill any first-borns in Sydney."

"But how do you know, Papa?"

"Because I do."

"He told you? Oh, but Papa, if He told you that, couldn't you have asked Him why He didn't make your first-born a boy?"

"We will drop this ridiculous subject."

No, you could not talk to Papa. There were lots of things she wanted to say to him. She almost said on that occasion: "Papa, perhaps it is something to do with your First Wife." But she dared not; there was something about Papa which could be very forbidding. But she knew there was a First Wife. She had heard Margery talking to Miss Kelly about it, talking in whispers in the way grown-ups do talk about a shocking subject, even when they do not know there is some-one listening who should not hear.

Margery whispered: "It fair gives me the creeps to go up to that first floor."

"That was where it happened, was it?" whispered back Miss Kelly.

"That was where it happened. And him and her . . ." The whispers were so low-pitched that it was impossible to hear from outside the kitchen door. Him and her? Who? Papa and Mamma, or Papa and the First Wife?

"Positive of it!" said Margery. "You only have to work it out. Miss Katharine will tell you that."

She herself tell them? How could she, when she did not know!

"Not," said Margery, "that I blame them . . . him or her!"

Blame whom? Papa and Mamma? Or Papa and the First Wife?

Exciting! Fascinating! Not that she thought much about it, for you cannot go on being excited about something that consistently remains a mystery. It was only when some overheard word came to her ears, or she was oppressed by the silence of the first floor where the guest rooms were, that she thought that the discovery of the secret would be the most exciting thing that could happen. At other times the thought of the Blue Mountains excited her far more.

Wando had told her about the Blue Mountains. Wando was very, very dark, with a wrinkled face and black eyes and hair and a chocolate brown body. He had fascinating feet with stubbed and broken toes; and he worked for Papa and went out with him and the men when they were going to make a journey. He called Katharine "Missy Kat," which made her laugh so much every time she heard it, that she enjoyed going to the little hut where he lived, almost more than anything else. She liked Wando, and he liked Missy Kat. He wore a pair of trousers that were too short for him, and a coloured shirt—because he was a Christian; but when he was alone in the hut he discarded the shirt and trousers and wore a bit of dirty rag round his middle. Katharine agreed with him that it was a good idea to discard the discomforts of Christianity when there was no one to see you. He fascinated her; he was very, very old, and, she believed, sad because he was remembering the days before the white men came to his country. Papa had told her about that, about Governor Phillip's sailing into Botany Bay with a transport of convicts. Papa thought it an exciting story; he often tried to tell her about it, and she would pretend that she thought it exciting too, because it was pleasant to see clever Papa looking rather like Martin telling Edward the story of Dick Whittington. He talked of pioneers

406

and the responsibility of being a daughter of a new and growing country.

"But I thought I was your daughter, Papa!"

"You are, but you are also a daughter of this great country."

Papa used to tell of the arrival of the first fleet, and the black men shouting "Warawara!" at them as they approached. She always meant to ask Wando if he were there, but she never remembered to; she was always more interested in the things he had to tell in his funny English. He had been a mighty hunter in his youth, and it was only now that he was an old man and the white men had come to his country, disturbing its ways, that he was content to live in a hut and accompany parties on expeditions into the hitherto unexplored bush. They were wonderful stories he had to tell of the days before the white men came. Katharine could catch at the excitement of the hunt. Wando had hunted with a spear, stalking the kangaroo, pitting his man's cunning against the timidity of the creature and its keen sense of smell. Wando, in sentences of one or two words, called up the thrill of the hunt. Katharine could feel his creeping closer to his prey, his body smeared with clay to hold in the smell of it. She could rejoice when the kangaroo was slung across Wando's shoulder. You cooked kangaroo in his skin, Wando told her, because it kept in all the juices of the meat. "Good! Missy Kat. Good!" he would say, smacking his lips; and his eyes would look back and back to those days before the white men came. She asked him, every time she saw him, how he had lost the two toes on his right foot. He could not remember, but when she asked he would look back and back and remember other things. Katharine liked to hear how one of his wives had fallen from a tree which she had climbed after wild honey, and had died. He had had four wives, and this matter of wives was baffling. Wando talked easily of them as though a man could have as many of them as he could get, and yet because Papa had had a First Wife, Margery and Miss Kelly whispered together, and there was mystery on the first floor.

It was Wando who told her about the Blue Mountains. Papa had pointed them out to her when she was quite a little girl.

"Why do you call them blue? They are not blue!"

Papa did not know. Papa was so clever that he only knew things which it was important for him to know. There was nothing exciting for Papa about the Blue Mountains; they were just mountains which hemmed him in. Beyond them there might be wonderful grazing lands; there might be oceans; there might be China. That was how Papa saw them; but to Katharine the most important thing about them was that they were blue. She discovered why they were blue; it was that curtain of mist hanging over them. It got bluer the more you looked. The Blue Mountains! The blue, *blue* mountains.

"Mamma, do you not want to ride over the Blue Mountains?"

"No one can. They are impassable."

"Will no one ever know what is on the other side of the Blue Mountains?"

"Very likely not."

"I would like to ride over the top of the Blue Mountains. Mamma, couldn't I try? I am sure *I* could ride over the Blue Mountains; I'd ride and ride until I got to the blue part, and then I'd be over the top . . ."

Mamma wasn't listening. Mamma's maid was dressing her for the evening. Mamma was big and glorious; shimmering and shining, with a green pendant hanging round her neck. Mamma was very important, but Papa was not quite so important, because of Mamma. She had heard that whispered once at a party. Whispering again! There are some questions it is better not to ask, because if you ask them, people are put on their guard, and then you cannot ask even questions which they will answer unthinkingly.

Wando knew a lot about the Blue Mountains. When she talked of them to him, his face wrinkled up and his eyes grew smaller and smaller; he didn't like to talk about the Blue Mountains. But she danced round him. Mamma and Papa could not be asked certain questions. Not so Wando. Wando should answer.

Beyond the Blue Mountains was a world none dare enter.

"I would dare, Wando! I would dare!"

"No, no, Missy Kat! No!"

His mouth worked; his flat nose wriggled; they did that when he was frightened.

"Wando, *what* is beyond the Blue Mountains?"

He told her, whispering as Margery whispered to Miss Kelly when she talked of the First Wife. A vast lake was on the other side of the blue curtains, and there lived fair people, people like gods.

"I will go, Wando. I will go and see them."

He shook his head violently. She must not go.

She did not believe anyone would not be glad to see her.

But in the mountains lived many evil spirits, and these evil spirits would never, never let anyone pass through their mountains.

"What would they do, Wando, if anyone tried to pass through their mountains?"

Wando's deep black eyes were pools in which were hidden this unmentionable knowledge. His silence told more than any white man's words could have done. She trembled with horror at the thought of what those evil spirits would do to anyone who tried to pass through their mountains.

What was it that fascinated her so much about the Blue Mountains? The horror and the beauty. Those wicked spirits had chosen a blue curtain for their mountains; not black nor hideously purple, but lovely blue.

She had gone back to her window. The sea was blue. There was blue in the gorgeous colours of the parakeets.

Somehow the Blue Mountains were fixed to her idea of an exciting day that must be exciting because she had awakened and thought it was Christmas.

She went into the boys' room and prodded them. They were all sleeping in different beds—all three of them. Edward and James were very much alike—one little and one big—but Martin wasn't like either of them. Martin was very quiet and dreamy; they said he would be clever. He was very pretty; people noticed him because he was pretty, and James because he was bright, and Edward because he was the baby.

She said: "I dreamed it was Christmas." And they all sat up and looked at her and thought of Christmas.

"I've been up hours!" she said loftily. "I've been flying."

"Flying!"

"I've been a parakeet—a lovely one . . . all blue and red, and particularly blue." She pretended to fly about the room, flapping her arms for wings. Very soon they were all out of bed, doing the same, which brought Miss Kelly in.

Katharine stopped being a parakeet, to think of Miss Kelly and Miss Kelly's brother who had been a convict. As a result of much questioning at opportune moments, Katharine had pieced together a good deal of Miss Kelly's story. Back in England, four years ago, Miss Kelly's brother had run amuck.

"Amuck! Amuck! Amuck!" whispered Katharine, who loved words for their sounds as well as for their meanings. If you broke into a confidence, to ask the meaning of words, a grown-up was liable to remember you were an inquisitive child, and grown-up people like to ask questions, not to answer them. Amuck? They said that Mr. Jennings ran the store where it was possible to buy any sort of goods you could think of. They said Governor Macquarie ran the country. Amuck must be something like a store or a country; only something bad, because running amuck resulted in Miss Kelly's brother becoming a convict; and Miss Kelly loved him so much that she followed him out to Sydney to have a home for him when he stopped being a convict. It was a very sad story, because Miss Kelly's brother had been sent to Van Diemen's Land where he had died. "Van Diemen's Land!" murmured Katharine, when she wanted to frighten herself. In the dark she said it to herself, when she was alone in bed at night. It made her think of red devils with cloven hooves and pitchforks made entirely of fire. One of Papa's servants had said: "Van Diemen's Land, Missy—that's hell on earth!" Surely hell in hell could be no more terrible than hell on earth. She tried to talk to James about it, but James was never easy to talk to. "It's only convicts that go there," said James. "But it's hell, James, hell on earth!" James thought that didn't matter because they were only convicts. But Miss Kelly's brother had gone there and he had died there. It made Miss Kelly terribly sad at times; it made her snappy. Mamma said: "You must be kind to Miss Kelly, because she has suffered a lot."

So Miss Kelly came in and said: "What is all this noise?"

"We're birds!" Katharine told her.

"You're nothing of the sort," said Miss Kelly. "You're a naughty girl and three naughty boys!"

Miss Kelly spoke in short clipped sentences. She dispelled any make-believe merely by talking of it. You could never be anything but what people actually thought you were, with Miss Kelly looking on.

"Now come," said Miss Kelly without a smile; she rarely smiled; she seemed to hate to see people laughing, and when they laughed it must remind her of her poor brother's going to Van Diemen's Land to be prodded with flaming pitchforks by the demons there, because naturally the demons would laugh while they prodded. "Breakfast in half an hour. Do you want to wake your poor Papa and Mamma?"

"They are not poor, are they, Miss Kelly?" asked Martin anxiously. "They're rich!"

Katharine tried painstakingly to explain to him what Miss Kelly meant, because she thought others cared as deeply as she did about getting to the truth of even the smallest details.

"She does not mean they are poor because they haven't

410

money. She means poor to get woken up too early in the morning."

Martin irritated Katharine. His mind flew from one subject to chase one that momentarily appealed to him more.

"Is Papa very rich?"

"Of course he is very rich!" said Katharine grandly.

"The richest man in the world?"

"Is he, Miss Kelly?" asked Katharine, now very interested to know.

"Of course not," said James, very superior. "That would be Governor Macquarie."

Katharine wished she had thought of that. Of course the richest man in the world must be Governor Macquarie.

"Is *he* the richest man in the world?" persisted Katharine. "Is he, Miss Kelly?"

Miss Kelly said: "Rich indeed! And very free with other people's money, if you'll be asking me. We must have roads here, buildings there . . . He'll be trying to make Sydney rival London. That's what he's after!"

Katharine wanted to say: "Why do you hate people who other people think are cleverer than other people, Miss Kelly?" but Martin was chasing a new idea.

"Miss Kelly, tell us about London."

"I'll tell you something else."

"What, Miss Kelly? Oh, what?"

"If you don't get dressed, and quick about it, there'll be no breakfast for you."

"We'd rather hear about London than have breakfast," said Katharine with dignity.

That made Miss Kelly angry.

"Oh, you would, would you! It's a pity you can't taste a bit of starving for a while, then you wouldn't be so ready to say No to good food."

"Miss Kelly, how do you *taste* starving?"

They all laughed, Martin and James throwing themselves on their beds in sudden amusement, lifting their legs high in the air and trying to touch the ceiling. Edward scrambled up and tried to do the same just as Miss Kelly put a stop to it. Poor Edward, he always wanted to imitate the others and was generally too late.

Only Katharine knew that Miss Kelly's sudden flush of anger meant she was thinking of her brother, so she did not laugh but said sharply: "Come on, you three! Get washed."

"Oh!" wailed James. "We want Miss Kelly to tell us about London."

Edward became so excited that he nearly choked. They all stared at him.

"Mamma . . ." he stammered. "Mamma . . . went to London." He looked up expectantly to see the result of his statement. Poor Edward! The things he said never meant anything.

Katharine walked out of the room; she was beginning to feel hungry.

The porringers from which they ate their bread and milk were blue. If you put your head right in, you could imagine you were in the heart of the Blue Mountains. The pieces of bread floating about in the milk, were pioneers trying to climb the Blue Mountains. The evil spirits had sent down a big milky lake to drown them. She must disperse the lake as quickly as possible.

"Katharine!" said Miss Kelly, turning the lake into a bowl of milk, and the mountains into a porringer. "Don't drink so fast! Milk needs digesting."

Miss Kelly gave them lessons after breakfast. Reading, writing, arithmetic, a little French and Latin. How dull were lessons as taught by Miss Kelly! The boys were difficult this morning; Katharine's dream of Christmas had upset them. The heat was intense. Katharine almost dozed. Miss Kelly gave the two boys dictation; it was all about Christmas in the Old Country, the snow on the trees, and the stage coach rattling down the road. It was very dull. That was not the sort of thing she wanted to hear about the Old Country. Edward was scratching on a slate. Edward was very silly; he could not make his letters yet. Katharine was supposed to be reading Monsieur Molière's *Le Misanthrope*, in French; she could not understand a word of it. Through the window she saw Papa and Mamma. They came out into the yard, and Papa was dressed for a journey. Mamma was very beautiful in a dress of muslin with green ribbons. Mamma was one of the most beautiful women in Sydney, she had heard people say. People looked sly when they talked of Mamma. Why? Why? That was the sort of thing she wanted to know; not Latin, not Greek, not French.

A happy couple. They kissed. Katharine had seen them kiss often. Papa kissed Mamma as though he didn't want to stop—a make-it-last-as-long-as-I-can sort of kiss.

She wished she were going out with Papa. How pleasant to ride along on her own mare, a present from Papa who said she rode well enough to be done with ponies! Where was Papa going? Why hadn't he taken her with him? A day which had

412

begun with a dream of Christmas is not the day to be spent idling over a lesson book.

A smell of coffee came up from below, reminding her of Margery. She sidled off her chair.

"Miss Kelly, I cannot read here; the dictation disturbs me. Could I go to my own room?"

"Yes," said Miss Kelly, "you may."

Katharine wandered downstairs, Molière under her arm. On the first floor she paused. First floor. First Wife. Did a first wife always have her room on the first floor? Silent it was on the first floor. Margery always hurried past it. If she came up, she liked someone to come with her; she would rather have Edward with her than no one. Katharine opened a door and peeped in. The toilet-room. The guests used that. Papa had had another toilet-room put on the second floor. Hip-bath and mirror and cupboards and table, with dusting powder on the table. Old haunting perfume. She tiptoed in, and as she looked at herself in the long glass, tried to think of the house without Mamma, and if Mamma was not there neither she nor James, Martin and Edward could be either, for they were all Mamma's children. Why did grown-ups try to keep so much from you? There were three doors leading out of the toilet-room. One she had just opened from the corridor; the other two merely led to two rooms, just ordinary bedrooms with big canopied beds. Nothing there to excite one! She went into one of the bedrooms.

A sudden sound startled her. A footstep in the toilet-room. A ghost? Yes, that was it; there were ghosts on the first floor. Not ghosts perhaps, but a ghost; the ghost of Papa's first wife. She was terrified; she ran to the bed. She got into it and drew the curtains. She peeped through them. Her heart beat so loudly that it was like the strokes of the blacksmith's hammer. The door was pushed open slowly, and Mamma came into the room. Mamma's face was working queerly; she had never seen Mamma look like that; had never known Mamma could look frightened . . . just like a child. One could not imagine Mamma like a child. Mamma looked all round the room. She was breathing queerly; her breath made gasping noises. Poor Mamma! Katharine forgot her own fear, seeing Mamma so frightened. Hastily she pulled back the bed curtains, but in that split second when the curtains began to move, Mamma's face went white and she caught her breath, so that it whistled like the wind did in the eucalyptus trees in the cove.

"Mamma!" cried Katharine; and then Mamma saw who it

413

was behind the curtains, and the colour came back to her face, and she came nearer, and Katharine did not know whether she was very, very angry or not.

"Did you think I was a ghost?" said Katharine.

"What nonsense!" retorted Mamma. "There are no ghosts."

"You looked very frightened."

"You were peeping out at me, you bad girl!" Mamma's voice was soft and loving, not as though she thought Katharine was a bad girl at all; so Katharine stood on the bed and put her arms round Mamma's neck, and Mamma hugged her suddenly and fiercely, and when Mamma did that Katharine loved her more than anyone in the world. It meant that Mamma loved her best too, even though she was not a boy and everybody wanted boys.

"Katharine, what are you doing here? Why aren't you in the schoolroom?"

"Because the boys are doing dictation, and I am studying in my own room."

Mamma raised her eyebrows, and when she did that she did it so funnily that it always made Katharine laugh.

"And I came downstairs and when I got to the first floor I thought I wanted to have a look at it."

"Katharine, you are always prowling about the first floor."

"What is prowling?"

"Well . . . just going there and peeping about. Why?"

"I don't know," lied Katharine, because somehow it was impossible to talk of the ghost of the First Wife to Mamma.

"You shouldn't do things without knowing why you do them."

"Do grown-ups always know why they do things?"

Carolan, shaken more than she cared to admit to herself, smiled at this disconcerting daughter who had evidently heard some gossip about these rooms . . . possibly about Lucille. What? And how could one ask a child without making it seem very important? Was she to be haunted all her life?

"I do not think they do, always."

Katharine brought her knees up to her chin, and rolled about on the bed that had been Lucille's. This was delightful. This was delicious. A tête-à-tête with the most exciting of all grown-ups, Mamma!

"Why do they do them if they do not know why?"

"Because they are stupid."

Stupid! So grown-ups were stupid as well as children. It was exciting; surely there was nothing you could not ask Mamma when she talked like that. Mamma was unlike herself today.

414

"Why is it so quiet here, Mamma . . . on this floor, I mean? Why doesn't Margery like coming here . . . even in daylight?"

"What?" said Mamma sharply. "Margery told you that!"

"She didn't tell me. She just doesn't. Why, she would even bring Edward . . . Edward . . . rather than come alone. Edward wouldn't know what to do if he saw a ghost. I don't suppose he even knows what a ghost is!"

Mamma stood up suddenly. The dignified Mamma, grown-up now, no longer ready to share a confidence.

"You are very silly, Katharine. If Edward knows nothing of ghosts he is wiser than you, for there are no ghosts, and let me hear no more of this foolishness. It is time you went back to your lessons. It is cold in here."

"But Mamma, I am boiling . . . It is hot!"

"It is cool after the rest of the house," said Mamma, and Katharine noticed that her hands were very cold.

"Come along," said Mamma, and pulled her off the bed quite roughly. And then Mamma's mood changed. Mamma did change quickly all the time. "What about a pick-a-back?" Katharine leaped on to the bed, and Mamma presented her back, and she put her arms round Mamma's neck and Mamma ran with her out of the room. Katharine was shrieking with laughter.

"Now, back to your room at once! And see that you learn your lessons." Mamma started up the stairs with her.

"Miss Kelly is in a bad mood today," said Katharine. "It is because I dreamed it was Christmas, and that made her remember about her brother in Van Diemen's Land, because he will never, never spend Christmas with her again!"

"Be kind to Miss Kelly, because she has been unhappy."

"You told me that before. I am kind to her. I see that the boys are too."

Mamma picked her up suddenly and they ran up the rest of the stairs just as though, thought Katharine, Mamma was afraid someone would catch them if they did not hurry.

It was a queer morning.

Mamma had dinner with them because Papa was not at home, and Edward spilled the contents of his plate into his lap.

Then Miss Kelly said that Edward deserved to be whipped, or at least to go without his dinner, which set Edward crying. But Mamma comforted him; she said it was not Edward's fault, and people should never be blamed unless the wrong things they did were their own faults.

Mamma took Edward on to her lap and fed him with a

spoon so that it was as though he had done something clever instead of naughty.

Then followed the drowsy afternoon. Mamma slept; so did Edward. Martin and James went off together. That left Katharine to herself.

She went down to the kitchen. She liked the kitchen in the afternoon. Margery usually dozed in her chair, and it was while dozing that Margery could be relied on to be even more indiscreet than usual. Poll always washed the kitchen floor in the afternoon. Katharine liked to watch her mop swamping the stones.

"Hello, young mischief!" said Margery. She was sitting there, her knees apart, a fat hand on each knee. Amy washed the dishes; Poll was getting ready to start on the floor.

"I dreamed it was Christmas," said Katharine.

"Glad I'll be when that's all over! There was never anything for making work like Christmas. I'd rather have twenty men about the house than Christmas."

"Twenty is rather a lot," said Katharine, pulling a chair close to Margery's.

"I'd manage 'em," said Margery with a wink. "And keep 'em in order—every man jack of 'em!"

That was where Margery differed from Miss Kelly. Miss Kelly dispelled illusion; Margery developed it.

"Would you make them do all the work, Margery?"

"That I would!"

"Mop the floor and peel potatoes?"

"You bet I would."

"Then what would Amy and Poll do?"

"They'd run round after the men—give 'em half a chance! Not that I'd say they was the sort to attract men—neither of 'em!"

"Wouldn't you, Margery?"

"No, I wouldn't."

Katharine knew about Poll's baby; she had got that out of Margery. "And don't you let on to your Ma or your Papa that I've told you," she had said.

"Why not, Margery?"

"Because it ain't right you should know such things."

"Why Margery?"

"You being only a child."

"How long will it be before I can know things like that?"

"Well, that I can't say. There's some as picks it up sharp, and there's some as don't. You . . . being your mother's daughter . . . There! Me tongue's running away with me."

At the time Katharine had been so intrigued by the thought of Margery's tongue running away with her, that she had forgotten the real issue. That was like Margery; you had to watch her or she would draw a red herring across the path, which afterwards you would discover was not worth pursuit. But in spite of this trick of Margery's she had many unguarded moments. Poll had murdered her baby because it wasn't right that she should have a baby. Amy had been sent out for hiding a highwayman. Amy was middle-aged and cheerful. She didn't talk very much about herself, but Margery liked to talk about her. Katharine heard quite a lot about Amy; how she had loved the highwayman, but how he was a rollicking, roistering type of fellow who had just made use of her, and when he was hanged by the neck, poor Amy had been sent for transportation for seven years for letting him use her house to hide himself and his plunder.

Margery could give her pictures of the Old Country that were far more real than anything Miss Kelly taught. Miss Kelly taught words; Margery taught life. Margery could be coaxed into telling of journeys with one of her husbands, a pedlar. Could there be anything more desirable than to be the wife of a pedlar? "What did you sell, Margery?" "Everything you can lay your tongue to, lovey!" Lay your tongue to! What a lovely way to express yourself! "Margery, I wish Papa would let *you* teach us, instead of Miss Kelly."

"Lor' love me! I ain't the scollard she is."

"Her brother went to Van Diemen's Land, Margery!"

"So I hear, poor soul."

"Do you know what it's like there, Margery?"

"It's the most terrible thing that could befall a man, I've heard."

What joy there was in talking to her! She suggested a hundred and one forbidden things. When she talked of men, her lips quivered and she pressed them together as though she was afraid something would slip out that you shouldn't hear because you were a child. She gave away so much that was exciting; how much more exciting must be those things which she suppressed! There was always the hope that she would tell more. Sometimes when she drank and drank she would say something, then clap her hand over her mouth or look over her shoulder and say: "Don't you get saying a word I tell you, to your Papa or Ma!"

Poll was slopping water all over the kitchen floor. Soon Katharine and Margery, perched on their chairs, would be marooned on islands.

"The sea's getting higher every minute, Margery."

"There now, is it? And then what'll we do?"

"We'll be drowned—or we may be rescued. Margery, have you ever been marooned?"

"No. But I've known plenty of sailors!"

"Sailors! Oh, Margery! Do tell."

"Sailors is much the same as other men, in a manner of speaking. They go off to sea though, and they comes home again—and that makes a bit of difference."

"Did you ever have a sailor husband, Margery?"

"In a manner of speaking."

"Did he go off to sea and come home again?"

"He did. And a bit too soon sometimes. A sailor ought always to let a woman know when he's coming home."

"Was he your first, Margery?"

"Oh, no, ducky! Not by a long chalk."

"Margery, my Papa had a First Wife, didn't he?"

Margery looked over her shoulder. Katharine took the glass from the table and handed it to Margery.

"Here, Margery, have a drink. I know Papa had a First Wife."

Margery drank and smacked her lips.

"Old-fashioned little thing, you are—no bones about it!"

Katharine knelt on her chair and leaned towards Margery; she put her face so close that Margery could see the fine texture of child's skin; like milk it was for whiteness, and she'd got a powdering of freckles across her nose, which made her skin look all the more fair. Dead spit of what her mother must have been at her age. And she'd be such another, with her wheedling ways. Little monkey! Still, Margery looked forward to her visits. It was pleasant to know the child came down so often to see her, to talk to her. She'd had a fondness for the child ever since she was born; had never taken to the boys one half so much. She put out a hand and touched the tender young cheek.

"Is it a smut?" said Katharine.

"No, not a smut." It made you feel funny, thought Margery. Here she was, a lovely bit of flesh and blood. Golly, it did something to you to see her; bright eyes, and what a tongue, eh! What a one for questions! There was no stopping her. What's this? What's that? It made you feel sort of powerful to know that you had had a hand in the making of her. But for you, things might have been very different. She might not have been sitting there now. Her mother might have gone

418

off with that Marcus, and the mistress might still have been. . . .

Margery shut off from that. Mustn't *think* like that . . . not with the child there, staring at you so close she'd see any flicker of your eyelids. It would be "Margery, what are you thinking of?" in a minute, if she knew anything! Besides, no one could say . . . All that was done with, had been done with eleven years back.

And now what had the little girl on her mind? She was a regular one for getting things on her mind. "I know Papa had a First Wife!" What did she mean? Margery knew she ought to turn the conversation, but for the life of her she couldn't.

"What's this?" she said. "What's this?"

"Papa had a First Wife!" whispered Katharine.

"Well, what of it? What of it? There's no law in this country to stop a man marrying again *if* his first wife's dead, that I know of."

"Oh," said Katharine. "She is dead then!"

"Of course she is."

"Margery, did you know her?"

"Know her!" said Margery. "Know her!" Purple colour was in Margery's cheeks. The children had to know some time, hadn't they? It was the talk of Sydney at one time. To marry so soon after . . . People were shocked. She wondered the master did it. But there was something headstrong about the master. Marrying like that two months after she died, and the baby born a cool three and a half months later—this Katharine here. No wonder the child felt something was wrong! No wonder people talked! No wonder they were still talking!

"Yes," said Margery, "I knew her."

This was success undreamed of.

"Oh, Margery, what was she like?"

"Sickly." Here, this wasn't the way to talk to a child, this wasn't. Oh, but things got dull in a kitchen. And since she'd married the master, the excitement seemed to die down. There they were like any other couple, eating together, sleeping together and having children. There was something in those two that overcame scandal, just as it would overcome most things that stood in their way. They fought all the gossipings, all the slanders. For a time Mr. Masterman was very unpopular. And *she* went about the house, carrying her child with the dignity of a queen. But there had been a certain triumph about her in the last months of her first pregnancy, as though she had worked for something and brought it off. That was the impression she gave. It wasn't until after the child was born that that room, where the first Mrs. Masterman had died, seemed to take on a special significance. It was only then that she made it into a guest room and moved up to the second floor.

Murder's a funny thing. It won't let you rest. It would make you feel a bit funny to have had a hand in murder. You'd keep remembering, thinking of the one you'd killed. I wouldn't like to be no murderer!

Did *she* murder the first Mrs. Masterman? Or did he?

Overdose of a drug she took for sleeplessness! Nobody knew where she'd got it from. Nobody knew she'd been taking it. When people took overdoses of drugs just in time to let their husbands marry girls who were in trouble, you couldn't help sitting up and taking notice. You couldn't help feeling this delicious creepy feeling all over you.

"Sickly?" prompted Katharine.

"Always ill."

"Did Papa love her very much?"

"Now how should I know?"

"You would know. Were you in the kitchen then?"

"Yes I was then."

"You must have known, Margery. You know everything."

Such flattery was irresistible.

"And what if I did!"

"Then you shouldn't say you didn't know!"

"If I have any cheek from you, miss, I'll get down the whip over the mantel."

"That's for convicts, Margery, not for me!"

"Well, and are you so far removed from convicts . . ."

"What, Margery?"

It was getting dangerous, but Margery liked danger.

"What do you mean, Margery? I'm not so far removed . . ."

"One man's as good as another, Miss. That's what I mean."

"A convict is as good as a free man?"

"As a *man* he might be."

As a man! What did she mean? Intriguing Margery!

"Oh, I *like* talking to you!" She put her arms round Margery's neck.

"Here, steady! Trying to strangle me?"

"You smell of grog."

"Well, and it's a good thing to smell of."

"My Mamma smells of violets."

"I've no doubt she does! There's some that gets on better than others in this world."

"Do you mean Mamma got on better than you? Is that why she smells of violets and you smell of grog?"

Sharp as a packet of needles, this child was. I wish she was mine. Golly, wouldn't I love her! A regular one she'll be when she grows up; she'll be the honey and the men will be the flies. I reckon I see a nice match being made up there for her. Madame Carolan will want the best for her daughter. And where would she be, eh, if the first Mrs. Masterman hadn't died at exactly the right minute! Did she do it? Or did she egg him on to do it? Not the master! I wouldn't believe that of the master. But her. . . .

"Your Mamma did get on better than me."

"You mean when the First Wife died, she married my Papa. If he had married you, would you have smelt of violets?"

Margery came as near to blushing as she could. The idea of the master so far forgetting himself as to marry her!

"There was never any question of your father's marrying me, you silly baby!" she said angrily.

"There was only a question of his marrying my Mamma?"

"Of course. What do you take him for! He was never one for running after the women."

"Wasn't he, Margery?"

"He married, and there was an end of it."

"No it wasn't, Margery. There was the First Wife, and then there was Mamma."

"You're too sharp by half!"

"Margery, where was Mamma when he was married to the First Wife?"

She was getting to know too much. If Margery let out that her precious Mamma was an ex-convict, there'd be the very devil to pay. And I wouldn't want to come up against Madame Carolan, no, thank you! At present there was a mocking affection between them, a little light blackmail practised by them both. Margery often thought, when the mistress came to the kitchen to give her orders and across the table their eyes met, Why, I could tell a few things to those children of yours. I could tell 'em how you first come to my kitchen, a shivering, lousy scrap with your loveliness hid in filth; I could whisper outside how you was always up in mistress's room —aye, and in the master's room too. I could give a few hints that it was more than likely you had something to do with that sudden death of hers.

And Carolan's green eyes said—I could tell what you were up to down here . . . James creeping into the basement . . .

The way you used to squirm and wriggle on that bed . . . in front of the others. Who is it now? Not James, for he's married to Jin, and she doubtless keeps him in order by showing him the knife she wears concealed in her clothes. But there is someone. The master would not want that sort of thing going on in his basement!

No, by God he wouldn't! And when it goes on upstairs it's different, eh? Even when it's necessary to put a poor sickly lady out of the way to straighten things out! Not that Margery'd tell. Why, she'd half murder anyone who hinted a word of it . . . anyone from outside. Her master and mistress were the best in Sydney, she'd maintain. And without a doubt it was upstairs Madame Carolan belonged, not down here in the kitchen. Still, there was no harm in thinking about it when you were in your own kitchen, even though sometimes it did give you a funny feeling in the pit of your stomach to think you had, in a way, had a hand in it.

But now this little imp had stumbled on something. Surely the most inquisitive child that ever was. So pretty though . . . you could eat her, bless her . . . and fond of old Margery too.

"Margery, where *was* Mamma . . .? *You* know . . ."

Now that would be dangerous. Keep off that!

"How should I know? A man's second wife don't usually put in an appearance till his first's dead and buried."

That satisfied her, made her pensive.

"She lived on the first floor, didn't she?"

"Who?"

"The First Wife."

"Well, yes . . . she did."

"I know what it is. Mamma's afraid."

"Afraid ! What of?"

Katharine leaned right over and whispered to Margery, because Poll's mop was getting nearer and nearer. "Of her ghost!"

Margery was very superstitious; she began to tremble like a jelly. Could it really be? What did the child know? There was something in the house . . . come to think of it, had been for a long time . . . She couldn't lay a name to it, couldn't explain it. Just something . . .

"Did she tell you?"

"Oh, no! She pretended it wasn't. You see, I was there."

"What's this?"

"I was hiding in the bed and I had the curtains drawn, and poor Mamma thought I was the ghost."

Margery drew a deep breath.

422

"You were trying to frighten your poor Mamma. I hope she spanked you hard."

"She didn't."

"She's saving it up for your Papa to do when he comes home."

"She isn't; she laughed. But, Margery, when she came in she must have heard me behind the curtains; she thought I was a ghost . . . the First Wife!"

"How did you know?"

"I did know, Margery. Perhaps . . . the First Wife lived down there, didn't she? And she wouldn't like Mamma being Papa's wife now. First Wives don't, do they?"

"You know too much!"

Margery got to her feet.

"Here, Poll, going to take all day to swab this floor? You're too slow by half! You'll be feeling the whip about your shoulders, my girl. . . ."

She wasn't really thinking of Poll, nor of the floor swabbing, nor of the whip. Madame Carolan had looked frightened, had she! Why? She wasn't the sort to show fear without a reason. The first Mrs. Masterman . . . Margery couldn't remember much what she looked like. Sickly. Fair. Suppose . . . Oh, just suppose . . . She had died sudden, hadn't she! People who'd been wronged came back to haunt them that had wronged them, didn't they? And Margery had had a hand in it . . . what you might call an innocent hand. She knew nothing of a drug. It wasn't likely she'd murder a woman just so as another woman could have her husband! But hadn't she thrown Esther to that Marcus, and because of that hadn't Madame Carolan gone to the master!

People would say, Don't be silly . . . 'twasn't none of your doing! But how could you know that a ghost saw things that way!

I ain't going to have much peace as long as I live in this house. And what do ghosts care for houses? If I went, mightn't it follow me? Oh, Lor', I'm frightened. Proper scared, that's me! I wouldn't have done it if I'd knowed how she'd take it. I wouldn't think anyone would kill themselves just because another woman was in trouble. Turn her out . . . that's what I'd have done; not took drugs!

"I believe you're frightened," said Katharine.

"You start thinking again, Miss Know-all!"

"Margery, do you think the First Wife is really angry about Mamma's being here?"

"No, Miss Nosey, I don't! And what's more, I don't want to

hear another word about ghosts and your Mamma. Don't you know ladies don't discuss such things in kitchens?"

"No," said Katharine, "I didn't."

"Well, it's time you learned. Here! You run along. I've got work to do."

'Oh, Margery, you haven't got work to do!"

"Whose kitchen is this? Do you want me to put you out and complain to your Mamma?"

"Oh, Margery, I thought you liked me here."

"There's a time for everything. You'll get your feet wet. We can't have Poll holding up her cleaning for you!"

"She usually washes all round us!"

"Well, she ain't today!"

Margery was seriously rattled. She hadn't liked the talk about ghosts. She was frightened . . . that's what she was.

"Get out, you little faggot you!"

By God, she thought, she'll be worming everything out of me before I know where I am. It ain't safe with a Miss Nosey like her about.

You simply could not stay in a kitchen where you so obviously were not wanted. Katharine walked gingerly, but with dignity, over the wet floor of the kitchen. She went out into the yard.

It was hot, but she did not feel the heat as Mamma did, nor as Margery did, nor Amy and Poll; she had been born to it. It would be pleasant, riding beyond the town. The sea was inviting; it was such a beautiful blue; but no, today was a special day. It was afternoon yet . . . and ages and ages before darkness fell. She could go far . . . explore! She loved exploring.

She went back into the house by way of the kitchen; Margery was still sitting in her chair.

"Ah! You're soon back!"

But Katharine would not stay where she was not wanted. Margery should not have an opportunity of turning her out twice in one day.

"I am not staying; I am going riding."

"In the heat of the day?"

"Call this heat?"

"Oh no, me lady, I call it midwinter!"

Katharine skipped upstairs. Even the first floor interested her but fleetingly. She wanted to be away. When she came down she was in her neat and modish riding kit, wearing the straw hat which she herself felt to be unnecessary, but which was worn as a concession to Mamma.

She went back through the kitchen. Margery softened to-

424

wards her. Regular little beauty! And of course she wanted to know. . . . Come to think of it, it might be rather fun to tell her. Take a bit of the tilt out of that head of yours, me love, if you was to hear that your fine Mamma was nothing but a convict when she first come out here!

"Here . . ." said Margery.

Katharine paused at the door, one hand on her hip, and in those clothes she looked the dead spit of what her mother must have looked sixteen or so years back.

"I'm in a hurry," she said.

"Indeed you are, me lady! I tell you it's too hot to go off riding. Wait till it cools off a bit."

"I don't feel hot."

"Here! Come back and have a talk with old Margery."

But no! Her mind was made up now. She wanted to feel her horse beneath her; she wanted to ride and ride. The time for confidences was past.

"We can talk any time."

"Oh, can we, Miss? It takes two to have a bit of conversation!"

"Goodbye, Margery! Goodbye, Poll! Goodbye, Amy!" And she was off, her red hair flying out under the straw hat, her sharp little chin as determined as ever her mother's was.

She rode out of the town away from the sea. Today she had what Margery would call the wind in her tail. It was all due to waking with that dream of Christmas in her mind. She had thought something really exciting was going to happen when she had hidden behind those bed curtains. She had a feeling that something might have happened, had she not called to Mamma. But then, she could not bear to see Mamma frightened.

It was hot, riding in open country, and when she came to a clump of trees she rested in their shade. Behind her the town lay like a toy town, the buildings all huddled together higgledy-piggledy, an uneven, untidy town; and beyond it the lovely harbour which Papa said was the finest in the world; and Papa ought to know because he had been to the Old Country, and said they had nothing like it there.

It was very lonely out here. There was, she knew, miles and miles of loneliness. She did not feel oppressed by the thought of that, although she did like to have people around her; she liked to watch them, to listen to them, to learn about them. She lay on the grass, musing. She looked, without noticing them, at the scrubby hills and the bush that ran right down to the water's edge. The silver barks of the gum trees were pretty, she thought vaguely. Far away in the distance she saw a long-legged kangaroo with a baby in her pouch. She watched idly. Kangaroos were good to eat, if you cooked them in their skins; you cooked them in cooking pits. Years and years ago, before Papa and the white men came, there was no township down there. Where did the black men live? She must ask Wando. Mamma did not like her to talk too much to Wando. Young ladies of Sydney did not talk to the natives, did not make friends of them. How could you *make* friends? Friends were . . . or weren't. You didn't make them. The kangaroo had leaped out of sight. Mamma and Margery told her about animals in the Old Country. There weren't kangaroos, nor koalas. Mamma had never seen those until she came to Sydney; nor had Papa. Fancy never having seen a kangaroo with a baby in her pouch, or two koalas clinging to each other, looking sillier than two babies, sillier than Edward! Fancy never seeing emus on their long funny legs, rushing about as though they were in a very great hurry like Papa, only not really like Papa because they were too scared to come near you, and Papa would never be scared of anything. He wouldn't be scared of a ghost on the first floor.

She stood up and stretched herself; she was tired of resting. There were hours and hours before dark. So she mounted her horse and rode on. Her thoughts were mixed, flitting from subject to subject. Miss Kelly and her brother; Margery—exciting Margery—who had been transported for marrying too many men. What an exciting thing to be transported for! She thought of Poll and her baby, and Amy and her highwayman; of Mamma and Papa and the First Wife, and the room which had been the First Wife's bedroom—that room at night with a moon peeping through the windows . . . showing what?

She was near enough now to see the outline of the mountains clearly. Beautiful they were, shrouded in blue mystery. She wondered what the time was. She had no idea except that she was getting thirsty. She was not supposed to go too far from home. She had set out, she knew, with some ridiculous idea of trying to make a way through the mountains; but with her thirst growing every minute, and her throat hot and parched, she realised that to dream in one's bedroom is one thing, and to make those dreams a reality another.

The wise thing to do was to go home.

She turned her horse away from the mountains. Around her were miles of bush, clumps of hills on which stood the tall eucalyptus trees. The brush was thicker here; there were few distinguishing features. A sudden fear came to her. Riding beside Papa, she knew now, she had always felt so safe because she had not even thought of safety. Margery said: "By golly, I wouldn't be the one for staying out after dark in this place! Felons can stay felons even though they may well be free men."

Loneliness! Alone in a world of bush and scrub and eucalyptus trees; somewhere before one, a mighty ocean; somewhere behind one, the vast impenetrable Blue Mountains. She could not really be lost. She was full of fancies today. She began to canter across the scrub. She had not noticed how rough it had been coming; perhaps it had not been so rough; perhaps she was not going back the same way that she had come.

After an hour or so there was no sign of the settlement, and her horse was lagging. There were the mountains, seeming nearer than when she had been going towards them. She seemed to see queer shapes behind that blue curtain; evil spirits who beckoned and laughed to contemplate what they would do to her if she dared set foot in their mountains.

She turned her back on them and rode on. She was hot and tired, and very dirty, and the changelessness of the scene was dispiriting. On and on she went without getting anywhere she recognised. She would be very late home, and Mamma would be cross.

She slipped off her mare, tied her to a tree and lay down under it. She must try to think which way she had come, to work out the way home. She thought now of the people Papa talked of—Bass and Flinders, Torres, Magellan, Dampier, Captain Cook—that glorious band, said Papa, through whose courage our land was founded. She had heard of them, she had read of their exploits; she had imagined herself sailing with them, and she had longed to; but this was different. This was loneliness; this was being lost. If only Papa were here, being lost might be quite an adventure. But that could not be, for the moment Papa appeared you would cease to be lost.

Lying on the ground, her ear close to the earth, she thought she heard the thump, thump of horses' hooves far, far away. She listened again. No doubt at all, but miles away, for they were so faint, and in the bush, so Papa said, you can hear for miles. She stood up and looked around her. There was no sign of a rider, only the interminable scrub and blinding sun, and the quivering curtain of blue on the mountains.

She put her hands to her mouth and called: "Coo . . . eee! Coo . . . eee!"

She laid her ear to the ground; she could still hear the thud, thud of hoofs. Did they sound louder, or was that just hope?

"Coo . . . eee!" she called again, and it seemed to her that, over the scrub, came an answering shout. "Coo . . . eee! Coo . . . eee!" she called again, and the voice called back. It was like a duet; she called, and the voice answered, and it went on like that for the best part of an hour. Once there was a frightening gap between her call and the answer, and she began to sob and laugh with relief when she heard the call again.

She watched the speck on the horizon until her eyes ached. It disappeared, and she thought she had imagined it. It came again. It did not grow any larger. It could not be a horse and rider. Then what was it?

"Coo . . . eee!" she called, and the voice called back; the speck grew a little bigger, and hope swelled up again.

It *was* a horse and rider, and she was astonished, as they came nearer and nearer, to see that the rider was a boy not much older than herself. He looked startled to see her, but he said casually enough, as though he spent his life answering Coo . . . ees in the bush: "Hello! You lost?"

"Well," she said, "I'm found now!"

He was attending to his horse, loosening the girths, removing the bit for the horse to graze. She felt irritated because he was more concerned for his mount than he was for her. Country manners! she thought haughtily, for she knew at once that he did not come from Sydney. She told him she did, hoping to command his respect.

He whistled. "That's a goodish way to come!" His cool blue eyes took in each detail of her well-cut clothes. "What made them let you out alone?"

"I often come out alone."

He raised his eyebrows. "Ever heard of bushrangers?" he asked.

"Yes, I have then!"

"Well!" he said, mocking. "Well, what would you say if I told you I was one?"

"I shouldn't believe you."

"Oh, and why not?"

"Because you're only a boy."

"There are boy bushrangers . . ."

"Well, if you were one, you'd have cut my throat by now or put a bullet through my heart."

"Look here," he said, crestfallen, "who's lost?"

"Nobody now. I was, but I'm found!"

"You're city smart, ain't you!" His skin was bronzed with

428

the sun; through slits, brilliant blue eyes peeped out at her. "Your mother shouldn't let you out," he said.

"She didn't."

"Suppose I was to kidnap you, and not let you go home?"

"What would you do with me?"

"Take you back to the station and make you work."

"You live on a station then? I tell you what—if you kidnapped me, you would be clapped in jail. My Papa would see to that!"

"Don't you be too sure. Who is your Papa?"

"Mr. Masterman."

The boy laughed at her dignity.

"He's very important," she persisted. "And a very clever man!"

"I bet he's not half as important as his daughter!"

"I don't know what you mean."

"I mean I don't care . . . *that*"—he snapped his fingers with a fine display of indifference—"for your father. And I'll tell you something else—I'm no bushranger. If you like, I'll take you back to the station and give you something to eat. We don't get many visitors."

"Are you a convict?" she asked.

"No. But Father was, and my mother was."

"Are they desperate?"

"Very desperate!" he said mockingly. He was a very fascinating, but very arrogant young person. He didn't mean half he said though, and that made it exciting because you had to separate the things he did mean from the things he didn't.

"Please take me there," she said. "I am hungry and thirsty." Which meant of course that she didn't care how desperate his family was.

"It's a long ride," he said. "Feel fit for it? But I can promise something good to eat at the end of it. They're killing a fat calf today, and there's plenty of meat."

"What is your name?" she asked him.

He told her it was Henry Jedborough, but he wouldn't tell her how old he was. That was his own grim secret. She had told him she was ten, and he seemed to think that was very little to be. He was only about her height, but broader, more sturdy; he looked strong, and his skin was almost as brown as a native's.

He told her that yesterday they had had a very successful muster. He loved a muster. As he talked she could almost see him, cracking his stock-whip, riding magnificently, darting here and there amongst the straying herds—bullocks and calves and heifers going where he insisted they should.

She told him that she had longed to cross the mountains. "But no one ever has," she said.

"They will . . . soon!" he said.

"There are evil spirits in the mountains," she told him. "And they have decreed that no one shall pass."

He laughed shrilly, mockingly, and his laughter both angered and humiliated her.

"You are a silly girl! You've been listening to natives."

"I did talk to Wando."

"And you believe that!"

"No!" she lied, blushing to the red roots of her hair.

"I am glad to hear it," he said. "There are no evil spirits in the mountains; it is the dangerous ravines that make it so hard to get across. But one day men will get across . . . My father will be one of them."

"Your father . . . the convict?"

"Ex-convict!" he reminded her. "He went on an expedition; it failed, but he says one day someone will find the way across, and then . . . and then . . ."

"Yes?" said Katharine breathlessly.

"We shall see what is on the other side."

"Do you think it will be very wonderful on the other side?"

"Of course! My father says we are shut off here, confined to a small space. He wants to find new land. My father always wants to find new places."

"He sounds nice."

"Nice!" He was scornful again. What could a little town girl know of the magnificence of his father!

She caught his excitement; she wanted to meet this man, the ex-convict who not only wanted to find new lands but set out with an expedition to do so.

She was a little disappointed in him when she saw him. He was lying in a hammock on a veranda; his shirt was open, showing a chest the colour of mahogany. His dark hair waved slightly, and his blue eyes peered out through even narrower slits than Henry's, and there were masses of wrinkles round them. They were very merry eyes, and it was a very merry face. But she had expected a giant, from Henry's talk.

Henry said: "Father, this is a girl I found. She was lost in the bush."

He rolled himself out of the hammock.

"Well, well!" he said, and looked at her as though he knew a lot about her. Then he said: "This is an honour. We don't often get visitors on our lonely station. Go and tell your mother to have an extra place laid for our guest, Henry."

Henry went in, and she and the man stood looking at each other, she smiling shyly.

"What is your name, little girl?" he asked.

"Katharine Masterman."

Something queer happened to his face then; his eyes seemed to open a bit wider.

"Of Sydney?" he asked in a voice that didn't tell her anything.

"Yes. How did you know?"

"Ah!" he said mysteriously. "You have a look of Katharine Masterman of Sydney."

"What do you mean?"

"It did not surprise me to hear you are Katharine Masterman of Sydney. Just that."

"Then perhaps you know my Papa?"

"No, I cannot claim that honour. I once knew your mother."

"She did not tell me."

"Did she not? That was a little remiss of her, I fear. You are astonishingly like her."

"Margery says that."

"Ah! Margery."

"You knew Margery too?"

"Well, yes, I knew Margery."

She clapped her hands. This was indeed coming among friends.

"Though," he went on, "it is many years since I set eyes on her."

"She did not tell me she knew you."

"Dear me! They do not appear to have done me justice in the Masterman household. How is your mother?"

"She is well, thank you."

"And what brothers and sisters have you?"

"James and Martin. There is Edward too, but he is only a baby."

"Hardly reached the status of brother yet then."

"What?" said Katharine.

"Come here and let me look at you."

He held out a hand and took hers; his merry eyes searched her face.

"You are doubtless hungry?" he asked.

"It seems a long time since I ate," she told him.

"I'll warrant it does. They are cooking some veal in there."

431

"I can smell it."

"And the smell pleases you?"

She lifted her eyes ecstatically, which made him laugh.

Henry appeared, and said: "It won't be ready for half an hour."

"Get a glass of something for our guest, Henry," said his father. "And bring me a drink too."

Henry disappeared, and when he came back carrying a tray, he was not alone; there was a woman, a pale, thin woman with an unhappy face and beautiful hair that curled and rioted about her face as if in defiance of its unhappiness.

"Esther," said the man—and he talked as though it was a great joke—"this is Miss Katharine Masterman, Carolan's girl."

Katharine wondered why the woman seemed to mind so much that she was Katharine Masterman, Carolan's girl.

Katharine stood up and curtsyed.

The woman said: "How . . . how did she get here?"

"Henry brought her. She was lost in the bush."

Katharine thought it was due to her to explain. "I rode out and I didn't realise how far I had come. And then I coo-eed and . . . Henry found me."

"Your mother will be anxious." The woman looked at the man. "You could take her back now. If you did, you could get her there before dark."

"Why, Esther," said the man, "Miss Masterman is very hungry. It would be churlish to send her away without food."

"Carolan will be frantic!"

"I wonder," he said, and he looked quite cruel then.

Katharine had not thought of that. She stood up. "I must go. Mamma will be worried."

The man stood up. He seemed to have thrown off his laziness now, and his eyes smouldered.

He said to Katharine: "Do not worry. It is too late for you to go now. You must stay the night here. In the morning I or my son will take you back. It would be possible though to get a message to your parents that you were safe."

She smiled. How clever of him! And how kind! For, much as she did not want Mamma worried, she did want to continue this adventure. There was more in it than being lost and found, than being hungry and smelling the good smell of roasting meat; there was more in it than meeting new people. There was something about these people that was exciting, mysterious; she sensed that as soon as the man began to talk, and more so when the woman came in. She was his wife, and

432

Henry's mother; he was her husband; they were like Mamma and Papa, but very different too. Papa looked at Mamma when she was in the room, as though he saw no one else; and Mamma smiled at Papa, and said that he was a very clever, busy man. But these two tried not to look at each other, and when they did look it was different somehow. Then of course there was Henry—quite the most exciting of the three.

The man and the woman went out and left her with Henry on the veranda.

"Have you any brothers and sisters?" she asked.

"Not real brothers and sisters."

"How can you have not real ones?"

"You can. You can have half-brothers and sister. They have your father, but not your mother."

It sounded very complicated.

"I've got a half-sister here. She is two years old and her name is Elizabeth. She lives here; she is the daughter of the servant."

Katharine was puzzled. The boy looked wise, and she thought he must be clever; and as she did not like to display her ignorance in front of him she asked no more questions.

The man came back, and stretched himself out in the hammock.

"She wants to go over the Blue Mountains," said Henry. "She believed that there are evil spirits there!"

Katharine blushed, and hotly denied it.

"That's just a native story," said the man kindly.

"I know!" said Katharine.

"She didn't . . . till I told her."

"Do not be so unmannerly, Henry," said the man. "I am sure she knew."

"Is it unmannerly to tell the truth?"

"Very often, my boy.'"

"You're a convict, aren't you?" said Katharine.

"I was."

"Were you very wicked?"

"Very!"

Katharine laughed, because it was very comical to hear a grown man say he was very wicked.

"What did you do?" she asked.

He was a wonderful talker—better than Margery—and his eyes danced with merriment as he talked. Never had the Old Country become so real for her. She began to see it as Marcus had seen it nearly twenty years ago. She saw clearly the cobbled streets of London, red brick buildings and old inns with their signs creaking in the wind and blistered by the sun; she saw nearby meadows and the clustering villages of Brentford and Chiswick, Chelsea and Kensington. Link boys, crossing sweepers, barefooted and hungry, and the great, riding by in their carriages; cock-fighting and the baiting of bulls and bears out at Tothill Fields; drunken people clustered round the gin shops; the bucks so gorgeously attired, the beggars with their sores and rags; pick-pockets and fools; street criers; here and there a sedan chair. The London of which he talked was an exciting one, filled with exciting people. There was Mr. Sheridan and Charles James Fox in league with the profligate Prince against the half-crazy king. There was the wild Princess of Wales. It was like something out of a story book, and yet wonderfully real. He made Katharine wonder whether even Papa was such an important man compared with these gorgeously apparelled and most amazing people of London Town.

Even when they were seated round the table he went on talking. He set out to charm Carolan's daughter, and he did so as successfully as he had charmed Carolan herself.

The meat was good and fresh, and Katharine was hungry, but it was not the food she remembered from that meal, but the talk and the lazy merry eyes of the man and the softness of his voice and the flow of his words. He could, in one sentence, make a picture full of detail. He did not hint by a word, a look or a gesture, that he was talking to a child; he made her feel important, convinced her that he enjoyed talking as much as she enjoyed listening, and he gave pleasure as naturally as he took it. His conversation was peppered with wonderful names that she was to repeat over and over to herself and remember for years to come. Seven Dials. Cripplegate. The Temple. Brooks's and Almack's. The Fleet. Coffee Houses. Chocolate Houses. The Blue Lion in Newgate Street. Islington. Chancery Lane. Covent Garden. The King's Theatre. Haymarket. St. Martin's. Turnbull Street. Chick Lane. Jack Ketch's Warren. The Charlies. Drury Lane. Bawdy Houses. Gambling Houses. London, London, London! The Old Country.

Besides this man, his wife, Esther, and Henry, there came to the table a man named Blake, his wife May and their two children—a boy and a girl; there was also Elizabeth, the little girl of two, who, Henry had said, was his half-sister, and who, when they had finished eating, sat on Marcus's knee and watched his mouth while he talked and talked.

Esther, Katharine did not greatly care for, because she tried to stop him all the time, tried to remind him that he was talking to children, which she did not seem to realise was just what they loved to forget. She kept saying "Marcus!" in a shocked voice which seemed to irritate Henry and certainly irritated Katharine almost beyond endurance.

But he took no notice of her and went on to describe the wicked things he had done in London, how he was one of the rogues who preyed upon those ladies and gentlemen in their fine clothes and carriages; and he told it so that you were on his side against the fine ladies and gentlemen, and somehow would always be on his side, whatever he did.

"You, my dear Miss Masterman, can have no conception of the extravagances of our pleasure gardens." Then he talked of Ranelagh and Vauxhall, and she *saw* the pleasure gardens and she walked in the avenues with him, she watched the fireworks and she was at the concert, and it was the most exciting time she had ever known. She drank hot punch and syllabub and shared oysters with this man, and Mr. Händel's music and Mr. Mozart's music was the background of the scene, for now and then he would burst into song.

He drank a good deal, and he told her then of how on one occasion at Vauxhall he had stolen the purse of a fine lady who had gone there to meet her lover. She dared not raise a hue and cry because it must not be known that she had gone there to meet her lover.

When he told that story, which was no more shocking than others he had told, Esther got up from the table.

"You are devilish!" she said, and burst into tears. And he just looked at her, cruelly, without saying anything, but Katharine could see he hated her and she hated him. She ran out of the room, crying, which made Katharine very uncomfortable at first, but the other children hardly seemed to notice, and guessing that the reason they did not was because they had seen it happen many times before, she did not care either; for after all, she would care only on their account, and if they did not, where was the sense in her doing so? She was rather glad Esther had gone; she had tried to spoil the fun anyway. They could be more rollickingly gay without her.

When the meal was over, they sat on, talking. Darkness had come and lamps were lighted. Then Elizabeth's mother came in and took the child away; she was a comely girl with a fat, stupid face, and the man Marcus kissed the little girl tenderly and the servant girl lightly, which seemed a very extraordinary thing to do, but none of the others appeared to think so. She tried to imagine Papa's kissing Poll or Amy. It was quite impossible!

They gathered round the table when it had been cleared of the food; two tame dingoes stretched themselves out on the floor.

Then Marcus took a map and spread it on the table, and she and Henry pored over it with him. There was Sydney, a big black dot, and there was the coast and the sea, and Port Jackson and Botany Bay . . . and then, all furry looking, like a great caterpillar, wound the Blue Mountains. And beyond the Blue Mountains was a blank space.

Oh, it was wonderful to lean over that table and to see his face with its wrinkled skin and merry blue eyes in the lamplight, to be there . . . one of them . . . to listen to him as he talked and pointed with his finger at the places, now and then throwing out a word for her alone. "What do you think, Miss Masterman?" "Do you not think so?" As though she were not only a grown-up but an explorer. She knew now why Henry adored him; she was not disappointed in him now. Once she cut into the most exciting conversation to say: "May I come here again? May I come often?" And he did not reprove her for interrupting; he seemed glad that she had interrupted, for he stretched out a hand quickly and gripped hers so that it hurt. He said: "Come as often as you like, Miss Masterman. Or perhaps I may call you Katharine. . . ."

He talked of how he and others had tried to cross the mountains; how they had hacked away at the brushwood, how they had camped in deep gullies, how they had followed what they had thought might prove to be a way over the mountains, only to be disappointed. He told of dwindling stores, of the necessity for return, of weariness, and cold and heat, and sleeplessness.

They adored him because at one moment he was a child with them, delighting in the things that delight children, and the next he was a man, and they man and woman with him.

The woman spoilt it all by putting her curly head round the door and saying: "It is time Henry went to bed; it is time she did too."

And strangely enough he did not protest, but folded up the map, and the lovely evening was over.

Katharine had a little room with a narrow bed in it, a basin and jug and a washstand and chest of drawers. The woman lent her a nightgown, and when she brought it in, Katharine could see that she had been crying. But Katharine was too tired to think much of her, and was soon asleep; and when she awakened in the morning, remembered where she was with a delicious sense of excitement. She washed hastily and went downstairs to find Marcus on the veranda, where the fat servant brought her bread and milk.

Marcus said: "We will ride back to Sydney as soon as you are ready." He seemed less happy than he had been last night, wistful and very sorry that she was going. When she had finished her bread and milk, and had eaten newly baked cakes, and drunk coffee, he said very earnestly: "I hope you will come again. It is not such a long ride out from Sydney, if you know the direct way to come. You must watch as we ride back, and take note of the best way to come."

"Thank you very much!"

"You are not sorry you were lost?"

"No, I am glad. I have loved it. I shall certainly come again ... often. May I come often?"

"It could not be too often for me."

"I am glad you like me."

"Does that mean you like me?"

"You are different from other people."

"Different from your father?"

"Oh, yes! Very different from him."

"Yet you do not dislike me? You must be very fond of him."

"Why, yes. He is very clever, you know. And very important."

"And he amuses you ... as I did last night?"

"Oh ... Papa is not like that. He does not talk ... very much. Except about the First Fleet and Mr. Bass and Mr. Flinders ... and then only a little. He does not talk like you do."

"And you liked the way I talked, did you not?"

She was puzzled. She did not know what he wanted her to say, but had stopped thinking solely about him because her thoughts had switched to Papa and Mamma. She hoped they had not been frightened.

She said: "He is the best father in the world."

"How do you know?" he said, just like Martin might have said it.

"Mamma says so."

Then he dropped the subject, and she was glad.

She said goodbye to Henry, who intimated very definitely

437

that she must come again. She said goodbye to Esther and Mr. Blake and all the children. Then she rode back with Marcus.

He talked fascinatingly as they rode, pointing out landmarks; he explained the difference in the grasses and the trees, and compared them with those of the Old Country. He sang songs he had known in the Old Country, and she was sorry when they came into Sydney.

Mamma came out into the yard. She was very white, and there were dark shadows under her eyes, and she stared at them as though they were ghosts.

"Hello, Mamma!" she called uneasily. "I was lost."

"Katharine!" said Carolan stonily, looking at the man.

Katharine slipped off her horse; she stood there holding the bridle nervously.

Marcus said: "Carolan, your little daughter was rescued by my son. Do you not think that a rather charming sequel to . . . everything?"

Mamma called to one of the men to take Katharine's horse. Mamma was white and haughty. Margery appeared; she had been crying. She screamed out when she saw Katharine: "Oh, my little love! My own little love!" And Katharine, frightened for some reason of which she was only partly aware, ran to Margery as if for protection, and Margery knelt on the stones of the yard and put her arms about her.

"Scared out of me wits, lovey! Why, you scared me out of me natural . . . Why, whatever was you up to?"

"I was lost, and Henry found me, and . . ."

Margery's body had gone taut; she was no longer thinking of Katharine; she was staring over Katharine's head at Marcus.

Papa appeared. His face shone with sudden joy when he saw Katharine, and Katharine knew then that they had had no message, and had been very frightened.

She ran to Papa; he lifted her up; she kissed him and went on kissing to try to explain by kisses that she would rather have given up her exciting evening than that he and Mamma should be worried like this.

Then Mamma turned her head and said: "It is all right now. She was lost. This . . . gentleman brought her home."

Papa hugged Katharine and said: "Bring him in! Bring him in!"

They went into the house, and when they were inside, Mamma took Katharine from Papa's arms, and her eyes were cold and very angry.

"Go to your room at once, Katharine!" she said, and her voice was like ice, and sharp like the edge of a knife; and Katharine went in shame because she knew she ought to have insisted on coming home, and that Esther had been right; that that jaunty, exciting, lovely man Marcus had not kept his word about sending a message.

She went to her room and waited there, feeling that something awful was going to happen. It was not very long before she heard Marcus ride away. She hoped they had been nice to him, for he had been very nice to her. She hoped they had given him refreshment; it would be awful if Mamma were not nice to him just because he had forgotten to send that message.

James and Martin came in.

"Where have you been?" demanded James.

"I was lost." What a glorious account of her adventure she had imagined herself giving James! And now she had nothing to say except "I was lost!" which they knew already.

"We had a search party!" cried James excitely.

"Lanthorns and flaming torches!" screeched Martin.

"We thought you'd been murdered, you see," said James cheerfully.

"I might have been," she said.

"Yes," said James with unnecessary melancholy, "but you weren't."

Miss Kelly came in.

"I wonder you're not ashamed," she said. "I never saw such a fuss. I think what you deserve is a thorough good whipping."

Miss Kelly bustled the boys out and turned the key in the lock.

It was some time before Mamma came in. Katharine threw herself against her.

"Mamma! Why am I locked up here? It wasn't my fault; I was lost . . . Anybody might get lost . . . And then I heard Henry's horse. It was exciting; I coo-eed and he coo-eed, and then he came and took me to his home."

"Yes?" said Mamma in an odd, stony voice.

"And then it was such fun, Mamma. Oh, he has been *everywhere!* And he told us, Mamma. He told us *all* about it. All about London and the Old Country. He talks differently from anyone else, different from Margery or Papa, or even you. He tells you things, and you see them, and oh, Mamma, don't you *like* him? Can he come here? He would like to. It's nicer here than there . . . and I think *they* quarrel a lot. She

439

looks at him as if she hates him, and he doesn't care a bit when she cries, and he kisses the servant, and there's an Elizabeth. Henry says he's got half-brothers and sisters. Henry's nice. Oh, Mamma, *can* they come?"

"Really, Katharine, I haven't the faintest notion of what you're saying. You are most incoherent. And it was very, very naughty of you to go off like that; and I am going to punish you for being so thoughtless. Your father and I were very worried."

"Oh, but Mamma, the man came. She said you would be worried; he said he would send a man to tell you where I was."

"Who is *she?*"

"The one they call Esther."

"Esther!" said Mamma faintly. And then: "Of course, no man was sent."

"Oh, but he said . . ."

"He is a liar," said Mamma.

"Oh, but Mamma, I'm sure there is a mistake. I know he said . . . I must ask him . . ."

"He has gone now."

"I am going there again, Mamma. They asked me. He and Henry said I must go again."

"You will never see them again," said Mamma.

Katharine was incredulous. She could find nothing to say.

"And," said Mamma, "you will stay here for the rest of the day . . . alone."

Mamma went out then. She had been pale, but now her face was flushed, her eyes hard as the glittering stones in the pendant she wore round her neck.

Katharine heard the key turn in the lock. She was angry with Mamma, angry with Papa even, poor Papa who had done nothing but be very pleased because she was home again. Still, she was angry with the whole world, for more than anything she wanted to see Marcus and Henry again.

"And I will!" she said. She went over to the Bible on the chest of drawers, the Bible which Miss Kelly had given her last Christmas. She laid her hands on it and swore as she did when she and James played Judge and Prisoners. But there was no jest about this; it was a solemn vow.

"With God's help, so I will," she said. Her eyes were resolute, her mind made up.

Carolan was dressing for her dinner-party. It was a very important dinner-party, a sort of coming out for Katharine.

She was seventeen. Carolan's thoughts must go back to a similar occasion nearly twenty years ago, when she was going to her first ball. A green dress she had worn; she was wearing a green dress now. How different though, this rather plump and still beautiful woman, poised and confident, the mother of five sons and one daughter, Mrs. Masterman of Sydney! How different from that slender girl who had gone down to the hall at Haredon to dance with Everard!

Audrey, her maid, was ready to do her hair. Audrey's eyes, meeting hers in the mirror, sparkled with admiration. She had rescued Audrey from the kitchen, much as Lucille had rescued her all those years ago, and the girl was her willing slave. She could hardly remember now what Lucille had looked like, and yet the memory of her was as evergreen as the fir trees which had grown so abundantly in the damp climate of Hardeon. There was everything to remind her in this house. Why did they not leave it? Simply because together they never broached the subject; they dared not. If she said to Gunnar: "Let us leave this house," he would know she was thinking of Lucille. And what they had been trying to do all the time, all through those eighteen years, was to show each other, without mentioning the subject, that neither of them ever thought of Lucille.

It was a ridiculous pretence; she knew he thought of her often. She knew the shadow of his first wife lay heavy across the happiness he might have enjoyed with his second.

Audrey said: "Pearls, Madam?" And she smiled her assent. Her smile was charming as it ever was. She always tried to be charming to the servants, particularly if they had been convicts. Behind each of them she would see a grim shadow of Newgate that could make hideous memories rush back at her, and whatever had been their crime, she would make excuses for them. Of Audrey she knew little except that she was sentenced to transportation for fourteen years, and had, by all accounts, been a desperate creature. And yet here was Audrey, almost gentle, pliable, eager to please. She never asked questions of Audrey; it occurred to her that the girl might not wish to talk, but because there was a daintiness about her which most lacked, she had taken her to be her maid, and Audrey was grateful.

Audrey clasped the pearls about her neck and stood back to admire.

"They are lovely, Madam!"

A gift from Gunnar—one of his many gifts. She was fond of him, though at times he irritated her almost beyond endurance. His ideas were so conventional that they bored her; she knew, almost to the phrase, what he would say on almost any subject. His conduct was absolutely what it should have been —except on one occasion; and how ironical it was that her tenderness for him should be just because of that lapse!

She smiled faintly at her reflection in the mirror. Ripe womanhood, full sensuous lips, and green eyes that flashed from mood to mood with a speed that could be disastrous. She was her mother's daughter; she belonged to that procession of women to whom numerous love-affairs were as natural as eating and drinking. But there was a certain strength in her which the others had lacked; perhaps it had grown up in the evil soil of Newgate, because that fetid air had nourished it. A glance from a pair of merry eyes, admiring, passionate—and she was as ready for adventure as her mother had been. But she had resisted every time, for she could not forget that her husband had jeopardised not only his soul but—and ironical as it might seem, this was of almost as great importance to him—his position here in Sydney, for love of her.

Gunnar was really a man after Lachlan Macquarie's own heart, and but for that eighteen-year-old scandal, what position might not Gunnar have held under the greatest governor New South Wales had ever known! Macquarie and his saintly Elizabeth had not been ruling when it happened, but there were those only too ready to tell him the story which they had preserved, as though it were something precious, through the reign of turbulent Bligh and the period of usurpation that followed before the coming of Macquarie. Gunnar admired the governor almost to idolatry; and the governor admired Gunnar; but there was that ancient scandal that had attached itself to poor Gunnar and dragged him down from the heights which, but for it, he would certainly have attained. It was not the fact that he had married a convict; it was the circumstances in which he had married her. There were many convicts, and once they were free it should not be remembered against them that they had suffered transportation. Everyone knew that the laws of the Old Country, and its conditions, were such as to breed convicts. A convict can become a respectable man in a new country—many of them had—for that reckless daring which may have driven them to crime, turned to good effect, can be the very quality needed to found a new nation. No, the fact that Mrs. Masterman had begun her life in Sydney as a convict was not really as important as that clinging scandal about Masterman's first wife.

And here I am, back at it, thought Carolan. Eighteen years

ago it happened, and I still think of it as though it were yesterday.

Tonight was Katharine's party, a joyous occasion. Katharine! Sweet daughter. Anything was surely worth while to have had Katharine. Five sons she had borne Gunnar, willingly doing her duty—one pregnancy following close on another—accepting the discomfort, the pain and the danger; and all because she was determined to do her duty, to give him those sons he had wanted. He had got them; he had paid dearly for them, and he should not be disappointed. Queer, that it should be Katharine whom they loved best of all. The daughter; and every time he looked at her, did he think as she did of those months immediately previous to her birth? Was it that that made her specially dear? No, no! It was the charm of Katharine; the sweetness of her. Carolan's daughter. Her eyes had lost that tinge of green, and were blue as speedwells you found in the lanes of the Old Country; her hair was a deeper shade of red; her chin determined as Carolan's had been twenty years ago, so that one was fearful for Katharine. The boys wer elike their father—calmer, assured; they possessed humour, though Gunnar had none, but that would not hinder their way of life. She could see them, years ahead, important men in the town, or perhaps in other towns, perhaps back in England. Martin and Edward both had a yearning for England. James would most likely take over his father's activities; and it was too soon to see what little Joseph and Stephen were going to do. The boys were safe, but of Katharine she was not so sure. Gunnar had wanted her educated in England; he had advanced ideas on education for such an unimaginative man. James was soon to leave for England, but Katharine she would not allow to go.

"But, my dear," said Gunnar, "she needs more than Sydney can give her. There are things she must learn, which she can only acquire at home . . . the way to behave—manners are necessarily a little rough here . . ."

"No," she said, "no! I should not have a moment's peace. How do we know what would happen to her?"

She had had a frightful vision of life's catching up reckless Katharine as it had caught up innocent Carolan. Newgate! The prison ship! But why should she be so caught, a young lady of substance? But how can you know what evil fate is in store!

She had her way. She remembered lying in the dark with him, holding him in her arms.

"Gunnar, I could not bear it! What happened to me . . ."

And he had soothed her and comforted her. Katharine should not leave her. It was for moments like that she almost loved him.

And now Katharine had grown secretive, her blue eyes full of dreams, her thoughts far away. You spoke to her and she did not answer; and she made no confidences in her mother. Sometimes Carolan thought she knew. Had it begun years ago when the child was only ten years old, and had disappeared one day and come back the next morning with Marcus?

The thought of Marcus angered her, and comforted her and hurt her. So insolent he had looked, standing there in the yard. She knew he had kept the child purposely to hurt her, Carolan, that he wanted to hurt her as she had hurt him. Insolently he had looked at her, hating her and loving her as she hated and loved him. Gunnar had stood there, exasperatingly unobservant, seeing in this man a kind friend who had looked after his daughter and brought her safely home.

It had seemed to her that Marcus's eyes had said something else too, that they pleaded for a moment alone with her; they seemed to say: "Carolan, Carolan, we must meet again. Where, Carolan, where?" And her heart had beaten faster with excitement, and her need of him then was as great as her love for her children. He had seen that, and hope had leaped into his eyes. But Gunnar had been there, seeing nothing, his voice calm, his manner slightly pompous as he thanked Marcus with the charm and courtesy a successful man can afford to give to one who is not so successful.

"My dear sir, we are deeply indebted to you. We shall never forget . . ." And because he was such a good man, because he had always striven so hard to lead the right sort of life . . . no, not because of that. Because of that one lapse when for her sake . . . She let her thoughts swerve. Not that again! Not that! But it was the reason why she had turned from Marcus and ever since not known whether she was glad or sorry. All she knew was that her life was full of regrets . . . regrets for . . . she was not sure what. Life was a compromise, when for people like herself and Marcus who knew how to live recklessly, it should have been glorious. Up in the heights, and perhaps occasionally—for Marcus could never be faithful to one woman even if she was Carolan—down in the depths. But never, never this unexciting, boring level.

And that day when Marcus had come into the yard with Katharine was a bitter day, for it had lost her something of Katharine. She had been too harsh with the child, blaming her because she had stupidly wanted to blame someone for that for which she herself was entirely to blame. "You shall never go there again!" she had said, and Katharine had answered with stubborn silence. If your daughter was so like you that the resemblance frightened you, you could often guess her thoughts. She had gone there, of course she had gone! She had felt the irresistible charm of Marcus. There was a boy, Henry . . . Esther's child. He would doubtless be as like his father as Katharine was like her mother.

The child often absented herself all day. She would ride off in the morning and not return until sundown. Where had she been? She would come back, flushed with sunshine and laughter, and happiness looked out of her eyes. And when there had been that talk of going to England, how stubbornly she had set her heart against it! "I do not want to go to England! I *will* not go to England!" Why? Because, if she went, she would miss those long days when she absented herself from her own home and went to that of Marcus.

Carolan had seen the boy, Henry. He had inherited that subtle attractiveness from his father. He was young and crude of course, but it was there, and Katharine possibly did not look for polish. Dark he was, dark as Marcus, with that quickness of eye; she had heard him call to someone in the town, and his voice had that lilting quality which belonged to Marcus's.

Katharine was young, only just seventeen. It might be that she thought she loved the boy, because it was the first time anyone had talked of love to her. So she had contrived to arrange parties for her, gatherings where she could meet charming people. That was not difficult, for Sydney was no longer a mere settlement. Macquarie had vowed it should take its place among the cities of the world, and surely he was keeping his word. From the Cove it looked magnificent nowadays, unrecognisable as that hotch potch of buildings it had been on her arrival. It was gracious and stately; large houses of hewn stone had taken the place of the smaller ones, and the number of warehouses had grown on the waterside to keep pace with the growing population and prosperity. Sydney would soon grow into a great town, busy and beautiful. There were young men of substance in the town who had shown signs of becoming very interested in the fresh young charms of Masterman's daughter; and not least among these was Sir Anthony Greymore, recently out from England, a young man, sophisticated and charming, wealthy and serious-minded enough to make a good husband. He surely, if anyone, could wean Katharine from Henry.

I will not let her marry Marcus's son! thought Carolan. I will not! Even though, for a time, she thinks her heart is broken. He will be like his father. I see it in him.

Audrey was looking at her oddly, comb poised.

"I am sorry, Audrey. I am fidgeting."

Audrey's eyes in the mirror worshipped her. Where else could a convict find such a kind mistress?

Gunnar came in. He had just ridden home. He looked tanned and healthy. He was in a hurry for he was late, but he would be ready at precisely the right moment when he must descend to greet his guests. He would never be late. His dressing-room would be in perfect order and he would know just where to find everything. How wrong it was to get exasperated over someone's virtues!

Audrey had finished her hair and the result was most attractive.

"You don't look much older than Miss Katharine, M'am. You might be her older sister. People could easy take you for that."

What flattery! She looked years older than Katharine and most definitely she looked Katharine's mother.

She felt an acute desire to be Katharine's age, to be going to her first ball where she would be told by Everard that he loved her. Had she known what was waiting for her, how she would have pleaded with him to let nothing stand in the way of their marriage! Had she never come to London she would never have known Marcus. She could not wish that. No, perhaps if she could live her life again, she would go back to that day when Margery had told her that Clementine Smith and Marcus were lovers.

She shrugged her shoulders impatiently. Had she not been fortunate? The life she had shared with Gunnar had dignity, security; and life with Marcus would never have given her either.

Gunnar came in from his dressing-room; he wanted to talk to her, she could tell by his manner, so she dismissed Audrey.

"Well," she said, playing with her fan of green tinged ostrich feathers.

He smiled at her, admiring her beauty which never failed to stir him, admiring her adroitness in dismissing Audrey without his having to tell her that he had something to say.

"I was late," he said, "because I met young Greymore. He asked . . . for permission to approach Katharine."

"And most willingly you gave it!"

She laughed, and he laughed too, though he was never sure

446

of her laughter. To him this seemed a matter of the deepest gravity; the betrothal of their daughter was surely no matter for laughter.

"I gave it, of course," he said.

"I hope she will accept him," said Carolan pensively. "I should hate it if she were reluctant."

"I was wondering if we should warn her, and tell her what our wishes are."

Dear Gunnar! Did he know his daughter so little that he thought they had only to tell her their wishes and they would immediately become hers?

"She may be difficult," she warned him tenderly.

"She is very sensible," he said. "And it is a good match."

She stood up then. He was sitting on her bed. She took his head and held it against her breast. He was always moved by these sudden displays of affection; they were so unexpected. Why should she embrace him now, while they were discussing this very important matter of their daughter's marriage?

She said: "You think everybody can be as sensible as you, my dear."

"Oh, I think Katharine has her share of common sense."

Oh, no! She wanted to say. There is no great common sense in our Katharine, because she has little of you in her; she is all mine. Reckless, adventuring. And yet there was a time when you . . .

"Gunnar," she said, "if she refuses him, what then?"

He said confidently: "We will talk to her. He is very eager. He seems to me the sort who'll not take no for an answer."

"She worries me, Gunnar. Sometimes I wonder whether she has not formed some attachment."

"But, Carolan, with whom?"

"How should I know!"

"But surely there would have been some evidence . . ."

He did not see the evidence of bright eyes, of that absent manner, of that shine of happiness. He would never see that. Blind Gunnar! How did he ever love blindly himself!

"I am determined," said Carolan fiercely, "that she shall make the right sort of marriage. I think she needs that sort of marriage. The boys will choose wisely . . . one feels that instinctively. Or if they do not, it will not be so important. But Katharine . . ."

She saw his face in the glass, and she knew he was thinking of the coming of Katharine; how she, Carolan, had talked of marrying Tom Blake; he was remembering it all vividly, for it lay across his life as darkly as it lay across hers.

447

She turned to him then, clinging to him in sudden tenderness.

"Oh, Gunnar, you have done so much for us all. You have made me so happy."

"My dear!" he said in a husky voice. But the shadow was still in his eyes. Lucille was there.

Margery knocked at Katharine's door and tiptoed into the room. Katharine was standing before her mirror, admiring herself in her blue ball dress with its masses of yellow lace. Audrey, before starting on Carolan's hair, had dressed Katharine's and it hung in curls about her shoulders. Margery clasped her hands together and rocked herself with delight.

"My little love! My little dear! The men will be at your beck and call tonight!"

"How your thoughts run on men!" said Katharine, and Margery cackled with glee.

She was more outspoken, this Katharine, than her mother had been. Not quite the same brand of haughtiness. Ready to enjoy a little joke. And up to mischief, if Margery knew anything!

"Pity *he* isn't going to be here tonight!" Margery nudged her.

"Who?" said Katharine defiantly.

"You know who! Him who you sneak out to meet, me darling. Tell old Margery."

"You know too much."

"Well, what's an old woman to do? The gentlemen don't come calling on me now, you know."

"You must not tell, Margery. You haven't told?"

"I'd cut me tongue out rather."

"Only sometimes I've thought that Mamma seemed to know. Margery, if you told I'd never speak to you again!"

"Not me, lovey! Not me! And if she was to know, what of it? Do you think she's never . . ."

She could silence with a look, the little beauty, and her with a secret on her conscience too! Old Margery had seen him. He was forever hanging about the yard, he was. And there was no mistaking where he'd come from; the look of him told you that. And his father all over again! He knew how to get round a woman, no mistake, and he'd got round her little ladyship till she was yearning for him. The things you could find out, if you kept your eyes open!

Margery finished lamely: "A pity he can't come here tonight! Pity he can't be introduced to your Ma and the master, and we can't hear the wedding bells ring out! That's how I'd like this to end."

"Parents," said Katharine, "have such ridiculous ideas!"

"Parents was young once, me lady!" Ah! That they was! And well I remember the two of them. Madam Carolan, flaunting herself in her mistress's clothes, and you, me lady, well on the way before you should have been. And that . . . what I don't like thinking of . . . and me having a hand in it, so's I'm frightened to show me face on that first floor. I wish we'd get out of this house. But ghosts don't mind where you go; they follow. And they don't need a carriage, nor a stage . . . not they! And as sure as I'm Margery Green there's a ghost in this house, though I ain't—and God forbid I ever should—clapped eyes on it!

"Yes, Margery, but they've got this Sir Anthony in mind."

"Ah! Marry him, me pretty dear, and you'll be a real live ladyship. There's some who wouldn't say no to that, I'll be bound!"

"I thought you'd talk sense, Margery!"

Sweet balm, that was. Madam and the master, they didn't talk sense, but old Margery did, according to this lovely bit of flesh and blood. Margery put her hand on the bare shoulder, though it was risking her ladyship's displeasure, for she was never one for being touched . . . except by some most likely . . . I never saw a child take after her mother more. And why not, and who are they to say her nay? What of them, eh? With the mistress lying in her bed, poor sickly lady! No, no, don't think of that, Margery; it ain't nice to think of. I wish we'd leave this house, but would that be any good? Ghosts don't need the stage.

"Look here, me dearie, love's a game for them that plays it. It's not for them outside to give a hand. That's Margery's motto."

"I agree, Margery!"

How her eyes flashed! Trouble coming, clear as daylight. Mrs. Carolan born again. Imagine telling *her* all those years ago who she was to love! Funny how people forget what they were like when they were young! Now Margery Green, she remembered all too well!

Katharine had dreams in her eyes; she was thinking of long days in the sunshine, riding out to the station; he came to meet her. At first he had pretended to think her just a foolish girl when together they had listened to Marcus. But when the Blue Mountains had been crossed, they both seemed to grow up suddenly. Marcus, deeply regretting that he had not been one of the gallant band that first crossed the mountains, told them the story in his inimitable way, and it was as exciting as though they themselves had found the road.

"No matter how difficult a project may seem," said Marcus, "stick to it, and you'll get across as sure as men got across the Blue Mountains!"

She had ridden out to them, and kept her secret; she had planned and contrived, and it had been worth it. How she loved the sunny veranda and the talk of the two of them! Marcus smoking his Negrohead, drinking his grog, watching them, loving them, talking to them, welcoming her into his home. Sometimes he called her Carolan. "That's my mother, you know. I'm Katharine." "Of course! Of course! I forgot. I used to know your mother once." And she had felt resentful towards Mamma, who, for no reason at all, had taken such a dislike to him, doubtless thinking him lacking in culture because he was not dabbling in politics, and did not attend the local functions, and was as different from Papa as it was possible for any man to be. Was Mamma perhaps a little snobbish? Her values were wrong surely since she tried to prevent her daughter's friendship with a man like Marcus. She knew that Mamma had come out on the transport ship; she could not help knowing. One of the girls at school told her; it was a great shock. It made her look upon convicts in a different way; at one time, she feared, she had thought them subhuman. "Are convicts real men and women?" Martin had once asked. She had been rather like Martin. But Mamma had been a convict, and Marcus and Esther. Convicts *were* ordinary people, and two of them—Marcus and Mamma—were among those she loved best in the world. So Mamma should not have been snobbish about Marcus. She felt a slight estrangement between herself and Mamma then, but afterwards when she drew from Margery the story of the First Wife, she warmed to Mamma again. Poor Mamma, a servant in this house where now she was mistress, and Papa unhappy with his first wife! What a different picture from the house as it was today, and how poor proud Mamma must have suffered! It was really a good thing when the First Wife died, and Papa discovered that he loved Mamma. Vaguely from a long way back she remembered a certain fear about the First Wife. What an inquisitive and imaginative little creature she must have been in those days! Probing; scenting mystery; drawing out Margery and Mamma and anyone who would respond in the smallest way! Then she had discovered Henry and Marcus, and the house with the veranda—and they filled her thoughts. She did not remember thinking very much about the first floor after that.

What would Mamma say if she knew she had been present at their musters! Papa too! But what a thrill to ride beside Henry! "You'd better keep close, young Katharine." That was Henry before he knew he loved her. "A bullock on the run can be pretty savage. Keep near me!" That moment when the bull dashed into the plain with the cattle at his heels—hundreds of them; she longed to join with them, with Marcus and Henry and Mr. Blake. She would one day. They would not let her at first; they said it was dangerous. She loved to hear the crack of the stock-whip, to see the skill with which they guided the cattle in the direction they must go. She was enormously proud of Henry. And then one day they let her join in, and it was after that that Henry gave her his first present, a stock-whip with a myall handle that smelt like violets.

She longed to stay at the station with them, to sit on the veranda with them till darkness came; to listen to the singing of the sheep-washers when their day's work was done, and to hear the talk of the knockabout men who came for the shearings or to do odd fencing jobs. She would have loved to come in after dark with Henry, just the two of them alone, and cook their own meals . . . beef steak or bacon, or perhaps, after a muster, a fat calf.

Marcus had promised them their own station when they were married. They could go to it now . . . if they were married. Marcus would put no objection in the way. It was possible to discuss all one's plans before Marcus. He never attempted to foil you; his suggestions were helpful, not destructive.

He said: "You'll be my daughter, Katharine. Fancy that! I wished you were my daughter right from the very first moment I saw you!"

He was a darling. If it would not have been so utterly disloyal to Papa—who really was the best father in the world—she would have told him she would have loved to have him for a father. A father-in-law was almost a father anyway. She flung her arms round his neck and kissed him when he told them about the station. He liked that . . . and yet, oddly enough it embarrassed him. He said: "Katharine, Katharine! My sweet little Katharine, I'd have given twenty stations for that." One didn't always believe all he said. That about giving twenty stations for a hug was just his way of telling you how pleased he was. Perhaps all of his stories weren't exactly true, but that didn't matter; he made them more exciting because he knew you liked them that way. He spoke her name oddly, slurring it, making it a mixture of Carolan and Katharine; there was a similarity between the two, and he had a curious way of rolling them into one. She loved him next to Henry and Mamma and Papa, and there really was no one like Marcus in the whole world.

Henry's mother she could never like, and she believed Henry's mother did not like her and did not really want Henry to marry her; Katharine believed she protested to both Henry and Marcus.

Not that anything would stop them. She and Henry were meant for each other; Henry was as sure of that as she was. When she had lain with her ear to the ground; when she had coo-eed over the bush, she had been on the threshold of a new life. Well, she knew that now! His dark eyes burned when he looked at her. He was eighteen. Papa would say: "Good gracious! How very young!" But Papa just did not understand.

She could recall—indeed she could never forget—the wonder of that day when Henry ceased to think of her as a little girl, and thought of her as Katharine. It was the day he had given her the stock-whip, and that gift represented more than the mere adventure of a muster shared; it was the adventure of finding each other. She was fourteen then. He was fifteen, but he seemed a good deal older; he had seemed a man when she first met him, and he had been little more than eleven then. They were shy at first, and Marcus knew why! He watched them with amused tenderness, and encouraged them to love each other.

She was sixteen when Henry said he loved her. It was there in that spot where he had first found her, and how deeply she had been touched by that sentiment which had led him to tell her there! They had lain on the harsh grass, and she had heard his heart beating, where once she had listened to the thud of his horse's hooves.

He talked of their life together, and she saw the station they would share; she loved the life he lived; it was the only life for such as they were. Fresh air, sunshine, and a new life beyond the Blue Mountains where the town of Bathurst was beginning to grow, and where the land was good, with grazing for millions of sheep.

So they talked and planned, and made love and dreamed of the life they would lead beyond the Blue Mountains.

Margery watched her and saw the dreams in her eyes, and whispered: "Tell Margery . . . Tell old Margery. Is it an elopement, ducky? You can trust old Margery."

452

Katharine shook herself out of her dreams, and shook old Margery by the shoulders.

"Stop it, Margery! Isn't it bad enough? How can I hurt them! I love them. How can I be happy . . . even there beyond the Blue Mountains with Henry . . . if they aren't happy too! How can I, Margery?"

"A new home, eh, t'other side the Blue Mountains? I don't like the sound of that, ducky. Why not nearer home?"

"Oh, Margery, don't be silly! We want to go there, and that's where the station is."

"The station! What station?"

"Our new home. Oh, Margery, you've no right to make me tell. It's a secret . . ."

"There, there, dearie! A station miles away . . . the other side of the Blue Mountains, eh?"

"It's wonderful land, Margery. Marcus . . . People say it was well worth all the trouble to discover. It's fine land. . . ."

"Two little 'uns like you two 'ull want a bit of looking after, lovey. What about taking old Margery along of you?"

"You wouldn't want to leave Mamma, Margery!"

"I might."

"You wouldn't, Margery . . . after all these years."

"There's things I ain't altogether pleased about in this house. I reckon it wants pulling down, and a fresh one built in a new place."

"Why, Margery? Why?"

"I feel like it. And how d'you think I'd be liking it, with you eloping off to the other side of the Blue Mountains?"

Katharine laughed and flung her arms round Margery's neck.

"Promise, not a word, Margery! Swear!"

"I swear!"

"Margery, if you were to break your word, I'd . . . I'd get somebody's ghost to haunt you for the rest of your days."

Margery shrieked and turned pale. Katharine laughed.

"Swear then, Margery. . . . Quick!"

"I swear," said the old woman.

"And, Margery?"

"Y . . . yes, Miss Katharine?"

"I'll see about it. We . . . we'll discuss it. I think it would be fun to have you around. I must go down now. Papa will frown if I am not there to help them receive the first of the guests."

She went to the door. Margery was still shaking; her face was the colour of cheese.

"Margery," she said, turning back, "do you believe this house is haunted?"

Margery did not speak.

"You do, Margery! I know you do, and I know by whom!"

"Don't speak of it, Miss Katharine! It's better not to. You don't know . . ."

"On the contrary, I do know!" She grimaced mockingly. "First Wife! That's it, isn't it?"

She went out, slamming the door.

Margery could not stop herself from trembling. Ah, she thought, my pretty dear, you think you're clever! You think you're smart. You laugh at ghosts, do you! Well, there's a lot you've got to learn, me dearie. You don't know what happened to the poor sickly lady. Margery looked furtively over her shoulder. "I was always fond of the poor lady," she said aloud, "fond of her and sorry for her." She paused, as though waiting for some response. There was none, and she continued musing, Oh yes, me fine lady, you ain't so clever! Ah, but when you're seventeen you think you know life; you think life is all living snug in a nice cattle station, and making love in the sunshine. Oh no, me darling, it ain't all that simple. And he's such another as his father, I'll be bound, from what I've seen. He'll like the women and the women will like him. Well, it's a different way you've chose from your lady mother, and I hope you'll be happy. And I'll be there . . . I'll keep you to that, me darling. I'll like to be there. I'll watch him for you, dearie, and then when you find love's young dream ain't as pretty as you thought, you'll have old Margery.

The candles were lighted in the drawing-room. It was bright with gay company, but how she longed for the shade of the veranda, and Henry, sitting close, leaning against one another whilst they talked of their home beyond the Blue Mountains!

Mamma was watching her closely, and there was that hideous Miss Grant watching Mamma as she was always watching her, slyly, as though she knew something, as though she had caught Mamma doing something wrong.

Instead of candles she saw tall eucalyptus trees; their barks shone bright silver in sunshine.

"Waiting is silly," Henry had said. "We can't wait, Katharine! I won't wait!"

Miss Grant sidled over.

"Why, Miss Katharine, how grown-up you're looking tonight! It seems only yesterday that you were but a little baby."

Poor Miss Grant! Homesick and angry, despising everything in the new country because of her nostalgia for the old. One imagined her coming over with her father, Major Grant, years and years ago. How dreary! Poor Miss Grant!

"Only yesterday!" she continued. "I remember well the day you were born."

"Do you? That is kind of you."

Mamma was looking anxious. Dear Mamma! How lovely she was, but strained tonight! She looked as if she were trying to catch what Miss Grant was saying.

"Kind! Oh, dear me no! The whole town was so interested . . ."

"In my being born? I suppose they were interested in all the babies."

"Not all, Miss Katharine. Not all! I said you were a very special baby."

"I'm sure I was most ordinary really."

Wouldn't it have been fun if Henry could have come tonight! She should have been bold and gone straight to Papa and Mamma and told them. Why should she not?

"You were a rather . . . shall we say a much-heralded little baby!"

What on earth was the facetious little woman talking about? She probably adored babies. People who were never likely to have any often did. She thought of herself and Henry having babies . . . lots of them. She smiled.

"Ah! You are amused. We did not think it exactly amusing!"

"I'm sorry," said Katharine. "What did you say?"

Mamma came over.

"Katharine, Lady Greymore wants to talk to you. Over there. She is waiting for you."

Lady Greymore said: "Hello, my dear! I must tell you that you look charming tonight . . . charming . . . La! How beautiful it is to be young! Your dress is most becoming. Come, tell me, was it your own choice? Or did Mamma help you? I'll whisper to you that you'll love the London gowns. They would make anything here look positively provincial!"

Katharine murmured that she was sure they would.

"And you, my dear, would be a great success in London. Of that I am certain. They would love you because you are *so* different. And when they heard that you had come from Botany Bay, they would be so amused! After all, it would be something of a joke."

"Why?" said Katharine.

"Why! Who in England has not heard of Botany Bay! But they do not expect lovely young girls to come out of the place, I assure you!"

"Doubtless they know little about it, and think they know a good deal!"

"La! What asperity! But it becomes you, child. . . . It becomes you. Here are the men coming back. And, ah! Anthony has seen you. He is coming over, dear boy."

He was very elegant; she was interested in his elegance; it was such a contrast to the manliness of the men she had known. Papa was always well dressed, always neat; but never, never had he aspired to elegance! As for Henry, she had never seen him in anything but riding kit, and a shirt open at the front. Marcus sometimes wore gay coats, but they were Sydney made and very sombre compared with this blue satin affair from London which Sir Anthony wore so carelessly, as though there were nothing very special about it. A faint perfume followed him as he moved. His snuff box was of silver and lapis lazuli, his eyeglass a pretty thing of light tortoiseshell. But he had pleasant eyes, very blue and warm too as they rested on Katharine. She liked him better than she liked his mother.

"Ah!" said Sir Anthony. "How I have looked forward to tonight!"

Lady Greymore moved away, leaving them together. He bent his head close to hers and he talked. He talked rather excitingly, in a way which recalled Marcus. He talked of the rich side of London life though, and it was that mingling of the rich and squalid that had made Marcus's descriptions so fascinating. He talked of gambling and balls, of the Regent growing fatter every day and indulging in amours with the grandmothers for whom he showed such preference. He gave her a picture of a spacious house in a London square, and lovely rooms that were really old as nothing in this country could be old; he showed her a picture of a gracious life, of entertaining clever people, of listening to and perhaps one day contributing to their wit. Politics and fashion, wonderful clothes which would be out of place in this settlement. It was a gay picture he showed her.

In the next room, which had been cleared for dancing, some musicians were playing Mr. Mozart's music. It was beautiful; she longed to dance; her feet tapped in time to the music.

"The dancing here," he said, "is years behind the times. In

London we have the new dances. . . . You will be enchanted by London, Miss Katharine."

"I do not think I shall go to London. Perhaps later. . . ." She smiled into a future. Henry, said Marcus, was made for prosperity; he was not content to ship his wool to London; he wanted to go there to hunt out the best markets. Henry said: "We shall go to London, you and I, and we shall see if it is as grand a place as they tell us." She pictured Henry and herself, walking hand in hand along the riverside; looking together at that frightful Newgate at whose name Mamma's face turned pale; visiting the chocolate houses; listening to the talk; riding about the town in a carriage. She had dreamed of London; but only with Henry by her side.

"Why should you not go to London?" He leaned so close that she could smell the wine on his breath; it mingled with the perfume in his clothes; she noticed his long white hands. One did not see such hands in this part of the world, idle hands, carefully manicured . . . women's hands! Her own were well shaped but burned brown by the sun, and the nails were short; useful little hands they were.

"Well, because my home is here."

"Why should your home always be here?" His hand was laid delicately on her arm, and she shivered though it was warm and caressing. "Would you not like to go to London? I shall be returning soon. I could take you . . ."

"Oh, no!" she said. "That could not be."

"Could it not, Katharine? It would be delightful . . ." His fingers ran up her arm. It seemed sacrilege that anyone but Henry should touch her. She shrank back.

"No, no!" she said. "You cannot mean . . ."

"I mean I will marry you, Katharine. I will take you back Home where you belong. You never belonged to this society of felons."

Hot blood ran into her cheeks. How dared he talk of her home like this! This stupid fop! What did he know of the men who had made this country! He talked of felons . . . slightingly, sneeringly. Marcus! Her own mother!

She said earnestly: "I would have you know that this country is being built by great men. They are pioneers. They came here to make a new land; my father is one of them." She had stood up. "Felons!" she said. "You talk of felons. Who was it who made these felons? Your England! Her wicked laws! Her cruelty! And she sent them here ingloriously, to fend for themselves . . . eleven ships, and five packed full with sick and starving men and women. England did that . . . and not yet forty years ago! And already here we have our own Sydney. It is young, but it will be great. We have crossed the Blue Mountains! New country is opened up. These men have had a hand in that . . . these felons, as you call them! And I would have you know that we are not all felons."

"Gad!" he said, amused and liking her fervour. "What a patriotic little soul it is! And, damme, it becomes you, Katharine. I'd like well to hear you make that speech in your own drawing-room."

"I mean it," she said, "and am I not making it here in my own drawing-room?"

"In your father's, my dear. Listen, Katharine. I'll go and tell your father now that you've promised to marry me. You need not look so frightened. I tell you, I have already spoken to him."

"You have spoken to my father!"

He came nearer, his lips close to her ear, his eyes burning.

"He is delighted to receive me as his son-in-law, my dear."

"But . . . I . . ."

"Ha! Ha! A spirited young lady, as I saw at once when I first made your acquaintance! Remember, Katharine? You were on horseback, and damme if I ever saw a woman cut a better figure. And you are sweet as honey, and lovely as a garden of English spring flowers! Damme, I can scarce wait to take you back!"

"I am not coming."

He rocked back on his heels. A very self-opinionated young man. He did not believe that any Sydney-born young woman, with parents who, though among the wealthiest in the town, were for some reason not so well received even in Sydney society as they might have been, could really say No to him. She was a coquette then, for all her frank looks. She wanted wooing, did she! Damme, he was ready enough to do the wooing.

He put his hands on her shoulders.

"You are coming. my love," he said. "I'm in love with you. You shall be my wife. I mean it!"

"No!" she said.

Margery was standing in the doorway, open-mouthed.

"Pray excuse me," said Katharine coldly, and went over to Margery. He stood, staring after her, fumbling for his eyeglass and his dignity.

Margery said: "Lor'!" and drew her into the passage, on the other side of which was the open door through which came the sound of music and laughter. "Come . . . quickly,'

458

said Margery in a hoarse whisper. "If your Ma was to know . . ."

Henry was in the kitchen. Katharine ran to him, and they clung together, kissing.

"How beautiful you are!" said Henry.

She laughed almost hysterically; Henry in lamplight was such a contrast to Sir Anthony, satin-coated in candlelight. She took his hand and kissed it. She found it difficult to stop kissing it.

Henry touched her white shoulder wonderingly; then the lace and the soft material of her gown.

"You are so beautiful," he repeated. "You are so beautiful!"

She said: "It is the dress. I would rather be in my riding kit, on the veranda with you."

He kissed her and they looked at each other incredulously as though they could not wholly believe in the existence of each other.

"Why did you come?" she asked breathlessly.

"I thought of you in there . . . dancing . . . being so beautiful that every man must love you."

"Stupid!" she said, and they kissed again, and his hands caressed her bare shoulders.

Margery was crying in the corner. The beauty of it! The beauty! Oh, to be young . . . seventeen and eighteen, and to believe love went on for ever! The lovely children . . . and me lord in there making love to her and wanting to marry her, and her wanting the other! Poor little soul! Funny listening to their lovers' talk. It didn't mean anything but "I want you! I want you!" They thought it did though, poor little innocents. You can't go on wanting for ever though, and what's a station beyond the Blue Mountains compared with a grand house in London Town! Muck and squalor, gaudy lights, and the poor and the beggars, and the lords and ladies. London! I hate you. London, I love you! Why is it, when you think of London, you get a pain inside you that nothing could ease but a sight of the wicked old city? If you was wise, me lady, you'd choose London Town. But love and wisdom never was two to go hand in hand. Your lady mother's right, and so is the master, and what are they going to do about it, eh? And who's going to win . . . you, me darling, and your rampaging lover, or wise Mamma who knows more than she'd like you to think she knows and your Papa who was born wise? And here's old Margery, watching and taking a hand. Who let him into her kitchen, eh? Who gives him bits of gossip, eh? It's nice to know you've got a hand in things . . . when you're old and there's nothing much left to you but a glass of grog at the kitchen table.

He stroked Katharine's shoulders and stooped and kissed them; he murmured again and again that she was beautiful and that he had forgotten how beautiful; and neither of them gave a thought to old Margery standing there, watching them with glistening eyes.

The door opened and Carolan came in, her eyes flashing fire, but behind the fire was fear for this daughter whom she loved better than anything in the world.

"Katharine!" she said, and Katharine swung round, all defiance, ready for the fight.

"It is time you and Henry met, Mamma."

"Henry?" said Carolan coldly.

Henry bowed.

Ah! thought Margery. He's not got the manners of the gentleman in the blue satin coat, but he's got some sort of charm, and you can see with half an eye where he gets that!

"Henry Jedborough," said Katharine, in a dignified manner. "We are going to be married."

Carolan turned pale.

She said: "This is rather sudden, is it not?" And her eyes, as they rested on the young man, were like cold green emeralds.

"No," said Henry, jauntily. "Katharine and I arranged it some time ago. We are tired of waiting."

"Yes, Mamma," said Katharine, "that is right."

"I do not recollect your having asked my permission to propose marriage to my daughter, sir. But perhaps you have spoken to her father?"

"No!" he said, hating her because he knew she meant "Who is this crude unmannerly creature who ignores all the rules laid down by decent society?" "We thought," he added, "that it was a matter for us to decide."

I know why she hates him so, thought Margery. In this light, where you can't notice the difference so much, he's the living image of his father.

"Katharine," said Carolan, ignoring him, "it was very ill-mannered of you to leave your guests. Go back at once!"

"Mamma!"

"Go back at once!"

"Mamma, please understand . . ."

"My dear child, this is not the time to conduct a ridiculous

460

cene. Mr. . . . Mr. . . . your friend can call upon your father omorrow. I must really ask him to go now."

Henry bowed. He had his dignity. He said: "Goodbye, my arling." And then, defiantly: "I shall see you tomorrow." And there in front of Carolan and Margery he took her into is arms and kissed her several times right on the mouth. She was quivering with desire for him in spite of the scene that ad just taken place, in spite of the spectators. That was how was when you were young, thought Margery. Love wamped everything; when young lovers kissed, they forgot veryone else. Ah! That was how it was when you were oung.

He said: "Darling, promise me. Don't let them . . ."

"No, no, no!" she cried.

"They will try . . ."

"They will not succeed."

"Remember . . . the station . . . the two of us . . . beyond ne Blue Mountains . . ."

"The two of us," she said, "darling, beyond the Blue Moun-ains."

He kissed her hands—he could not tear himself away.

Carolan was stamping her foot in fury.

When he had gone she looked coldly at her daughter.

"Go upstairs at once," she said. "People are wondering hat has happened to you. I am ashamed . . ."

Katharine was ready to obey. She loved her mother very early, for indeed they were much alike, those two, and they ad been very close until this Henry came. She went slowly ack to the music and the guests, but she had a remote look in er eyes for her thoughts were with Henry galloping home nder the stars.

Carolan turned on Margery.

"You arranged that meeting, did you? Did you?"

"Now, now," said Margery. "What's all the excitement? If young gent comes knocking on my door and asks for Miss atharine, what should I do but ask him in?"

Carolan, as always, was indiscreet when angry.

"I believed you arranged it, you wicked woman!"

"Here!" said Margery truculently, for, as she told herself, ne was all on Miss Katharine's side, love being love and the uff that makes the world go round. And, she reasoned, it's rd when someone who was as ready to love as most, forgets She thought: I don't like this house. There's ghosts in this ouse. I'd like to go with them two young ones, that I would.

461

My goodness, there'll be some fireworks there. She ain't going to lose her lover like you did, Madam Carolan! He ain't going to let that happen. Perhaps children is wiser than their parents, because, if they wasn't, how would things get moving on at all? I'm for the young ones . . . whatever you say. And she's promised I'm to go with them and he won't say no. I'm his friend. Haven't I shown him I'm on his side! And he's his father all over again and don't mind handing out a bit of flattery even to an old woman. He's made that way, and my little lady will want someone to look after her, I'm thinking. That's my home with them, on the other side of the Blue Mountains, so I ain't afraid of you, Madam Carolan, that I ain't! And I knows too much about you to pretend I am!

Carolan was looking at her arrogantly.

"I said that you probably arranged it. You let him in. You doubtless suggested he should come in. You meddling old woman!"

Margery felt sorry for her. If you know human nature, she was thinking, you know what's behind words. What she means was—"You meddled in my life!" And that boy was the dead spit of his father, and she was thinking back years and years and wanting his father, never having forgotten him, never having forgotten how, through her own pride, she had lost him.

Then Margery was angry with her, for she reasoned, had not Madam Carolan seen what interfering could do, and yet she wanted to interfere with them two lovely young things, wanted to tear them apart when they were yearning for one another, wanted to thrust the little dear into a pair of blue satin arms just because there was a grand title and money there!

"I believe in helping young lovers!" said Margery boldly. "And Madam, I'll tell you here and now, it ain't for you to go criticising what I might do."

That started Carolan; her lips quivered with anger.

"You are insolent," she said.

"Oh, Madam," said Margery, seeing herself safe in that station with her two young lovers, "have you forgotten what it's like to be in love? It ain't so long ago since . . ."

"Insolence!" cried Carolan, her eyes flashing with rage.

"Ah! Now you're like the poor shivering mite you was when you first came into my kitchen. Head full of plans, that was you. And the way you treated that poor boy's father, and the way you went to the master, and then . . . and then . . .

462

Margery could not say it. But she lifted her eyes upwards to the first floor, and there was terror in Margery's eyes, and the terror communicated itself to Carolan, for her pride collapsed before her fear. She was as superstitious as Margery.

Margery thought afterwards that something icy touched her, and even when she found that Henry had left the door open she still thought it must have been that poor sickly lady's ghost.

Carolan recovered herself.

"That will do!" she cried, and she turned and walked slowly back to her guests. Yes, there were ghosts in the house. Whatever your idea of ghosts, they were there.

Margery came up the stairs and knocked at the bedroom door. If the master was there she would make some excuse. He was not there.

Carolan was in front of her mirror fixing a lace collar on her gown; Audrey was hanging clothes in a cupboard.

Carolan looked up; her eyes smouldered as she was remembering last night's scene with Margery. "Yes?" she said coldly.

Margery sidled over and turned her back to Audrey. She said in a soft voice: "It is a letter that was brought for you."

She held out an envelope across which was scrawled "Mrs. Masterman". Carolan took it.

"It was brought to me kitchen this morning."

How long ago? wondered Carolan. Had Margery found some means of opening it and read it?

"The kitchen?" said Carolan casually. "That's an odd place to deliver a letter. All right, Margery. Thank you."

As soon as Margery had gone, Carolan tore open the letter.

"Dear Mrs. Masterman," she read. "Would you be so good as to grant me an interview? I think there is much to be discussed concerning our children. Perhaps Katharine would tell you where she was once lost and where Henry found her. Those two young people have made that spot their meeting place; could we make it ours? I shall be there this afternoon at four o'clock. If you are not there this afternoon, I will be there tomorrow, because I hope so much that I shall see you. William Henry Jedborough."

She crumpled the letter. How like him! What insolence! He had determined that Katharine should not marry Henry

463

Jedborough; what good did Marcus think he could do by this meeting? Did he think he could be so persuasive? He was ever one to over-rate his powers.

She had not seen him since that day he had ridden in with Katharine. She had said she hoped she would never see him again. This marriage was impossible. How could the two families unite! Esther and Marcus! What memories! At all costs Katharine must not be allowed to marry Henry.

She shivered, thinking of last night's scene in the kitchen, with that insolent Margery almost blackmailing her, and Katharine going back to the guests and acting as though she were a being from another world, until one wanted to slap her. But Anthony Greymore seemed to have found that will-o'-the-wisp mood attractive. Oh, Katharine, you little fool with your romantic ideas of love and life! Here is position, wealth, security . . . and you would throw all that away for a station in a wild country where bushrangers might deal death to you and your family one dark night. You want love, you say; Sir Anthony loves you, and you, foolish child, ought to know that it is wiser to accept love than to give it. And your Henry, what of him? He is his father all over again. How long will his love stay warm for you, my dear?

Oh no, this folly must be stopped; because I love you, Katharine, better than I love anyone else in the world. It is not because I cannot bear to meet Marcus that I want to stop this marriage; it is not because I hate Henry's mother for taking Marcus from me; it is for your sake, my dear . . . for your sake only.

She tore the note into many pieces. I wonder what he is like now. He will be over forty, past his prime. I am thirty-six. What years and years ago since I first saw him, and he stole my handkerchief! Thief! Rogue! Philanderer!

She thought of him in his room at Newgate, she standing at his shoulder while he fed her with pieces of chicken. She remembered the proposal he had made then. She thought of Lucy's looking in at the door, and Clementine Smith on the boat, and she was as angry with these two as she had been when she had discovered his relationship to them.

In the glass Mrs. Masterman looked back at her, smooth-faced, well-preserved, a lady of dignity; behind the mask of Mrs. Masterman, Carolan Haredon peeped out. Carolan Haredon was still there in spite of Mrs. Masterman.

She saw Audrey's reflection in the glass.

The girl's face was placid, a mask as concealing as the mask she herself wore.

"Audrey," she said on impulse, and the girl came swiftly to her.

"Audrey, I have often wondered what brought you here. Forgive me, Audrey, and do not answer if you prefer not to. It may be that you do not wish to speak of terrible things."

Audrey's grey eyes filled with tears.

"You are so kind, Madam."

"Kind!" Carolan laughed at herself in the glass. Not kind, no! Selfish, and sometimes cruel and scheming and . . .

"I wouldn't have believed anyone could be kind like you are," said Audrey. "Not if it hadn't been for her. She talked to me . . . she talked to me special, she did. She said, 'Never despair, Audrey . . . Life can't be all cruel,' she said. 'That wouldn't be human nature. There's good and bad, bad and good. Look for the good, Audrey!' She spoke to me special."

"Audrey, you were at Newgate?"

Audrey nodded. She began to shiver. Carolan shivered too. The memory was such as to make one shiver after nearly twenty years.

"Tell me, Audrey . . . Tell me . . ."

The story came out by degrees. It was an ordinary enough story; Carolan had heard many like it in Newgate, and on the convict ship. The daughter of unknown parents, left on the doorstep of a lodging-house, where she was taken in because she might be useful; five years old, scrubbing floors, seven years old a fully fledged drudge; blows and curses; learning to steal, food first, then other things; then running away and eventually ending up in Mother Somebody-or-other's kitchen. The usual story of crime and violence. An innocent child turned into a criminal by a brutal system. She had been in the bridewell; she met people in the bridewell who said they would help her when she came out. They did help her—to go lower.

Carolan was fascinated by the expressions which crept over the girl's face as she talked. Depravity, cunning, lewdness . . . another Audrey posed before her. Her placidity was a veil which she lifted, and something horrible peeped out.

"And finally Newgate?" said Carolan, for she wished she had not started this.

Carolan had a picture of the girl's facing that crowd of wild beasts. She thought of Esther, naked before them, of Kitty's going down, of herself and poor Millie bloody with battle. But this girl would have been prepared; she would have been one of them. She would be no innocent when she went to Newgate.

465

Audrey covered her face with her hands.

Carolan said: "And you drove from Newgate to the ship. It was horrible. My poor Audrey! Perhaps the most horrible . . . because free people laughed at you and did not care. But do not think of it any more; it is too depressing."

Audrey uncovered her face, and the veil of placidity was drawn over it again.

"We drove in a closed carriage. She said we must . . ." Audrey was herself now, the quiet, discreet maid.

"Who said it?" asked Carolan.

"She did."

And Audrey told the incredible story about a lady who must surely be an angel. Carolan had not suspected Audrey of lying before.

"She walked in one day," said Audrey. "The turnkey opened the door and he said: 'Lady, you go in at your own risk. There's wild beasts in there!' And she walked in . . . like an angel with the most beautiful smile you ever saw in your life, M'am. And she picked up one of the children, and he hadn't got no clothes on at all, M'am, and his face was half eaten away with sores, and she picked him up like she was his mother. And she was beautiful, M'am, though not as you're beautiful. But beautiful different, M'am . . . beautiful like an angel would be . . ."

Audrey was romancing. If you had spent horrible weeks in Newgate, you knew it was no place to harbour angels. The poor child had had an hallucination.

"Audrey, finish your work and leave me. I wish to be alone."

She picked up the fragments of Marcus's letter. What impudence! Of course I shall not meet you. And what would you do if I did? You would flatter; you would tell me you had never forgotten me, doubtless. You would . . .

She tried to still the absurd fluttering of her heart. It was not Marcus of whom she was thinking, she assured herself, but of that absurd flight of fancy of her maid. Newgate did something to you, turned the brain. If you stayed there too long, doubtless you would suffer from hallucinations.

A lady . . . like an angel. She walked into that den of savages and she picked up one of the babies, naked, with his face half eaten away with some disease. Surely an angel . . .

"Audrey!"

Audrey came over and stood before her.

"Who told you this story of a lady who was an angel?"

"I see it . . . I see it myself, M'am! He says to her: 'Lady,

466

you go in at your own risk,' he says, and she walks in. And her skirt rustled like an angel's wings, and we was all afraid of her and somehow glad. And she picks up one of the babies . . ."

"Did anyone else see this . . . vision?"

"But M'am, they all see. They was all there . . . She wasn't no vision, M'am. She was Mrs. Fry!"

"I have never heard of Mrs. Fry," said Carolan.

"You will, Ma'am! The lady . . . another what come . . . said you will. She come and read to us sometimes . . . and then there was the needlework, and she said: 'One day everybody will know about Mrs. Fry, know what she's done for you poor souls.' "

Why should one waste one's time talking to a crazy maid! She slipped the torn pieces of paper into her pocket. I shall not go. Of course I shall not go!

Katharine was missing all day. She was with her lover of course. Carolan was tired and weary. She retired early and gave instructions that Miss Katharine was to come to her when she returned.

Katharine was sullen, already defiant, ready to forget the care of years for the sake of Marcus's son.

"I wonder you're not ashamed, chasing all over the countryside after that young man!"

"I am not ashamed, and do not chase after him. We met."

"What do you think Sir Anthony will say if he hears?"

"I do not know, and I do not care!"

"You are a stupid girl, Katharine. Have you thought of what Sir Anthony is offering you?"

"Oh, Mamma! As if I wanted to be offered anything! Do not be so dreadfully behind the times. I suppose, before you married Papa, you decided it was right and proper that you should, and everything was just as it should be. People aren't like that . . . so much . . . nowadays, thank heaven!"

Carolan's face was hot with shame. It was almost as though Lucille Masterman was in the room, laughing at her. All right and proper! That was funny. If Katharine knew it. And it was all for her I did it! Oh no, Carolan, for yourself as well. No, for my child; I could not have my child born without a name. I did all that for her, and see how she repays me? She deceives me, she flouts my authority! She is threatening to run away with a boy who will never be any good to her, because he is his father's son. And Marcus and I will be related in some ridiculous way, and I shall have to see him, and . . . and . . . It was for her I did it—this ungrateful girl, this wayward

467

daughter. If she marries Henry Jedborough, it is the end of peace. It is Marcus coming back into my life. She must not marry Henry!

"You cannot marry without our consent," said Carolan coldly, "and I assure you you will never have it."

"Do you imagine you can keep us apart?"

How like me she is! How her eyes flash! This is Carolan again, with her first love, Everard.

"We shall refuse our consent, your father and I."

"My father would give it if you would. He would help us, I know."

"Your father is all in favour of your marriage to Sir Anthony."

"But you could make him in favour of my marriage with Henry."

"As if I would! You are a stupid child. You know nothing of the world."

"Does one need to know the world in order to know whom one wants to marry? You will be telling me next that unless one has been in England one cannot pick one's mate!"

"Don't be so stupid, Katharine!"

"It is you who are stupid, Mamma."

"My head aches. You are grieving me very much. When I think of all I have done for you. . . .!" The old plaint of the defeated mother, she thought, fighting for that place in her child's affection which is lost to a lover.

"Oh, Mamma, please! I did not ask to come into the world, did I?"

No, she did not. It was I who wanted her; it was I who used her before she was born, to get what I wanted.

"Katharine, you know how deeply your father and I feel about this. Cannot you realise that we know better than you do?"

"No, Mamma, you do not know better. It is for each person to manage his own life, surely. Because you made a good job of yours, it doesn't follow that you can make a good job of mine. Mamma, I do not want to go on deceiving you."

"Oh no? You did that very successfully, for how many years?"

"Only because it was necessary. Please give your consent to our marriage, Mamma . . . darling Mamma! We have loved each other so much, you and Papa and all of us. I am going to marry Henry; let us be happy about it."

"My dear child, you talk romantic nonsense. It is your happiness we think of. You know how that boy has been brought up. You know what his father is—a convict!"

"Mamma!"

"I was different, I tell you! It was a mistake. Good gracious, child, do you believe your own mother to be a felon?"

"No, no, Mamma! Dearest Mamma . . ."

"It is very different with him. He was a thief. He was here before. He escaped and was sent back again. I know his record."

"His record, Mamma, is his affair. It is Henry I propose to marry."

"But he is Henry's father!"

"Mamma, if you had done something terrible, you would not expect people to blame *me!*"

What did she mean? What did she know? It was that wicked old Margery? Did *she* feel ghosts in this house?

"Oh, Mamma, I know you will be reasonable. You won't blame Henry because of what his father did?"

"I will never give my consent to your marriage with that boy."

"You must know that we shall never give each other up."

"I should advise you not to do anything rash. You are our daughter; you are seventeen years old; your father could have him sent to prison for abducting you."

"Oh, Mamma, you could not be so cruel, so . . . so wicked!"

"There are many things I would do if I were driven to them . . ."

"Mamma, you frighten me."

"Ridiculous child! Why should I frighten you?"

"You must not be cruel to Henry, Mamma!"

"I hope you will be sensible, darling. You have no notion of how exciting life in London can be, if you have money and position. Suppose your father insisted on your marriage to Sir Anthony! You would be grateful to him to the end of your days."

"If Papa knew how unhappy I should be, married to Sir Anthony, he would never force me to it . . . unless you insisted."

"My dear child, do not stare at me like that."

"You look different . . ."

"Stupid! Well, leave me now. It is for your father to decide."

"No, Mamma, it is you who decide. You could persuade him, and I know he would want me to be happy. You could tell him how there is one way of making me happy."

"You are stubborn, Katharine. Go to your room. My head aches. Think of what I have said to you. Think of what will be best for us all."

Katharine went to the door. She looked dazed, as though she were seeing Henry dragged from her. Van Diemen's Land! It's hell on earth, and hell on earth is surely as bad as hell in hell!

"Audrey!" Carolan called, when Katharine had gone. "My head aches. Sprinkle a little perfume on a handkerchief, and lay it across my forehead."

Audrey gently did so.

"Thank you, Audrey."

Sleepily she smiled, and thought of Gunnar, the cold man whom it was so easy to rouse to sudden passion, even now. Queer faithful Gunnar! She had chosen him and the house with its comforts. She had turned away from the station, back of beyond, and quick hates and quicker love. And she did not know now whether she had chosen the right way. No way is right—perhaps that is the answer. Here she was, a beauty at thirty-six; she did not eat recklessly of the sweets of life, as poor Kitty had done; she was plump, but not over-fat. How would she have grown in the station? A slattern? That wild life would make demands on a woman, take toll of her beauty. And Marcus ever had a roving eye. He would never have been true, and she would have hated him for that, and perhaps she would not have been true either, for she was hot-tempered and impulsive, and would have wanted to pay him back in his own coin.

How should you know which was the right road for you—and no road was sunshine all the way!

But she wanted so desperately to have done something fine with her life. She was full of memories tonight. There was something Esther once said about her being a pioneer; and she had answered that she would have liked to have been the Good Samaritan, but she greatly feared that she would have passed by on the other side of the road. It was only when she fell among thieves that she cared about other victims.

And yet a woman had walked into that den of savages, and she had smiled, and her smile was the smile of an angel, and her dress rustled like the wings of an angel, and she picked up a naked child, suffering from some hideous disease. Without fear she had done these things, and only a saint could go among those caged beasts and be without fear. What power had she?

"Audrey! Audrey! Come here."

Audrey came and stood by the bed.

"Bring a chair, Audrey, and sit down. I would hear more of this Mrs. Fry."

Audrey kept telling the story of her coming. It was like a miracle. Dead silence, and her standing there. An angel. And she picked up the little child. And he was naked and his face half eaten away . . . Only those who had lived in Newgate could understand that that was a miracle. Carolan, her face pressed against her pillow, saw it clearly, as though she had been there when it happened.

Audrey stumbled over her words, but she gave a picture of a changing Newgate. People who were taken in now did not suffer quite so intensely, as Carolan had suffered. Change had been worked by an angel in a Quaker gown. Audrey talked of the readings, of the sewing; how it was possible to earn money while you were in Newgate. There had been the visitation of this angel, and she had spread her wings over the prison and given her loving care to those sad people.

"Tell me about her! Tell me about her! What does she look like?"

"I couldn't say . . . She's different . . . M'am. That's all you know . . ."

"Different? Different from me? Different from you?"

"She makes you feel you ain't all bad, M'am. She makes you feel you might have a chance."

A chance? A chance?

"What sort of chance?"

"I dunno. Just a chance . . . that's how she makes you feel. She's different."

"Is she beautiful?"

"Not like you, M'am. Not that sort of beautiful. She's different . . . I dunno. She makes you feel you've got a chance."

"Why did you not tell me about her before?"

"I dunno, M'am. You didn't ask. She come to us, M'am, when we was waiting on the ship, to sail, and she talked to us . . . she talked lovely."

"What did she say?"

"I dunno. She made you feel you wasn't all bad. She made you feel you'd got a chance . . . And it was 'cos of her we'd come down closed, they said. She wanted us closed in. She said it ought to be . . ."

Carolan said: "Leave me now, Audrey. I want to sleep. I have a headache." And Audrey went.

It was all coming back vividly. The arrival in Newgate, the fight, the talk, the smell, the ride to Portsmouth. Mamma,

Millie, Esther—so young and pure, praying in that foul place —and the whale-oil lamp flickering in the opening high in the wall. The ship. The deck. Hot morning, and coloured birds of brilliant plumage, and the horrible man with the eyeglass, and Gunnar . . .

What was the good of having lived! I wanted to be a saint. I wanted to be like Mrs. Fry. I would have gone there; I would have been unafraid. I would have picked up the little child. I . . . I . . . I could have made them feel there was still a chance. But what have I done with my life? What indeed!

She began to shiver. "You should have been a pioneer. You could have been, Carolan!" No, Esther, no! I should have passed by on the other side of the road.

But I wasn't all bad. I should have been a good wife to Everard. I should have cared for the poor and I should have understood their troubles and helped them. Perhaps if I had married Everard I should have been different. I might have been good—not wicked. I might even have been like you, Mrs. Fry.

"Marcus!" she cried.

He leaped from his saddle and tied his horse to the tree. She noticed his hands; they were brown with the weather.

He said: "I knew you would come!" with all the old confidence, and as though years had not passed since their last meeting. "Carolan! Carolan! Why, you have scarcely changed at all!"

"Rubbish!" she said. "I am years older. I am the mother of six children."

"Well, Carolan, Carolan!"

She remembered his old habit of repeating her name; it still had power to move her.

"This is a great day in my life!"

The old flattery that meant nothing. He would flatter old Margery just because he could not help flattering women.

"Are you glad to see me, Carolan? Do you find me changed?"

He had come forward; he had taken her hands; his eyes were older, with experience, with weather; but the charm persisted.

"Naturally! Since I have come a fair ride to see you. But we did not come to talk of ourselves."

"Did we not?" He was still holding her hands. "Not such an uninteresting subject! Carolan, how has life been treating you, Carolan?"

"Very well, thanks. You too, I think."

"Very badly, Carolan, since I lost you."

"Oh, Marcus, you are too old for that sort of talk, and I am too wise to listen to it. It is of our children that we must talk."

"My Henry," he said, "and your Katharine. What a sly old joker life is, Carolan! Would you have believed eighteen years ago, when we looked forward to our happiness, that one day we should meet in this wild spot to discuss the marriage of my son to your daughter?"

She was determined not to fall into that reckless mood which he was trying to draw round her like a web. She felt strong in her pride and her dignity and her knowledge that she was Mrs. Masterman of Sydney.

"It certainly does seem ironical, but as it happens to be a fact, shall we say what we came to say? Why did you want to see me?"

"To beg you to put no obstacles in our children's way, Carolan. They are so young, and the young are so lovely, so helpless. It would be unbearable if they too were to lose their happiness. Could history repeat itself so cruelly? We must prevent that happening."

"You are still the same," she said, angry without quite knowing why. "You talk, and your words must not be taken seriously. You are suggesting, of course, that we lost our happiness; we did not. We are both well pleased with ourselves."

"You found perfect happiness, Carolan?"

"Oh, let us stop this absurd, sentimental talk! Who ever found perfect happiness yet?"

"But if you cannot find it, Carolan, it is something to think you see it in your future. I thought that, Carolan, eighteen years ago in old Margery's kitchen."

"When you decided to marry Esther? How is Esther?"

Real pain seemed to come into his eyes, but of course he was an adept at endowing each mood with a semblance of truth.

"No," he said, "not then! It was when I thought I should marry you. Oh, Carolan, Carolan, what a witch you were! You bewitched me. I had to obey you. I dreamed of you all day and all night. I believe I never stopped dreaming of you."

She looked beyond him to the mountains. She thought of them as Katharine's mountains, because Katharine had loved to talk of them when she was a little girl.

"Listen, Marcus," she said. "I love my daughter, more than anyone in the world, I love her, and I am very unhappy because she is angry with me. She is going away from me. If she were your daughter, would you not want the best possible for her?"

"Indeed I would, Carolan."

"Well, understand this. There is a man who would marry her. He has everything—money, position. He is kind and tolerant, and, I think, very much in love with her. He can take her to England; he can make her happy. But she is obsessed, and it is your son who has obsessed her. She sees no happiness but with him, and I will not have my daughter spoil her life!"

"Spoil her life, Carolan!" he said earnestly. "Why should she spoil her life?"

"You know the life as well as I do. What is it, for a woman? She would have to live in the wilds; she will meet scarcely anyone. I can see her in London, sparkling—for she has a merry wit of her own; I can see her a dazzling beauty, for she is only budding and will bloom gloriously. London is her proper setting. Money . . . Position . . . that is what I want for my daughter. How do we know what will happen here? This is a new country. I have heard stories of the terrible things that can happen on lonely stations. Men are more desperate here; laws are less rigid. No, no! She would very soon forget your son. Oh, I imagine he is very like you were once; I imagine he knows how to charm a young girl. He will hurt her, I know he will . . . as you hurt me, as you must have hurt Esther and your Lucy and Clementine Smith and God knows who else. I want her to have security. Who knows better than I what can happen to a woman who is unprotected and . . ."

"Carolan, Carolan, where is your good sense? She will be secure enough with Henry. He will love her, I promise you. He will look after her."

She was emotional; it was not so much of Katharine that she was thinking, but of herself and Marcus, and tears of self-pity welled into her eyes, for his charm was potent as ever. And she thought of the years immediately behind her, and the ghost that had haunted her for eighteen years—and of what wild, free happiness might have been hers for the taking.

He came to her and slipped his arm about her. He had seen the tears in her eyes.

"Carolan," he said, "we are still young."

She spun round to look at him, and he threw back his head and laughed. "Carolan, Carolan! I am just past forty. Is that so very old? You are thirty-six—surely in your prime. Carolan, look at those mountains! Are they not beautiful? Do you feel them beckoning you? They are wild, they promise adven-

474

ture; there is new country beyond them. Carolan, Carolan, why should you go back to Sydney? Why should you, why should you, my darling? This is linking up, my dear, linking up with eighteen years ago. You are mine, and I am yours . . . that was how it was then; that is how it is now. That cannot change."

"Marcus!" she said. "Marcus!"

He caught her to him and kissed her; she kissed him wonderingly.

"It is strange," she said, "to feel young again. It is years since I felt young." She had lost control for a moment, but she was resolved it should be for no more than a moment. She wanted to recapture that feeling of recklessness, she wanted to know again what it meant to love without thinking . . . just to love. She had had that moment; she would remember now.

"That is all," she said.

He shook his head.

"Carolan, come away with me. Why should we not? You would have come with me . . . once."

"Once!" she said. "But so much has happened since then."

"A moment ago," he said, "I thought you were still my sweet and beautiful Carolan whom I loved in your father's shop, and in Newgate, and on the ship and in Margery's kitchen. You broke my heart when you went to him."

"And you mine when you went to her!"

"It was nothing, Carolan. Did you love him?"

"I am fond of him," she said.

He kissed her angrily. "Why did you spoil our lives?"

"It was you who spoiled our lives, Marcus."

"No, it was you . . . you with your conventional ideas."

"It was you with your philandering, your lies, your cheating . . . How do I know that even now you are not cheating! You may be laughing—'Oh, this is funny! I am amusing myself with Mrs. Masterman of Sydney!' "

"Do not speak his name."

"It is my name I speak."

"You are Carolan, nothing but Carolan! Why do I love your daughter? Because she is so like you! Why was my life brighter when she came and sat on the veranda and talked to my boy, Henry? Because she is so like her mother."

"Why do you always say the things I most want to hear?"

"Because I love you."

"Oh, Marcus, it is too late to talk of love."

"It is never too late to talk of love. Carolan, never go back to Sydney! We will go to England . . . to London. It will be a different London from that wicked city in which we met. We will conquer it this time, Carolan."

"It is too late. Do you think I would leave my children and my husband?"

"If I had twenty children I would leave them for you!"

"Please, Marcus, do not talk of it any more."

"If I talk enough you will understand how it is we cannot throw away this chance of happiness."

"There is no chance, Marcus. We lost our chance eighteen years ago."

"My darling, while there are boats to carry us away from this place, there is still a chance."

"I would never leave my family."

"I am your family. I am your home. You are mine and I am yours. You must understand that."

"But Marcus, people change in eighteen years. I have changed."

He kissed her; he held her against him and he laughed with joy.

"You have not changed; you are my own sweet Carolan. You will never go back. Always I have vowed that if I could talk to you, if I could but hold you like this, I would never, never let you go again. I am no longer young, Carolan, I am old in wisdom. Never shall I let you go again, my darling. I will keep you by my side always. You are my comfort, my love, my darling!"

"I should not have come," she said sadly. "I am only making you unhappy, and myself unhappy. I was resigned. I will never, never leave my husband—I have sworn that, Marcus."

"What oaths you have sworn for nothing, darling. You are mine—you cannot deny that!"

"These oaths I have sworn in the dead of night, when I wake up trembling, or when I have been unable to sleep. I have sworn, Marcus. He lies there beside me; sometimes he is sleepless too, and I wonder what he is thinking. I have said 'I will never leave you, Gunnar. I will do all I can to make you happy.' It is because of that . . . because of what happened, Marcus. I have never told anyone, but I will tell you now because I owe it to you, Marcus. I must tell you why I cannot go away with you. How I long to! I cannot pretend any more; I have always loved you. I could have killed you and Esther . . . but there is no one but myself to blame; how well I know that now! Listen, Marcus. I am a murderess. That is why I cannot go. Did you ever hear talk in Sydney? Did you hear how Lucille Masterman died? I was to have his child, Marcus, and I was alone and afraid, and I was brutalised; Newgate did that to me—or so I tell myself! Perhaps it is just an excuse; perhaps if you are strong, nothing can maim you.

"She used to take a drug, Marcus. I knew about it; so did Gunnar. I used to think it would be so easy for her to take an overdose. She did not want to live; I did . . . desperately. I wanted a good life for my child. How do we know what motives prompt our actions? I tell myself I did it for my child; but did I? Did I do it for myself? He was so kind to me; he said I should go away to discreet and sympathetic people, but I laughed at that; I laughed it to scorn. No! I said, *you* must marry me; we must have a real home for my child, or I shall marry someone else. You remember Tom Blake would have married me then. Gunnar loved me; loved me as you would not believe he could love anybody; he wanted children, and she had cheated him. Marcus, do not look at me like that! Put your arms around me, hold me tight. She has haunted me since; she will go on haunting me. Sometimes I feel she will drive me mad. She was so weak, Marcus, and she did not greatly want to live. You see, the bottle was there; it should have been so easy. She had bought the stuff from an ex-convict who dealt in illicit medicines. She used to drug herself to get some sleep. She always imagined herself ill. And I think she knew how it was with me; I did my best to tell her . . . without doing it in so many words. I put the idea in her head that it would be so easy . . . just an extra dose, and then she would sink into that deep peaceful sleep of which she had talked to me."

Marcus took her by the shoulders, and looked into her eyes.

"Carolan, you . . . you killed her!"

She threw back her head.

"Yes," she cried, "I killed her! I killed her! No, no! I did not pour it out into the glass and give it to her; I did not kill her like that. I do not know who did that. Perhaps she took that overdose herself—perhaps he gave it to her. Sometimes I picture his going into her room. 'You look tired, Lucille!' I can hear him saying it. 'Have you not some medicine that will make you sleep? Sleep a little; it will do you good. I will get it for you . . .' You see, if he did that, I drove him to it. I taunted him with pictures of myself married to Tom Blake. I carried his child, and I threatened to cut him off from it. He is a strange strong man; I do not know whether he would do that; I have never known. Often I have thought it possible. It has been between us all our life together. Did he? I ask myself, but I have never dared ask him; I am afraid of the answer. But Marcus, listen. Whichever it was, whether she took that overdose herself, or whether he gave it to her, I am the murderess, for I created that situation which made it the only way out. For my daughter, I said! But it was not for my daughter —it was for myself."

She was sobbing wildly in his arms. She was laughing; she was crying.

"You see me, Marcus. I am wicked. There is no goodness in me. And I so wanted to be good, Marcus. Audrey has told me of a woman, a wonderful woman. Marcus, she is changing Newgate. Were we to go there now perhaps we should not recognise the place. That is what I like to think . . . We should not recognise it. She is a saint, this woman. How I envy her! I say to myself 'That is what I might have been!' And what am I . . . a murderess!"

He said: "Carolan, Carolan! How wild you are! What absurd things you say! You have not changed at all. You are still the same Carolan, the same sweet Carolan."

"Please do not say my name like that. I cannot bear it. Do you not see that I will never leave him? You see what I have done. You have haunted my life; you will continue to do so. Oh, yes! I have thought of you constantly, longed for you . . . No, no, please do not! It is useless. I cannot be happy with him because of you. I couldn't be happy with you, for always I would remember what he had done . . . or perhaps he did not do . . . but he is good and has a strong conscience, and he suffers just as though he had done it, because he knows why she died. She died because of what we had done, and he knows and I know it."

He said: "Carolan, I could make you forget."

She answered: "Oh, Marcus, I am afraid for my sweet daughter. She is headstrong, as I was. Sometimes I think that the women of my family are doomed to sorrow. There is some story about my grandmother; my great grandmother too. And then my own poor Mamma; she has told me the story of how she lost her lover to the press gang. How different her life might have been had my father not been taken by the press gang!"

Marcus held her against him, stroking her hair.

"The press gang is done with, Carolan. It ended with the wars."

"My Katharine will never lose her lover to the press gang then!"

"Oh, Carolan, Carolan, do you not see a new world opening before us? We are going on . . . on to better things. You tell me even our old evil Mother Newgate is changing her manners. Slowly but surely, my Carolan. There is something here. Let us not think of our own little tragedies, darling. Look on . . . to our children and their children and their children . . . generations of them . . . going on and on! The press gang gone, Newgate changing! And what changes will our Katharine and Henry know in their lifetimes!"

"Marcus, you see what I mean . . . I want to make sure of safety for my daughter . . ."

"You cannot make sure of safety for anyone, my sweet Carolan."

"But you can! You can!"

"No, darling. They will work out their own lives. We cannot interfere. People should never interfere; it is only the time in which we live that should influence us, and times are changing, Carolan. What if your mother and father were young in these days? No press gang to ruin their lives. Mother Newgate is changing her face! Who knows, some time there may be no Newgate at all, no possibility of the innocent, such as you were, being caught up with the law; no need for the weak, such as I was, to break the law. Carolan, Carolan, do you not see a wonderful world lying ahead of us?"

"You talk wildly, Marcus. You always did. There is much cruelty in the world still. There always will be. How can we overcome all the poverty and cruelty and injustice?"

"Look there, Carolan! Look to our own Blue Mountains. How long ago is it that we thought there was no way across that mighty barrier? Impassable! people said. The natives told absurd stories of demons who had sworn we should never pass over their mountain. But we did, Carolan. We are across; and on the other side is a fertile country, undeveloped yet, undeveloped as the future. But it is there, and it is wonderful, and it is worth the heartbreak and the struggle to get across. That's how I see it, Carolan, the way across the Blue Mountains to a beautiful future. Our grandchildren, Carolan . . . Our great great grandchildren . . . they will have their difficulties, as far removed from us as it is possible to be. There will always be a range of mountains to.be crossed perhaps, but the struggle is worth while, Carolan, when you get to the other side."

"They want to live beyond the Blue Mountains," she whispered.

"Let them, Carolan! Oh, let them! Perhaps you are right;

479

perhaps she would be wiser to marry her knight and go to London Town. But it is not for us to say. The future does not belong to us, Carolan, but to them. They must have freedom; we must give them that. You understand, Carolan. You do understand?"

"I am glad I came, Marcus."

"Do not go back, Carolan. Why should you? To a haunted house! I will make you forget there was ever such a woman as Lucille Masterman. You did not kill her! My child, you are not to blame. If she killed herself, who is to blame but herself! If he did it, let him take the blame. Come to me, Carolan. I will show you happiness."

"You have shown me that our children must choose their own happiness, Marcus," she said, "and that is a good deal. I shall think of what you said. I shall always think of it."

"You will go back, Carolan?"

"Yes."

"You broke my heart once. I mended it very roughly. Will you break it again?"

"No, Marcus, it was never broken. You will go back, and you will enjoy many moments in your life; sometimes you may think of me, and perhaps you will believe then that I alone could make you happy. You have not changed at all, Marcus. Your heart is strong—it will not easily break. I shall go back and be the same haughty, arrogant, though sometimes gracious, Mrs. Masterman. This afternoon I have cried like a foolish girl, but that is only a part of me. I am part foolish girl, part arrogant woman. I am soft, I am a schemer. Do not ask which is really me; I do not know. I yearn to be a saint like Mrs. Fry, and I am only a murderess. I could have been the saint perhaps; I was the murderess. I was not strong enough. Events have made me what I am; they have made you what you are, Gunnar what he is. We are weak people, all of us. But now there is no press gang; Newgate is changing. There will be other changes, Marcus. And it will go on like that . . . always . . . for a hundred years, for two hundred years. However difficult the mountain range is to cross, it can always be crossed. I'll remember. Goodbye, Marcus. Goodbye!"

She did not look back at him as she mounted her horse. She held her head high and rode away, back to the house in Sydney, back to Gunnar and her family and the memory of Lucille Masterman.

She turned after a while though and saw him, a lonely figure against the background of the Blue Mountains.